I0661423

Be My First

CANDY QUINN

PATHFORGERS PUBLISHING

Contents

INNOCENT TEASE

Karen's Sugar Daddy

Book Themes: Billionaire, Virgin/First Time,
Breeding/Impregnation, DaddyDom,
Spanking
Word Count: 10952

T he three of us gathered into our family mansion's foyer. We were standing side by side, as our father had called us down for something very important.

Olivia sat on the stairs, annoyed by the whole situation, while Christine had her eyes glued to her phone.

Me? I was worried. This was totally unlike father. If there was any good things to tell us, he would just send us a text, or maybe a phone call. He wouldn't demand we all gather in person.

I tried to look on the bright side. Maybe he was getting re-married. Unlikely; father was just a wreck in the past few months. Why was he such a wreck? I really had no clue. He was always evasive when I asked.

He had taken care of us, and we were living in the classiest of accommodations, the Van Hansen Mansion. It had our name on it so you knew it was important. We had landscapers, maids, cooks, and everything that came with fine living like that.

Well we did. Father had been laying them off, saying he caught them stealing or slacking off. He never replaced them. I had to take to teaching myself how to cook, which honestly, I didn't mind excessively much. It was just odd after being pampered all these years.

Father stepped in from a side room. He looked terrible, no jacket, and his tie was barely on him properly. His steps were heavy as he came to the front of us. "My beautiful little girls," he began. There was a sobby tone in his voice.

"What's the matter, Father?" I was first to ask. "Just tell us. The anticipation is killing me."

He was crying. My sisters perked up at it. "Did someone die?" Olivia said.

Christine elbowed her. "Don't be so brash."

"This obviously isn't good news," Olivia replied.

"I'm broke," he sobbed out. "I'm broke. I have nothing. I have less than nothing, I'm in crippling debt, even."

All three of us startled at his words. "I thought we were doing fine," Christine asked.

"I didn't want to alarm you girls. I thought I could turn everything around. I can't now. I'm out of options. I have to sell the estate, everything in it."

"What about my college fund?" Christine said. "I was supposed to head to Europe in the fall."

"There's nothing, sweetie. Nothing."

I didn't know what to make of any of this. I was fresh out of high school myself, graduating only a month ago, and a few months north of eighteen. I had no doubts about what I was - a rich bitch. Like Christine, I was going to have the luxury of a few years to find myself before deciding what I wanted to do with my life. Or so I thought, anyway. Now? I wasn't so sure.

"We're going to be kicked out of the house at the end of the month," he continued.

"Why did you wait so damn long to tell us, Daddy?" Olivia

was pissed and was right in father's face. "We needed time to prepare for all of this."

"I thought I could fix it, girls. I really did." Father was devastated. Tears, whimpering. I had no doubt that he truly did try. A series of bad investments, making wrong deals, I didn't fully understand how he made his fortune in the first place. "The person buying the house is going to be by in an hour to take a look at it."

"Is there anything we can do, Father?" Christine said, standing in front of Father. "Anything we can sell to stave this off? We need time."

"What I owe is far more than selling a TV or a personal collection will deliver, girls. I'm sorry. I've failed you as a father."

I rushed over and gave him a hug. "I still love you, Father. I know you meant the best."

I hated seeing him like this. Part of me, though, just didn't want to face the music. I was toast. I had average-ish grades so I wasn't getting any sort of scholarship. We didn't have any rich friends, so there was no one to run to in that regard. What on earth was I going to do?

Was I going to be waiting tables in mere weeks just to be able to afford ramen or whatever it is poor people eat?

There was a knock on the door. It opened quickly after. My father turned to face the intruder. "You can't just barge in..."

"I can. I own this place," the voice was quick, and to the point. "Or will soon, anyway."

Flanked by a few assistants, the man that came in caught my attention, and caught my attention quick. He was tall, his blonde hair short yet wavy, styled perfectly. He had a fine goatee, groomed and not the least bit ratty. His suit fit perfectly, outlining his fantastically shaped body.

Despite him looking about forty, this guy was hot. He was absolutely stunning, and my eyes never left him as soon as he had entered the room.

"I believe in coming early, see how the place is naturally before people dress it up," he said, walking by. His stride was strong, confident. "It looks like this place is well kept regardless. Cheers to that."

Father broke from my arms even as my eyes didn't break from the intruder. "You could have let me get my daughters out of here first. They don't have to see the place they grew up in bought like it was nothing."

"Calm yourself, Van Hansen. I just want to make sure I'm getting what I'm paying for. I don't seek to be hostile in my business deals." He glanced over the house, and then over to us three sisters. He shot a glance at Olivia, at Christine, and then over to me.

His gaze lingered on me, and mine lingered on him. Before I shyly looked away from him, not wanting to look into his eyes.

The intruder stepped forward, and offered me his hand. "Hello, little lady. You look beautiful today. The name is Tyler Warren. May I ask yours?"

"K - Karen," I stuttered out.

"Karen? A gorgeous name for a gorgeous woman," he took my hand up, and then kissed it. I was frozen solid by the gesture. "George, I have to say you've raised some wonderful daughters."

"Get away from them, Ty. You can exploit my misfortune for some real estate but this doesn't mean you can womanize my daughters." Father's tone was quite a bit more angry suddenly.

Ty did so, stepping back. "I'm not the womanizing type. I just saw something I liked and wanted to let her know. I'm very selective in who I pursue."

"My daughters aren't for you, Ty."

"Don't be hostile, George. I'm going to depart, I can take it on good faith that the other rooms aren't missing ceilings or walls or stained with horrible and gaudy art." He walked back to the door, ready to leave as swiftly as he arrived. "Take your time in preparing your departure, I take no joy in destroying a family's home."

My father was silent.

"As for you, Karen," he turned slightly and shot me a glare. Could I have been even more frozen in shock and anticipation than I was. "Everything will be fine. Calm down, little girl."

I swallowed a gulp of air as he stepped through our threshold.

When the door closed, I almost collapsed in shock.

"You okay, Karen?" Christine put a hand on my shoulder.

"Just - just fine, I'm okay. Really."

T retreated to what was currently my room, and collapsed on a massive pile of stuffed animals. A soft, cushy bed of them, that I'd collected ever since I was an actual little girl. I thought about how much my collection would have been worth, but I remembered what my father had said about their relative value to what he had owed.

Shame. I was overwhelmed with shame for reacting to this situation like that. This man walks into my home, a man who was exploiting our families sudden ruin, and I'm sitting there dumbfounded.

Because I find myself so ludicrously attracted to him. Honestly, he was the first person I've ever seen that did those sort of things to me. All the boys I encountered in high school were goofy looking idiots who just didn't do anything for me. Maybe I had a thing for older men?

Ty Warren was one hell of an older man. He was powerful, his handshake told me he was someone who would be in control. I wished for him to be in control of me.

I shook my head. This was just some rich asshole, I had to remind myself. Still, a man like him... My hands were taking on a mind of their own, drifting down my dress. What did he have beneath that suit? Never being with a man before, I had more than enough research to know what I wanted still. A strong, powerful fame, firm yet smooth muscles, not too hard, but not too soft. Then for those hands to pick me up, ravish me, care for me.

Down my body, under my skirt. Under my panties. Find their way to my most tender of parts. To be teased there.

He called me little girl, but I still wanted to be treated like a woman sometimes. The way he looked at me, that was the way a man looks at a woman. I slid my fingers past my nub and into my slit, continuing to do so, imagining a man there. Imagining Ty there. Imagining something so much more powerful than my fingers there, making every sensation I felt be so much more. My body being ravished as I was fucked, feeling the presence of another right there was I was being taken higher and higher toward ecstasy.

Him pounding my pussy, faster, harder, bringing me to greater and higher heights of bliss.

Letting the orgasm come and wash over me so intensely.

It was sweet, cumming like that as I leaned back even more.

The shame hit again right after, remembering who I was thinking about. The closest thing I had to a villain in my situation. I stood, straightened my clothes, grabbed a small towel and wiped the sweat off my brow and anywhere else. As far as my father knew, I was probably still his sweet baby girl who didn't have a single carnal thought in the world.

It didn't matter I was eighteen. In some ways, I was still a child – and a woman. It was a weird place to be, but I guess all girls have that period. Being faced with poverty looked like it was going to make me into a woman real quick, whether I liked it or not.

The doorbell sounded as I was leaving my room. I looked around the foyer and it seemed I was the closest one to respond to it, since our butler was laid off weeks ago. I darted down the stairs, and opened the door. There was a man in a black suit standing there, holding a massive teddy bear. It wasn't a cheap looking one either, myself being a sort of stuffed animal aficionado.

"Karen Van Hansen?"

"That's me, yes."

"This is for you."

He handed me the large bear. It was softer than anything I had felt before. It was also heavy, so much so I had to plant it on the floor inside the house after holding it up for a short time.

The courier who delivered the bear stayed standing tall at the door. "That was a gift, courtesy of Mr. Warren. Ms. Van Hansen, you are cordially invited to dinner with him. He wishes to spend more time in getting to know you."

I swallowed. "He's asking me out on a date?"

"That would be the vernacular summarization of his request, yes. He requests an immediate response, as the event is scheduled for tonight."

I turned around and glanced back into the house. This was the man who was benefiting off of my father's misfortune. Would I be betraying Father by accepting this?

Because I wanted to go. Ty Warren had an interest in me and I had one hell of an interest in him.

The gigantic silk teddy bear certainly helped things too.

I made a quick glance around the mansion. No one was around. My answer would remain private, and no one would know that I agreed to all of this. I took a deep breath, and turned to the courier. "I'll go. Yes. I'll go, where, when does he want me?"

"He will send a car for you at seven o'clock tonight to take you to restaurant of his choosing. Also, he has requested you wear this," he stopped, and darted back to the black car that he had shown up in. Opening the door, he pulled out a dress. He brought it back to me, and presented it to me. I accepted it.

"I have to wear this?"

"Those are the terms of the engagement as he relegated them to me."

The dress was ridiculously ornate and worth far more than anything else in my collection. It was pink and frilly. "What if it doesn't fit?"

"It will fit."

"How do you know?"

"Mr. Warren gained access to your father's accounts as part of paying for his debt. This includes receipts with tailors used by your family over the past year. He had it sculpted to your exact measurements. It will fit."

So much for privacy. "I guess that's how he figured out my collecting of stuffed animals too."

7

"Yes, the receipts for your purchases. He knows everything about you and likes what he sees."

"I guess I'll be ready at 7," I said, looking at the dress. It really didn't look like it would fit me, and it looked like it was designed for someone half my own age, but somehow still having my ample bosom. It was a really strange collision of design.

"Perfect. Mr. Warren will be quite pleased."

"Do I need to tip you or something?" I was still looking over the gown.

"I am compensated more than well enough. Mr. Warren is a fine boss. Good Day, Ma'am." The courier turned and walked away from me.

It was weird as hell. I had this new dress, I had this stupidly expensive new stuffie, and I had a date with someone it seemed I was willing to betray my own father for.

I had a date with Ty Warren.

As the weirdness of my encounter with the courier faded, that fact became more and more prevalent.

I had a date with Ty Warren. My first date.

God, I hoped that I didn't screw this up.

I was no stranger to having a personal driver. I *was* a stranger to riding with a dress so short that it would immediately show off my panties if I didn't sit in a certain way.

The courier was right though. The dress fit. All too well, really. Were the eyes of Ty Warren on me longer than I really knew? The car pulled up to the restaurant, and the driver was quick to play classy chauffeur and grab the door for me, quicker than I could get settled and do it myself.

Restaurant Samuel. I didn't know who this Samuel was but the way everyone was dressed told me that this was definitely the furthest thing from McDonalds that one could possibly imagine. The difference being while they wore black, white, brown, with the occasional red and blue, I was stepping out in something entirely different.

He was there, waiting. Ty Warren. His handsome body dressed in a black blazer, a white shirt. It all had it's own style to it, though, not something you'd get off the rack at any place. He had his wealth and he was going to flaunt it, knowing it would take something special to show himself off to someone like me.

"Karen, my dear, you look so... pretty in that dress."

It was an oddly immature word to use, like he was a polite relative rather than a date. And the dress wasn't typically my style by any stretch. It was a bright pink, not even a subtle one, like one shade of intensity under calling it hot. Dragging behind my feet were frills, and lots of them. They were long, some of the fabric was see through and showed off my legs. They stopped just short of dragging on the floor, making the whole get up look slightly undersized. Ty approved though.

Boy, did Ty approve. He hooked his arm into mine and took me right past the line of people waiting to get in. "Restaurant Samuel is one of the most esteemed establishments in town. Reservations are commonly booked up months in advance."

"Were you planning on taking me on a date back then?"

He walked up to the waiter, who was big enough to double as a bouncer. "Two, Timothy."

"Right away, Mr. Warren."

He led us in, and I glanced back at the line. They were furious that we were simply able to cut ahead so easily. "No, my desire to have you is much younger than that. Pull the right strings, make the right investments though, and planning is just a hurdle you can bypass."

I was led to a corner of the restaurant, near the stage. Ty pulled out the chair and offered it to me, and I gladly accepted it. I was still overwhelmed by him, the way he touched me, the way he was controlling me, guiding me through everything.

The waiter stepped up. "May I get you two some drinks?"

"Ah," Ty said, "A glass of brandy for me, and a Shirley Temple for my little girl here."

Little girl? I raised an eyebrow. Wasn't he going to ask me what I wanted?

"And what may I get for you for your meal this evening?"

"A filet mignon. medium rare, asparagus with your finest sauce. That would be just right for her."

The waiter nodded. "Yourself, sir?"

"Prime Colorado Lamb Duo Porterhouse, of course. Medium Rare as well."

"Sir," he said, scribbling it down and departing.

"Don't I--" I started to speak.

He placed a finger up on my lips. "Karen, you will enjoy the selections I have made for you. You seem offended that I did you the honors."

"I didn't even get to see a menu."

"You don't need to worry yourself with such adult manners."

"I'm eighteen-years-old. I can handle ordering off a menu. And a Shirley Temple?"

"Alcohol will spoil your youth. Never mind that you're not even legally allowed to imbibe."

"I wasn't a peasant before this. Places like this one here? They wouldn't card me if I asked for a vodka shot and told them to leave the bottle."

He laughed. "Still throwing a fit like a child. I knew you would be perfect for what I desired."

"What is this what you desire? What's going on, Ty?" I was shaking my head. "Yeah, you're attracted to me. But everything, the giant teddy bear, the dress, ordering for me just now, this isn't typical. This isn't how it goes in the movies."

"Nothing ever goes like it does in the movies. Have you ever even been on a date before, my little Karen?"

I blushed, and turned my eyes away. "Well, yeah, of course."

"It's not nice to lie to Daddy."

My eyebrow perked up again. "Daddy?"

"Karen, I am a man of great success. With this success comes getting what you want. When you always get what you want, you start to develop very specific tastes. You want something out of your woman, out of your lover."

My interest was piqued when he mentioned the word 'lover'. "Like what?"

"I want someone with enough of their childhood demeanor

still alive, but is still a woman. You, Karen, are a woman. A shapely one that any man would love to have. Looking over your family's finances though, you haven't fully embraced growing up yet. A woman, yet still a little girl. You are perfect, Karen. Perfect to attend to, to take care of in every way imaginable."

"Because I have a stuffed animal collection you think I'm going to just be your little girl?"

"You aren't interested?"

I froze a second. I wasn't fully sure what he was describing. I wasn't completely filled in on every bit of subtext in his words. There was one thing that was perfectly clear, though.

It meant being with him. It meant being him in ways he would care for me, and caring for me in very adult ways. "I'm intrigued."

"Then I will make you mine, Karen. You're going to be my little girl, with everything that entails. My so very spoiled brat... that is what will make Daddy very happy."

The food was brought out, along with the Shirley Temple.

I took a gulp of the drink - it was better than I expected, not even really knowing what a Shirley Temple was. Seemed to be a mix of fruit juices and soda. I could live with being restricted to this.

As I reached for the knife and fork for my food, he put up a finger. "Oh? What's wrong?"

He reached across the table and pulled my plate over to him. "Let me get that for you."

Ty took the knife from his side, and asked for my fork. I handed it over, again curious to where he was going with all of this.

Cutting into the meat, a little bit of juice escaped as he carved out a chunk of it. "Open wide, little girl."

I obeyed, as he delivered the food right into my mouth. He let me savor it, licking up the meat and its juices, little it dribble down my throat. Glancing across the table, I saw that smirk on his face. How delightfully twisted of him. I bit the meat off the fork and pulled my lips away, chewing it.

"Chew it up real well, little girl."

It was as good as 'Daddy' promised. I wondered if the pleasures that would follow if I went with Ty Warren would be far more than simple culinary ones...?

He took me by the hand as he led me from the restaurant. "Little girl, we are retiring home for the evening."

"Oh, are we?"

"Oh, yes. Let me show you what awaits you." His grip grew firmer as he brought me to the limo and let me step in.

I was curious to say the least, about what was going to come next. What was with all of this Daddy stuff?

He brought me to one of the tallest buildings in town. I came from money, yes, but he seemed to be on a whole different level than my family was.

The whole time, Ty Warren held me close to him. It wasn't a simple hand hold, but he encouraged me to hold onto him, to hug him like he was the very giant teddy bear he had bought me today. Resting on him almost as we rode the elevator high, all the way to the top floor of the building. The doors opened in front of two ornate double doors. He pulled out a key, unlocked them, and opened them for me, leading me in.

I was met with a gorgeous view of the entire city below. An amazing sight to say the least. I took it in for a moment, before Ty spun me around and laid a deep kiss on me. A rush of adrenaline hit me as he did so, his tongue invading my mouth and mine almost following his automatically. One hand running through my hair, the other going down my back. The kiss, my very first, seemed to be lasting an eternity - an eternity I was enjoying so very much.

When it finally broke, my eyes were locked with his, and his were very much driven and determined. "If you are to be my little girl, there are going to be rules you must follow in this relationship."

"What rules?"

"You must obey, Karen. You must obey Daddy. You will do as I say, and you will do so without objection. You are to be mine, you are to be my... Kitty. Yes, Kitty, that is much more fitting of a name for my little girl."

I blushed, not being called that for more than a decade.

"I must obey no matter what?" I wasn't sure what to make of this as he explained.

"If you have strong objections to something, it will be discussed. For day to day things though, you will listen to Daddy. You will wear the things Daddy tells you to wear, you will go to bed when I tell you too. You will be my little girl. Do you understand, Kitty?"

He wanted complete control of me. It wasn't something so simple.

"In return for your obedience, I will treat you like the princess you are. What you have experienced so far today is only the tip of the iceberg in what your obedience to Daddy will bring. I want nothing more than your absolute happiness – as well as your absolute obedience."

So much was going on in my brain at that moment. What he was proposing, what it meant, and everything else that was going with it. How we wanted to control me... how he wanted to make me happy.

I wasn't sure of what to make of it. The fact was I didn't know what I wanted to make of my life either. I was an eighteen-year-old with an uncertain future. I didn't know what I wanted, I didn't know where I was going. He was offering me something very clear, and in a haze of uncertainty, that sounded like paradise.

"Yes," I said.

"Yes, what?" He grinned.

"Yes...Daddy."

"Good girl. Why don't you get ready for bed then?"

"Oh?" I raised an eyebrow.

He broke away from me, and walked over to a box left on a nearby sofa. The entire room really was full of the best things money could buy, the carpet super soft even through the heels he had ordered me to wear. He opened the box, and produced a nighty. It was even shorter cut than the dress he had given me, and looked so opaque I could see him through it. "This will look beautiful on my little girl."

"It does look very comfortable."

"How about you put it on for me?"

"Okay," I said.

"You need to take off the clothes you're wearing right now, first."

I swallowed. Of course it did. I slipped off the heels, confirming that yes, the carpet was very much super soft. Why was I suddenly bashful? I knew that this all involved something more than what he was saying. I knew it involved another first time I hadn't yet given up.

Reaching for the bottom of the dress, I started to hike it up over my head, revealing my underwear below.

I glanced over at Ty, and a frowned formed on his face. Oh god, what if he didn't like my body? "What - What's the matter?"

"Daddy is going to have to buy you some new panties and bras. What you have now is unacceptable for my little girl. Take those filthy things off right now."

I frowned, and reached around and unhooked my bra, and let it fall by the wayside. Ty was right there, picked it up, and tossed it into a nearby wastebasket.

"Come on, let Daddy see his little girl."

I didn't notice that I had instinctively rushed to cover myself. With great willpower, I pulled my hands away from my breasts, and put them at my side.

"There we go," Ty said. "Beautiful. Nothing that should be covered up, especially by any garbage fabrics like that. You deserve only the best, my little girl. Get that other thing off your body. Now."

Blushing, I started to slide my panties down my legs. They were a heap on the floor, and again, he snatched them up and threw them up in the garbage.

He stepped back. "Absolutely beautiful, just as I suspected.

You're the right one for me; the right one to be my little girl, Kitty."

I smiled, and let him devour my body with his eyes.

"As foolish as it is to cover up such a wonderful body, let me see you in this, my little girl."

He handed me the nighty. I let it slip on over my body. It was as silky as it looked, it tickling my nipples as glided over my body. So soft, so nice – I could definitely get used to this.

I showed it off to him. It was just long enough to not obviously show off what was between my legs, but not much longer than that at all.

It didn't take long for him to grab my ass and pull me close, and following it up with another one of those delightfully deep kisses. I was lost in him. He was overwhelming, so much of a man, so much of everything. Even if it wasn't going so far past the aspect of making out as it was at this point, it was hitting all the right buttons inside me, giving me what I was yearning for, asking for, wanting so much of.

"I don't think I'll be able to keep my hands off of my Kitty," he said, breaking the kiss.

He took me by the hand, his grip tight and firm, one that said he was going to protect me and care for me no matter what was going to happen. Ty led me to his bed, huge and soft, and laid me down on it. His hand opened and slid down my body, using the garment to tickle me, let my nipples perk up underneath it. It felt as good as him letting his fingers caress my breasts bare, a wonderful sensation as he came between my legs. Still kissing me, he slid a finger past my clit, and into my slit.

"Knew you'd be as innocent as you appeared to be. Daddy's angel. You were saving it for me, weren't you?"

Again, I blushed. I had a feeling that my innocence wasn't long for this world.

I shuddered as he flicked my nub and started to fuck me with his fingers as he led me along with that sweet, sweet kiss. I broke it to gasp, as he didn't stop. He kept on going, watching me shake, watching me coo under his touch. Sure, I had touched myself down there before, but a man down there doing these things... it was so much more. I could tell Ty was hardly inexperienced, and knew exactly how a woman liked these things.

Waves of ecstasy traveled through me, and I watched as his smile only grew. Sure, there were many childlike things about what he was proposing. This here, though, told me he was completely aware I was a woman, and I had woman-like needs.

His eyes left mine as his head drifted down my body and parted my legs further, pushing my nighty up more. He kept a steady petting of my clit as he rained kisses down my body and over my legs, and then topped what his fingers could give me by laying a kiss right on my clit, and sucking on it hard.

Ty licked and sucked, his rough face brushing against my thighs as he did so. He massaged my thighs as he ate me, just spreading the joy of everything and anything as he continued down there. I cooed a bit louder, and arched my back a bit as he kept up his worship of me. His tongue was just as skilled as his fingers if not even more so and I was tossing and turning quickly under his control. I gripped the blankets of his soft king bed, and arched my back in response as he continued his dedication completely.

I was loving it. Everything he was doing. He had me where he wanted. I was panting, breathing, heavy, and completely ready to explode in utter bliss.

Then, rudely, he stopped.

He grinned as he rose up, staring over my body.

"No, not yet. You don't get to cum until I do. Kitty, my little girl, we're going to seal our deal simply. If you want me to be your Daddy, and you want to be my little girl, you will give me your virginity."

He stood tall. Long ago he had done away with his jacket, and all that remained was that collared shirt that contoured his muscular body so well.

"So, my Kitty, do you want to give Daddy your virginity tonight?"

There was a brief pause. I always thought it'd be with someone I loved. A boyfriend, one I'd been with for months. Not someone who I met the same day, not to someone who I was now calling Daddy, and not someone anywhere near under these circumstances. This wasn't a typical circumstance by any measure, but Ty Warren wasn't a typical man.

"Yes, Daddy. Please, show your little girl what it's like."

That smirk. It only grew wider.

He began unbuttoning his shirt one by one, revealing the bare chest that was hidden underneath. He tossed it to the side, and then quickly shifted to undoing his pants, and letting them, as well as the boxer briefs that were hidden underneath, be pushed to the floor.

It was then I saw his masculinity. Strong and mighty, and I was suddenly having second thoughts about the logistics of our encounter.

Ty was there though. Back on top of me. Kissing me.

I knew that it would be all right. The way he interacted me, the way he caressed me, the way he touched me, I knew his words were nothing but true. He wouldn't do anything that would hurt me. He wanted to bring me joy, not agony. Love was in his movements. It was a different kind of love than I expected, but it was love nonetheless.

He brought the head of his cock to the lips of my pussy, and teased them slightly. He slowly but surely began to push in. I was so aroused, and so much in need of stimulation at that point that I could tell I was gushing for him, aching for him, needing him, and ready for him.

I was so ready for him that there was barely any pain as Ty slid into me, even though I'd always heard it hurt. But I guess I was just so wet, and all those years of anxiety were gone just like that... all because of Daddy's magic.

Instead, I felt a massive rush of bliss. God, it was so strong, so intense having him inside of me, making me feel foolish for having the slightest bit of doubt about him.

He held me tight as he began to fuck me, his embrace so overwhelming. He started slowly, letting me get used to him even more. "You're perfect for me little girl. A perfect, tight fit. You're happy to be Daddy's little slut aren't you?"

"Yes, Daddy," I muttered between gasps as he fucked me

harder. Quicker. Faster. Every penetration bringing another level of sweet ecstasy to me. I called out for him. Louder. My voice wasn't muffled and I was quivering around him, crying out, enjoying Daddy for everything he was going to do to me.

My fingers ran down his back as I held on to him as he fucked his little girl. He was fulfilling everything I ever wanted out of my first time and then some. Things I never even knew I desired, but he'd teased my most taboo fantasies to the surface... and then fulfilled them. I never expected a man doing this to me to feel so damn good. I could barely hold on any more.

He listened to my cries, and it seemed Ty almost knew my body better than I did. He was slowing down again. "What is it this time?" I whined, so desperate to cum on him.

"Don't take that tone with me. You ask nicely."

I knew exactly what he meant. "Please."

"Please what?"

"Please, make me cum," I said.

"Hmm? What does my little Kitty want?"

"Please make me cum, Daddy," I finally spat out.

"As my little girl wishes."

He reached between my legs and flicked my clit, and combined it with a sudden, rough, and utterly determined pace. I was screaming for him, and that's exactly what he wanted me to do. To be screaming his name, to be screaming Daddy.

So much intensity hit me and washed over my body at that point, I was lost to bliss. So much, so fast, and it was all because of him.

He kept on fucking me, making sure I felt every bit of intensity for as long as I possibly could.

I could barely feel anything but the ecstatic ache as he finally pulled out of my pussy, his own cock aching and ready to blow.

Blow he did. Cum erupted out of him, lashing up and over over my body and splashing onto my chest and my face. I squinted some, but I was enjoying my own orgasm too much to truly care.

I was panting, exhausted by what he had done. I was ready to pass out, not caring about the mess that was on my body and my flesh.

Ty was there though. He moved quickly. "I'm sorry I made such a mess, little girl. Daddies do that sometimes when they don't want their little girls to swell up just yet."

Swell up just yet? What did he mean by that?

"Here, let's get you all cleaned up." He had a warm rag on hand, and started to wipe his mess off of my chest. Off of my face. After everything I had experienced, it was absolutely sweet, a perfect cherry on top of everything else. He lifted my head up from resting, and laid a final peck on my lips. He then pulled me into his bed, and took me into his arms, cradling me.

All I could do was look up at him and smile.

It was unusual, yes. I liked it, though. I was his, I was Daddy's, to use, to command, to care for. I was going to get used to this very quickly.

Thoughts of un-little girl things like Daddy fucking me hard and fast again bounced through my head as I fell asleep in his arms.

＊

When I came to the next morning, I was buried in the softest of sheets and blankets. I rubbed some of them against my face - this was of some exotic fabric. Probably not even silk, but something even more rare with some six digit thread count or something like that.

The only thing that would've been nicer to wake up in would have been Ty's embrace.

Ty, though, was already up and about. He was redressing, buttoning up his shirt. "Good morning, Kitty."

"Morning," I said, still shaking the cobwebs out from waking up. Also, the whole wonderful experience that I had blissfully indulged in the night before. That was still shaking me up, still not able to believe that it happened.

"I have important Daddy business to attend to this morning,

unfortunately, or we'd be repeating last night right now instead of later."

I grinned at his words.

He pointed to a small book on the nightstand next to the bed. "You'll find the number for my driver there, as well as the number for the house chef if you desire some food."

"Thank you," I said.

"Thank you who?"

"Thank you, Daddy." It was getting a whole lot easier to say as we went.

"That's better. Today, you're going to return to your former home and collect your personal affects, anything that you don't want to leave behind. You're moving in with me now."

I swallowed a gulp of air. "I'm moving in with you? Already? Isn't this all moving too fast?"

"Your father is being evicted from the mansion. You need a place to stay. Besides that, I don't do things the normal way. I do things my way. Haven't you figured that out yet, little girl?"

There was little disputing that fact. "Okay. I'll tell my father and sisters where I'm going. I'm sure they'll be rational and understanding given everything we're going through."

Ty didn't respond, he just focused on getting his tie just right for whatever business things that he had to do.

"You're seeing who?" My father's voice raised.

"Ty. Ty Warren," I said, suddenly feeling a whole lot more meek.

It had been such a good morning too. I had a fantastic breakfast made by some chef whose name was so French that I couldn't pronounce it. Ty had presented me with brand new clothes to wear home, and my ride home even included a stop by for gourmet ice cream.

I didn't even know ice cream could be gourmet.

The feel good morning came crumbling down as I walked

into my father's home. He was wondering where I had been all night.

I told him, and it didn't go over well.

"That greedy miser scumbag? No daughter of mine is going to be seen attached to someone like that." He was shouting at me. My sisters were on the floor above, looking down at the two of us in the foyer.

"Father, he wants to take care of me."

"He wants to rub all of this in my face is what he wants to do. He's trash, Karen. He's why we're in the situation we're in. I forbid you to see that man again."

"Father, I'm an adult, I can make my own decisions."

"If you have any respect for me as a parent, Karen, you'll listen to me anyway. I won't let him lord you over me."

"I'm not a possession for people to lord over others," I said. I mean, unless I want to be. It's a free country.

"Karen, please. Don't torture your father like this."

He was standing firm in front of me. I was angry that he was reacting like this - but he was my father.

He did want what was best for me. He was blood, he was family, he loved me.

I couldn't just throw away that bond because of things like money. Or the pleasures that Ty delivered to me again and again. I couldn't just shun that, could I?

Sighing, I nodded. "Okay, father. I won't see him again."

Ow. I didn't expect that inner pain to hit me so hard for saying those words.

"Thank you, Karen." His words felt empty, worthless.

I suddenly felt a huge surge of despair coming on. I didn't say anything else to my father, and instead bolted to my room and dove into my bed. Tears began to flow.

Why was I sobbing? I barely knew Ty. It was just one night.

Was it everything I was potentially losing out on? I did want to know more. How would he take care of me, in so many definitions of the word?

It was for my father. He was already going through a rough

time. I didn't have to make it worse just because I was a hopeless horny teenager.

I couldn't bring myself to call Ty and tell him off. It wasn't easy, and it wasn't like Ty didn't have this intimidating presence about him. He was a man who was used to always getting what he wanted.

There was another gigantic teddy bear waiting for me the next morning. With some effort, I dragged it into my room before anyone noticed. There was a note card attached to it - "Call me - Ty". I still couldn't do it.

Not even as another day passed and the courier showed up with a diamond necklace. He asked for my response. I told him I couldn't give him one.

Why was I such a coward? I told my father I wouldn't betray him for Ty. But I couldn't tell Ty that.

Again, I hid the gift away.

The third day, I couldn't hide the gifts anymore. "Karen!" Olivia called out. "Flowers. Again. The fourth time today."

Bashfully, I descended the stairs to collect them. Olivia just shook her head as she walked past me. At least she wasn't judging me for all of this. This time there was an ornate fruit basket, complete with fruits I couldn't even name if you asked me to.

Taking it and retreating back to my room, I reached for my phone. I brought up his number, and my finger hovered over it for what felt like an eternity.

Not like this. I couldn't just call him, tell him we were through.

Even though we had only one date, and one night together, Ty wasn't typical. He deserved better than being broken up with over a phone call.

The doorbell rang again. I immediately knew that he had sent something else my way. He was driven on spoiling me rotten even if I was disobeying him. I made sure I looked decent, and prepared to go. The courier who sent me more than likely had orders to bring me to him if asked.

I had to face Ty. I had to tell him it was over. Then, maybe, after a few weeks of crying into a pillow, I could move on.

The ride to the top of the penthouse felt like it was going to take an eternity. The whole time my hand was hovering over the stop button, ready to request the ground floor and run away from all of this again.

I had to stand firm though. Continuing to languish in this purgatory state with Ty wasn't good for either of us, and it made me feel like kind of a bitch to be leading him along like this.

I reached the top, and I waited for the doors to open. He was there, waiting for me.

"Kitty, you've been a naughty girl ignoring my advances like that."

I couldn't look him in the eye, even as he approached me. "We can't do this, Ty."

He paused a moment. "And why not? You more than enjoyed my company. I could divine that much from the sounds you made."

"It's not me. It's my father."

He laughed. "Really?"

"Really what? He doesn't want me seeing you."

"I didn't think George would be so petty."

"He's blaming you for his troubles."

"George got himself in debt. I was buying his home to help him out of it."

"He still blames you. I'm sorry, Ty."

"Kitty," he started.

"I'm Karen."

"No, you're my Kitty. My beautiful, precious Kitty. I want you to ask yourself something. If the Daddy that spawned you won't let you follow your heart to a Daddy you love, is he really all that much of a Daddy?"

"It's not like that. I know sometimes emotions don't make sense. Like how I feel about you doesn't make any sense. I can't blame my father for thinking like this, but that's how he's thinking."

Ty moved forward, and pulled me closer to him. Despite me being there to put an end to our game, I didn't mind it. Not how my head was buried in his chest, and how he was stroking my hair as he talked. "So you love your father."

"Yes. He's never done me wrong."

He laughed.

"What's so funny about that?"

"I'm sorry Kitty. I made assumptions. I've seen so many husks of men who dared called themselves fathers that I made a poor judgment of character regarding yours. I figured he was the type who was fine in letting the dominant male figure in your life be the butler. I mean, you call him Father, not Daddy, even."

"He thought Daddy was juvenile and didn't let me or my sisters call him that."

He laughed again.

"You see why I can't do this then?"

"No, I don't." He pulled me closer. "I still want you Kitty. That's without question, and I will have you. I'll just reassess George, since you still hold him dear to you."

"And that means?"

"Instead of buying his home, I'm going to bail him out and cut him a check so he can pull himself back together. A gift he can call a loan if he decides that offends him. I don't want my Kitty worrying that her family is struggling as I spoil her rotten."

I looked up at Ty. He was smiling warmly. I'm sure father would be far more forgiving of my choice of man if he wasn't in such dire straits himself. "Thank you," I said.

"Now there's the matter that you've been very bad hiding from me like this. That isn't what we agreed to, my Kitty."

"I'm sorry about all that."

"Hmm?" He had a huge grin on his face.

"I'm sorry, Daddy. I won't hide from you again." I tried to hide my own smile. He was making everything all right, of

24

course. I was going to be able to please both my father and my Daddy, after all. "I made a mistake and I was bad."

"You're damn right you did, little girl. Making me worried sick about where you were all this time. You need to be taught a lesson."

My eyebrow raised. "I do?" I was suddenly confused by what he meant. He had been treating me like a spoiled child all this time.

"Come with me."

Somewhat roughly, he lead me by the arm across the room to his bed.

"Bend over, Kitty. Over the bed."

Still confused, I remembered what I had agreed to that night. I would obey Daddy no matter what. Obviously, I had failed at that majorly, so I had to get back on the right track.

I leaned over the bed, wondering what was going to come. Was he going to fuck me from behind? Fuck my ass?

I could almost hear the air break as he wound up and rained down a mighty slap across my ass.

It stung. Hard. I let out a gasp, and shot a look back at him.

"Kitty, you need a good spanking so you realize what you've done and so you understand that you're to obey Daddy. I only want what's best for you."

He followed this declaration with another mighty spank from his hand, my flesh shuddering all the way up, making me gasp again.

A third, stinging through me.

"Up. We're not done yet." Ty sat on the side of the bed. "Across my lap, little girl. Now."

My ass was already hurting a bit from the strength and velocity of his slaps. It wasn't enough to dissuade me from obeying though, and I nodded, laying across Daddy's lap. Across his strong, firm legs, and wondered what was to come next.

Yes, it hurt, but I was still amazed I was willing to take more. That a dark part of me wanted more.

I got more.

As I laid across Daddy's lap, he unleashed another spank.

More intense than the last, zeroing in on the same spot, aiming to make me really feel sore from everything that was happening.

Another lash, another shot of pain through me.

I was panting, whimpering, but he wasn't done yet.

Far from it.

He pulled my panties down my legs, tossing them away. I wasn't even going to have their flimsy protection anymore.

Through the corner of my eye, I watched him reel back his hand again, and let it rush down and sting across my now naked ass.

A little harder, a little more intense, I let out a whimper from the strike.

"My little girl is a slut isn't she? She's soaking wet and enjoying this."

I closed my eyes, and found myself nodding. Why was I enjoying this? This hurt.

Having him though – having Daddy – spank me, was hot. I didn't understand why, maybe it was the thought of having his hand so close to my intimate parts. Whatever it was, he wasn't lying. I was incredibly aroused by all of this.

Ty started raining down the hands across my ass swiftly, the sound of hand against flesh echoing through the room again and again.

My ass was sore, and every spank was more painful than the last. It wasn't long until I couldn't help it – there were tears in my eyes.

It wasn't much longer before he finally stopped. The sound of slapped flesh was replaced by my soft whimpering.

It was then Daddy pulled me up, and took me into his arms, using his strength to turn me around, holding me close in his arms.

"It's okay, little girl. I do this because I love you."

He was massaging the sore spot on my ass, letting the warmth of his hand soothe the pain he had caused. Feeling so close to him after all this, it was odd. It was comforting.

I finally understood why he did that. There was a great pleasure in simply being cared for so closely, being taken care of like this.

"You're mine, Kitty. I will take care of you, I will give you anything you desire, just as long as you accept that you're mine."

I nodded, enthusiastically.

"I need more than that after all of this, Kitty. You told me that before, and then you ran away from me for days. I need you to give me something that you can't run away from. Something that will make you mine forever."

I blinked. "What would that be, Daddy?"

"Your womb."

My eyes went wide.

"I need an heir. I've never felt something stronger than what I feel for you, my Kitty. To finish your punishment, you will promise me your fertile body without protection or other interference."

"You want me to have your child?"

"That's what I said, yes. I want my little girl to also be the mother of my children. No matter what follows, spoiling you won't ever stop. No matter what happens, I will care for you, spoil you, and you will always be the mother of my children as well. I want a woman who can be many women at once, and you are that woman. Do you think you can do that for Daddy?"

Ty Warren never screwed around in pursuing what he wanted. He didn't relent in asking me to dinner, he didn't wait in taking my virginity, and he wanted me to move in immediately. Now he was demanding I have his children. To an outsider looking in, I'd have to be insane to agree to something so quickly.

Love though, never goes like that. Love lets you know things are right even when all logic tells you otherwise. Ty was the one for me, and he knew that.

I knew that.

"Yes, Daddy. Anything for you."

He kissed me for the first time since I returned. It was a deep, powerful kiss. His tongue led mine, and the embrace felt like it would last forever – and I wouldn't have minded one bit.

Unfortunately, it did, but fortunately, for something greater to soon to replace it. He slid me off to the bed, and started to strip himself down, revealing that sculpted chest to me once again. His belt undone, his legs followed, and I remembered why it was so damn hard to turn him down. Ty Warren was hot and he was mine.

I leaned back on the bed, kicking my shoes off, and hiking my dress up. My panties already taken care of, I was more than ready to take Daddy on.

Down to only his boxer briefs, he was on top of me, with another deep kiss. He was ravishing me, his hands exploring me, making all my flesh light up in anticipation for more. We had been apart for days, and the built up need and desire for me was so strong and apparent inside him. He was going to fool around much, he had to have me, his boxer briefs sliding down his legs.

I felt his erection loom over my pussy lips, Daddy's intimidating cock wanting to go in to where it belonged. His body heat against mine, it was so overwhelming as I spread my legs for him and allowed him to get even closer to my body. I wanted him and I was more than ready for him.

When he pushed in, I almost came, my own need so great from being deprived of him and the fire that the spanking had created inside of me.

He was swift in creating a steady pace as he stared into my eyes, fucking me gently yet firmly. I was his dirty girl and didn't need to be treated so dainty like a virgin anymore. At least when he was treating me like a woman and not a little girl, any way.

Every penetration brought such wonderful electricity shooting through me, building it higher and higher. Kissing me on the lips, the chest, he explored my body as I explored his and all of his muscles. God, having him underneath my fingertips just drove the point home that being his little girl was what I wanted all along even if I didn't know it.

Harder, faster still, I called for him. I moaned for him. I soaked in the rising tide of bliss, yearning for more and more as he fucked me so fast and so completely. I yearned for what was to come, my legs closing around his hips, which only made him fuck me harder.

Ty drove home the fact that my pleasure was his top priority as he moved a finger to my clit, massaging it in tune with every way he fucked me. Just his cock alone felt so damn good, the tandem of his skillful finger and him fucking my pussy was absolutely wonderful. I was quickly being overwhelmed by him, and whispered into his ear. "Please, Daddy, more."

"Let's fuck you nice and deep, little girl," he said with his usual devious grin.

He left me briefly, only to urge me to turn myself over, plant my feet on the ground. I did so, and tensed myself for something great and mighty to follow.

Ty's need, my need, it didn't let him delay for too long, his cock finding my pussy lips again swiftly. With our new position, he thrust himself in deep and it was such a sudden and delightful spike of pleasure that washed over me. I wasn't there yet, no, but I was close – damn close.

Daddy wasted no time setting his pace. He slammed into me with such a wonderful rhythm, making me moan through the smile on my face with his dedicated and relentless pace.

Then he massaged my ass, still sore from the vicious yet delightful spanking he had given me only moments before, adding another level to the array of sensory delights he was giving me.

The main attraction, though, was still his cock inside me, pounding me, its head inching deeper inside me without every penetration. He had pulled out at the last moment last time, but there would be one of that this round. Like a piston, he was making me shake with delight through a combination of orgasmic wonder and anticipation of what was still to come.

I was his. It was absolutely clear of that, I was his little girl and as long as he kept fucking me like this, I would be perfectly happy with that.

Louder moans, stronger energy building inside me, I wasn't going to last much longer before orgasm took me.

I welcomed it. Stronger than ever before, the bliss shuddered through me as I screamed out for "Daddy!". My hands were tearing the thousand dollar sheets off the bed as I arched backward in utter bliss from all the pleasure that Daddy's cock had visited onto me.

As I bent back, he was there to meet me, muffling my ecstatic screams with another kiss. So close to him, I could hear him groan. "You're too fucking tight for me," he murmured. "I'm marking you as mine forever with this – making you mine, my little girl, the mother of my children. The woman who will be my everything. Beg for it."

I was barely coherent, still moaning loudly.

"Tell me what you want from Daddy."

He was going to hold himself until I begged, the bastard. He had me right where he wanted me, and I had to submit. "Fill me up, Daddy. Please. I want your baby."

My body's muscles were spasming with need and desire all shuddering through me again and again. Even then though, I could feel my pussy wrapping around him, urging him even deeper inside, urging him to claim far more than my virginity, to claim my body, and make me swell with his child.

His body more than accepted my body's invitation. I could feel his cock shudder and spasm, and begin to erupt inside me. Pulsing, I wondered what was coming.

Even greater bliss, that's what.

An eruption of seed inside me, a strange yet absolutely pleasant sensation of being filled up, as if there was an emptiness inside of me that I never even knew was there. There was so much of it too, it felt like I was overflowing.

We stayed entwined with one another for a short while, sharing a kiss ever so often as his cock finally faded in strength. Slowly, he withdrew himself, some of his seed escaping down my thigh. He used a finger to pick it back up and press it back inside me, giving it a second chance to get the job done, and make sure Daddy's words came true.

I was nearly useless, exhausted from everything he did, ready to drift off to sleep.

Ty used his strength to pick me up, take me into his arms, and bring me into the bed proper. He laid down with me, letting my head rest on a pillow, but keeping me in his embrace. All throughout, he stroked me tenderly again and again. "Rest, little girl."

I obeyed, happily.

———— ∾ ————

M y own room, it was decorated in a light pink, wall to wall. It wasn't my choice, but I wasn't going to complain. I walked in, tenderly, my belly swelling with child now and I wasn't going to risk the product of my love for anything.

There was a slim, velvet box sitting on the belly of one of my newest gigantic teddies.

Everything had been smoothed over by Ty. Spending money was nothing to him if it meant making me happy, and when my father got the check, he was suddenly a lot more supportive of my relationship when he realized just how generous he could be.

The generosity to him, though, was a one time thing. The generosity to me? Was never ending.

Every day was a new gesture of love, be it things or something else, a constant reminder that he was always thinking of me.

I picked up the velvet box, opened it up. There was a diamond necklace within. I slid it out, found a mirror, and began to slip it on. It fit perfectly, of course. Everything always did, everything was perfectly tailored to me.

The necklace was studded, and it felt incredibly close to my neck, almost like a collar. I watched my grin curl, realizing that perhaps that was his intent, just another way of claiming me as his own.

As I admired my newest gift, he appeared behind me, and I almost jumped in fright.

"I can't believe how sexy that belly you have makes you," he said, as he wrapped his arms around me. "I'm sorry, but I have to have you now, little girl."

He spun me around and laid a deep, powerful kiss on me. It was enough to make me ache with need for him too. Daddy pushed me to one of the bigger teddies, and tore down my dress with his might. It was typical for him, a replacement was just another beautiful gift that he could give me.

Kisses raining down my bare body, a massage to my growing stomach. He was going to make love to me right here, a burning passion of his I didn't think would ever be quenched. He was going to make a mess of the teddie that we were on, but he knew steam cleaners that wouldn't ask too many questions.

"I'm going to have to keep you like this as much as possible, my Kitty. You're mine,"

As he ravished my body in every which way, fingers in my panties, kissing on my lips, and made me yearn for what was to come, all I could do was simply smile.

Ty Warren was a man I would gladly call Daddy for as long as he would let me.

Sugar Daddy Student

Book Themes: age gap, virgin, breeding, sugar daddy, millionaire

Word Count: 8330

The lights are dimmed down low, except for the spinning array of sparkly lights from the strobe machine.

Scattered orbs of colored light dance across the walls and dusty furniture pushed off to the sides of the room. Shadows of distorted dimensions grow and writhe as people come and go from the improvised dance floor.

The pulsating glow matches up with the driving bass beat of the music playing.

I can feel the musty old wooden floor of the fraternity house thrumming with vibrations under my feet.

The beat pulses up through the pointy spire of my stiletto heels. I feel it in every white cord and buckle of my white strappy heels, all the way up my calf.

The music is so loud, so intense, it's almost like a second heartbeat thumping next to my own. I love this song. It's a remix with a great rhythm for dancing, and that's primarily what I came here to do tonight: dance, drink, and look hot.

This music is the soundtrack to my life, and the frat house makes a perfect setting for another episode of my own personal soap opera.

I'm surrounded on all sides by my friends, who would form the cast of my life as a TV show. We make a pretty gorgeous picture, the five of us all dancing close together on the crowded dance floor.

I have my hands up in the air, one open with fingers waving, the other gripping a drippy red plastic cup of watery party beer. I feel a bead of sweat roll a ticklish straight line down my back. I feel dewy and hot all over, as the combined body heat of the dancers keeps the temperature up.

Exhilaration pumps through my veins. My body is coursing with endorphins from dancing, laughing, and drinking. I'm three beers deep on an empty stomach and it's got to be pushing two in the morning, but I've never felt so alive. I shimmy my shoulders and roll my hips, swaying side to side as my feet move to the beat.

I let the magic of the moment wash over me, rinsing away any self-consciousness. I have no reason to be nervous. I know how good I look right now, with my curvaceous, petite frame undulating to the music.

I'm wearing a slick, form-fitting satin dress in a bright shade of bubblegum pink. It shows off my deep cleavage and pushes together my ample, soft breasts so they look even more spectacular.

The hem falls barely to the middle of my thigh, which makes it easy to entice the boys with a flash of my long, shapely legs or, if he's lucky, a glimpse of my lacy black thong underneath.

A delicate gold necklace encircles my graceful, slender neck and draws attention to my collarbone and shoulders. I toss my long, wavy brown hair over my shoulder with a carefree giggle. I cast my gaze out across the room, fluttering my long lashes and flashing my catlike hazel eyes at some of the cuter-looking guys skulking around the walls.

From the kitchen I can hear the occasional shout or cheer out of the people playing beer pong. Tucked away in the dark corners of the room or strewn across the furniture are pairs of tipsy lovers. People are entwined, fully focused on each other, too hazy-headed to care what's going on around them.

Whether they've been dating forever or just met tonight, the couples are heating up. Chatting evolves into holding hands which transforms into kissing which morphs into making out passionately on a stained futon in the middle of a party.

I must have done the same thing countless times, although I never let it get too far. Some guys come here to get wild and play beer pong, just get up to mischief with their buddies.

But others arrive with the sole purpose of watching the hot girls and trying to hook one of us to take home. I didn't come here tonight to find a mate; I learned long ago that this environment is more of a free-for-all than a potential meet-cute. At least I can enjoy the thrill of dancing sexy with my little group.

In front of me is my best friend and roommate, Paisley, who's wearing a similar outfit in black. We like to coordinate when we go out sometimes, just for added cuteness.

We're both fashion students, so it's in our blood. The other girls in the group I don't know as well. In fact, we pretty much only hang out in situations like this: hazy, boozy, and loud.

We don't get a lot of time to actually chat or get to know each other, but that's okay. We don't have to be confidantes; we can just be dance partners.

My friends and I are in the very center of the big, open-plan downstairs living space of the fraternity house. We are the crux of the party. We provide the pretty faces, nubile bodies, and enthusiastic woo-hoos that keep the shindig rolling high and hot. My friends and I are like a pretty centerpiece.

We draw the eye, we set the scene, but you're not supposed to touch us.

However, we'll make you really, really want to.

There's a feeling of sensual chaos in the air. Like anything could happen at any moment, all doors are open. People kissing and rutting against each other, fully clothed and unashamed.

The DJ is playing only the sexiest, hottest beats. I run my fingers back through my soft brown hair and shake it out as my body sways and spins under the whirling strobe lights.

I can sense the many sets of eyes locked on me from around the room.

Guys are watching my every move, their eyes taking greedy notice of the way my hair swishes down my back and my tits jiggle deliciously when I dance. I raise my arms over my head and turn in a slow, swinging circle to show off my perky, round ass.

I look good enough to eat in my pink satin dress, and I love knowing that these guys get off on watching me. I can feel their longing, how they pine for me from a distance.

They imagine how they would touch me, how they would dance up behind me and drape their arms around me, marking me as 'taken.' They fantasize about the smooth, filthy words they could whisper in my ear and how I would blush or giggle in response.

These guys, my fellow college kids and classmates, would leap at the chance to be with me, even for one night. But that's just part of the fun-- delaying gratification. I love to be a little tease. I love to keep them coming back for more, *craving* for more.

It's easy to get swept up in the hedonistic flair of the evening. We're college kids who need to blow off steam, forget about our classes and GPAs and exams. We need to cut loose, let our hair down, and dance the night away.

We showed up around midnight, and my girls and I have been working the room ever since. I look around at my beautiful, happy friends and can't help but grin. I bat my eyes at a cute boy leaning against the wall with a flask in his hand.

He's instantly intrigued, his eyes panning up and down my body with desire. I tempt him with a swish of my hips and hold his attention by smoothing my hands down over my full breasts spilling out of my dress. My nipples poke against the slinky fabric and creates delicious friction. I lick my lips and give my audience a little wink.

To amp up the sex appeal, I move up closer behind Paisley and begin to grind against her. She looks over her shoulder at me with a smirk and plays along, the two of us swaying in sensual tandem.

I take her hands in mine from behind and lift them up over our heads. I play with her hair, tossing it around as we dance together. Another of our friends catches on and comes up behind me to join in. The guys are all watching us slack-jawed and half-stiff as we tease them from the dance floor.

They can't look away-- a group of beautiful girls dancing provocatively together? It's almost too good to be true. It's soft-core porn for our pervy audience, and we know it. Guys my own age are so easy to please. Too easy, to be honest. All I have to do is shake my ass and they're putty in my hands.

I long for a man with more substance. With panache. A guy who can take control, who can make me feel like a woman and a naughty little girl at the same time. But I won't find him here.

None of these guys are mature or interesting enough to hold my attention for long. They're fun for a little tease, a little ego boost, but nothing more. My friends are always going home with hot guys from parties, but I always go home alone, no matter how many dudes ask me out.

I'm a virgin, and I guess you could say I'm a little bit picky. When I find the right guy, I'll know it. But until then, I might as well go home alone. Like tonight, for example. Once the music starts to slow down, the hype wears out, and exhausted party-goers start to file out, it's time to leave.

I give Paisley and the girls a big hug and a promise to text them in the morning, and then I slip out into the cool autumn night. Rubbing my arms to keep warm, I hurry across campus back to the dormitories.

Maybe I should be more careful walking alone at night, but until I find the perfect prince to escort me home, I'll take the risk. I have enough liquid courage in my body to carry me across campus tonight anyway.

I'm still feeling tipsy and dizzy-happy when I reach my dorm room. I rush through taking off my clothes and makeup, getting ready for bed, and then I crawl under the crisp sheets and turn off the light. As I drift off to sleep, my thoughts of the evening spill over into my dreams.

I find myself dancing just like before, only this time there's nobody else around. I'm spinning and swaying alone on the dance floor in the middle of the frat house in my pink satin dress. At least, I think I'm alone. But suddenly, there's someone standing in the corner of the room.

But instead of a run-of-the-mill cute frat dude, there's a ruggedly handsome man with strong hands and hypnotic eyes.

He watches me dance with a look of pure possession. Like he's a wolf eyeing up a dainty mouse for dinner, he knows I already belong to him. He beckons to me with a curl of his finger. I am helpless against his command, not that I would want to fight it. I dance closer and closer to him.

Every spin brings me a few inches nearer to the man. He's tall, he's strong, and he's ready to take me on. Everything I am. All of my flaws and all of my goodness.

My heart is pounding. Every inch of my body is burning with desire. Finally, I'm close enough for him to reach out and touch me. The moment his fingertips collide with my bare skin, I feel like I'm flying. It's pure ecstasy. He pulls me in close and leans down to kiss me. His lips are so close I can almost taste him.

BEEP. BEEP. BEEP.

My eyes flutter open to stare up at the ceiling in my dorm room. The threads of my steamy dream feather away into nothing as reality sets in. My ears are bombarded with the egregious beep of my alarm clock. I hoist myself onto my side and flail my arm out to whack the off button. Ah, blessed silence. I rub my eyes and look at the clock blearily.

My heart skips a beat.

"No," I murmur. "Oh no. Not again."

It's nine o'clock. Which means I slept through my eight o'clock alarm, and it's been going off for an hour. So clearly I did *not* get up and go to my eight-thirty algebra class. That's another absence. Another strike against me, in a time when I'm supposed to be *improving* my academic standing. I grab my phone and wince at the screen. More bad news: multiple missed calls from my parents.

"Uh-oh," I groan.

On top of everything, my head is pounding. I'm hungover, dehydrated, and exhausted, but I need to take care of business. I drag myself into a sitting position and call my mom back. It rings a few times while I chug from the water bottle on my nightstand, and then my mom picks up. I can tell from the very first syllable that she is not pleased.

"Taylor Marie Snow, where in the world have you been?" she greets me.

"Do you mean, like, this morning? Or just in general?" I ask.

"Both," says my father, chiming in over her shoulder as he does.

"Uh, well, this morning I was here, in my dorm, asleep," I explain. "As for--"

"Don't you have a class right now?" Mom interjects.

I grimace. Here we go. "Yeah. I overslept," I answer meekly.

"Unbelievable," she hisses. "Taylor, we were calling to talk to you about this letter we got from the college. Something about you being on academic probation?"

I wince so hard I might just curl in on myself.

"Shit. I mean, damn it. Sorry," I sigh. "I was hoping I could get my grades back up before you all had to know about that."

"And you think sleeping through your math class is the way to do it?" Dad cuts in.

"Well, I didn't do it on purpose," I reply.

"But I bet you didn't go to bed at a reasonable hour," says Mom.

True.

"Probably because you were partying with your friends," says Dad.

Also true.

"Taylor, we sent you to college to get a degree, not to waste time," Mom lectures. "And money. Our money."

"I'm sorry. I'll try harder," I assert.

"You've already had lots of chances to do that," Dad says. "But you don't seem to take your education very seriously."

Again, true, but I definitely won't say that.

Mom concludes, "If you want to party your way through life, you're going to have to find somebody else to pay for it."

My stomach drops.

"Hold on. What?" I splutter.

"That's right," Dad says. "We're sorry, sweetheart, but until you start showing us some real improvement, you're on your own."

"But what about my credit card?" I ask. "And my phone bill? What about tuition?"

"Taylor, if you don't go to class, why would we pay tuition?" Mom points out gently.

I'm stunned. "I can't believe this," I mutter.

"It's for your own good," Dad insists.

"You'll have to stand on your own two feet," adds Mom.

"You'll figure it out, honey," says Dad.

Mom says, "We have to go. Call us after you've had a good think about this."

Click. The phone drops from my hand as I stare into space. My head aches like crazy. My stomach is churning. I feel betrayed. Where the hell am I going to get the money for food? For classes? How can I get a degree if I can't pay my tuition? I wrack my brain for solutions. I could get a job, I suppose. I told myself I was going to focus on school instead, but I couldn't get that right either. It's just that... I don't really like school. I don't like being on my own. I want someone to take care of me, make sure I'm safe and loved. I want to be somebody's true love.

But right now, I'll settle for being somebody's employee.

I have never been job-hunting before, but I remember some professor mentioning that there's a bulletin board in the commons with local job listings pinned. So I hoist my hungover ass out of bed, get dressed, and make the short trek across campus to the student commons. I squint over the hundreds of listings, scanning for anything that sounds reasonable. I don't have a lot of qualifications to work with, but I do find a tiny, simple ad that draws my attention.

Wealthy gentleman in search of a housekeeper. High pay. Audition required. Text number below. Attach current photo with your message. Thank you - CW.

The word 'audition' seems odd for a housekeeping job. Wouldn't it be an interview? And what does he need a photo for? But on the other hand, the words 'high pay' intrigue me. I may not be good at math, but I know how to clean. I've been doing household chores since I was a kid. Should be easy money. At this point, I'm in no position to turn down an opportunity.

So I take the leap: I text the number a short message along with a selfie from my camera roll. Within minutes, I get a response. My heart is racing as I open it.

You're perfect. Audition for me tonight at the address below. 7 PM.

"Yes!" I exclaim, doing a little fist pump as I grin down at my phone.

I did it! Now, if this isn't proof of my motivation, what is? But I won't call my parents to fill them in until I know it's a sure thing. Which, I guess, will be tonight. It does seem slightly odd that we're doing the interview-slash-audition tonight instead of tomorrow during the day, but maybe he knows I'm a student and I have class to attend. Oh, and sooner the better, right?

Either way, I return to my dorm with a spring in my step. I go to the rest of my classes, counting down the seconds until I'm free. I rush to get ready, chatting with my roommate while I get dressed for the evening. I put on a simple, professional-looking black dress and nude heels, brush my long brown hair, and put on a little shine of makeup. I book a cab and give the driver the address. I sit back and watch out the window as we roll across town.

We leave campus and the student-dense part of the city, out past the bustling streets and the suburbs. I watch the countryside fly by and admire the golden, red, and orange leaves on the tree branches. Every now and then, we pass a big, old-fashioned house. The neighborhood is somewhat rural, but expensive. The houses only get grander as we drive, until finally we pull up to the address. I step out in complete awe of the massive, beautiful old house looming over me. It's situated right on a picturesque lake, with the lovely forest stretching out around it. I can't imagine what a place like this costs. This 'wealthy gentleman' must be loaded.

I'm impressed as I stand in front of the stately front door. I give it a solid knock and wait, my heart beating a mile a minute. Soon, the door clicks open and parts to reveal a man who looks just like the man of my dreams. The literal man from my dream last night-- the one with the hypnotic eyes and the magic hands!

He smiles warmly. "You must be Taylor."

"Yes, sir," I answer. I sound breathless, because I am.

A flicker of something like lust clouds his eyes for a split second, and then he beckons me into the house. I follow him in and he locks the door behind me.

"Welcome to my home. I'm Cliff Wilcox. It's wonderful to meet you in person. I'll give you a brief tour before the audition," he offers.

"Okay, sure!" I chirp back, still stunned at how insanely hot he is.

My body is yearning to get closer to him, to break the professional boundary we haven't even fully gotten to establish yet. But I force myself to remain calm while we explore the giant house. My eyes are wide as I look around the elegant interior. Everywhere I look, there are signs of wealth. The mid-century modern sofa, the gilded lamps, the stained-glass feature in the cabinets. Every item looks to be either modern designer or stylish vintage. There's art on the walls that probably cost more than my entire tuition. Opened white French doors separate the foyer from the cozy living room. I'm so impressed by my surroundings. Yet, his home is warm and inviting despite the upper-crust furnishings. There's a crackling fireplace with beautiful photographs and paintings on the mantle above it. I see signs of actual living-- a book dogeared in a chair, a coffee mug in the sink, a stack of paperwork on the dining table. He's ridiculously rich, but he's a normal guy otherwise. I feel more and more comfortable here with him by the minute. He's just so damn gorgeous and so charming, too.

He takes his time showing me around, and then he brings me into a guest bedroom. It's simply but beautifully decorated.

"It's time to prepare for the audition process," Cliff says. "In the closet to your right, you will find your uniform on a hanger. There's an en suite bathroom through that door if you need it. I'll wait in the hall for you to get changed."

"Right," I reply.

He slips out and I immediately rush to the closet, curious to see what's inside. I expect to find some miserably uncomfortable, unflattering cleaning scrubs. To my surprise, it's actually a black lingerie set with flimsy white apron and red heels. I put on each piece of the ensemble and look in the bathroom mirror.

"Oh my god," I mumble.

This is not a typical housekeeping uniform. This is lingerie with an apron thrown in for good measure. There's something else going on here, something more to this innocent-sounding ad for a housekeeper. Why would he mention being 'wealthy' in the ad? Why did he need a photo with my text? It dawns on me.

I'm not just here to take care of his big, beautiful house. I'm here to take care of his big, beautiful cock. But I'm just a virgin! I don't know what I'm doing! I swallow hard as I walk up to open the bedroom door and show him my outfit. I'm nervous that he won't like what he sees, or that he'll be disappointed to learn how inexperienced I am.

But when the door falls open and Cliff turns around to look at me, all my fears fly out the shiny bay window. He looks me up and down voraciously and shakes his head, letting out a low whistle of awe.

"You look absolutely divine," he compliments me. "The uniform suits you."

"It's not quite what I expected, but I'm eager to work," I insist.

Cliff walks up and hands me a feather duster. "There. Dust something."

I bite my lip nervously as I start lightly dusting off the bookshelf on the wall. As I do so, I throw in a little extra-- I bend over and poke out my juicy ass while I dust. I look back at Cliff over my shoulder and the look of predation in his intense green eyes makes me feel all tingly. When he walks up behind me and grabs my waist, I nearly melt in his touch. His huge hands smooth down my waist and around to grope my ass. I playfully back up against him and he leans in, the two of us grinding on one another. I can feel his cock stiffening long and hard against my ass. Cliff's hands move up my narrow waist to my arms and around to caress my ample breasts. I moan and rut back into him to ask for more. I know it's naughty, I know it's definitely inappropriate for a boss-employee relationship, but I can't help it. I've been lusting after Cliff since the second he opened the door, and now there's nothing to hold me back.

His hands gently grip my shoulders as he spins me around to face him. I feel a rush of exhilaration when his green eyes lock on mine and a devilish smirk crosses his handsome features. Cliff snaps his fingers and points to the floor.

I drop down to my knees in front of him. My heart is pounding. My mouth salivates at the possibility of what's to come. I peer up at Cliff longingly.

"You say you're eager to work," he purrs as he slowly unzips his trousers. "I have your first assignment right here."

I gasp at the size of his cock as it bounces free of his boxers. My eyes go wide and I open my mouth wider, splaying out my tongue. Cliff strokes his massive length in front of my face, and I can hardly wait to taste him. He lets go and uses both hands to gather my long brown hair together, grabbing it like a ponytail. Or like a set of reins. The tighter he grasps, the harder he tugs, the wetter I get between my soft thighs. I lean in close, breathing in his manly scent. I run my tongue up and down the side of his cock while my hand pumps his length, letting myself get acquired to this new sensation.

Then, without any more hesitation, I pull the thick head of his cock into my warm, wet mouth. I flick my tongue along the underside and moan with pleasure at how deliciously tight he feels in my mouth. His enormous size stretches my cheeks and lay heavy on my tongue. I push down further, inch by inch, until the tip of his glorious shaft brushes at the back of my throat. It's a ticklish feeling, but not uncomfortable. In fact, as soon as Cliff starts to rock his hips and gently thrust down my throat, it's all I can do to keep from dripping my sweet honey all over his perfect wood floors.

"Touch yourself while you suck my cock, Taylor," he commands roughly.

I do as I'm told. I drop my hand between my legs and rub my achy, tingly clit through the lacy black lingerie. I moan around Cliff's thickness as I bob up and down. I'm really getting the hang of it now, loving the forceful rhythm of his cock ramming down my throat again and again. Drool drips down my chin. Come slicks up my fingers as I climax through my panties.

"Good girl," Cliff coos. "Just like that. I'm almost there."

He tightens his grip on my hair and pumps his cock harder and faster down my throat. I hollow out my cheeks, relax my jaw, and let him pound my pretty virgin mouth until his body tenses up. I feel him losing his grip. I suck him off with more gusto, eager to make him come. I'm desperate to please him, to give him whatever he wants.

"Fuck, I'm coming," he groans.

His cock spurts hot, salty seed down my throat. I gulp down every drop, licking his massive cock clean. I then look up at my new master with big, innocent eyes. I wipe my mouth and smile up at him sheepishly. He lets my hair fall around my shoulders again and takes my chin gently between his thumb and forefinger. He tilts my chin up and smiles down at me.

"That was excellent work. You're a perfect fit for this position," Cliff says.

He offers me his hand and I take it, getting to my feet.

"Really? I did good?" I ask, eyes shining.

Cliff nods. "Very good. Let's make this official. You're hired. You will report to work every day after classes. From here on out, you won't need to hire a cab. I will send a car to pick you up. You're working for me now, Taylor. Your life is about to change."

"It is?" I breathe.

"Stick by me, Miss Snow, and you will never want for anything again in your life," he assures me with a confident grin. "For this evening, I'll hire you a car for the ride home. You need to get some rest, prepare for tomorrow."

"What happens tomorrow?" I ask.

"Let's just say you'll get a taste of what a life with me has to offer," he says cryptically.

And with that, he ushers me into the guest bedroom to change back into my black dress. We say our goodbyes, Cliff sends me off with a kiss on the cheek, and the hired car takes me back to campus. By the time I fall into bed, I'm dead-tired. I drop off into a dream, where I luckily get to see Cliff again. This time, we get a little bit closer. A little steamier.

Until I wake up the next morning for class. But knowing that I have alone time with Cliff to look forward to makes the day feel so much brighter. I skip off to class humming and smiling. I feel on top of the world when I walk into class and sit down next to Paisley. We chat a little while we wait for the professor to show up. I tell her about the housekeeper ad, about meeting Cliff--although I spare some of the filthier details. I half-expect her to disapprove or call me crazy, but instead, Paisley is super supportive.

"Holy shit, girl," she whispers. "You're not a housekeeper. You're a sugar baby."

"Wait. What? Is that's going on?" I gasp.

She laughs. "Of course, silly! He doesn't want you to clean, he wants you to be his girlfriend. Treat him like a king. And in return, he'll shower you in gifts and money."

"How do you know all this?" I ask.

Paisley smirks. "Let's just say I've dabbled a little in my time. But your situation is different. It sounds like you really like this guy."

"I do," I admit. "He's almost old enough to be my dad, but he's so sexy."

"Not to mention the money," she says with a wink.

"So you approve? You think it's a good idea?" I implore.

"Hell yeah, girl. Your folks cut you off, you need cash, and this sexy older man wants to give it to you. Sounds like a win all around!" Paisley gushes.

Between her excitement for me and my own excitement for the evening to come, I stare at the clock throughout class. Watching the seconds tick down to the moment of truth. Finally, class lets out for the day. I check my phone to find a text message from Cliff. My heart is pounding as I open it. He's here, waiting for me!

I rush to the parking lot and light up like a firework when I see Cliff behind the wheel of an absolutely gorgeous black Aston Martin. He steps out to usher me into the passenger seat, a gentleman as always.

"Hey there, gorgeous," he greets me.

"Hi!" I reply excitedly.

He slides behind the wheel. I look over at him in his designer shades and sleek navy blue casual suit, drinking him in with hungry eyes. Every one of my senses is on fire just being close to him. He's dressed impeccably, and he smells like the finest bourbon mixed with the fresh scent of a dense forest in rain. I stare in amazement. Watching his strong, veiny hands on the leather steering wheel. Seeing the light glint off his shiny luxury wristwatch. Hearing the purr of the Aston Martin's engine as it rolls us into the center of the city.

"So, am I cleaning today?" I ask innocently.

Cliff smiles over at me. "Not quite. When was the last time you bought yourself something nice, Taylor?" he asks.

I blush. "Well, the other day I bought a fancy frappucino with whipped cream."

"Consider today an upgrade to that," he says smoothly.

We pull to a stop on a street famous for its high-priced designer shops and boutiques. The kind of stores I have no business visiting, even before my parents cut me off. I would normally feel out of place in a designer boutique-- I know they know I can't afford anything. But with Cliff, it's a totally different experience. He puts his arm around my shoulders and guides me with confidence. He has the money to be here, and the swagger to let everyone know it. He has a commanding presence.

People notice him and respect him on sight. Being with Cliff makes me feel invincible. We walk into one high-end shop after another, and every time, we're flocked by sales associates hanging on Cliff's every word. Women fawn over him. Men respect him. Cliff is the centerpoint of every room he walks into, but even more remarkably, I seem to be the centerpoint for him.

Cliff dotes on me, follows me around the shops, encourages me to try on obscenely pricey, luxurious clothes. He hand-selects jewelry for me. He makes sure I am happy, hydrated, and having fun the whole time. The sales associates bring us trays of champagne and hors d'oeuvres while I flounce around in luscious gowns, killer shoes, and elegant lingerie. We spend hours shopping and racking up a bill that makes my eyes water, but Cliff doesn't bat an eye. This is pocket change for him, just another day of luxury. He pays me so much attention, our conversations flowing like a waterfall. I'm wildly attracted to this slick, generous, charming master of a man. He makes me feel so secure and adored, and I can't deny my intense desire to be alone with him again. I'm having so much fun, but I can think of even more enjoyable activities to do together.

Apparently, Cliff is on the same page. Because at the final boutique, while I'm trying on clothes, I'm surprised to see my handsome hulk of man slip into the dressing room with me. He places a finger over my lips to quiet me as he pins me back against the wall. I'm fully naked, and Cliff reaches down to cup my mound with one large, strong hand. His thumb finds my clit and begins to gently circle it. He presses his lips to mine as a sigh escapes my mouth. I rock against his hand, feeling my body bloom for him. His lips trail down my jaw, my ticklish neck, to my chest. Cliff flicks his tongue over one of my perky pink nipples and I have to bite my lip to keep from moaning. He suckles my nipple and tweaks it gently between his teeth while his thumb rubs circular, tight strokes on my sensitive clit. My legs start to shake.

Cliff stands up straight to whisper roughly in my ear, "Feels good, baby?"

"Mhmm," I mumble.

Keeping his thumb on my clit, he slides one long finger inside my tight, virginal cunny. He has to use his free hand to cover my mouth as I whimper and sigh. His intense green eyes lock with mine as he fingers me upright in the dressing room. His finger sliding in and out of my pussy feels so divine, and the rhythmic strokes on my clit bring me closer and closer to coming.

I can still hear the muffled sounds of the boutique beyond the velvet curtain-- the music playing, the click of stilettos on hardwood, the cheery murmur of conversation. We're hidden, but only by a curtain. We're not supposed to be in here together, and we're definitely not supposed to be doing this. But instead of being scary, I'm turned on by the risk of getting caught. It adds an edge of extra sinfulness to the delicious pleasure burning through my body.

"Come for me, princess," Cliff commands in a soft whisper.

He immediately swallows my moan in a kiss as my cunny gushes sweet, slick juices all down his hand and wrist. My thighs tremble violently through the orgasm and Cliff keeps me steady. He pulls out his fingers and sucks my honey off just as we both hear the sales associate approaching in her clicky heels.

"Miss Snow, can I be of assistance?" she asks, barely a few feet from the velvet curtain separating us from her.

"Nope! I'm good. Super good here," I answer quickly.

"Yes, ma'am," she says, and clicks away.

I release a deep breath and Cliff chuckles. He kisses me on the cheek, pats me on my bare ass, and whispers, "Get dressed. It's time to go home."

Still dripping wet and tingly all over from my sneaky climax, I put on my own cutesy pink dress, white socks, and wedge heels. We make our final enormous purchase of the day, and we head back to the car, laden with shopping bags. Cliff somehow manages to hold everything and my hand at the same time without looking insane. I don't know how does it, but he possesses this infinite coolness. He's always in command, even without trying. It's addictive and exhilarating to be around him, especially since all of his charms are focused on me.

We chat as we ride back to his place, and when we get there

we go into the kitchen to start cooking dinner together. We sip expensive vintage wine, listen to music, and sing and dance around the place together. Cliff is a masterful dancer, and I follow his lead perfectly. Our bodies come together like interlocking pieces, and our shared connection shows in our spins and twirls and dips. We sit down for a delicious dinner in his formal dining room.

Nearing the end of the meal, I gush, "I feel so spoiled."

"Good. You deserve to be spoiled," Cliff asserts. "Today was just a taste of what's to come, Taylor. I can give you anything. Everything."

"My tuition?" I venture quietly.

He nods. "Tuition, books, accommodations, food, bills, clothes, nice things-- whatever you want. I can make it happen. I made my fortune in real estate a decade ago. I've been building on that empire ever since. These days, I have plenty of time and money to spend however I want. And what I want, princess, is you," Cliff concludes.

"How did I get so lucky?" I wonder aloud.

"You answered the ad," he chuckles, taking a sip of wine. "You're exactly what I hoped for. Better, even. Taylor, I never expected to feel quite so strongly as I do."

"I feel the same," I agree enthusiastically. "Ever since we first met."

"I intended to take things slowly," he says. "But when you showed up, I knew that plan would go out the window. I can't resist you, Taylor. I can't deny you anything."

"You can have whatever you want. You can take me," I insist. "Anytime, anywhere."

His green eyes seem to almost glow with lust. His fist tightens on the table. I see his jaw twitch. I slowly stand up and walk over to him, slipping my dress straps off my shoulders. Cliff watches me approach with pure predatory desire. I tease him with a flash of my panties under my dress, then lick my lips at him. He reaches out for me with his strong arms, pulling me into his lap. I grind my ass against his bulging crotch and let out a moan when I feel his hard, long cock stiffening underneath me. Cliff holds my hips while I sway and rock against him. The friction makes us both feverish for more.

He spins me around and stands up in a swift movement. He wraps his arms around me and leans in for a deep, powerful kiss. My knees buckle underneath me. My heart explodes like a spray of fireworks. I feel that soul-level rush of warmth and longing for Cliff, like I'm one half calling out for my other half. He cups my face in his hands and strokes my hair. When we finally break apart, his green eyes are bright. Full of meaning without words.

I say what we're both thinking.

"I'm ready," I whisper. "I'm a virgin, Cliff, and I don't want to be one anymore."

"I'll be gentle with you," he promises.

I give him a naughty smile. "You don't have to."

With that, Cliff scoops me into his arms and carries me off to the bedroom. As soon as he sets me down, we start stripping off our clothes. I slip off my pink dress, kick off my shoes and socks, unclasp my bra, and tug down my panties. Cliff gets naked and walks me back to the luxurious king-sized bed. He lays me back on the silky sheets and climbs on top of me, his lips and hands exploring every curve and sensitive spot of my body. I writhe and whimper with pleasure under his touch. He kisses my neck and sucks deep, delicious bruises there I can't wait to admire in the mirror later. His hands grope my tits, my plump ass, my cinched waist. He dips to nip and suck my breasts. His tongue teases my nipples until they're rosy and swollen. Every ticklish spiral of pleasure shoots straight down between my legs.

When Cliff moves down to devour my pussy with his mouth, I cry out with delight.

"I've never felt this before," I gasp.

His tongue swivels around my clit, then slides up and down my dewy folds. He dips to lunge his tongue inside my tight little hole, then licks and suckles his way back up to my clit. I arch my back and rub against his face while he laps up my slick juices. My hands grasp the bedsheets tightly on either side. The pressure inside of me builds up fast, and before long, I'm gushing honey all over Cliff's masterful tongue. He groans his approval and licks up every drop while my cunny clenches and convulses with orgasm.

"Ohh my god," I pant. "I need you, Cliff. I need you inside me."

"That's right, baby," he growls, his hand stroking his cock long and slow as he positions the swollen head at my slick hole. He rubs it in a teasing circle that drives me crazy with desire. I arch against him, begging for more.

"Please, Cliff," I whimper.

"You want your sugar daddy to pound that pretty little virgin pussy?" he purrs.

I nod vigorously. "Yes, oh yes!" I gasp.

"I'm going to take your virginity. I'll make you a woman tonight, Taylor," Cliff promises.

"Please. I need it," I beg.

"Yes, baby. Yes, you do," he grunts as he pushes the thick head of his cock inside of me.

I mewl and pant with the combination of pain and pleasure shooting through my body. Cliff holds me close and kisses me softly while he pushes into me. His enormous cock stretches the tight walls of my cunny, spearing me open inch by inch. I clench around him and wrap my legs around his waist, my eyes locking with his. Neither of us are playing games-- we know what we want, and we're eager to get it.

"Fuck, you're so tight," Cliff groans. "Feels so fucking good."

"Nnngh, yes," I hiss.

He rocks back and forth slightly, and every thrust pushes his glorious shaft deeper within me. My pussy is so wet and achy with need. Every cell in my body is ringing, dangling over the edge. Every touch, every twinge of delicious pain gets me high. Cliff grabs my wrists in one hand and pins them over my head. His other hand grips my thigh as he slides in and out of my cuny harder and faster. He pounds into me so deep I can feel him striking through my hymen. There's a flash of searing pain, and then it subsides into a deep, dull ache that only makes the pleasure more intense.

"Good girl," Cliff fawns over me. "So fucking good for me."

"Your cock feels so good inside me," I moan.

"This pussy is mine. This womb is mine," he growls.

"Oh yes. All yours. Every inch of me belongs to you, sir," I agree.

"I'm going to pump you up with my come, Taylor. Can you take it?" he grunts.

"Yes! Fill me up! Put a baby inside this virgin pussy," I cry out.

Cliff's hips snap back and forth faster now as he hammers my cunny with his thick, hard cock. The head strikes again and again at my g-spot, a place I never knew really existed. But I know without a doubt what that the incredible, earthy pleasure I feel is. Cliff knows exactly the right angle to hit deep and true. I gaze into those beautiful green eyes while he fucks me hard. I lift my pelvis as much as I can to meet his every powerful thrust. The friction of his pelvis and soft, curly hair against my tingly clit feels so damn good. I feel the ache of my arms and wrists where he has me pinned, and it adds to the concoction of pleasure. And then there's the love, true love, pooling in those green eyes. He fucks me like he means it, like he's been waiting his whole life for this moment. And maybe we both have. I never found a man who made me feel this way, and I can tell I've changed his life, too.

Our bodies crash together in perfect but wild tandem, as we both spiral out of control. Lust builds higher, restraint ebbs away to nothing. Before long, we are rutting like wild animals in heat. The headboard bangs rowdily against the wall. The mattress shakes. Every thrust makes a resounding smack of his heavy balls swinging against my juicy ass cheeks, added to the slick squelch of my dripping cunny. I'm so wet there's a puddle forming underneath me in the sheets. We're so close now. Hanging on by a thread and so wrapped up in each other, we can no longer tell where he ends and I begin. We're interlocked now and forever.

"Almost there, baby," Cliff grunts.

"Me too," I breathe. "Fuck me harder."

With a growl of desire, Cliff rears back and shoves inside of me. His cock slams into my g-spot over and over again as he pounds my drenched pussy. I moan with every stroke, whimpering his name and incoherently begging for more. He thrusts harder and faster as he loses all self-control. Cliff uses my pussy like the fuck toy it is. He lets go of my wrists and uses both hands to grip my hips. He holds me in place while he fucks me harder than before.

"I'm coming!" I squeak out as another orgasm rushes over me.

That's all it takes to send Cliff over the edge. He lets out a deep bellow of pleasure, and I feel him tense up. His cock twitches inside of me, pumping long spurts of precious seed deep inside my fertile, virginal womb. He ekes out every drop, with the help of my cunny clenching around him. I squeeze him dry before I unwrap my legs and let him go. He withdraws and lays beside me, holding me in his powerful arms. We sigh and whisper sweet nothing words to each other as we come down. He strokes my hair, I listen to his steady heartbeat.

"I hope you realize you're never getting rid of me now," I giggle.

Cliff kisses my hair. "I wouldn't dream of letting you go, Taylor. I wasn't joking when I said you belong to me."

"I know. And I love it. I want to be yours, now and always," I gush. "You're everything I want, Cliff. I've been so aimless and lost all this time. School wasn't enough for me. The guys my own age weren't enough for me. But you? You tick every single box I had and then some."

"You're the most beautiful, charming, loveable woman I've ever met. I mean to spend every day from here onward doing everything in my power to keep you so, so happy," he pledges. "You deserve the world, and I intend to give it to you."

"I'm falling for you, Cliff," I confess, my cheeks flushed.

He smiles and kisses me softly. "I'm falling, too. But we'll catch each other."

I grin against his lips. "Always."

From that night, the two of us are inseparable. Even though he dutifully pays my tuition and bills (and then some) for the rest of the school year, it doesn't take long for me to figure out that college just isn't for me.

I would rather spend my precious time traveling, shopping, cooking, dancing, laughing, singing-- anything with Cliff.

He's the most fascinating and sexy man I've ever known. At first, my parents are skeptical of my choice to drop out and be with Cliff. But after one elaborate, fancy dinner at Cliff's house, my parents immediately fell for him, too.

He's impossible to resist, and my parents love knowing I'm well taken care of. Especially now that I'm pregnant! I'm due in the summer, and I can't wait to build my family with the man of my dreams.

From sugar daddy to real daddy, I'm excited to see where our path of love together takes us.

Being His Gymnast

Book Themes: age gap romance, forbidden romance, virgin, breeding
Word Count: 7907

The bright white lights above me cast an eerie shaft of illumination across the stage.

I feel swept up in the magic of the theater, the drama of the great scarlet curtains drawn back with golden tassels.

The glossy but well-worn wooden planks of the stage creak ever so softly beneath me with every soft step.

Every mottled whorl of the wood is a new texture on the sensitive bottoms of my feet, barely softened by my flexible acro shoes that feel more like socks.

The ceilings overhead are vaulted to such a lofty height that it's more of a sky than a ceiling. I can hardly make out the scarlet and gold damask design, like I'm trying to see the surface of the sun. There's a luxurious, opulent art deco design to the theater which lends a vintage touch, and the expert mood lighting makes for an ethereal ambience.

The audience is broken up into three levels, including VIP seats that flank the vast walls.

The seats seem to stretch out endlessly in each direction from the stage, but the whole audience is cast in dark shadow.

I blink out into the darkness, my eyes partly blinded by the white glow from above. It's chilly in the theater, and if I were an audience member I would need a cozy coat to stay comfortable. But here on the stage, the lights keep me warm, even hot.

Teeny beads of sweat gather at my temples as I peer out into the vast blankness of the crowd.

My heart is thumping so hard in my chest that it aches a little, but the adrenaline pumping through my veins makes me feel more alive than ever before.

I have goosebumps covering my arms and legs, but I'm lit with a glow from above and within.

The lights shimmer across my heavily-sequined ensemble. It's a form-fitted silvery crop top and matching tight athletic shorts paired with a ton of body glitter.

The outfit is over-the-top, as most of my costumes are, but it does a good job of showing off my petite, curvy body.

I can almost feel the eyes of the crowd honing in on my perky, round breasts, my taut ass, my long, elegant legs. They love to see my long lashes flutter and my full lips pout as I emote onstage and play perfectly whatever role I'm cast.

My long, dark curls are bound in a high ponytail, the locks sweeping around my shoulders. I tilt my sweet, cherubic face up to the light and close my eyes. I suck in a low, slow breath and find my center.

I sense the rows of interested eyes staring at me, waiting for my first move. People are always eager to see me succeed-- or fail.

But I rarely fail. I'm a professional, I'm a devotee, I was made for this stage. The endorphins are flowing, my body is tingling from head to toe with anticipation and barely-restrained energy.

My feet are itching to dance across the stage.

My body is ready to bend and sway and enchant the crowd

with my grace. I am laser-focused on the task at hand. I am intensely aware of every little cough, sigh, or murmur from the crowd in the initial silence.

I listen for the telltale swell of the music that cues me into motion like a magic spell enchanting my body. When the hail of violins and cellos harkens me out, I raise my arms above my head slowly in preparation.

Passion and peace arise in equal measures inside of me as I begin to move across the stage. My feet make quick work of the space, running, tiptoeing, leaping, and twirling in perfect rhythm with the dramatic music.

I arch my back and twist myself around. I curl in tight like a rosebud and arch outward like I'm blooming under a loving sun.

All the while, I feel the delicious thrill of being watched. I am more than an entertainer, I am a spectacle to be desired. Eyes locked on the swerve of my body, the shape of my movements, the passion in my every nimble step.

I know it's more than art that keeps their gaze drawn to me. Admiration borders close to lust, and lust dances right along the line of obsession.

I've had countless admirers over the years, even though I'm only nineteen. Men see the way I move my body and they can't help but wonder what else I can do. If I can arch my back and do a split onstage, they can only fathom what my body is capable of in the bedroom.

I am the silent star of many a wild fantasy that will never come true, and even though it can be intimidating to know that, I can't deny how it makes me feel. I love being wanted.

I love being coveted.

Even the one-way nature of the dance turns me on. No matter how deeply I entice my audience, no matter how advanced their fantasies around me become, it will never come to fruition.

They lust after me endlessly and there's nothing I can do to stop them-- not that I want to. I draw energy from their lust. I use it to fuel every backbend and leaping twist.

But sometimes... I do wish I could reach out across the vast expanse between the stage and the crowd and make contact.

As I land a particularly twisty backflip, I glance out into the audience. To my surprise, there's a pillar of light streaked through the darkness now, illuminating one seat in the very center of the theater. I can make out the shape of a tall, broad-shouldered man sitting there in an elegant suit.

He has dark hair, streaked with a dignified peal of silver and swept back from his handsome face. He has a strong jaw and high cheekbones, and eyes that could entrance me right back. He emanates strength.

He radiates charisma. I find myself desperate to know everything about him.

I'm drawn to him like a moth to a dancing flame, even though I'm the one dancing.

In fact, I feel as though I'm just dancing for him. This mysterious, handsome stranger with the hypnotic eyes might as well be the only person in the audience. I turn all of my focus to my mystery admirer. I feel his eyes on my breasts, my waist, my taut little ass.

He's drinking me in like a tall glass of cool water. I lick my lips and run my hands down my body-- slowly. I make sure to luxuriate over every curve and swell of my petite frame. I feel the sharp edges of sequins under my fingertips and the heat growing between my thighs.

A glistening drop of sweat rolls down my back as I arch forward. I stretch my arms to the floor and lift off, balancing myself on my two hands with my legs in the air.

Using every stitch of self-discipline in my muscles, I gracefully drop my legs forward in a slow flip. I reach up and easily pull my hair loose from its tie as I stand up straight.

I toss my hair so that it shakes out full and wavy to frame my pretty face. I sway my hips and sweep my arms around myself. My hands caress my breasts.

I feel their fullness in my palms, roll my perky nipples between my fingers until I feel the tingle deep inside me. Every touch is like a gentle jolt to my pussy. It's not long before I'm slick and soaking through the tight crotch of my sequined dance shorts.

Every time I look into the crowd, my admirer seems a little bit closer. He's in the third row, then the second, then the front. His eyes never leave me. There's no one else around.

I can't even see any other faces. Nothing stands out to me but him. Something about him tells me he is important. He's a man with a lot of connections.

He could take me and turn me into a magnificent starlet. A dazzling queen of the stage. He has the power to control the theater like a puppeteer, to place the moving pieces as he sees fit. He could turn this Midwest wannabe into a bonafide international dance and gymnastics icon.

I just have to seduce him first. As I slip one sleeve of my silvery crop top off my shoulder, he stands up.

He starts walking up the steps to the stage. My heart is pounding, but I keep going. I take another step, slip off the other shoulder.

He stands before me now, tall and strong and dignified. His face is both handsome and unclear, like my eyes won't let me memorize his features completely.

I yearn to please him.

I long for his sweet approval. I cross my arms, grab the bottom hem of my top, and peel it up over my head. My breasts spill out and my nipples stiffen up in the cool air. I fondle my full tits as I step closer to him, licking my lips.

"Can you stick the landing?" he asks in a deep, resounding voice.

I feel the vibrations through the floor. I nod. "Of course. I can do anything you want."

"Arch that back for me. Let me see how flexible you are," he commands.

He reaches out with one muscular arm and I rest my back against him while I bend backwards. His other hand drapes across my bare chest. His palm lays flat against my thumping heart while he inspects me with his intense gaze.

I'm trembling and dripping with desire for him. I am so

tightly wound, so in need of release, and I know he could give it to me. I have to prove myself worthy, and he will give me the whole world. His hand is moving down my chest, down my smooth, flat stomach to my slick, aching mound.

I sigh and push up into him in a wordless plea for more. He's folding over me, his lips nearly an inch from my bare skin.

Just then, the world goes shaky. The ground beneath our feet rumbles like the shifting of tectonic plates.

The mystery admirer disappears and I am alone on the stage for a moment before my eyes flutter open wide.

"Please fasten your seatbelts. We are experiencing light turbulence," chimes a cordial female voice over the airplane intercom.

I hastily click my seatbelt and grip the armrests on either side of me. I look around at the crowded airplane cabin. I grab the little bottle of water in my cup holder and take a swig.

I stare out the window at the heavenly puffs and swirls of white clouds through the deep blue sky.

I sigh as I tilt my head back against the seat. It's only a short flight of a few hours from my hometown in Ohio to the big, sparkling, surreal city of New York.

But I've been frantically practicing, planning, and panicking about this big move for the past few weeks since I found out it was a sure thing. By now, I'm already exhausted enough to fall asleep thirty minutes into the flight.

I check my watch. My heart skips a beat when I see the time. There's only about forty-five minutes left in the air before we land in the Big Apple. I must have slept like the dead. Well, except for the content of my dreams, which was very much alive.

In fact, I almost feel as though the emotions and sensations in that fantasy world are more real than this plane right now.

The connection I felt with that handsome, older stranger in the crowd seems too visceral to be make believe.

If he's a figment of my imagination, I need to start spending way more time in my own head. Even if he isn't real, the effects he had on my body are definitely real.

I'm still tingly all over and slick between my thighs. I keep my legs tightly closed with my travel blanket over my lap.

My eyes dart around nervously for signs of anyone looking at me funny. My dream was so engrossing, I hope I didn't moan or sigh in my sleep.

It's silly, but I always have this weird worry that people can read my mind-- especially when I think dirty thoughts. The truth is that I'm just an innocent nineteen-year-old virgin who hardly knows enough about sex to fantasize in the first place.

I've spent pretty much my whole life devoted to my craft. Long hours practicing backbends on the balance beam or memorizing choreography for the stage.

Quite frankly, I haven't had time to mess around. I wish I could meet a guy like the sexy older man from my dream, someone who could teach me what I've been missing all this time. Until then, I have to keep my little desires to myself.

I look around and see, with relief, that nobody's paying attention to me. It's pretty loud in the cabin anyway.

It's a busy afternoon flight, filled with jetsetters, businesspeople, moms with whining children, even a group of young men who look like a sports team of some kind.

All absorbed in their own little worlds.

I lean back in my seat and relax. A smile spread across my face when I look out the window and see New York City shimmering like a flicker of light in the water.

As we fly closer and closer, the scintillating cityscape comes into view. My jaw drops at the lofty skyscrapers, the glistening windows and metal siding of the buildings, the twisting streets that traverse the bustling metropolis below.

I feel a flutter of nervous excitement. It's all coming together! My dreams of making it in the world of gymnastics and dance, of becoming a real star, it's so close I can almost taste it.

After years of hard work, I'm finally going to train with the best of the best, a talent scout and former athlete-turned-coach named Nick Thomson.

He's world-famous, ridiculously successful, and well-connected.

He's worked with the best of the best, and he knows the

industry backward and forward. I've never met him, never even seen the guy, but I remember his name.

He's the guy all my idols have worked with. He's the one who catapults potential into stardom. And now it's my turn to gain from his power.

As the plane descends for landing, my excitement shoots through the roof. By the time we're disembarking, I'm so giddy I nearly forget all my luggage. I'm grinning ear to ear as I roll my carry-on through the bustling NYC airport.

Everywhere I look, people are moving at top speed, all on a mission. Back home in Ohio, it's a slower pace of life. I've always been the odd one out, the girl who tries too hard and won't take time off. But here, everyone seems to be that way.

City folks walk with a purpose, and I do my best to join them. My heart is soaring as I go to baggage claim, grab my pink suitcase, and keep it moving.

I can see all around me people are reuniting with each other. Family members cheer and hug each other. Couples run to each other's arms and catch up in a passionate kiss.

It's a beautiful sight to behold, but it gives me a little twinge of homesickness. There's no family, friend, or lover waiting to scoop me up. I left everything and everyone I know back home.

But when I see a sign with my name, Carly Kittredge, emblazoned across it, I light up. Holding the sign is a man so startlingly handsome, I do a double take.

He's tall, built like a powerful athlete, and dressed like a stylish New Yorker. He's also nearly old enough to be my father, a fact which definitely draws me in.

I've always preferred older guys, and this one is a perfect specimen.

He has dark hair streaked with glimmering silver, green eyes that enchant me from a distance, and a calm assuredness about him. I instantly feel a connection with him.

The fact that he really resembles the literal man of my dreams isn't lost on me. But could it be-- this is *the* Nick Thomson? How did I not realize how gorgeous he is?

I walk up to him with a shy wave.

"Mr. Thomson?" I pipe up.

He nods. "Miss Kittredge?"

"That's me!" I chirp back.

He smiles at me, and I melt at his dimples and the soft crinkles at the corner of his eyes. He offers a handshake, but being a nice Midwestern girl, I instinctively go in for a hug. Instead of making it weird, he embraces me fully. From the second my cheek touches his strong chest, I'm a goner.

There's a connection between us that is instantaneous. Suddenly, I don't feel so homesick. His warmth, his strength, his demeanor-- everything makes me want to be close to him. Always.

Oh god. One second in, and I'm already falling for my coach.

"It's good to finally meet you. We're going to do great work together, I can tell," he assures me in a voice velvety smooth and deep. "You can call me Nick. Or even Coach."

I hope there aren't actual hearts coming out of my eyes.

"I'm so excited to be here. It's truly an honor," I reply breathlessly.

"Thank you. The feeling is mutual," Coach Nick remarks. "Come on, let's get out of this stuffy airport. The city awaits."

He offers me his arm and I happily take it. He grabs my suitcase with the other arm and leads me through the crowded airport to the gleaming exit. We step out into the free air and a sleek, very expensive, black luxury sedan rolls up to the curb.

"Is that your car?" I ask, shocked.

"Yes," he answers.

"Then who's driving it?" I ask.

He chuckles. "My chauffeur. Louis."

Coach opens the back passenger door for me and I slide in while he puts my suitcase in the back. Louis, a jolly-looking man with wispy white mutton chops, smiles at me in the overhead mirror. I smile back bashfully.

Coach slides in next to me and closes the door. The car pulls away from the airport pickup and out onto the road.

"It's about an hour or so drive with traffic," Coach points out. "You can get comfortable, even rest your eyes if you'd like. I know you've been training hard, and we're going to work even harder together."

"Oh, I don't think I could keep my eyes closed when there's so much to take in," I gush.

"In that case, Louis, turn on some music," Coach Nick requests.

I'm on cloud nine as I watch the landscape changing outside the window. Even the view from the highway is intriguing to me. I've never been far from home.

The farthest I've gone before now was Chicago one time for my sixteenth birthday.

Sinatra's silky vocals and brass set the mood while we drive through the city to the Brooklyn Bridge. I am fascinated by the world outside. I can't get enough of the architecture, the fashion, even the grunge and grime of the city enchants me.

It's a whole different world from the suburban life I've been living.

As we cross into Manhattan, I'm awash in noise and color. Everything is teeming with life, from the gigantic billboards, the honking cars, the traffic lights, people laughing and shouting, music blasting from windows and cars.

It's a smorgasbord of sensory overload and I love being drenched in it all.

I shake my head with amazement as I stare out the window.

"I can't believe this is my real life," I murmur.

"Believe it. You're really here," Coach says warmly.

I turn to look at him, happy tears in my eyes. "I've worked so hard for this. It's like a dream come true," I confess.

"Your audition tapes were very impressive. You beat out hundreds of other top-notch candidates to win this partnership with me. You deserve to be here, Carly," Coach Nick insists. His green eyes are bright with passion.

"Thank you, sir. I intend to prove it every day!" I assert.

"That's what I like to hear. Now, we only have a few short weeks together. But you are already so advanced, we'll have no problem getting you ready for the upcoming season of competitions and auditions. You'll be perfectly positioned to sweep the field, be a real contender on the international stage," Coach Nick explains.

"I'm ready to work," I assure him.

He smiles and nudges my shoulder with his. "I believe it."

After a long, exciting ride through the city, we arrive at a luxurious apartment building that stretches way up into the sky. Louis pulls to the curb and retrieves my luggage while Coach and I step out onto the sidewalk.

"Thanks, Louis. I'll take it from here," Coach Nick says, taking my suitcase.

Louis leaves to park the car, and Coach leads me into the building, past a smiling doorman. The interior of the building is even more beautiful than the outside somehow. Everything is bright white and modern, slick fixtures and clean lines everywhere I look. We take the elevator up to the top floor-- the penthouse suite. My heart is hammering like crazy as Coach leads me into his apartment.

"Holy cow," I breathe, looking around at the impressive space.

"So, this is my home. You'll be staying with me, since our work will involve early mornings and late nights. In order to reach maximum potential, we'll have to keep close. This is an intense partnership, but I think you already understand the value of hard work and dedication," he explains as he leads me on a tour of the place.

Every room is more luxe and elegant than the former. A full chef's kitchen. A lofty living room with vaulted ceilings and wide, bright windows. Two full bathrooms with incredible golden fixtures, clawfoot tubs, rain showers, the works. He shows me a private gymnastics and dance studio tricked out with everything we could possibly need.

"Wow. An in-home studio," I gasp.

"Of course. My home also comes with access to the gym, pool, spa, and sauna on-site," Coach says. "And here is your bedroom."

He opens the door to a gorgeous, neat room with a queen-sized bed and a lovely sitting area. There's a walk-in closet and a bay window overlooking the city.

"It's beautiful," I exclaim.

"It's yours for the time being," he says. "My room is on the other side of that wall, so I'm close by in case you need anything."

I'm suddenly intensely aware that we're just two good-looking, athletic, passionate adults standing in a romantic bedroom. Alone together. With that unmistakable connection crackling between us like a live wire. I can feel his body heat. I can smell his manly scent. His presence is doing strange, wicked things to my own body. I wonder if he can tell. But before the tension reaches a screaming peak, he steps away with a glance at his watch.

"My apologies, Carly. I hate to leave you so soon after your arrival, but I have a meeting with an important corporate sponsor in about half an hour across town," he says.

"I'll be fine! I'm just going to unpack and relax a little bit," I assure him.

"Perfect. Make yourself at home, help yourself to anything you find in the kitchen. I will be back sometime tonight. If the meeting runs late, don't feel obligated to wait up for me," Coach says. "Again, it's wonderful to meet you, Carly."

He slips away, leaving me to wander around the penthouse in a giddy daze. I unpack, I explore a little more, I make myself a sandwich made of the most upscale ingredients I've ever seen outside of a fancy restaurant. I take a long, leisurely soak in a clawfoot tub while listening to music. I take my time drying off and lounging around in a fluffy white robe provided for me. After a while, I video-call my family back home. I have a great time catching up with my mom, dad, and two older sisters. I walk around and show them some of the penthouse, which they all find deeply impressive. My sisters, both athletes in their own right, are excited for me but a little bit jealous. My mom reminds me to be careful, my dad tells me to work hard and do what Coach Nick says. I'll have no problem doing that-- in fact, I would do just about anything Coach wants. In or out of the studio.

When I hear Coach Nick arrive back at the apartment, I

quickly hang up the call with my family and listen for his footsteps. I realize that it's been several hours, and it's now dark outside, although the city continues to glow like dense stars in the darkness.

I hear Coach walking across the apartment and the soft jangle of keys. I hop up off my bed and hurry out into the hall to intercept him as he comes toward the bedrooms.

Not only am I eager to hear what the corporate sponsor had to say, but I can't stay away from Nick. Even though he wasn't gone too long, and I only just met him anyway, I can't deny that I missed his presence.

It's hard not to get attached, especially when he's my only known contact out here in the big city.

He looks somewhat surprised to see me, and I'm delighted to see him. He's dressed sharply like earlier, only now his tie is loosened and swept over one shoulder and his jacket is folded over his arm.

His black undershirt barely conceals the powerful, muscular chest and arms underneath.

There's a rugged edge to his charm right now, and it's doing dirty things to my body. I fold my arms over my chest and shrink in on myself a little, suddenly feeling exposed even though I'm wearing a modest set of print pajamas.

Like he can read my X-rated thoughts when I look at him. Like he knows I'm wet between the thighs for him.

What is wrong with me? He's not supposed to be my lover. He's my coach! He's a father figure, not boyfriend potential. I'm a young, innocent virgin with career ambitions-- what am I doing falling all over myself for a guy a decade and a half older than me?

"Oh, you're still awake. I thought you might be asleep by now after a long day of travel," he greets me warmly.

"I didn't want to miss you," I admit.

He smiles. "You don't have to stay up past your bedtime for me."

I blush deeply. "I'm nineteen. I'm more of an adult than you think," I blurt out.

Coach raises an eyebrow and takes a step closer, looking

intensely at me. His eyes burn right through to my very core. Like he can see every part of me. Unclothed, unhidden.

"You're right. You're certainly not a child," he agrees softly.

There's that same tension between us again. We're both holding back. Just barely.

He clears his throat. "Anyway. Tomorrow will be a full day of work."

"Practice?" I ask.

"Eventually. But first, you need to settle in and decompress. Get used to the city, find your bearings. I can help you with that. But for tonight, just get some rest," he insists.

"Okay. See you in the morning?" I pipe up.

He reaches out and touches my shoulder with one large hand. I feel his body heat like a shock of electricity. I'm tingly and hot all over from that one light touch.

"Goodnight, Carly," he says.

"Night, Coach," I reply.

He gives me a nod and disappears into his bedroom. I watch the door close. Then I slip back into my own room and climb into bed, pressing my ear against the wall. I can hear him moving around in his room. Footsteps, kicking off his shoes, humming under his breath. I smile when I note that he actually has a very pleasant voice. And then it dawns on me that he's taking his clothes off. I hear the faint jingle of a belt buckle, then the whip of a zipper. I picture him getting naked, putting visuals to the sounds I catch through the wall. I imagine his brawny chest and sculpted arms. I want to run my fingers along the ridges of his abs. I want him to fold me up tight in his powerful embrace. I reply the moment of our hug in the airport. The way he took me into his arms so instinctively. He sensed that I needed a hug and he leaned in. I remember his heart thumping under my cheek. The first time I inhaled his masculine scent that drives me wild.

Through the wall, I hear him get into bed. The mattress squeaks faintly and I hear the soft rustle of bedsheets, then the flick of a lamp turning on. I sink down into my pillows with my cheek still turned to the wall. My hand trails down the front of my pajama pants. I cup my tingly, aching mound in my palm and stifle a moan as I listen to Coach in bed. I picture him listening to me the same way, both of us silently fantasizing about the other. We're a world away, and there are canyons of professional boundaries between us, but at the same time... he's right there. Just on the other side of the wall. If I were to go one door further down the hall, we would be together. Maybe together in *his* bed. So close, yet so far.

But what I can't see, I can imagine. I picture him sliding his hand inside his boxers, stroking his magnificent cock. I lick my lips at the idea of tasting him. I wish I knew how it feels to choke on his rod, feel him push down my throat and come all over my pretty face. My fingers circle my overstimulated clit while my mind runs wild. I hear a rhythmic rustling of bedsheets-- like he really is touching himself while I do the same.

Just a wall away.

I caress my full breasts, I insert one dainty finger inside my dripping cunny. I rut against my own hand while I listen to Coach's soft breaths and sighs. I let out a little moan of pleasure when I gush come all over my fingers, and I barely try to conceal it. In fact, I hope he hears me moan.

In this moment, I'm so fiery with desire, I don't care who knows-- I'm hopelessly attracted to my new father figure, and I wish he would march into this bedroom and take my virginity. I drift off to sleep with my hand still tucked into my pajama pants, and my dreams take the shape of Coach Nick and me, alone together on a stage again. This time, we get a little closer.

In the morning, I awaken to the smell of coffee and omelettes after a restful night. I peel myself out of bed and into some cozy workout clothes, then head down to the kitchen.

My jaw drops when I turn the corner to find Coach Nick cooking breakfast in nothing but a white towel wrapped around his waist, his silver-streaked hair still damp from a morning shower. He turns to smile at me and I force myself to look normal.

"Morning. Sleep well?" he greets me.

I slide onto a stool at the eat-in counter and he sets a plate of food in front of me.

"Mhm. Wow, that smells incredible," I reply. My stomach yowls in agreement.

"Egg white omelette with spinach, veggies, and pesto. You drink coffee?" he asks.

"I would get it in an IV drip if I could," I answer.

He chuckles. "Likewise."

He slides a steaming mug of fragrant, high-quality coffee next to my plate.

"So what's on the agenda for today?" I ask between bites. "Balance beam? Pilates?"

"How about a luxury shopping trip and a French restaurant?" he suggests.

My eyes go round with wonder. "Wait. Really?" I breathe.

Coach nods, looking pleased with my reaction. "Just a day to decompress. Get used to the city. Plus, you'll need new, top of the line gear, not to mention formal outfits for events. How's that sound?" he asks.

I'm positively brimming with excitement. "Oh my god. Heavenly."

We quickly finish breakfast, get cleaned up, and dressed for a lovely day out in the city. I'm still in shock as Louis drives Coach and I all over Manhattan.

We hit up every designer shop on each block. We buy formal gowns, leotards, upscale skincare and makeup, new acro shoes, a plethora of glittery costumes, handbags, perfumes, even a pair of sleek heels that cost more than my whole wardrobe combined. Everywhere we go, people know Nick Thomson.

He's a VIP in every club, it seems. His list of connections is endless. And when I'm beside him, people treat me with more respect than I've ever felt. I stand up straighter.

I feel taller, stronger, more confident with every moment I spend by his side. Just before we head to the restaurant for our reservation, we dip into one last boutique.

I look around at all the lacy, naughty lingerie on display. Crotchless panties. Bondage sets. Roleplay ensembles that make me blush.

"Anything you want is yours," Coach says.

I've never picked out expensive lingerie before, but with my newfound self esteem, I manage to pick out a few sets that really show off my curves. I look at myself in the gilded mirror of the dressing room and feel a swell of self-love.

I look like a dream. I look like a girl who's good enough to stick any landing, and land any hottie.

Too bad the only one I want is off-limits. But then... why are we in a lingerie shop together if our relationship is purely professional? Why do I feel a deep yearning whenever he looks at me with those deep green eyes?

When we sit down at our candlelit, white-clothed table for dinner, my heart is thumping like crazy. The man across from me is everything my heart desires.

He's handsome, clever, witty, kind, and hard-working. He respects me and builds me up-- I've only known him for twenty-four hours and I already feel ten times more confident. And we haven't even hit the studio yet!

"How are you feeling about your stay in the city?" he asks as he pours a glass of wine.

"Really good. I mean, today was a total whirlwind. I had so much fun," I gush.

"Good. I'm glad I could kick off our partnership on a high note. We have a lot of work to do together, and we will starting tonight. But I wanted to establish trust and comfort between us first. Besides, I know how hard you've worked to get here. You deserve a little pampering," he explains.

"I hope I can prove I'm worth it," I confess.

"I believe in you. I'm fully invested in your future. In *our* future together," he says.

I tell him, "Thank you again. For the opportunity. For everything."

Coach leans forward, his eyes locked on me.

"I've been working this industry for a long time. I've partnered with the best of the best. My success has brought me wealth and power, but there are more important things. Trust. Teamwork. True human connection," he muses. "I feel that with you."

After a pause, he continues, "I want you to know that I will take care of you, Carly. As long as you're with me, your every need will be met."

The waiter arrives to take our order. Mushroom risotto for me, steak for him.

Our conversation flows back to our plans for the evening. After a relaxing day of shopping in the city, we return to the penthouse for a little one-on-one studio work.

During the drive back, I could hardly focus on anything besides how close he was to me. His leg mere inches from mine. His heat radiating, calling me closer.

When we step into the studio, that fire is still burning bright. Coach directs me to the low-height balance beam for warm-ups. He walks me through several reps, explaining the process as we go. He's detailed and methodical, but his demeanor is more encouragement than command.

He knows just what to say to get me to move my body a certain way. He can speak with just a look, just a glance.

We're falling in sync. Mentor and protege, perfectly attuned to each other. He pushes me further than I would normally go, but he always has my best interests in mind. He's always ready to catch me should I fall.

But every time he touches me, I feel it like a searing handprint. My body is aching for him. I respect him as deeply as I want him, and I know the feeling is mutual.

I feel the way he watches me as he puts his hand on my lower back to steady me. I feel his eyes soaking in my curves in my form-fitting leotard.

He tries to step back, always keep his distance. But he can't resist. Again and again, we find ourselves dangerously close, with only a worn thread of propriety left between us.

"Take a break. You're working hard," he urges me.

Panting, I sit down on the balance beam with my legs hanging off. Coach saunters up to me, standing between my legs with his hands on my shoulders. He peers deep into my eyes.

"How do you feel?" he asks gruffly.

I lick my lips. My heart is pounding. I'm positively soaking through my leotard. I wonder if he can tell, if he can smell the desire on me. My eyes flit downward. There's a stiffening bulge at the front of his trousers. He's trying to hold back, but his body betrays him.

"I don't want to hold back anymore," I murmur.

He frowns slightly. "You're doing great, Carly. You pushed to your limit."

"I'm not talking about gymnastics," I clarify pointedly.

The realization of my meaning dawns on his handsome face. He runs his hands down my thighs. I can see some kind of inner battle playing out in his eyes. He's reaching for something to restrain him. He's waiting for me to change my mind, to pull back.

But I don't.

"You have so much to teach me," I begin softly. I slip one strap down my shoulder.

"Carly, be careful," he warns.

"Or what?" I whisper. "I trust you, Coach Nick. You said you'd take care of me. You said my every need will be met."

He cups my face with both large hands. I tremble with delight at his touch. I pull down the other strap and peel down my leotard. My full breasts pour out and he caresses them in his hands. I roll the suit down my taut stomach, over my hips and thighs.

I push it down my legs and kick it to the side, sitting naked on the balance beam. He leans in close enough to kiss me, but he stops just before touching.

"What is it you need?" he murmurs.

"You. All of you," I whisper. "Inside of me."

He can't resist any longer. He bumps forward and we collide in a passionate, forceful kiss. He strokes my hair, my face. His hands trail down my back and caress my dainty waist. His tongue pushes into my mouth while his hands push my legs apart.

He reaches two fingers down to rub my clit while his lips trail down my ticklish neck. He leaves little nipping kisses in his wake, tiny bruises to admire in the mirror tomorrow. His fingertips massage tight, perfect circles that make me quiver all over.

When he bends down to dive his tongue between my legs, I nearly fall off the balance beam.

But my new daddy, Coach Nick, holds me steady while he devours my slick, gushing cunny. I'm dripping all over his magical mouth.

His lips nip and suckle my clit while he laps up my juices with his warm, wet tongue. Every tiny movement sends me shivering with delight. His hands rove up to play with my tits. I arch my back and grip the beam tightly while he licks my pussy. I find myself grinding against his face and whimpering for more.

"Oh my gosh," I gasp. "That feels so good."

Coach moves faster, sucking my clit with more pressure. I can feel the tension knotting up inside of me. My body tensing for a climax.

"I'm almost there! Ohh, I'm coming!" I cry out.

My cunny gushes sweet nectar all over his tongue, and he slurps up every drop. As I'm coming back to reality, Coach lifts me off the beam and sets me on the mat.

He kisses me deeply. I reach out to touch his erection through his trousers.

He rocks against my hand and suddenly, I know what I need. I drop down to my knees in front of him and eagerly start unzipping his front. He strokes my hair and gathers it in his fist.

His cock pops out, tall and stiff and glorious. My mouth is watering already when I lean in to taste him with my tongue.

"That's my good girl," he purrs.

I love the feeling of his thick cock pushing into my mouth inch by mouthwatering inch. He makes my cheeks ache with his fullness, and when he rocks back into my throat I cough a little. But I quickly recover, and it's not long before I'm bobbing up and down on his cock like a pro.

Coach rocks his hips to meet my mouth. Every thrust into my throat makes me slicker between the thighs. I reach down and rub my aching clit while I take Coach's cock down to the root.

He uses my hair to hold me in place while he fucks my throat, and just before he's about to explode in my mouth, he pulls back.

"Lie back for me," Coach commands.

I do as I'm told, splayed out and waiting for him. He tears off his shirt and trousers, kicks off his boxers, and returns to the mat to pin me down. He dips to kiss me. I arch up to meet him, wrapping my legs around his waist.

He's stroking his massive cock and positioning the thick head at my virginal slit. I push into him, begging for him to fuck me.

"I'm ready. Please. I need you," I implore.

"You can have whatever you want. Anything, Carly," he growls.

"Fuck me, Coach. Fill me up with your come. I want you to make me a woman," I insist. I tighten my grip around his waist to show him I'm serious.

My offer is one he can't refuse.

Coach Nick rears back and shoves inside of me in one long, swift motion. I cry out with the onslaught of incredible pleasure and pain as he pounds my cunny hard.

I feel his cock push through that thin, tiny barrier that kept my innocence.

He holds me and kisses me as he spears deep inside my cunny. Just like before, we're perfectly in sync. He fucks me hard, but he knows my limits. He understands without a single word exactly what I need and how to give it to me.

Coach doesn't treat me like a delicate flower or a silly child. He knows what my body can handle. I'm an athlete, and a damn good one.

"Oh, it's so deep," I gasp.

"Just how you want it," he grunts.

"Mhm. Deep and hard. Don't hold back," I dare him.

He takes the bait. After all, we are both athletes, with a competitive edge.

His cock spears deeper and harder into my fertile, virgin pussy. Coach scoops me up without missing a single thrust and flips us both over so that I'm on top. He grabs my hips while I ride him.

I lean forward and sigh at the delicious friction of his pelvis bumping against my clit. Between his cock hitting my g-spot and the pressure on my clit, I can't help but come again.

"Oh, Coach!" I squeak.

"That's right, Carly. Ride that cock," he groans.

He tightens his grip on my waist and holds me in place while he fucks me hard, thrusting up into me with so much force, all I can do is hold on for dear life.

His cock strikes deep within me while those wild green eyes are locked with mine. I feel the raw strength rippling through his body beneath me. He's fully in control. I am safe in his hands, right where I'm meant to be.

"Fill me up," I whisper. "Please. Give it to me."

"I won't hold back," he promises.

And with a few more violent, passionate thrusts, his cock spurts hot, sticky seed deep inside of me.

I bounce up and down on his twitching shaft as he comes, my own juices mingling with his as we fold together on the mat.

When he's emptied every last drop inside me, I roll away onto my back, still panting. Coach pulls me into his arms and showers me with kisses.

"How do you feel now?" he asks softly, his lips against my cheek.

I turn to quickly kiss him on the lips and giggle, "Better than ever."

"We've established some new *training* procedures in the studio tonight," he teases. "We'll have to pound out the details, but I think it'll be a satisfactory program for us both."

"I think you're right, Coach," I agree with a wink.

He laughs as his fingers lovingly brush the hair out of my face. We spend the rest of the night in bed together-- his bed. From that night onward, we share a bedroom. And pretty much everything else, too.

Every day with Nick is a new adventure.

We train together, we sleep together, we eat together, we dream of a beautiful future together.

As it turns out, my sweet, dedicated coach has been missing something in his fabulous, high-class lifestyle: me. I needed a guide, someone to believe in me and teach me how to succeed.

A father figure... but something more than that.

I trust him with my whole being, and I love him with my entire heart. I can't wait to start building our little world together, starting with the baby growing inside of me.

Our baby.

Our future.

Coach Nick shows me that I really can have it all.

Being His Student

Book Themes: age gap romance, dean/student, virgin, breeding, exhibitionism, punishment
Word Count: 8071

I roll my pretty hazel eyes as I sit in the empty hallway.

There is an antique grandfather clock at the end of the hall. I can hear it ticking dutifully, counting down how many minutes I have been waiting here. Judging by the sunlight streaming in at a dark golden hue, it must be getting to mid-afternoon.

I groan and shuffle impatiently in my seat. I've never been very good at waiting for things. I tend to get what I want when I want it.

And very rarely do I ever have to do anything outside my desires.

I guess you could say that makes me spoiled, and I guess you'd be right. I don't like being bossed around. I don't like being boxed in. Nobody makes decisions for Avery Winston--I'm in control of my own life.

Although, it doesn't feel that way right now, as I'm being forced to sit in this stupid hall and wait to pay my dues. I prefer when I make the schedule, not someone else.

Not even the sensible and sexy headmaster, in front of whose office I'm currently parked. Waiting for my disciplinary meeting.

My punishment.

But I'm not quivering with fear.

In fact, it's quite the opposite.

I feel a sense of anticipation. Adrenaline is running through my veins. The sting of punishment runs so closely along the stroke of pleasure.

I'm a bad girl, and I need to be corrected.

Everything about me screams "teenage troublemaker."

I'm freshly eighteen, and technically a virgin, but I'd like to think my dirty mind makes me more mature than I look.

I know how I look. I know my appeal. I'm in my boarding school uniform, but I don't make it look frumpy. I don't hide my body, I don't shy away from my own curves.

I'm supposed to wear my gray, black, and white plaid skirt down to my shins, but I used my daddy's credit card to get all of my uniform skirts tailored.

Now they barely reach to mid-thigh, and that's saying something, considering how long my legs are. I'm supposed to tuck my starchy white button-up shirt into that skirt, but instead, I undo the two bottom buttons and use the loose fabric to tie a cute knot, so that the shirt is cropped to show a little flash of my narrow waist.

I undo the first two buttons, as well, so I can put my ample cleavage on full display. On top of that, I'm meant to wear a boxy gray fleece (which I conveniently 'misplaced' within a week of enrolling here) and a modest black blazer.

Even the blazer is improved with a little tailoring and rolling up the sleeves. Add to the ensemble some woolly gray knee-high socks and black mary-janes, and a black headband in my long, brown hair, and I look like I could've stepped right out of some perv's schoolgirl fantasy.

I'm leaned back in the rickety wooden chair, my arms folded

across my chest in a pouty position. I sit somewhat sideways in the seat with my legs crossed tightly and one foot tapping out a restless beat.

I'm not nervous so much as intrigued.

After all, I'm no stranger to punishment at the hands of older men.

My own father has tried to discipline me in all kinds of ways-- grounding me, lecturing me, taking my credit cards, getting my car towed so I can't drive it... you know, all the stops. Not that it's ever been very effective.

Dad doles out the punishment, but he's never there to enforce it. Not like he really cares that much anyway. I've always been able to weasel into or out of anything with just a bat of my lashes or a sweet word. It's only too easy.

Daddy never stays angry for long-- in fact, he rarely interacts with me on any level for very long.

He's a very busy man, always jetting around the world for important meetings to schmooze with other boring, uptight, old-money socialites. When you get so little attention from the one person who's supposed to shower you with affection, it makes you desperate. I'm always desperate for attention, whether it's negative or positive.

I look forward to the punishments just like the rewards. Maybe that means I'm a little warped, but oh well. I'm a bad girl and I deserve to be disciplined. At least, I hope I will be. I mean, what's a girl got to do to get a little attention around here?

I sigh dramatically and look around me. It's really a beautiful, picturesque setting if I let myself think about it.

The boarding school is situated in the midst of a vast plot of forested acreage in the idyllic New England countryside, with tons of space for outdoors activities, competitive sports, events.

Out the wide window across the hall I can see rolling green hills fringed in the distance with a dense tree line. The school buildings are all stately brick buildings with vaulted ceilings and vintage touches throughout.

There is a beautiful conservatory flourishing with green plants, herbs, vegetables, flowers. The school library is a dinosaur of an old structure with walls and walls of every kind of book imaginable.

Tall ladders reach to the topmost shelves, while a spiral staircase leads down into the restricted archives in the belly of the building. The dorms are private, secure, cozy, and draped with tapestries and beautiful decor to keep the students feeling inspired and at home.

Far out across the grounds, there are stables for horses and a private lake for rowing, swimming, and fishing. The on-site gymnasium is state-of-the-art, and even the cafeteria is elegantly designed.

The whole boarding school drips with prestige and deep, deep pockets. This is the kind of place where every student is some kind of heiress or trust fund baby.

I'm no exception. I've had pretty much every material desire or shallow whim fulfilled since I was old enough to start demanding what I want.

But it turns out that gifts are not an equitable surrogate for genuine attention.

I keep looking for that attention wherever I can get it. Daddy couldn't handle my needs anymore, so he sent me here to 'straighten out'. Jokes on him, though, because I've set my sights on a new father figure. As I sit here outside his door, I glance up at the golden plaque hanging there proudly.

His name is emblazoned across it in bold, classy lettering: HEADMASTER DANE GRAHAM.

My heart flutters just thinking about him in there, on the other side of the door. Sitting at his desk with that furrowed brow, that concentrated look on his handsome face.

I picture his large hand raising to his head, his long fingers running through his thick, dark blond hair streaked with white. I want to know what's inside that pretty head. What is he thinking about? Is he thinking about me?

Headmaster Graham is gentle, and patient to a fault. I've been trying so hard to break him, to get a rise out of him.

There's nothing sexier than a calm man suddenly losing his

restraint. It's not that I want to see him crack under pressure. I just want him to get real with me.

I want to break down this teacher-student wall between us, bring him down to my level, get down and dirty with him. I don't have bad intentions, I just want to do bad things to him.

The more I think about him, the more turned on I get. Even though I'm sitting in the world's least comfortable wooden chair, meant to bruise my tailbone and make me dwell on my regrets or whatever, my body is tingling all over.

I imagine what fate might befall me when that office door opens. Maybe my punishment won't be boring-- it'll be sexy.

I picture him calling me into his office, locking the door, and turning to me with those soft gray eyes hard with lust. My mind is filled with images of him grabbing me and forcing me to bend over his lap. If I close my eyes, I can almost feel his wide, flat palm smacking my bare ass.

I can hear the echoing slap, feel the sting of a red handprint on my ass cheek. Just another temporary tattoo, another piece of evidence to treasure in my reflection.

Maybe it'll go even further than that. I wonder if he'll order me to get down on my knees, to gaze up into his blazing eyes as he shoves his cock down my willing throat.

My mouth salivates at the thought of giving the headmaster head. A million fantasies splinter off in my mind, ricocheting in every sensual direction.

I'm so entranced by him, so desperate for him, that any touch will be enough to send me reeling. I've been watching him from afar since I was sent here a month ago.

Normally, it only takes me less than forty-eight hours to get a new guy wrapped around my dainty little finger. But the head-master has his guard up.

He's used to dealing with... difficult young women. Spoiled rich girls who need to learn discipline. Girls like me. But I'm going to be more than he expects. I'm going to blow his mind, one way or another, until he's mine.

My body warms to the idea of being near him. My soft, petal-pink nipples stiffen to perky peaks underneath my starchy white blouse. I go without a bra so he can see my arousal. I'm not ashamed. I want him to know what he does to my smooth, virginal, beautiful young body.

I'm getting slick and tingly between my legs, and every time I rub my thighs together I can feel the friction stimulate my clit. I tilt my head back against the wall and close my eyes. My hands drop to my full breasts. I cup their fullness and fondle my nipples until I have to bite my lip to keep from moaning.

My body is begging for more, for deeper.

Closer.

Harder.

I need the release so badly, especially since I never get any privacy around here. At home, I was left alone all the time, free to masturbate and be as filthy as I wanted. But here?

I am always surrounded by other girls. In class, in the library, at lunch, the communal bathrooms, even in the dorms at night.

My bed is a cute little four-poster twin in a row of identical beds. There are five other girls just in my dorm room. If I'm seized by a delicious fantasy in the middle of the night when I'm too horny to sleep, I have to touch myself so silently and softly under the sheets so nobody hears me. I can never fully let loose like I need to.

Although, I can't pretend like the risk of getting caught doesn't amp up the thrill. Even now, another student could come wandering down the hall. The headmaster could pop his head out of the office at any time. I could easily get caught in a compromising position with myself. That only makes me wetter.

I rock and undulate my hips while I squeeze my thighs together. My fingers stroke my nipples and trail down to rub my achy mound through my short skirt. The delectable friction of my pussy lips grinding together, stimulating my tight little clit-- it's almost too much. I almost hope someone walks in on me.

Getting caught would be so fucking hot. I would get in trouble... and then my favorite new father figure would *have* to pay attention to me!

The pressure is building up ever higher inside of me as I rub my clit and touch my tits right here out in the open. I'm gasping breathless on the edge of coming when I hear the click-turn of the office door handle from the inside.

The excitement I feel trumps the desire to come. I hastily smooth down my blouse and skirt, sit up straight, and smirk up at the headmaster as he parts the door and looks out. As soon as his stony gray eyes land on me, a wave of understanding crosses his gorgeous features. I can't help but flash a naughty grin.

He knows I'm a troublemaker.

This isn't my first rodeo, and certainly ain't his. He steps out into the hallway to address me. I find myself licking my lips as my eyes pan slowly up his enormous, powerful frame. He's so tall and broad-shouldered, he could intimidate even the most brazen rebel. Even me... well, almost.

But I'm not shaking at his hulking size and authoritative demeanor. I'm just turned on. I want to brush my fingers through that thick blond hair, trace the impressive shape of his jaw, feel those hard pecs underneath layers of professorly digs.

Headmaster Graham wears a modernized tweed suit complete with tailored trousers, vest, suit coat, and a scarlet tie.

All business, but still sexy.

He looks at me with exasperation, shaking his head.

"Here we are again, Miss Winston," he chastises.

"It's a date," I retort audaciously. "Wouldn't miss it for the world."

"It's not..." he trails off, pinching the bridge of his nose.

Those gray eyes flick down to me again and I feel an electrical shock through my body. His gaze burns with intensity.

Either he's really mad at me and I'm in trouble, or he's really into me and I'm in trouble.

I'm perfectly pleased with both options.

Either way, I can't wait to get him alone in his office. But first, I need to up the ante. As always.

I hop to my feet and stand very, dangerously close to the headmaster. I stand on tiptoe and stretch my arms up over my head, letting out a sensual-sounding groan of satisfaction. When I lower my arms, I accidentally brush against his shoulder.

"Oopsie," I giggle, biting my lip.

Headmaster Graham stares down at me. There's a wordless conflict between us. His nature is gentle and understanding, but he's also in charge here. Gentleness hasn't worked on me yet, and he's well aware.

Usually I can use my rebellious ways or feminine wiles to make men stand down. I'm sweet and harmless-looking, just a sexy little schoolgirl who can't possibly do anything wrong. That's been my schtick.

But Headmaster Graham knows better. He's an authority figure and he's not afraid to stand up to me if needs to. He has the patience to deal with an endless supply of rebellious young female students. But there's something holding him back when it comes to me, and that's what fascinates me.

That's what keeps me trying to seduce him, and today I am ready to take my mission to the next level.

"Step into my office with me, Miss Winston," he commands in a low voice.

"Yes, sir," I reply enthusiastically.

We walk through the threshold into a cozy, dimly-lit office decorated with the same stately, vintage touch as the rest of the school. Huge, glossy mahogany desk.

A bay window overlooking a stretch of verdant fields edged by forest. A white candle flickers on a shelf. Hefty, dusty tomes line the shelves on the walls, and an old-fashioned green glass lamp is the only spot of light besides the fading sun.

I happily follow him in, my heart pounding and my endorphins rushing like a river in my veins.

I'm in trouble, but that's the point. It's the vessel by which I arrive at this place: alone in a room with the object of my seduction. I've been crushing hard on him since day one of my exile here at boarding school. I need to be punished, to be called a bad girl, to be disciplined by this sexy hunk of a headmaster.

I know it's filthy, but I can't stop lusting over the fact that he's almost old enough to be my dad.

I'm just a dainty, delicate, virginal eighteen year old.

Ripe and lush and ready to be plucked by a lucky, lucky guy.

Who better to tame my wild streak and make me a woman

than Headmaster Graham? I love knowing I have the power to keep his interest. To seduce him away from his moral responsibility.

It's dirty, it's bad, but it's what I desire more than anything.

Headmaster Graham folds his hands on the desk in front of him, peering at me with furrowed brows.

I chew gum and lean back in my seat while he starts listing off my crimes.

"Avery Winston. You're in my office for..." he pauses, picking up a stack of forms filled out by other professors and staff.

He reads off, "Skipping class, sneaking off campus, running in the halls, stealing from the cafeteria, using foul language in the classroom, turning your exam into a paper ball and throwing it across the room, violating dress code, giving Professor Halford the middle finger, and breaking curfew."

I tick off each infraction with my fingers as he lists them. "All of the above, guilty as charged," I declare. I blow a perfect pink bubble and it pops.

Headmaster Graham solemnly holds out his hand. I lean in and, never breaking eye contact, spit the gum into his open palm. As he tosses it in the trash, he adds, "Chewing bubblegum during a disciplinary meeting."

I grin, pleased with myself. I prop up my heels on the corner of his desk brazenly.

"So, Headmaster," I tease, "what are you going to do to me?"

He stares at me hard. His jaw tenses, his hands clench a little on the desk between us. I lick my lips and twirl my hair around my finger as I wait patiently for him to make his next move. I can tell I've struck a chord.

His eyes flit down to my chest for a second, then up to my lips.

I wish I had x-ray vision so I could see through this mahogany desk. I want to know if the headmaster has a hard-on for me, just like I'm dripping wet for him. I can sense his feelings shifting from regular frustration to the sexual kind. I'm going to make this hard for him in lots of different ways.

He won't be able to resist me for long.

It's a big risk for me to take-- trying to seduce the closest thing to a father figure I've had for the past month. But what is he going to do to me if I fail?

Expel me?

I only have a month of school left until graduation anyway, and even if Headmaster Graham did kick me out, Daddy would hire the very best tutors to get me through to graduation and then some. He may not pay much personal attention to me, but the resources and funds he has to offer are endless.

So I'm barely nervous at all when the headmaster launches into a somewhat scripted lecture.

"Miss Winston, you have only been here at the Academy for a month, and you've managed to fracture more rules than any student before you," he begins.

"I've always been an exceptional student," I remark.

Is that a flicker of a smile on his face? It's gone as soon as it arrives. He clears his throat and gives me a disapproving frown instead. He's trying to keep this professional, but I won't let him.

As he opens his mouth to go on, I lean back in the armchair and spread my legs.

"Here at the Academy, our students must adhere to the standards and regulations found in the pupil handbook. This is not a regular public school, Miss Winston. Your antics won't be tolerated here. I know you're close to graduation, and you may be feeling impatient about ending the year, but this final month is a crucial time period for your grades and your future," he says.

"Mhm. Totally," I reply. I give him my full attention as I slowly unbutton my white blouse even further to reveal more of my cleavage.

Headmaster Graham hesitates for a moment, then goes on, "If you want to make a change, this is the time to do it. This final month could be an opportunity for you to really turn things around, look to your future, figure out what path you want to take."

"You think so?" I ask. I let one of my sleeves drop off my shoulder and I hike up the hem of my skirt to show more of my milky white, smooth thighs.

The headmaster is barely holding back now. Those stony gray eyes are desperately looking everywhere but at me... but he can't help it. His gaze passes over my bare shoulder, the swell of my breasts, my exposed midriff, my soft thighs.

"I think you have more potential than you let on," he says, his voice a little rough. "You just need a little guidance."

"Will you teach me? Will you be my guide?" I ask him sweetly.

He starts, "Of course. We can work together to--"

He trails off as I spread my legs wider and bite my lip. I flash him my lacy, soaked-through panties. His eyes are wide and locked on me. His jaw twinges. His face is slightly flushed. He draws a long, deep breath. The headmaster is holding back, but he's like a rubber band ready to snap. I have him right where I want him.

"I'm ready for my discipline now," I purr. "In fact, I have an idea."

Headmaster Graham looks wary. "What is it?"

"Well, it seems like many of my crimes involve my mouth. Cursing, chewing gum, talking back, stealing food. Seems like I have a little oral fixation," I point out. "And if the punishment is supposed to fit the crime..."

I slowly get to my feet and start making my way around the desk. Headmaster Graham stands up, too, and looms over me. His full height and hulk turn me on even more. I feel so dainty and vulnerable beside him, like a little mouse before a tiger. His mouth is set in a hard line and those gray eyes are burning bright when I look up at him coyly.

"What are you doing?" he murmurs.

I place my hands on his broad chest and stare into his eyes as my hands move down the front of his body, over his taut stomach, down to the growing bulge at his crotch. He sucks in a tight breath. At first I think he might push me away, but instead he just gathers up my long, glossy brown hair in his fist as I drop to my knees in front of him. My heart is racing, every cell in my body is going haywire. It's really happening! My mouth waters, my pussy drips, and I'm aching to taste him.

"This meeting is about discipline," he insists again. "You're here for your penance."

I smirk as I unzip his trousers. "Well, then, don't hold back," I goad him.

"Is this really a punishment? Or a reward?" he growls.

"That's up to interpretation," I tease back.

I work his stiff, massive cock out of his silky boxers and my eyes go wide. He's absolutely gigantic, way bigger than I expected. Granted, I'm a virgin so I have little to compare to, but even I know he's hung like a horse. I wrap both hands around his shaft and begin to slowly work him up and down. I love the way his smooth, warm skin glides smoothly under my palms. I feel him getting thicker and heavier as I pump his length. Headmaster Graham lets out a low groan of approval when I reach my tongue out and flick it over the engorged head.

"You are a bad girl, aren't you?" he hisses.

I look up at him and see him gazing down at me. His gorgeous gray eyes are cloudy with lust and locked on me, watching my every move. His lips are slightly parted, his jaw slack. He strokes my hair and keeps it neatly gathered in his fist, out of my way.

"Open that pretty little mouth," he commands.

I obey, opening up wide. I splay out my tongue and dutifully let him slide his thickness into my warm, wet mouth. I moan around his cock as he takes inch by inch. My cheeks ache with his massive size and the tip of his cock brushes the back of my throat. I feel a ticklish little twinge, I almost cough, but I manage to keep my composure. His shaft feels so good in my mouth. I slide my tongue up and down the underside while I bob on his cock. He grips my hair tighter and guides me back so that his cock slips out of my mouth with a wet smack.

"Spit on it," he orders.

I spit a bubbly string of saliva onto the head of his cock and start pumping him faster with one hand while the other gently massages his balls.

"That's it. Very good," the headmaster murmurs.

My spit slicks him up so I can work his length with ease, but I can't resist tasting him again. I need one of my holes filled at least, and right now, my mouth is aching to take him.

I suck his length into my mouth inch by inch, taking him down to the root. I choke myself on his cock as his hand guides me by the hair. He pulls me back and pushes me down again and again.

"Open up your throat and stay right there for me, Avery," the headmaster grunts.

I feel a thrill through my body when he says my name. It sounds so musical on his lips. But it's nothing compared to the delight I feel when he hold my head in place and starts fucking my throat in earnest.

I loosen my tension and let him pound my mouth, slipping in and out. His hips snap forward and back as he keeps me steady. He isn't holding back now-- he's giving in to what he needs. He's using me like the little sex doll I am, and it feels so fucking good.

"I'm going to come all over that beautiful face of yours," Headmaster Graham grunts.

"Mmmhmm," I moan around his thick cock, urging him to come.

I want to taste it, I want to feel it on my skin. I want to know I have the power to make this powerful man lose control. He twists my hair a little and cups both sides of my head. He holds me stiffly in place while he thrusts erratically, forcefully. Like he can't hold back for another second. My mouth feels too good, my throat belongs to him.

"I'm right there," he groans. "Oh, fuck."

"Nnngh," I whimper as he pounds the back of my throat.

"Ohh yes. Avery!" he gasps as he slides out of my mouth.

His cock spurts hot, delicious streaks of come across my cheek and chin. A few drops hit my lip and I lick it up eagerly, never breaking eye contact with the headmaster.

He pumps his shaft with one hand, eking out every last precious drop onto my innocent face. He releases my hair so that it falls in loose, messy waves around my shoulders.

Just as he's grabbing a handkerchief from his desk drawer and starts dabbing at my face, we both jump at a loud, sharp knock at the office door.

"Headmaster, it's Kathy. I have those files you asked for this morning," the secretary announces through the door.

"Shit," he mutters, hastily wiping my face and throwing the handkerchief under the desk.

He pulls me to my feet as the secretary knocks again.

"Headmaster Graham?" she repeats.

"Just a moment," the headmaster calls back. He leans in close to me, his eyes ablaze with passion. In a voice so quiet I can barely hear him, he says, "Listen, we need to discuss your future, Avery. We cannot let *this* get in the way of your grades and my job. We have to figure something out."

"I'm always available for more discipline," I answer sweetly.

He raises an eyebrow as he pushes me toward the door. "We'll discuss it later."

"What about tonight?" I suggest. "Come find me at midnight."

He sighs, "It's inappropriate for me to go to the dorms at night. I'm a grown man and headmaster of this school; I can't just waltz into a room of vulnerable, sleeping female students."

I assure him with a wink, "Oh, I won't be in my bed anyway. You'll just have to track me down elsewhere. I could be almost anywhere, though, hmm? Even, oh, I don't know, maybe the restricted section of the library."

"The archives? Students are not allowed in there without supervision," he hisses back as he reaches for the door handle.

"Well, I guess you'll just have to supervise me, then!" I chirp back as he pushes open the door to reveal the secretary standing there with an armful of manila folders.

Headmaster Graham clears his throat and proclaims in an authoritative tone, "I hope this disciplinary meeting has made an impression on you today, Miss Winston."

"Oh, totally! You can see it all over my face," I tease back, grinning from ear to ear.

The secretary does a double take at me as I push past her. She seems befuddled by the inconsistency between the headmaster's stern words and the look of pure devilish delight on my face. I delicately push past her and start to skip down the hall. She stares after me quizzically.

"The files, Kathy?" Headmaster Graham reminds her.

She turns her attention back to him. He ushers her into his office as she twitters on about some bureaucratic detail she needs him for. In the final seconds before the door closes, the headmaster gives me one last look. I stick my tongue out and give him a flirty little wave. He shakes his head, an almost imperceptible smile on his face, and closes the door. I giggle and scamper off, bursting through the double doors and out into the courtyard.

I breathe in the clean, fresh air and listen to the birds singing in the trees. I admire the beautifully-curated campus grounds as I stroll along back to my dormitory. I pass by brick buildings adorned with strands of green vines growing up the walls, blooming in little patches of white and purple flowers here and there. It's a lovely late afternoon, and I'm on top of the world. It may have taken me the whole month I've been here to do it, but I finally seduced my headmaster. Now that we've crossed the first professional boundary with that luscious blowjob, what's to stop us from going all the way? I'm confident he'll meet up with me in the archives tonight. He's had a little taste, and I know he wants more. Just like I do. I want my new favorite father figure to take my virginity and make me a woman.

I have a little time to kill until then, though, and I haven't had the time or motivation to make any good friends here at the Academy. I've only been here a month, most of which I've spent getting in as much trouble as possible, so building friendships has been low on my list of priorities. I take out my cell phone and look at it for a moment, thinking. I decide I might as well try and call my dad. I can check in and see if he has anything disapproving to say about my newest set of charges. He should have at least gotten an email about my disciplinary meeting with Headmaster Graham. Maybe this will get his attention.

I click his name as I lean against the outer wall of the dorms. I listen to the line ring and ring and ring, then go to voicemail. I try again. Ring, ring, ring, voicemail. With my heart sinking, I give him another few tries. No answer. No anything. I sigh as I looking down at my phone sadly. For a moment, that old loneliness sweeps back in. That feeling of abandonment I could never really shake. It's funny-- Daddy makes sure I have every material desire, but the one thing I really want he can never give me. His heart. I've spent my whole eighteen years trying to get his attention, trying to make myself important in his world. It's never worked.

But now, I don't need his attention anymore. I found a better place to seek validation. I found a new daddy to take care of me, to punish or reward me like I deserve. Besides, what's better than a father figure you can rely on?

A father figure you can rely on *and* have passionate, mind-blowing sex with.

I mean, it's an obvious choice. Maybe that makes me a little bit dirty, a little bit messed up. But oh well. I am who I am, and if my daddy didn't want me to turn out like a messy, horny slut, he should've paid attention to me years ago.

I turn off my phone and put it in my blazer pocket. I walk into the dorm and go upstairs to rest and prepare myself for the crazy night ahead of me.

Many hours later when night has fallen, I find myself in the library archives. I arrived about an hour ago to watch the night shift librarian close up for the evening. I've always been a night owl with a considerable rebellious streak, so I've already spent a few nights staking out the library's security measures to find the best way to sneak in after hours. The librarian didn't suspect a thing. It's eerie down here alone in the archives. It's a large, dimly-lit room with walls, cabinets, and displays of old records. Dusty old books line the walls. A brassy light fixture hangs in the middle of the room, and a steep, creaking staircase leads up into the main library. It's not totally spooky, though. Actually, I find the cozy darkness and the walls of rich history comforting. Even romantic. I walk around the room inspecting various eccentricities as I count down the seconds to midnight. I feel a twinge of nerves, but mostly excitement. I've been holding onto my virginity for what feels like forever, waiting for the right one. The one who deserves me, who can rock my world like *I* deserve. I knew I wouldn't find that in a guy my age. But the headmaster? He's just the kind of daddy I need.

At just past midnight, I hear the creak of footsteps on the stairs. I freeze up, staring with wide eyes at the stairs. My heart is pounding as I wait to see if it's the headmaster or possibly the librarian come back to catch me in the act. Every step makes my heart beat faster. When the figure steps into the low light and I see the headmaster's hulking, handsome frame there, I light up. He came! And he looks like he stepped right out of my fantasy world. Gray eyes burning with need, his white-streaked hair pushed artfully back out of his face, and those lips begging to be kissed. He stands there with a solemn look on his face. I can sense that he's restraining himself. He's waiting for me to make a move. Go time.

I slowly saunter over to him with my eyes fixed on his. With every step I take, I strip off more of my clothes. I kick off my mary-janes. I drop my blazer to the floor. I undo each and every button on my blouse before tossing it aside. By the time I get to Headmaster Graham, I'm clad only in my bra, panties, and knee-high stockings. He peers down at me with one brow raised, like he can hardly believe I'm real. I smile softly and reach up to grab for his tie, but he flips the script in an instant. Before I can touch it, he jerks the tie loose over his shoulder and cups my face in both hands. I can hardly breathe as he leans in close and kisses me-- hard.

I moan into his mouth as he kisses me. Fireworks explode in my heart. I feel tingly and ecstatic all over, like there's pure electricity running through my veins.

The headmaster tears off his coat. I reach to unbutton his shirt while he unclasps my bra and lets it drop. My breasts spill out, my nipples perking up in the cool air. I drop my hand to rub his bulge between us, but the headmaster grabs me by the shoulders and walks me backward.

He yanks down my panties, throws them aside, and pins me against a stately white pillar. I moan as he wrenches his leg between my thighs. I rut against him while he kisses my neck.

His lips trail down my ticklish throat to my chest.

His teeth graze my nipple while he fondles my breasts, my ass, my dripping cunny. I rock against him, loving the friction on my overstimulated clit.

"You showed up," I breathe. "You really came."

"Now it's your turn to come," the headmaster growls.

He drops down to his knees and lifts one of my legs over his strong shoulder. I stare down at him in amazement as he dives in between my soft, dewy folds. I cry out with shock and pleasure as his tongue swathes over my clit.

He suckles the tight bundle of nerves until I'm trembling all over. He slides the rigid tip of his tongue up and down my flower, lapping up my honey as he works me closer and closer to the edge.

"Oh my god," I whimper. "It feels so good. Nobody's ever touched me like this."

"Mmm," he agrees with his handsome face between my legs.

I have to brace myself against the pillar while he devours my pussy. My leg is shaking, I feel like I might collapse at any moment, but the headmaster holds me up.

He supports my body while he gives me the wildest pleasure I've ever known.

His tongue is warm and wet, and he knows exactly how to use it. He circles my clit with his tongue, then sucks the whole bud into his mouth, alternating between these two delicious sensations until I can't hold back any longer.

"Oh! Headmaster, I'm coming!" I squeak.

My cunny gushes hot honey all over his lips. He laps it up eagerly while I twitch and moan through the waves of climax. But he's not done with me.

Oh no.

Far from it.

While I'm still recovering from coming, he stands up and

kisses me again. I can taste my own juices on his lips and it turns me on. He strokes my hair and holds me close.

His hands rove down my body. He smooths along my waist and slips around to grope my juicy ass. I rock against him, feeling his stiff cock hard on my thigh.

"You've been a very, very bad girl," he snarls between kisses.

I gently bite his bottom lip and pull back to murmur, "Are you going to punish me?"

He leans in to whisper roughly in my ear, "I think you need a little discipline."

Headmaster Graham grabs me and spins me around, pinning me against the pillar with my ass poking out. I brace my arms against the marble while he smacks my bare ass. I let out a peal of thrilled laughter and peer back at him over my shoulder, daring him to do more.

I feel him push my thighs apart. I hear his trousers unzip and then there's the sensation of his swollen, thick cock pressing at my slicked-up pussy.

"That's more than a *little* discipline," I purr back.

"You're more than a little naughty," he growls.

I shake my ass, rubbing against his hard cock. His length slides up and down, dragging from my pussy back to my tight ass. I whimper with impatience, pouting for more. The headmaster smacks my ass again and I shiver delightedly.

"Are you ready for me, Miss Winston?" he hisses.

I nod enthusiastically. "Yes, sir!"

The next moment, everything in my body goes wild. His hard cock pushes into my tiny, tight little virginal cunny. I cry out and grasp at the pillar, feeling sweat roll down my spine as the headmaster pushes inside of me. With every inch, I feel a twinge of pain edged with indescribable pleasure.

My cunny clenches around his massive shaft as he rocks deeper and deeper.

He rears back, almost fully pulling out, and then slams back in hard. I cry out and nearly collapse when a white-hot sting of pain shoots through me.

The headmaster catches me in his arms and holds me steady

while he pushes past my virginity. I ache and tremble while he clutches me, his cock spearing deeper and deeper inside of me until finally he shoves through.

I feel a tiny trickle of blood roll down my thighs, mingling with my pleasure honey as the headmaster pounds me from behind.

"Is this what you wanted, little girl? A big, strong man to pound your pussy?" he snarls.

"Oh, god yes!" I squeak.

The headmaster reaches around to rub my clit while he fucks me hard.

With every thrust of his hips, his balls slap against my ass. His cock strikes deep inside of me, hitting a delicious spot that makes me see stars.

Every stroke gets me higher and higher. I push back into him, meeting every thrust so that my ass bounces. He slaps my ass and plays with my clit while his cock strikes my g-spot again and again.

"Ohhh, it feels so good," I gasp.

"Come again for me, Avery. Come all over daddy's cock," he rumbles.

I do as I'm told. My cunny explodes slick honey, gushing down my thighs and dripping all over the fancy marble floor. The headmaster pounds into me harder and faster as he loses control.

He's barely holding back now, just pumping his hard cock into my tight virgin cunny. I'm giddy with satisfaction, with feeling whole.

Like the dutiful good girl proving my obedience, my devotion, my promise to be his and only his.

"I'm going to make you mine," he murmurs. "You belong with me."

"We belong together," I whisper.

"Yes. I'm going to give you everything," he hisses between his teeth.

I can feel his body tensing up. His muscles are growing tight. He's exhibiting as much self-discipline as he can to keep from coming. Even though he's bearing down on the edge, he still manages to not only keep my trembling body steady, but his fingers remain soft and rhythmic on my clit.

All of his attention, all of his focus is fully on me. The headmaster holds his own desire at arm's length to maintain my pleasure. I feel warm all over.

"Avery," he says in a soft, rough voice.

"Sir?" I reply.

"Are you ready for me?"

"Yes! Yes, sir!" I gasp.

"That's my girl," he grunts.

With one arm supporting me and the other between my thighs, the headmaster lets himself lose control. His thrusts grow more and more erratic.

I bounce back against him and he holds me up while he pounds me from behind.

Every push brings us both closer to the edge. We're moaning and panting together, my cunny dripping slick juices down my legs and his. I feel the sting of his handprint on my ass and the delicious ache of a bruise on my waist.

My body is shaking and delicate now, but strong in his arms. I feel his fingers caress my clit in soft strokes while his cock strikes deep inside me. The pressure is building between my legs again. My knees buckle and my thighs shake.

"Avery," my headmaster groans.

I feel his cock pumping inside of me as his hands both grasp my waist. The sensation of my headmaster filling my fertile virgin pussy with his seed sends me over the edge.

"Oh! Headmaster Graham!" I gasp as I come all over his cock.

He strokes my hair and holds me through our shared release. My come mingles with his and adds to the puddle on the floor beneath me. My headmaster whispers gentle words of comfort, little nonsense whispers that soothe me. He withdraws from me and I start to collapse, buckling at my knees.

But he sweeps me into his arms with one swift motion. Like I weigh nothing at all. Like his arms were built to hold me.

I smile up into his handsome face. I could get lost forever in those gray eyes, like an endless foggy morning. The faint lines at the corners of his eyes make me feel warm inside.

There's so much affection in his gaze, and when he smiles back at me I feel like I could melt. He gently sets me down. I'm steady on my feet. He kisses me softly on the lips.

When he pulls back, he murmurs, "You can call me Dane."

"Yes, sir," I reply instantly.

We stare at each other for a split second, then laugh. He leans in and rests his forehead against mine.

My heart flutters like a dragonfly.

In my mind, I picture the golden plaque on his door. Headmaster Dane Graham. I grin.

"I mean *Dane*," I murmur.

He hands me my skirt while he puts on his clothes. He brings me my blouse and starts buttoning it up for me. I gaze up at him adoringly.

"You broke the rules for me," I blurt out.

"I see the potential in you," he says with a wink. "But you're going to need ongoing discipline, if you know what I mean."

"I definitely do," I giggle.

"And you can call me whatever you want, Avery. We have time," he assures me.

"How much time?" I ask.

He cups my cheek. "As long as you like."

I turn to kiss his palm. "Forever?" I breathe.

Dane pulls me into a tight embrace. He kisses the top of my head. I look at him expectantly and he laughs.

"Forever," he confirms. "Now, let's get you and this place cleaned up before the morning shift librarian gets here."

From that night on, the two of us are intertwined. For the last month of classes, I split my time between studying and sneaking in alone time with Dane. As it turns out, I'm actually a pretty good student. All I needed was a little one-on-one guidance.

It's a little hard not to be obvious about our love, but we have a lot of fun sneaking around together until graduation. It's our little secret for a while, but once I graduate, I move right in with Dane.

My father, still too busy to notice me, didn't even attend my graduation ceremony. But it doesn't matter. It doesn't ache like it did before.

Now, there's a different face I look for in the crowd, and he's always there for me.

Always smiling back, always waiting to take me into his arms and into his bed. Every day, we fall harder and farther into love. He takes care of me.

He makes me feel so safe, so complete. We're building the most beautiful, bright life for ourselves, and he's already given me the greatest gift.

There's a sweet little light growing inside of me, and I can hardly wait to introduce my baby to the world.

Because now that I've found the love of my life, the world isn't such a scary place anymore. I don't need to rebel. I don't need to act out. I have everything I've ever wanted and it feels so, so good.

Christine's Sugar Daddies

Book Themes: Billionaire, Virgin, Breeding/Impregnation, Menage, MFM, Anal, Double Penetration
Word Count: 12230

I saw it coming from a mile away. A little bit of empathy goes far, sometimes. This was far from the first time I saw our father crying.

"I'm broke," he sobbed. "I'm broke, I have less than nothing, I'm in crippling debt, even."

It was the first time he had done it in front of all three of us, and looking how Karen reacted, she was very surprised. Olivia was too, but she always tried to cover it up with some bitchy exterior. I knew my sisters all too well, and sometimes better than they did.

This suit came in and started crushing on Karen. She didn't know a thing to do about it, and was probably flipping out. Usually, I would console her.

Nothing changed what father said however. It was true – and I couldn't help my sisters until I helped myself.

After the family meeting broke up, I headed back up the stairs. I was worried as the rest of them. Father was paying for my tuition at the best school in the state, Ivy League level. It was one of the ways I knew something was askew with his finances – he didn't pay in full, instead opting to pay by semester.

This semester was drawing to a close, and the next one was coming. I had gotten a mail or two about sending in payment for the next, and father was evasive when I did ask.

I was supposed to be the smart one. The one that would be the professor, and now, I wasn't even sure that I could stay in college instead of standing in a checkout line ringing up some guy's groceries.

Opening the door to my room, I already had my friend in there lounging on my bed, her eyes barely breaking from her phone to acknowledge me. She had kindly waited here when my father called for the family meeting.

"So who died?" she said.

"You're as bad as my sister sometimes," I replied, taking a seat at my desk.

"You do have that dour doom and gloom look on your face. I doubt your dad was telling you about the new puppy he got."

"Bea, quit it. Yeah, it's bad."

"How bad?"

"I'm going to have to drop out of school because I can't pay for it bad."

She put down her phone and glared at me. "How? Isn't your family stupidly rich?"

"Was. My father just broke into tears like it was the worst thing to ever happen. Basically told us we're losing this mansion soon and because he delayed so long, we literally have no savings."

"So you're completely broke?"

"Yeah. Broke enough that I have to go get a real job on top of dropping out of school."

Bea sighed. "You're young and pretty, Christine. You don't

have to worry about that if you do the smart thing – and you're also smart, so you're going to do the smart thing."

"What's the smart thing?"

"You're not getting kicked out from the university immediately for being poor. There's time. There's a big frat party tonight. You should go there and flaunt your stuff, you know."

I raised my eyebrow at her. "What are you implying, Bea?"

"Go get yourself a sugar daddy."

"You can't be serious."

"Completely," she said, sliding off my bed. "A girl like you can have any man. To come to a school like this you have to be loaded. Even a scholarship usually isn't enough. A lot of these guys already have millions themselves and would buy you the rest of your education in a second if it meant getting you to spread your legs."

I turned away. I didn't want Bea to see me blushing.

"Oh wait, I forgot, you're Christine. You want to wait for true love, like it's going to be in a movie where you fall in love instantly and have a big beautiful wedding night."

"It's not like that. I just," I stammered, trying to think of a good excuse.

"You're a virgin at twenty, Christine. You're three years through college and you haven't even had a boyfriend beyond that one that turned out to be gay."

"Hank's a nice guy. He said he needed me to make his mother happy."

"Yeah, but he didn't fuck you. Nothing is perfect. Nothing happens like in the movies. When love comes your way, it's going to be in a weird ass package and you're going to have to accept that. Til then, have fun, and take advantage of your relationship status."

"There you go again. I could just go get some student loans, Bea. I don't need to whore myself out."

"You're studying anthropology. You going to pay student loans back on that?"

I cringed. I could, it would take decades though. It was a luxury of being born rich – I could pursue whatever I found interesting, and not worry about its career viability. With what I was studying now though, I would have a life of living in crappy apartments and eating far more ramen than any person should ever have to.

Bea put her hand on my shoulder. "Not saying you need to go fuck everyone, but you have options, Christine. Don't go being prideful trying to score a scholarship, and be forced to rough it by doing all this studying while working part-time at Starbucks."

It would be so much easier if I could have kept living how I did now, being the model student with all the privileged free time in the world to study.

Plus I would actually have a boyfriend, with all the benefits that would entail.

I had enough lonely nights with a spicy book and my fingers to realize that yes, that's something I would very much enjoy having.

"Christine, tonight there's a big event at this party I'm going to. They throw an 'auction' for charity. Donate all the proceeds to the local animal shelter."

"What are they auctioning?"

"Girls."

My eyes went wide. "Isn't that illegal? Like, the thirteenth amendment is all against that."

She shook her head. "Don't be dense. It's for 'dates'. Rich frat boys throw money to get dates with girls they find attractive. The girls sign up for it. You should sign up for it."

"How is raising money for charity remotely helping my problem? I mean, I love puppies too, but..."

"Seriously, stop being dense. There's usually an unspoken agreement behind it. They plop down big bucks for charity, and the girl shows them their contribution are greatly appreciated." She elbowed me. "If you know what I mean."

"I don't... oh, yeah that."

"See, I knew you could stop being dense."

"I still don't see how getting me laid solves the problem."

"Well it's fun for one. And there's a high tendencies that the auctioned and the buyer aren't just a one night stand. Like, they become an item a lot. The guy is giving massive amounts to charity while telling you he thinks you're sexy in one swift move, it's a pretty solid pick up line, and he's already invested in you. Even if you don't think he's the greatest guy in the world, you could wrap them around your finger easily."

There was some logic to what she was saying. Don't flat out say what my issue was. Be a doting girlfriend. When it comes up, like it inevitably would, they'd protect their investment. "Alright. It sounds unethical as hell, but I'll do it."

"And if all else fails, Christine, just tell them they don't have to wear protection. You're on the pill."

"I'm not?"

"Don't be dense."

"You mean lie about that? That's extremely unethical!"

"Yeah, and these guys have more money than they know what to do with. You aren't really hurting anyone. Besides, you wanted kids at some point anyway, right?"

"Yes, but, urgh, you're really Machiavellian sometimes Bea." I did always want a family. Just not in the way she was proposing. It was yet another way to take care of my problems though. They'd give me a nice giant settlement for me to make the problem go away.

"I do my best. Come on. We need to make sure you get the highest bid possible."

The house was packed, and this was turning out to be as big of an event as Bea had advertised it to me as. There was no shortage of hot guys walking about, and no shortage of them making themselves considerably less hot as they did something stupid like shotgun a beer down their throats right afterwords.

I watched the process unfold in front of me. A girl would walk up and onto center stage. A bunch of cat calls happen. Dudes start throwing out numbers in the hundreds and low thousands range. Eventually only one bidder is left and he walks off with the girl. The girls mostly seem pleased, but I guess being as drunk as the bidders were only helps things. It wasn't my usual scene, but I could understand the appeal.

"The next girl coming to the stage is going to be," the MC announced, pausing a moment, likely to read a name, "Christine Van Hansen! Come on up Christine?"

I walked forward, trying to put on my best strut like Bea had told me to. The MC put on some ballad from Leo Rose as I walked forward, the crowd hooting and hollering as I progressed. I was wearing a dress that did much in showing off my ample cleavage and didn't go too far down my legs. It was again, Bea's decision. I never had an eye for fashion so I let her pick, and she told me that this highlighted all of my best attributes.

I blushed as I looked around the room, all eyes on me. Bea wasn't lying when she said guys would find me attractive. I never thought I was hot shit or on the other extreme self esteem issues due to my appearance, I thought I was average. For tonight though, it didn't matter how hot I looked. It mattered how hot the boys thought I looked.

"Christine here is a first here tonight at our auctions, because at age 20, and despite being here for two years," the MC then dropped to a hushed tone, "she's a virgin!"

A chill went down my spine as it was announced. I glanced around and saw Bea waving at me. This was her doing. She probably thought it would get people to bid higher for me and generate more money for the shelter. I thought it might attract the wrong kind of guy, personally.

I shook my head as people hooted and hollered my way, telling me that they would gladly be my first, shouting out immature things like they were going to pop my cherry good or that I was so nice to keep myself pure for them.

"Let's start the bidding at one hundred dollars for Miss Van Hansen's company."

Someone quickly rose their hand at that.

"Two hundred, do we have two hundred?"

Another hand.

"Five hundred!" Someone from the crowd shouted out.

"Eight hundred!"

"I'll take her for a thousand!"

It was all increasing so suddenly and so quickly. Of course, they were college dudes with huge disposable incomes. What else did I expect?

One bold voice echoed out from the crowd. "Five thousand."

The entire room suddenly went silent. No girl was bid on for over fifteen hundred all through the night before me. I looked toward the source of the voice. It was a tall individual, a chiseled jaw, clean cut. He had dark shabby hair just over his eyes. His clothing was black, a black jacket over a black suit, but no tie, and wearing jeans underneath. I had to say if he was paying five thousand for me I would have expected a whole lot worse of results.

"All right, five thousand. Do we have anyone who can beat five thousand?"

"Ten thousand." Another voice said, stepping out beside the dark clothed man. He didn't look too much different aside from blonde hair. Were they related? Brothers?

Dark hair shot him a glare. "So you wanna go to war over this Darren?"

"Yeah, I want her." The supposed Darren nodded.

"This is where we're playing that hand then, aren't we?"

"Yeah. Winner gets her first."

"Twenty thousand," the unnamed darker brother spoke up.

What were they on about? Getting me first? I just looked on in confusion.

"Forty thousand," Darren bid.

"What we're just going to keep doubling each other like that?"

"Keeps it interesting."

"We're not here to practice multiplication tables, Carson. One hundred thousand."

I just stood in awe. These two were brothers, fighting over me.

"Well folks," The MC joined in, "Thanks to Christine, the dogs are going to eat mighty well for awhile."

"A quarter million," Carson countered.

"A half million." Darren said, staring at his brother more than he was bidding on.

"They're going to be eating Filet Mignon," the MC added.

"Just go with a million. That's where we'd say we stop, right. That's what we agreed to, huh, Darren?" They looked like they were about to break into a brawl.

"Two..." Darren took a deep breath. "Fine, I'll have your sloppy seconds. I'll win her over that way, and show her how much more of a man I am than you, 'big bro'."

I just blinked.

Darren looked my way and walked toward me. "We'll be getting to know each other very very soon," he said, taking my hand and kissing it, his anger at his brother quickly replaced with flirtatiousness at me.

"Well, is anyone going to beat a million dollars?" The MC asked. "Going once, going twice."

The room was still in shock from what occurred.

"Sold, to the man who either really wants this woman or really really loves animals."

Carson walked over to the MC and scribbled out a check quickly.

"God, I hope this thing actually clears."

"It will."

"Then enjoy your million dollar woman."

He walked forward, taking my hand and leading me off the stage. There were murmurs now, but it was still mostly quiet.

"Woohoo, you go girl!"

Thanks, Bea.

As soon as we were out of earshot and I was alone with my purchaser, I had to speak up. "Really? A million dollars? Listen, I'm not plagued with low self-esteem or anything like that, but I'm not worth a million dollars."

"Isn't that for me to decide?" He smiled at me and offered me a handshake. "Carson York. I'm going to be the man who wins your heart."

I blinked. "Isn't that a bit ambitious given we've only just met?"

"I've seen you around the campus, Christine. I don't think it's a stretch to say I got a good feeling about us. Although I had no idea you were a virgin."

I cringed again. "My friend told them to say that."

"You're not a virgin?"

"Is that any of your business?"

"Well, yeah."

"I don't have to sleep with you, you know. It's for my time, not to fuck me, no matter how much you paid."

"Pride. Yeah, you don't have self-esteem issues then. But I do like that. I don't like my women to be doorstops."

"Good, that's something nice about you."

I kept walking, he followed as we left the frat house. Bea's words echoed in my mind though. No matter what I thought about this guy, I needed him. Either for him to be my sugar daddy or at least knock me up.

The latter one seemed so utterly wrong and deceptive, I repeated to myself.

"What's with you and your brother?" I asked as we kept walking.

"Darren?" He paused. "We're brothers. We butt heads. We compete. We both happen to be highly successful. Honestly we're still going to this school almost as a competition to who can get the most pretentious title. Right now, he's winning. Dr. Darren York."

"He doesn't look like a doctor."

"Can't deny he's brilliant. Got an early start. It's in business, by the way, so don't go having a heart attack near him."

"Same for you?"

"Hey, I did it first. Little brother follows big brother, wants to get out the shadow and cast the shadow on me for a change."

"Ok. But what does that have to do with me?"

"Everything." He placed a hand on my shoulder and turned me around to look him right in the face.

He then kissed me.

Not just a peck, no. His hand ran through my hair and pushed me deeper into his lips, his tongue invading my mouth. Oddly, I felt compelled to go with it, and follow his direction. There were definitely some sparks there as our kiss suddenly broke. "You liked that, didn't you?"

"Maybe," I said, blushing.

"Me and my brother compete over everything. Business, sports... women."

"Wait, I'm just some notch on a bedpost?"

"Oh no, there's no fun in that. I'm sure we'd both pull some big numbers if we competed that way, but that's not how we play."

"Then how on earth do you compete?"

"We share."

"Share?"

"We take a woman. We both have her. We let her choose who she prefers to be with."

"What if I don't want to 'have' your brother? What if I only want you?"

"Then I've already won, haven't I? The way I see it, you win either way. I don't hate my brother in the least. He's a fine person. Bit rough at times and hard headed, but I'm just better, in my admittedly biased opinion."

I closed my eyes, turning away from him, trying to think for a moment. "So you want me to fuck both you and your brother?"

"Only if you want to. If a relationship is to bloom between us, I don't view it as betrayal if it's with him. At least until you have to decide, anyway."

It was madness. All I wanted was a boyfriend, and someone to take care of the whole money issue.

And yet...

"I can't say I'm not intrigued."

"You're twenty years old and in college. There's no better time to try something like this."

"Alright, Mister Competitive. Give me your best shot."

"With pleasure."

He led me back to his place. A fine mansion in its own right, in walking distance from the fraternity. Huge gates, well maintained gardens, it really did put my father's mansion to shame. Carson, and likely Darren, likely had access to more funds than my father could ever dream of possibly having. The interior didn't do much to dissuade me of that notion, fine art and other various doodads gracing the walls and hallways.

I wasn't here to see his house. I was well accustomed to luxurious homes, and maybe I'd even have one of my own in the future. I was here for Carson.

"My brother and I have very different ideas about making love. He's abrupt, rough. Tries to call it passion. My definition is very much different."

He led me to his bedroom, in which there was a king size bed with four pillars on every side of the mattress.

He tossed off his jacket as he walked toward the bed.

A tinge of nervousness hit me. This was it. My first time. It wasn't like how I envisioned it happening. I expected more candles, maybe some flower petals. I was always the more hopeless romantic.

Carson was approaching me, met me eye to eye.

He kissed me again.

This. This was okay. It wasn't like the movies, no, but I definitely couldn't deny my attraction to Carson – or his brother for that matter. Even as he guided me in our embrace, the kisses meeting my face, I was constantly reminded of the fact that he wanted to share me, just to prove how much better of a lover he was.

I had to hope that this wasn't all bravado and he was actually terrible. As his hands ran through my hair and down my back, I was realizing that to be quite unlikely. Everywhere he touched me, gooseflesh appeared. He was good at this, damn good at this. Deft and delicate, I only wanted more from him, and let my own hands roam him back. He was firm and strong, and even through his shirt I could tell that he was incredibly ripped and strong.

Carson then used that strength to sweep me off my feet and carry me to the bed, planting my back on it, and covering me right behind him. He whispered into my ears, his hot breath tickling them as he spoke. "Ever since I saw you, I knew I had to have you, Christine. I had to have you first. I would have broken the rules for it."

"Rules?"

"Me and my brother put a cap at one million, but I would have bet a billion for you."

His continued to devour me with his kisses, them raining down my cheeks, my mouth, down my neck and across my chest. He reached around my body and found the zipper that was keeping my dress in place, pulled it down, and with it, the garment as well.

Carson took the revelation of more of my flesh to ravish it, and make more the tiniest hairs on my body all perk up. He outlined my breasts with his fingers, my bra still protecting me from the best of his touch, and he proceeded to continue to use it against me. My nipples hardened, yearning for more of his touch, but I was denied, his hands going down my back, all across my thighs.

He was making my entire body want him. Every single nerve inside of me yearn for more of his touch. It was the move of both evil and genius at the same time.

My tormentor only briefly glanced over my panties, even though I knew he wouldn't ignore what laid underneath forever, but he was only going to drag it out further. Anticipation was powerful, and Carson was all about abusing that power to its absolute fullest.

His teasing continued, and I unhooked my bra, trying to encourage him to go forward. Luckily for me, he actually took the cue, pulling it off me and reveling in my naked breasts in front of him. Carson smiled, his approval comforting as I'd never shown them to anyone who should have been attracted to them before.

Doubling down on his admiration, he laid a kiss on my chest, and let his tongue roam around my nipple, and they were more than ready for his stimulation. The littlest bits of bliss were forming there under his licks, and it only got better as he showed my other breast the same attention, running his fingers softly over the teat that his tongue was neglecting at the time.

Even steadier, his hands slid down my naked body and toward my valley. Carson continued to suckle me as he slid his fingers into my panties, and saw how despite my initial confusion and protests, I was hot and ready for him already. "You're an awfully dirty girl for a virgin," he said.

"I have a very active imagination, and you're just making me imagine what's coming for me very shortly."

"Well I shouldn't disappoint you should I?"

He ran a finger suddenly over my nub and I damn near almost came from that alone. He continued, his finger deftly circling around my labia, letting the shock of his brief touch set in before doing it again. His fingers slipped into my slit, teasing me even further, and his kisses left my breast to cross my abdomen and down to my panties. Carson teased me even further through the fabric of my underwear, sucking on my clit for them, and letting me yearn for it to be gone.

My own hands reached for the band of my underwear, trying to push them down. All Carson did in return was grin like the asshole he was, then help me get rid of them. Bare in front of him, I was now completely at his mercy.

Carson was going to make sure that I wasn't going to regret it. He took in the sight of my naked body, nodded, and then flung off his own shirt. His chest was as good looking as it felt moments earlier, but I only got to see it briefly before he dropped to one knee, and then the other. His hand slid down my body from between my breasts back to my valley, before gently easing my legs apart. Carson's head drifted between my legs with a grin, as he was out to enjoy everything about me. Taking in my scent, then shocking me as he began to lick up my arousal, sucking it up like it were sweetest nectar on the planet.

It threw me off, the sudden surge that jolted through me did.

It kept coming as his tongue pressed against everything tender down there, and started building the fires of lust inside me. No longer content with me simply enjoying the little things that he was doing to me, he was out to give me the absolute best, something that up to this point, I had only enjoyed by my own hand before this, and Carson was quickly proving his tongue was far greater than my fingers.

He continued to build at my ecstasy. Every lick around my labia, every little fuck with his tongue, every suckling of my clit, it was all orchestrated by him so damn well. His hands roamed my body, to keep the fire alive there and unify everything in my core. He wanted me to cum, and he wanted me to cum so damn hard.

It wasn't going to be long before he got his wish and I got my wish to. As much as I resisted the growing bliss inside me, pulling his hair, crossing my legs around his head, I was quickly heading toward that climax and fast.

When it hit me, it hit me hard. Every muscle tensing then releasing in bliss. So intense, so powerful, I moaned so loud for him as he was devouring me so completely. He didn't even stop as I screamed for him, wanting my orgasm to be sung out as loud as it possibly could be.

By the time he finally stopped, I was a panting, sweating, and highly satisfied mess. In my ecstatic haze, I watched as he stripped himself the rest of the way down and showed me his very well sculpted and toned body, with his hard, erect cock at the forefront.

Carson climbed on top of me, and gave me another kiss, as well as a look that told me he wasn't done yet. There was going to be even more to come for me. "I'm going to take you, Christine. Make you mine. Going to make it so you won't even want to touch my brother."

The thought swirled around in my head. The words that his brother took a very much different approach to love making. I wondered what it could be, as Carson was so dedicated and driven to my pleasure. What could Darren do that was all that different?

I couldn't think about that now. No, not with Carson over

me, kissing me, and making me realize what I had at exactly this moment was good – damn good.

He brushed my clit again as he brought his cock to my pussy lips, right on the outside, ready to make me no longer a virgin. Despite my one orgasm already, I was still wet, and I was still hungry for more if we was offering it to me.

"I'm ready," I said, nodding enthusiastically for him.

He nodded back, and started to press forward inside of me, spreading my pussy lips as he entered. I cooed as he did so, feeling him fill me up so much.

Anticipation was driving me mad. Both of his – and my creation. I was afraid of all the rumors I heard that it would be terrible.

Truth be told, I barely felt any pain. I was aroused by him, so wanting him, I think my body just wanted him in, not caring one bit about any of my hymens protests and just letting him through.

Carson didn't rush me. Not one bit. He let me adjust to having the full might of his girth inside me before he slid himself out, and back in, and began the full proper fucking motion. He kissed me, he hugged me, he caressed me, and suckled my tits, it was all part of his worship as he created a rhythm with his cock.

I was loving every single moment of it. My entire body was alive with lust, from my skin to my nethers. I could only sit back and moan, with the occasional counter brush of his firm body. I did enjoy touching him, but I enjoyed the way he touched me so much more. His pace only grew faster and more rapid, and every time I noticed this change, he grunted and groaned himself, my body jerking at his cock, urging him to fuck me deeper.

Moaning, I relished it, feeling my legs unconsciously close around his body as he stayed on top of me. I realized that it was his bare, naked cock against inside my pussy. My unprotected, potentially fertile pussy. I thought about the risk of what was happening, but strangely trusted Carson to be able to control himself. After all, no man who was this good at making me climax could be inexperienced enough to spill his seed so suddenly. He would know when he was cumming.

I realized the irony of that thought with all the other girls through history who accidentally got knocked up. Even then, I remembered Bea's words and how that wouldn't be the worst thing in the world.

Harder, faster, now so sure that I was adjusted to him, he was fucking me like a man possessed. Every penetration let bliss shudder through my body, and all I could do was hold on, relishing all of it. I called out for him, and he only took it to another level in response. "God, you're so fucking tight, Christine. Never fucked anyone who felt as good as you do."

Even in my haze, his compliment made my smile curl a bit at the end.

"Fuck, I don't see how any man could last with you."

I was coming up to my climax once more by his hand, and it didn't help that he had reached between our body and began to massage my clit, all while never letting up fucking me. I was shaking, and ready to explode. One final flick, combined with one final thrust, was all that it took to send me over the edge, shaking in bliss and orgasm from his fucking.

So much more than the first, I was sent screaming, loudly. I knew we were alone in this place so I took advantage of it fully, calling his name as every nerve in my body flared with exquisite delight.

Carson never stopped. I could hear him grunting, trying to control himself, drag out by own utter bliss even longer, but he was nearing his climax too.

Even as my legs lost strength and dropped from around his back though, he wasn't stopping. He picked up my legs, folded me deeper, and kept fucking me. Carson grit his teeth. "Fuck, Christine, so fucking good."

The loudest grunt I heard from him that night was followed by him being forced to slow down, as I felt his balls pulse against my skin, his cock buried so deep inside, pressed to the hilt. Everything pulsed, for that matter, and he came. Burst after burst, every bit of his seed was being fired off inside of me, splashing against my cervix and making my eyes roll back in my head further.

I liked it. I really did like the feeling of him cumming so deeply inside of me. It was a wonderful finish to the blissful climax he had already given me.

Carson was in no rush to pull out. As the haze of orgasm cleared, it became obvious what he just did.

"You came inside me," I said, as he was still inside me.

"Yes." His voice was flat, obvious, like he couldn't understand why I would question that.

"I'm not on the pill. Or anything else."

"I knew that was likely."

"Is this where you tell me you had a vasectomy?"

"Nope. Never had one of those."

"Then why did you cum inside me? Why are you still inside me? I have to get it out." I was becoming increasingly panicked by the notion.

"I'm claiming you as my own," he said. "Part of how my brother and I compete is by seeing who has the stronger seed."

I looked at him like he was insane. Finally, he started to pull his cock out of me. Drips of cum followed his cock, but he pushed it back into me. "Why are you doing that?"

"Best chance of success."

"What if I don't want to have your child, Carson?"

He shrugs. "It was an unspoken part of the deal. If you don't want to fuck me, that's fine. I'm willing to treat a woman like a goddess, but when it comes to sex, we do it my way, and I don't use protection. It takes away from the natural, primal nature of it all. It ruins it for me."

I breathed deeply as he massaged my messy pussy, still stewing with his seed.

I reminded myself that this is what I wanted, right? I wanted a way to make sure I was taken care of, and right now, he offered me multiple ways of making it happen.

"You're free to get up and run to the bathroom if you so desire now. I'll miss fucking you though, and all the fun we'd have as you swell with my child."

God, I did enjoy everything he just did. "It's fine. I was just really, really, surprised that you approached it like that." I managed a smile.

With my approval clear, he climbed to bed beside me and took me into his arms. Embracing me wholly, he held me close, a hand over my pussy, almost seeming to want to keep his seed inside me all night.

Thoughts of what he did drifted through my head as I began to doze. Thoughts of Carson, and thoughts of Darren, and what was going to come with everything that had happened – and that was going to happen.

Over the night, Carson's grasp on me weakened, so by the time we finally woke up, I wasn't locked into him. I shrugged, and thought it worked for the better. I rolled out of bed, stretched a bit. I wandered off to the bathroom, and did a few things there that don't need to be said. Still naked, I walked out into the foyer of Carson's home, trying to collect my thoughts.

I still felt his seed inside me, even if I couldn't feel it running my hand down there.

A set of hands grabbed me from behind. The grasp was similar, yet different from the set of hands that I had experienced before. They were still strong, firm hands.

I turned around inside the grasp to see the man who had grabbed me.

It wasn't Carson, with his unkempt dark hair.

It was Darren, a much cleaner blond man holding me.

I almost jumped out of my skin, feeling so naked and vulnerable – because I was – in front of a man who wasn't my lover.

Yet.

He was dressed in a pair of sweatpants and not much else. His chest was ripped, with little hairs all over. If I wasn't so petrified of his sudden appearance, I would have been very happy to have him this close to me.

Instead, I stammered like an idiot. "Uh, um, what are you doing here?"

"I live here too. My brother and I share this place."

I swallowed. It wasn't the only thing they said they were sharing.

"I see – and heard – my brother have some fun last night. He told you everything, didn't he?"

I nodded.

"It's my turn then."

He introduced himself to me with a kiss. Harsher, stronger, and dare I say far more passionate than his brother. Darren forced his tongue into my mouth, and made my tongue follow his. He pushed me against a wall as he did so, pressing his body against my own, engulfing me with his powerful presence.

Darren broke the kiss by yanking my hair away from his head. It stung at first, but there was an oddly sensual aspect of what he was doing. "See, me and my brother have different opinions of what women want sometimes. He thinks they want to be worshiped. Me? I think more than a few think they get enough of that already. They want something very different – they want passion, something they won't get typically."

I listened to his words with an eyebrow raised, curious to what he meant. "Like what?"

"Like maybe they want to treated like the sluts they are."

Putting a little strength behind it, he pushed me down to my knees, never taking his eyes off mine. He shoved his sweatpants down and out came his cock, hard and very much ready for me. He grabbed my hair and guided it toward my lips.

"I heard the way you screamed last night. Those weren't the screams of a princess. They were the screams of a whore. Suck it."

I blinked.

"Suck my cock. You know you want to."

Looking up at Darren, there was definitely a fire to him. He was definitely sexy. My heart was pounding. Carson was so sweet, so caring, why was his brother so different?

I couldn't say I wasn't intrigued. I couldn't even deny his accusations of me being a slut were untrue. After all, he was talking down to me, pulling my hair, and had his cock in my face. Yet I still felt like I wanted him, even after enjoying what his brother did so damn much.

Obeying Darren, I licked the tip of his cock. Licked his head. It felt weird doing this; Carson didn't even ask me to. I let my tongue run down his cock, up and around it. I was virgin only a day ago, but I wasn't completely naive in the realm of what people did behind closed doors.

Or in the hallway of a mansion owned by two sexy brothers.

"Lick my balls, Christine. Lick them good."

I nodded, doing as he asked, tasting the flesh. It wasn't as bad as I expected it to be, and the adrenaline that was starting to pump through my head only intensified my resolve. I took them into my mouth even, and started to suck on them. Darren's head draped back with a silent groan. I was getting his approval despite his harsh words and it oddly brought a smile to my face.

Leading my tongue away from his balls, I went up and down his shaft, letting him enjoy the delicate job I was doing.

The problem was, Darren wasn't a delicate man.

Again, he took me by the hair, and thrust his cock through my lips.

Sudden, strong, powerful, I was overwhelmed and almost gagged on him. I was driven to please him however, licking him and sucking him as he fucked my face. So sudden, so rough, the adrenaline started to really pump, along with my own imagination running wild and making parts of me far hotter than I would expect from such treatment.

My eye contact never broke as I looked up at his sick grin, which only broke so often so often for a grunt or gasp of his own when the pressures of me sucking his cock was proving to be just too much for him to handle.

He was legal, as Carson said. Even if I wanted more of Carson, he said I was allowed to experience Darren too. It's not cheating, and as a young and sexually curious woman, I wanted to please Darren so he would show me just what his brand of love was.

If it felt anything like Carson's it would be well worth it.

Sucking, licking, fondling his balls as all of this happened, Darren was only a man and was soon struggling to hold himself back from the charms of a first time cocksucker.

I wasn't surprised when he pulled my head off his cock. "You really like that don't you? I knew you'd turn out to be my slut after all."

He followed his words by pulling me up to my feet, and bringing me in for another rough yet delectable kiss. Everything was so powerful, so passionate with him.

When it broke, he was still staring deeply into my eyes, the hand not on my head going down my body and to my pussy, where he shoved his fingers in. "You're already dripping wet for me. I knew it."

I shuddered as he fingered me, flicking my clit as if the sounds I made when he did so were purely for his amusement.

That I enjoyed the feeling of that he was doing was secondary to him, it seemed.

"I'm going to fuck you, Christine. I'm going to fuck you harder than my idiot brother ever could. You're going to scream for me. Louder than you did for him. Isn't that what you want?"

Breathing deeply, I nodded. God, I really was a slut.

He shoved me over to the bannister that I was looking over when he first accosted me. His hand was still over my pussy massaging it, preparing it.

Unlike Carson, he wasn't going in slow. Darren instead impaled me on his cock.

Strong, powerful, it was a hell of a change, an intense burst of delight rushing through me as he fucked me. He was in me to the hilt, and let me adjust to him after a short time before starting to fuck me – and fuck me hard.

The echo of flesh rang through the hallway, and every penetration caused me to sway forward, my breasts bouncing with each fuck. I held on to the bannister as he did so, trying to contain the wave after wave of delight that was being sent through my body.

Darren slapped my ass as he continued his rhythm, nursing the spot he hit me only to slap it again. The small bits of pain only brought a smile to my face, another piece to the wonderful sensory pile he was building.

Faster, my back started to arch from his penetrations. He took it as an opportunity to hold me by my breasts, taking my nipples into the hand, and roll them in his finger tips. It stung and I called out, but he didn't stop. Why was I still smiling? That hurt.

It was all part of the design. The passion, the roughness. Carson was tender, Darren was rough and passionate. Everything he did only amplified the feeling of his raw, bareback cock inside me. How he fucked me, how I moaned for him.

Screaming for him. I don't know if I screamed louder for him than I did for Carson, but I did scream for him. He was good, and he was quickly bringing me to a whole new level of orgasm and ecstasy from what he was doing. As he fucked me, he reached between my legs, and just like his brother, he found my clit. His approach wasn't to massage it, though, but to assault it.

What was a steady rising tide soon became an uncontrollable flood in my body. Tears in my eyes, there was no way that I was going to be able to go much longer. It was too much, too fast, too great.

It exploded inside me. Everything from my core outwards surged in wonderful and blissful orgasm. From head to toe I felt the goodness spread over me, and I was singing his praises.

Even deep within, I could feel my pussy spasm around him, pulling at him, jerking him forward, as if that's what he wanted all along.

Underneath my screams, he had to have been struggling to keep himself together. He was grunting, slowing down in his onslaught, leaning down over me, the sounds he made tickled my back.

He was cumming.

Again, just like his brother, he didn't pull out. No. He kept himself buried deeply and to the hilt, letting his seed rush out of his balls and through his cocks and directly into my womb. Not caring if I would have objected as he filled me once again to the brim.

Again, I couldn't help but relish the feeling after it all. I wondered if I'd ever be able to accept a guy with a condom after this, knowing it would be denied this blissful feeling of a pussy full of cum.

Panting, he held onto me tightly, holding me up even after my own strength failed to keep me up on the bannister.

"You're fucking amazing, Christine. Just fucking wonderful. God, I haven't had a girl enjoy it that much in a while."

"I guess I am as much as a slut as you said I was," my tone somewhat somber.

"Don't say it like it's a bad thing. I love me a good slut who wants me to abuse them in all the right ways."

Slowly, he let me down, pulling out after it was far too late to prevent anything. Just like his brother, he pushed the little bits of seed that escaped back in.

I was resting against on the floor as he pulled his sweatpants back up. "It's almost noon. I have things to do babe, but I'm going to make sure I fuck you again tonight. You're welcome in our home as long as you like and I definitely hope you hang around."

Darren walked away, to do whatever it is a Darren does.

Carson then stepped out of his room, towel in hand, and threw it to me. "Oh, I see he's going to make it interesting for me. Shame, I guess I have to keep sharing you. Wipe yourself off, take a nap, because I'm going to want another go too tonight."

I took the towel, wiping the sweat off of my brow and the rest of my body. As I reached down between my legs, Darren's seed was still freshly there. My eyes closed, thinking of the implications. They both wanted to keep fucking me. They both wanted me pregnant, so that they could claim their sperm was the superior stock. It was a blissful thought, knowing that it was going to continue.

Good things don't last forever though. I looked toward Carson, gathered my breath and spoke through my exhaustion. "Do I have to choose?"

Carson knelt down before me. "Well yeah, that's the point. I know you want me though. Let's give you, say, a week, and then you'll know for sure."

"A week?" I said, wistfully.

"Yeah. You'll be sore and sick of his shit by then." He pointed down to the mess that was leaking out of me and onto the carpet – his brother's seed. "We'll determine who has the better sperm later, but I'm not sharing you for nine months, Christine. I want you all to myself."

I wasn't so sure of that. Deciding? It wasn't going to be an easy task.

W hat came next was a delight. I didn't think about things like the decision between the two brothers that would be inevitably forced upon me, and instead simply enjoyed what was being done to me. Every time Darren fucked me roughly against the wall, over a counter, or just fucking took me on the floor, I screamed for him. He fucked me hard. He filled me to the brim with his seed.

Inevitably, Carson would be there to care for me. He would wipe me off after Darren's rough ravishing. Treat me like a princess, eat me out if I wasn't dripping with his brother's cum. I would cum again and again with him, and he too would be flooding me with seed.

My whole day was an endless fuckfest where I was cared for, used and abused, and everything else. My plan about trying to con them into paying for school for me was the furthest thing in my mind, and even the ideas that they would eventually knock me up at this rate was second to the wonderful, seemingly endless sex I was having.

Sure, Carson was sweet. Darren was so damn right though. I was a slut, through and through. The two brothers had awakened a powerful libido inside of me that I don't think I would be able to stifle again so easily. The thought of losing one of them and not having a cock on demand was an utterly devastating thought.

The days went by, each as blissful as the last. I kept the thoughts of what was coming out of my head, and just simply enjoyed the attention for everything that it was. It was a hell of an introduction into the world of sexuality. The end was coming though, and it would be unavoidable.

I was sitting alone in their kitchen, drinking some coffee, trying to wake myself up after another wonderful yet incredibly exhausting day. Dressed for a change, I wondered for how long I would be, hoping for the fuckfest to continue.

"She's all about me, bro," Darren said, his voice coming off from the distance.

"She's going to get tired of your games," Carson replied.

The two came into the kitchen. They were both dressed for business, and whatever they had planned for that day. They too poured themselves coffee and each one of them sat beside me.

I suddenly felt incredibly nervous, staring at the table, not wanting to make eye contact with either of them.

"So, Christine," Carson began. "I've had such a wonderful week with you."

"So have I," Darren added, running hand through my hair. "No one has made me enjoy making a woman scream quite like you do."

"I think I enjoy you both so damn much that I can't imagine a world where I don't have you now," I said, somewhat suggestively.

"We're not sharing you forever, Christine," Carson responded. "We came here today because it's time for you to choose. Do you want me to keep treating you like a goddess?"

Darren suddenly grabbed my hair. "Or do you want me to keep fucking you like the whore you are?"

I was silent in response, Darren's grip loosening when he realized I wasn't all that into it at that moment.

"What's the matter?"

"I can't," I said. "I just can't just choose between you."

"Of course you can, Christine. One of us treats you like

garbage, the other wants to worship you." Carson shot a twisted gaze over at his brother.

"It's not garbage. It's how she wants to be treated," he spat back.

"It's two great flavors of the same great thing," I continued. "Sometimes I want to be tenderly fucked, but sometimes I want something raw, and animalistic. Both of you are so damn good at what you do, but I can't just push the other away and accept the other."

"Seriously? You're trying to play the we're both awesome card?" Darren stood up out of the chair. "Look in your heart. It'll tell you the truth."

I closed my eyes, and did exactly as he said. "No, I can't."

Carson shoved Darren. "You've probably made her all stock-holmed and whatever with how you fuck her."

"You suggesting I'm abusing her?"

Carson glanced toward me. "Come on, Christine. I'll take good care of you. You can tell my asshole of a brother off."

"Oh you want to go make it like this, huh?" Darren shoved his brother away from me. Their bravados were flaring in full force.

"You know how our scuffles always end little brother."

It was becoming clear to me that as much as I enjoyed it, it wasn't about me.

"Let's go, I'll let you have a free shot."

"Oh stop it!" I screamed out, unable to cope with the nonsense anymore. I shot up. "Stop fighting, stop yelling, stop this literal dick-waving contest!"

Surprisingly, that worked. They calmed down and were both staring my way.

"I've had it. I think I love you both and everything you do to me, but it seems you're not doing it because you want me as much as you want to beat your brother. Clearly, what I really want isn't important as much as just validating your egos."

When forced to confront my feelings, I was exhausted, and I'd be exhausted no matter how much coffee I would drink.

"You're brothers, and you're very close to one another no

matter how the two of you act. I'm going to be seeing the one I don't choose often because of that. A constant, heart wrenching reminder of what I can't have, and I don't think I'd be able to take that."

With another deep breath, I rose.

"If I can't choose both, then my second choice is going to be neither."

I started walking toward the front door of the mansion.

"Christine, wait!" Carson called out.

"Look what you did, asshole," Darren replied.

"What I did? It's your fault!"

As I exited the building and I was sure the door was closed behind me, I started to cry.

A few weeks passed, and I barely even noticed. They consisted of moping around my room, feeling sorry for myself, and hating myself for blowing it.

The pregnancy test sitting on my desk had a positive reading. Apparently they had zeroed in on me at my most fertile. My mission was accomplished. I'd be set for life, even if I needed a paternity test to be so. I cringed, realizing that they would still get to play their stupid game and beat their chest that their sperm won or whatever it was they saw in it.

Not like it mattered. Apparently the Van Hansen family was going to be just fine. A mysterious donor infused our estate with more funds than we ever had before. I didn't think about the mystery too much, since both Karen and Olivia had brand new boyfriends who adored them and were worth far more than my father could ever dream of being. Our family was going to be just fine, I was going to be just fine even if I didn't want to go the route of hitting Carson and Darren up for money for the next eighteen years.

So everything I had enjoyed had been for nothing.

The pain I was feeling? Also for nothing. Was it even all worth it? The sting in my heart told me no.

Still, I pulled myself up to my feet, determined to do the one thing that would take my mind off of heartbreak. Studying. It was seven in the evening, but the college's library stayed open into the wee hours of the morning. I could bury my nose in some books for brief relief.

I took off walking, trying to keep my mind blank. Even if the library was open into the twilight hours, it didn't mean that it was packed to capacity for all of that time. It was sparsely populated. I had my favorite spot inside of it, a little private cubby where no one could bother me. It was at the far end of the hall, past the conference rooms.

Grabbing my book, I began my journey. Only I wasn't making it alone. "Christine, long time no see, beautiful."

I froze. It was Darren. Of course, he was a student here too, if a ludicrously wealthy one.

"You're the last person I want to see right now."

"Oh come on, babe, don't be like that."

"Am I the second to last?" Carson's voice perked up as he stepped beside me. "Do I win via you speaking a cliche?"

"This is why you both need to fuck off. I don't want to be part of your stupid contests anymore."

I kept walking past them, trying to drive my point home. Them being here was going to make forgetting they existed a pain in the ass.

Carson ran ahead of me. They weren't going to give up easily were they? He opened a door. I was about to turn around and head somewhere else, but Darren took me by the shoulders and showed me that all the muscles he had were hardly just for show.

Even with his strength, he was trying to avoid hurting me as he guided me into a conference room, and Carson came in, closing the door behind him.

"I don't want to deal with you two anymore. Why can't you get that?" I said, closing my eyes, wishing a three-year-old's logic were true and that would make them disappear. "I'm not going to choose between you. That's that."

"Christine, what if we told you," Carson began.

"That you can have us both," Darren finished.

Opening my eyes, I saw that they were both in front of me. Close, I could feel each of their body heats. Each of them took one of my hands.

"I don't understand," I said.

"Shall we make it clear, bro?" Darren nodded.

"Let's."

Carson kissed me. Deep and delicately as he always did. Even as I was protesting and telling him to fuck off moments before, I couldn't resist my body's natural reaction. It wanted his affection, his kiss.

Darren snapped me away from his brother and kissed me too. God, my body missed him so much too, even as he yanked me forward so he could thrust his tongue into my mouth deeper, forcing me to relish his rough nature.

The kisses broke. "We're brothers, Christine," Carson started. "Rivalry is what we do."

"The weeks without you though, well, it made us realize that we couldn't just move on," Darren said. "I just liked the way you screamed for me too much, and I knew I wasn't going to get that with any woman. I don't want to go searching for that next one in the million."

"The competition is void. It's stupid and pointless if it costs us fun, and maybe love?" Carson raised an eyebrow. "You win. You get us both. You're a girl worth sharing, Christine."

I couldn't believe it.

It became a lot more real soon after though. Carson laying a kiss on me, and Darren yanking at my shirt. With a bit of umph, he tore the t-shirt off of me, just to more quickly get at what was underneath it as I was being kissed by his brother. He pulled at my bra, snapping it off me, then roughly sucking on my teat.

The two pushed me onto the long table of the conference room, ready to ravish me. The delicate kisses of Carson were contrasted by the roughness of Darren sucking on my tit, and his hands roaming down, pulling at my jeans. He snapped away the button and then forced his hand down my panties.

"She's already fucking wet and we barely even touched her. I think she is too much of a slut for just one man, Carson."

"If that's what it takes to make her ours, then that's what we're going to do," his brother replied stroking my hair. "Get these clothes off her. I have two weeks of pent up lust that she needs to feel. Maybe I'll get a bit rough."

"Way ahead of you," Darren replied, stripping me of my shoes, socks, and yanking my jeans down my legs. In the blink of an eye, I was completely naked before the two men of my dreams.

Hands were caressing my body all over, with the rare twist of a breast and the spanking. I reached out and caressed them back, as they weren't going to let me be the only one naked for long. Soon, all three of us were as bare as the day we were born, Darren on top of me kissing me, and Carson dropping between my legs and giving me a kiss someplace else entirely.

After weeks of being so deprived of him, having him down there was a miracle. He was licking up my juices and sucking on all the right tender parts as he continued to do what he did best. I was reliving my memories again and so suddenly as he continued to massage my clit, and give every bit of my pussy the love it deserved.

Darren on the other hand had other things in mind. He shoved my face toward his cock, and at this point, he didn't even need to say it. I knew what to do. I licked him. I ran my tongue up and down him. I sucked on his balls, all before doing my damnedest to suck his cock the normal way. All before he pulled me back and started to fuck my face, and fuck it hard.

Even with the distraction of Carson eating me, I thought I did a commendable job of it really.

Carson wasn't going to let his brother get all the attention, either. He flicked my clit every time he thought I was paying his brother too much attention, and apparently he thought I was giving him too much attention way too often.

He was building that orgasm inside of me quick, weeks of being deprived and not even being able to cum by my own hand anymore, he was making the wait all worth it. It was becoming something harder, stronger than ever before with Darren making me suck his cock as I was being eaten out. The heightened sexuality of having two men on top of me was stroking my own ego and making the situation all the more sweeter.

It wasn't long before I was moaning around Darren's cock. It was an odd symphony of orgasm and flesh and I think Darren was liking the muffled sounds of my delight. Making it all the sweeter for him as I sucked the precum right off the tip of his cock.

I came. It would have been loud if I hadn't been silenced by Darren, but it was so sweet realizing that I'd be able to have each of them again, and that now i was going to be able to have both of them at the same time.

"Shall we switch?" Darren said.

"Let's," his brother responded.

Already shaking with orgasm, I was welcome by Darren only wanting to force me to do so again. Unlike his brother who was simply content with taking his time and building me up to orgasm, he came at me like a ravenous beast. He was licking my pussy, yes, but in a powerful, intense way, and not letting my poor clit even rest for a second. I wasn't going to get the chance to come down from the highs that Carson had brought me, no, I was going to go right back up there.

I reached out and pulled the elder brother closer, jerking his cock, bringing it to my lips. He never made me blow him before; I guess it held too much against his ideology of treating me like his goddess. I took him into my mouth, and made sure every bit of that hardness was getting attention, like all those times he did so well in worshiping me between the legs.

Again, the other brother was being quite the distraction. Making me coo and moan as I tried to do my part in our menage a trois. Sucking, being sucked, it was all a chain of bliss, of moans, of grunts, and of everything else. One thing I knew though is they knew how to control themselves far better than I did, because their erections were firm ad strong, while I?

I was moaning and screaming like the novice I was. Darren's rapid fire approach quickly sent me high and loving it every step of the way.

Soon, I was left in a sweaty, panting heap, and I still hard two hard cocks that needed release, and they were going to find it inside of me.

"Wanna try something new?" Carson said, elbowing his brother.

"Don't want to take turns, huh?" His brother replied, winking.

"You brought the lube. It was your idea."

"Oh, hell, I'm not complaining at all."

Pushing myself up with one arm, I raised an eyebrow. "What are you two up to?"

Carson took my hand. "Christine, sweetie, if we're going to both fuck you at the same time, we're going to open you to a whole new world."

"I'm interested."

Carson laid down on the table beside me. "Ride me, Christie."

I nodded, and summoned my strength to do so. Taking his cock in my hand, I began to lower myself onto him, placing a hand on his chest. A deep breath, and I began to bounce on him, slowly.

What I didn't expect was for Darren to come up behind me and touch me on the ass. His hand was freezing – and it was because there was something on it. Oil.

Lube.

It quickly warmed up when he touched me, but he didn't relent. He was circling that oil all around my asshole. One finger, pushing into my pucker.

Odd. That was the only word for it. I wasn't all that discouraged by it though, and instead felt very much intrigued by what he was doing to me. He kept slathering that lube all around my ass, pushing deeper in, making me get used to it. Doubly odd, was that his brother's cock was still inside me. It halted me trying to fuck him, but it didn't seem like Carson minded.

He watched as I coped with all of these brand new sensations Darren was visiting on me. Two fingers, he was stretching my asshole further, like he was training me for something. My eyes went wide as I began to suspect what they were doing. A shiver went down my spine, but Carson caressed my side. He didn't get his jollies off on pain or hurting me. He knew I would be okay, even if may have been hardly the traditional way people make love.

Besides, that went out the window when he decided he was going to let his brother fuck me too. We were deep in the weird territory, and it was good.

It was a strange sort of pleasant as Darren fingerfucked me in the ass, as if he were awakening some odd nerves down there. I was intrigued, and just like everything else the brothers had done to me in recent time, I wanted to go further. Moaning slightly, I glanced back at Darren.

He stared at me slyly. "You want me to fuck your ass, don't you? One cock inside of you isn't enough, you slut. You gotta have two at once."

I nodded, confessing to my wanton sluttery.

"Hold her tight, Carson, cause I'm coming in."

Darren slid his fingers out of my ass, and his brother, pulled me down deep on his cock as I bent over and presented my ass in as easier to access manner.

Has hands wrapped around me and I felt his girth pressing at my back door. Slowly, he began to press himself in, and it was intense. By far the most intense thing I had ever experienced as he spread me apart, pushing himself deeper into where he was never meant to go.

Combined with the size of Carson's cock already buried deep inside my pussy, I was feeling so pulled apart, so full. Taking two men like this though, it just stroked my ego in all the right places that I was this wanted.

Then they started to fuck me.

Back and forth, Carson pulled out then rammed himself back in my pussy. Darren did the same with my ass. There was never a time where a cock wasn't buried deep inside me, and never a time when one wasn't rubbing against all of my tender parts and driving me wild. Every nerve inside of me was firing in such a delightful way, electricity shooting through me again and again with each of their penetrations.

I could see them struggling too, my pussy and ass being made so tight by the other brother's cock. Everyone was being so overwhelmed with orgasmic energy, and each one of us never wanted this to stop.

Carson held me steady by my hips as Darren took my breasts, tweaking them, contributing further to the sensory overload. With everything being as it was, I knew none of us were going to last long. I wasn't a tantric sex master, I was only a woman, and there's only so much of a woman can take from two young studs inside of her.

I was shaking, I was moaning, I was struggling to let it drag out a little longer, knowing the longer I resisted the greater the payoff would eventually be.

Pointless, because Carson is an asshole and let his thumb come for my clit, massaging it and stimulating me further, when I was already overstimulated already.

I let out out a shriek of delight as a tsunami of utter bliss crashed over me, my body unable to resist the pleasure that was being forced upon me anymore. The feeling was so strong that I briefly felt like I was going to die, and if death felt like this, I was perfectly okay with it. Instead, I was simply in heaven, relishing this moment to its fullest, knowing that it was likely to come again.

My lovers, the brothers, were right there with me. Darren grabbed me tight, pulled me close as he thrust into me, his grunts rushing past my ear. Inside my asshole where it was stretched to the limit, I could feel his cock shudder, and begin to spew his seed inside me. It was an odd, but not unpleasant feeling being filled up there. It was hardly something I never wanted to feel again, and I was welcoming the next time Darren, or his brother, wanted to fuck my ass.

Carson, though, had his cock buried in a much more traditional place. There too, I was still feeling every little thing that was happening down there, his cock pulsing, and him firing his seed inside of me. As much as I enjoyed having my ass fucked, the feeling of having my pussy filled with a man's cum couldn't be topped. I wanted to feel this again and again, no matter the risks.

Unbeknownst to the brothers, they had turned me into their little breeding whore.

There was an orgasmic haze among all of us. Slowly, Darren pulled out of my ass, and helped his brother guide me down to the table where I was laying there, a sweaty and cum soaked mess, their seed leaking out of both of my holes.

"Damn, I was trying to save myself for your pussy, but your ass just wanted my cock too much, Christine," Darren said, leaning down and giving me a kiss on the lips after all of this. "Guess my brother gets a leg up on the knocking you up part."

I laughed. "I'm already pregnant."

Carson and Darren shot one another a glare, and there was a bit of surprise among them.

"What did you expect to happen when you both kept blowing such huge loads inside me?"

"It's probably mine, you know," Carson said.

"Fat chance," Darren snapped back.

"Does it matter?" I again said, with some effort.

The brothers again shared a moment. Darren took a breath and spoke up first. "No, it doesn't. You belong to us, now, Christine. We're going to make full use of you. You better get used to all of this. The fuckings, the anal, the being pregnant, because this is your life now."

"I couldn't have said it better myself, brother."

All I could do was laugh. I remembered how I had this plan of enrapturing a man to take care of my uncertain future. Of trying to snare some rich guy into being my baby daddy to do so if that didn't work.

It did, though. It all worked too well. I had two lovers, two brothers, willing to give me everything I could possibly want and then some. I had succeeded far beyond my wildest dreams.

As my two lovers laid beside me, it didn't matter where we were.

It felt good. Real good.

Sugar Daddy Camgirl

*Book Themes: age gap, virgin, breeding, sugar
daddy*
Word Count: 8812

O nce I'm sure my bedroom door is locked, I saunter across the room and kneel down on a fluffy white rug at the foot of my bed.

In front of me, there's an open laptop and a set of chunky pink headphones.

There's a modest little purple vibrator on my right.

Behind me on the nightstand is an old-fashioned alarm clock glaring midnight in ghostly green. There are thick white pillar candles lit and glowing on every surface throughout the room, giving it an elegant ambiance. Soft, sultry mood music plays from the record player in the corner. But across the house, all is silent save for the low, constant hum of the air conditioning. It's the ideal white noise to block out the naughtiness about to go down in the cozy privacy of my room.

This is a private show; there's no space for the peanut gallery.

Everything I need is already here. They are already waiting for me. I'm willing to bet they've been counting down the seconds.

My hands reach up to tug my hair free of its taut, no-nonsense ponytail. The stress of the day comes tumbling down as coppery waves splash out around my milky-pale shoulders and fall around to frame my pretty, angelic face.

I sigh as my achy scalp starts to tingle with relief. Finally, the hair can come down along with the rest of my tension. Tonight is all about release. I slowly trace my fingers back through my thick mane of fiery auburn hair and shake it out so it's slightly teased up and extra sexy. Bedroom hair, but not bed head. Sexy, but not sloppy. Not yet, at least. It's still just the opening act.

Keeping my eyes locked on the target of my seduction, I twirl a long lock of hair around my pinkie finger. I tilt my head to one side and smile coquettishly.

A soft giggle falls from my lips and I wiggle my perfectly-manicured fingers in a little wave. I slip one strap of my lacy black camisole over my shoulder and mouth the word *oops*. As if it was an accident. As if any of this is coincidence. I know what I'm here to do.

My big blue eyes are wide as I sit awash in the glow of the laptop screen, scanning the cam chat. I hear the bling of new notifications, new members joining the virtual room.

There are already a ton of my regulars here, and another one logs on every minute or so. The list of names grows longer, and the chat populates with typed messages. Compliments and greetings roll in, quickly followed by requests.

I pick up the bubblegum-pink gaming headset on the fuzzy rug in front of me and slide them on over my ears. I bite my full, plush bottom lip gently, feeling the delicious sting of my teeth.

I want to remind my audience how soft my lips are, how plump and juicy they would feel to the touch. I want each and every man to salivate over the thought of kissing me, tasting me, feeling my pretty pink tongue push into his mouth.

I raise my finger to my mouth and suck it in, hollowing out my cheeks as I slide it in and out. All the while, my eyes are locked on that little webcam pinhole with the flashing red light.

A flood of pervy messages comes in. Requests for me to take my clothes off, to blow a kiss, to say something filthy. I move the mic piece closer to my mouth, so that my lips are almost buzzing against it when I speak.

"Tips speak louder than words," I remind my suitors in a low, smoky voice.

Ding, ding, ding!

Notifications pour into my ears as more members join the chat and start sending small but heart-skipping tips. Five dollars here, ten dollars there. Most of their money comes with a request, but some of it is just like confetti raining down.

"Oh, you want to see a little more skin?" I tease.

The screen is filled with messages like:

You're so sexy!

I want you so bad.

I'm so hard for you, Nina.

These guys think of me as a pretty, ditzy bimbo who lives in this little square screen on their computers. They definitely don't think about me as a complete person with a life, but that's okay. I play the role they pay me for. I can pretend to be naive and innocent if that's what a paying customer wants. They get off on my bimbo act, and I get off on taking their money.

It's a win-win. Besides, I'm genuinely sweet to them. My curvy but petite body combined with my ginger hair and pretty face is more than enough to draw them in, but my sparkling personality keeps them coming back again and again. I win just as many tips with kind words as I do flaunting my plump breasts, flat tummy, and juicy ass. I know how to chat these guys up just enough to make them feel wanted, but keep them at arms' length so they're always wanting more. I thrill them with my spicy side and enchant them with the girlfriend experience. I make them feel welcomed and appreciated. I listen to their troubles and give encouragement. And if a pep talk from a pretty girl isn't enough to brighten their day, a flash of my tits usually does it.

I pout at the screen and murmur, "I wish you were all here right now."

The responses flood in:

> Me too!

> What would you do if I was there?

> Want to touch you all over.

Still, as filthy as we get, there's still a computer screen between us. It's more about the fantasy than the fulfilment, and that's what makes me irresistible to them.

They can look, but they can't touch.

I'm a virgin, ripe and pure for deflowering, but I'm out of reach. Not that some of them haven't tried to get me offline, but I don't allow that. I keep the two worlds separate: my industrious days and my steamy nights.

During daylight hours, I'm just Nina Clarke. But starting at midnight and ending whatever time I can reach before falling asleep, I'm Naughty Nina.

She's my camgirl persona, the sexed-up version of myself I sell every night, and business is booming. Maybe even busting. I need cash, and this is a quick, mostly painless way to get it. Occasionally, I'll have to deal with an overly friendly or rude customer, but in general, my clients worship me.

I'm exhilarated by the hustle and the rush, even if the guys themselves are pretty dull. Most of my arousal, my playing-along, is just for show. I've gotten very good at pretending to be way more turned on than I really am. All they see is a hot girl moaning, teasing, touching herself for their pleasure. They're easily fooled, and most of them seem flattered to even get an iota of my attention, even for a price.

> Show us your tits!

> Take your panties off!

Play with your vibrator!

They *are* a little demanding. Virtual dollar signs pop up on the screen, though, and I jump into action. I give my audience a little more to ogle.

I slide my other strap off my shoulder and let the lacy camisole slip down a little, showing more of my deep cleavage. Underneath it, I have on a matching black mesh bra and panties, along with sexy white thigh-high socks and a choker around my neck. I lean forward and subtly push my tits together to make them look even bigger and juicier.

I know these guys are drooling by now. The tips keep coming in small tidbits, enough to keep me going on this hours-long striptease but nothing unusual.

It's just another sexy night in the office. That is, until a long-time lurker with the username Deep Pockets starts typing a message in the group for the first time since I started doing this a couple months ago. I expect just another low-level tip and request, but instead, the dollar amount that pops up on the screen is well over the average. My eyes widen with wonder. He just dropped a hundred.

Good evening, Nina.

"Hey there. You definitely have my attention, Mr. Deep Pockets," I purr.

I can see a flurry of the other guys typing furiously. The jealousy is palpable.

Who's Mr. Moneybags?

Big spender in here…

What the hell?

The new guy sends me another hundred. My jaw drops. He messages again.

> How are you doing tonight?

"Much better now that you showed up," I flirt shamelessly. "How are you?"

To my shock, a third hundred dollar notification goes off. It's like music to my ears. I lean in, excitedly awaiting his next message.

> I'm well. But I think some privacy would do us good. Do you agree?

My heart is racing like mad. The other guys are still competing for my attention with their pervy requests and petty cash, but I'm focused on Deep Pockets. He wants to go into a private chat room with me! That means I'll be making more money per minute on top of whatever extravagant price tag he racks up by the end of... whatever he wants to do with me.

I've only gone private a few times in the couple months I've been moonlighting as Naughty Nina.

It's expensive for the customer, and most can only afford a few minutes of alone time with me, tops. Even the ones lucky enough to afford it aren't blessed with charm, too. They get me alone just to show how awkward, inexperienced, or sleazy they are. I play along, but I'm faking it all the way.

But there's nothing false about my enthusiasm for Deep Pockets. He's not afraid to drop serious cash, and that gets my juices flowing.

I have to say, the way he takes charge is a turn-on, too. He does it in such a dignified, confident way. He doesn't even consider the others competition. This is a man who knows what he wants, and he can afford to take it. If that happens to be me, then I'm one lucky girl.

"Let's take this private," I respond into the microphone piece. "Sorry, boys. I'll be back tomorrow night."

Deep Pockets replies.

> Better luck next time

The next moment, a separate chat room bubble pops up on my screen and I nearly smash my keyboard in my haste to open it. There he is--Deep Pockets. Just his name and mine on the screen. Every second tallies up cents on cents. Minute by minute, dollar by dollar. But that's not good enough for my newest, most intriguing suitor. He drops another hundred with his first message to me.

> I've had my eye on you for a while. Happy to
> finally make your acquaintance.

I smile at the webcam and murmur into the mic, "I noticed your username before, but you never said anything. Clearly, you have the money. Why wait so long to make the first move?"

> Call me old-fashioned, but I wanted to be sure.

I cock my head to one side. "Sure about what?"

> What I want. Who I want. But I know now.
> You're perfect, Nina. You're what I've been
> looking for all this time.

Even a seasoned pro like me can still blush.
"I can totally give you what you need," I whisper.

> Show me.

His command makes me feel wet between my thighs. This is serious. The vibe with him is so different from anything else I've felt so far. I reach down and pull my camisole up over my head. I let it drop to the side, revealing my full breasts in my black mesh bra. My rosy pink nipples are visible through the tiny holes in the fabric.

Deep Pockets sends two hundred. My whole body is tingling with anticipation now. I've already racked up more cash from this one guy than a week's worth of entertaining the other guys. I lick my lips at the camera while my dainty hands smooth down over my plentiful chest.

"You're very generous," I point out.

You're very worth it. True beauty ought to be worshiped.

"I just wish we could be closer," I sulk, poking out my lower lip.

There's another notification in my ears. A message pops up on the screen. My heartbeat picks up when I see that it's a video invite. Deep Pockets wants to show himself! I've never had this happen before. I swiftly accept the invitation.

The screen opens up to another video square like the one I'm in, only this window has a very different picture. I enthusiastically soak up every detail. I can see him from the neck down, his face obscured out of frame. He has a broad set of shoulders, thick arms, and a barrel chest. He's dressed in a white button-up shirt and dark gray fitted trousers.

He's sitting in what looks like a sumptuous, dark leather armchair close and center to the frame, and what little I can determine of the background seems quite elegant. There's only the faint amber glow of a lamp on the glossy wooden side table beside him to hint at the fancy furnishings surrounding, but I am fascinated.

I stare at his muscular body, his dignified posture, the size of his hands in his lap.

No wedding ring, I notice. I'm already salivating over him when he taps into the microphone and speaks, low and vibrational, right in my headphones.

"Hello, Nina."

His voice is deep and sumptuous, a gruff purr in my ear. I feel goosebumps all over. My nipples stiffen to peaks and my pussy aches between my legs.

"Hi, Mr. Deep Pockets," I reply. "You're very handsome."

"I'm even better in person," he says smoothly. "I bet you are, too. But for now, let me see that gorgeous body of yours. Take your bra off."

I reach around to unclasp the bra and it falls to the floor. I push it aside and start caressing my full, bare breasts with my soft hands. I fondle and squeeze them while I moan, letting my fingertips trace ticklish circles around my perky nipples.

"Beautiful, Nina. Now, take off those panties for me," he commands.

I tug my panties down and sit on my ass, lifting my legs up to slowly pull the lacy panties down my legs. I kick them off with my toes and center myself in the frame again.

"Show me your pretty little pussy," he orders.

I gradually spread my legs open wide and lean back against the end of my bed to give him a fuller view of my body. My fingertips stroke at the sides of my labia as I peel myself open, showing him my dewy, irresistible pink flower. He scoots forward a little, on the edge of his seat.

"Good girl. Spread her open for me. Perfect," he groans. "Now, touch yourself for me, Nina. Put your fingers on your clit."

I dutifully obey, letting out a soft sigh when my fingertips start massaging rhythmic motions around my clit. The taut bundle of nerves is so sensitive to my touch. I can hardly keep from twitching and moaning as the tension within me grows tighter. I gaze into the webcam, eyes wide and lips parted, waiting for my next order.

"Grab that vibrator," Deep Pockets says. "Turn it on."

I pick up the tiny purple vibe and flick it on. The vibrations tickle my fingers.

"Put it on your clit and hold it there," he instructs.

"Yes, sir," I reply obediently.

I press the vibrator against my clit and nearly jump out of my own skin at the shock of intense pleasure, almost too much to bear. My other hand slides up my body to tweak and pull at my nipples. The pleasure is building ever higher within me. My muscles tighten up, my pussy aches with every thrum of the vibrations through my body. The need to release is overwhelming.

"Oh my god," I murmur.

"Tell me how it feels, Nina."

"It feels... oh, it feels so good," I whimper.

149

"Yes, it does. You feel so good you want to come."

"I do. I'm so close, Mr. Deep Pockets," I confess weakly.

My swollen clit is pulsating. Endorphins rush through my veins. I'm about to burst.

"You've been a very good girl. You deserve to come, don't you?" he teases.

"Yes. Oh, yes, please," I beg.

The constant whir of the vibrator on my cunny is too much to handle.

"Come for me, Nina."

His deep voice, his filthy command, and the bling of another few hundred dollars on the screen push me over the edge. I tilt my head back and my eyes roll shut as I press the vibrator hard on my clit. I cry out with pleasure as my pussy erupts, gushing slick juices all over the vibe and my fingers. There's a tiny wet puddle forming on the white rug beneath me.

"Excellent. Beautiful, Nina," he growls in that sexy voice.

I'm still hazy-headed when I turn off the vibrator and open my eyes again. Pure electrical pleasure burns in every cell of my body. I've never come so hard in my life. I stare at the webcam, clearly rendered speechless. My mysterious benefactor laughs softly.

"I've had a wonderful time tonight. I'll be seeing you."

My heart skips. "Wait! Don't go yet," I plead. "What's your name?"

"Deep Pockets. For now," he says cryptically.

With one last hundred-dollar bonus, he logs out of the chat room. Gone forever, or at least until he shows up in my stream again. I'm stunned to see the grand total of how much he paid me for less than a half hour of my time. Obviously, his username is accurate. But it's more than just the money; there's something about him. Even without seeing his face, I'm magnetically drawn to him. I want to feel those big hands on my bare skin. I want him to bend me over his lap and spank me like the naughty girl I am.

But for now, I close my laptop, get ready for bed, and slide under the sheets. My body is still tingling from my powerful orgasm as I close my eyes and snuggle into the pillow. My final thoughts before I drift off to sleep are of a luxurious room with a leather armchair and a fabulously wealthy, impossibly sexy man...

The next morning, I awaken to the soft clanking of pots and pans in the kitchen down the hall. I roll over and blink blearily at the alarm clock.

It's barely seven o'clock, and after my late night I could sure use a couple more hours of sleep, but I climb out of bed anyway. When Grandma Doris gets up, I get up. It's just part of being her full-time caretaker. I stand up, stretch, and trudge down the hallway flanked with family portraits all over the walls, some as recent as last year and other photos many decades old.

There's a lot of history in this house. I grew up here myself, being raised by my grandmother. I moved out at eighteen to go to college, but I moved back in a year ago when I graduated. Grandma Doris is fiercely independent and always has been, but even she finally admitted that she needs some help around the house. She's my number one, and we've been close my whole life. It makes perfect sense for me to be the one to help her.

I walk into the sunny, bright kitchen with a smile on my sleepy face. Grandma Doris is at the stove, stirring a pot of buttery, salty grits. She's a slightly hunched woman in her seventies, with a mop of curly white hair, the same blue eyes as me, and a flowery apron over her purple muumuu. She slowly turns to look at me with a sparkling smile.

"Good morning, sweet pea. How'd you sleep?" she asks.

"Great. Like a baby," I answer. "How about you? Have any interesting dreams?"

"As a matter of fact, I did. Nina, it was so strange. I looked in the mirror and all my teeth fell out. Can you believe it?" she chuckles.

"Hope it's not a prophetic dream or you might have to get used to the idea of wearing dentures, Grandma," I quip back.

She snorts. "As if! I'd sooner dump this pot of grits on my head."

"Well, don't do that," I giggle. "Here, let me whip up some scrambled eggs to go with it."

We fall into step beside each other in the kitchen as we always do. When I was little, Grandma Doris was head chef. I remember shelling peas and shucking corn while she gave instructions from the stove. I recall Christmas mornings spent cooking up french toast casserole or a special festive quiche, or my favorite triple-chocolate cake on my birthday. I have so many memories of cooking, laughing, and gossiping with my grandmother in the kitchen. Only nowadays, I'm the one who has to take charge. She's not as spry as she once was. Now, I'm the one rushing around to cook while she spills things, forgets ingredients, or complains about her achy feet. Not that I mind. She's taken care of me for over twenty years, and I feel honored to return the favor.

She can do most things on her own, more by sheer force of will than anything else, and she was resistant to my aid at first. But now, we have a good balance. She lets me help her, and I let her believe she's the one helping me. Giving me a place to stay. Making me grits in the morning. But we both know the reality: she needs me. Try as she might, she can't keep up with the housework or the bills anymore. Money is tight these days, and since I spend my days pretty wrapped up in taking care of Grandma Doris, I haven't been able to find a job that works with our schedule. Hence the birth of Naughty Nina. After weeks of researching ways to make money from home, I decided to give camgirl work a try. It's been enough to keep us afloat, and for that I am grateful, but I wish I could do more. This old house is big. The property taxes, the mortgage, the monthly bills on top of grocery spending, pharmacy trips, and visits to the doctor... it's a lot.

But today, my load feels a lot lighter. I made enough money last night to support us through the next few weeks. After breakfast, I slide into the usual routine of chores, errands, and looking after my elderly grandmother. It's a normal, busy day, but every time I get a moment to spare, my mind inevitably wanders back to Deep Pockets.

I wonder what he's doing today. I ponder where he could be. Connecting over the internet like this, there's no telling how far away he lives. He could be across the planet or right next door. The latter thought gives me a thrill. I know I should be cautious, and I should keep my expectations low. It's best not to get attached to any of these guys. What are the odds that he'll come back for more? He already dropped so much money on me, surely that isn't a sustainable spending practice for him. Unless it is. In which case, he truly does have deep pockets.

After a long day of chores, caretaking, cooking, and cleaning, Grandma Doris and I watch game show reruns and sip hot cocoa on the couch until it's time for bed. She shuffles off to her room and I go to mine. I do my usual nightly routine, counting down until midnight when I go live as Naughty Nina. I light my candles, set up my sex toys and headset. I apply some subtle makeup, brush out my auburn waves, and put on a skimpy, cutesy satin nightie in a deep shade of blue. This time, instead of sitting on the floor, I bring my laptop to my bed. I pull up the chat stream, take a deep breath, and log in as the clock ticks midnight.

My heart is pounding as I turn on the webcam with a coy smile. I absently comb my fingers through my hair as I watch the chat members arrive one by one. They log in, drop a little tip and a greeting, and I respond with the usual flirtations. For a few minutes, it's just the usual suspects and me. My hope is sinking. Maybe last night *was* just a fluke.

But then I hear another notification and my eyes light up with joy. Deep Pockets has logged in. Tonight, he wastes no time. He drops a hundred dollars and sends a message.

Good evening, Nina. Come to me.

He disappears from the main chat room and an invite to a private chat pops up. I click it hastily, not even saying goodbye to the other guys. It's a shame for them, but they just can't compete with Deep Pockets. As soon as the private chat room expands, my heart skips to see the man himself perched in the same distinguished leather armchair in that fancy sitting room. He's wearing a gray shirt, black belt, and black pants. I can clearly see a bulge at the front of his trousers and I'm eager to see what's underneath.

"You came back," I say brightly.

"Of course I did," he replies. "I know what I want."

His voice comes through deep and rough-edged. It makes me shiver with delight. He wants *me*. Another hundred ka-chings in my ears.

"Take off your nightie," he commands.

"Anything for you," I purr.

I pull the nightie up over my head and toss it aside, turning back to the camera in just my bra and panties. I stroke my hands down the swell of my breasts, my flat stomach, and down to my pelvis. I scoot back against the pillow behind me and spread my legs wide.

"Good, Nina. Now start touching yourself, but don't take off your panties yet," he growls.

With my eyes locked on him, I slide my hand between my thighs and begin lightly rubbing my pussy through the damp fabric of my panties. I moan and arch up into my palm. Warm waves of tingly pleasure roll down my body and make my toes curl.

When I see Deep Pockets unzip his pants and take out his massive, glorious cock, my jaw falls open. His shaft is beautiful. At least eight inches long, thick, and ever so slightly curved. I lick my lips as he starts slowly stroking his enormous length. I'm so wet at the sight of him, I'm soaking through my panties.

"Oh my god," I breathe.

"Use the vibrator," he commands me in a gruff voice.

I obey, picking up the vibe and flicking it on at the lowest setting. I press it to the damp spot growing in my panties and immediately goosebumps form on my skin. Pure wild pleasure shoots through every part of me. Coupled with the delicious view of Deep Pockets stroking himself, it's barely a minute before my first orgasm.

"Ohhh, I'm coming," I whimper.

"That's right. Come for me, Nina," he hisses.

Pleasure courses through my whole system. Deep Pockets sends another hundred.

"I wish you were here with me," I pout.

"What would you do if I was?" he prompts me.

My eyes are mesmerized by his enormous hand moving smoothly up and down his thick shaft. I'm nearly drooling with desire. It's killing me that he seems so close, yet so far.

"I would get on my knees and suck you dry," I tell him boldly.

He groans. "I would give anything to fuck that perfect mouth."

"And you'd come down my throat," I add greedily.

He murmurs, "Or all over your pretty face."

"I want you so bad," I confess.

"I need you, Nina. All to myself," Deep Pockets groans. "Turn up the setting."

I do as I'm told. The vibrator hums deliciously against my clit. My free hand plays with my breasts while I rock against the vibrations. The tension is building fast.

"I'm about to come," I gasp.

"Do it," he orders. "We'll come together."

"Oh my-- nnngh," I moan as my pussy gushes everywhere. My panties are slick now on both sides, fully soaked through with my juices.

Onscreen, I watch him stroke his cock faster and faster until finally he spurts a long, impressive stream of thick white come through the air. A drop of it even splatters on the webcam, and he swiftly wipes it clean. My pussy pulses through waves of pleasure while Deep Pockets pumps every last drop. I've never seen anything or anyone so sexy. I feel the need to be close to him like a deep ache of the soul. I want to be in that room with him. I want to be the one licking up his come, making him moan and sigh and feel oh so good. I'm intrigued now, as I watch him clean up and resume his throne.

"I'm enjoying our nights together," I gush.

"Me too. I could easily make a habit of this. Nina, I want you all for my own. I don't like to share, and I can afford not to. You need money, and I need you. I would block off all your time if I could. And I think it's time for something a little more real," he begins.

"What do you mean?" I ask, eyes wide.

"I know you're a virgin, Nina. You've mentioned it in the chat room before," he remarks. "I am willing to pay any amount you dream up to be the one who deflowers you. You deserve a wonderful first time, and I can give you exactly what you need."

"Wow. That's one hell of an offer. But how can we do that when you're so far away?" I ask him confusedly.

He chuckles softly. "We live in the same city, Nina."

"But how do you--"

"I have my ways," he answers. "I'm asking you to meet me in person. Tomorrow."

"Wh-what? In person?" I splutter. Nerves take over instantly.

"Don't be nervous. We can take it slow, test the waters. We will meet someplace public, somewhere you feel safe," he explains.

"Like the park? There's one around the corner from my place," I blurt out.

"Noon. I'll be there," he says.

And before I can say anything else, he logs out. I stare at the screen in disbelief for a minute as my brain catches up on what just happened. Holy shit. I'm meeting a guy I met online tomorrow. In *person*. Oh my god! How am I going to sleep tonight?

The next day at noon, I find myself pacing back and forth under a gigantic oak tree at the park around the corner from Grandma's place. I was up half the night with excitement, and it was tricky arranging time for a date without Grandma Doris figuring out what's up, but I'm here now and I'm ready. I'm wearing a flirty, swishy white sun dress and strappy wedge sandals, along with a floppy sun hat with a yellow ribbon.

My hair falls in perfectly tousled red waves around my shoulders, and my dress falls to barely mid-thigh.

I look cute, but nothing can prepare me for the sight of my mysterious suitor sauntering up to me in the bright glow of sunshine. I recognize him by his size and build, as well as his sleek but casual clothes. He's dressed in a starchy white button-up, dark gray jeans, and black boots. In his hand, he carries a picnic basket with a baguette and a bottle of champagne poking out the top. Upon seeing his face for the first time, I think I might actually swoon.

He looks to be in his late thirties or early forties, with a thick head of dark hair that falls in charming heartthrob curls around his forehead and temples. He has dark brown eyes that sparkle with wisdom and light. There are soft lines at the crease of his eyes and a smile on his soft lips that makes me immediately feel at ease. My nervous butterflies calm to a still as he walks up and offers his hand.

"It's wonderful to meet you," he says in that deep, velvety voice I've come to adore.

"Enchanted," I agree breathlessly as I peer up at him and shake his hand. "Mr...?"

"Wood. Darren Wood," he introduces himself.

"Nina Clarke," I reply.

"Beautiful day for a walk with a beautiful girl," Darren says.

My cheeks flush hot pink and my heart pounds like crazy.

He doesn't release my hand after we shake; instead, we just start strolling hand-in-hand across the rolling green fields of the park. Birds sing and squirrels chatter in the trees. Branches sway and swish their leaves in the gentle breeze. We can hear the faint laughter and shouts of kids playing in the distance. We mosey along the pathway to a pond, which is beautifully green with lily pads and rushes growing up out of the clear water. Darren opens up the picnic basket to roll out a thin checkered blanket, a baguette, some strawberries, and a little golden container of luxury chocolate truffles from a local upscale patisserie. We sip ridiculously expensive champagne out of plastic flutes and munch on chocolate and berries as we watch the sun glittering across the pond. I can't help but think of the sharp contrast between this whimsical daytime date and my secretive, online nocturnal antics. It feels weird-- in a good way-- to be falling in love in the sunshine rather than feigning interest under computer glow.

"So, I have to know..." I begin slowly.

Darren smiles and nods. "Where I got the money? I'm a day trader. A good one. I've built my fortune over two decades, and now I'm just coasting. I've always focused on my career, on making money to make myself comfortable, but also to spend on worthwhile causes."

"Like what?" I prompt.

"Various charities. Paying off other people's debts. Funding scholarships, donating to social programs. Anything to feel like my fortune is being used, not squandered," he explains.

"Where does that put me?" I ask playfully.

Darren grins and leans in closer, his lips so close to mine.

"You are a worthwhile cause," he whispers. "But between you and me, there's a little bit of selfishness when it comes to you."

"Oh, really?" I tease.

"I want you all for myself, Nina," he murmurs. "So I can do this whenever I want."

His hand comes up to cup my cheek as he presses his lips against mine. Explosions go off in my mind, my heart must be about to take flight, and I'm burning all over. His lips are so soft, yet forceful when he kisses me hard. I moan into the kiss, letting him stroke my face and brush the hair back from my temples. He sweeps off my floppy hat and sets it gently aside. When we finally break apart, I'm breathless and pink-cheeked.

"Wow," I mumble. My lips tingle where he kissed me.

"And what about you?" he asks softly. "What is your purpose?"

"I take care of my grandmother. I need money to pay the bills and make sure we can keep living comfortably," I admit. "Not the most glamorous reason."

"I think it's wonderful. Further proof that you're beautiful on the inside, too. But oh, that outer beauty..." he trails off. He looks down at me greedily.

I'm already wet between the thighs. I look around the park. There's nobody nearby in any direction. I can see and hear people in the distance, but right here on this picnic blanket, we have a tiny slice of privacy. I intend to use it.

"There's something I've been wanting to try ever since last night," I venture.

Darren leans back and looks at me with one dark brow raised. "Oh? What's that?"

With my eyes still locked with his, I slowly reach out and unzip his jeans. Darren watches me pull down his boxers enough to let his enormous shaft bounce free. I gasp and moan at the sight of him, and I can hardly wait to taste him. Darren sweeps my long red hair into one hand to hold it out of the way while I pull the thick head of his cock between my lips.

"Oh yes. Take it," he groans, letting his head fall back.

I wrap one dainty hand around his shaft and pump up and down while his cock stretches out my cheeks. I whimper with delight at how heavy he is on my tongue, how silky smooth his skin feels. I flick my tongue along the underside and around the sensitive head. I lick up a salty, delicious drop of precome. The taste drives me wild with desire. I hollow out my cheeks and focus on taking him in one inch at a time until finally, his rod is poking into the back of my throat. I start to cough, and Darren gently strokes my head, whispering soft words of encouragement.

"Good, Nina. Just like that," he murmurs.

At any moment, someone could come walking over to the pond and discover us in a highly compromising position, but instead of worrying me, it thrills me to think we could get caught. The risk only adds to my pleasure.

He starts to gently lift his hips to meet my mouth with every thrust. I feel him knocking into the back of my throat, sliding up and down my tongue. I moan around his thickness as he starts to fuck my mouth in earnest. Darren's cock pokes into my throat with a wet gulping sound again and again as I bob up and down.

He holds my hair tightly in his fist and uses it as a gentle guide. He pumps into my mouth a few more times before he tenses up.

"I'm coming," he hisses between gritted teeth.

I moan with delight as his cock bursts a stream of hot, salty come down my throat. I swallow down every last drop and lick his cock clean. Satisfied, I roll back on my knees and wipe my mouth with a grin. Darren zips himself up just as another couple comes strolling by. We give them a cheery wave, and once they disappear around the corner, we burst out laughing.

"That was close," I giggle.

"Dangerously so. Maybe we should go somewhere a little more private," he suggests. "My place is only ten minutes away."

"You mean to tell me the guy of my dreams has been just down the road from me this whole time and I never knew?" I gasp.

Darren smiles wide and kisses me on the cheek. "Serendipity."

"Must be," I agree warmly.

We pack up and head back to our respective vehicles. I slide behind the wheel and follow Darren's luxury sedan across town. I call Grandma Doris on the way to let her know I'll be out for a few more hours. To my relief, she doesn't mind at all. She's too busy watching her soap operas to miss me too much yet. The scenery gets more and more elegant as we approach Darren's home. The neighborhood is full of stately, expensive houses with perfectly manicured lawns. High-class vehicles fill the garages and driveways. Darren's house is the biggest and most beautiful on the whole block.

"Holy cow," I breathe as we walk up to the front door.

It's a romantic old Victorian, with a gigantic wraparound porch and balcony. The interior is just as lush as the outside, filled with highbrow furnishings and pricey art pieces. I'm in awe with every step, but Darren makes me feel right at home. We spend the afternoon hanging out and talking about everything. He tells me his hopes, I share my dreams. He gives me a secret, I share one, too. The age gap of nearly twenty years hardly enters my mind. I've always been an old soul, and Darren is the most gently commanding man I've ever met. He puts me at ease with his kindness, and he makes me feel safe with his power.

In the evening, we go into the kitchen to make a romantic dinner together. While we cook, we listen to Sinatra on his antique record player. We put a delicious chicken with potatoes and carrots into the oven to be slow-roasted. We pour glasses of wine and sip them while we laugh and kiss. Darren sweeps me into his arms and we slow dance, my cheek resting against his heart. I can't stop smiling, and my soul is full of love.

"You know, I never expected this," I whisper.

"What?" he murmurs, his lips against the top of my head.

"This feeling," I answer, struggling to explain myself. "I know we just met, but I feel so connected with you. And you treat me so well."

"You deserve it. I have the money to give you anything you need. I can give you a beautiful life, Nina. What good is a fortune without someone to spend it on?" he answers, nuzzling into my hair.

"I felt it from the very start," I go on, pulling back to look in his dark eyes. "I know this is supposed to be a business transaction, but... I can't help how I feel."

"I feel the same way. You don't have to hold back with me," Darren growls.

"Not now, not ever," I whisper back as I stand on tiptoe to kiss him.

He takes my hands in his and gazes into my eyes. I can feel the desire burning like a bonfire between us. I'm tingling all over just standing close to him.

"I want to give you the world," he says fervently.

I bite my lip. "There's something I want to give you, too," I breathe.

We both know exactly what I'm talking about. My virginity. That prize I've been holding onto for all these twenty-two years, waiting for the right one, the right time. Now he's here, and even if he wasn't offering me an insane amount of money for it, I would be ready. Darren Wood is everything I want in this world, and I can't wait any longer to make him mine.

He flicks his eyes over the stove clock, then back to me.

"That'll roast for at least two hours," Darren points out.

"We have time," I mutter.

With that, Darren scoops me up into his arms. I let out a peal of surprised laughter as he damsel-carries me out of the kitchen and up the stairs.

"Where are we going?" I giggle.

"You'll see," he answers, pushing open a door at the end of a long hallway.

He sets me down gently as we step into the room I recognize from our nights on webcam together. It's a small, lush personal library with shelves of books lining the walls up to the ceiling. There's a big, stately leather armchair with a mahogany side table holding an antique lamp, an expensive fountain pen, and a stack of books recently combed through. The moon glows like a white crescent in the night sky out the wide window.

As I gaze out across the lawn, Darren walks up behind me and drapes his arms around me. He kisses my cheek and makes his way to my ear. His warm breath tickles my neck, making me giggle and shiver. Goosebumps spread across my skin as I turn to face him. Darren catches my face in both hands and leans in to kiss me deeply. His fingers gently brush through my fiery red hair. He unbuckles his belt and I slip off my dress.

It falls in a heap at my feet and Darren's hands explore my bare breasts. He plays with my tits and teases my perky pink nipples until I'm squirming in his grip. Darren dips down to kiss me again, his lips trailing down my neck, over my collarbone and down to my breasts. He tugs my nipple between his lips and flicks his tongue over the sensitive tip. I arch my back and tilt my head back, my hair sweeping down my bare back. Darren holds me in his strong arms while I tug his shirt off to reveal his broad, powerful chest and sculpted abs. Despite being almost twenty years my senior, Darren is the sexiest, fittest man I've ever seen. I can hardly believe my eyes as my fingertips trace his abs and move downward. I unzip his jeans and he pulls them down, stepping out of them as he kisses me again. I peel off my panties.

Darren steps back to pull off his boxers and I lick my lips to see his massive cock standing hard and erect. Waiting for me. Darren takes my hands as he sits down in the leather armchair. He pulls me down into his lap so that I'm straddling him. His hands smooth down my back and grope my thick, bouncy ass. He gives it a loud, powerful smack that makes me moan with heady desire. I'm dripping wet already as I rub myself against his thick length. We rut together, just enjoying the friction between us as we kiss.

"I'm ready," I whisper to him. "Take me, Darren."

"Anything for you," he murmurs back roughly.

He strokes his cock a few times and then positions the engorged head at my slick, achy hole. I hold my breath as he guides me down, letting me spear myself on his glorious cock. My mouth falls open in a gasp as he pushes into me inch by inch. My cunny twinges and clenches around his thickness, and I start to rut back and forth.

"Oh yes. So good, Nina," he grunts.

"Oh my god," I whimper. "It's so big."

"And you're so wet for me, baby. So perfect," Darren murmurs.

He braces my back with both strong arms while he leans forward to suck my nipples, his cock now pushing against that little barrier inside of me. It hurts in a deep, aching way, but it also feels unbelievably good. Like nothing I've felt before. I roll my hips, starting to ride him harder and faster. I'm moaning by the time he shoves through my hymen, and when his cock pounds into my g-spot, I see stars.

"Ohhh, Darren," I pant breathlessly.

"That's right, princess. Ride that cock for me," he growls.

His hands rove down the narrow slope of my waist. He slips one hand down between us and I gasp at the sensation of his fingertips rubbing my clit. The combination of my stimulated bundle of nerve endings with the pounding pleasure deep inside of me makes me come within seconds. I cry out as my pussy gushes hot juices all over his fat cock.

"Just like that! So good, Nina," he grunts.

I whimper, "I'm so wet."

"You're perfect. You feel so fucking good," Darren growls.

"Your cock-- fills me up-- so good," I choke out between pounding thrusts.

Darren is losing restraint now. He's fucking me hard and fast, spearing into my virginal cunny again and again. I'm on top, but he's in control. His large hands grip my rounded hips as he pumps up into me. I ride him harder, bouncing up and down on his glorious shaft. Darren holds me steady while I lose control, giving in to my own needs.

"Take what you need, baby. Come for me," he encourages gruffly.

His fingers circle my clit in perfect rhythm with the beat of his thrusts. His cock pounds my cervix while my thighs start to tremble. I'm losing control all over again.

"I'm almost there," I moan.

"Me too, Nina. Don't stop. I'm going to fill you up with my seed," he growls.

"Oh yes! Please," I beg, bouncing up and down on his cock.

Darren smacks my ass again, and the delicious sting of his hand pushes me over the edge.

"I'm coming!" I burst out.

"Oh fuck," he groans. "That's my girl!"

He seizes up, his hands tightening on my hips while his cock spurts hot, precious seed deep within my virginal, fertile womb. I feel every little explosion, every drop leaking into me deep inside. It feels so fucking satisfying, like I'm finally whole for the first time in my life. My come mingles with his, dripping onto the armchair as we hold each other through the afterglow. Darren strokes my hair as we come down, both panting and exhilarated.

"How do you feel?" Darren asks softly after a few minutes.

"Incredible. That was amazing," I breathe.

He smiles and kisses my forehead. "Yes. Yes, it was."

I grin. "I don't think I've ever felt this happy."

"I feel the same way," he says. "I knew I was making the right choice when I messaged you. I could just feel it."

"I'm so glad you did. I just wish you'd done it sooner. All that time, lurking but never saying a word..." I sigh.

He strokes my cheek with two curled fingers. "I had to be sure. And I am. You're the one I've been waiting for, Nina. You're the one who shows me the true meaning of life."

"And what is that?" I ask.

"Love," Darren answers. "It's love. All the way. Love is what put you in front of that webcam to begin with, and love is what will set you free. *I* can set you free. If you'll let me."

"Mr. Deep Pockets, I think it's pretty clear by now that I'll let you do just about anything you want with me," I reply playfully.

"What about dinner?" he suggests.

He gestures vaguely toward the door, toward the delicious smell of roast chicken and vegetables wafting up from the kitchen downstairs. My stomach yowls. I nod vigorously. Darren laughs and helps me to my feet. He gives me a big, fluffy robe to wear. It swamps me, with the sleeves hanging off by a couple inches. Once we're decent, we head down to the kitchen for a romantic, delectable first dinner together.

From that night on, it's a balancing act between spending time at home with Grandma Doris and spending time with Darren. I'm only able to wait until after the third date to introduce him to my grandmother, and to my delight, the evening goes swimmingly. Grandma Doris is instantly enamored with my handsome, respectful, wealthy older beau. One time, she even makes an offhand comment about how if she was only "thirty years younger..."

We love spending time together, alone or with Grandma Doris. After a while, though, she tells me I need more freedom. More time for my own life, for my swiftly flourishing relationship with Darren. So he does something I never expected: he hires a wonderful, sweet, attentive live-in nurse to help look after Grandma. She gets to stay in her beloved home, I know she's safe and taken care of, and Darren makes sure to take care of me. Which is a good thing, because it doesn't take long for me to find out I'm pregnant! It's the most incredible news I've ever received, and I can't think of a better man to start a family with.

Darren is the most romantic, considerate man I've ever known. Not only does he spoil me with expensive gifts and luxurious trips all over the world, but he makes my heart sing. He loves me passionately and protects me like it's his sole purpose.

For the first time in my life, I get to slow down and enjoy new things.

Like falling in love.

Like moving in with Darren.

Like waking up every morning to see his handsome face next to me on the pillow. Our world only gets brighter and happier day by day. My belly grows rounder and our hearts grow fuller.

From Naughty Nina to pampered princess, I have the love of my life to thank for saving me.

For loving me.

And finally, for setting me free.

The Billionaire's Obsession

Book Themes: BDSM, Begging, Bondage, Blind-
folds, College Student, and Risky Sex
Word Count: 13041

For months, he'd been waiting for just this moment. Where his hand could trace along the hollow of her throat and feel her swallow in fear and nervousness. Where he could see the little goose bumps jump up all along her flesh in his chilly bedroom. Where her lip trembled as she wondered what next awaited her.

This moment had been such a long time coming. For a year, he'd been watching her. Every morning, every afternoon, he saw her walk by on the way to school, and from the first day he knew he had to have her. He'd spent so much money on getting his room just so - buying all the leather straps and collars and harnesses, the silken sheets. Hell, he even splurged on a new king size bed with a canopy.

And why shouldn't he? He'd made it rich, right from the safety of his computer chair, and it gave him ample time to watch her, to follow her, to go over his plan for her again and again, deciding what he'd do once he lured her in.

She went to the local college and he was older than her, and already divorced. His wife had left him just before he made his fortune, and he couldn't have been happier for her timing.

It had given him more time to work on his goals, and he looked better than ever. When he wasn't working or spying on the sweet Aubrey, he was exercising, running. Getting fit, strong.

So that when he had her, he could keep her.

Two days ago he'd struck up a conversation with her at her favourite coffee shop. Sometimes she went in the middle of the day, off campus, to drink some horribly sugary concoction, all by herself. Almost every time he'd seen her, in fact, she was by herself. Certainly it wasn't because of her looks. The girl could have been a cheerleader if she didn't seem so out of place in her own body. She had an awkward, cautious way of moving, and you could tell she was conscious of it.

Her height was average, her hair long and dirty blonde.

He thought of those silken strands filtering through his fingers, prickling against her scalp as he made her look at him.

She always wore loose fitted tops and skirts, but her legs were divine, and her outfits just added to the intrigue. Throughout the winter it was even worse, with her large coat, scarf and hat, but it had only made him more smitten.

He'd thought of stripping off those layers, one after another, discovering what prizes she hid beneath it all.

It had been easy to approach her in the overcrowded cafe, asking if he could share her table just for a little while. His head had been spinning and he couldn't quite recall all the details of the conversation, which he cursed himself for, but eventually she told him it had just been her twentieth birthday. When he bought her a cupcake, she'd broken down in tears.

He was the only person who had wanted to celebrate with her.

She couldn't afford the tuition at any of the better schools and was stuck living with her parents until she could graduate and move into the big city for work.

"Well if you want," he'd offered, never before having felt such a thrill, "I could offer you a place to stay. Rent free, until you graduate, of course. I have a spare room."

"I couldn't," she'd protested, her green eyes seeking out his matching pair. "I couldn't do that to you." Maybe there was some hesitation, some caution. It was wise of her, but he simply smiled as if it were all up to her.

Surely his height and build could be intimidating. But he'd hoped that his green eyes, his carefree stubble, his strong jawline would balance that out. Make him seem ruggedly handsome rather than dangerous.

"Listen. I know what it's like, having parents who don't appreciate you." He spoke slowly, with measured beats, in a controlled tone.

She wiped away her tears as he spoke, her lower lip trembling. He wanted to bite it. To kiss her so hard she'd stop shaking and melt into him.

"I have a nice house, good neighbours. You'd have your own room and all that. Privacy." He leaned back in his seat, nonchalantly, reaching into the breast pocket of the fine tailored jacket and retrieving a business card holder. Unclasping the fine platinum holder, he took out one of the thick pieces of cardstock with his name, business, and phone number on it.

"You don't have to decide now. But if things get too tough at home, it's an option, okay? I work from home, and that's my cell number. If you need me, I'll come running."

Her caution melted away, her slender shoulders slumping with gratitude, and she nodded. His heart beat faster and his loins began to stir at the image of this wary vixen.

"I'll think about it," she'd said, and he gave a calm smile as if it was all up to her.

He watched as she swallowed, traced her pink tongue over her pale lips and left a slight sheen behind. Her cheeks were a bit flushed, her outfit a bit too heavy for the crowded cafe, but it left her looking like a porcelain doll, so artfully painted.

As he stood from the table he was thankful his jacket hid the bulge in his pants. He leaned down and his index finger went to her chin, making her look into his eyes. He held her gaze for a few seconds before he spoke, "Happy birthday, Aubrey."

Tears glittered in her eyes again and a smile formed on her wet mouth. "Thank you, Ryan."

I t wasn't even a full four hours before he got her call, and he went to pick her up in his black Audi. It was all dark at her address, and for a few minutes he wondered if she was yanking his leg.

It wasn't a great neighbourhood. The grass was overgrown in most of the lawns, and there was a broken down vehicle in her driveway. He momentarily wished that he hadn't just waxed the car earlier that day, making it sparkle under the few street lamps that still flickered in and out. It stood out too much, was too flashy in the poor neighbourhood.

But when she quietly closed her front door, an oversized duffle bag in her hand, eyes widening at the sight of the car, he knew he'd done the right thing. Silently, he slid from the driver's seat and walked over to help her with her bag, like a gentleman.

This was the start of something amazing, for both of them. She just didn't know it yet.

" I 'm not sure about this," she protested as she heard the camera flash go off again, her arms bound behind her. She was still dressed in that oversized white shirt, the black skirt pooling around her legs as she kneeled before him. A soft, leather collar was worn tight around her throat and she wouldn't stop swallowing, as if to make room.

She'd already accepted more than a couple of drinks that

night as they celebrated her final midterm exam. She'd been living with him a few weeks, and he couldn't have been more elated with the company, the companionship. It had started out as lust, as a passing curiosity, but had quickly exploded into something more. A friendship of sorts.

When he'd told her that he made and sold bondage equipment online, it wasn't a total lie. He was the middle man, an intermediary for a bunch of fetish sites. But he didn't make it, and he certainly didn't need a model for his newest designs.

But she was cautiously curious, and that'd been enough. When he asked if she'd be willing to take some pictures - totally clothed, totally anonymous - she'd been afraid but that temptation gleamed in her eyes.

When he'd offered to pay her, to help her gain her independence, it was what toppled her over the edge.

"You look great, Aubrey. The collar fits you perfectly." He smiled as he looked down on her, the camera separating them yet making him feel so in control. So in charge. "We'll take it slow and just do what makes you comfortable," he reassured her in his deep voice and she nodded.

"I've just... never done anything like this." Her eyes were blindfolded, her arms bound, her throat collared, and he'd never seen her look more perfect. Her pristine skin looked so fresh and clean after her shower, and even though it was the middle of the night, both of them were wide awake. Alert.

Not even the wine could inhibit this, not when there was such electricity between them.

"I promise, no one will know it's you. I really appreciate this, you know. And I'm sure the $500 will go a long way towards a lease, eventually."

She stilled her uneasy fidgeting for a moment at the reminder of why she'd really agreed to do this, and she gave another nod.

His cock throbbed in his pants.

He could scarcely believe that this was happening, that all his dreams were coming true, and the grin across his face widened as he dropped to one knee in front of her. He could smell that light vanilla perfume on her, see every little detail of her skin as his eyes greedily devoured her blindfolded form.

"This will be the easiest money you can ever make, Princess. If you don't watch yourself, you might get addicted."

The way her back arched at the word 'princess' made his loins jump again, responding so acutely to that odd mix of emotions he sensed within her. The submission in her, craving to be coaxed out.

Ryan didn't touch her, though. Not then. Even though he wanted to, he only appreciated every bit of her body in its fully-clothed glory, up close and personal. She was bound and helpless, but he didn't want her to fight. He didn't want her to struggle.

No, he wanted something grander. He wanted to possess her. To get in under her skin.

The next day, he doled out 25 crisp $20 bills, placing them into her hand with a wink. She was already feeling more comfortable, now that he'd proven his word and not taken advantage of his bondage shots. She'd come out of it unscathed. Untouched.

He almost felt like a father, paying her allowance, and when he watched her head out to classes there was a noticeable skip to her step.

She'd be back, begging for more before she knew it.

The day passed horrifically slow. Every moment was spent pining for her, poring over the pictures from the night before. The way her creamy skin was caressed by the light, the contrast of the dark, textured leather against her slender neck.

She was a prize, and he couldn't help but touch himself as he stared at her.

His favourite was one where he was looking down on her slightly, and there was a pensive look on her face. Her plush lips a bit pouted, her cheekbones prominent beneath the blindfold, her collarbone peeking out from the loose blouse.

It was an innocent picture, but one he felt captured her. That struggled desire, that curiosity, the line between being a girl and a woman so tentatively crossed.

She was more perfect than he could ever have imagined, and he smiled in anticipation of more.

"Ryan," Aubrey started, and his heart began to thud. The way his name rolled off her mouth was exquisite, and he looked at her curiously over the dinner table. Just like they were family.

"Yes, Aubrey?"

"Last night..." She swallowed and his eyes were drawn to the way the motion made her slender bones flex and move so fluidly. Everything about her seemed designed so carefully, so lovingly. It was hard for him to believe that her parents didn't appreciate how lucky they were to have her.

"Go on, Aubrey. I won't be mad, I promise." His green eyes flashed at her and he took a sip of tart wine.

"It was weird, wasn't it?" Oh, how delicately she phrased that, as if she truly didn't believe the words. As if she wanted his reassurance.

He stood from the fine wood dining chair, closing the distance between them and staring down at her. Careful, he reminded himself. Play it slow. Get inside.

His large hand reached out, gently cupping her jaw and letting her look up at him with those wide, expressive eyes. They looked almost fake, so vibrant a shade of green they were, and the bit of mascara she wore brought them out even more.

"I don't think it was weird at all. Modeling is a fine profession, and I think you have what it takes, if you don't mind my saying." He smiled at her, leaning down and pressing his nose to the top of her blonde hair, smelling his own shampoo in her soft tresses.

He lingered there, the smell of his soft cologne wafting towards her nose before he pulled back slightly. "You are a gorgeous young woman, and I think those photos I took of you were some of the best I've ever taken." The compliments he paid her were genuine, and he let the truth seep out of him just a touch.

She looked cautious at first when he touched her, when he kissed her. It was hard to get a read on why, but the relief in her gaze spoke to her own darkness. His heart leapt when it occurred to him that it was something she kept hidden, deep inside, and his gentleness was teasing it to the surface.

"But it's not really modeling," she protested, and he knew what she was asking. *It was sexual, wasn't it? The collar, the bindings, the blindfold...*

She wasn't ignorant to the sensuality of the display, and his heart pounded. He wanted her, but he needed to bide his time. To wait. To be patient.

His fingers trailed through her hair, tucking it behind one of her beautiful, fragile ears, and he leaned down on one knee so he could look her in the eyes. So that he could see her reaction in vivid detail.

She sat primly with her knees together and her billowy skirt flowing over her legs to shield them.

"It's a special type of modeling," Ryan said, cautious of his words. "And it takes a special type of person to get good at it."

"But people will see them and..." she struggled for the words. She was still a newborn fawn, needing his guiding hand. To train her, to teach her about this strange new world she was so frightened of, so curious about.

"No one needs to see them if you don't want." Ryan's face softened, and his voice was so calm and reassuring.

"But I already spent some of the money!"

He realized she was practically in tears, her eyes glittering with all of her pent up emotions, and he couldn't help it. He pulled her to his chest, into the finely tailored dress shirt, into his personal space.

His hand stroked along the back of her head and she started to sob louder, harder, and he kept petting her, cooing. Easing her through a rollercoaster of emotions he could never hope to comprehend.

But when at last she pulled away, his shirt soaked, her face red, he kissed her forehead once more. "Listen," Ryan said softly, "that money is yours. I don't need it, and if I just spent $500 to give you a little piece of mind, I'd do it again. You don't have to do anything."

She looked at him through blurred eyes, and he saw something there. Something lurking at the back of her mind that needed coaxing out, luring out of its hiding spot. Something that only he could see.

"But if you want to have me take your photos again, I would like that very much."

So many things raced across her face he had a hard time keeping up, but he knew that she wanted it. And wasn't that what someone like him was able to do? Find those hidden fears and drag them into the light of day, confront them? Make them go away, if only for a while?

And Aubrey's eyes were haunted with things she wouldn't yet name.

"I don't know," she said cautiously, and Ryan wondered what she saw when she looked at him.

His hand trailed from her head down to her shoulder, squeezing it.

"It would be good for you." His voice was commanding, with a bit of a hardness to it that belied his gentle gaze. "And there is nothing wrong with wanting it."

Her body stiffened a bit and she stared at him in shock, as though he'd just read her mind. Her mouth parted and he saw that soft, pink tongue within. Oh, how he longed to suckle that, to bite it, to make her body and mind contort as pleasure and pain mingled and danced.

"Tonight you may rest up, but tomorrow, after class, I want you to come right home to me. I'll be waiting, Aubrey."

"Yes, Sir." The words were out of her, instinctually. As if they'd been beaten into her as the correct response when given an order, and it sent an illicit thrill through him. She was a natural. He'd known it from the moment he first saw her.

He smiled, kissing her forehead once more, hand lingering on her soft, feminine flesh a moment. "Good girl."

L ying in bed that night, knowing she was just down the hall, was sweet torture for him. He only made it worse by denying himself his own pleasure, but still he stroked himself, picturing her form tussling up the sheets he'd carefully picked out for her.

When he'd first shown her the room that was to be hers, she looked like she might faint. His house was beautiful, he knew. He was useless when he came to decorating, so he'd hired a professional and had everything redone.

The only thing he'd really specified was that the rooms all had to feel a bit different, to have their own personality. His room was warm, antique. The home was already old, and it had a fireplace opposite the foot of his bed which he'd had refurbished, and all of his furniture was a dark cherry wood against the burgundy walls. Gold accents dotted the room, brightening it slightly and making it seem quite ostentatious.

But her room, the guest room, was cozy and inviting. Bright blues and crisp whites made it seem like something out of a dream, a relaxing getaway. With the mirrored closet at the side of the bed, though, and the four-post canopy, it was designed with purpose.

His room was punishment, hers was pleasure.

She'd sunk into the soft mattress and cooed her subdued, disbelieving delight. As if making too loud of a noise would frighten this fantasy away.

He thought of her as she was at that first moment, as that astonishment washed over her that this is how she could live. That this could be hers, if only for a while.

In her eyes he saw her thinking of the way she'd toss and turn trying to get used to the new quiet, the lack of barking dogs and yelling neighbours. Of the way she'd think of him, of what he'd seen. Of how vulnerable she'd allowed herself to be after only a couple of drinks and a little bit of persuasion.

Of how much she wanted what he could do to her.

He let out a soft sigh as his cock brushed against the silken sheets, caressing his body and easing his tense muscles. How could he do it? He'd gone over this a thousand times before, hadn't he? His mind was cluttered with thoughts of her in the bed, so soft. So inviting. So needy.

He thought about stealing into her room, touching his hand to her slender thigh, feeling out her form as she tried to drift to sleep. She'd tense, but then, finding it was him, relax. Welcome it. Welcome the lack of choices, no longer having to decide what was right and wrong.

He would tell her, and she'd never need to worry.

Ryan moaned again at the thought, and his body tightened momentarily. She was so beautiful, and his cock throbbed in his hand.

But he forced his hand from his thick member, willing himself to go to sleep. He wouldn't let himself cum, not yet. He had to practice control over himself if he had any hope of dominating her.

"How did you sleep?" she'd asked him that morning, and they both knew. They had matching blurriness in their eyes, a twin slowness to their motions. Neither had slept well.

"I'll sleep better tonight," he replied, and his lip twitched into a smirk. "You will too."

Her eyes widened and she bit her lower lip into her mouth, but her next gesture was the one he'd longed for. It was so simple, such a gentle motion, but the way she nodded said it all.

B y the time she arrived home, he felt calm. Certain.

When he saw the tears in her eyes, though, his heart missed a beat. She looked so soft and sweet, and he wanted to coddle her, to make all her hurt disappear at the same time that he wished he'd been the one to cause it.

Ryan opened the door for her and then locked it behind her, not presuming to take her in his arms. He had to hold back, to resist the pretty little tears on the young woman's face.

"What happened?" he asked, his voice dark and gritty and edged with need. She couldn't have changed her mind. Not after how willingly she'd bent to him. That fickle fawn, uncertain of how good he would make her feel.

Instead of answering, she thrust out her hand, her phone revealing a text message.

At 1:09 pm her father had sent her a message asking when she was coming home.

At 3:48 pm, he'd told her never to come home again if she wasn't going to answer him.

And five minutes ago, the final text. *'Don't you dare come crying to me & your mother when you get your stupid ass knocked up & on drugs. You are dead to us.'*

Harsh, especially considering she still had him listed as 'Daddy' in her directory.

Ryan brought her into his arms, letting the phone drop to the desk beside them.

Aubrey's slender form pressed into his, and that delicate body quaked with the sobs that shook her. She seemed to lose all vestiges of her maturity, resorting to seeking comfort in his arms like a bawling child.

Her slender little fingers curled and sunk into his back as she loosed her tears into his shirt, her dirty blonde hair masking what little of her face wasn't pressed to his chest. She couldn't bring herself to speak, just sobbed and cried so helplessly, like a child lost from her parents.

Though she very much was in some ways.

His broad, strong hand stroked through her blonde hair, her

tresses entangled between his fingers and making his heart and his loins swell from such new, titillating sensations. Her slender body pressed to his, her scent filling his nostrils.

He let her cry until at last no more would come out of her sobs, and then he let her slump from his now-wet, blue shirt.

"Aubrey, it will be okay. Trust me."

Her pale face was highlighted by red puffy eyelids as she looked up at him, seeming to have little more moisture within her dainty form to give up to her distress. Tears still stained her cheeks, rolling down to the top of her upper lip.

"I couldn't respond," she choked out, all that crying only seeming to accentuate her beauty, making her look more vulnerable, more needy of him. More pained. Just as he wanted her. "I was in class. And... I just needed a break from them... that's why... why I came here," she said, looking away, fighting off another sob as another tear threatened to roll past her lips, her fingers digging into his shirt deeper. "And I didn't tell them where I was," another sob cut her off, "because I was afraid they'd come for me."

His thumb caught her tear, tracing over the bow of her mouth. He looked at her so seriously, so intently, and he knew how he could cure her. How she could work past all this pain and angst and find that inner peace.

He just didn't know if she was ready.

But staring down at her puffy face, her trembling lips and quivering body, he knew he had to do something. And there was only one way he knew of that always made the pain more manageable.

"I can make this go away," he said, his voice husky despite how calm and even it was.

Her long lashes curved upwards, so thick and dark, threaded together by some remnants of her glistening tears. She glanced aside, then back at him, her puffy eyes framing those bright emerald gems at the center.

"What do you mean?" she asked, her voice broken by the sorrow that still lingered beneath despite her confusion.

She quivered before him, shaking like an inexperienced

dancer on unsteady legs, her slender limbs buckling so that her knees banged together just above her stockings.

He stroked her still, caring and considerate. Perhaps that was why she regarded him with both caution and desire, because he reminded her of what she'd always longed for at home but was never able to receive. Comfort. Compassion.

He looked down upon her, his body strong and firm against her slender and shaky one. "Sometimes, feelings get a little overwhelming. Ever heard the expression 'bringing a hammer to your thumb to distract you from a missing limb?'"

His hands held her shoulders, supporting her frame. "I can help do something similar. Bring your pain into focus, into a manageable level, and you can deal with it one little piece at a time."

Aubrey's beautiful green eyes nervously strayed from his, but they flitted back again and again as she stood before him, unable to even stand upright and steady without his support. She looked so utterly lost, and he could read the conflict on her face as she bit down on her lower lip, letting her white teeth sink into that pale pink flesh.

"Like... with that... stuff... you pictured me with?" she said, her voice soft and airy, so very weak. A struggle for her to get her words out in that moment.

"That's part of it." His voice was so certain, but it wasn't cold. He couldn't be cold with her. It started out as a fantasy, a crush of having her. But she'd been in his home for nearly a month now, and in that time he'd seen into her soul. She was an open book, so obvious to his expert gaze, and she wasn't soley a conquest any longer. She was Aubrey, and she needed him more than she knew.

"But when we play with those things, for real, you will have the real power. The power to stop it." He paused, letting those words hang in the air and sink into her for a moment as he looked at her, squeezing her shoulders in his hands. "It takes some trust, though."

She was so very delicate, like a porcelain doll in his strong arms. She sniffled, relinquished her hold on his shirt to wipe her sleeve over her cheek, moving away some of the drying tears.

"You don't trust me?" she asked, clearly misinterpreting what he'd meant in her naïveté. Perhaps already she'd come to trust him so much, to see him as a charitable and kind man, that her trust in him was a foregone conclusion? That instead she worried of herself coming off as a foolish girl not yet worthy of his trust.

Oh, she was so sweet and tender, and he chuckled as he shook his head.

"I trust you'll be a very good girl, and an absolutely lovely subject." One of his hands lifted from her shoulder, lightly running his thumb over her jawbone. It was strange how much fairer she was than he, as though she were still so innocent and clean.

"If you trust me to take your pain away, I will," he reassured her.

This was all so unreal, he reflected, to touch her smooth, clear skin, to feel her delicate jawbones beneath a soft layer of flesh. She felt too good to be real, like a work of art crafted by countless artisans to portray the very best of her kind, to be exemplary of all the finest that femininity possessed. Or perhaps he was merely growing more smitten with her over time rather than losing the enchantment he held all these months.

"Of course I trust you," she sniffled, her eyes growing watery again, her lips pursing and trembling as she looked on the verge of more tears.

"No more of that," he chided gently, cupping her face in his hand. He took a deep breath in. "You are the most beautiful woman I've ever seen, and I want to help you."

Her cheek fit so neatly into the palm of his hand. That delicate jawbone touching to his flesh as she looked up at him, blinking away the watery tears that were forming in a flurry of eyelashes.

"I... I don't want to let myself hurt anymore," she resolved, biting her lower lip, a rosy hue filling her cheeks as she belatedly realized what he'd said. "The most beautiful?" she repeated, so sweetly disbelieving.

He nodded, slowly, before lowering his left hand to her right wrist, wrapping his fingers around it. It was a motion both firm and gentle, and he caught her pulse quickening through the fragile flesh. "Come with me," he said, guiding her down the hall, past the framed pieces of art and into that warm, antique room of his.

The fire was dimly lit, the light casting odd shadows around the room, and he went to the candles at the side of the bed. They boasted of scents that were masculine, like leather and tobacco and the outdoors, and he thought it suited the room nicely. He lit the trio with his back to her, letting her ease into the foreign room.

Aubrey followed after him like a lost little girl taking the direction of an older man, her pleated skirts swaying as she swept into the room. All her pain and sadness was held at bay as she darted her big, emerald eyes about the chamber, soaking it all in so curiously. In all her time as his roommate, she'd never seen his room.

The smell of the candles, of the fire, they all filled her dainty nostrils and she stayed close to him, clutching her hands together beneath her petite bust, anxiously wringing her hands together.

"This is your room?' she asked in her soft, weak little voice. "It's so... so beautiful," she remarked, a bit awed and intimidated by the vintage style that dominated the room. It all served to only make her feel like an even younger and more lost little girl, so out of her element. So out of her league in this lair of a rich, strong man.

Her room was designed to comfort, his was designed to keep her on edge. To purposefully make her feel small and uncertain. He smiled over her shoulder at her, realizing it was doing its job. "It is. All real heartwood, too." He placed the candles on the elegant nightstand and turned to face her.

"If you want me to stop, at any time, you just say 'Sunshine', okay? 'No', 'stop', those won't count, okay? I'll just keep going until you say sunshine. Say it," he ordered, his voice stern.

That frail little princess stiffened at the authority in his voice, her waifish figure twitching and standing a little more erect as her gaze locked onto his. Those green eyes of hers betrayed not fear at the command, but something else. The total focus of attention. The eagerness to obey.

"Sunshine," she said quickly and breathily, her pale, slender fingers knitted together as she pressed them up beneath her chin, as if it was a prayer.

"Good girl," he said with a smile, fancying that he was doling out affection and compliments as easily as commands. "You can stop me whenever you need. Even if it's just for a break." He was still quite in control, but he didn't hide the compassion or the concern in his voice.

He found himself walking a fine line between offering what she needed and frightening her off. And he couldn't do that, not when she was so near, trembling like a little leaf and so ripe with sensuality that was only starting to stir from its sleep.

"I'm going to blindfold you now, Aubrey."

She had grown a little stiller as authority edged into him, but the thought of having her sight taken from her made her quiver harder still. "You'll... you'll be careful with me... right?" she asked, gnawing her lower lip, those white teeth sunk deep into her pink bottom lip as she fidgeted, one leg rising up so that her calf rubbed against the back of her knee.

"Of course. If I'm not, you can stop me," he reminded her, reaching for the bed stand drawer and opening it, withdrawing a black, silk blindfold. "It's quite soft," he chimed as he closed the distance between them. His heart was thudding so fast, and all he really wanted was to shove her down, to take her then and there, but he knew he couldn't. Not yet.

He wouldn't rush it with her. It would be sweet torture for them both, and the way she kept biting her lower lip made him all the more certain.

He reached his hand up to her lower face, cupping her jaw and using his thumb to roll her lower lip free. It was so red from her worrying upon it, and he had to wrestle back the urge to suck it into his mouth.

"You better stop that." His voice was husky, marred with

183

arousal, but his eyes betrayed his humour as he rose the blindfold to her face.

"Sorry," she murmured in a meek, soft little voice, already sounding so sweetly obedient, as if she were meant for such a life. Meant to obey.

When she gently pressed her soft, lightly pinkened cheek into his palm, it only stressed the point even more so. Her delicate scent of vanilla wafting off her beautiful young figure as he leaned in around her with his own strong aroma. Already she was marked by him, his own more masculine scented hair products mingled into her soft, luxurious hair.

He couldn't have chosen a better candidate than her. She was everything he could have dreamed of, so... malleable.

He wrapped the blindfold around her face, tying it tightly at the back of her head. He smirked a little as it mussed up her thick tresses, but he smoothed them down gently, and just like that she was perfect once more.

He took her hand and carefully led her to the bed, urging her to settle upon the slippery, silken sheets. "I want you to lie back in the middle of the bed, Aubrey."

She moved with such tentative little steps, her fingers curling about his much thicker ones for comfort as he guided her to the bed. She bent her legs, pushing her knees up onto the silk sheets, bunching her skirt up along her calves and the argyle socks she wore. She still had on her jacket from walking outside though, and had to shoulder it off to expose her bare arms and the white blouse beneath before laying back down.

With her hair splayed across his pillow, eyes covered up and hands at her sides, she looked like a serene sleeping beauty. Those black mary janes pushed out to the side as she gnawed her lower lip once more, worrying the pink flesh.

He didn't mind that she was tracking in the outdoors into his sanctuary. He instead relished the little bits of imperfection, the small things he didn't account for.

Over and over he'd fantasized over this scenario, and to see her deviating from what he'd imagined in subtle little ways sent thrills like he'd never known through his body. It was *her*. The imperfections defined the moment, he realized as he moved away, and it would have seemed fake if she acted too perfectly.

He went to his bureau, grabbing his camera from the top of it and walked back to the foot of his bed. She'd always dressed in such loose outfits, and to see the secrets hidden beneath the baggy cloth was like entering heaven, into a realm he felt so at peace in.

The sweet little woman, so eager to please him, her keeper. Her benefactor.

"I want you to lie still for a little while," he asked in a husky voice, his throat tightened by his own lust.

Her head tilted to the side, her delicate little chin angling towards his direction as he moved. "You're not going to leave are you?" she asked, sounding almost heartbroken at the prospect of him going. Though of course, he had absolutely zero intention of doing so.

Otherwise she obeyed, her slender form motionless atop his big, posh bed, her slender limbs so still. As if she were the doll she resembled, frozen in time where some young girl had laid to rest in her doll house.

He exhaled and let his hand click the shutter, capturing the moment forever. Anticipation swirled heavily between them, and he could see those little tells in her body, he read her so easily. She needed someone like him, and she was lucky he found her.

It was a blessing, then, that he coveted her for himself.

He clicked the camera shutter again, from a slightly different angle, keeping the flash off so as to capture the feel of the room. The dark ambiance, the dancing shadows, the strange tint of the fire reflecting off her pale flesh.

"Take off your shoes, sweetie. You're messing up the bed."

"S-sorry," she murmured, her cheeks burning a bright red from the realization she was staining his expensive bed sheets with her outdoor shoes. She bent her lithe legs back one at a time, the muscles in her calves straining and bulging a little as she reached down, undid the clasps and pulled off one, then the other, before trying to reach down and set them at the foot of the bed.

She underestimated the height of the bed, and they dropped with a bit of clatter. "Sorry!" she repeated, her voice a little high pitched from anxiety, worried about displeasing him.

But that gave him the excuse he needed, and he placed the camera aside as he strode towards her. His fingers reached out, encircling her wrists, and he tut-tutted. "You're going to have to learn to be more careful, little girl," he chastised, his voice dark.

Never could he recall being so turned on, so desperate for her, and the feel of her delicate wrist in his hand was exquisite.

Her stockinged feet curled up beneath her pert little rear, and she bit down upon her lower lip once more as he took hold of her wrist. Anxiety was written all over her beautiful, porcelain face, and she hung her head a little, still blinded because of the mask.

"I'm so so sorry," she pleaded, sounding so meek and pathetic, so injured by his reprimand as if she'd failed a very important test. Not understanding that he'd hoped for her to give him the excuse.

But that made it all the sweeter, and his pulse quickened as he sat upon the bed, his larger weight pulling her towards him. "You don't apologize like that," he said. "You crawl into my lap like a good girl..." He could barely believe he was saying the words. That they were finally coming from his lips. "Stomach down."

She froze.

Her whole body went stationary for a moment and he feared he'd gone too far when her lips parted as if to speak, only to shut and remain silent.

The seconds were excruciating, and he feared she'd say that word. That one, simple, bright word that would bring this all to a stop and risk everything he'd planned for.

She was the one to break the tension, however, and to his unimaginable delight she shimmied across the bed and did just as he commanded. Pressing her slender form over his lap, her stomach to his thighs as her pert little rear pushed up behind her beneath her pleated skirt. "I'm sorry," she murmured softly.

There was no hiding his arousal from her, even though he still wore his finely tailored pants. He was fully dressed, but for his shoes, and that made him feel more in control. More empowered over the trembling leaf of a woman pressed so helplessly to him.

Her sweet apology just made things all the more sensual for him, and he rubbed his heavy hand down along her spine. He touched her, through her clothes, and it was everything he'd dreamed it could be. She was warm, almost a bit sticky in the heated room as the fire danced beside them, and he could note her scent more easily in the air.

"Pull up your skirt, sweetie. It's time to show me how sorry you are."

Her first inclination was to obey, and that made his heart sore with want. Her arms immediately moved to do as he said without any thought, and only hesitated afterwards as the thought of the impropriety settled in.

"I-- but..." she muttered, but before he could administer further admonishments she acquiesced. Her hands lowered down and she shakily grasped the edge of her frilly skirt, drawing it up slowly to reveal the round, pale flesh of her bottom.

Those cheeks of hers suited her body--not large, but perky all the same. Round and oh so smooth, with her white panties nestled between the plush cheeks. The cotton fabric cupping her mound, showing her slit betwixt her thighs.

He could do nothing for a moment but stare, to drink in that soft, youthful flesh.

His hand stroked over her spine again, feeling out her form as he stared, letting her stew. To settle into the discomfort of the situation, to make her uncertain and off kilter. She would be waiting for what was to happen next, the inevitability of his strike, but still he wanted it to be unexpected.

He lifted his hand from her blouse, and simply caressed her with his eyes, going over her form with such affection that was as invisible to her as everything else through that blindfold. Things she didn't know existed. Those hidden secrets gave him the greatest pleasures, and when he brought his hand down on the fleshiest part of her ass, it was sudden and hard. The crack resounded in the sparsely furnished room, and even stung his hand a little.

That nubile flesh rippled with the impact, so soft and supple. Those twin clefts jiggled as her body tensed and her voice rang out in a high pitched little squeal at the strike. She was so tender, so delicate, and she pressed against his manhood harder as her spine arched and her stomach jutted down further.

Yet she didn't try to get away, didn't protest, just squealed then whimpered, gnawing her lower lip as her bare cheeks showed the outline of his hand in ruddy pink.

He rubbed that tender cheek, encouraging the blood to the surface, marring the pure white of her flesh. Oh, how did anyone become so perfect as she?

He felt over the heated flesh, but didn't tease lower. He didn't stroke the places he truly lusted for, nor did he pull her panties from the cleft of her ass. He wanted to, but he held himself back as his member throbbed beneath her slim stomach.

Again his hand cracked down, and again she whimpered and straightened in his lap.

"What do good girls say?" he growled out in his lust-laden voice.

Aubrey jumped, her whole body twitching atop his lap as he struck her again, a yelp escaping her pouty lips as she wriggled and writhed. Her body squirmed a little as her pert rear smarted from the twin strikes.

"I'm... I'm so sorry!" she called out, not sure what else she could say, her long, slender legs sticking out behind her. Her fingernails dug into his thighs as she squirmed atop his lap in her pain.

But her squirming only made his cock throb harder, and his breathing got louder. "You were a bad girl," he admonished, bringing his hand down again with another hard smack and leaving his palm on the smarting flesh. "But I can forgive bad girls."

She twitched and her nails dug into him harder, her wail this time louder as she seemed to border on more tears. Though this time they were not tears from emotional anguish, but just raw, physical hurt on her tender, sensitive flesh.

Though the more she wriggled and struggled atop his lap, the more it tantalizingly swayed her perfect little rear. That round swell of flesh waggling before him so delightfully.

"Forgive me, pleeeaase," she whimpered out pathetically.

It was hard to resist not bringing his hand down again, punishing that tight little bottom of hers further. It was so sweet, and the way she wiggled was divine. His head felt a bit heavy, her loins throbbing so desperately as she cried and squirmed against his hardness, but he rubbed her ass in a tender manner.

It was still tortuous, to have that sensitive skin rubbed so roughly, the threat still lingering in the air. He listened as she cooed and sobbed, her shoulders pinched and her ass tensed as she awaited the next blow that never came. He rubbed her for a long few moments, waiting for her to settle down, and his cock with it, and when finally she soothed, he stroked the back of her head with his free hand.

"That's enough crying for now, little pet," he growled. "But I don't think you've learned your lesson yet."

Her breathing hitched a few times but she ceased her crying at his command, proving an obedient pet indeed.

That delicate body shivered a while before stilling, calming atop his lap, her bare bottom red and exposed still. "I haven't?" she squeaked out pathetically to him. She didn't know what to expect, acting so lost, even if she gleefully crawled into his hands.

The fact that she couldn't see, was denied that right to take in what was happening with all of her senses, that just made it all sweeter. She was reliant upon him, and he stroked her ass affectionately. His other hand curled her long, blonde hair between it, feeling to soft strands out.

"No. But I will teach you. Climb back onto the bed."

She had tensed up the moment he'd tightened her hair between her fingers, but with that command she relaxed. Her nails no longer dug into his thigh so much and she tentatively pushed herself up, her slender body rising, lifting up off him. She tottered off his lap and back to the sheets to sit sheepishly, resting her weight back upon her elbows, her knees bent and pointed up as she waited.

He massaged himself for a moment, trying to relieve the

tension in his pants, to calm his hardness, but it was useless. There was no fighting it. Not with just how perfect she was, how compliant. It was time to push her, to see how far he could take her.

To see how far she would willingly go.

She still hadn't uttered that safe word, despite how he knew her ass must sting and burn. His hand still tingled, after all.

"Aubrey," he said as he stood, moving towards the foot of the bed once more and picking up his camera from where he'd left it. "I want you to pull off your panties."

Again, he watched attentively as her first instinct to obey took hold, but then... hesitation set in. Her arms froze midway to her undergarments.

"My... my panties?" she murmured softly, those full lips quivering a little as she tried to look in his direction, unable to find him precisely because of her lack of sight. "I-- I don't know.." she murmured sheepishly, gnawing her lower lip once more, but despite her apprehension, he could sense that she was teetering at the edge of capitulation, so close to giving in.

She just needed a bit more of a push.

But it was so sweet to watch as her body changed, those little motions so subtle and appealing as she struggled with his command.

"Don't you want to be a good girl, pet?" he asked, and his voice was hard, almost mocking. Daring her to not follow his instructions, to disobey.

Her ass still stung, and she sat as she did to try and take pressure off it, hoisting her weight up on her elbows. It was too fresh of a reminder, and though she waffled, hesitating a moment longer, he then watched as she lifted her pleated skirt, reached in under it to her hips, and hooked her thumbs into the waistband.

She wriggled her hips from side to side and kept her thighs together, barely about to tug the panties down between them, but she couldn't hide it all despite her attempts at propriety. He caught a glimpse of her pink little cunny, the puffy labia dainty and sweet betwixt her legs before she lowered her skirt again.

"I do," was all she said to him, her cheeks burning a bright red.

He didn't even take a picture. He was too caught up in capturing the moment with his mind, committing every single motion to memory. He saw the brief flashes of bare skin, of forbidden flesh, and it sent his thoughts into a haze.

The fire crackled behind him and a bead of sweat trailed down under his finely tailored shirt. "Good girl," he rewarded his pet, but his voice was tight. Constricted. He cleared his throat, trying to get back his sense of command and dominance.

"I want you to lay back, and spread your arms to either side of the bed."

Her legs were pressed so tightly together that as she lay down flat, he never got another glimpse of her slit, nor the little tuft of wispy blonde hairs above it. She obeyed, though, splaying her arms out to the side, leaving her panties discarded on the edge of the bed, twisted and pretty as she did as he told.

He swallowed and took another picture, leaving the camera as he walked to her left side. He kneeled at the bed, his fingers trailing over her bare arm. The underside of it was so fair, with blue veins just barely visible beneath the surface. He traced them, feeling the soft pulse quicken at his touch.

Licking his lips, he turned her arm over, his gaze following the light hairs along her forearm. They glistened from the orange light of the candles and fire, the downy hair so soft. He reached beneath the bed and with a soft clatter, removed the heavy chain and soft leather from beneath the bed skirt. He caressed her arm once more before he spoke. "Do you trust me?"

Her spindly limbs tensed at the sound of those chains, and she lifted her head off the bed just a fraction of an inch, still so blind to the world around her. Her lips parted and she looked as if about to ask him what the noise was, but instead she licked her pink lips and nodded to him so very briefly, and he had a tantalizing suspicion that she knew.

"Yes sir," she said meekly, just a wisp of her usual soft voice available.

He caressed her again, bringing his mouth to her wrist and

pressing it there for a long moment, tasting her skin. He nuzzled her flesh before pulling away, bringing the soft leather to her hand. He held her fingers in his, guiding them along the dark leather, feeling out the rich texture of the material.

"This won't hurt, sweetheart," he said softly, taking her dainty wrist and wrapping the binding tightly around it. He secured it in place and kissed each of her fingers in turn.

Her soft little breaths caught a few times as he kissed upon her delicate skin, her slender fingers twitching as he treated her with such care. She seemed to expect more, some hurt, some pain, but instead he merely wrapped those bindings about her and gave her such tender affections.

It made her shiver and fidget just a bit, rubbing her thighs together as she waited restlessly for the hitch. The catch to all this. She was feeling the same buildup he had clung to for all this time.

He walked to the other side of the bed, repeating the same motions with such tender affection, teasing her skin with gentle caresses. When that one, too, was secured, he moved to her foot. He didn't ask, this time. Instead, he reached across the bed and caressed over the top of her foot, down over her instep, tickling the arch through her stocking.

Each motion was so slow, so sensual, and when he got to her ankle and began coaxing her legs open, her foot towards him, it all seemed and felt so natural.

Though he hadn't asked, she never resisted. Her legs parting as he pulled them gently to the side to tie them down, her shaking seeming to still while he strapped her limbs to the bed. Perhaps the lack of control brought her comfort, or perhaps she simply had less room to quiver as she was tied down.

Either way, her beautiful, pale form looked at ease as he ensnared her, trapping her to the bed, her white blouse betraying the outlines of her perky little teats, aroused and stiffened through the nearly see-through fabric.

As he finished with the last foot, he stood back to admire his work. To admire her.

Never had he seen someone so beautiful, who had been so worth waiting for. Holding out for. He knew how lucky he was for her to be so perfectly crafted for him, so much so that it made him wonder if there truly was a greater power looking out for him.

For both of them.

He knew that she needed this, needed him, just as badly, and as he watched her body still and calm, he knew that they'd both feel whole after this evening.

He crawled onto the bed, careful not to hurt her slender legs as he moved between them. He knelt over her, his body weight shifting the mattress a bit as he hovered, staring down at her face. His gaze caressed her nose, her mouth, over her throat and down over the buttons of her blouse.

His fingers crept over her thighs, never disturbing the skirt, but instead going towards the first button on her blouse and pushing it through the sewn hole.

She'd remained so calm and quiet through it all, but as he popped that first button she gasped, softly and quietly. Her shoulders shrank inwards and she seemed to want to retreat within herself, but instead she stilled, calmed herself, her breathing having grown as he lowered her top, to show her milky white skin down to the pale white peaks of her breasts, cupped so tightly by her thin, fabric bra.

It was torture for him. He wanted to tear the shirt off, to ravish her, but even now, when he'd come so far, he refused himself that pleasure. No, he didn't want her for the moment.

He needed to *possess* her, always. And he wouldn't get there by pushing her to the limit.

Instead, he brought his mouth to her collarbone, letting his lips trace over the delicate skin, his bristly stubble contrasting to the softness of his kisses.

And against her smooth, blemishless skin, his coarse jawline was like a scrub brush. It made her gasp and squirm a little, shifting away from him, but unable to move more than mere centimeters away from his hungry mouth.

A soft little whimper escaped her lips and she faced away

from him, in the process leaving her slender stalk of a neck and shoulder vulnerable to his devouring mouth.

He moved up to the newly offered flesh, his nose teasing and soft as he trailed it up towards her ear. He breathed against her, letting out a soft moan that he'd so long held back as his hand went to caress her face. "You're beautiful," he murmured before kissing her neck flushly, his tongue flicking against the pale skin.

His words and the feel of him each made her gasp and quiver, her body unable to move, but she seemed content to sink into the bed and let him press against her. She bit down upon her lower lip to stifle her soft little moan as he kissed at her pale neck, enjoying the warm affection even as she was powerless to do anything else. Never did her plush lips threaten to spill out that one word in her arsenal.

The only one that could put an end to all of this and make their world come crashing down.

He teased her skin, exciting it with his tongue and his soft little gusts of breath as he kissed lower. His thumb went towards her mouth, coaxing her lower lip from between her teeth. "Let it out, Princess," he huffed as he kissed the valley between her nubile breasts.

Instead of calling for him to stop with that safe word, she arched her spine, pushing her tiny chest up towards him as she gave a shuddering moan and capped it off with a whimper. Her little body shivering as if cold. Though as his lips grazed her supple breast flesh she murmured, "No. Stop. It's not right."

"It is," he whispered back, his hand trailing down her body, along her ribcage, peeling back the blouse a bit more. He was so mind-numbingly hard, and his fingertips brushed the edge of her perky breasts. "And you don't have a say. You're my good girl, aren't you?"

Her teeth sank back into her worrying lower lip again, the poor girl unable to keep herself from gnawing at that poor abused morsel of flesh. "It's wrong," she protested softly, her meek little voice so weak. "You said you'd take care of me," she whimpered, her chest heaving a little quicker. "This isn't taking care of me." Her voice grew strained, vanishing into nothingness though her breathing only grew heavier.

"Oh sweetheart," he breathed out over her chest, looking up at her worried face. "I will. I just didn't realize how impatient you were." His voice was nearly a growl as he kissed lower, along her taut tummy, his fingers playing along her smooth, bare thighs as he hitched the skirt up, unveiling that sweet prize.

She could do nothing to hide her sex from him, the delicate, roused flower parted as her legs were pulled to the side of the king-sized bed.

Though being unable to resist didn't stop her from trying, and she did her best to clench her thighs inwards, to hide the glistening, needy little slit before his view. But she couldn't do it, not with her legs tied so taut. He had her under his control and she whimpered at her powerlessness.

"No!" she protested weakly. "Not that! Please no!" she offered up, squirming so feebly beneath him, only making her ripe young body to shimmy and shake deliciously before his gaze.

But he reminded himself that every time she said no, she wanted it. She had the right word that could make him stop, but her refusal to use it betrayed the true depth of her desire, and he gripped both her thighs in his powerful hands.

He squeezed the tender flesh between his fingers and he groaned loudly, almost growling with lust. "But princess, you smell so sweet."

His rough grab, his lewd words, it made her squeal and dig the back of her head into the bed. Though no physical action she took could tear him away from her, could rob him of the arousing aroma of her cunt. How deliciously ripe and ready it smelled. The sweet scent of her nubile body so strong off her slick little slit.

She tugged her legs at those shackles that bound her, "Get off! Get away from me!" her voice getting so girlishly shrill at the end.

"No, sweetheart. I can't do that." His dick throbbed so hard as he brought his nose to the soft little bit of fur that topped her mound, inhaling her scent so fully. It made him almost dizzy with arousal, but as his tongue flicked out of his lips and touched that warm, forbidden fruit, he nearly came.

Before she could even protest, his tongue ventured out again, his fingertips working in closer as he coaxed her clit from its hiding spot.

She very nearly jumped out of the bed, and would've if not for the bindings, he swore. That tiny little bud was so sensitive she reacted almost violently at his touch, but by the time he stroked her again she gave a moan instead of a squeal.

Already his little pet was learning so fast.

"No!" she panted out, her slick honey upon his tongue. "No that's too sensitive! Not there!" she protested.

But he didn't speak, didn't reassure her or try to warm her up to the sensations. Instead he toyed with her, running his tongue over that tiny bud, down her length just to get a taste of her. He kissed her, more frantically, hungrily, his fingers prying apart her slickened labia and devouring her with such need.

He was losing control over himself, and he damn well knew it. But there was no more holding back, not when he was finally tasting her juices, feeling her body respond to him with such repressed need. Her desperate little 'no's, repeated over and over just thrilled him more, and he sucked her little clit so needily.

She was like a puppet to him, every little lash of his tongue able to make her jump and flail and struggle at her bonds in futility. He played her like that, more of her slick honey coating his tongue and lips as he lashed at her feminine gash.

Aubrey seemed almost to sob, the sensations too much for the young girl. "No no no no no nonono!" she chanted. "I can't take it, I can't take it!" she pleaded, biting down on her lip. "Stop, no more please!" she begged.

And he did, not because she told him to, but because *he* couldn't take any more. He was breathing hard and frantically as he stared at her glorious little pussy. Her clit still throbbed, wanting more despite Aubrey's protests, and he slipped his thumb up against it, pressing against the sensitive bundle of nerves.

"What's wrong, sweetheart?" His voice was husky and he licked around his lips, tasting her sweet scent along them.

She squealed so loud it was very nearly a scream. That pressure of his thumb on her poor clit, it was too much for her to handle as her petite body strained against its bindings.

"Stop!" she wailed, then her breathing sounded once again like sobbing. "No more! It's too--ah!" she protested. The sweet young girl was too unused to such intense sensations. Had she even touched herself before? The thought of that shy little fawn exploring herself riveted him with arousal, but it was hard to imagine she had with how flushed she was, how much she cried out at his every touch of her cunny.

"Oh, baby," he chastised. "I want to make you feel good. Haven't you ever done this before?" He ground his thumb there, daring her to say the safe word as his other fingers delved lower, playing with the entrance of her cunny. "Haven't you had a man do this to you?"

She was a panting, writhing mess before him already, she strained upwards, struggling against her binds. "No. No!" she cried out, her perky tits slipping from her cheap bra to show the pink little areolas and stiff buds of her nipples as she squirmed. "S-stop!" she whined before breaking into pathetic little sobs.

'It will make you feel good, baby doll. And it'll show me what a good girl you are. Make all the pain go away." He caressed his middle finger up over the seam of her cunny before oh so slowly letting it sink into her. Her muscles were clenching and spasming and he knew how close she must be as he ground his thumb more urgently against her clit.

His mouth, though, delved for that freed breast. He was ravenous for her body, and perhaps he was being too hasty, too hard, but he sucked that stiff nipple, bringing it between his two rows of teeth and putting some pressure on it as his middle finger reached for that cluster of nerves, hidden within her.

Her throat was growing hoarse with all her cries and pleas, that tight little cunny so slick and warm, wrapped about his digit and squeezed it delectably. She was so tight, such a sweet young thing even as she flailed about against her bindings in futility. No longer able to form coherent words as he suckled her perky tit in his mouth, torturing that sensitive nipple as he toyed with her virginal little cunt below.

He growled against her puffy, pink nipple, his thumb and middle finger working in tandem as he felt her body grow so still and then arch. She squeezed his digit so intensely as the orgasm rocked through her, starting in her belly before spiraling out along her body, uncoiling like a spring. He kept torturing her all through it, sucking and fingering and pleasuring her form despite her protests, despite her little acts of defiance.

She never got to relax, never got to still as her breathing grew so ragged and hoarse. She instead only weakened and flailed more importantly than before against her bindings as he tortured her sensitive loins and nipples.

"Stop," she muttered breathily. "No more... please," she whimpered, sobbing as her head pressed back into the silken bed sheets, her shoulders lifted up off the mattress itself.

He pulled his fingers from her ravished cunny, bringing them instead to her nipple and smearing her juices upon that thoroughly sucked, puffy mound. "But darling, I haven't had you yet. I'd be so disappointed if I didn't get a chance to take your flower. You saved it for me, didn't you, like a good girl?"

Her face was flushed, some tears streaming from beneath her blindfold, and her body was in such a heightened state of arousal. So much of her slick, honeyed fluid running down her inner thighs. Yet she gnawed her lower lip in such a familiar manner all the same.

"I did," she whimpered out in such a slight gasp, bobbing her head just the slightest bit.

"What a good girl you are," he husked, licking her fluids off of her nipple, savouring the taste. His free hand went down to his leather belt, deftly undoing it, followed by the button and zipper on his fine trousers. "I promise, my little princess, this won't hurt. Not with how wet you are."

He placed his forearm at her side, his fingers lightly resting along her bicep as he moved up along her body. His mouth was inches from hers, and he knew she must have been able to catch her own scent so near as her nose crinkled. "You taste like heaven to me, princess, and you look even better."

He pushed down his boxer shorts, finally removing his heavy, throbbing cock from their confines. He needed her so bad, and there was already precum leaking from the swollen helm as he brought his member to her pussy.

Rubbing himself against her clit, he teased her slightly as he brushed away some hair from her ear. "Do you know what this is, pet?"

A very visible shudder travelled through her svelte frame and she nodded to him, biting her lower lip hard as she whimpered out an "mmhmm" to him. Even as naive as she seemed, blindfolded from reality, she knew what that hot, hard flesh that brushed against her sensitive quim was.

There was no mistaking it. Not a hint of deception in his intent.

"I'm going to take you, little girl, but I want you to ask for it." His voice was so laced with lust, his breath still scented with her juices. He robbed the head of his cock over her clit again, then back to the entrance, and back again. It was threatening, teasing, and he was hardly able to contain himself from simply pushing in.

"Say, 'take me, Daddy,' and I will push my cock into you. I will make you feel things you never dreamed of, make you see things you never imagined. I will make you whole. But first, you have to say it." He kissed her throat again, sucking her flesh hard and threatening her with bruises as his hand tightened around her bicep.

"Or, you can beg me not to, and I'll do it anyways, but it will be so much worse, my little doll."

He didn't notice it at first, but she had completely frozen at his mention of the word 'daddy'. She seemed to be pulled out of the moment by it.

Had he gone too far?

She'd broke down crying because of texts from her father. Her daddy, after all.

The moment of silence dragged on, her lips quivering as she

was about to speak. Was it the safe word upon her lips? He wasn't sure, but he didn't press any further, just holding himself there as he waited for her decision.

Her nails dug into the silk sheets and leather bindings and she murmured, "Take me daddy," as his cock coated itself in her slick honey still.

The relief he felt that he hadn't pushed her to the limit was quickly stripped away by something far grander. The anticipation, the buildup, how torturous it had been on him, and as he finally began sinking himself into her, he felt whole. Remarkably, spectacularly whole. He didn't hide the moan that erupted from his chest, he didn't quiet the soft, "Good girl," that fell from his lips. He simply pushed himself into her slowly.

Even with how wet she was, how hard she'd cum, how aroused he'd made her, she was still so tight. A virgin! And surely, it was risky. Unprotected, unhindered, he enjoyed her with full sensations that sparked through his body.

"You're so tight, princess," he managed out between suckling upon her neck, his cock sliding up inside of her spread body.

She shivered and convulsed as he filled her, gasping and moaning from the intense sensations. His manhood filling her so completely, that only her extreme slickness saved her from the hurt of being thrust open so wide upon his girth.

"Daddy," she mewled out in her pleasure, embracing their roles. Embracing him, if not literally, as her tight little cunny clung to his shaft as he pulled away, as if trying to tug him back inside of her warm, fertile depths.

God, that word upon her lips almost sent him over the edge. He'd denied himself pleasure for so long, and as he once more hilted himself within her, he stilled. Nestled in her depths, he let her muscles contract around him, squeezing and milking him with such naive, innocent skill.

She wanted this, needed this so bad. Rewarding her, his kisses trailed up along her jawline and against her ear. He moaned, licking along her sensitive flesh, "I forgive you, my sweet little girl. I'll always forgive you."

Aubrey broke into open sobs, but he felt their nature. Felt

the relief in it as her chest heaved and she tried to press herself to him, to embrace him as best she could, her warm cunny wrapped about his manhood so tight.

"Thank you," she murmured out breathily, "Thank you daddy!" That tight little virginal cunt so snug about his prick, squeezing such pleasure out of his long-deprived manhood as he pumped into her body bare.

He nuzzled her ear with his nose before he brought his mouth to hers, sharing that sweet tang of her pussy with her quivering little mouth. They needed one another, and in so many ways. Ways that he had barely scratched the surface of, and as he put his weight atop her body and kissed her, it was with a passion neither of them had known they possessed.

He embraced her, wrapping his arms around her back and pulling her into his chest as he bucked his hips over and over again. He was so much larger than her dainty form, but she'd shown him her strength, her will to succumb and be healed by him.

Aubrey took the pummeling of his hips bashing to her inner thighs, the dull smack of his balls against her pert ass cheeks below. The wet slap of his groin to her wet cunny. Her moans and cries echoing through the chamber as she was left to his mercy.

"Yes, yes--" her voice hitched in between smacks of their lips. "Oh daddy," she whined, overflowing with need, her spine arching, her body tensing so much such new and overpowering sensations flowed from him as he plumbed her depths with his thick cock.

"I could never be mad at my baby," he promised, kissing her mouth and down her chin, tasting her flesh so eagerly. "Do you want me to cum in you, sweetheart? Wouldn't that feel so nice?" Just saying the words sent a jolt of pleasure through him and he thought he was going to lose it then and there, to spill into her without warning.

Without hearing her beg for it.

She'd surrendered herself to him completely, and the very notion of thinking for herself was now foreign. In so short a time she'd given herself up to just being his, and she gasped out "Yes" immediately, her cunt spasming tighter around his dick in response, compelling him to heedlessly empty his load into her fertile depths.

"Cum in me daddy," she begged, "please! Don't be mad at me," she whimpered, needy and so hungry for him.

Her sweet, seductive, sinful words sent him toppling over the edge, heedless of how risky it was. She was so fertile, so youthful, and even so he unleashed himself inside her. His eyes flew open and he gaped, taken aback by how powerful his orgasm was as it crashed through him.

Every part of his body tingled, every limb was alight with sensation as he groaned out her name, loudly. He rammed himself into her so hard, so fast, so unforgiving that he thought he might hurt her and though he tried to hold back and remain in control, there was no hope of that.

Torrent after torrent of cum pulsed into her as he bucked up against her depths.

"Aubrey," he gasped, bucking his hips again. "My good little girl."

All the while her legs kicked, her body flailed and she cried out, another powerful flood of pleasure coursing through her limbs and then back to her heated core as she wailed out, filling the room with the cries of their matched orgasms.

He'd emptied his loins into hers, filled her waiting cunny and left her panting and dewy beneath him, her pristine form sullied by his lusts and their mutual pleasure. She whimpered, her depths sore from his pounding. "Oh daddy," she mewled, "I love you."

He stilled within her, hugging her so tightly as his body was finally spent within his young lover. His sweet Aubrey. He kissed her neck once more and let out a relaxed sigh as he whispered into her ear. "Daddy loves you, sweetness, and he'll never leave you unsatisfied."

He caressed her face, her neck, before he finally shifted and removed himself from her feminine depths, leaving her gaping and empty without him. "You must be so stiff. I'll release you and you can curl up in my lap, watching the fire, okay? Do you feel better?"

That familiar sight of the pretty young girl biting upon her lower lip presented itself to him, but it was somehow different. It wasn't nervousness so much, it was just bashfulness in the after-glow of sex. A timid shyness.

She gave a slow nod to him and kissed beneath his ear. "Yes daddy. Thank you," she cooed softly to him.

After over a year of waiting, she was finally, blissfully his.

The Fertile Pet Maid

Book Themes: Dominance and Submission, Pet Play, Barely Legal, Virgin, and Breeding
Word Count: 9122

I f you told me I'd be working for the very man that put my father out of work, and my whole family into poverty, I'd have called you crazy. But it's funny what a few years and the burden of debt can do to you. I already had to drop out of college to look after my ailing father, and I needed work to keep the lights on.

That was how I ended up working at his office. I mean, one of his offices. He was a big capitalist, owned more companies than I had digits to count 'em on I'm sure! And I was just another 'human resource' in the data entry pool. That is... up until the day he came striding in, looked us all over and let his dark gaze rest upon me.

"You," he said, hooking a finger at me, beckoning me into my manager's office, which he commandeered on the spot for our impromptu meeting.

Oh, how I loathed the man... though his gorgeous, dark good looks made it so hard to keep my anger up as he stood there behind the desk in his black suit and maroon tie, a light neatly trimmed layer of beard hair that was oh so fashionable.

Though really, when was getting called into the boss' office, being singled out, ever a good sign? I mentally went over everything I'd done that day, and I knew I was a good worker. Hell, it wasn't that revenge didn't come to mind once in a while, but I liked to think of myself as above that.

More respectable.

"Yes, sir?" I asked as he shut the door behind me, my hands awkwardly at my sides, brushing the edge of the black dress he insisted we all wear.

It was so rare that I actually saw the man himself, always jet setting around the world on business trips I'm sure. Probably shutting down more factories like my father's, and shipping them off to the third world.

"Interested in a substantial raise?" he asked me, sliding his hands into his pockets as he looked me over. His well-tailored suit did wonders at showing off his cut physique, and so without giving away anything at all I could still imagine the ripped muscles beneath his suit.

That just made me hate him more, though, but in that weird way that wasn't comfortable. How could someone be rich and gorgeous and still be so damned cruel?

It wasn't fair.

It especially wasn't fair how my body responded to the thought of a raise, my blue eyes going to his. I'm sure they were sparkling, and my spine was a lot straighter.

"Yes," I answered. Best keep it simple with a guy like him, right?

He wet his lips, taking his time as he inspected me like another of his possessions.

"My previous maid has retired, I need someone to keep up the maintenance of my condo. It's a full time gig, especially since I'm gone for such long stretches. It'll require moving into the maid suite and being on call 24/7, but your pay will be doubled," he said with such curt efficiency.

My head reeled from the prospect, but before I had a moment to even ponder it, he asked.

"Interested?"

I just stared for a second. He was gone, like, all the time, so why did he even need a maid? And what did he mean being on call 24/7? In case there was an emergency dusting?

Then the second part of his statement finally sunk into my thick skull and I was nodding.

Double pay?

I'd give up my life for that, easily enough.

"Very good," he said and reached into his coat to pull out a small card and slide it across the table to me. "This is my address, and on the back is the time and location of a fitting appointment, for your new uniform. Be there on time. I don't wish to drag this process out any more than necessary," he said in that firm, authoritative voice of his.

New uniform?

Who's even going to see me in his condo?

I ran my fingers through my bleached hair as I reached out for the card, looking it over. "When do I have to move in by?"

Not like the moving part would be that hard. I had to move around a lot the last three years and pruned almost everything down to the necessities.

"Immediately," he said as he began to walk around the table, studying me. "But you won't start work until your uniform arrives."

He pulled open the door and stood aside, waiting for me to leave.

"What are you waiting for? That fitting appointment is..." he checked his watch, "in just twenty minutes."

Panic sank in then, but I nodded and rushed off.

Ready to start my new life as a domestic servant...

The fitting was not what I was expecting. It wasn't some dreary sort of office-oriented uniform dispensary or something, but rather a swanky, upper scale clothing store. Where the shirts cost more than I made in a year!

It almost made me turn on my heel and run right out until I remembered I wasn't the one paying.

The older gentleman who fitted me was professional, albeit thorough and then... off I went.

I went home, bagged up my things, told my family about the promotion — in as little detail as possible, sticking to the point about 'double pay' — then headed over to his penthouse condo overlooking the city. I wondered if rent was included. It better be, because I wasn't prepared for just how swanky it was.

I was so bowled over by it the vista before me, and the expensive furniture, that I missed the first few things his personal assistant said to me.

"Are you getting all this?" he asked, looking at me, brow raised.

"Sorry, what was that?" I said anxiously, brushing back my hair behind an ear.

"Just follow me," he said impatiently, and led me off to the right and down a round stairwell. He took me down to another level — there were apparently at least three! — and led me to a secluded section. My residence, it seemed.

"Here's your room," he said, pushing open the door giving me a brief glimpse of the lovely but sparse area before he moved onto the next door. "Bathroom," he indicated, then last, "kitchen and living area. There's room for guests, but you can't have any. Got that?" he said, but didn't wait for the answer. "Good."

No guests? That was odd.

I arched my brow, but he didn't look like the kind of guy that wanted to deal with any of my questions. He was probably too busy handling all of my boss' bullshit.

I looked over the room again, though, and felt a strange sense of emptiness. It wasn't what I'd expected, after seeing such a luxurious place, but I supposed servant's quarters were never as nice as the Master's.

"How does he like things done? Can I speak to the last maid?"

"No," he said firmly, staring at me through his round glasses, the stick-thin man so severe looking he seemed to rival my boss, but without any of the good looks. "She's moved back with her family and is not to be disturbed. If there are no more questions, you can relax in your new suite for the time being. Once your uniforms arrive, you'll be expected to start cleaning up. Fetching groceries will also be your duty, you'll find the list on the tablet in your closet. Make sure you do regular inventory checks on what's in the kitchen. Understood?"

It was really, really hard not to roll my eyes.

Instead I smiled as I grit my teeth, trying to look pleasant.

"I never got your name," I said brightly.

"Martin," he said in a clipped tone of voice turning back around and leaving me there. "Good luck," was all he said as he climbed those stairs briskly and vanished. Leaving me all alone in the spacious penthouse.

I unpacked my things, which didn't take as long as I expected, and then settled in for a long wait. Luckily, my living area came with just about every form of entertainment I could hope for, the smart TV had access to every streaming service imaginable, with a private computer desk, my own tablet and an expensive phone to boot! All with pre-made accounts intended just for me, with a sticky note that detailed my password and security details.

Though I didn't get long to relax, before a jarring buzz filled the air around me, and my new devices alerted me that it was someone at the front door. By the looks of the security feed that came through my tablet, it was a parcel delivery.

I rushed on up to the door, since it was apparently my responsibility, and answered.

"Hello!" I said a little breathless, having climbed the stairs more enthusiastically than I intended.

"Here's the clothing items Mr. Romy ordered," he said, then held out a digital signing device. "Just jot your name here, ma'am," the young fellow said before the transaction was quickly done.

And I was left alone again.

I took the package to my room and opened it. What lay inside shocked me! Oh, it was a uniform alright, several of them in fact. But...

I stared, and I knew my jaw was dropped, but I couldn't help it. I felt embarrassed just looking at the package and I quickly shut the top of the box again.

There had to be a mistake. The black dresses that ended just below my ass was one thing. I mean, he had a kink, obviously, but with a guy that rich how couldn't he fetishize the power he had over people? Making them dress and act and talk like he wanted, as if we were all little puppets.

But these outfits wouldn't even give me that much coverage!

I walked away from them, fuming! My brain working wildly as I tried to come to terms with what I'd signed on for. Maybe it wasn't too late to go back to the office... though the more I thought of him, the less I figured he'd put up with one of his peons changing her mind.

I wasn't sure how much time passed with me on the couch, glancing back to my room where the outfits waited, but eventually my phone and tablet both warned me: the boss was due back in an hour, and it was expected I'd be there to greet him. For inspection.

A shiver ran through me, of disgust and... secretly, a little titillation.

Though the idea of getting dressed up in some skimpy maid outfit for the guy who fired my dad and put us all in the hole overwhelmed all else. I was thinking what I'd say to the man, about his nerve! When a call came in, it was Martin.

"Has the package arrived yet?" he asked crisply, no pleasantries.

"Uh, yes, but—"

"Good. I'd suggest you get dressed and get ready. There's several versions there, for different occasions. One for wearing in your leisure time, in case you get called to duty abruptly. It's similar to the usual uniform, but more comfortable, relaxed," he said with such calm, casual certainty.

"Wait... I don't think I can wear *any of this*," I said, cutting him off.

Silence took over for a while.

"You'd best get over that quickly, miss," he said to me. "If you wish to keep your job, I suggest you stuff your qualms in a sack. Otherwise, get out immediately and I'll let him know he needs a replacement."

I went over to the box again, looking at them and feeling my hands tremble.

Not only would I be out my new job, but I wouldn't even have another job to go back to. And let me tell you, if anyone in town was hiring except the guy who fired my dad? I'd already be working there.

"I'll do it," I said softly, a sigh upon my voice. Though Martin had hung up almost immediately upon my acceptance. It was clear I wouldn't get a lot of sympathy from him. He was probably too busy busting his ass for Mr. Romy to care about anyone else.

I squeezed myself into that outfit, just as I was ordered to. Though the stockings, heels and ridiculously-short miniskirt were a challenge, it was the top that snugly hugged my bosoms and made my cleavage bulge out that really was the toughest part. But I suffered it, because I had to, and made my way up to wait by the door for Mr. Romy's arrival.

He came home himself that evening, looking as handsome and hard-nosed as ever. His gaze went to me immediately, and he shut the door behind him as he let his briefcase thunk to the floor.

"Very nice," he said in a gravelly voice, and for once I actually heard what approval sounded like from my boss.

But I just felt like running and hiding. I looked at the briefcase and wondered if I was supposed to bring that in. The job didn't really come with a list of duties other than the few that I'd been told, but more than that, rich guys always wanted their staff to be mind readers.

I shifted in my heels, my hands clasped behind my back. I thought it'd make me look professional but instead it just made my chest stick out more.

"Thank you, Sir."

He took his time sizing me up, but he kept such a calm, cool aura about him all the while, somehow avoiding the disposition of a letch like I was more used to dealing with.

"I approve. You'll get your raise, Miss Tish," he said to me, pushing his shoulders back and looking at me expectantly. "Well?" he asked.

I blanked.

"Excuse me, sir?" I said, and that made him furrow his brow in irritation.

"Didn't you study your new duties?" he asked. "On your tablet?" and I suddenly turned blood red, realizing I must've missed some other things. "Surely Martin told you," he said.

He didn't, I didn't think, but I stared up at him blankly.

"Grocery shopping. Taking an inventory. No guests..." I trailed off, trying to think of what else Martin had told me.

His brows furrowed and he looked irritated.

"Take my briefcase to my office, set the table for supper and await further instructions," he commanded me firmly. "After tonight, I'll expect you to go over the details in the tablet, understood?"

It was less a question like when Martin said that word, and more of a command itself.

My cheeks went hot and I grabbed for the briefcase, my knees trembling a little as I went up the few stairs into the main area, going towards where I figured his office was. I regretted not looking around more earlier, but it felt strange, being in someone else's house all by myself.

It took me longer than I'd hoped just to find the office, what with how big his place was! But at last, the spacious room was in my sights and I laid his case upon his hardwood desk, taking but a moment to admire the very old-fashioned style of the decor as compared to the more modern look of the rest of his place.

I came out then, rushing to the table, when I found him doing something I'd never thought I'd see: cooking.

There he was, tie and jacket gone, sleeves rolled up to his elbows, working at the stove with such intense focus.

I'd just assumed he had someone to do that as well.

And secretly I was grateful that wasn't another one of my tasks.

I stood for a moment, my head cocked to the side as I drank the sight in. He looked good, and it was nice to see him, without being seen. To study him and let my eyes roam over his hair, his trim figure, the way his forearms bulged from out beneath his dress shirt.

I had to keep my head clear, though. But honestly, it was hard. I was dressed up like some tramp, and you'd have to be someone way more moral than me not to feel exposed and a little turned on. You can't dress up like you would in the bedroom and not feel a bit of that bedroom allure.

I licked my lips and was so aware of the sensation before I pushed it aside. I hated this man. I hated that he dressed me up like a doll.

I just had to keep reminding myself of that.

I walked into the kitchen, looking at the cabinets.

"Place setting for one, Sir?"

"Yes," he said, absent-mindedly, paying me only a tiny morsel of his attention as he focussed himself upon his cooking. The frying pan sizzling as he set to work on whatever culinary creation he had in mind.

Finding the things I needed to set the table was the most troublesome part, but once I was done... I wasn't quite sure what came next. I stood there, a little awkward and confused until his voice came out of the kitchen.

"Grab a bottle of wine from the rack, the one on top," he

instructed, not burdening me with the fancy names and boring dates of his wine collection.

When at last it was all done though, he came to the table with his food as I stood there. Not sure what to do with myself as I imitated a living statue.

Though as he began to eat, his eyes would drift to me again now and then.

"Do you have experience in those kind of heels?" he asked me out of the blue, in between bites of his stir fry.

Was I trembling that much? I thought I had it under control.

Honestly, it wasn't the heels that were bothering me so much, though they were way higher than I anticipated. But it was everything else. Nerves.

I brushed my hand over my stomach, smoothing out the fabric though just for an excuse to hide my eyes from him.

"I'll get used to them, Sir. I promise," I raised my eyes, hoping I looked resolute.

He laid down his fork, and wiped his mouth, gesturing to me.

"Stand closer to me," he instructed firmly.

I did as he told me, but it put me within an awkwardly close distance of him, right up against my towering boss almost.

"This isn't an easy job," he said to me, looking up over my body before resting his gaze upon my face once more. "But the rewards will scale with your effort. Doubling your pay will just be the start, as long as you're willing to put in the commitment," he said smoothly, his voice losing some of that edge. But only a little.

"How does that sound to you?" he asked.

"I've always worked hard," I managed, though I had to wonder why my voice sounded so weak. I swallowed, licking my plush lips and tried to be more confident. "I'm sure I won't let you down."

Though honestly, I had no idea what I was agreeing to. But I needed the money, and if I needed to dress in a skimpy costume to earn it, I'd do it.

He raised his one arm up, and placed his hand upon my

lower back, rubbing there... and brushing against the round swell of my rear.

"I knew I had a good feeling about you," he said, touching me so brazenly, feeling my flesh through the thin silk and lace fabric of my uniform. "You'll adapt in no time, I'm sure. Now," he said, continuing to talk before I could object, "are you hungry?"

There he speared his fork through a piece of chicken and broccoli, looking at me with a brow raised in anticipation of my answer.

My stomach being up with my chest, both of them tight with nervousness, made me want to say no.

But Mr. Romy wasn't the type of guy that wanted me to say no.

I instead nodded, my head spinning as I looked at that bit of offered food. It really did smell and look divine, but I was too worried about the precariousness of my situation.

And of what he really wanted.

I wish I'd looked through that list of duties to see if 'let me grab your ass' was on it somewhere.

"On your knees then," he said so firmly, so matter-of-factly. I was a little dazed, but his strong hand upon me guided me down, and I knelt beside his seat as I was ordered. His cruel disposition had vanished, or rather shifted, he was commanding still, but it had a different air to it then...

"Part those luscious lips," he instructed, and I felt like a fool as I obeyed, and he very slowly offered me the food, placing it upon my tongue for me, leaving me to pull it from the fork.

"Good girl," he husked in approval.

What the fuck was happening in my life?

My mind was spinning, and I had to close my eyes as I chewed. I knew this wasn't right. I mean, I knew he wanted to play puppet master, but this was a whole other level.

Part of me wanted to just get off the floor and run home, find something else. Anything else had to be better and less degrading than being fed off my boss' fork, kneeling on the floor at his side.

So why did I stay put? And why wouldn't my body do what I wanted it to?

That cruel man who held my fate — and that of my families — in his hand, speared another forkful of food and fed it to me in turn. His hand stroking over my back, as if I were some dear pet and not a grown woman and employee.

"There you go. It's nice to have some pleasant company for dinner for a change," he said, smiling wryly as he continued the bizarre, demeaning ritual.

I shifted, my knees digging into the marble tile of his condo, my body trembling in barely suppressed rage, laced with desire. I was making myself sick, honestly. What type of person could even think of how great his thighs looked beneath his pants, or how strong his hand felt as it tenderly caressed my body?

I definitely should not be thinking that.

I should be thinking about getting the fuck out of here. No wonder his last maid quit.

So why wasn't I moving? Why was I just staying?

Because this isn't bad.

Shut up, subconscious.

I looked up at him, a furrow in my brows as I swallowed the latest bit of food.

His steady hand continued the ritualized feeding, while I watched his handsome, stern face contort to one of pleasure and amusement.

"You're a very good girl," he said in a breathy murmur. "I have a feeling you shall exceed in this new position of yours." With that, he laid down the fork, the meal at an end as he smiled at me. "Now, clean up," he said, in an almost patronly tone of voice.

Part of me was relieved, mainly the knees, because the floor was so hard! But I got up, took his dirty dishes and brought them away from the dining table in front of that massive window into the kitchen.

When I returned, he was gone, however. And I saw nor heard no sign of him the rest of that night.

My first night with my boss was so bizarre, but after that I had the time to read over the instructions in full. Martin had neglected to tell me about it, but the tablet contained an extensively detailed list of everything required of me, from taking his briefcase and placing it on his desk, to how I should arise early to set out some eggs on Sunday and Thursday mornings, to prepare for him to cook with.

Why they had to be set out early on those days, I couldn't fathom that night.

But the coming morning, a Thursday, I got to see what he did with it at least.

There was no mention of him feeding me, or him touching me upon the list at all, but when he served up his home made waffles for breakfast, it became clear that little event was to happen on repeat.

"Come here," he said as he sat there with the morning light shining upon him and his dark hair. And by his tone of voice, I could tell... he wanted more than for me to merely come closer. "I bet you're hungry," he said, as I looked down on the thick waffles, sprinkled with colourful fruit.

I had to admit, they smelled and looked divine.

I'd spent all night thinking about what I was going to do. Half of me just wanted to tell him to stick his job up his ass.

Then I thought: hey, if I wanted some revenge, knowing these weird little things could only help, right? A weird, sexual scandal could really hurt him, I reasoned with myself.

Funny how elated and relieved I felt when I decided that. Revenge was a dish best served cold, not with a strange tingle between my thighs.

But I knelt at his side without needing to be told, biting in on the corner of my plump lower lip.

"I am, Sir," I said like the obedient lap dog I apparently was.

"Good," he said, and he served me up a neatly pre-cut square of waffle with fruit and syrup, feeding me once more as he pet my hair this time. Luxuriating in the long, blonde strands.

"You can claim the satin cushion from my office for this from now on. No need to risk bruising your precious little knees," he said, half-amused, but half pleasant, as if some part of him wanted to be nice to me despite how cruel his nature was.

This was weird. I knew it was weird.

My mind must have been fucked up, because he was doing messed up things to my body and brain. I swallowed, and it tasted so good.

But his hand felt better.

As the meal went on, a tiny bit of syrup spilled from a bite of waffle onto my chin, and he took up his fancy napkin and gently dabbed it away.

"Hold still," he cautioned as he cleaned me up, removing all trace of that sweet syrup. "Very good girl," he remarked with a smile, a certain glint in his eyes that made me both worried and pleased.

That was how our days went for a while, me setting up his things, cleaning up his home — though little actual cleaning was necessary since he lived alone! — and then kneeling upon a satin cushion at his feet as he fed me for each meal he was home. He bizarrely never made any move to push things further, just his strong hand stroking my hair and my back, on down to my rear.

I just chalked it up to some weird power play. He just liked feeling in control.

I had no idea how to deal with it all, I was lost. My feelings were in turmoil and I nearly stormed off several times, until the end of the week... when I saw my pay deposit.

Not only did he pay me double as he'd said, but he'd tripled it. And I was paid not only for the typical work hours, but every hour I spent at his place. If I put up with his strange behaviour for just a while, I could quit and leave a wealthy woman, I told myself!

Though as time went on, it became clear, he had no guests, not even his assistant would come by. It was just him and I. I grew so used to the quiet and loneliness, that I was cleaning his room one day and became completely startled by his presence!

There he was, sat down on the balcony, bottle of wine beside him as he stared off out over the city scape.

I gasped — and maybe even squealed a little — and he calmly spoke to me.

"Bring me a bowl of fruit, Miss Tish," he said.

"Sorry S-Sir! Right away Sir," I said, and I hustled off, the ruffled plaits of my skirt bobbing as I went downstairs to get him that.

When I returned, he was just as I left him, and I placed the fruit before him.

"Sorry Sir, I had no idea you were home," I explained about my earlier fright, and he looked at me, studying me quietly.

"Getting used to the quiet, are you?" he asked in his gravelly voice.

"I suppose," I said, though honestly, I never quite got used to it. Just expected it. Even when he was home, he wasn't a big talker.

It was hard to hate a man that looked as good as he did and played things so close to his vest.

I stood just a few feet from him, the warm summer breeze loosening my hair from its barrette. Blonde tresses tickled my cheek and I swept them behind my ear.

"Are you feeling well?" I asked.

He looked out over the city and only glanced back at me, not answering my question, at least not right away. The pause lingered a while, and I wet my lips anxiously.

"What's on your mind?" he asked me.

I reached across my stomach, suddenly feeling uncertain. What was on my mind? I felt like I'd disconnected, become so invested in just work and money and...

And desiring those soft strokes of affection, and his kind words.

I looked out at the city and shrugged my shoulders before looking back at him.

"Just concerned by the... break in routine, I guess."

I'd had no contact with anyone but him all week, and it was starting to take its toll, truth be told. But I didn't want to let him know that.

"Is that all?" he asked, brow raised in that questioning way that made me want to spill every secret I ever held to him.

It got me to confess to something I never meant to.

"Do you... do you intend me to do... y'know," I said.

"What?" he asked pointedly, plucking a grape from the bowl and feeding it to me, touching his thumb to my plush lower lip in the process. I chewed and took my time before answering.

"Sexual... things," I said, my cheeks burning blood red.

"Is that what's on your mind?" he asked, looking not amused nor even upset, just... unfazed by it all. "Would you like that then, hmm?" he asked, and he let his free hand trail low, grasping my round rear through my skirt rather pointedly.

I swear, I was on fire. My skin felt so hot, and my heart was racing.

What'd I just say?

I couldn't look at him, because I did. Because I fucking did, and that was a horrible thing for me to want. It wasn't even about revenge.

It wasn't even the fact that I hadn't had a boyfriend in ages.

It was about all the things I was afraid to admit in myself. That I liked it.

"I..."

I couldn't speak, or eek out more than that one word, that one letter.

"It's okay if it is," he said with that handsome smile of his plastered across his chiselled face, his hand giving my rear a firm squeeze. "But no, I wasn't intending to take such liberties with you... beyond the pleasure of viewing your shapely form," he said, his smile evolving into a wry smirk.

Come on, Tish. This couldn't be your idea.

The things he was making you do!

So why did I believe him? And why was I the one that brought it up?

I fluttered my eyes, and was so aware of his hand on me. I hated this man, I told myself over and over again. He'd cost me so much.

He was arrogant and strange.

But I was drawn to him.

His strong hand wandered low, and I felt vulnerable... like I'd give into him and his cruel charms at any second. But then something popped out of my mouth, some way to deflect that I both instantly regretted and felt grateful for.

"Is this how things were with your former maid?" I asked, and my face burned red.

It only got worse when he laughed at me.

"Bertha?" he said and laughed again, shaking his head. "Oh no. Oh my no," he took such amusement in my question as he took another sip of his wine.

"Why not?" I asked, confused, embarrassed.

"She was more than twice my age, and took care of me since I was a boy. It wasn't like that... like this," he said, looking me over again, with that hint of lasciviousness.

"Why is it like this with me then?" I continued blurting out things I didn't quite want to say, but did all the same.

"Because I saw you around the office. And my mind... burned with questions. Possibilities," he said, his eyes going wide as he looked at me.

"Like what?" I asked.

"Like what you'd look like in a skimpy skirt and high heels," he responded immediately.

Something in me was unravelling. I'd just assumed he'd been a playboy. That he had burned through more maids than I could count, that they couldn't handle his strange demands and behaviours that my body seemed to enjoy and my mind hated that I responded to them so eagerly.

My breathing was high in my chest, my breasts rising and falling quickly.

"But you acted like this was all, like, second nature to you!"

"It is, in a way," he said with that wry little grin on his face that made me want to slap and kiss him all at once. "I'm just acting on impulse. My desires," he said, continuing to stroke the curve of my ass, feeling out the sumptuous flesh.

And it made sense. It wasn't like these little sexual nitpicks were included in the itinerary left for me, after all.

I'd just assumed he hadn't wanted a record of all his plans for me.

I shifted in my heels, my ass growing a little rounder as I put the weight on my leg, looking at him with such mixed feelings.

But mostly, they were all quickly becoming clouded by lust. Desire.

He was the man I hated and wanted most in the world. Maybe working for him so long and realizing he wasn't a complete monster had softened me. Whatever it was, I was throbbing between my legs, and I just wanted to run and hide.

"You never saw me?" he asked, brow raised again in that way that sent shivers down my spine to where his hand rested on my ass. "I could watch you shake your rear about that office all day. The loveliest woman in all my offices. Such fire, such determination," he said, and his appreciation for me dripped from his words so sincere. "You had a passion for life, to get through and make something of yourself."

His appreciation for me came as such a shock, and not just because I was unaware of his attention all that time!

I drew in my lip and knit my brows, but my mind was moving at a snail's pace. I couldn't believe the things he was telling me. That this wasn't just a thing he did.

That I wasn't latest in a line of many desperate women, eating off the floor as he fed them.

As he fed me.

How could I be the only one in all of his little capitalist empire?

Without even realizing he was doing it, he had taken up another grape and offered it to me, like his adored little pet. His intense gaze upon me as I chewed, studying every little thing about me.

"I want you," he said at last, firm and forward. "I want to bend you over this table and claim your body, as well as your soul," his voice taking on a gravelly edge. But his words were making me dizzy, literally dizzy!

"I— but..." I struggled to get out my words, but he had no hesitation slipping his hand in under my little maid's skirt, touching the bare cheek of my rear.

"I don't want to hear a no," he said, eyes half-lidded.

I wanted to give in, quickly, completely. But part of me was still obstinate, stubbornly resistant.

"I can't," I said, my throat dry as I watched his reaction to my refusal.

"Why not?" he said, dark and ominous.

"I don't want to just be your... your play thing. Not knowing how casually you toss off your employees," I said, all those years of angst over what happened to my family bubbling out. My throat had went dry from it, and I desperately tried to swallow and wetten my throat.

I didn't have enough money saved up, not yet, not for all I needed to do. Fear gripped me, but it was more than the loss of the job, and I knew it. How could I lie to myself about what was really scaring me?

The idea that he'd let me walk away.

He stared at me, his brows furrowing at first, but then softening as he reached out a hand and slid his long fingers along my cheek, caressing my smooth skin with his hard pads.

"I've offended you," he said, as if realizing his actions had done me some harm without his intending.

"What? No," I managed, but my knees were trembling and my voice sounded weak and distant. Where was all that fire he saw in me? That determination?

Wilted by his stupid charms. His sexy body. His irresistible smirk.

"No, I have," he said, as if able to read my mind, understand the old hurt there. It made him ponder, think a while, licking his lips before he spoke up again.

"I'll undo whatever I've done. All of what I've done," he said, rectifying his statement as he looked me back over. "As long as you'll be mine," he said, his gaze so intense, his desire palpable.

There wasn't any undoing it though, was there?

I stared at him, and I knew he had to have figured out that he'd been right. I was being pretty obvious about it as I worried my lip, feeling that tremor of anxiety run through me.

"My dad..." I finally managed, taking in a deep breath. He liked my fire? He'd get my fire. "You put him out of a job, even though I'm a slacker compared to him!"

That revelation must've shocked him. He didn't seem to realize it was all so personal to me.

"I'm so sorry," he said, eyes wide. But then... his hard form filled with a certain determination, and he puffed up his chest and knit his fingers back through my blonde hair and leaned in, placing a hard kiss upon my lips. His tongue probed between the two moist morsels, and he held me locked into that embrace for some time, until...

"I'll fix that, regardless of what you say. But I want you," his voice turned to a growl with those last four words. "I want you so bad, Tish. And I need you to be mine. Don't say it... show me... show me and bend over this table like the good girl I know you can be."

My heart was racing, and though it had started out in anger, that bruising kiss turned it into something else entirely. I could barely breathe, and my world suddenly felt so narrow. Like all there was was he and I, and the patio didn't open up to the wideness of the world.

It was amazing. I'd kissed a couple boys growing up, but not like that. Never like that.

His kiss was hard and determined, but had such passion behind it. Not the sloppy over eagerness, but the purest need.

My lips fell open as I tried get catch my breath, my blue eyes slowly working their way to the table.

Could I actually do something like that? What type of person was I if I said yes?

If I agreed to be spanked by my boss? By the same arrogant man that fired my father and put our family into turmoil?

So why did I believe his words that he'd make it right?

And why was all my reasoning being thrown out the window, even if I knew it was wrong?

He rose up from his chair, those strong arms about me, lifting me up and tipping me back over the table as he kissed me so deeply. He had such strength in those arms, and I knew it came from his long sessions in the private gym I so often cleaned up for him. Even bent over like that, he held my ample figure in his grasp as if I were nothing.

"You're too perfect to let go," he murmured in the brief gap that our lips broke their seal, in which I was too dazed to even realize it.

He could have anything, anyone he wanted. So why me?

It made sense, if I was just next up in line for his little experiment in humiliation. I could understand that. Respect it, even, in some weird, twisted way.

But the idea that I was somehow special or different to him? That was throwing me through a loop.

And the fact that all my blood seemed to be rushing throughout the rest of my body and avoiding my brain wasn't helping my situation. I was quickly getting caught up in his charms, letting my guard down. I was weakened by his strength, and I wished I could just let everything else go away so I could enjoy this.

Enjoy him.

But I didn't want to betray my family.

So why did I move my face towards him, my lips pressed against his with such a slow, insistent tenderness?

I was entangled in his powerful grasp, lost against his hard body and passionate embrace. Those long, strong fingers sinking into my flesh, holding me by my hips and shoulder, until at last he laid me down on the table, hovering over me as he plucked a few more kisses from my pouty lips, and moved on down towards the frilled collar of my uniform at my neck.

"I want you to be mine, in every way," he growled, like some beast in heat, drawn to me.

I was losing my mind, losing my everything, but I couldn't

fight it forever. I was going mad with desire, and my body needed what he was offering. That touch, those weird rituals, the strange behaviour...

It all spoke to me in some way I could never understand, and I'd fantasized about this moment since I first knelt at his table like some pet.

"Oh God," I murmured, my voice sounding so strained.

He rose up, looked down upon me with such a fiery intensity in his eyes. Such a hard man, with such a passionate desire, and he made me want to give into him. That was his trick. That was what made me submit so readily to him, he kindled a desire in me to do what he wanted, as he wanted it.

With his strong hands upon my form, he twisted me about, pressed my ample chest into the table and looked me over, with my short skirt flared upwards.

"Be a good girl and lower your panties," he growled in command.

I'd never done anything like this, not ever. Not even thought about doing it.

Even in my wildest fantasies, I couldn't have conjured up what those words could do to me and how readily I wanted to obey.

My fingers found their way to the waistband of my panties, and I knew that I should stop it all and just walk away, pretend none of this ever happened.

But it did happen. It was happening. I wanted it more than anything, and I was lowering my panties down over my thighs with a youthful glee, and a womanly excitement.

It was so wrong, and I felt the fabric slip down over my calves, gathering around my high heels and leaving me so exposed to the man who made me want to obey, even when I knew it was wrong.

I could feel the cool air graze my nethers, and I shivered with excitement, nervousness. I could hear him working his own belt, the sound of metal and leather, and then the cloth of his pants parting.

I only dared look behind in the glass reflection of the doors, see that towering man there, ready to take me as he pulled down his trousers and revealed his thick, sizable manhood, so rock hard with desire.

"I'm gonna fuck you raw, my pet Tish," he growled hoarsely. "Gonna pump you so full of my cum you'll be knocked up twice over," he pledged as he trailed his thick, purple crown along the seam of my cunny.

I was always a good girl. Always knew to avoid the very thing he was promising to do to me.

But he made me weak. Drew out my secret desires, the ones I wouldn't admit to myself let alone anyone else, and then display them in front of me so blatantly. With such expectation.

He was the type of guy that you never said 'no' to, and all of my good sense was gone and in its place was a girl I didn't recognize. A girl that pushed back against his cock, begging him with her body as a foreign, "Yes..." escaped my lips.

It didn't take much to make him oblige, that gentle little nuzzle of my quim to his manhood, and he was spearing his way into me. A single, rough thrust and he imbed his pulsating pillar deep into my warm, waiting canal.

"Yes!" he roared out, throbbing thickly, stretching my narrow, virginal canal wider with his entry. "You're so damn perfect! The way you feel with your pussy wrapped around my dick," he growled, reaching up, taking hold of my ponytail as he tugged back his hips, pulling the clinging walls of my cunny with him before he thrust back in.

I wondered if he even knew he was my first, if he knew what he was taking from me. What I was giving him. There was a sharp sting, and my body tensed and tightened as he stole my virginity.

I'd never heard him curse like that before, and the idea that I had unhinged a man that was always in control, always so put together... it was a rush. A high unlike any I'd experienced, and I was crying out in unison with him. Pain and pleasure mingled.

I hadn't realized how badly I wanted and needed him inside me until I had it, and suddenly I felt whole. All of my worries and fears slipped away and in their place was just warm, welcoming love and passion and desire.

I slammed my backside against his hips, and his cock hit against a sensitive part of me, sending a jolt of sensation through my entire body. My fingers grasped onto the heavy table, holding myself up as he took me so hard and with such need. The pain ebbed and gave way to a dull ache, and then to nothing more than sweet bliss.

"I've never felt so good as I do now that I'm fucking you," he growled to me, winding my hair about his fingers as he thrust, burying his shaft deep inside me with each thrust. He smacked my ass cheek with his free hand before grabbing hold of my hip to aid in his motions. "You feel so damn good around my cock, pet," he husked into my ear.

I shouldn't want him to think of me as a pet, as a thing he kept and took care of, but that was what I was.

And that was what I wanted to be.

I moaned again, my large breasts flattened into the table as my legs spread. I tilted my hips a bit more as he impaled me on his thick shaft, and he delved into me deeper.

The table squeaked as I held onto it tighter, my words peppered with cursing as he fucked me raw. It wasn't what good girls did. It wasn't what I did.

But I didn't want anything to separate us. Not now.

His two hands were holding me, guiding me, and he was thrusting with such rigor. I was captivated by the reflection of our bodies moving together in the glass. The way he pumped his organ into me, filling me up and making my ass cheeks ripple with each impact.

"Take it, take my cock... take me!" he said with such force, but I could feel the yearning in his words. How much he wanted me to accept him, not just physically.

His fingers sank into my fleshy ass cheek, and he swelled inside my raw cunny.

The man who had the entire world, and all he wanted was to take me in such a primal way. My body was trembling, responding to his so acutely. He hit the right tempo, his sac slapping against my clit and threatening to send me over the brink.

But when his fingers wrapped tighter into my hair, tugging on those blond tresses as he went in harder, that was what did it. Maybe I get off on degradation. Whatever it was, I couldn't stop it as every nerve in my body went on fire. My knees were trembling and quaking, and I'd likely have fallen if I weren't pinned between his body and the table.

"Sir!" I screamed, because I couldn't think of his first name at the moment, but I wanted to let him know. Needed to tell him. "I'm cumming!"

But he had to have noticed the way my pussy tensed along his cock, the muscles drawing him in and beckoning him to do the thing he shouldn't. The thing I shouldn't want him to do.

I did, though. Oh, how I wanted him to fill me with his cum, to claim me as his. To bind him to me for eternity.

"Cum on my cock, Tish," he growled, demanding what was already the inevitable. The flood of warm honey coating his length, running down to his sac and adding a wetness to the loud slaps of against me. Though it slowly changed.

As I screamed out my ecstasy, he barreled towards his own. His organ twitched and grew harder inside me, his moans and groans deeper, heavier.

"I'm gonna make you mine, pet," he growled again, and I knew it was coming. He was cumming. And I didn't pull away, didn't fear it. I accepted it as that handsome, powerful man took hold of me and hammered away to his own release, the two of us exploding into a jumble of exploding nerves, the two of us lost to bliss as his virile seed flooded my fertile womb.

The thought, the awareness of what was happening, gave me the sweetest orgasm I could've ever dreamed up. I was soaring, my entire body seeming so disconnected and yet connected at the same time.

My throat was soon coarse, my begging and pleading for him to cum in me mixed with cursing and panting and praying for more. For this to never end.

I didn't want to come down from the high, but as he

pumped those last few streams into me, and slowly stilled, I desperately tried to catch my breath.

Mr. Romy stilled atop me, breathing heavily as his tool twitched and spurt its last inside me, and I laid beneath him. So satisfied... flushed and deflowered. But happily so.

He leaned in, kissed my neck beneath my ear, licked up to my earlobe and suckled it softly. He put one of his arms about me and squeezed me tightly as we lay there atop his balcony table.

"Stay with me... in my room," he husked into my ear lowly. "I'll keep my promises. I'll make everything right. Just be mine," and his plea was so genuine, so needful. He wanted me still, even after having spent his essence inside me.

I trembled, pushing in against him, needing his warmth. The feel of his body against mine, encompassing me.

I brought my hands to his, feeling them as they still gripped my hips, and I shivered gently, because I wanted it. Oh, I wanted it bad.

Before I could stop myself or think rationally, I was nodding.

The story of Mr. Romy and me didn't end there, though. Even if part of me felt no matter what he said, it would. I was always told men say hasty things in the passion of the moment, but despite how bold his promises to me were... he kept them.

Perhaps it helped that the maid uniform he had made for me needed some altering in just a few short months, to accommodate for the growing bulge in my belly. Or how once I was sleeping with him each night, I could coo such sweet words into his head, and fill him with an appreciation for my feminine gentleness.

Whatever the reasons, when he cradled my pregnant form, with our child fast on its way, I got to do so guilt free. Not only did my father get his job back, but all the old workers did when he opened up a new facility in town, with better wages and safer conditions than ever before.

The irony of the fact that I was into degradation and used it to get others the respect they deserved didn't go unnoticed. And every mealtime, when I kneel at his side, patiently waiting for the food he lovingly prepared, I appreciate that — and him — a little bit more.

Sugar Daddy Influencer

Book Themes: *age gap, virgin, breeding, sugar daddy, billionaire*
Word Count: 7883

The California sunshine beams down on the wooden roof of the beachside bar and glitters across the golden sand.

It's a stunning, clear day here in beautiful Malibu, and there's so much to take in. The crystalline water lapping at the sandy shore, with the sapphire sky reflected above it, not a cloud in sight.

There's the plaintive call of sea birds flying through the air in curved formations. They swoop and dive for bits of french fry or bread in the sand, waddling on their spindly legs.

Further out, I can see flocks of them swerving around the surface of the gleaming white-capped waves in their search for fish to nab. They don't have a care in the world, just coasting along on the delicious balmy sea breeze.

Down the beach I can see the enormous outcroppings of reddish-brown cliffs emerging like behemoths from the earth.

I make a mental note to explore those cliffs when I get a chance; the area should make a perfect photo spot, and I'm always on the hunt for new, exotic places to snap pictures.

The beach is spotted with little groups of sunbathers, swimmers, and people wanting to see and be seen.

Candy-hued rainbow umbrellas brighten the scene here and there, and no matter which way you look, there's always someone conventionally beautiful to behold. Women in bikinis and beach dresses, flaunting their curves.

Men in swim trunks or even speedos, spread out on towels, sunning themselves like exceptionally vain lizards. Malibu is a magnet for the rich and beautiful, many of whom are here today, crowded around the small but charming tiki bar.

On either side of me, the bar is populated with gorgeous girls and boys. All of them young, stunning, and camera-ready. I am no exception-- I'm one of them.

I flash my bright, naturally-straight pearly whites for a photo. I raise my tropical coconut drink to my lips and pose like I'm taking a sip. I make sure to pout my lips a little, to emphasize how full and luscious they are.

I need everyone on the receiving end of these photos to be overwhelmed with my charm, my sex appeal. After all, that's how it goes, right?

Sex sells.

It's how I picked out my ensemble for this not-quite-impromptu beach bar shoot. I'm wearing a skimpy, trendy scarlet bikini that accentuates my round, plump breasts, waspish waist, curvy hips, and juicy butt.

However, I know there's an art to being 'effortlessly' sexy: instead of giving my audience a full view of my killer body in this bikini, I wear a flowy white beach dress over it. The dress is ruffled and light, fluttering in the salty breeze. It's modest enough to turn my bikini look from hardcore to softcore, but it's revealing enough to keep viewers reeled in.

The delicate golden necklace I got as a brand deal is nestled cozily at my collarbone, showing off my chest and slender neck. My long legs draw the eye, up to my white dress or down to my strappy wedge heels that make my calf muscles pop.

A pair of dangly earrings, also gifted to me for a brand deal, nestle into my long, thick mane of beachy blonde waves. Two artfully-messy locks of golden waves frame my face on either side.

I tilt my head and bat my long lashes as another camera phone flashes. I bite my lip, relieved to be wearing my favorite non-transferable red lipstick, from a high-end brand I would never be able to afford years ago.

I scrunch up my nose and poke out my tongue for another picture, hoping my youthful expression and pretty, freckly face will draw in a lot of views.

My manicured fingers pluck the colorful toothpick umbrella out of my drink and tuck it playfully into my blonde hair. I lift my phone and pose for a selfie, then immediately check my gallery to assess the photo.

The picture shows me, looking radiant and dewy with the California sun beating down on my bare skin. The salt in the sea air gives my hair extra curl and volume. There are several bar-goers in the picture behind me, all good-looking in their own right. Some of them pose for their own pictures, even tapping me on the shoulder to get me to turn and look in the right direction.

That's one thing always on my mind: angles. Always looking for the most flattering angles. The most flattering light. The most exciting backdrops and props. It's a lot to keep track of. I take a deep, needy sip of my tropical drink, feeling the booze flow through me and assuage my nerves a little. Why are my nerves so shot when I'm just chilling at a beachside bar in one of the most enviable vacation spots in the world?

Well, because I'm technically not on vacation. I mean, for all the world it looks like I am, but that's just part of the act. That's the hard work of it-- making it look effortless. Making my life, my persona, my experiences feel both magically exotic and fully authentic. I'm always working, even when I look relaxed.

My gorgeous smile and passion for luxury travel are my trademarks, so I have to get that right. Even though I'm surrounded by friendly faces, I'm on my own. I'm here to work, to get the photos and content I need to post on my social media accounts for my massive following. They hang on my every picture and caption, flocking to comment, like, and subscribe.

Leaving compliments and declarations of love under each photo set, demanding always more, more, more. My audience can't get enough of me, and I need their support to keep jumping from one project to the next.

Even though I'm here acting and looking the part of a wealthy heiress with no responsibilities or fears, I don't come from big money. This isn't my world, I'm just masquerading through it.

It's not all glamour, either. I'm naturally shy, but I have to play up my personality for the cameras. For my fans. For my reputation. So when a guy on the bar stool beside me starts getting a little too close for comfort, there's little I can do but smile. I'm not famous for sticking up for myself. I'm famous for being beautiful and easygoing.

"Hey, I recognize you," the guy says, leaning in to whisper in my ear.

I can smell the rum on his breath and I have to force myself not to physically recoil.

"Really?" I reply, as if this isn't a conversation I've had a million times.

The guy grins and nods, his eyes looking me up and down with no shame. He's clearly tipsy, and whatever boundaries he may have had sober, they're gone now.

"Yeah, totally. You're some kind of actress or model, right?" he asks.

"Sort of," I answer. "But not quite."

He squints at me for a moment, thinking. Then realization dawns on his face.

"Ohhh! You're that internet girl. That influencer. Vanessa Cherry!" he bursts out.

I smile. "That's me."

"Oh shit. You were in Costa Rica just last week, and now you're here. What's next? Bali or south of France?" he goads me.

"Not sure yet," I answer truthfully.

I try not to let the question get to me, but it makes me nervous to be reminded of how precarious my lifestyle is. I never really know where I'm going next. It depends on whatever brand deal, sponsorship, or promo event I get invited to. And the only way to keep getting invited is to keep showing up. Keep playing the game. Paying attention to the numbers, the algorithm, the trends. I need to emulate what my fans want. I don't go where I choose-- I go where I'm invited. This isn't an extended vacation, it's my life. Never knowing where my next flight will take me or where my next meal or bed will come from gets exhausting. But I can't quit now. People rely on me for my travel posts or even just my flirty selfies. Besides, I do love traveling, I love connecting with fans, I just wish I had a little more control.

"Well, if you need a tour guide to show you all the cool spots around Malibu, I'm totally your guy," says the tipsy man beside me.

"Thank you. I think I'll be okay on my own, but I appreciate the offer," I reply politely.

No sooner have I fended him off than a whole group of shirtless bachelors flock me for photos. They hang on me, their arms around my shoulders, their hands on my lower back or my waist. They're always like this, trying to touch me and get as close as they can. I'm used to it, but at the same time, you never really get used to the invasion of personal space. These guys feel entitled to my attention and time. They feel entitled to touch me without permission. When they pose with me for photos, they always find a way to grope me or get too close. I can smell their mustiness. I can feel their sweat on my skin. I see their eyes rake over my curves. They see me not as a human, but as a commodity. A living doll meant to look pretty and please a crowd. Besides, a photo with me is guaranteed to blow up on social media. My fans swarm me for a little taste of my fame. I'm a golden goose, and they want in on the feast. They fire off questions and comments so fast I can hardly keep up.

"Damn, baby, where are you staying tonight?"

"I have your photos saved on my phone!"

"How long are you in town?"

"Can I get your number?"

"You're even sexier in person."

"I'm your biggest fan, can I get a kiss?"

"You got a boyfriend?"

I volley the questions with a breezy smile or a generous giggle. I manage to extricate myself from their groping hands and roving eyes. I take a deep breath as I polish off my mai-tai and leave the fancy glass on the bar counter. I turn and start to walk away from the tiki bar, giving the crowd one last flirty wave goodbye. Everyone waves and shouts their goodbyes enthusiastically before they start whispering to each other about me. It's expected. As long as they're talking about me, right?

I start walking toward the water to dip my toes. The salty wind whips around my face and lifts my blonde waves. I love the feeling of sand between my toes and salt air on my tongue. I'm finally starting to relax a little when I'm rudely interrupted by the same guy who tried to hit on me earlier. By now, he's gone past tipsy and straight into sloppy. He grasps a sweaty beer in one hand while he reaches out to touch my arm with the other. I take a step back, dodging him.

"Where d'you think you're going, gorgeous?" he slurs.

"Just dipping my toes in the ocean. You seem a little wobbly. Maybe you should go back to the bar and sit down," I tell him in the sweetest voice I can manage.

"Only if you come with me," he replies. "But I can think of better things to do."

"Is that so?" I answer. I look around frantically for an escape route.

He steps closer and alarm bells start going off in my head. This guy seems to have misconstrued my upbeat attitude as interest. In him. Somehow, this always happens. All I have to do is smile at a guy, and suddenly he thinks I'm his property.

"Don't run away from me. I know you want it," he says.

He waggles his eyebrows and reaches out to grab my arm. As soon as his sticky fingers close around my wrist, my heart starts pounding. Panic sets in.

"Please let go," I insist.

"What, you think you're better than me because you have a zillion followers? Big deal! I have followers, too. And money. And clout. You should want to get with me," he declares.

"Leave me alone," I assert.

I try to rip my arm away, but he holds tight. I see anger flash in his eyes.

"You're a fake, that's what you are. A fake and a tease!" he accuses. "You think you can flirt with me for the camera and then just walk away?"

I'm desperately searching the beach for someone to intervene as the guy drones on.

"I've heard the rumors, you know. That you're not really rich, you're just some backwoods white trash who's faking it for the internet fame!" he hurls at me.

My stomach churns. I don't know how he figured it out, but he's right. The rumors are true. He could totally ruin my reputation if I don't do what he wants. I'm about to give in when suddenly, a slightly older guy in sleek, beachy loungewear comes swaggering up to us. My eyes are drawn to him instantly. He has the dark, tousled hair of a soap opera heartthrob and the bone structure to match it, visible even with his designer shades on. He's tall, with broad, strong shoulders and an assured smile on his handsome face. He's walking right up to us. I feel a rush of relief looking at him. Somehow, I understand that I'm safe now. The older man steps right up and slides his arm around my shoulders, peering down at the pervy guy over his shades.

"Oh, honey! There you are. I thought I'd lost you in the crowd," he says in a deep, commanding voice.

"Who the hell are you?" the first guy demands.

The older man smiles. He looks pointedly at the guy's hand on my wrist.

"A friend of Vanessa's. Now, would you kindly remove your

hand from her arm? Or would you prefer that I remove it for you?" he warns.

The pervy guy's eyes go wide. He pulls his hand back as though he'd been burned by a hot stove, and takes a few staggering steps back. He holds up both hands-- one holding a beer-- in surrender.

"Hey man, not looking for any trouble," he says.

The older guy smiles wider. "Great. Then get a move on."

With one last longing look at me, the perv slinks away back to the bar. Defeated.

I turn to stare at the older guy in awe. My cheeks are flushed and I have butterflies in my stomach. He's strikingly attractive, not to mention the cool, in-control demeanor he gives off. Even though I'm usually the celebrity, I find myself stumbling over my words like a heart-eyed, starstruck fangirl in front of him.

"Oh my god. You're a lifesaver. Thank you," I gasp.

"Anytime. That guy was a creep," he answers. "Luckily, he's a coward, too. Would've been a real mood-killer to have to kick his ass down the beach."

Normally, I'm not the one to be impressed by tough-guy talk, but it's different with him. Because it's not empty words, it's the truth. There's no doubt in my mind this guy could and absolutely would fight someone to defend my honor. I feel a little swoony just thinking about it.

"I'm glad it didn't come to that, but I owe you big time. I thought he'd never leave. How can I repay you? Can I buy you a drink or something?" I offer.

"You don't owe me anything, Miss Cherry. In fact, I'd like to make you an offer," he begins smoothly.

I cock my head to the side. "What do you mean?"

"We both know what kind of lifestyle you live," he goes on. "Takes a lot of cash to jump from one exotic location to the next. Costs money to dress designer, too. And all those expensive hotel rooms. Not to mention you have to deal with guys like *that*."

I'm speechless. He smiles and keeps going.

"I bet it wears on you after a while. Doing everything yourself but only doing it for other people. You go to all these beautiful places, and you're surrounded by beautiful people, but at the end of the day, it's a job. Not an easy one, either. I see how hard you work. I see the effort behind those effortless photos and captions. You're good at what you do, but you don't have to do it alone. Not anymore," he explains.

He whips out a white envelope and hands it to me. I frown at it.

"What's this?" I ask, taking it with hesitation.

"I've had my eye on you for a while, Vanessa. What I have in mind is a mutually beneficial arrangement. I can make your dreams come true. I can take the stress out of your life so that you can actually enjoy it. All you have to do is be mine," he concludes.

He leans in, gives me a kiss on the cheek, and pats the envelope in my hand.

"I'll be hearing from you soon," he says warmly, and then saunters away.

I stare after him in pure shock for a moment. Then I decide to head back up the beach to the resort where I'm staying, envelope in hand. I manage to slink away from the bar without another tipsy perv following me, and once I finally retreat to the privacy of my room, plop down on the bed and open up the envelope. A few items come falling out onto my lap.

"What even?" I murmur, my eyes going wide.

There's a wad of cash strapped with a pink ribbon. Like a gift. My hands shake as I flip through the stack of hundreds. It's a lot of money. Thousands of dollars.

"Holy cow," I gasp.

But that's not all. There's also a room key almost identical to mine, proving that my mystery benefactor is staying in the same resort, as well as a slick, silvery business card. I inspect the card, reading off Leo Pierce, travel writer. It dawns on me suddenly that this guy is no ordinary joe-- he's famous, too! I've definitely heard his name before, and it's always said with great reverence. He's a guy who knows the industry well, and he writes beautifully. And judging by the pile of cash in my lap, his skills are paying off.

This is more than enough money to pay for the rest of my stay here in Malibu and then some. Leo Pierce, famous writer, critic, and world traveler, wants to join forces with me. I remember his wording: all you have to do is be mine.

My heart is racing. This is an offer I can't refuse.

I flip over the business card and find a phone number. I immediately send a text message.

I'm in.

The response comes within seconds.

Perfect. Come to my room tomorrow at noon for our first adventure.

I lay back on the bed, squealing with excitement. The rest of the day can't pass by quickly enough; I'm so excited for tomorrow! It's a massive relief to know where my next meal is coming from. I get to keep doing my thing, and Leo will fund it. He said he would make my dreams come true... and I believe him. I drift off to sleep, and my dreams are filled with desire.

The next morning, I wake up smiling. I spend the morning getting ready and anxiously watching the clock. I put on a romantic pink dress and comfortable, cute shoes in case our 'adventure' requires steady footing. I braid my long blonde waves into two plaits, one over each shoulder, and add a floppy white hat. Just before noon, I hurry to the elevator down the hall and ride up to the top floor-- the penthouse suite where Leo is staying. My heart is racing, my palms are sweating. After dreaming about him all night, I'm eager to see Leo again. I wonder what my new sugar daddy has in store for me.

I have the room key he gave me, but I still knock politely at his door. I hear footsteps approaching and then the door swings open. Leo lights up to see me, and I feel like I'm floating an inch off the ground just seeing him. He looks me up and down and smiles.

"Well, hello. You are insanely beautiful," he remarks.

I blush. "Thank you. You look very handsome, yourself."

It's true. He's wearing simple, high-end black joggers, a gray henley with the sleeves rolled to his elbows, and athletic sneakers. The ensemble shows off his killer physique, and he somehow manages to look just as chic in athletic wear as he would in a slick suit. Gone are the designer shades, so I can get lost in his warm brown eyes with flecks of pear-green in them. I even adore the teensy faint lines at the corners of his eyes. There's infinite kindness and wisdom in that gaze, and I find myself entranced by him.

He steps out into the hallway and offers me his arm. "Shall we?"

I nod happily. "Let's go! But, uh, where are we going?"

"Taking a gentle hike up to a scenic, secluded spot. Most people don't know about it yet, but with a little cash lubrication, you can get the locals to tell you where the good spots are. It's beautiful there, and quiet. You can shoot some content there for your followers," he points out.

"Wow, that sounds great!" I chirp back.

To my delight, it turns out to be a hike up to the same cliffs I admired from down the beach yesterday. The weather is perfect for a hike. The sky is blue, there's a gentle breeze, and there's nobody around up here. We can see and hear the faint sounds of beachgoers down the way, but up here it's nothing but us and the wind. We chat as we steadily climb our way up.

"So you're a travel writer," I begin.

"Yes. I've written various columns and articles over the years. Shot some reels for a couple TV shows, I've done podcasts, photoshoots, the usual. My work has taken me all over the world. I've been to every continent except Antarctica, but as soon as they open a restaurant there, I'll be the first to make a reservation," Leo jokes.

"Wow! You've been everywhere," I reply.

"Judging by your social media posts, so have you," he says.

I smile wistfully. "I've been lucky. I never even left my home state until I started this whole influencer thing," I reveal.

"Where's home for you?" he prompts as we walk out onto the plateau at the top of the cliff sides.

"Alabama. My accent isn't very strong these days, but when I call home, you can hear it in my voice," I laugh. "My mom and sister are still there. I send them money whenever I can."

"How'd you get into this industry?" he asks.

"Well, I was eighteen years old, walking to work as a grocery cashier when this talent scout stopped me in the street. I thought he was joking at first, but he offered me a brand deal for this luxury beachwear line. It seemed like a one-off thing, but when I posted about it online, it went viral. Overnight, I got a ton of followers and offers to fly me out for various ads and deals. It started with flying to New York and L.A. Then it was London, Madrid, Berlin, Hawaii-- all these places I never even let myself dream about because it seemed so out of reach," I sigh.

"Sounds like you've really made it," he comments.

"But it's stressful sometimes, pretending to be someone I'm not. I fly to these amazing locations, but I'm no heiress. Every flight is for a work trip. My photos make me look like a socialite jetsetter, but I'm actually just a regular traveler on a budget," I shrug.

"Not anymore," Leo tells me. "Stick with me, and you'll never have to think about a budget ever again."

"You're so kind. But why me?" I ask honestly.

Leo takes my hand and gently leads me closer to the edge of the cliff so we can look out over the water, the beach, the horizon beyond. It's a breathtaking sight.

"Wow. So beautiful," I murmur.

"It is. But part of the beauty is having someone to share it with," he says. "Traveling alone is rewarding. It's an adventure. But traveling together? There's nothing better. As for why I chose you..."

Leo turns to me and sweeps me into his arms. He leans in and kisses me full on the lips. I melt into his embrace. Even though we just met yesterday, it feels so right. My body warms to him instantly, blooming for him like a flower in the sunshine. His lips are so soft, even with his stubble rough against my skin. He towers over me, and it's clear who's in control. With the wind whipping around us and the sea crashing waves against the cliff below, Leo's hands explore my body. He smooths down my narrow waist and around to cup my taut, round ass. I moan and arch into him, feeling the stiff bulge at the front of his pants.

Leo's lips trail down my jaw to my neck. He kisses and teases my ticklish skin with a graze of his teeth while he hikes up my pink dress. I inhale sharply when his hand cups my mound. I lean into his touch eagerly. My heart is pounding, the adrenaline is coursing through my veins. His finger strokes teasing, delicious lines up and down my cunny through my soaked panties. His fingertip rubs my clit with the added friction of the fabric in between, and it drives me wild. Nobody has ever touched me like this, and it's overwhelming. I tilt my head back and sigh as his fingers work their way under my panties, slipping them aside. Leo rubs my sensitive clit with the flat pad of his thumb while two long fingers tease my hole. His lips move down my neck to my chest. He slips one spaghetti strap off my shoulder so that the dress sinks lower, revealing one plump breast. My nipple stiffens in the cool air, but Leo pulls it between his lips and flicks his tongue over it, sending spirals of pleasure straight down to my core.

His tongue circles my nipple in tandem with his thumb massaging my clit. I feel so tense inside, like a taut string about to snap. I'm hanging on the edge of coming, just like we stand on the edge of the cliff.

"Mmm, it feels so good," I whimper.

"You want to come, don't you, sweetheart?" Leo coos, lifting his head.

I nod vigorously. "Yes, oh yes, please."

"Look into my eyes, Vanessa," he commands.

I meet his gaze and hold steady, even as I blush deeply. I feel so vulnerable, looking him in the eyes while he fingers my cunny. He holds me and plays my body like a beloved instrument while the salty breeze wraps around us. The pleasure mounts higher and higher inside of me. I need a release so badly.

"Please," I whisper.

His thumb moves harder and faster while his fingers pump inside of me. I'm breathless and gasping. My legs shake. I feel weak all over, but Leo holds me up. And just when I think I can't hold back anymore, Leo murmurs his permission.

"Come for me, princess," he commands.

"Ohhh, Leo!" I squeal.

The most powerful climax of my life rips through my body. My pussy gushes slick honey all over Leo's hand as my knees buckle beneath me. I shudder violently as my juices run down my sticky thighs. Leo massages my cunny through the waves of orgasm, and just when I think it's over, another climax comes stumbling after. I all but collapse in his embrace as I whimper and twitch in pleasure.

"That's my girl," he grunts. "Feels good, hmm?"

"Nnnngh, so good," I moan.

"Want to feel even better?" he purrs. "Look out on the water."

He turns me to face the sea, the wind whirling my hair around my face. I smile with exhilaration as I squint over the glittering waves. With his arms wrapped around me from behind, Leo points to a white yacht. It's beelining for the shore, crossing from dark blue into paler turquoise shallows. A trail of churned white water follows in its wake.

With his lips at my ear, he whispers, "That's our ride."

I light up. "What? Are you serious?"

He chuckles and nods. "Yep. But first, let's snap a couple photos here for your feed."

Leo helps me set up the right lighting, angle, and poses for at least several days' worth of content. We capture tons of lovely photos of the scenic views and, of course, me. Then we pack up and head back downhill to the beach for our boat ride.

To my surprise, Leo hops aboard and helps me up with the ease of a seasoned sailor. The current captain hands off the keys to Leo with a respectful nod. The captain departs, leaving Leo behind the wheel of the boat and me, standing on the deck in awe. I whip around with a big smile and my arms up.

"Is this for real?" I shout over the rush of wind and water.

"Get comfortable," Leo replies coolly. "We're going to take a little ride."

I sit down on the cushy seat and gaze out over the scene. The sunbather-dotted shore shrinks away as we ride out onto the choppy blue waves. I sprawl out on the seat and, once we're far enough from the beach, I whip off my dress. Lying in just my bra and panties, I warm myself in the California sun. I roll over onto my stomach and look back at Leo coquettishly. To tease him, I give my ass a little smack and it jiggles deliciously. While he's stuck behind the wheel, I take out my phone and camera to start snapping photos. I capture the aquamarine water, the crystal-blue sky, the flare of sun glinting off the side of the boat. I take selfies with loose strands of my wavy blonde hair fluttering romantically in the wind, or facing into the sun with my sleek shades on. I pose and blow kisses for the camera, getting content to post later.

Once we're far enough out, we drop anchor and Leo can relax his duties as captain. To my delight, he takes over as photographer. He picks up the camera and starts directing me.

"Stand there at the end of the deck. Lift your arms over your head, but make it delicate. Extend your left leg and pop your hip. Now give me your most genuine smile," he instructs.

Looking right at the man of my dreams, it's easy to give him that. He snaps photos at lightning speed as he moves closer, giving more instructions.

"Beautiful, Vanessa. Bring your arms down again and pose like you're gazing over the water. Perfect. Now, turn just your head and look at me with those pretty green eyes," he says.

As I look at him hard at work behind the camera, bending over backwards to help me secure my career, my heart swells with fondness. Leo is not only the hottest guy I've ever met, but he's got a beautiful soul, as well. I feel safe with him. He's old enough to know what he wants and strong enough to demand it. But he's soft when I need him to be. Passionate when that's even better. My body tingles as I remember how good he made me feel up on that cliff. As he walks closer with the camera, I adapt my poses to be more sensual. I bite my lip, cock my head to the side. I pose so that my cleavage is pushed together, and I wiggle my ass to taunt him. I watch him lick his lips as he approaches and lowers the camera to look at me straight on.

"Ready for a new pose?" Leo purrs.

I bat my lashes at him and smile. "I'll do whatever you want."

"Kneel down and look up at me," he instructs.

Oh my god. Is this really about to happen? I excitedly drop to my knees. I gaze up at him longingly. Holding the camera in one hand, Leo reaches to cup my chin daintily with the other.

"Now open your mouth. Let me see your tongue," he commands.

I splay out my tongue and say 'ahhh', which makes him smirk.

"Very good girl," he coos as he strokes my hair.

He tilts the camera down and tugs down his joggers and boxers so that his enormous, stiff cock bounces free in the salty air. My mouth salivates as I await my first taste eagerly. He strokes his massive length slowly, moving closer to my tongue. I widen my mouth as much as I can and gently suck the thick head of his member into my mouth. I run my tongue up and down the soft underside, flicking around once I reach the tip.

My pussy tingles when I taste his precome, salty and bitter at the tip of my tongue. I moan around his thickness and he pushes deeper in, bit by bit. He strokes my hair and murmurs soft words of encouragement while I take him down to the root. His cock pokes the tickly back of my throat and I start to cough a little. Leo pets my hair and I regain composure. I love the weight of his cock on my tongue, the way he pushes my cheeks open and fills me up. He slides in and out faster and faster. My saliva bubbles at my lips and dribbles down my chin, making everything more filthy and sloppy. I feel like a dirty girl when he snaps photos of me with his cock down my throat, and I can hardly wait to check out the images later. Granted, they won't be going on my feed, but... they'll occupy a place deep, deep in my heart. Maybe lower.

Leo's hips rock back and forth as he fucks my warm, wet mouth. I moan when he slams into my throat again and again. I can scarcely remember to breathe, but I don't care. I'm swept up in the messy glory of the moment, desperate to make him feel oh so fucking good. I take his cock like a champ and I can feel him tensing up, getting close. I use my hand to swivel up and down his length while I focus my lips on the sensitive head. Over and over I let him slip out with a wet pop and use my palm to slick him up with my spit and his precome all over again for the next pump. Before long, Leo is thrusting hard, his hands stroking my hair and holding me steady while his hips snap back and forth, pummeling his cock down my throat.

"Oh yes, just like that," he grunts. "I'm right there, baby."

"Mmmm," I moan, my mouth stuffed with cock.

The extra little vibrations of my voice sends him over the edge. With a few more short, frantic thrusts, Leo comes down my throat. His cock twitches in my mouth and I choke down every precious drop of his seed. I lick him clean when I'm done, and when he finally puts his cock away, I can't help but pout.

"You like that," Leo points out.

"I *love* it," I gush. "I can't wait to see what else we can do together."

"There'll be time for that later," he says cryptically. "For now, I think we should grab a celebratory drink and watch the sunset. Your fans will love a shot like that."

We get cleaned up and head to the lower deck. Leo pours us each a cocktail from the surprisingly full mini-bar, and we take our drinks back up top. We settle into the seat together and watch the sun slip toward the horizon. Bright peals of pink, orange, and gold streak the sky, casting magical hues across the water. It's quiet and serene. We might well be the only people for miles around. I sip my cocktail and soak in the warmth of the moment with Leo. I can't stop stealing glances at him, and the feeling is mutual. We can't keep our eyes or hands off each other. We sit so close I might as well be on his lap.

"You know," he begins thoughtfully, "there was a time when I thought I loved the anonymity of travel. The temporary nature of everything. Never staying in one place for long, never staying with one person for long. I've been almost in love a hundred times, but the feeling is fleeting. I used to think that was something the matter with me, but I see now I was just waiting for the right person. The right girl to make me stop what I'm doing, forget my itinerary, and throw caution to the wind. I've been all around the world, searching for beautiful places and incredible experiences. I thought I'd had it all. But no place on Earth can compare to you, Vanessa."

"I feel the same," I tell him fervently. "I know we only just met, and we're trying out this business partnership. But I have to be honest, Leo. I don't want you to ever leave. In one day, you've shown me more joy than I've felt in years of solo travel. You make me feel safe and wanted and oh so sexy. I don't want to explore the world without you. The next time I step on a plane, I want you there beside me."

"I'm done with flings. I'm finished with running away before anything sticks. I'm ready to commit. I'm done chasing-- I just want to be with you, everywhere," he says.

"What about here?" I ask.

I set down my drink and look at him intently to show I'm serious. Leo puts down his drink, too, and cups my cheek in his hand. I lean into his warm palm, my lashes fluttering.

"You're a virgin," he assumes correctly.

I nod. Softly, I answer, "Never found the right one, either. Until now."

"I want to take such good care of you," Leo growls.

"You already do. But I know what I want tonight," I assert.

I stand up and let my dress slip off my shoulders and slink to the floor. I reach back to unclasp my bra. My breasts spill out, full and perky. Leo's jaw twinges with self-restraint as I drop my panties and stand fully naked before him. I open my arms and do a little twirl.

"I'm yours, Leo. All of this, all of me belongs to you. So, tell me, what are you going to do with me?" I ask playfully.

Leo stands up and pulls me close, his lips colliding with mine in a passionate kiss. His hands reach up to stroke my hair. His tongue pushes into my mouth and I moan. He drops one hand to cup my mound, then swivels me around and cradles me back onto the squishy boat seating. He moves between my legs and pushes my thighs wider apart before diving in, tongue first, to devour my slick cunny. I arch and moan under his machinations. His lips nibble and kiss my clit while his fingers work inside of me. I prop up on my elbows to watch him eat me out. Leo's perfect tongue circles and massages my clit until I can't hold back any longer. I come all over his tongue and he growls his approval, licking me clean.

"Mmm yes," I whimper.

While my pussy is still twitching with pleasure, Leo positions the thick head of his cock at my drippy hole. I wiggle against him, begging for more. He whips off his shirt, revealing his powerful chest as he bends to kiss me on the lips. I can taste myself, and it only turns me on more. I get so wet watching Leo take off his pants and boxers. I lick my lips at the sight of his cock. He returns to me and grabs my thighs, hooking my legs over his shoulders. He gazes deeply into my eyes as I feel his cock slowly push inside my tight, clenching cunny.

"Ohh. Oh my god," I gasp.

"That's my girl. Hold on," Leo murmurs sweetly.

He holds and comforts me while his enormous shaft spears deeper inside of me. Inch by inch, I feel him splitting me open in the best way. The pain mingles delightfully with pleasure until it's all one big soppy mess. I cling to his shoulders for dear life as he begins to thrust deeper. He rears back, sliding almost completely out of my cunny, only to shove back into me with one swift, forceful motion.

I cry out and Leo bends to swallow my cry in a kiss.

"Oh, it feels so good," I gasp.

"You're mine, Vanessa. This pussy is all mine," he snarls.

"All yours. Nobody else can make me feel like this," I gush.

I bite my lip hard and lift my hips to meet his thrusts. Leo rests his forehead against mine while he pounds my pussy. He's gentle, but in control. He's forceful, but he never forgets about my pleasure. Even when he's fucking me so hard I can feel his cock hit my cervix, I feel so loved and seen. Leo cares about my pleasure. He reaches down between us to rub my clit while he fucks me. I can hardly breathe, I'm so overwhelmed with bliss. There's no one but the stars above to watch us make love. There's only the sound of water lapping against the side of the boat and the wet smack of Leo's shaft plunging into my silky wet depths.

"Damn, baby, you feel so good," he growls.

I sense him stiffening up around me. His grip on my soft thighs tightens up. His thrusts become more purposeful, more forceful. He pounds my pussy with short, violent strokes. His dark eyes lock with mine and I get lost in them while earth-shattering pleasure soaks around me. I come again and again, my pussy clenching around his fat cock. I lose track of how many times as one orgasm piggybacks into the next one. I gush and groan and writhe under his touch. I'm so overcome with bright feelings. My body is a-glow with endorphins. My heart is galloping along at breakneck speed. Leo holds on tight as he loses control bit by bit. I squeeze tightly around him, keeping him close so he can never let go. His cock slides in and out of my tight, virginal cunny with wet slaps, his balls swinging against my ass.

I never knew how badly I needed to be fucked like this, to be used and rocked and filled up. I'm desperate to feel him come inside me. I'm salivating, and my pussy drips with desire. My come runs down my legs and puddles on the boat seating. Leo kisses me deeply just as I feel him lock up. His hips thrust a few more violent times and then his cock spurts his precious seed deep, deep within my fertile womb. I cross my legs around him, holding him there while his come fills me up. Only once I start to feel his juices and mine slowly leak out of my cunny do I finally relinquish my grip.

Leo kisses me on the lips while we come down together. Slowly, Leo withdraws from me and sits up. He strokes my face and hair, then pulls me into his arms, holding me close under the stars. The waves rock us gently side to side as we gaze at each other in pure adoration.

"Safe to say I'm no virgin now," I giggle.

I nuzzle closer to his chest, listening to the steady thump of his heart.

He pets my hair and kisses my head. "You're my girl now."

"I love the sound of that," I sigh happily.

"Me too," he agrees. "I think I'll call you that forever. How's that sound?"

"Perfect!" I chirp. "Now, what's next?"

"Well, for tonight I'm going to steer this baby back to shore. Then you are going to come up to the penthouse suite and spend the night with me," Leo explains.

"And what about tomorrow?" I prompt him eagerly.

He grins. "We can do whatever you want. Go wherever you want to go. Hell, if you want to hop on a plane and get the hell out of Malibu, we'll do that. Spain, Japan, Australia, Thailand-- wherever you want to go, Vanessa."

"My followers would *love* to see the architecture in Barcelona," I muse aloud.

"Spain it is!" he replies with a hearty laugh.

"But honestly, I don't care where we go. As long as we're together, it'll be the trip of a lifetime," I declare.

"I thought I knew everything there was to know about traveling the world. Turns out, I missed the number one lesson: that every experience is better when shared with the one you love," Leo says. "One day with you is enough to prove that right. You've changed everything, Vanessa. For the better."

We spend the next few days exploring Malibu-- well, more like exploring each other.

After that, we hop on a plane to Spain. Turns out, traveling with Leo is a blast. We get each other. We're always laughing, always kissing, always plotting out our next big adventure. We make one hell of a team.

He writes, I write.

He snaps photos, so do I.

His readership grows and grows, and my influencer persona takes off into the stratosphere. People love the newfound spark in my work, and that's all because of Leo.

We traipse around the world together, falling deeper in love with every stamp of our passports. We make love in luxury hotels and on deserted beaches. Every day is a brand new dream, and I have never been so happy.

I can hardly wait to embark on the next great journey of our lives: becoming parents together! As we hold hands in first class and wait for the plane to ascend, my free hand rests on my growing belly. I look out the window at the fluffy white clouds and blue skies as far as the eye can see.

It looks like heaven.

With my true love at my side and a whole lifetime of joy and adventure before me... maybe this is heaven, after all.

Off Limits: Teacher

Book Themes: virgin, teacher/student, age gap,
spanking, BDSM, exhibitionism
Word Count: 7053

I lie flat on my back in bed in my dorm room, staring up at the ceiling while the rain patters against the window outside. It's Friday afternoon.

Most of the dormitory has cleared out already.

Students have gone home or off to visit their boyfriends at other colleges. As for me, I'm currently taking a quick break from packing up my stuff for a trip to my hometown to stay with my parents. It's only a weekend trip, but I have big plans.

Big, secret plans which have led to my low-grade panic over what to wear. Judging by the number of half-assembled outfits draped throughout the room, it looks like I'm packing for a week rather than a weekend.

My suitcase sits open on the floor by my bed, and so far there's only a few pairs of stockings and panties inside it. I have a ways to go yet. But right now, it's kind of impossible to focus.

My mind is miles away. And more than a year ago, drenched in vivid memories that I revisit often. The details are preserved forever in my brain, like scenes from a favorite film.

I can see it so clearly: my senior year of high school.

Sitting in the very back row of a classroom, pink bubble gum between my teeth. I blow a bubble slowly, I pop it. I start over again. All my friends are nearby, clustered close like a pack of wolves and I'm the leader.

They all hang on my every word, but I'm no tyrant. I rule my clique with sweetness, not an iron fist. That doesn't mean I won't break the rules, though.

I'm no goody two-shoes. I have my cell phone out in my hands, right in the open in the middle of math class. Every now and then I send a text message or snap a cute selfie to post. Even under the horrible fluorescent lights of a high school classroom, I look cute from any angle.

I toss my long, honey-colored hair over my shoulder and undo a couple buttons on my school uniform blouse to reveal my cleavage. I lick my lips and take a photo. The tiny lens-clicking sound draws the attention of my teacher, Mr. Galloway.

His sharp green eyes focus on me from behind his black-rimmed glasses. My heart stops when he looks my way.

I don't even try to hide what I'm doing, even though I know full well that students aren't allowed to have our phones out in class. It's, like, the number one rule.

On top of that, my friends and I like to pass notes and whisper during lectures.

We can't help it-- there's just so much material to gossip about!

Who's dating who, who's cheating on whom, who's moving to another school, it goes on and on. We could chatter about anything, always cracking jokes and giggling among ourselves in the back of class. Some people might call us bad students, but we all make pretty good grades. It's just that, well, there are more exciting things going on in our lives than the quadratic formula.

Plus, I love it when Mr. Galloway turns his attention to me.

Even for a moment. His eyes on my face, my body... it makes me tingle all over.

Most students, even my friends, actually pay attention in his class because he's a good, well-liked teacher. He's younger than the rest of the teaching staff, he's clever, he's passionate, but most of all: he's gorgeous.

Tall and broad-shouldered, he's always wearing button-down shirts with the sleeves rolled up to show off his sexy, muscular arms. That tweed vest can't hide his powerful upper body, and his fitted trousers barely conceal the outline of his enormous cock.

And I swear I can see his cock twinge when I show off my cleavage.

My brown eyes lock with Mr. Galloway's green, and I can feel the tension crackling between us from across the classroom. I lift my finger to my lips and slide it into my open mouth. I suck on it hard and simulate moving my head up and down while I stare right at him. It's a bold move, but what can I say? I've always been pretty fearless.

I see his jaw tense up as he grits his teeth. He's trying so hard not to look at my chest. He knows I'm not old enough. I'm off-limits. Mr. Galloway manages to tear his gaze away and turn back to the chalkboard to write out another long, boring formula.

I sigh and lean back in my chair. Even just that split second connection is enough to get me hot under the collar. And between my legs. I wonder if he Mr. Galloway ever knew that I'm actually quite good at math. I was just way more interested in him.

A rumble of thunder rattles the window slightly in my dorm room, bringing me back to the present moment. I turn my head to look at my open suitcase and the absolute tornado of clothes scattered across the room. I hoped my trip down memory lane would be restful enough to get me motivated into packing again, but now I'm *so* turned on thinking about Mr. Galloway.

For a virgin, I sure have a lot of dirty thoughts.

Especially about him.

I've had a massive crush on him since I took his math class in high school. I thought going off to college, meeting hot guys my age, and the whole party girl experience would cure me of my obsession with Mr. Galloway.

Wrong. No frat guy can match up to my sexy math teacher, looking like a cross between a dashing hero and a brilliant bookworm. I wish he had responded to my not-so-subtle flirtations the way I longed for.

I imagine him looking straight at me with those soft green eyes, walking toward me slowly. Loosening his tie, running his fingers through his thick dark hair as he approaches. I would put one foot up on the desk, the other on the floor, with my legs wide open to entice him closer. To show him I'm ready.

"Oh, Mr. Galloway," I murmur.

My hand trails down my body, feeling my soft breasts and my tight stomach, and further to slide underneath the waistband of my cotton shorts. I stroke myself through the silk of my panties, feeling myself get wet as I think about my teacher bending down over me. He would put one hand on the desk, the other reaching down to lift up my plaid skirt. I hear him commanding me in that low, imperative voice to touch myself while he unzips his trousers.

In my dorm bed, my fingers massage my clit through my soaked panties. My other hand caresses and gropes my breasts. I gently tease my sensitive nipples under my tank top until they're perky pink points. My pleasure is getting more intense by the second, and any second, my roommate Dakota could come walking into our shared bedroom and catch me in the act. But then, I've always loved a little risk, a little exhibitionism. I imagine flashing Mr. Galloway my panties, showing him what he could have if he reached out and took it.

"Ohhhh," I whine.

My body shivers and I get goosebumps all over as my pussy gushes honey all over my panties and fingers. I shudder through the first heavenly waves of orgasm before I hear the telltale jingling of the room keys-- my roommate is back! I hurriedly clean myself up with a nearby towel, slide off the bed onto the floor, and resume packing just as she's stepping into the room with a bag of what smells like freshly-baked cookies. She's a sweet girl, and she tends to stress-bake when she has a big test or something. This morning, she had her first exam.

"Hey, you're still here!" Dakota greets me cheerfully. She tosses the paper bag onto the floor next to my suitcase. "Chocolate chip and oatmeal raisin."

"Both?" I giggle.

She smiles sheepishly. "I was, like, *really* stressed out. I made both batches in a total daze while I was studying for the exam. I haven't even tasted them. For all I know, they could be totally inedible."

I bravely take a bite of what looks to be chocolate chip.

"Mmm. No, they're perfect. Just like your grades. I'm sure you aced that exam, Dakota," I assure her. I start folding up more outfits to stuff into my suitcase.

She heaves a sigh. "God, I hope so. I have to see my stepmom this weekend and she'll be pissed if I don't get an A," Dakota laments as she flops back onto her bed.

"You skipped that frat rager last weekend just to put in extra study time," I reply.

"I know."

"And you've literally been reciting bits of essay in your sleep," I remind her.

"I *know*."

"So don't worry, girl. You've got this," I conclude. "Now, eat one of these delicious cookies and help me figure out what to pack."

She slides onto the floor, too, and grabs a cookie. "I guess it depends on what you're packing for, right?" she offers helpfully.

"Just the weekend, believe it or not," I laugh.

"Yeah, but what are you gonna do over the weekend? Just vibe out and watch game show reruns with your mom at your parents' house or are you, like, going on a date or something?" Dakota probes, looking for a fix of gossip.

"I'm going to visit my old high school," I admit.

Dakota's eyebrows shoot up and then she wrinkles her nose.

"Oh no. High school was terrible for me. I definitely

wouldn't want to go back and visit," she replies, shaking her head. "But I bet you loved high school, right?"

I smile and shrug. "Well, it was a pretty good time, I guess, but it's not so much the high school experience I miss. I can leave it in the past, where it belongs. But there is a certain teacher in particular I want to go see," I tell her.

"Aww. That's so sweet," Dakota beams.

"Mhm. Totally sweet," I agree, only half-lying.

My intentions are definitely more spicy than sweet, but that's not a story I want to explain to Dakota right now. For the time being, the details of my plan are still secret. I have a bit of a reputation for recklessness, for being too brave, for bending the rules too much. I don't want anyone to know what I have planned just in case they might try to stop me. In fact, I know they would try to stop me. But that only makes me want it more.

"So what's the deal with this teacher? Did she inspire you in some way?" Dakota asks.

I think about my orgasm five minutes ago. He definitely inspired that.

"I guess you could say he's inspired a lot of my dreams," I answer.

My sex dreams, I don't add.

"Wow. That's awesome. I hope you get to have a good long chat with him," she remarks.

"Thanks, I hope so, too," I reply sweetly.

I'm actually hoping for a lot more than a chat, but we'll see what happens. Dakota and I gossip and talk about upcoming parties and events while we finish up packing our respective suitcases for the weekend. When we're all done, we lock up the dorm room and head down to the parking lot.

"Have a good time with your teacher!" Dakota says as she hugs me goodbye.

"Oh, I will! See you Monday!" I chirp back.

She gets in her SUV and I slide into my slick little car for the long drive back to my hometown. It's about a couple hours, just long enough for me to get lost in thought as I roll down the highway. I think about what kind of a girl I was back in high school. Only a year ago, and yet it feels like another world.

I've never been the quintessential "good girl" but I've never been naughty enough to land me a reputation as a "bad girl" either. My parents did a good job raising me. They are both kind, hard-working people who did everything to make sure I was taken care of. Maybe we didn't have every little thing we wanted, but we definitely had what we needed plus a little more. I'm an only child, and the apple of my parents' eyes. I keep a good grade point average but I'm never top of the class. I wasn't the prom queen, but I had lots of friends.

I remember the bell ringing at the end of math class. My gaggle of friends and I making our way down the row of desks to the doorway, giggling as we go. And then, clear through the din, we all hear Mr. Galloway's strong but soft voice.

"Melody White, can I speak to you, please?"

My heart stops.

"Ooooh," is the collective response from my nosy classmates.

"What did you do, Mel?" whispers my friend.

I shrug. "I guess I'll find out. Don't wait up for me."

My heart is pounding and my hands are clammy as I slowly walk up to Mr. Galloway's desk. He's standing with his arms crossed over his chest, looming tall and powerful over me. I never noticed until now just how much bigger he is. I feel positively dainty in front of him. He stares me down, not saying a word until the last student has filed out and the door closes. He puts both hands on the desk in between us and leans in closer. I can hardly breathe, I'm so nervous.

Then, he sighs, "I think you know why I've called you up here."

I go rigid. Is he going to bring up my cell phone usage? Or my flirtatious behavior?

"I-I don't know," I mumble.

"Your grades are slipping, Melody, and that's a real shame," he says. There's genuine compassion in his tone. "Because you are so much smarter than this. Trust me, I can tell."

I blush deeply. "I think you've got me wrong, Mr. Galloway. I'm just not good at math."

"I think you're afraid to grab onto your own potential. You're so busy with boys and gossip, you forget that you're a smart girl underneath it all," he says sagely.

Damn. Is he onto me? For real?

"Look, I love teaching, I love seeing my students learn new things and gain confidence in themselves as a result. I want that for you, too. I believe in you, Melody," Mr. Galloway affirms.

My heart swells just thinking about it. It's one of the most memorable times someone went out of their way to make me feel supported, to make me feel smart and worthy. I guess I'm not so different now, just older and more mature. The tenderness in his words coupled with the passion of his tone, his body language...I didn't understand it fully then. I was more naive than I am now. But he was so invested in me. It's a sweet memory because he was sweet to me, and it's a sexy memory because he was so close and I could feel his body heat from across the desk. But it's also bittersweet because I let him down. I made mediocre grades in his class because I was so engrossed in trying to steal his attention or pretending I didn't need it.

Plus, it is infuriating that at the end of the day I *am* good at math, but I squandered that grade because of a soul-deep crush on the teacher. I've grown up a little since then. One year at college has taught me the importance of making good grades-- and good impressions. High feels so long ago, but Mr. Galloway is still crystal clear in my mind. Probably because I've fantasized about him, like, a bajillion times. He's always number one in my heart.

Not for lack of trying, though. I've dated around a lot in the past year, but none of the guys my age satisfy me. I'm reckless and wild enough on my own, so trying to build a relationship with an equally unhinged college guy just doesn't cut it. I need a more mature partner. Someone who can handle and manhandle me. Someone to rein me in, correct my wrongs, teach me how to be a good girl-- a good grown-up.

Someone to make me a woman.

I know those aren't lessons I'm going to learn from some sloppy frat guy I meet at a party four games of beer pong deep. I need to aim a little older. Who better to slip into that role than the literal man of my dreams (and fantasies)?

Although, I've changed quite a bit since I was his student. What if he's changed, too?

I wonder if our connection will feel the same? I wonder if he'll look at me with the same forbidden lust as before? I have been pining for him all this time. I can barely spare a thought about anything or anyone else. I'm aching to see him, to be near him again.

As my car rolls down the driveway of my parents' house, I'm hit with a rush of warm familiarity. Nothing like coming home. I smile at the simple townhouse with my dad's perfectly manicured lawn and my mom's colorful little garden plot near the porch. I recall many lazy Sunday mornings and hazy summer nights hanging out on the porch swing, listening to the cicadas singing and the wind rustling through the trees. I step out of my car and grab my rolling suitcase, pulling it behind me as I make my way up the path. My eyes flit up to the second story bay window and I remember so vividly clambering out of that window to slide along the edge of the roof and drop down into the bushes below. It was my primary method of sneaking out back then, when my parents said I couldn't go to a party because it was a school night or something. I've always been very determined. Stubborn, some might say. All I know is that I know what I want and I'm not afraid to grab for it.

I hoist my suitcase up the steps and knock at the door. Barely five seconds later, the door pops open to reveal my mom and dad beaming at me joyfully.

"Sweetheart!" Mom coos.

She throws her arms around me while Dad grabs my suitcase. She just about squeezes the life out of me. I squeak, "Hi Mom. Hi Dad."

"Hey there, kiddo. Good to have you home. Come on in, girls. Weather guy says it's supposed to start raining any minute now," Dad explains.

We shuffle into the house and my mom shepherds us to the dine-in kitchen for dinner. As we sit and eat my mom's "famous" lasagna, they ask me about classes. I tell them about my good grades, how I'm keeping up with my homework and maintaining a social life at the same time. They gush about how responsible I've become, how proud they are of me. I'm very lucky. My parents have always been this way: unconditionally supportive. They made sure I felt totally safe and provided for, but they also gave me space and freedom to be myself. To explore and rebel and play the naughty teenager every once in a while.

They are over the moon to see me tonight, and I'm pleased to see them happy. But I can't help but feel a little guilty about the real reason I'm home to visit.

"So, what are your plans for tomorrow?" Mom asks.

"I'm going to visit my old stomping grounds," I reply.

Dad chuckles, "Really? Feeling nostalgic in your old age?"

"Ha-ha," I reply, poking out my tongue. "I know there are a couple of my old teachers who grade papers and do lesson plans in their classrooms on the weekend. I figure I'll just drop by and say hello."

"You can tell them all about your first year at college," Mom suggests.

"We'd love to hear more of your college stories, too!" Dad agrees.

We jump into a long discussion about my friend group, how I met everyone, some of the little adventures we've gone on together. I do have a solid circle of friends at college, just like in high school. Mostly I'm just glad we're on a different topic than what I plan to do on my high school return tour. I feel comfortable talking to my parents about a lot of things, but I bet they'd still prefer I spare them the details on this one.

After dinner, we part ways to go to bed. I mosey on upstairs to my bedroom, which looks just as it did a year ago when I was still living here. I open up my suitcase and set out my prospective outfits for tomorrow. Then I get cleaned up, change into panties and an oversized t-shirt, and crawl into my four-poster bed. I'm exhausted from the long drive, and I feel sleep creeping over me as soon as my cheek hits the downy pillow. I drift off into deep slumber and find myself standing in a dream.

I'm in what looks like a college classroom, but instead of a professor, it's Mr. Galloway at the front of the room. He beckons me up to the chalkboard with a curl of his finger. I walk on air, my bare feet squishing into soft cloud as I approach. My handsome teacher seems to only get taller and more intimidating the closer I get. When I reach the board, I see a column of algebra equations in front of me, waiting to be solved. In my hand is a little white nub of chalk.

"Every right answer is an extra ten points to your test grade," he instructs. "Every wrong answer is my ruler on your ass."

He flips up my skirt to reveal my bouncy, bare ass cheeks. I let out a surprised squeal and look back at him. I decide I don't give a damn about my test grade. I write out the wrong answer for every formula, and I receive a swat of Mr. Galloway's wooden ruler on my bruising, bright-pink booty. It stings so good, and it makes me so wet between my thighs.

When I wake up the next morning, I'm dismayed to look in the mirror and find that my butt is, in fact, bruise free. Perfectly smooth, milky white skin. Oh well. At least that means I'm a perfect canvas for whatever might happen today.

My heart stops. Today's the day! I'm going to enact my plan.

I take a long, hot shower and take my time getting ready. I put on makeup, I comb out my glossy locks, and I step into a set of lacy black lingerie. I put on a black top and a flirty plaid skirt, along with thigh-highs and some kitten heels. I throw on a breezy black trench coat over that, so I can hide my risque ensemble under the guise of being prepared for rain.

I'm tingling with excitement and nerves as I head downstairs, say a quick good morning to my parents, and go out to my car. I slide behind the wheel and start the engine. My mind is whirling with doubts as I sit in the driveway.

What if my plan doesn't work? What if Mr. Galloway isn't even in his classroom? What if he spends his Saturdays at home now and I wasted a trip? What if I get caught?

Or worst of all-- what if my plan backfires? What if he

doesn't feel the way I feel? I shudder to think that I've been misinterpreting his intentions all this time. It would be so embarrassing to take a giant leap of faith and be *wrong*. But then I remember the way he used to look at me. The twinge in his jaw. The clench of his fist. Even the outline of his cock through his scholarly trousers. He couldn't resist looking at me even in the middle of a lesson. Oh god, that unspoken tension. How will I ever get closure if I don't try?

I summon up the courage needed to pull out of the driveway and roll on down the road toward my old high school. It's a short drive, since this is a small town and everything is pretty close together. I smile at the familiar sights and sounds as I make my way to the school. Memories rush back to me when I pull up to the old parking lot. In a town like this, there's little security. We trust each other. We know each other. And since it's a Saturday, I find a parking space without any trouble.

I get out of my car and look around, marveling at how small everything seems now, with the new lens of a years' time. I feel like I've outgrown this place. Like a pair of too-tight shoes you used to wear every day. The buildings that felt intimidating back then look small and modest to me now, as a college girl. Living on a university campus has expanded my world. And yet, it's easy enough to still feel like a high schooler as I walk the halls. I can slip back into who I was. I feel the familiar rebellious spirit inside me, wanting to break free. Wanting to break a rule.

Luckily, I'm already en route to do that.

I come across a couple other former teachers of mine as I trek to Mr. Galloway's building, and the interactions are pleasant. But I'm on a mission. I quickly volley their polite small talk with smiles and easy answers to keep moving on. My heart is pounding like crazy when I reach the classroom door I've been searching for.

With my cheeks already flushing pink and my body positively zinging with anticipation, I lift my hand to give a soft knock. Chills run up and down my spine as I wait for an answer. I hear footsteps approaching and I tense up as the door handle turns. The door creaks open.

My heart leaps into my throat as soon as I see him.

Mr. Galloway, somehow even more handsome than I remember him, standing tall and broad-shouldered in the doorway in front of me. There is a new tiny, silvery streak through his dark hair near his right temple, but those bright green eyes are exactly the same. He peers right into my soul when we lock eyes. He looks stunned to see me. Like he can't believe I'm real.

In the moments before we utter a word, those eyes sweep down my body. The trenchcoat disguises most of my shape, but I may as well be naked judging by the intensity of his stare. I can feel that same forbidden lust emanating from him I felt a year ago, when it was truly forbidden. He likes what he sees, and so do I.

Mr. Galloway is a real man. I can almost feel his wisdom, his quiet strength, his easy confidence. All gifts he's accrued over the years. I think he must be around thirty, maybe a little older. Still young by most people's measure, but more than a decade older than me. The thought makes me tingly wet. I'm tired of dealing with boys. I need a man. I need *him*.

"Melody White," he says. "Come in."

"Are you surprised to see me?" I ask as I step into the room.

I get goosebumps when he closes the door behind us. We're alone, although someone could just open the door at any moment.

"Yes, I am. I assume you must be visiting from college," he says.

He leans against his desk. I walk over to him and lean against the student desk in the front row, letting my trenchcoat start to slip down my shoulders, revealing more and more as Mr. Galloway fights to maintain his composure.

"Mhm. I came home just to see you, actually," I assert. My heart is thumping so hard I'm afraid he might be able to hear it.

"Me?" he murmurs.

I tilt my head to one side and let my coat drop down. It drapes over the desk behind me and I stand up straight. Mr. Galloway's eyes can't help but rake in my delicious cleavage and my killer curves. I twirl a lock of my hair around my finger.

"Yes, you. It's always been you," I tell him. "No one else can teach me what I need to know. It has to be my favorite teacher."

The straps of my black tank top slip down my arms as I step closer to him. There's barely a foot between us now. His jaw is tensing, just like it used to.

"What are you doing, Melody?" he growls roughly.

I lean in close enough to feel his heat, to smell his familiar manly scent. My mouth waters. My pussy is soaking wet just being near him. I bat my lashes up at him innocently.

"I'm here to learn," I murmur.

I reach down to cup his cock. I'm pleased to find it rock hard and monstrously huge. Just like I dreamed. He sucks in a tight breath and glares down at me. I stand on tiptoe.

I whisper, "So teach me."

Something in Mr. Galloway cracks. He steps away and crosses to the door in a few long strides. He locks the door and turns back to me, a fire lit in those green eyes.

"If it's a lecture you want, you'll get one," he grunts.

He grabs me and kisses me on the lips. I feel fireworks bursting in my soul. I melt into his touch. His hands rove around my body, exploring every swell and curve. He squeezes my narrow waist, my rounded hips, my juicy ass. He caresses my breasts and slips my tank top up over my arms, tossing it aside. He lets out a low growl of approval at my sexy, lacy lingerie underneath. He leans back on his desk and pulls me flush against him so that I can feel his hard cock spearing into my pelvis. I rock into him, moaning and whimpering with need.

"I never properly punished you for being disruptive and inattentive in class," Mr. Galloway growls.

He spins me around and bends me over his knee. He flips up my skirt, just like I fantasized about, and gives my bum a loud, echoing smack. I cry out with pain and delight. I jiggle my ass to beg for more. Mr. Galloway responds with several more hard slaps that I'm sure will leave a heavenly handprint on my butt. I'm already excited to look at it in the mirror later, admire how he's marked me up and made me his own. Just like I plan to be... forever.

"Please, I need to be corrected," I play along flirtatiously.

"Texting during lectures," he hisses.

I yelp with pleasure as his hand cups my drenched mound underneath my skirt, through my lacy panties. He rubs in a wide circle, applying the magical amount of pressure to make me arch my back and push back against his hand.

"I never punished you for seducing me during class, either," he snarls in my ear. "But I think that infraction requires a harsher sentence, don't you agree?"

"Mmm, yes. Make the punishment match the crime," I egg him on.

He gently pushes me back and I watch his fingers deftly unzip his trousers. He pulls out his massive shaft. It's every bit as beautiful as I hoped. I ache to feel him inside me, to smell him, to taste him, to be so full of him that I might split open.

He snaps his fingers and points to the carpet. "Get on your knees, Miss White."

"Yes, sir!" I obey happily.

I kneel down, mouth open and tongue splayed out. I want to be the perfect student now. I have to make up for how bad I was before. Mr. Galloway stands up. His hand strokes his long, glorious rod in front of me. I'm dying to taste the glittering bead of precome at his tip. I reach out a tentative tongue to lick it off.

From there, I'm hooked. I lean in and tug the full thickness of his cock between my lips, groaning at the aching stretch in my cheeks. His cock slides back and forth, in and out, and I bob on his shaft like my life depends on it. I hollow out my cheeks and force my throat to relax so that when his engorged head rams into my throat, I don't even gag. I just moan and slurp him up eagerly while my pussy drips honey all over the classroom carpet.

"Mhm. Just like that, Melody. Suck that cock for me," he groans.

His hand sweeps my long hair up into a messy twist so he has better control.

"Follow my instructions," he commands. "Take a deep breath and stay right there."

He tugs my hair to move me back and forth, then to hold me in place while he pounds my throat hard. I moan around his thickness as saliva slips down my chin and breasts. My throat makes a wet squelching sound every time he fucks my mouth. I can't help but play with myself while he fills one of my needy holes. My hands massage my breasts, tweak my perky nipples, and rub my soaked panties. Mr. Galloway notices.

"Poor little Miss Bad Girl needs her pussy eaten," he coos.

He pulls back and his cock pops from my lips. I'm disappointed to not have his load down my throat, but that's not the ultimate mission here. So I wipe my face and look up at him eagerly to await my next command.

He tugs me to my feet, sweeps a stack of papers off the top of his desk, and bends me over it with my legs up in the air. I prop up on my elbow to watch in amazement as he dips down between my legs. He hikes up my flouncy plaid skirt and slips my barely-there panties aside. I hold my breath while he bends down to breathe in my feminine scent. Then he dives right in-- devouring my pussy with his lips and tongue and that warm, wet mouth that makes me see stars. He suckles my clit while his fingers work their way inside me. I clench and convulse around his digits when a powerful orgasm shivers through my body. Goosebumps show up on my skin. My heart races so fast, and I feel lightheaded with pleasure.

"Nothing has ever--touched me-- in there-- before!" I squeak out between twinges of climax. Mr. Galloway stands up to loom over me while his fingers still circle and tease my clit.

"A virgin? A beautiful, sexy, ravishing little minx like you is still untouched?" Mr. Galloway growls in my ear. I get chills just from his closeness.

"Mhm! But I want you-- I want you to touch me there!" I plead. "Not just with your fingers. I want everything. All of you."

"Are you sure what you're asking for, Melody?" he rumbles.

I bite my lip and flutter my lashes as my hands slide down my body seductively.

"All of this... every curve, every hole... it belongs to you, Mr. Galloway. It's been yours all along, but now nobody can tell you not to take it," I purr.

I spread my legs out wide just to show off my glistening, virginal pussy. He licks his lips while his hand idly strokes the enormous length of his thick cock.

"Come on, Mr. Galloway. I know you want to. Just take me," I prompt him softly.

He glances at the door with the small rectangular window in the center of it, then at the window on the far wall. If someone wants to catch us in the act, they could easily do so. But that little lick of risk only makes us hotter.

Mr. Galloway grabs both my legs and holds them out as he lines up his twitching, juicy cock at my slick hole. I rut against him, pleading for it. He pushes inside with a groan of pleasure and relief, like he's been dreaming of this exact moment for so long. I have to play with him.

"How does it feel, Mr. Galloway? How do you like that pretty little virgin pussy?" I tease him playfully.

"Feels even better than I imagined," he grunts.

"Oh, you imagined me?" I gasp. "Ohhh, fuck, that feels so good."

He begins to rock back and forth, his hips slowly pistoning his cock in and out of my aching cunny. I stretch and clench around his thick shaft to try and accommodate such size in such a tight, inexperienced space. He rears back, pausing a moment before he slides effortlessly back into me-- hard. He strikes against some place inside of me so deep and secret and magical, I almost can't believe what's happening to me. Surely I'm not allowed to feel this good. I'm a bad girl, after all! I'm getting my punishment, but it feels like a reward.

"You're all mine now, Melody," he snarls.

"I don't want anyone else," I pant. "I'm done with boys. I want a man."

"I'll show you a man," Mr. Galloway hisses.

He rubs my clit with two fingers while he pounds into me hard and fast. I cry out and he claps a hand over my mouth to muffle my whimpers of pain and ecstasy. His cock pummels deeper inside of me, tearing apart that tiny barrier that marked me innocent. He fucks me like I'm a real woman, like this pussy can handle the pounding he gives it. I'm overwhelmed with the intensity of my pleasure. Wave after wave of blinding-white bliss seizes through me, one orgasm stumbling into the next until I lose count. Hell, I may lose my mind, too.

"I'm going to come inside your little pussy," he grunts at my ear.

"Yes. Oh yes, please," I whimper eagerly.

"You want my seed to fill you up? You want me to knock you up and show the whole world exactly who you belong to?" Mr. Galloway growls.

"Yes! Yes!" I choke out between clenches of pleasure.

"I'm so close now, Melody," he murmurs.

His cock spears me so hard and fast I can feel his balls slapping against my ass. His hands grip my thighs so deep they're going to leave marks. My cunny is dripping, soaking, slippery wet with desire. Every plunge of his cock into my achy virgin cunt makes me dizzy. The pleasure is more than I can bear. He reaches up with one hand and gently presses against my throat while he pumps me full of his come. His hips snap back and forth, striking my g-spot again and again as he deposits his precious seed deep within my womb. I can feel it in my soul-- he's going to do what he says. He's going to make me pregnant. I wrap my legs around his waist to hold him there. To hold every drop of him inside of me.

"I don't want to waste a single drop," I whisper.

He kisses me on the lips and murmurs back, "We'll have every chance to do it again."

My heart flutters with joy. "You want me, too?"

Mr. Galloway laughs softly and strokes my face. "I think that should be pretty evident at this point, Melody," he assures me. "I can't deny that I've wanted this for a long time."

"Me too. I've dreamed of nothing else," I confess. "You believed in me even when I didn't. You have been in my every fantasy since the day we met. I don't care if that's wrong to say. It's the truth, and we both know it."

Slowly, he pulls out and steps back. As he brings me my clothes and my coat, he kisses me on top of my head and gives me a hug. "I'm not going anywhere, Melody. You and I-- this is an equation that just makes sense," he promises me.

"I'll visit every weekend," I say. "And whenever else I can."

"I'll come to you, too," he says, pulling on his own coat. "Now, come on. Let's get out of here. You and I have a lot to discuss."

"Another lecture, Mr. Galloway?" I pipe up.

He chuckles and pulls me in close for a passionate kiss. Then he cups my face and gazes right into my eyes, just like he used to when we were still just teacher and student.

"I was thinking more like dinner at a restaurant. A real date," he suggests. "And you can call me Stephen. I think we're on a first-name basis now, don't you?"

I giggle, "Yeah, I guess so! But Stephen..."

"Yeah, Melody?" he asks as he opens the classroom door to lead us out into the afternoon, into freedom, into our first outing as a couple.

"Can I call you Mr. Galloway sometimes? You know, in special occasions?" I ask, batting my eyes again. He gives me a wink and a warm smile.

"Yes, Miss White. I think we can maintain our scholarly formalities in the classroom, hmm?" he says suggestively.

I grab his hand and give it a tight squeeze. I'm grinning from ear to ear.

"Yes, sir!" I reply.

The two of us walk out together, finally hand in hand, and free to love each other the way we want to. Hard, dirty, and passionate. I can tell I'm going to learn a lot.

Being His Model

Book Themes: age gap romance, virgin, stripping, breeding
Word Count: 7848

I am a beautiful, aloof angel floating in a bright white cloud. The angled shafts of light that beam down from the high ceiling cast me in a heavenly glow. My long blonde hair is arranged in a half updo. The bulk of it is elegantly piled on top of my head in artistic twists like tiny golden rosettes, and strewn with tiny interlocking braids.

Flowers of varying species and color adorn my wispy, wavy romantic locks as they cascade over my shoulders and down my back. With every softest swish of my body from side to side, my hair bounces and swings like a stack of flaxen thread.

The wind machine at the far end of the set tilts a perfectly-aimed vent of cool air toward me. The manufactured breeze gambols those delicate wisps that hang at my temples and frame my symmetrical, rounded face like a gilded picture frame.

One naughty tendril floats down the center of my face and

lands on my lip, where it becomes affixed to the three layers of lip product tacky on my pout.

I wrinkle my nose and give it a soft puff of breath to dislodge the hair and it drifts obediently back into place at my hairline.

Knowing I need to keep my look fresh and gorgeous from every angle at every second, I transition my puffer lips into a soft pucker for the camera.

I purse my full, plush lips all glimmering with silky gloss. I raise one dainty white-gloved hand to rest against my smooth, rosy cheek while I blow a slow-motion kiss for the multiple camera lenses pointed at me like the barrel of a gun.

The cameras flash, crackle, and pop all around me. It's almost enough to make you dizzy, to knock you flat. Sometimes that's how it feels to be a model, to be an attractive young woman in Hollywood: blowing kisses into the face of something with the power to make or destroy you.

Like cuddling up to a monstrous beast that could either devour you or keep you warm.

You want to love this city.

You *do* love it, accepting its flaws and faults along with the glitz and glamour.

You have to take the grimy backstreets and the sleazy producers along with the scenic views of the Hollywood sign.

The shady handshake that lands you a glittering smile on the silver screen. It's all smoke and mirrors here, and it can quickly morph into an intimidating funhouse if you're not prepared.

But LA is my turf. I grew up here, and I grew up in the industry. I know how to face the mirrors that stretch and distort my image and still see my true self in the reflection.

It's taken a lot of self-criticism, a lot of skin-thickening, and a whole lot of fake-it-'til-you-make-it mentality to get me to this place of soft success. I can wear any garment, no matter how bizarre the couture gets or how incomprehensible the styling looks, and I make it work. More than work-- I make it *sizzle*.

Right now, I'm cultivating a lot of sizzle for someone dressed in what essentially looks and feels like an origami sculpture turned into something vaguely wearable. It's certainly a runway look, not an ensemble you would wear on the streets.

On almost anyone else, it would be a frighteningly unflattering look. But I use my well-honed posing skills and cool confidence to bring heat to this frigid white outfit.

It's flowy and possibly sexy in an avant-garde way, though not at all revealing. It's a two-piece couture ensemble. The top is a paper-white blouse with a fitted, almost corset-like bodice that laces up the front. It has a wide scoop neckline that shows off my elegant shoulders and neck, plus hanging, majestic bell sleeves that I can swipe around me like alabaster bat wings.

The top is paired with a matching white, flowing maxi skirt with a full swing and papery crinkle to it. Standing barefoot, I reach a willowy natural five-foot-nine, but today I tower a little bit in chunky beige designer heels.

Add in a tiny, delicate gold necklace with an itty-bitty heart charm on it, and that's the editorial look for today's fashion spread.

It's certainly no lingerie set, but my sex appeal is still undeniable.

The paper-white fabric is just transparent enough to hint at the delicious swell of my breasts. The opacity only barely conceals the rosebud-pink color of my perky nipples, and the espresso-colored mole on my left hip.

Not even the full, swingy skirt can conceal my rounded, sculpted ass. I work hard in the gym to maintain my natural gifts, and it pays off. I pinch the skirt and lift it slightly to extend one long, toned leg toward the camera while I lean away slightly. It's yet another basic modeling trick to make myself look even more ethereal and elongated.

The camera guys hurry to snap photos of my exposed knee and calf.

Then I raise my arms slowly over my head so that the long bell sleeves slope around me like a fairy stretching up into the air. In the process, my tiny waist and toned midriff are on display, and once again, the cameras go crazy.

Crackles and jolts of light, a rain of soft encouraging

murmurs and approving grunts. The lights burn down on me against my stark white canvas backdrop.

The set is located in a historic old house here in Los Angeles, a popular set for fashion and boudoir shoots because of the maximalist, eccentric vintage interiors.

This room is some sort of small ballroom, with vaulted ceilings and paintings in Rococo pinks and golds. Of course, there's the white canvas behind me, but the rest of the room is a marvel of architecture. Not that anyone's looking at the house's old bones-- they're looking at me.

Every photographer, producer, makeup artist, stylist, assistant, and lighting guy in the room is focused. I can barely make out their faces in the fuzzy halo of camera lighting, but through the haze I hear one new, unfamiliar voice as deep and smooth as the color blue.

"Turn around for me, Chloe," he instructs.

I do a slow rotation to face the white canvas backdrop, with the plunging backline of the dress on full display. The cameras pop off like before, only this time I hear more murmuring from the set.

Between the faint, pumping mood music and the wind machine, I can't discern much of their whispers.

But I know the tone. They're impressed. They're intrigued. They're falling in lust with every bare square inch of my milky white skin they get to see. Even if it's just a flash of my stomach or my spine, they're salivating for it.

They all want a piece of me. That's a good thing. If they want me, I'm desirable, and desire is marketable.

Whoever told me to turn around knows his stuff. Knowledgeable, confident, *and* he has a sexy voice. Now *I'm* intrigued. But I shouldn't be. I know better than to fall into this trap. I am not on the market for a new boyfriend.

I'm at work.

I'm a career-driven young model who cares way more about landing a major runway spot than going out with yet another vapid Hollywood hunk who's all brawn and no brains.

I don't mean to sound jaded, but I've been in the modeling

game since I was a child. Most of my friends are models, too, by circumstance. All of them end up dating guys in the industry. When there's so much overlap in interests and desires, it's hard not to date within that clique.

Besides, it's almost too easy to meet people in LA. I don't even have to try. Wherever I go, men follow. Guys literally corner me, throw themselves in my path, slide into my DMs, haunt my public appearances like horny ghosts.

Anything to get me alone. To get me off. Just like these guys on set. They hide behind their professionalism or behind their cameras to get up close. Part of the dance is that I have to let them think for maybe one iota of a second that they might win me. It's a seduction dance, even fully clothed.

The truth is that I'm still a virgin at nineteen.

I've only even been kissed a few times, and it never went any further. I'm extremely choosy about romantic partners. First of all, I'm a successful model in Los Angeles. Many of the men I meet are, frankly, not in my league.

Not that I'm shallow, but I don't have the time or energy to deal with the kinds of melodramatic, narcissistic, immature guys I meet in my line of work. Male models who think they're heaven's gift to womankind.

Neurotic actors who preen and obsess over the press, the paparazzi, their publicist. And don't even get me started on musicians. Talk about moody and self-obsessed. The last date I went on was with a singer-songwriter who spent the whole time talking about his album... which was a bitter, heartbroken serenade to his ex-girlfriend. Who was also a model. For obvious reasons, it didn't work out.

There's a reason why I've pretty much given up on dating in Los Angeles, why I'm focusing on my career. I'm over all that.

The mystery guy with the deep voice suggests, "Now run your fingers through that beautiful blonde hair for me."

I lift my hands and work my fingers through the unpinned waves of hair splashing around my shoulders. I toss it back with a glance over my shoulder.

Again, a manic flurry of camera activity.

I feel powerful... and a little bit turned on, to my surprise.

It's a new feeling. I'm used to feeling pretty, feeling professional, feeling competent on set. I'm accustomed to the fawning fans and sleazy set guys who think they have a chance just because they got to see me work it. But sexy? Aroused?

I never get that sensation.

Especially since my mom has been my manager for all of my career. In fact, she had it drawn up in my contract that I don't do nudity. That made sense when I was just a little girl, when all of Hollywood was pushing me to grow up too fast, to be sexy too early, to trade my wide-eyed innocence for a smoky come-hither stare. My mom always told clients that I refuse to sell out.

My schtick was to get by on my professionalism, talent, posing, and industry know-how. To lean toward a restrained, modest beauty rather than a teased-out sensual allure. I have tons of friends who model nude, and I respect and envy them for it, but it's never been a real option for me working under my parents' names.

My father, James Elmwood, is a famous American filmmaker, but he's always too busy filming, writing, producing, and jetting all over the globe for film festivals and award ceremonies to spend much time with me.

My mom is a French former supermodel named Claudette Cartier. She's been my momager, best friend, and confidante my whole life. Even before I became a model in my own right, I used to travel on set with her. I grew up behind and in front of the camera, and my mom has been right by my side the whole time. She taught me all I know. I don't just work with her, though.

I've been living under her roof, too. It's hard to envision yourself as a real adult when you still live with your mom, especially when she runs off pretty much any guy who looks at me for too long.

The man with the deep voice speaks up again. "Give us a little pout."

Chills spread across my pale, smooth skin. My heart races a little faster. I push out my bottom lip and bat my big, powder-blue eyes at the cameras as I cup my face in both hands. The camera guys fire off another round of flashing shots.

I hear my mysterious mentor say, "Just like that. Perfection, Chloe."

Ooh, something is changing inside of me. I'm clearly not a little girl anymore. I'm nineteen, and suddenly attention from men-- especially older men-- affects me differently. Lately, like today, I notice my body responding to the crowd's desire. Instead of feeling mildly disgusted, I'm thrilled.

I feed off of their lustful energy.

I draw power from their obsession. Most of them probably looked me up on the internet beforehand. To see what I look like. To start drooling before I even walk in the room.

They know what to expect from my years of solid fashion, editorial, and runway work, but if there's one comment I always get, it's that I am more beautiful in person. I can't lay claim to that myself, but it often comes up. Knowing that all these well-connected, wealthy, jaded guys still see something so irresistible in me makes me feel powerful. Just a glimpse of my bare skin makes them weak. I'm feeding off their vibes, but there's one soul in particular I'm trying to impress.

It's like I'm doing a private performance just for him. I'm feeling myself, striking all kinds of sexy poses. The guys on set are frothing.

"Oh, right there. Perfect."

"That's the look."

"Very alluring! Hold that pose."

"Work it, girl."

"Just a little more, Miss Cartier."

"Show us those big blue eyes."

Then the man with the deep blue voice says, "Beautiful. Embrace your playful side."

I turn and gather the skirts in both hands and lift it slightly, my eyes wide and focused straight ahead like I'm taking a measured step. In the process, I show off more of my legs, and lean forward enough to give a hint of delicious cleavage.

"Excellent, Chloe. That's a money shot," the deep voice purrs.

Despite my professional composure, my body tingles to hear his voice. My nipples are stiff and begging to be played with. My pussy is slick between my thighs.

Adrenaline courses through my veins. I let one cavernous white sleeve slip off my shoulder as I give the camera a coquettish smirk. The set guys yearn.

"Oh, fuck yeah."

"Gorgeous, just gorgeous."

"Keep it coming."

I love getting them all hot and bothered, not even in a sexy outfit. I have these guys wrapped around my finger. But when the man with the deep blue voice steps forward closer to the light, I'm the one fawning. He looms taller and broader than even the equipment wranglers with their bulging biceps. He's dressed in impeccable but casual designer digs.

He's at least ten or so years older than me, with dark hair that's gone delightfully salt and pepper.

"Don't be shy. You're a natural," he tells me coolly. "You know what to do."

This man makes me rethink everything. He makes me question why I'm here. Is it to model or is it for the validation of a good job? Is it to make this mysterious, sexy older man proud of me? He shows me I need more than modest campaigns and tame outfits. It made sense when I was young, but now? It's time for me to sex it up a little bit.

I get off on the idea that all these men are probably on the edge of cumming in their pants every time I make eye contact. I'm performing for that salt-and-pepper prince, but I get a rush of exhibitionism having all the other guys here to watch. I've always thought of myself as a late bloomer and a sex object, but this man makes me feel empowered.

Like I'm a sexual subject, too.

I have the confidence and strength in me to ask for what I want. Maybe I should start owning my power. Maybe I should be brave... and a little bit reckless for once.

Just as I'm about to really ramp up the heat, I hear a familiar loud voice coming from all the way out in the hall.

"What a beautiful set! But did you remember to have that fancy alkaline water on hand for Chloe to drink between shots? I know how hot it gets under those bright lights," chatters the woman in a clipped French accent.

My heart sinks. It's my mom, come to pick me up for lunch at the end of the shoot. Even though she's technically not my manager anymore as of last week, she's still tagging along and micromanaging whenever she can. Old habits die hard. Mom is such a cockblock.

Before she enters the room, the man with the deep blue voice steps closer and I finally get a full look at him. My eyes are wide as I try to drink him in, memorize every detail. He's handsome in that slick, California-suntan kind of way, like an old-timey movie star but with modern sensibilities. I'm entranced by his dimples and his intense, icy-blue eyes.

He hands me a silvery business card with the name VINCENT WEST, AGENT on it.

"We make a good team. I'd like to get you alone. Meet me for dinner tonight," he says suavely. "I'll text you an address and send a car. Wear something that makes you feel... you."

"Okay," I breathe.

He smiles, showing off his dimples and perfect teeth. "See you tonight."

He slips away and disappears through the crowd as my mother flounces onto the set, dressed in designer from head to toe. The vibes on set change instantly. All the guys stand up a little straighter, wipe the horny smirks off their faces. They go from pervy to professional in two seconds flat.

My mom instantly takes charge, like she always does.

"Bonjour. Could you bring me a cappuccino? Thank you. And you, adjust your lighting a little. You're casting a shadow on Chloe's upper lip," she instructs, with the royal air of a queen.

"Yes, ma'am."

"Of course, Ms. Cartier."

Mom continues to give me instructions, too, to strike more modest, traditional fashion poses.

All the while, the whole set essentially grovels at her feet.

Not only do they respect Mom as my mother and manager, but as a talented, beautiful model in her own right. Even now in her fifties, she's still landing enviable campaigns. She has a decades-long international reputation, not to mention a list of powerful contacts a mile long.

I would have been a success just based on my own skill, but my parents' connections definitely clear the path. Still, I'm excited to finally strike out on my own.

The photoshoot comes to a wrap, and my mom swoops in to help me get changed and ready to leave. After a good half hour of Mom and the stylist team picking the braids and flowers out of my long, lustrous blonde hair, we can finally slip out.

As we step out into the lovely Los Angeles sunshine, Mom links her arm through mine.

"*Bonjour, mon chou!* How was the photoshoot without me there to help?" she asks. "Did they give good direction? Were they respectful?"

"*Oui*, Mama. It was good. Everyone was great," I answer.

"So many men on set! It was starting to look like a fraternity house in there," she jokes.

I chuckle. "Yeah, this was a detailed shoot."

"I'm sure you got many wonderful shots. I can't wait to see them! Now, let's grab a bite at the bistro before your fitting at three," she steamrolls onward.

We walk a couple blocks to a trendy, tucked-away cafe. My mom, ever a Parisian, orders a *jambon-beurre* and a mineral water. And ever a momager, she orders me an arugula salad with brie and pecans.

Once the waiter slips off, I raise an eyebrow at Mom. She gives me a sheepish shrug.

"*Pardon, mon ange.* I may not be your manager anymore, but I am still your mother. You need your greens," she insists. "And since you no longer live with me, I can never be too sure that you're getting your nutrients!"

"I promise I still eat my vegetables at the new apartment," I assure her with a laugh.

"Don't let your roommates convince you to eat *bon bons* every night," she warns.

"Mom, I live with two fitness models. I don't think that's going to be an issue," I remind her. "If anything, *I'm* probably the bad influence."

"My Chloe? A bad influence?" Mom snorts. "Impossible."

"See? You have nothing to worry about," I remark.

"I know, I know. You are a beautiful, brilliant baby bird who has left the nest. You don't need your mama bird to boss you around anymore," she admits.

The waiter returns with our food and we dig in.

"How goes the search for a new manager?" she pries.

I bite my lip, remembering the business card in my bag from Vincent.

"Good. Actually, I have a dinner meeting set up for tonight," I spill.

She puts down her sandwich and stares at me expectantly. "*Oui*, go on. With whom?"

"An agent named Vincent West," I tell her.

Mom claps her hands in excitement, her eyes lit up. "Vince? Oh, I thought that was his fancy black Porsche parked outside the set!" she says.

"You know him?" I prompt, leaning in.

"Everybody knows Vince. He has a stellar reputation as a hard worker. Some people in this industry are just lucky, but Vincent West earned his way to the top. He is subtle, but he knows how to turn a nobody into a household name," Mom gushes.

"Wow. Good to know," I respond in awe.

I sensed that Vince was a man of power and connections, but nothing like this. I can see why he gave such clear, good direction on set-- he eats, sleeps, and breathes this stuff.

As Mom and I continue chatting over lunch, my mind is spinning with anticipation for tonight. I can't wait to meet up with Vincent West.

If I can impress him and make him my new manager, my career is set. But it's more than just that; I want to spend time alone with Vince. I'm already addicted to the exhilaration and desire he made me feel on set this morning, and I'm craving more.

We head to a fitting appointment for an upcoming fashion shoot, and then Mom and I part ways.

She goes back to the picturesque villa in the Hollywood hills I used to call home, and I return to my much smaller, much more modest apartment across town.

Luckily, my roommates are both out at auditions, so I have a couple hours to myself to get ready for my meeting. I take a long, hot shower to cleanse the gunk out of my hair and scrub my skin clean of all the makeup caked on for this morning's shoot.

I blowdry my long blonde waves and put on some simple, dewy makeup to bring out my full lips and sea-blue eyes. I squeeze into a form-fitting black dress and nude heels, paired with a classic trench coat. I look sexy but refined. Perfect.

Just as he said, a black car arrives to pick me up. I slide into the cushy back seat and stare out the window at LA traffic as we ride across town.

We end up in an elegant, upscale corner of the city, an area that almost reeks of big money. I come from a family of wealth, but not like this.

The chauffeur lets me out in front of a restaurant with plain black lettering and a modest front door under an awning. I walk in and immediately the maitre'd leads me back to a corner table.

There's already a basket of fresh bread and a bottle of wine on the white tablecloth. Vince stands up to greet me and shake my hand. My heart is pounding like crazy. The simple touch of his hand on mine makes me shiver.

Chills erupt across my skin and I have to remind myself to take slow, deep breaths so I don't look like a total mess. The connection between us is still there, burning hotter than before. Now, there's so little to distract us.

It's just Vince and me, essentially alone. Almost in private. I wonder if he can sense the lust building inside of me, the draw to be close to him, to touch him. I know he's off-limits, but my body doesn't understand.

"So glad you could make it, Chloe," he says as we sit down. "And such an honor to have seen you at work, in your element this morning."

I blush. "Thank you. I truly appreciated your input this morning," I confess.

"You take direction like a pro, but you only need a light touch. You know what you're doing. You're a natural. I was very impressed," Vince says.

He flashes that brilliant smile with the symmetrical dimples again and I nearly swoon.

"So, here's the deal: you and I make a good team. We know that already. Between your raw talent and beauty and my experience as an agent in this crazy town, there's no stopping us. You have the look, you have the skills, you have the drive. Claudette has done a great job of managing your talent, but I think we can both agree it's time for you to level up," he explains.

"What does that entail?" I press him.

He smiles and runs his fingers back through that sexy salt-and-pepper hair.

"We're going to rework your squeaky clean image, give you a little edge. After all, you're no child anymore. I want to see you in lingerie. Maybe even nude," Vince suggests.

"Oh, wow," I answer.

"Don't worry-- I will be present for every shoot, every meeting. I will make sure no one touches a hair on your head or an inch of your body. I will protect your honor, your dignity, your ability to say no. I will find opportunities for you, and I will do everything in my power to catapult you to stardom. But at the end of the day, it all comes down to what you want, Chloe. I can give you anything you desire, you just have to tell me what it is," he concludes.

I wish I could tell him what I *really* want. Him.

"We'll be working closely together, then," I begin.

He nods. "Yes. I'll be there whenever you need me. In fact, I'm more concerned that I might become too involved," he muses thoughtfully. "I'm a consummate professional. I usually have no problem keeping my distance and severing the partnership when the contract has ended. But with you... I'll admit you might be more difficult to relinquish."

"Why is that?" I ask breathlessly. Every thump of my heart aches.

He smiles and cocks his head to one side. His glacier-blue eyes move down my body, drinking in my curves. For once, I don't feel disgusted by the attention-- not with him. I wish he would always look at me like this, with that lick of red-hot desire in his icy gaze. His body is longing for mine the same way I ache for him, and we both know it.

I'm not only flattered, I'm turned on.

This guy is closer to my dad's age than mine, and he makes me feel both sexy and safe at the same time.

Admittedly, my own father is too swept up in making Hollywood magic to even have a full conversation with me, so the attention from Vince feels even more gratifying. At the start of our dinner, he turned off his phone and put it away to focus on me. Ever since, he hasn't so much as glanced at anyone or anything else beyond our table. He makes me feel important and strong, like I can do anything. I can ask for anything.

Vince leans in closer, his lips at my ear. I forget to breathe as he whispers, "Have you seen yourself, Chloe? Do you know what beauty like yours does to a man like me?"

I'm absolutely slick between my thighs. I wonder if he knows.

I finally manage to choke out, "I don't know. I want to move my career forward in a more adult way, but what if I can't be sexy?"

Vince smirks devilishly. "Oh, trust me. You're already there. But I can help you. I can teach your body how to feel sexy. I can teach you all kinds of things."

"Will you show me?" I purr. "Now?"

Never breaking eye contact, Vince rests one large hand on my smooth thigh under the table. I suck in a tight breath as he slowly moves his way up my thigh, under the skirt of my black dress to cup my soaking cunny through my silky panties. He slips his fingers underneath and begins to lightly, slowly stroke up and down my slick slit. I moan softly and rock into his hand, my eyes flitting around to make sure nobody is watching us. My heart is racing a mile a minute. The restaurant is mostly empty, but there are enough people around to make it risky. We could get caught at any moment if someone was to look closely. I spread my legs apart under the table while Vince finds my clit with the flat pad of his thumb. He rubs it in tight, delicious circles while his fingers slowly push inside of me.

My mouth falls open in a gasp, but Vince deftly leans in and captures it in a kiss. His fingers pump in and out, making soft, wet noises with every stroke. He murmurs against my lips, "That's good, Chloe. Embrace it. Let yourself feel so, so good."

"Pressure... building up," I hiss. "I'm almost there."

His thumb presses harder on my clit and his fingers move faster inside of me, sliding in and out with my juices dripping down my thighs.

I tilt my head back as an orgasm crashes over me. I bite my tongue to keep from moaning, and Vince works my pussy through every last shaking wave of pleasure. When he finally withdraws his fingers, he raises them to his lips and licks them clean just before the waiter comes walking up.

"May I interest you in a dessert menu this evening?" he asks politely.

Vince smiles and shakes his head. "No, thank you. My sweet tooth is satiated. Could we get the bill, please? One check."

"Yes, sir," the waiter says, and disappears into the back.

I'm still wide-eyed and giddy with endorphins when Vince turns back to me with a cocky smirk on his handsome face. "Our synergy is unmatched, Chloe," he remarks.

"I agree. You seem to know exactly what I need... out of a business relationship," I add.

I'm half expecting him to take me home tonight, but to my disappointment Vince sends me off in another hired car. At least when I climb into my bed tonight alone, I have a lot to think about. A lot of dirty thoughts, to be precise.

By the next morning, my mind is a cesspool of fantasies and desires. I could hardly sleep from excitement, and even my dreams are filled with Vince. Clearly, this man doesn't sleep either, because he's amped up my career overnight.

It's day one with Vince as my agent, and by noon he already has me all the way across town in a makeup trailer, getting prepped for a major perfume ad.

This is a far cry from my usual modest fashion shoots-- this time, I'm wearing a set of extremely high-priced, high-quality lingerie. We're shooting in a bathtub filled with sparkly fake crystals. Expensive, delicate jewelry adorns my neck and ears. My hair is down and flowy, teased out for maximum volume.

My makeup is fierce, much more seductive and grown-up than my usual look.

There are a ton of men on set, already ogling me in my skimpy lace bra, panties, knee-highs, and choker. But Vince is right there beside me, making calls, directing cameras and lighting, and handling everything like a real pro.

Even when the moment comes, all the prep is ready, and the cameras are bearing in on me in my luxurious crystal bath. For the first time in years, I feel excited but nervous for a job.

Having my beautiful body on display is new for me, but Vince stands right behind the camera guys just like before, giving instruction and encouragement.

He guides me with a simple word or look in his eye. I can see some of his own lust peeking through the professionalism, and that keeps me feeling sultry.

The camera guys and staff are all overjoyed to be the first to shoot the famously modest Chloe Cartier that everyone has been waiting to see naked, waiting for me to be old enough to ogle without guilt. But it goes beyond that; everyone is impressed at how I'm killing the shoot. I hit all the right angles and poses. I play up my own, long-buried sex appeal.

Instead of feeling degraded by the circumstances, I feel empowered, and that's because of Vince. His presence makes me feel organically sexy and turned on, rather than having to fake it for the cameras.

All my little kisses and pouts and seductive stares belong to Vince. I may be looking at the camera, but he may as well be the only guy in the room.

It's not just a shoot, it's a striptease for the man I really want. I'm having so much fun, but I can't wait for the shoot to be over so I can be alone with Vince again.

When the camera guys call it a wrap, Vince and I are both feeling super high and exhilarated as we walk out. He takes my hand and gives it a squeeze.

"Well, safe to say that was a major success. Everyone on set couldn't stop talking about how good you were. I heard the producer say he can't wait to process the photos," Vince reveals. "And they want to hire you on for the rest of the campaign, too."

I stop and gawk at him. "Oh my god. Really? They said that?"

"Are you surprised? You blew their minds, Chloe! Mine, too. You stepped outside your comfort zone and it paid off. I'm so proud of you," Vince says warmly.

"Wow. I can't believe it's all happening so fast," I breathe.

He slides an arm around me as we slip into the back seat of his Porsche. The chauffeur pulls off and Vince leans in to kiss me on the cheek.

"You did a phenomenal job today. I'm already plotting your next move," he says.

"Really? Oh, I'm so excited. Please don't make me go home yet-- I couldn't relax even if I wanted to. Can't I just go to yours? We can... we can strategize," I plead.

"And celebrate," he adds.

"Yes, definitely that!" I chirp.

"We can sleep when we're dead, right?" he agrees with a soft laugh.

The whole ride back to his place, we can barely keep our eyes and hands off of one another. The exhilaration of a wild success right off the bat coupled with our explosive desire is enough to get us hot around the collar.

We all but run into his building, jump into the elevator, and press the button for the penthouse.

On the ride up, the tension breaks.

Vince grabs my face and kisses me hard on the lips.

I moan against his mouth and press into his body, feeling his cock stiffening between us. Just as he's shoving his hand down the front of my designer jeans, the elevator door slides open and we bust into Vince's penthouse.

Still kissing me, he scoops me into his arms and carries me off to the bedroom. He tosses me gently on the bed and starts stripping off his clothes.

I prop up on my elbows to watch as his powerful chest, bulging arms, and washboard abs come into view. I lick my lips when he unzips his trousers and kicks off his shoes.

His cock is straining massive and thick at the front of his boxers when he climbs into bed with me. I can hardly resist.

"I think I need another lesson on how to be sexy," I pout.

He leans back on a pillow and looks at me with his blue eyes shining with lust.

Vince strokes my face and gives me a gentle downward push. I know what he wants, and I want it just as badly. With my mouth salivating, I pull his cock free of his boxers and reach out to taste him with the tip of my tongue. I moan at the heat and softness of his skin, and I can't help but pull a few more inches into my mouth.

His thickness stretches my cheeks and weighs heavy on my tongue, and when his full length pokes at the back of my throat, I go almost dizzy with desire.

I never knew how good it could feel to have this sexy, powerful father figure sliding his thick cock in and out of my pretty little virgin lips.

My spit rolls down his cock and I pump his length with my hand in tandem with my mouth. I can feel every tiny twinge of pleasure he gives me, I hear every soft moan or word of encouragement.

"Just like that, Chloe," he groans.

I splay out my tongue and lath it up and down while I suck him off. I love the way he feels in my mouth, but when I feel his hands grab my hips and reposition me so that my pussy can grind on his face, I almost lose my mind.

His hips flick up to pound my throat while his tongue circles my clit. He devours my dripping cunny, his tongue plunging in and out of my tight little hole.

His lips envelop my tingly clit and suck it hard while I can't help but roll my hips against the sweet friction of his mouth. It feels so good he almost distracts me from my own task-- but not quite. I suck his cock with enthusiasm.

I bob up and down eagerly, and every drop of salty precum is precious on my lips.

"Good girl, that's right," Vince growls. "Come for me, princess."

He increases the intensity of pressure on my overstimulated clit and I feel my cunny burst hot, sweet honey all over his face. He laps up every drop while my thighs tremble and shake over him. I pump his cock faster and harder, eager to give him the same release he gave me.

But before I can get him all the way there, Vince stops me. His cock slips out of my mouth and he flips me over, pinning me down on the bed.

"You're a fast learner," he growls.

"You're a good teacher," I purr back.

Vince cups my breasts in both hands while he kisses me deeply. His tongue dances in and out of my mouth. His lips are soft, even when he kisses me hard.

His fingertips toy with my perky, tingly nipples. He rubs them into tight peaks and twists them gently until my pussy is gushing, aching for more.

I gaze up into his eyes with longing.

"I'm a virgin, Vince," I confess. "But I don't want to be."

"Be careful what you ask for. I can't deny you anything, Chloe," he grunts.

I can tell it's taking all his strength to hold back. He wants to fuck me so badly.

He wants to split me open with that fat cock and fill me up

with his precious seed. I can see the battle in his mind-- he knows he's supposed to take care of me.

Protect me. Defend me like a father protecting his own daughter. Vince is meant to be a father figure to me, and he is, but we can't help it if it's more complicated than that.

"When you know, you just know," I breathe.

"I said you could have anything you want. All you have to do is ask," he reminds me.

"Well, then," I begin, "I want you to fuck me, Vince. I want you to take my virginity and turn me into a woman. Teach me how to be sexy."

"That I can do," he grunts.

"And I want you to come inside me, Vince. Make me your own. I'm all in," I admit.

He leans down to kiss me while he strokes his glorious cock. "Me, too. From the second I saw you on set. Beautiful, ethereal, but lost. You needed me."

"I need you now, too," I assert. "And always."

He rubs the thick head of his cock around my slicked-up opening. I moan and arch my back to meet him. I lick my lips as his cock slowly pushes inside of me.

My eyes grow wide at the dull ache of his thick shaft spearing me open from the inside. My tight, virginal cunny clenches around his fat cock as he sheathes himself inside me entirely.

I cry out and grasp at him.

Vince is there for me, as always. He leans down and cradles me while he fucks me slow and deep.

His cock pushes past that thin barrier inside me. There's a flash of alarm and pain, and then pure bliss. I toss my head from side to side with rapture as his cock pounds my pussy hard.

His balls slap against my ass, and Vince's hands explore my body.

He teases my nipples, caresses my breasts, grips my narrow waist. He smacks my ass with a resounding slap that makes me cry out with stinging pleasure.

"Oh, it feels so good," I whimper. "Don't stop."

"Wouldn't dream of it," he growls back.

Vince grabs my arms and pins them at either side of my head, then slides his hands up my wrists. He interlaces his fingers with mine, sweetly pinning me while I wrap my legs around his waist.

Vince kisses me and whispers sweet words as his cock pounds my fertile womb. I can feel him tensing up, starting to lose control. His strokes are irregular now, even though the intensity of his gaze never breaks.

"Fuck, I'm going to make you all mine, Chloe. All mine," he groans.

"Please, oh yes. Fill me up," I beg.

"I'm going to knock you up so fast," he grunts. "I can't resist you. I can't deny you."

"Never let me go, Vince. I know what I want-- it's you. Always," I plead.

He fucks me harder, his fingers tightening around mine. He dips down to kiss me with surprising softness, even as his shaft spears into that deep, delicious spot within me. My g-spot, pounded again and again by my agent's glorious shaft.

I know I should feel guilty.

He's older than me, meant to be a father figure, a mentor.

And he is, but he's so much more. There's no stopping the tide sweeping over us both.

We can only cling to one another through the tempest of unmatched desire. Vince fucks me deep and hard, and with every stroke of his cock sliding in and out of my wet cunny, I'm closer to the edge, too.

"I'm going to come again," I gasp. "Oh, Vince!"

"Mmhm. Good girl, Chloe," he hisses between his teeth.

My cunny twitches and gushes around his cock as he pounds me faster. I tighten my grip around his waist. I stare intently into his eyes. I mouth the words, Come inside me.

With that, he loses all sense of restraint. Vince growls my name, "Chloe!" and then his cock bursts a steady stream of thick, hot come deep inside my fertile, virgin womb.

I feel every pump of his shaft and I hold him in place while we come down together. He rests his forehead against mine, both of us breathing raggedly in the afterglow.

Once we're done, he gently leads me into his bathroom, which is essentially just a small spa. It's got every tricked-out furnishing imaginable.

Vince runs us a hot bubble bath and we slide into the tub together amid the fragrant, iridescent bubbles. I recline back into him, my back against his strong chest.

He gently combs through my hair with his fingers and washes it while we just talk and enjoy our closeness.

"I've never been this happy," I admit.

"Me neither," he confesses. "I've spent so much time in this industry. I've met so many beautiful women, and I've never once had difficulty staying professional. But you? Chloe, you took me by surprise."

"I feel the same way," I gush. "This has to mean something, right?"

He kisses me softly and strokes my cheek. "Yes. I think so."

"I hope you know I meant every word," I tell him. "I'm yours."

"Me too. I'm yours, now and always, Chloe. Dream team forever," he chuckles.

And it's true. From that moment on, we spend every possible moment together. Sure, my roommates are confused at first as to why I suddenly move out.

But once they meet Vince, it makes sense. Everyone gets it when they see us together. He looks like he could be my dad, or at the very least a much older brother.

But age doesn't matter when true love comes along. Months later, we finally wrap on the massive, international perfume ad.

The campaign is a wild success, and Vince has to field requests for my talents left and right. Business is booming, I've never been more fulfilled, and I am very excited to take a break from everything. Modeling will always be my first love, and I have big plans to return once I'm ready.

But today? I have something more exciting to do.

A photoshoot that you won't find in any magazine or billboard.

A shoot just for my family and friends to see. It's just Vince, me, and the tiniest baby bump starting to show on my belly.

It's a perfect time to step back from the cameras and slow down for a while, really savor every day of this beautiful pregnancy. There will be plenty of time to do everything I want to do. And now, I don't have to do it alone.

I have my king, my agent, my everything by my side. A life with Vincent and our growing family? That's what I'd call picture perfect.

Olivia's Sugar Daddy

⌒⌒〜⌒

━━━━∞━━━━

Book Themes: Billionaire, Virgin, First Time,
Rough Sex, Breeding/Impregnation
Word Count: 11965

━━━━∞━━━━

"I'm broke," the old man cried. "I'm broke, I have nothing. I have less than nothing, I'm in crippling debt, even."

Tears were running down his face, and I expected him to fall down onto his knees in a mess in some overacted melodrama.

Sure, he was my father. Sure, I loved him. I just never saw him like this before, with him turning into some sad sack of tears and misery.

It didn't change the fact that what he said was true. The hints were there, yes, our staff going from a grand army to a skeleton crew, to then not even having that.

Some suit came into our family's mansion. Made a bunch of grand gestures. Ogled my sisters and I. Sure, he was attractive, but I wasn't too focused on him. I hadn't even had my hair done and Dad would have freaked if I started dating the guy who was buying our house.

No, in my mind, I was terrified. I liked my lifestyle, I liked having my occupation listed as socialite. My father's failures suddenly were going to turn that occupation into waitress if I didn't act fast.

As the family meeting ended, I bolted up the stairs to my room, thinking about the dress that I was going to wear that night. Something sleek, something sexy, something that would tease and deflect the fact that I wasn't as hard of a bitch as I seemed.

Sure, my wardrobe was draped with black dresses and high heels. Maybe I wore make up in a way that said I was a bad girl. Truth be told? I think I liked the attention more than anything else.

So many times I went to the Cleopatra, the fanciest bar in town, just to strut my stuff. Horny rich bastards slathering over me, offering to buy me drinks, trying to get close enough to touch instead of just looking, but I never let them.

I was a tease. The most hardcore and devoted of teases. Ever since I turned twenty-one I'd been going there in something sexy, and every night I returned home – alone. On purpose.

Despite my seductress nature, I was a virgin at twenty-one. I laughed at the irony whenever I thought about it.

I pulled out the dress for tonight, it had to be doubly special. Something that didn't go too far past my ass, and showed off a lot of leg. Black, low cut, playing the brinksmanship game with my cleavage as well but still remaining classy. I had lots to choose from. I settled on something that had a bit of a boob window.

Shoes were next, settling on some heels to really drive the leg thing home.

Because tonight, I wasn't just playing games like I usually did. Tonight, I had to enrapture some rich bastard.

I shuddered. I was becoming what I feared most. Some moneygrubbing bitch. With eviction looming though, I didn't have much choice in the matter. I had to string someone along.

Again, I was disgusted thinking about who it would probably

be. The older and more decrepit they were I supposed, the less amount of time I would have to put up with them before they finally had a heart attack and keeled over, leaving me their fortune.

The alternative was getting a real job, trying to go back to school. A prospect with no definite success.

Looking at myself in the mirror as I finished applying my makeup though, I realized that I looked good. I was confident despite my inexperience. This was going to work, no matter how much I hated the fact that, yes, it was going to work. I'd meet the man who I would marry tonight.

Closing my eyes, taking a deep breath, I grabbed my phone and dialed for a cab.

The Cleopatra was where it was going to happen.

The doorman didn't even stop me for an ID as I walked past. I was well established as a regular so all he did was nod. I usually threw a flirt at him, but tonight was more about business, and as nice as the doorman was, he wasn't what I was looking for.

The people I was looking for were up the stairs and into the bar room proper.

The Cleopatra was immaculate. Huge windows which gave a view of the city below. Waiters and waitresses desperately trying to stay on top of the requests of the clientele, carrying out huge platters of food and drinks – mostly drinks. Of the alcoholic variety.

The clientele? No one was in an item of clothing that wasn't worth at least three digits. I'd put good money that it'd also apply to minor items like a woman's stockings or hair decorations. Suits, jackets for the men, a few daring to only go with collared shirts. Even looking at the women, I took notes about fashion to steal and alter for my own use later on – if my mission was successful anyway. Besides, if confronted, I'd use the word inspired. Sounds nicer than steal.

Every single one of them was worth seven digits or would be by the time they'd be thirty-years-old. Stock brokers, lawyers, entrepreneurs, all jobs where you didn't get to being successful by playing nice. Honestly, I hated the lot of them. Caring for money more than humanity.

Money was so very nice though, so I had to work fast. I had to bite my tongue, find some loveless relationship at least long enough to secure my own future. If it got out that my own fortune was ruined, they'd all see me as a gold digger and want nothing to do with me.

I found the corner of the main bar, where all the singles lurked. I scooted up on the stool and did my damnedest to look seductive like I always did. I had my routine, get attention, get people to buy drinks for me. That was all the ego rush I needed, usually. With the stakes raised, I only had to hope that my desperation didn't shine through.

"Hey, Candy Cheeks," a voice said, breaking through the background.

Candy Cheeks? What kind of pick up line was that? I turned to face my newest 'suitor'. Sure, he had good hair. He was traditionally attractive, dressed well in a gray suit. He wasn't ugly. The way he smiled though? I instinctively wanted to punch him in the face. I resisted, for the combination of not wanting to be arrested and needing an asshole like him.

"Mind if I buy you a drink for your time?" He sat on the stool next to mine.

"Oh sure thing handsome," I said, putting on my own fake smile.

"Man, what a day," he began. "Cornered a market. Got a monopoly on it now. Gonna make me rocket up the Forbes list."

"Oh really," I said, passively. These assholes just want to endless talk about themselves over and over again, never shutting their mouths on the matter.

"People need what I'm selling if you catch my drift and this is going to turn me into a full fledged billionaire," he went on. "Bartender! Get me a beer and the lady some Balkan vodka!"

"Vodka?" I said.

"You'll love it," he replied, his punchable smile growing more punchable. "So anyway, it seems like I got it all, you know? All except that soft luscious lady in my life." He snidely glanced my way.

The bartender slid the drinks towards us.

Just looking down at the vodka, its subtle fumes were making my eyes burn. I wasn't some veteran in drinking, only legally being able to do so recently. Vodka was super strong, especially the authentic stuff that the Cleopatra would carry. Actual stuff from the Balkans, stuff that would put hair on my chest even though I was a woman, and would make me a dribbling incoherent mess in no time flat.

I glared at my 'suitor'. He had clear nefarious intent, getting me something so hard when he was drinking something so utterly not. I slid off the stool. "I don't think I'm up to vodka, I'm sorry. Enjoy your illegal monopoly."

"See? I show some charity to a butterface like yourself and this is how I get treated?" I cringed as I started to walk away from him, but he didn't shut up. "You don't even belong in this bar, bitch, I should have you thrown out!"

I cringed at his words, there being truth in the second part of his rants. He wouldn't go that far. He'd just go try to prey on someone else. I pushed him out of my mind.

Then I saw him.

Actually handsome. A solid jaw, dark hair hanging over his eyes. piercing yet as dark as his hair. His sleeves were rolled up, revealing a strong forearms, slightly furry.

He had a light wine at arms reach, and seemed as bored of all of this as I was. He had vacancies to both sides of him. Mystery man looked around the room, shaking his head, until his gaze spun around and met my own. He froze for a moment, and looked me up and down.

All while I was staring right back at home.

My gaze snapped away, realizing how aggressively awkward I was being.

"You want to have a seat next to me, or do you want to keep standing there randomly gawking at me?"

Blushing, I accepted his invitation and climbed up on the stool next to him.

"A drink?" He said with a kind eyebrow raise.

"Sure," I replied, trying not to come off too weirdly.

"What'll it be?"

"Not vodka. Anything but vodka."

He laughed. "Two beers please!" He said, raising a hand to get the attention of the barkeep.

"That's a better start than my last encounter already."

"You mean that guy?" He pointed over the bar, where my former 'suitor' was already at work with another girl. Luckily, it seemed she wasn't having much of him either. "That guy's a prick. He's the whole reason I don't come to this place."

I glanced at my new crush. "Yeah, I haven't seen you around before."

"Cause it's the first time I've been here. My latest attempt and mingling and hopefully finding the whole true love thing."

"You want something real, huh?" I said, sipping the drink as it was slid in front of me.

"Who doesn't?"

"People who are dead inside and believe love is a lie," I replied. Realizing what I was in here for, I couldn't say I didn't see how they would be driven to believe that.

"See? I like that. That's genuine. Most people around here are so full of themselves, and if they're not full of that, it's just a bunch of hot air covering the fact that they're only a millionaire instead of a billionaire and that's the worst thing in the whole damn world."

I laughed. "They don't let anyone in here besides those types. Self-loathing millionaire?"

"Billionaire, but as I said, doesn't matter. I don't hate myself. I just hate everyone in the same tax bracket as me."

"I understand that."

"You know how it is though. If I want to find something that actually resembles love, I gotta stay in that tax bracket. I can't imagine me or the girl I search for being able to get over the whole sugar daddy or gold digger implication of the relationship."

I coughed, shiftily looking away. "Money complicates everything."

"There's something about you, and I don't think we've even exchanged names. I'm Daniel Carter. May I ask what yours is?"

"Olivia," I said, stopping myself for letting out my last name. What if this guy knew of my family's recent troubles and the ruin that we had suddenly encountered?

"Olivia, eh? That's a beautiful name." He sipped his beverage. "I just don't think I'd be able to get over the feeling that they'd only be interested in me for my money and my money alone. I mean, you end up with either them snatching half your fortune in betrayal or I get them to sign some pre-nuptial saying I don't trust them to not do that. I rather just not be in such a situation."

"Yeah," I muttered. "I'm surprised a guy like you hasn't found someone already. I'd think that you'd have your open choice of any woman you wanted, no matter how big her bank account is."

Again, he laughed. "It isn't that simple. Sure, if I just want to get off, I can get anyone. I want more though. I've developed certain tastes that not everyone goes along with."

"What, do you like girls to call you Daddy or something?"

He shook his head, amused. "Nah, nothing like that. It takes a very special woman to really get me going. They need an edge to them. I don't know why, Olivia, but something tells me that you might have that edge."

"Oh?" My eyebrow raised again. "I'm curious. I just considered most of the guys in this bar to be super vanilla. Inherit your money, never have to think, never let your imagination roam."

Even as a virgin, just the whole pump the penis in the vagina thing until he splooges thing seemed kinda bland. There needed to be context, more to it. I guess it was why it was so easy for me to stop at flirting to get my rush. Daniel, though, was definitely different, even without what he was hinting at. What he was hinting at? I had no idea.

"My imagination is why I have my success. No trust fund here, just a good idea, the drive to make it happen, and the wisdom to sell it off at the right time. I never have to work again if I don't want to, but I'll see where life takes me. Tonight, I think it might be taking me with you, Olivia."

A rush of adrenaline hit me, as I pondered everything that he was suggesting to me.

We kept talking for a time. About our lives, about everything else. All the while I kept being evasive about my family's circumstances, not wanting my incoming destitution to be known.

"God, I hope I remain the anonymous billionaire. I don't want to be known like that. Besides, all I need is some stupid scandal getting out from a bunch of people that don't truly understand what's going on and what it all means," he said, still only on his third drink. We had been talking for hours at this point.

"Keep going, you can't just say that without details," I replied.

"People just don't understand why I like the things that I do. They think one thing and immediately just make a million and one assumptions about the person and everything. That they're some sort of Patrick Bateman style psycho who gets off on violence, or that they're just some abuse junkie who is a massive misogynist."

"What do you mean, then?"

"See, even with you, I don't want to come out and say it. I think you'd like it. I also just think I tell you, you run away screaming and miss out on something great."

My interest was most definitely piqued as he spoke about things. I wanted to learn more about him, I wanted to do more with Daniel Carter. Somehow, someway, I found the one dude with money at the Cleopatra who didn't make my stomach twist and turn at the idea of doing more with him than cashing his checks.

"Show me, then."

"Hmm?"

"Show me. Show me what your into. Daniel, I can't say much more than I am open minded, especially when it comes to you."

The grin that formed on his face was definitely genuine. He took me gently by the hand, placed a pair of hundred-dollar bills on the counter, and stepped away from it. I followed him with curiosity, wondering what would come next.

"I rented the executive suite from the hotel above the Cleopatra just in case I found such a woman who was curious enough to follow me further." He led me into an elevator, and pressed the button to the top floor. "I want to take you tonight, Olivia. Ever since our gazes met, I knew that you were going to be something special, and I hope that this inkling is more than just a one night stand for you too."

"Not even a first date, huh?"

"I see this as cutting to the chase; if we aren't sexually compatible, why waste our time with one another?"

The door opened to the top floor, and the executive suite was as exorbitant as I thought it would be. Daniel let go of my hand as he undid a few buttons on his collared shirt. I did the same, kicking off my heels and enjoying the plush carpet underneath my feet.

"Olivia," he said, flatly, our eyes meeting directly. "If something happens you are absolutely not comfortable with, tell me these words clearly: Green Apple."

Green Apple? I was confused, but not enough to get back up on that elevator and flee Daniel. No, this was going to be the night that I went beyond teasing. Way beyond teasing.

I wandered a bit through his suite, looking out the window, split between enjoying the view and pondering what was going to come. My first time, and what on earth was Daniel going on about?

"Olivia, some men are content with nothing more than the sweetest romance. Tender kisses, nothing more than soft touches between you and your lover. Me? Not so much."

His footsteps hit the carpet behind me, and I soon felt his presence. Swiftly and suddenly, he spun me around, taking my hair into his hand roughly, and then kissing me so very deeply. He didn't hold back. Not one bit.

There was force in his movements, powerful and sudden. Even as he kissed me, it was like he wasn't giving me my first kiss, but instead taking it from me. His tongue was pushing in, demanding that my own follow.

The way my adrenaline started pumping, well, I was shocked to say that I actually liked what he was doing. Direct, strong, and dare I say, manly.

Our kiss breaking, he kept my eyes locked on his, using my hair as a lever. "For me, though, I'm looking for something more primal. Savage. This is what is so easy for someone outsider to look in and call me a chauvinist, someone who just hates women and wants to exert power over them."

I blinked at him, not quite fully sure what to make of it.

"Exerting power, yes, that's part of the fantasy. But I love women. I love a woman more when they love each and every little cruelty I give to them as if it were a pleasure."

"You think I'm going to like having this done to me?"

"I've been talking with you for a few hours. You're a bit of a tease aren't you?"

I blushed in response. "Maybe a little?"

"I theorize that you've been waiting for a guy like me to come along, reach out, and take what he wants. You want someone to be rough with you. Poor little rich girl never had any real adversity in her life, so you want someone to at least give you the fantasy of it."

"Are you my shrink now?"

He simply laughed. "It doesn't matter, really. Just remember what I told you. It's not fun for me unless you're having fun too."

The smile faded, and he yanked me around again. The pain was there as he almost dragged me to the room, toward the bed, and then shoved me down onto it, making me bounce as I hit it.

It was by far the nicest bed I've ever been roughly tossed on to. Also the first, but...

I had to say I definitely wasn't expecting this. Daniel climbed on top of me, held me down and kissed me deeply again, roughly.

No matter how weird it was, I reminded myself that it was for my future. No matter how much I liked how he kissed me so hard on my neck that I think it might have left a mark.

Daniel kept going. He reached down to my dress, silky and

fancy, and just tore at it. Brute strength, tearing it down the middle like it was tissue paper. "I think I'm going to enjoy ravishing you," he said, taking in the sight of my body, now effectively clad only in my bra and panties.

All I could do was blush more, wondering if my smile was ruining his fantasy.

His hands sprung into action, yanking my bra across my breasts, another move I wondered if it was going to leave a mark tomorrow morning. He roughly handled me, twisting them, teasing them. I winced here and there, but still found myself into it through it all. Not content with proxy stimulation, he used those buff arms to pull at and break my bra. God, was he going to leave me with any functional clothes in the morning?

The way he took my nipples into his hand, tweaking them, twisting them. It stung, yes. The blood still rushed to them, my arousal rising steadily from his movements. Even as I gasped, cried out softly from the pain, I was entranced, wanting to experience anything and everything that was going with what he was doing.

"A little pain can give way to a whole lot of pleasure," he said, as he latched onto my breast with a mighty and powerful kiss. It was a powerful suck, and that suck turned into a bite.

"Ah," I said, wincing a bit. It didn't change much about the situation though. That nipple was hard, and I could feel other parts of me getting more and more ready to experience Daniel's unique brand of rough love. The other breast soon got the same treatment, and it's hardness, the coolness that his saliva left behind as he used my body so roughly it left me aching, yearning for more and more.

With his hands and mouth, nothing he did was gentle, everything being a bit uncomfortable on top of wonderful. He rose up again, and proceeded to slap me across the face.

Following it by holding my cheeks and shoving another deep kiss down my throat. It was strange, it was cruel, and I wanted more of it above all. It seemed so reckless and unloving, but the adrenaline, oh, he was so right about the adrenaline.

As he was kissing me, his long arms reached down to my

panties, fondling me through the fabric. It seemed as if he were only doing it to get a reaction out of me, something that would make me agonize, and feel shame that I was enjoying being used like this. As the hard kiss broke, he looked me right in the eyes, "You're such a little slut that all of this is making you sopping wet, isn't it?"

I couldn't help but nod softly, knowing a lie was pointless. I was a dirty slut, and I wondered what he would think when he learned I was somehow paradoxically a virgin and a slut at the same time?

Even as I enjoyed the little ripples of delight going through my body as he used me, he wasn't content with my nervous smile and shameful coos.

He pulled at my panties, only this time I was able to throw up my legs to let them slide down my body before he so unceremoniously destroyed them. He instead flung them across the room, not giving a damn once he had me fully naked in front of him.

So bare, so vulnerable at that moment, I looked away from him. I knew that he was into me, but never before had I been like this in front of man.

The whole roleplay seemed to suddenly stop. "You can't be serious."

"Wait, what?" I raised an eyebrow, pushing myself up. I looked up and down my body. Did he suddenly find me hideous. "What's wrong? Is it me?"

"No, no, Olivia. You're absolutely beautiful."

"What did I do?"

"The way you're acting. Your lack of eye contact. You're way too anxious for the type of girl you act like. You're a virgin."

I couldn't look at him, feeling embarrassed by the fact somehow. It felt like a point of pride to many women, yet his tone made me feel like it was shame. "I'm sorry. Do I have to leave?"

"What? No!" His response was sudden and quick. "I just can't believe you're a virgin. You're sex on two legs, the world's biggest flirt, and you're a virgin letting me bite your breasts, tear off your clothes and everything else?"

"I'm liking what you're doing," I said, scratching my hair, nervous and feeling even more vulnerable and naked. Which was something, given my actual nudity.

He let out a brief laugh, and smiled once more. "If you want your first time to be like this, who am I to say no? Just remember the words I told you."

Apples of the green variety were the last thing on my mind.

Daniel didn't hesitate for long before he resumed his assault. Another harsh yet sensual kiss, his hand running down my body, slapping my breast. There was an admiration that went along with the minor violence. "Still have no idea what you were waiting for, a body like this could get anyone."

"I didn't want anyone. I wanted something more. I wanted someone," I stopped myself from saying rich. "I wanted someone genuine. Real. Someone who wasn't just a greedy husk or a human being."

"Nice flattery," he smiled, his grin looking ever so slightly evil. "You're mine now, Olivia. There's no stopping me now."

Unless I wanted it to, anyway - and I sure as hell didn't want it to stop.

My pussy now naked and bare, his fingers slithered down there, over my clit, and thrust themselves into my body. I was already so wet for him, so ready for something far thicker and more virile than his fingers. The fantasy though, gave him control, as was the nature of it.

What he wanted to do I was sure wouldn't end up disappointing me.

I wasn't wrong, but I was very surprised.

His movement was swift and sudden, and his fingers started rubbing my clit.

Fast. Rough, beating the thing like it owed him money.

The surge through me was just as sudden. Electricity shot through my body, shuddering through me again and again as he rubbed my nub.

It was a tactically focused attack and my inexperienced body was reacting just like he had planned all along. I was moaning, my back arching, it was happening quick. The way he was touching that most sensitive part of my body was making me uncomfortable, but natural response quickly outweighed it.

Ecstasy was flooding over me and fast. I fought it, not wanting to cum so easily but I couldn't help it. I wasn't able to resist it and I screamed out as the sudden explosion hit me and washed over my body so completely.

I fell back onto the bed, already panting, cold sweat going down my brow. Only then did he finally stop rubbing my clit with such ruthless abandon. "You... you asshole," I managed to murmur.

"Oh? You're blaming me that you cum so quickly from a little fingering? Bitches like you, Olivia, are the type who cum from anything. Guys roughing them up, guys simply laying a finger on their pussy. Jesus, you really are a slut."

"Just a little fingering?" I was almost angry at his words. Almost.

As feeling returned to my body post-orgasm, I pushed myself up, watching as Daniel finished tossing away his shirt and letting his black dress pants fall to the floor. All that was left was a tent in his boxers and that didn't last too long either as he pushed them to floor, letting his cock spring out, erect and more than ready for whatever devious thing he was planning on doing with it.

He reached for my head, and yanked me forward. It hurt a bit, but the adrenaline pumped through me and made me realize I didn't mind it all that much. One foot on the bed, he brought my face towards his cock. "If you wanna be with me, Olivia, you're going to learn to suck my cock just the way I like it."

I flashed him a devilish stare, my eyes lowering and settling on the mighty rod that was in front of me. The heat radiated off of it to my face, and I had to admit, I was a bit intimidated.

"Lick it, slut."

I swallowed, and slowly obeyed, pushing my tongue out of my mouth and licking the head of it.

"Lick it like you like it, and I know you do."

Obeying, I licked it up and down, roaming his shaft. He groaned ever so softly from my worship. He still had his hands on my hair, using it to control me, still pulling at my roots with a good deal of cruelty with everything that he was doing. He urged me down towards his balls, shaking them into my face.

"Suck on them. Suck on them like you're an idiot and you think that's the best way to get the cum out of them."

Again pushing me, I opened my mouth and took his sack into my mouth, having him lay them on my tongue, forcing me to lick them. To suck on them. Heavy and strong, he was more than full of seed, all of it ready and yearning to escape their prison. Sure, it wasn't going to escape from this, but Daniel was liking what I was doing anyway, sucking on him so hard, so completely. His head fell back, another soft groan from him as I kept up my driven and dedicated worship of him.

The scent, the sweat, it was all the essence of his sheer manliness and I couldn't help but liking it even when I clearly shouldn't of. In a way, it was a giant metaphor for everything he was doing. Slapping me, pulling my hair, using my own body against me, and generally abusing me, I should have hated every single thing about it. Having his balls shoved down my throat?

Didn't matter. Liked it anyway.

He pulled his balls out of my mouth, despite my best efforts at pleasing him.

"Open up, slut," he demanded.

I obeyed and was suddenly welcomed with a sudden cock shoved down my throat. He didn't waste any time, throwing me into the deep end with this – with a deep throat. I fought my temptation to gag as my lips rolled over his cock and towards his balls once more.

He pressed himself deep, daring me to gag, and I sputtered.

The rush. That's what all this was. All that talk about the primal nature of it all became very clear to me. Adrenaline plays such a big role, and adding a bit of roughness and what may be violence into it just made more of it pump through me. Sure, my heart would be pounding if I was just trying to suck his cock normally, but as he tried to make me choke on it, I got all the excitement I would have gotten from that and oh so much more.

Daniel didn't let me choke on him for too long, again

yanking his cock out of my mouth only to drive it back in. I struggled to do something besides gag, trying to suck on him, trying to lick him, trying to enjoy him even more.

He continued to act carelessly, being so rough yet so driven in his movements. He wasn't hitting my face with his cock and balls enough to leave any marks but he was definitely doing enough of it that I would feel it. He went faster and faster, and with every cycle I strove to please him despite his roughness. Even as he thrust deeper, even as he pulled on my hair harder, beating my face with his cock, my lust was still burning for him.

"Suck it harder," he demanded.

I muffledly protested, wanting to say that I was doing my damndest, but all that came out was "Mmmf mmvrrmf."

There were tears in my eyes yes, but I didn't really know why. Everything that was happening was like some sort of sensory overload. Pain, pleasure, it was all the same.

He kept fucking my mouth like an animal, and I wondered how much of me could he really take. He didn't take long to give me an answer. "I'm not ready to cum just yet." He again denied me his cock, pulling it out of my mouth, and pushing me back down onto the bed. I hit it spread eagle.

"I still got things I want to do to you, slut." Daniel's words were always accompanied by that satanic smile. He was having the time of his life, knowing that I hadn't yet put a stop to his fun – and that I was liking the way that he was treating me. He climbed on to the bed with me, his hand going to my clit, still sore from the rough way he had forced me to cum earlier. "This cunt belongs to me now, you understand? I can do anything I want to it. Finger it, fuck it, and lick it."

He dropped his head between my legs and laid a kiss on my nub, and sucked on it. Hard. A jolt of delight shot through me just then. Daniel licked up my juices, sucking on my labia, pulling on those lips, stretching that skin, but was always back there to make sure the pleasure outweighed the discomfort.

Thrusting his tongue inside me, trying to fuck me just as swiftly and as hard as he had done with fingers moments ago, he was devouring my pussy. Pulling at my clit and every sensitive part down there he was doing well in making me toss and turn under him again. Even as I started to bend to try to cope with the growing ecstasy inside of me, he held me down, making me squirm even more underneath of his devious touch.

It was weird that he was so good at eating me out, as I never thought it was possibly to roughly eat pussy, but Daniel was all about surprising me. Left and right, he was showing me a whole new and wonderful world tonight.

Too much was coming my way though, no matter how much I resisted or Daniel helped me fight my bodies natural tendencies. Every lick of my pussy, every suck on my clit, every fucking via his tongue it was all building up to something even stronger than the lightning fast finger fucking he gave me. Pressed hard into the bed, I just twisted in place as the orgasm hit me, a thick thundering wave washing over me again and again, every bit of utter bliss as I screamed his name.

As I came down from this high, I watched as Daniel looked on, seeing my predicament brought him such great amusement. "Such a slut. You know what? I'm not going to fuck you like a virgin. I'm going to fuck you like the filthy slut that you are."

I swallowed. Despite how much pain and discomfort had been involved in Daniel's unusual style of lovemaking, I was still anxious about the whole hymen thing, hearing so much about it being terrible and how there would be blood gushing everywhere.

So far though, everything had ultimately been great. Daniel was very experienced, so I decided to nod and accept it. "Fuck me," I said, softly.

"Oh, you're asking for it now?"

I nodded. "Please fuck me," I repeated, panting, not even remotely recovered from the first orgasm let alone the second that I had enjoyed tonight so far. Here I was, begging him for a third. Maybe I really was, unironically, a slut?

A hand still on my chest, he climbed onto the bed with me, forcing another brash kiss on my lips. His body's presence against mine was so strong and so overwhelming. More nervous than ever before, I felt him loom closer to me, his cock, still rock hard and ready for me, looming at my pussy lips, and ready to push through. "I'm going to take you, Olivia. Going to take you so fucking hard."

My eyes closed, I prepared myself for what was to come.

He thrust himself inside me. Suddenly. I had his entire cock buried within me, to the hilt, my pussy lips spreading to accept him so easily.

My eyes opened in surprise.

Daniel leaned down and whispered into my ears, the heat of his breath teasing them. "You're so fucking aroused by all this like the dirty bitch you are. It only hurts when girls aren't properly warmed up to it – like cumming twice on my fingers and tongue like the slut you are."

I couldn't help my laugh, my anxiety all for naught. He started to fuck me, a bit slowly at first, giving me the slightest bit of leeway to adjust to having his cock inside me, but he didn't wait long before pounding me, hard. His hands held down my hands, forcing me to take all of the impact of what he did again and again. Every penetration built on the last, making me lust for more and more of the electric energy he was forging inside of me.

Faster still he hammered his naked cock into me, making my legs rise up around him as he fucked me. Again, I tossed and turned to deal with the growing ecstasy and orgasm that was stewing so much inside me. He grit his teeth wanting me to only scream louder, trying to go deeper into me, pounding me like I was nothing more than meat designed for him to fuck.

Even that, though, wasn't enough for Daniel's insatiable lust for rough fucking.

Withdrawing from me, ever so briefly, he took me by the wrists and urged me to turn over. "I need to fuck you harder, deeper. I need to make you truly feel the power of a cock fucking you as you scream with lust from the first time by a man fucking you like the filthy, disgusting slut you are."

Now face down on the bed, he didn't waste time reintro-ducing his cock into the equation. Daniel thrust himself back into me from behind, squeezing my ass as he did so, and this time he made his words true, fucking me deeper. More than before, I felt him going so much further, to the point that I don't think I could have taken a man much bigger than he was. It was almost on top of everything else, Daniel was physically perfect for me.

My ass in the air, he fucked my pussy with even greater speed and abandon, quickly building up my next orgasm to be even something greater than everything that had come before it. This time though, he was pressing my face into the bed, muffling my moans of ecstasy with his strength. Every cycle of our lust was rubbing my sensitive breasts and body against the bed. Everything all coming together, the friction of my body against the blankets, his touch, the roughness of the way he was handling me, it was all blending together. Adrenaline pumping more than ever before.

I wondered why I had waited so damn long to find a man as he fucked me, but reminded myself none of those empty souled assholes could do anything like Daniel. Even in my inexperience, I knew that as absolute fact.

Holding tight, gritting my teeth, my back arched and I let out one last delightful scream.

"Scream for me, my little slut."

With it, came a grand burst of bliss. All the way through my body, I was shaking from the wonderful, powerful feeling that Daniel had delivered to me tonight. It dominated me so completely, and what a feeling being dominated was.

"Yes, yes, sing for me."

I did just as he asked.

"Fuck, you're so tight for a slut. Can't take much more of you Olivia. I should just bust my nut inside of you, shouldn't I?"

My mind lost to bliss, I found myself subconsciously nodding at his words, wanting him, despite knowing that it was something so risky.

"You'd like that wouldn't you? Be a useless breeder slut on top of it all, taking unprotected loads from guys you just met."

He kept fucking me, even as I had peaked, dragging out the bliss a little bit longer.

"No, my seed is too good for a cunt like you," he said, grunting. He pulled out his cock, and it looks that my body was finally too much for his. His manhood shuddered, spurting out blast after blast of cream, exploding outward and onto my back. It felt like so much being rained down on me. Did guys always cum this much?

I was weary and sore from everything that happened, but I was happy. There was a definite pleasantness to every ache that I was experiencing.

The puddle of cum on my back did make me yearn for him to have came inside me, making me wonder just how that would have felt on top of everything else he had done to me.

A warm rag touched down on my back, wiping up the remains of the seed. It was Daniel, still naked, but taking a more tender touch now. "You okay there, Olivia? I get a little out of hand sometimes."

I flashed him a smile. "I'm fine. Sore, but fine."

"You're the best fuck I've had in ages. It's wonderful when you find someone into it as you are."

I blushed through my cold sweat and exhaustion, him wiping me down. The cooling rag against my flesh just felt so good as a follow up. "Surprised at myself, really. That I liked it. But I did, and I guess that's what matters."

As he cleaned me up, he took me into his arms, such a massive contrast to how he was calling me a bitch and slapping me merely minutes ago. "I didn't mean it, by the way."

"Hmm? Didn't mean what?"

"My seed being too good for a cunt like you? Not at all. I just figured I should play it safe."

I nodded. "Yeah, I supposed so. Knew that's what you meant. I wouldn't have minded risking it though."

"What, are you trying to get knocked up on your first time?"

"What if I am?"

He shook his head, amused. "Baby crazy already? Maybe you are one of those girls who are just after me to score some sweet child support money."

I laughed again, but this time, incredibly nervously. "What? No. Of course not. Why would I need to do that? My family is very well off, I don't need to go and seduce guys for a quick pay off."

Daniel stared at me. "I was joking."

I kept laughing nervously. "So was I."

"Forget about it. That was just amazing, Olivia. I'm going love using you like my personal fuck doll."

He held me in his arms, closely, and kissed the top of my head. It was sweet, it was romantic. It was everything I wanted in a guy, and I wished something like this could last forever.

Daniel whispered into my ears as he embraced me. "Stay with me tomorrow. I want to learn so much more about you, why you just might be the one who I thought I would never find."

I let out a deep breath and didn't respond. I didn't want to think of what would happen when the truth shined through.

My eyes opened slowly, adjusting the rudeness that was the morning sun. My body still ached from the night before, but it was an ache that reminded of just how blissful the night before was. I pulled myself up, and heard the water running. Daniel was in the bathroom, showering. I contemplated getting up and joining him. A blinking light in the tattered remains of my clothes though caught my eye. My phone.

Casually I walked over to it and fished it out of the fabric. There were several voicemails from my father. My mind was rushing with what could possibly be so important that he called so much, simultaneously reminding myself I was a genius for setting my phone to vibrate so he couldn't have interrupted Daniel and I or our rest.

Still, he was my father and I couldn't completely ignore him. I figured I should listen before attempting to ambush Daniel with more sex.

"Olivia? Where are you. All my little girls are gone. What's going on?"

The water stopped. My chance was missed. Thanks Dad.

"Please, call me back. Let me know. We need to stay a family."

A deep breath, there were a dozen of these. I figured they were all the same thing. I started to delete them, one by one, focusing on trying to get through it as quickly as possible.

Daniel stepped through the door, wearing only a towel, my attention shifting from my phone. "Ready for some more, slut?" He said, dropping his towel, raising an eyebrow, and revealing that he, at the very least, was definitely ready for more.

Not done with what I was doing, I reached over to put the phone down without looking at it.

When gravity was suddenly a bit too strong, I realized my arm wasn't long enough to reach the nightstand. Instinctively, I tried to correct myself, trying to catch my phone before I accidentally dropped it on the floor.

In a panic, I became a klutz, slid off the bed, mashed some stuff on my phone as I tried to get a hold of it, as it slid across the room, and I started to hear my father's voice – on speaker phone.

"Why did you girls abandon me? You girls are all I have left since the money's all gone. Karen? Olivia? Christine? Where are all of you? Please. We can make it through these tough times as a family."

I froze as my father unwittingly revealed my ulterior motive to being with Daniel.

He stared at me, as shocked as I was, not saying a word.

Every word he said about being afraid that someone would only like him for his money echoed inside my mind.

I picked up my clothes, or what was left of them, the phone included. I covered myself the best I could.

Then I ran for the elevator.

"Olivia?" Daniel called out.

I was to the elevator, the door opening, and me scurrying inside. I mashed the close button as well as the first floor one.

"Come back here," he said.

It was too late, the doors closing before he could get to me.

I froze in place, trying to put on my panties. I didn't care how ridiculous I looked. Nothing would hurt me more than him acknowledging the sheer betrayal I had enacted against Daniel.

When the elevator touched down, I darted out the door. I'm

sure people were looking at me, the mostly naked girl in the torn tatters of a dress running barefoot through the Cleopatra's lobby. I didn't care. The shame of exposure was microscopic from the shame I was fleeing.

I would never return to this place, I decided, as I hailed for a cab. The little bit of money I had would get me home. It would get me away from Daniel.

What was next for me? I had no idea. My mind was blank and didn't even want to ponder a future where I didn't get to experience his rough yet loving touch again.

T blew it. I absolutely positively blew it. I laid on my bed in my room, like I had spent much of my time doing the last few days. There wasn't a terrible lot to do as a soon to be poor girl anyway, so I just decided to let my thoughts of my own foolishness haunt me.

It was only a matter of time before I'd be kicked out of this house and made to go get a real job. The thought was terrifying, but not as terrifying as the idea of how long I would have to wait to get a chance to be with a man like Daniel again. It was special the things he did, and it wasn't something you just went and did with anyone with the confidence they wouldn't go too far.

He's the man I've been waiting for for so long. This wouldn't have been a problem even last week. If only I'd met him sooner...

A literal one in a million man. Would I ever be able to find someone as hot as him, as knowledgeable as him, and as perfect for me ever again?

A knock was on the door. This was the fourth time today. I pulled myself up and off the bed, and headed down to answer it. It was a guy, this time with flowers.

"A delivery for Karen Van Hansen?"

I sighed. "Karen, get down here!"

At least my little sister managed to score an admirer. Good on her. The size of the bouquet told me she was definitely succeeding where I had failed.

I stepped away as my sister stormed down, bashful that more stuff had come for her. She had little to be ashamed of, unlike me.

I puttered around the house. I wondered if this pain would ever go away or would I continue to just anguish about this forever. Time heals all wounds, but time takes well, time.

The door was knocked on again. Jesus, couldn't Karen answer the door herself? "Karen! Answer the damn door."

I was almost to the refrigerator when the knocking resumed. Desire to not be an asshole won out over boredom hunger so I decided I'd answer the door for Karen. Again.

I opened it up and wasn't greeted by the same courier who I had ran into almost a dozen times by now, but instead two police officers.

"Are you Olivia Van Hansen?"

I nodded, confused. "What's the problem officers?"

They stepped behind me, grabbed me by the arms and pushed them together.

"Wait, what?"

"You're under arrest, Ms. Van Hansen."

"What did I do?"

"Indecent exposure at the Cleopatra a few days ago. An anonymous tip was sent in."

"You can't be serious. You know what happens in that place right?"

"It doesn't give you the right to break the law, you're coming with us."

The officer pushed me forward and I had no choice but to follow. All of this and now I was also being arrested? This was insane!

T hey kept me handcuffed the entire time. Shoving me into the car, for the long ride to the precinct, and even out of the car. No matter how much I told them I'd cooperate and work with them peacefully, they kept up the harsh treatment. It wasn't like I hurt anyone running nearly naked through the hotel. No kids could have possibly saw me because no one would bring their kids to a place like the Cleopatra.

I was sat down in a room. Cold as ice. There was one cop in dress clothes pacing around me. Besides him, there was a steel table and a glass mirror. I wondered if it was a window from the other side. I wasn't dressed for this, being in a t-shirt and sweatpants I had been wearing bumming around the house, and some sandals. I didn't look like the billion dollar princess I expected to be treated as.

Which was fair, since I wasn't one anymore.

"Are you trying to interrogate me?" I said, squirming in my handcuffs. "You think I'm going to lead you to some huge conspiracy of streakers who only run through high class hotels?"

"Cute," the officer said with a sarcastic smile. "What you did was wrong, lady."

"I guess, but I don't see how treating me like a murderer is going to do anything?"

The door the room swung open, and I immediately glanced over to see who it was.

Daniel Carter.

I swallowed. He was well dressed, no jacket, but a tie, and he was carrying a metal briefcase. "Officer," he said, nodding his head.

"Mr. Carter, she's ready for you."

"Thank you, Officer."

The cop left the room, and closed the door behind him, leaving me in a terrifying situation.

I was alone with Daniel and I had nowhere to run to escape him.

"Olivia," he said, flatly.

"Daniel," I said, nervously.

"Do you know how hard it was to find you? I realized you never even gave me your last name. I had to hire a private investigator to find you again, trying to find the only Olivia in this city with your beautiful face, your soft hair, your luscious lips, your sexy curves..."

"I get it."

"That's what the private investigator said too."

"I didn't know if you'd be able to figure out what'd been going on with me. I was afraid you would have heard that the Van Hansens were ruined and you'd tell me to fuck off."

"Maybe I would have."

I nodded. "I didn't want you to know I was destined to be in the poor house, okay?"

He paced around behind me. "I've gathered that. So, that's what you were at the Cleopatra to do, then? Find some rich schmuck, earn his trust, make him your sugar daddy?"

"Yes, that's what I wanted to do." I answered his questions honestly, knowing that I wasn't exactly in a good place to be lying and stringing him along. "I didn't know what to do otherwise. I thought it would be someone who probably deserved something like that anyway."

"You don't think I deserve being lied to?"

"No. You didn't seem like all the other assholes who were in the bar that night."

"So you went along with me anyway, despite still having that intent?"

I nodded, not wanting to outright say it.

He took a deep breath, still pacing behind me as I sulked.

"Relationships are about both sides bringing something to table. When money is involved, one ends up supporting the other, so the other better bring something worthwhile."

"I can't bring anything," I said. "I'm broke. I'm sorry, Daniel, I didn't..."

"Olivia, tell me. Was the whole night an act? Did you just pretend to like all the things I did to you? Or were you faking it?"

He planted his hands on the table and were staring directly into my face.

"Were you, Olivia? Just all part of your plan, right?"

"No," I said, this time with a bit of firmness. "I wasn't faking that. I liked each and every single thing you did. Maybe slapping me, spanking me, torturing me felt so good because I was being bad. But I enjoyed it. I liked all the rough stuff you did to me."

Daniel didn't respond immediately. He looked away from me for a time.

Then when his eyes returned to mine, it was with a kiss.

A strong, passionate kiss.

I was overwhelmed, him running his hands through my hair pulling me back, some of that trademark roughness shining through.

"I decide if I object to being the sugar daddy in this relationship. You bring you and your wonderful body to the table."

He pushed me forward down onto the table and forced me to stand, throwing my shirt up and over my head. It fell loose, and I smiled as in my slacker ways, I wasn't wearing much of anything underneath it. Daniel proceeded to use my newly bare breasts to take them into his hand and pull me close to him. Tightly, he pressed me against him, rolling my breasts in his hands, slapping my breasts, teasing the nipples and flicking them. They were already hard from the coldness of the room, but he was warming them up real quick.

"What about all that stuff about not wanting to be loved for your money," I said, before he forced me let out a soft moan.

"You want me because I do terrible things to you, Olivia. That's enough for me." He pulled my hair, forcing my face back and shoving his tongue down my throat with such a powerful intensity. "You're the type of slut I've been looking for and I'd pay anything to have you call my name out when I abuse you."

Helplessly, I was folded across the table, the handcuffs still in place. I had a strong suspicion they wouldn't be coming off my wrists any time soon.

"You like all this, don't you? Being ravished like this? Having your breasts hit and twisted?"

I nodded enthusiastically as continued to take his frustrations out on my tits, as he slid his hands down my body to my hips.

"Look at you, dressed in easy access clothes like this," he said, pushing my sweatpants down my legs and my panties right behind. "Just waiting to be fucked at a moment's notice. That's solid slut behavior, isn't it?"

With my clothes no longer in the way, he cruelly leaped into action, those deft fingers of his sliding down my body and going between my legs.

Everything that had suddenly happened, hearing him accept my situation, well, they were a load off of my shoulders. It was a rush to realize that after all my woe and worry, that I was going to get to have Daniel do things to me again.

And he was going to do those things to me right in that inter-rogation room.

He pressed his fingers against my pussy lips, and slipped them in again. "Already dripping wet for me too. You just love driving the point home of how much of a slut you are, don't you Olivia?"

"I'm your slut," I murmured right before he thrust his fingers into my pussy.

God, he was at it again. Pumping his fingers in and out of me like a machine. I couldn't stop him, not like I would want to anyway. I was immediately cooing and moaning for him as he manipulated by nub and used it against me, causing me to squirm on that cold steel table.

The handcuffs added a whole new dimension to it. I was literally just a torso he could do anything he wanted with, and he was choosing to fingerfuck me like this. He was building me up higher and higher, fingerfucking me even faster. I was screaming out for him as I wiggled the little ways I could in my predicament.

He slapped my ass, the sound echoing through the room as he did so. Daniel was going to continue to find new and creative ways to torture me and bring me to even greater heights. How on earth was I suppose to cope with all of this?

"You like this don't you. A filthy gold digger who just wants to cum everywhere, even in a police station?"

Daniel never stopped pumping his fingers in and out of my pussy and over my nub. I was curling into him as he did so, nodding furiously, agreeing with every word that he said. The energy inside me was rising so fast and so suddenly that there was no way I was going to last much longer with the way he was using me and abusing me.

I moaned and I screamed out his name, giving him everything that he wanted as he gave me everything I wanted – a strong burst of bliss shuddering through my body. Limply, I fell forward, but I knew that he wasn't going to leave me only with a fierce fingering.

"That's not enough for you, is it? You want more, don't you slut?"

Limply laying on the table, I watched as he undid his dress pants, pulling them down around his thighs and letting his erect cock shoot out, so very close to my face.

"Suck on it. Like the dirty slut you are, Olivia."

I nodded, sticking out my tongue and licking it, urging him to bring it closer to I could do exactly what he was asking of me.

Arms still bound, he shoved his cock into my mouth, and I licked him as he did so. Grabbing my hair, he didn't waste much time before fucking my face, and there was little I could do to stop him, only heightening the adrenaline rush from being treated like this – and feeling so bad for enjoying that I was being treated like this.

There was nothing I could do but sit back and take the abuse he was delivering to me. Every thrust of his cock, every forceful inch of his flesh as it passed my lips. I just embraced my own defilement as he fucked my face, and felt his rod only get harder as he continued to use and abuse me so roughly. So rough with my hair, all I was for him at that moment was a set of lips and a tongue.

Degradation had never been such a rush for me, but Daniel was making it so.

I could hear his grunts as his cock shuddered with the intense pleasure I was clearly giving him with only mouth and him fucking it.

"No, slut," he said, stopping, halting his cruel assault on my face. "You want my cum somewhere else, don't you?"

He stroked his as he walked behind me, as I was still bent over the table. He went to my pussy, rubbing it, it still sore from the sudden orgasm he had delivered to it moments before. His dick was perched outside my nether lips.

"This is what you want, right, slut? My naked, unprotected cock inside of you, nothing between it and your young, fertile pussy?"

I nodded, not fully understanding the subtexts of his words. God, I really was the slut he was accusing me of being.

He thrust inside me, and the first penetration after being denied him for so long was almost an orgasm in itself. He wasted no time putting his hands on my shoulders and making sure he was fucking me as deep as he possibly could with each and every thrust.

Daniel pulled me closer, his hands shifting down to my breast, twisting them, and spiking a competing jolt through me as he he kept up his rhythm. I called out with a moan, which he responded to by making his rhythm even faster.

"This is all you wanted, really. A guy fucking you unprotected. You want me to impregnate you right here in this interrogation room, don't you?"

I kept nodding. I think I would have admitted to murder if it kept him going. Everything he was doing was building up to something intense, something so much stronger than what I've felt before.

There was something different about the way Daniel was fucking me this time. Did my actions incite some true anger in him? They probably did. He was a rational individual though, so he didn't let it dominate him. Maybe that's why he was drawn to this sort of thing so much. Anger doesn't go away, so he channels it into sex.

Harsh. Rough. Primal. It was all energy Daniel was fucking me with. It hurt a bit, but the pleasure far outweighed any pain.

There was something else with it too that was different. The way he was talking. Impregnating me, flooding me with his seed. He was measuring himself last time, showing restraint and control.

This time? There was no such thing.

It was a raw, driven fucking, with far more purpose than making me cum alone.

Although that was still a pretty big part of it.

Daniel reached for my face, squeezed my cheeks, still fucking me, guiding my moaning face to his. "I'm going to give you what you want you little gold digging slut," he said. "A little bastard. That way you can try to claim child support. That's all a slut like you wants, right? To be fucked and taken care of."

There were tears in my eyes as I nodded so affirmatively, and I didn't know how much of his assessment I was agreeing with. I wanted this. With him, with Daniel fucking me the way I was sure no man could ever really possibly do so well.

Everything was coming together. I was on the brink of utter bliss, and I wasn't sure what my body was waiting for. The feeling inside me was so incredible and immense, it was almost torturous that I wasn't getting that final release just yet.

"It's not going to be like that. No, no child support, cause you're going to stay with me, Olivia, and let me fuck your sweet pussy whenever I want, and do whatever I want to it. That. Includes. This."

His hands firmly gripped my hips, and I felt his cock begin to shudder within. It began to pulse as it fucked me, firing burst and burst of hot seed inside of me, splashing against my cervix as he did so.

It was just what I needed for the final release.

I was sent to heaven just then, and I let out a scream so loud that not even the heavy metal door was going to stop everyone hear how nastily I was being fucked right now. Every surge of seed he fired into me only spiked my orgasm even higher. Just then, I was absolutely overwhelmed with the thoughts of everything that was happening, that I had succeeded, and that Daniel had just said he wanted to make me his, care for me and give me all the fucking I could ever desire.

It was beautiful, it was perfect, it was the product of our unusual lust.

Panting, voice hoarse, I could barely hold myself up over the table anymore as Daniel kept his cock buried inside of me.

"You're mine, now, Olivia. You'll always be my personal slut."

He let out a deep breath, tragically withdrawing his cock from me. I felt his seed start to leak out and go down my leg. It was such a sweet yet somber feeling, a reminder that my body was nothing more than a depository for his cock. It felt so sinful, so wrong to think of myself like that, while also feeling sexy to do so at the same time.

It made no sense, really. The human brain is weird, and I decided that if I couldn't make sense of it, I might as well enjoy the weirdness, embrace it. After all, those weird emotions are what landed me Daniel.

Out of my sight, I felt him futzing around with the handcuffs, undoing them. "You had the key the whole time, didn't you?" I said.

"Hey, I like you better handcuffed. Maybe I'll restrain you even more next time."

I smiled as I rubbed my wrist, restoring the feeling to them.

Daniel then picked up the metal suit case he had brought in with them, flicked the locks, and opened it in front of me. Inside was a beautiful dress, much like the one he had destroyed in our first fling days ago. Beside it, a set of heels. Missing? A pair of bra and panties.

I guess those were superfluous anyway when I had a man with an appetite like Daniel.

"Dress yourself. While you're my filthy breeding slut in private, in public, you will be my girlfriend and possibly much more than that."

Helping me, my body still weak from the wanton fucking he had given me, I slid the dress on, and strapped on the heels.

I stood before Daniel, and he offered me his arm. "Shall we? I've made dinner plans. I figured you'd be hungry after all that."

"Oh, I don't mind."

"Then maybe I'll tear that off your body again and ravish you like an animal again. Fuck, I'm tempted to do that right now." His words were honest, and even though he had covered himself once more, I got the idea that his cock was already ready to escape and fuck again. "Sadly, I only brought the dress. I lack foresight sometimes. Forgive me."

Together, we walked out of the room. His seed was still leaking out of me, a line of it moving down my leg as we walked past the police officers, who likely had heard the whole thing. Hell, with that 'mirror', they may have even been watching.

I had no doubts Daniel had bought them off as part of his plan to take me back. When you're worth a billion dollars, there's little you can't do.

As he left the precinct, he took me by surprise, lifting my legs and kissing me deeply. My lack of panties may have given some random onlooker an unintended show.

I didn't care. I had the richest, sexiest man on the planet.

I had succeeded what I had set out to do. And I got something so much more – I had won.

T placed my son in bed, tucking him in. He was an easy one, really. Not giving me a whole lot of trouble. Which was good, because it meant I still had more time for me.

Which meant more time for Daniel.

I stepped out of the room, still rubbing the new ring on my finger. It was an engagement ring, and the date was set.

My appreciation of my new jewelry didn't last long, as a strong arm pressed me against the wall.

His presence was so overwhelming. "All this time, with you being pregnant, and how I've had to be gentle, it's been driving me absolutely mad."

I could only smile as he fished under my dress, and got rid of those unneeded panties, tossing them down on the floor like the trash they were.

"It's a damn shame you're so fertile, Olivia. I'm going to ravish you, knock you up again, and then I have to back off. Life is too damn cruel."

"I could go on birth control," I said, not too enthusiastic.

"And deny us of the high? No. It's just something we're going to have to deal with. To feel you, raw, unprotected. I want to feel that adrenaline as I breed you like the filthy animal you are. Then do it again, and again, and again."

He wasted little time shoving his cock inside me as I was pinned against the wall. Every time it felt so absolutely wonderful, and knowing it was mine forever was such a marvelous thing. All I could do was smile and laugh, knowing that it ruined his roleplay. I couldn't help it. I loved this – and I loved him – far too much.

As he pounded me from behind, I knew I loved all the wrong things, and ironically, there was nothing wrong with that.

Punished by the Principal

Book Themes: barely legal, virgin, breeding,
teacher/student, creampie
Word Count: 5475

I shouldn't be here. I'm not dumb, I know that sneaking around after hours is going to get me in trouble. But I can't help it. There's only three weeks left of class, and if I don't find out now, it's going to bug me for the rest of my life.

See, my Principal is best friends with my dad, and a couple nights ago, I heard my dad cussing his friend out something fierce.

"How can you spy on Haley like that, Rick? She's just turned 18."

"Oh come on, Hank. I didn't mean nothing by it, but you can't tell me you haven't noticed—"

"Rick! I don't like where this is going, and if you don't stop what you're doing right now, I'm going to have to take action. Those pictures on your hard drive are inappropriate!"

"It's just innocent," Rick protested, but I could see the way his lip curled into a smirk, and I knew it wasn't.

I hoped it wasn't. I'd always had a crush on him ever since he was little, and he used to treat me like a grown up instead of a kid. And now that I'm not a kid, his lips put bad, bad thoughts in my head.

But hearing them fight like that was strange, especially over me. I haven't been able to stop thinking about it, about what Rick might have on his computer. So I decided to stay late after school today and sneak into the Principal's office. How hard can it be?

I know it might not even be on this computer. Maybe it's at Rick's home, but dad hasn't brought me over there since last summer for a BBQ and I know how weird it'd be if I just showed up out of the blue trying to get on his computer.

Nervously, I bite in on my lower lip as I walk through the school halls. It's creepy at night. Even with the lights on, and the janitors here and there, it feels too quiet and abandoned. Like the ceilings are too high and the walls are too wide, and yet it's almost claustrophobic, like everything's closing in on me.

I try to reign in my fear and continue my walk towards the end of the hall. I remind myself of why I'm here.

To find out what pictures Rick has of me.

Earlier that day I'd gone into the secretary's office and when she wasn't looking, I put a little piece of tape over the door hole so it wouldn't lock all the way. When I finally get to the door, I gratefully find out that no one noticed, and I slip into the inner office.

I stare at the nameplate on his door. Principal Rick Wood. All the others called him Mr. Dick Wood behind his back, but I never did. Mostly because I was afraid that if I did, I'd moan out the word or something like that. I didn't want anyone to know how much I thought about his dick.

I turn the knob and push the door in, but it makes a surprisingly loud noise and I cringe and stop. But I hear nothing, can't see anyone around. So I continue and push on into his office.

The light from his monitor is still on, which means he

must've forgot to turn it off when he left work. But all the better for me, because it means that I can get onto his computer more easily.

And it's doubly good, because I see he hasn't logged out of his account! No guessing his password. Which is good, because I have no idea how I'd go about that. I wasn't thinking straight, or planning ahead, clearly!

I sit myself on down, the chair squeaking noisily, but no sooner than I start moving the mouse about to click through folders do I notice the dark silhouette of a tall, broad-shouldered man looking in from the door.

"This kinda thing gets a girl a whole ton of detention... or worse," came that dark, gravelly voice that was so familiar.

Oh crap! He must have heard me come in through the receptionist's door.

"It's not what it looks like!" I protest instantly, the words coming to my tongue no sooner than I'd thought it. I push myself away from the computer as if it's hot lava and I somehow won't get in trouble if I'm not touching it anymore. My blonde bangs brush against my forehead as I shift, and suddenly I'm more aware of everything.

Of the smell of him in the air, the rich cologne filling my senses. It's so dark, but my eyes adjust slowly, and I can see how good he looks in his suit, the way he's undoing the collar of his button down shirt.

He steps towards me slowly, purposefully, placing his two palms upon the desk and leaning forward. I can feel his dark gaze on me, boring through me as he sizes me up, licking his lips slowly.

"Y'know, if you were anyone else... I'd be about to expel you, Andrea," he says to me, each word a deep, husky delight on my ears as he says them.

"No," I whimper, my shoulders slumped, my school outfit crinkling. I'm hot beneath my blouse and vest, and my skirt suddenly feels itchy around my thighs. I can't let my dad find out I was sneaking into his best friend's office at night, that I would have been expelled if he didn't know me so well!

Those perfect, masculine lips of his quirked up into a wry smirk, and as he sizes me up again, I feel downright trapped. So I stand up to leave, but he so casually steps in my way, blocking the only route around his desk with his tall, towering form.

"Andrea," he says, my name rolling off his tongue so smoothly as he reaches out and cups my chin and cheek, stroking his thumb along my smooth skin. "Where do you think you're going? We haven't come to any arrangement here yet," he says.

My nose crinkles, and his eyes twinkle. He's teasing me. I know that look better than any. It's like he caught my hand in the cookie jar and now he's asking what I'll do for him to not tell dad.

"What kind of arrangement?" I ask, and I'm surprised by how lusty my voice is. I feel scared, sure, but he keeps stroking my cheek, and I can feel my body start to flush.

"Well," he begins, taking his time as he looms over me, his natural musk tinged with some light manly aroma of cologne. My eyes are the perfect level to stare at the bare triangle of his hard, masculine pecs. "I can't very well let you off with just a warning in lieu of an expulsion Andrea, now can I? Some kind of punishment or service has to be rendered," he explains slowly, those long, hard fingers of his knitting back into my hair.

When did it get so hot in here? I swallow hard and lick my lips before lightly crossing my arms beneath my heaving breasts.

"I'll wash your car for you every day after class," I promise, knowing very well how much he prizes his car. His dad gave it to him years ago, and he's looked after his Cadillac like it was his child. I guess since he never married, he needed something to care for.

"Wash and polish my car, huh?" he says, brow raised, sounding sceptical of my proposal. "You think that's all it's gonna take to wipe the slate clean, lil' girl?" he taunts me, goads me as those dark eyes of his flash wide a moment and he looks down over me. "I think we'll have to step things up a notch, don't you?"

I'm dying to know what pictures he has of me, but that look in his eyes...

I'm a virgin. I've never been interested in other guys, especially not those my own age. But Mr. Wood is so sexy, and way out of my league. So why does it look like he wants me? Why does he keep looking at my pink-lipglossed lips? Every time I lick them, he looks at them almost enviously.

There's no way.

Is there?

"Like what?" I manage out finally, my voice soft and cautious.

He brushes his fingers back through my blonde hair, stroking it as he tilts his head and admires my face with that warm smile. A warm smile that contains a hint of something else entirely. Something more than warm. But hot.

"You're telling me a beautiful young woman such as yourself doesn't have any ideas, Andrea?" he asks, and I can hear a bit of that suave charm in his gravelly voice, and it's melting my knees.

But he called me beautiful. The word is slow to seep into my mind. Usually he'd call me cute, or pretty. Never beautiful.

I tilt my head and feel his thumb brush against the shell of my earlobe. He strokes it tenderly, and it sends something straight through my core.

"Mr. Wood?" I murmur curiously, "What should I do?"

He doesn't remove that hand from my face, but his other one comes up, grasps my hip and holds me. Keeps me from floating away. Or that's how I feel anyhow, with him looming over me so closely, holding and caressing me.

"Whatever it takes," he says with a certain gravel to his voice, leaning down towards me, until I realize his lips are within a hair's breadth of touching mine.

I can almost taste the cinnamon mint on his breathe, and I don't know what to do. I'm like a startled animal caught in the headlights.

Yet at the same time, excitement thrums through me. For so long I've fantasized about him, wanted him to just... take me. And now he's so close, I could just... lean forward and kiss him.

But when my mouth touches his, I'm shocked by my brazenness! I didn't mean to actually do it!

Whether I meant to or not though, he takes the kiss, and deepens it.

His head tilts, and his tongue lashes along my lips, parts them and probes into my mouth just a little. He's holding my face and guiding the tempo, making me swim in a sea of excitement until...

He pulls away, and looks down at me with that dashing smile of his.

"You can't kiss your way out of this entirely, young lady," he says with such smooth authority, his hand on my hip running around until it's skirting the top of my bottom. "But maybe a few spanks and I can see through to letting you off with this... and we can get back to that kissing," he says, just as his palm slides down around the curve of my ass.

Oh God. I wonder if he can feel how hot I am?

If he just moved his fingers just a little further, no doubt he could sense the heat that's radiating from between my thighs. I want it so bad that I'm distracted from his words.

"Spanks?" I ask with some confusion. I haven't been spanked since I was a little girl, and certainly never by someone not my parents. That was always a childish punishment thing.

So why does the thought of him spanking me turn me on?

That hand of his strokes over the round part of my rear, and it's done so softly, so tenderly, but it feels like such a tingling tease of what he's saying.

"C'mon now, Andrea. Bend over this desk here and we'll sort out your punishment," he says, and his hand leaves my face at last, but only to reach down, take hold of my hand and guide me to his desk. He's placing my hands to the top of that hardwood, doing it all so tenderly, but I can feel the strength in his grasp as he slides his hand back to my waist and hip, and pushes me into a bent-over position.

I'm in a daze, and feel so prone bent over, my skirt hiking up over the backs of my creamy thighs. My stockings end right above my knees, and my flesh is so vulnerable and bare. But I can't find the will to protest or stop him. I don't know if it's just fear of being caught, or wanting to make amends.

In fact, the only thing I do know, is that the longer his hands are on me, the harder my pussy throbs with need. Why would punishment turn me on like this?

That big, strong hand of his is stroking over the swell of my pert rear again, and I can hear him step around me, switching sides. The pathway to the door is open now, but I can't will myself to move. Not even as he squeezes my cheek.

"Alright sweetie, that's a good girl, it'll all be over soon," he husks, and not long after the first crack of his palm lands, smacking over my skirt against the flesh of my rear. A firm, crack of his palm, so easy and casual for him, but enough to make me gasp out loud.

It's so much different than the spankings I took before. I don't know what it is. Maybe just my feelings for him, my desire, but it's almost like the stern punishment is a reward instead. A juicy treat of humiliation and pain, and his hand on a part of me that he should never touch.

Whatever it was, it only does me better with the second spank he lands on my rear, and I swear my gasp is tinged with a bit of a moan. But he does it again, and there's no denying it then.

"Now now," he says, stroking his hand over that part of my rear he'd just struck three times! "I think this skirt is making things too easy on you," he muses, and I feel his long digits curl in around the edge of my skirt and slowly hitch it up higher. Higher. Until my pale butt is exposed.

"This is more like it, don't you think?" he asks, leaning over my, his gravelly voice so close to my ear as I feel his hand taunting my cheeks.

Oh my God. I've wanted and dreamed about this for so long. His hands touching my bare, sensitive skin that now buzzes with sensation.

It makes me buck towards him like some mindless animal, wanting to feel his touch so damned bad. Even if it stings, it's still his hand touching me. My dad would kill us if he knew. Oh, and if he could read my thoughts, I'd be killed twice!

"This is so bad," I say, but it comes out like a delicious groan of desire.

"Perfectly suited for a bad girl," he says right back to me without missing a beat, and his strong hand strokes along the curve of my ass, skirting the crack of my cheeks only barely... but he pauses low, and I know he can feel my feminine heat there. It's so strong, my desire too strong.

"Fitting punishment for snooping around like such a bad, bad girl," he says with such devious delight, right before his hand smacks my rear again, but this time it's harder. Or maybe it's just the lack of clothing separating us, but his bare hand hit my cheek and makes me cry out in time with the sharp crack.

I gasp, but he's right. I am a bad girl, and I deserve to be punished. This is just more than I ever could have dreamed of or anticipated. It's more of a forbidden treat than anything, and then I feel like the dirtiest girl alive for thinking that.

But I can't help envisioning his fingers going between my thighs, pressing into my white panties...

Instead I get another, harder, slap across my rear and I cry out louder than ever! He follows it up with another, and my butt is stinging, but then... then he's caressing the red hot flesh so tenderly. Gingerly exploring that smooth skin.

"There there. You're a bad, naughty girl Andrea," he says in that deliciously dark rasp of his, "but you're in good hands. I'm going to take care of you. But not before I mark you and lay claim to this pretty lil' body of yours, starting with this sweet ass," he growls out the last of his words, before smacking me again, then again and then the spanks blur together until...

Until he's cradling me, stroking my stinging flesh again and...

He's doing it.

I can feel him sliding his fingers between my cheeks, over the fabric of my panties. Feeling the fiery warmth and dampness over my pussy.

I almost feel drunk or like this is all a dream, the haziness of the pain dripping away and instead replaced by the purest pleasure I've ever know. Sure, I've touched myself once or twice, but

I've never been touched by a man. Especially not a man twice my age and best friends with my dad!

I can hear his breathing in my ear, deep and husky, tinged with such lust as he rubs me through my panties. He's ravenous for me, I can tell even before he bites my neck then kisses it, making me tilt my head to the side to make room for his hungry mouth. That thin stalk so sensitive to his ravishing mouth, but the feeling of him petting my pussy down below is so distracting.

"Mmm, you're an even badder girl than I thought," he growls, and then I feel his finger hook into my panties, grazing over the raw flesh of my femininity as he peels them away from the source of my wetness. "Damn, your little cunt's so wet from this spanking, Andrea," he says, tugging down my panties, dragging them down my thighs to my knees, then letting them slip further down.

"Does any of this even count on punishment if you were getting off on it like this?" he asks me, bringing his hands back up to cup my slick, naked mound.

I don't have answers for him. The first time a man's ever done anything like this to me, and I'm helpless against my lusts. I never anticipated I would let it go this far, but now I don't want to stop. I need to feel him inside of me, even if it's just his fingers, and I spread my legs slightly.

"I'll do anything you want, Mr. Wood," I moan out truthfully.

"That's right, you will," he growls into my ear, and his hands slip away from me and I feel him pull back. But when I peer over my shoulder, I see him undoing his belt, hear it jangle as he pulls it free, then the buttons of his pants come undone.

"You know all about safe sex, don't you Andrea? Come on, tell me," he says as he pulls his pants down, and hooks his thumbs into the waistband of his boxer-briefs. The tight, black cotton hugging that thick bulge which snaked left.

"Always use a condom, and abstinence is the only safe sex," I recite from my lackluster sex ed classes. But when I'm watching him undress, I know abstinence is not an option.

"That's right," he says just before pulling down his briefs, and letting that thick, long shaft topple out so rigid and huge. That veiny length pulsating with such desire as the purple tip glistened with precum. And then those balls, heavy and big, dangled beneath as he nudges my feet wider, causing me to spread my legs.

"And have you been a good, clean, safe sex girl, hmm?" he asks me, taking hold of my two butt cheeks and prying them apart.

I feel anything but clean, but I understand what he's asking.

So do I lie? Or do I tell him that I'm a virgin?

I lick my lips, not sure of what to do, and then I feel another crack on my bare ass. My skirt is up around my waist, my panties dropped to my maryjane shoes, and I feel so vulnerable and yet... it's good. Really good. I arch my back, digging my palms into the hard wood of his desk.

"Answer the question," he demands sternly, and I know I shouldn't be caught in a lie. Not now.

"I've... abstained."

He goes silent for a moment, and I can tell he's shocked, not sure if he should believe me.

"You're lying," he says, but I can feel his finger exploring along the seam of my slit, and then... probing on in. Parting my labia, he dips his middle finger into my cunny and I can feel myself wrapped about that digit. And I moan.

"Damn, you weren't lying... you're tighter than a stubborn knot," he says with such growling approval before plucking his finger out of me and sizing up the glistening digit. He pops it in his mouth and tastes my honey, giving a deep, throaty 'Mmm'.

"Well then sweetheart, you learned all that safe sex stuff for nothin'," he says, and I feel him hefting his thick cock to guide the tip along my moist slit.

"What?" I murmur, looking over my shoulder at him, watching as he suckles on it. I want him so bad, but I don't want to get pregnant!

He unbuttons his shirt all the way, and as I peer back I get an eyeful of his broad, bare chest. The toned muscles, the hard pecs and ripped abs, and then... his manhood. So big and hard as it presses against my most private of places.

"That's the price for being a bad girl tonight," he says, and slowly he begins to pierce my virginity. That thickness of his sinking in, stretching me wider than I've ever been before, and him groaning with such pleasure as he does it. "Or are you sayin' you don't want me in you?" he growls, taking hold of my hips so tightly.

"I do!" I protest instinctually, and even though I was going to follow it up with a big 'but!' he pushes in and my words die on my tongue. He's so big, and even though I'm wetter than I've ever been, it stings as he takes my virginity, making me into the bad girl he thought me to be.

He moans so lewdly as he pushes on into the hilt, filling me up completely as our debauched sounds of pleasure fill the air. And I can feel him inside me, pulsating, stretching me with each new throb of desire.

"Ohhh fuck yeah," he growls, his fingers sinking into my flesh so tight it almost hurts, but it keeps me anchored and in place to have him grasping my hips and waist like that. "You've got the tightest, sweetest little pussy I've ever been in, sweetheart," he rumbles to me.

He stays there for a few moments, letting me get used to his size, to the fact that there's a man inside me! And then the throbbing pain dulls, and is replaced by something much nicer. He grinds against me, not moving in or out, but with each rotation of his hips his body collides with mine, his hips pressing into my tender ass.

My breasts flatten into the wood as he holds my ass up in the air so that I have to go on tip toes, even in my shoes, and then he begins to pull out.

But he doesn't pull out all the way, and I can feel his thick crown snugly inside me still before he pushes back in, and starts to build up a slow budding tempo. His deep, husky moans filling the air.

"Mmm," he gives a long, deep moan. "I can feel your lil' pussy lips clingin' to me as I slide back... like they don't want me

343

to go," he says, smacking into my ass a little as his pace grows. "This tight lil' pussy of yours needed a nice hard cock so bad, huh? Makes you willin' to be such a naughty girl," he husks, his breathing growing heavier.

I know the risks, I know that what we're doing is so wrong, but he feels so right. Like I'm meant to be here, pinned between him and his desk, with nothing between us. It's even better than I fantasized, and I push my ass into him, wanting him deeper.

"You feel so good," I gasp, shuddering when he fills me completely.

"You feel like heaven, you devilish girl," he growls back at me through his own heady lust, but everything is getting lost in the slap of flesh. The way his cock plunges in deep, fills me up, stretches me wide and makes my toes curl with bliss.

My stinging cheeks are taking a beating from his thrusts, but I can barely feel it as he pumps into me. His heavy balls swing up, smacking my clit before he reaches in under, and those long fingers of his find that sensitive bud themselves.

"Ohhh, you feel so good sweetheart... but now it's time for you to cum on my cock," he says with such an insistence. Like I have no choice in the matter.

But it's not like I could hold back, even if I wanted to. His fingers... Oh God his fingers. It's like every nerve in my body is being caressed all at once, and when he strokes along my soaking pussy, I begin to tremor. I've never felt anything like this, and he rubs a bit harder, more insistent.

I buck forwards, the sensation almost too much! He has me pinned to the desk, though, and there's no real escaping him. Ohh, not that I want to!

"Ah!" I gasp out, and his rough fingertip swirls around my clit. "Ohh!"

And then there's fireworks going off behind my eyelids, and my pussy clenches his dick so hard that he can barely pull out.

But as pleasure explodes within me, I don't think he's trying too hard to pull out. He pumps into me, the gush of my honey flooding around his shaft, then coating his balls as they smack wetly against my body.

His deep, growling moans fill the air with my squeals and cries, and he's pumping me into the desk so hard.

As I lose all control and become a spasming, twitching mess, he takes over. He bends down, ceasing his thrusts long enough to take my leg and twist me around. He lifts me up, puts me down onto my back atop his desk and places my calves against his shoulders.

"That's it," he says, licking his lips as he starts to pump again, reaching his two thick forearms out as he undoes my blouse, one button at a time.

I can't help but knock his pencil holder to the ground, folders under my ass as he holds me in position. I can see his face in the dim light as he opens my blouse to find my red, lacy bra that I had to hide from my dad whenever I needed to wash it.

My breasts heave as he fucks me deeper, so deep that I almost feel like I'm going to black out!

But then he reaches out, grasps my breasts with his two powerful hands, sinks his fingers into the twin mounds. His greedy grasp pulls the bra away, to get at the stiff nipples, to maul and manipulate them as he continues to pump his hips and pound his dick into me.

"You'll be doin' more than just wash my car from here on out, lil' girl," he growls so possessively as I watch his ripped chest ripple with his motions, his abs and pecs glistening with a thin sheen of perspiration.

We're wrapped in each other like a game of twister, but so much better. Though at his promise — or threat? — I shudder again. My stiff nipples are clasped between his fingers and thumbs, and he pinches them hard enough to send a jolt of pain and pleasure through my entire body. My pussy tightens around his cock, and he feels so good, I've long forgotten about my worries of getting knocked up. All I know is that I don't want him to stop yet!

I watch him pound into me, more and more powerfully, all that hard muscle and sinew rippling as he makes me body quiver and quake. He's a beast as he takes me, thrusting so hard and fast now as my pussy is stretched out around him. And all the while he's fondly my breasts, squeezing and manhandling them, teasing my stiff nipples.

"Oh fuck... I'm gonna cum in this tight little cunt of yours," he growls, and reluctantly relinquishes one of my breasts to reach down and tweak my clit again. "Cum with me," he demands.

And his finger on my clit is all it takes for my mind to go numb and forget all about how he definitely should not cum inside me.

Instead... I like the thought. Of making my dad's best friend, my principal, cum in me. It'd be the ultimate rebellion, and I start grinding into him, but I'm already so sensitive. It only takes a second before I gasp for air, and the waves of pleasure come crashing down on me.

I can hear him moan out loudly, and he's grasping my body so tight as he fucks me through my orgasm.

"I am gonna pump you so full of my cum," he growls amid his huffs and moans of pleasure, "I'll take you away and make you my lil' breeding bitch if that's what it takes!" And no sooner than those filthy words were out of his mouth, he was ploughing into me one last time and exploding.

Thick gouts of his virile seed shooting into me as he lets loose such a gravelly, long moan. His hips bucking as he spurts more and more of that creamy load, filling me up to capacity and then some.

"Take it!" he growls, twitching as he blows his load into my raw, unprotected pussy.

My pussy is vibrating against him as jolts of pleasure go through me, and I hear something heavy crash to the ground as I flail desperately against the sexy older man.

When I finally come down from my erotic high, I'm gasping for air, covered in a thin layer of perspiration.

When the last of his cum flows into me, he falls over on top of me, his hard chest crushing atop my breasts as his lips find mine. We're making out, our chests heaving as his tongue invades my mouth and we lay there atop his desk, sweaty and entangled.

Somehow, kissing him like that is even more intimate than having sex, and my arms wrap around him. I'm scared he's going to leave. That after this moment, he'll realize what we've done, and how wrong it all is, and he'll run. For just a few moments longer, I want to savour him in all his masculine glory.

A few weeks have passed, and here I am. Staring down at this pregnancy test, letting it tell me what I already know: I'm pregnant.

I rub a hand over my belly and head on out. Mr. Wood is waiting for me in his car, and I can see him there, smiling my way. I head on over to his Cadillac, and slip into the passenger seat.

Immediately his hand is on my bare thigh, and he's leaning in to kiss me on the neck. But I'm a bit tense.

"What's the matter?" he asks, concerned.

"Mr. Wood... I'm pregnant," I say, hanging my head a little.

He pauses, but then laughs and squeezes me thigh.

"Of course you are babe," he says and nips my earlobe. "That was my intention all along," he says with such devious delight.

"But what'll I do?! I'm too young!" I protest.

"You'll move on in with me baby," he says, rubbing my thigh, letting his hand drift on up between my legs close to my pussy. "And when that belly grows big I'll make it bounce, and keep you forever," he declares possessively.

I glance up at him, biting in on my lower lip. He always knows just what to say to make me feel better, and dad... he'll come to accept it in time. After all, Mr. Wood is his best friend, so who wouldn't want the best for their daughter?

Off Limits: Will Pound

Book Themes: virgin, breeding, age gap, daddy's best friend, exhibitionism
Word Count: 6422

The blazing Hawaiian sunshine gleams across the surface of the pool. My eyes are dazzled by the dancing lights in every chlorine-blue ripple.

Sweat beads down my neck, rolling in a straight streak between my perky breasts.

I let out a long, low sigh as a fragrant breeze rolls across my stretched-out body. I am lying by the pool on a super-comfy and stylish lounge chair, my nubile young body barely concealed by my teeny tiny bikini.

It's a pretty shade of bubblegum pink, which is my go-to favorite hue. It suits my girly-girl style. I usually wear a lot of flouncy summer dresses and floral skirts matched with crop tops. I may be a virgin still, and barely broken eighteen just a few months ago, but that doesn't mean I have to dress like a prude.

I know how much my body has blossomed in the past several

years. I know how perfectly bouncy and plump my breasts look in my little pink string bikini top.

I am fully aware of how round and juicy my ass looks in my thong bikini bottom.

In fact, now that I think about it...

I stretch out my arms and legs languidly, feeling the midday sun warm my smooth, soft body. I turn over from my back to my stomach and rest my head on my arms.

I can feel the eyes of men all around me, from all angles of the pool area. I give my cute butt a little wiggle so they have something to really look at.

I hear a low whistle from across the deck and it makes me smile to myself. I can't deny how good it feels to know they all want me. It's been this way ever since I hit puberty and started getting curves.

Everywhere I go, boys and men look at me like I'm the juiciest steak they've ever been served. I can sense them salivating over me. Lusting for me. Building fantasies around me in their filthy heads. And now that I'm eighteen, I'm on the menu.

After a few minutes of tanning my back and bum, I slowly sit up and reach into my little poolside duffel bag for a bottle of sunscreen. Safety first, you know.

It's time to reapply. But it's also a great opportunity to draw in even more attention. They all watch me squirt out thick white sunscreen into my hands and gradually, sensually massage it into my skin.

I slide my soft palms over my curves, rubbing circles into my breasts and stretching out to apply more to my legs and arms. A stranger comes up to offer to help me lotion up my back, but I sweetly decline. He walks away somewhat defeated.

Sorry, guy.

You're not the one I'm trying to impress.

I shake my hair out of its messy bun and it falls in loose, beachy blonde waves around my shoulders. I comb my fingers through it while I sit on the lounge chair waiting for my sunscreen to soak in.

With my eyes sufficiently hidden behind my pink heart-shaped sunglasses, I'm free to glance around and see who's looking at me. I'm gratified to find that pretty much every red-blooded male in the immediate vicinity is either flat-out staring at me or trying to do that oh-so-obvious half-glance thing guys do. I'm not fooled for a second.

There may be hundreds of people at this resort, but right now, I'm the main attraction.

Once my sunscreen is set, I stand up to my full height of five-foot-three and slowly saunter toward the shallow end of the pool. With every step, my hips sway, my ass jiggles, my tits bounce. My blonde hair ruffles and plays in the soft Hawaiian breeze.

My tongue darts out to wet my full lips as I tilt my shades down and reveal my baby-blue eyes, fringed with long lashes. I poke one toe into the water and goosebumps prickle up on my skin. It's just cool enough to feel really, really good against my sun-warmed skin.

As I make my way down the concrete steps into the cool blue water, I see that the man I care about, the only one whose attention I truly crave, is looking my way. Just like I planned.

I give him a flirtatious smile as I sink into the water. My blonde hair floats around me like the locks of a mermaid as I slowly breaststroke across the pool to the deeper end.

Everywhere I look, I'm surrounded by opulence. This resort is exclusive, reserved only for the rich and beautiful elite who can afford it. There's enough collective wealth just between the pool and the tiki bar to buy a small country. But none of that fazes me. I have eyes only for one man.

The object of my seduction is only a few yards away from the deep end, seated at a table with a fancy white tablecloth. He's wearing aviator shades, but I know he's looking at me. And that tablecloth may hide him from the waist down, but I bet he's hard underneath it all. I bet he's drooling for me. His hands are itching to feel my barely-legal softness under his calloused fingertips. By the time I reach the far edge of the pool, I can see his jaw tightening ever so slightly. His hand on the table is curling into a fist. I push myself up out of the pool, beads of water dripping off my smooth skin as I rise up. I gracefully climb out and back into the sun's heat. Water rolls down my body in rivulets as I toss my damp blonde hair over my shoulder and start sauntering up to the table.

I take my time as I walk. Every step brings me deeper into my own fantasy world. All I can focus on is him, and all else falls away. I feel his eyes burning into my body. I've felt him looking at me for a long time, only then he was still afraid to look. He's known me forever, watched me blossom from a skinny, naive little girl into a curvy, sensual young woman. Still, I can tell he's hesitating, trying to hold back. He's telling himself it's wrong, it's taboo, it's not allowed. I'm off-limits. But doesn't that just turn him on more? It makes me feel tingly between my legs. It makes me want to throw caution to the wind and say fuck the rules.

I can't help but imagine what would happen without that invisible boundary between us?

What if he was rubbing himself under the table? His strong hand slowly stroking his long, hard shaft as his eyes drink in my every soft curve and swell. Because he can't help himself. I picture him reaching up for me as I get close enough to touch, my wet body dripping all over him. But he wouldn't care. He likes me wet.

I can almost feel his hands caressing my sides, following the curve of my hips to slide around and grope my ass. I would lean down with my hands on either armrest and kiss him deeply on the lips. I would taste the faint tang of rum, smell his masculine scent mingling with the floral breeze. And then he would grab me and pull me down into his lap. My legs would sprawl out while his hand dove between them to cup my soaking warm mound. I would whimper and tilt my head back on his shoulder. Let my hand drop to his crotch and rub his thickness through his linen trousers while his fingers slip under the soaked fabric of my bikini. I'm dripping wet all over, but somehow even wetter underneath. I would arch my back and moan, grinding my ass against his hard cock to tease him while he touches me in the place no one has ever touched before. It's everything I've ever wanted. Nothing could ever pull us apart, now that we've finally found our way to each other, to where we've always been meant to be.

All of these sexy, romantic thoughts swarm my mind as I walk up to the table. We both have our shades on, like we're both pretending not to be as enraptured by the other as we really are. My fantasy is just a dream for now, but with the way his powerful body is turning toward me, tensing up, tunnel-focused on me... well, maybe it will come true.

But before I can get close enough to break the barrier between us, we are sorely interrupted by the sudden appearance of a tall, lanky man in a Hawaiian print button-up. He's carrying two oversized tropical drinks with little umbrellas in them and wearing a goofy grin that makes his eyes twinkle brightly. He looks positively delighted by everything going on around him, but he brings a very decidedly unsexy vibe to the table.

Ah, my dad.

"Got your mai-tai right here, Will! That bartender is a hoot and a half. Yours is the one with the pink umbrella, buddy," he says cheerily.

"Thanks, Jim," says the object of my desire, the recipient of my so unfairly-interrupted seduction attempt: William Pound, my dad's business partner.

Dad slides both drinks onto the table, only sloshing a little bit of it in the process. Then he does a double take at me and grins even wider. He gives me two finger guns and makes little pew-pew noises, like I'm a child. Somehow, he fails to realize that I am now an adult, officially as of a few months ago, and he doesn't have to treat me like a baby anymore. Not to mention, he totally foiled my plan to seduce his business partner, and doesn't even have the decency to notice I was doing it. He's that oblivious about my age and maturity level. He can't even fathom that his own little girl might have deep, tingling desires for Will, a man closer to his age than mine. A man who should be more like an uncle to me than a Prince Charming, but you know what they say. The girl can't help it.

"Callie! There's my sweet pea," he croons. "Looks like someone took a dip!"

"Just a little cooldown," I reply.

"Poor thing, you're soaking wet," Dad says, handing me a towel.

The accidental double entendre isn't lost on me, and judging by Will's body language, it isn't lost on him either. I can see now even through the tint in his aviators, his eyes are locked on me. On my body, following every curve like it's the most fascinating story he's ever read. I almost hesitate to wrap the towel around myself and hide away what he wants to look at so badly. But my dad is watching, so I cover up and settle for a pout instead.

"I want a fancy umbrella drink," I sulk.

"Well, you may be eighteen but as far I know the drinking age is still twenty-one here in beautiful Hawaii, sweet pea. But I bet you that nice man behind the bar would make you a virgin daiquiri if you ask politely," he tells me.

Oh, you mean the nice man who's been eye-fucking me from the tiki bar all afternoon? Is what I want to reply, but I bite my tongue. There's no point with Dad, he refuses to see it. I'm at a crossroads: he sees me as a child, but the rest of the world sees a beautiful, enticing young woman in charge of her own sexuality, her own needs. I know Will sees that in me, even if he's trying so hard to fight it.

"Order anything else you want, too, Callie. I hear they have really good calamari here Use the black credit card," he says.

He slides me the credit card with a fond wink, then turns back to Will and immediately starts talking business. My shoulders slump a little. As usual, I'm dismissed with a little payout. Dad has been using money and gifts in place of attention for years. He dotes on me and makes sure I have everything I want-- as long as he gets to pretend I'm still his little girl. I'm annoyed that he interrupted my moment with Will, but there's no salvaging it now. They're totally engrossed in their business tactical discussion.

I sigh and walk away toward the bar, my father's limitless credit card in hand. If I can't have the attention of the one I want, I guess I can settle for idle amusement with the guys at the tiki bar. There's a group of them, all probably in their early to mid-twenties. For some girls my age, this is the perfect group. Chiseled young guys with all their bravado and raging hormones and their constant elbowing to be top dog. Fighting with each other to get to me first. They all watch me walk up. They don't even hide it. When you're young and rich like the clientele here, you can get away with anything.

I toss them a charitable smile as I sidle up to the bar counter. They all crowd around me, vying for my attention. Compliments, pick-up lines, icebreakers; they will try anything to make me look their way. The bartender abandons his conversation with another patron mid-sentence to slide over to me with a big grin on his face.

"Aloha, beautiful. What can I do you for?" he asks smugly.

"Just a sparkling water," I tell him.

"I can buy you something stronger," offers one of my admirers.

Another one pitches in, "I can buy you an island."

I consider half-heartedly playing along with them for a while, just toying with them until I get bored and move on. But I don't want to waste my time or theirs. I know none of them can give me what I need. I don't want some immature guy my own age who won't know how to treat me right. I want an older man, someone wiser and stronger and in control. Someone who can take care of me and teach me what it means to be a woman.

Specifically, I want William.

He's probably only about ten years younger than my father. The two of them have been friends and business partners in the elite yachting industry for a long time, ever since I was a kid. My dad is the showman, the salesman. He's the guy who will talk the client's ear off with soupy descriptions and charisma. Will is behind the scenes, reading the legalese, following the fine print. He's the money guy, the quiet contemplator. My dad may be the face of the business, but Will is the powerhouse.

It's always just been my dad and me. Everyone in the business knows me as Jim's spoiled little princess, his beautiful pride and joy. His associates are always calling me "cute" and asking what grade I'm in now. I hear Dad on the phone with them, and to hear him talk, I might as well have just graduated kindergarten instead of high school. As if I'm not an adult now, with adult needs that my father could never wrap his head around. I'm still a virgin, because I've been saving myself for the right guy. Only I've had the guy picked out for a while now.

Will. There is no other for me. He's trustworthy, he's kind, and he is always in control. He knows so much about the world. He's good with his hands. He's brilliant. And then he dares to be drop dead gorgeous on top of all that? No wonder I'm obsessed with him.

I abandon the tiki bar, to my suitors' dismay, and walk back to give my dad his card. As I walk up, I can tell that Will is doing his best not to stare at me. I wish I could just drop my towel and show him what he's missing. What he could so easily have if he just reached out and took it.

"I'm heading to the spa," I tell them. "Thanks for the drink, Daddy."

"Have fun, Callie. And don't mention it!" he says as I give him a peck on the cheek. "Oh, and don't forget to meet us for our dinner reservation tonight."

"Eight o'clock. I'll be there. See ya," I chirp.

"See you tonight, Callie," Will says.

His deep, rumbling voice is enough to get me all slick between my thighs again. I bite my lip, wishing I could stay. But I just wave goodbye and flounce off to the spa. God knows I need this massage anyway. As I walk through the luxurious hotel, I barely notice the gorgeous tropical surroundings, the elegant architecture, the stylish decor. As always, I turn lots of heads. People stop what they're doing to look at me. Mostly men, but sometimes women, too. My towel does little to conceal my luscious curves, and it barely reaches my mid-thigh. But it's not their attention I want. I need Will.

Even when I lie down for my massage, I can almost imagine it's Will rubbing my sore shoulders and back instead of the middle-aged female masseuse. What if it were his fingertips circling my tight spots? Stroking my skin, touching me with healing warmth.

By the time the massage ends, I'm in a haze thinking about Will. Not ready to go back to the hotel room yet, I head into the sauna and sit down in the comfortable heat. I look around. No one else is here. The sauna is totally empty. Feeling emboldened, I strip off my towel, then my bathing suit. I sit in the steam with my muscles all loosened up, my body relaxing as I stretch out. I let my hands graze down my ample chest, my taut stomach, my soft thighs. I imagine Will here, kneeling between my legs as I sit on the wooden bench. He would spread my thighs apart and breathe me in. I would run my fingers through his thick dark hair while he devours my pussy. I imagine his tongue sliding up and down along my wet slit.

My heart is pounding as I drop my hand down to touch myself. I'm alone now, but someone could walk in and catch me at any moment. I rub my clit and pretend that Will's tongue is circling that tight little bundle of pleasure. I grope my breasts, tweaking my nipples and playing with them like William would. I can almost feel his enormous hands caressing me all over while his tongue flicks around my clit.

"Mmmhn," I moan. "Will."

I pick up speed, slicking up my fingers with my dewy flower as my body tightens up. The pleasure inside me mounts higher and higher. I see him so clearly kneeling before me. I imagine his deep voice whispering my name, moaning little vibrations through my aching cunny as he eats me out.

"Ohh, Will!" I squeak.

I shudder as a much-needed orgasm passes through my body. I tremble through the waves of bliss until I can hear people approaching. I hastily wrap my towel around myself again in time for them to come into the sauna. But I pay them no attention. I've decided that nothing is going to stop me from getting what I want. It's time to pump this seduction into overdrive.

Will is the only man who can give me what I need, and I'm going to get it.

I shower off in my hotel room, which adjoins Dad's master suite, and then I get ready for dinner. I put on in a flirty beach dress and strappy sandals. I apply just a touch of glowy makeup to play up my soft features, and off I go to the fancy hotel restaurant for my dinner date with Will... and my dad.

As soon as I walk up to the table, I can see the change in Will's demeanor. His hulking, powerful body stiffens up when I sit down beside him. Our legs are almost touching. I can feel his heat. I can smell his masculine musk. I wriggle a little closer, just to tease him. I want him so hot, so worked up he can't resist me.

Will looks at me sideways, just a glance, but a powerful one. My eyes lock with his and something electric passes between us. A connection. An understanding. Meanwhile, my oblivious dad just beams at me happily and continues chattering on about our big day tomorrow.

"Callie! There's my girl," he greets. "So anyway, picture this: crystal turquoise water, bright Hawaiian sun glittering on the waves. Our client, Mr. Bixby, is looking for a true sailor's experience but without the, you know, dirt and grime of being a sailor."

With my heart pounding, I leap into the next step of my seduction plan. Under the table, while Dad is still talking, I nudge Will's foot with mine. I rest my hand on Will's thigh. I feel him tighten up, but he doesn't make a move or sound as I move my hand closer to his crotch.

"We can give him the glamor without the grime," Will answers in his deliciously deep, gruff voice. I can sense an edge there. Like he's trying to hold something back.

It doesn't take more than a simple touch to figure out what it is. I bite my lip with delight as I feel his cock straining through his trousers. He's hard as a rock. He twinges under my fingers and he shivers when I begin lightly stroking him over his pants. His voice becomes more strained as the conversation goes on and I rub his glorious shaft up and down. Will does a remarkable job of hiding his arousal, but he can't hide it from me. Not when I can feel it. Yet, he's still in control, despite my teasing. At any moment, he could stop me. He could order me to stop and I would instantly fall into submission to him. But it's not until Dad goes to the bathroom while we're waiting for the check that Will finally breaks composure.

He turns to me and grabs my forearm to stop me from rubbing his cock. Our eyes lock and he leans in close. His grip on my arm demonstrates his strength and his restraint in equal measure as he whispers fiercely, "You're crossing a line here, Callie."

My heart is racing. I murmur back, "You want me. I see it when you look at me."

"Not in front of your father," Will retorts.

"Then let's be alone," I suggest.

"You don't know what you're asking for," he growls.

"Yes, I do," I insist.

I take his hand and place it on my lap. I arch up into his palm, pressing my mound against his hand. He inhales sharply, and for a second it looks like he's going to tear my clothes off with his teeth. Then he rips his hand away and glances toward the bathroom.

"Shit. He's coming back," he grunts. "We need to talk. Alone. I'll come to you."

After dinner, we part ways. I go upstairs with Dad to our adjoining rooms. After a little while, he gets in the shower. At almost exactly that moment, there's a soft knock at my door. I rush to answer it, and before I can say a word, Will comes barging in.

He grabs my face with both hands and kisses me hard on the lips. I'm tingling all over. I'm speechless as he spins me around and pins me to the wall. He shoves my thighs apart and hikes up my dress to reveal my bare cunny. Will shoots me an almost anguished look.

"You didn't wear panties to dinner?" he murmurs.

I open my mouth to reply, but he claps a hand over my lips and shakes his head.

"No. Not a word. You just listen," he hisses.

He keeps his hand over my mouth while the other hand strokes my slick pussy. I whimper and moan as his fingertips circle my sensitive clit.

"You want to break the rules, hmm? You want to play like a

big girl? You're done messing around with boys, huh?" Will snarls in my ear.

"Mmhm," I mumble.

"Sweet little Callie wants a big cock inside her tight little virgin pussy," he whispers roughly. "She needs a real man to make her come."

"Nnngh," I whimper.

Waves of pleasure roll through my body. I push into his hand. His fingertips stroke an endless pattern of figure eights on my clit. I tense up and he moves faster.

"That's right, princess. Come for me," he commands softly.

He has to brace me against the wall to keep me from collapsing when the most intense orgasm of my life thus far rips through my petite frame. My legs shake, my heart races, and I see fireworks bursting behind my eyes. Pleasure unlike anything I've ever known radiates from my aching clit throughout every cell. I'm floating, weightless.

We hear the shower cut off. We could be caught any second.

Will releases me and steps back. He lifts his fingers to his lips and licks off my sweet honey. I'm still dazed as he turns to leave, with the parting words, "See you tomorrow. Be good."

The next afternoon, I'm standing on the top deck of a massive, glorious yacht out on the Hawaiian waves. It's nothing but blue seas and blue skies for as far as the eye can see. Dolphins dance in the distance. Seabirds call overhead. There's a sweet balmy breeze whipping around my flowy dress and carrying my hair in floaty blonde locks. I look back to see my father wining and dining the wealthy older client, Mr. Bixby. Taking the yacht out for a spin to show off its amenities and strengths in real time is my dad's signature move.

It's a sleek, elaborate yacht with two full bedrooms, a chef's kitchen, dining room, two living spaces, a gym, a small pool, and many other details that make it a floating paradise. Currently, we have just a few staff members onboard, but it has space for a much larger crew and company. Will and I have been more or less trailing behind the little tour of the lower deck, but there's a buzzing intensity between us that cannot be broken. Whether we're on opposite ends of the boat or standing right beside each other, it feels the same. That gnawing, desperate need to be closer, to rip off any barriers between us and let temptation take control.

Meanwhile, Dad and Mr. Bixby are already hitting it off, as expected.

"As you can see, the master bedroom down here is hardly less than you'd get at the resort," Dad showboats enthusiastically.

"It's downright opulent, Jim. I love it!" Mr. Bixby declares.

"Well, then, let's break out the cigars! You know I always keep a stash of your favorite on the top deck," Dad says with a wink.

He leads Mr. Bixby back down the hall and up the stairs, leaving me alone with Will. We turn to look at each other as their voices fade out to silence. Finally, the tension we've been holding all afternoon snaps.

We collide in a mess of limbs and desperate kisses, moving slowly backward toward the king-size bed. Will sits on the edge and I climb into his lap to straddle him. As the yacht gently sways on the waves, I rock against him. Our bodies move in slow rolls, grinding as close as we can with the barrier of thin fabric between us. Will gently bites my lower lip and I moan. His hands feel me up greedily. He caresses my back, my narrow waist, my soft breasts. My nipples are perky and tingly against his palms, and when he starts rolling them between his fingers I get all slick between the thighs. Will's tongue probes into my mouth and I let him eagerly.

His cock strains hard underneath me and I ache to be closer. I rut into him with my pussy soaking through my lacy panties. I'm leaving a mark on his pants, I'm sure. That could get us caught. The idea thrills me to my core. Is that wrong? Is all of this wrong?

It doesn't matter. I couldn't stop now even if I wanted to, and I don't. I know what I want, actually. I shimmy back and stand up for a moment, looking into Will's eyes. I drop down to my knees and peer up at him innocently. He gives a quick glance toward the open doorway, then back to me. Without a word, he unzips his pants and pulls down his boxers. I salivate at the sight of his massive cock hard and ready for me.

Will cups the back of my head as he guides me to his cock. I flick my tongue out to taste the salty pre-come at the tip. He sighs when I take the engorged head into my mouth. I play around with my tongue while I use my hand to stroke his shaft. Will strokes my hair to coax me closer. I take him even deeper into my mouth until he's pushing into the back of my throat. I gag a little around the thickness of his shaft, but I recover quickly. He slides out, then pushes my head down again.

This time, I'm better prepared. I loosen up my throat, revel in the weight and girth of his cock rather than fear it. When he tickles my throat, I get all tingly deep inside my cunny. I need more. I moan around his cock as I bob up and down. I slide my tongue along the underside as he slowly fucks my mouth harder and with less restraint. His hand twists in my hair while he pumps his hips. I whimper and drip on the carpet as his cock spears down my throat again and again. Saliva trickles down my chin. He moves faster, murmuring half-nonsense to me.

"That's so good, Callie. Mhm. Take it all-- just like that," he hisses.

With a few more erratic thrusts, he seizes up and pulls back. His cock pops out of my mouth and explodes thick come all over my lips and cheek. I lick up what I can and hastily wipe off the rest with a nearby throw blanket as we hear voices approaching again. Will zips himself up and we're both standing a cool few feet apart by the time Dad and Mr. Bixby come back in, clutching a bottle of champagne.

"There you two are," Dad beams. "Come up top to celebrate!"

"Celebrate?" Will prompts.

"You've made the sale, boys," Mr. Bixby declares.

"We're headed back to shore just in time for dinner," Dad adds as we head up to the top deck. He starts pouring glasses of champagne for the three of them.

Will makes some excuse to get out of dinner tonight, but Dad is so wrapped up in his new best friend he hardly notices anyway. Will slips me a sip of champagne and leans in to whisper in my ear, "Meet me at the steps down to the beach. We'll talk."

A couple hours later, I'm standing where the concrete steps meet the sand. The sun is sloping over the horizon, streaking the sky with purple, pink, and gold. Wind ruffles my hair as I look out over the water. I hear the most beautiful sound. A deep, familiar voice saying my name so softly it may as well be the breaking of a wave downshore.

"Callie."

I turn around and I'm immediately swept into William's arms. He hugs me tightly and kisses the top of my head. He slides his hand down my arm to my hand, interlacing his fingers with mine. With the other hand he lifts a bottle of wine. There's a blanket draped over his arm.

"Let's walk," he commands gently.

"I'll follow you anywhere," I reply. And I mean it.

We take our time walking down the beach. The dark, vaguely volcanic sand crunches under our footsteps. There are a few other groups out on the beach, but the crowds have disappeared. The sun is setting and nightlife beckons most of them to land. But Will and I walk farther out, and talk the whole way. We talk about the yacht, the island, my dad, the past, the future... everything. No one else is around, we've walked so far. We stop and lay out the blanket in the sand as the sun makes it final display across the horizon.

"You're too young for me," Will says. "That's what people will say."

He takes a sip of the bottle and hands it to me.

I shrug and tip it back. "I don't care what people say. I'm old enough to know what I want. I've had enough of guys my age, but it's not just that I want an older man. I want *you*, Will. Just you," I emphasize.

He leans over to cup my face, peering into my eyes. "I can give you everything."

"I can take it," I whisper back.

There's a pause. He gazes at me, sizing me up. And then he pounces.

Will kisses me hard, his hands stripping off my dress, then his shirt, his pants. We cling to each other, rolling on the blanket as he kisses me. His hands rove up and down my body. He pins me down and kisses his way down my neck to my bare chest. He flicks his tongue over my nipples while his fingers stroke between my thighs.

I sigh and rock against his hand in a silent plea for more. He lines up the head of his cock at my slick opening. I wrap my legs around his waist to lock him there as we stare into each other's eyes. He circles my tight hole with the swollen head of his massive cock, waiting to spear me open. I give him a little nod and he presses in. I toss my head back and he kissing biting bruises into my exposed neck while his cock pushes inside my tight, aching cunny.

I feel an explosion of pleasure tinged with a little dose of pain as he splits into me where nothing has ever touched. I feel my pussy clenching around him as he works me open. I bloom for him like a flower, both of us moaning and clutching at one another in the disappearing light. His cock sheathes entirely inside of me, brushing into a soft place within me that feels like a kiss of heaven. He rears back and pushes into me harder this time.

I cry out. Tears burn in my eyes. Will kisses them away as he plunges harder and deeper into my virgin cunny. With every stroke, I feel myself gushing wetter and wetter. It becomes less painful, more blissful. Until finally, I'm shuddering through a climax. My pussy convulses around his thickness as Will swallows back my every sigh and whimper.

"Oh, Callie. Good girl. That's so good," he coos.

"Nnngh, Will!" I squeal as he pounds me harder.

"How does a real man feel inside your little pussy?" he murmurs in my ear.

"So--so good," I pant.

"You want me to pump you full of my seed, princess?" Will growls.

"Oh god, yes!" I whimper. "Please!"

He grabs my legs and hikes them up over his shoulders, giving him an even tighter angle. He fucks me hard and fast, pummeling my g-spot with his glorious cock. I cry out in absolute ecstasy as he makes me a woman. I know who I belong to, and I know who I will always belong to. Especially once he gives me his greatest gift. I've never wanted anything the way I want this.

I clench around him, coaxing him to come inside me. Begging him with my little sighs, my pleading gaze, my pouting lips.

"I want it," I whimper. "Please give it to me."

"You're mine. All mine," he growls.

"Forever. I was always yours," I promise him breathlessly.

"That's right. My sweet Callie," Will grunts. "Oh, fuck. Stay right there."

He grabs my thighs and holds me in place while he pounds my pussy mercilessly. I feel myself clench and shiver through another climax as he hits that delicious spot inside me again and again. He hurtles closer to the edge with every hammering stroke. He stares into my eyes, deep passion burning between us as he tenses up. His cock explodes with hot, precious seed deep inside me. I squeeze with every ounce of strength I have to keep it in as he slowly withdraws.

Will caresses me and whispers soft comforts to me as we come down together. The sun has sunken below the horizon now, and the only light comes from our phones and the distant fuzzy light of the resort. We hold each other in the near-darkness for a while, just reveling in the moment. I feel his come leaking out of my cunny onto the blanket as he holds me close.

"So what's next? Do we sail into the sunset together?" I tease gently.

He laughs, a deep, wonderful sound. Will strokes my messy hair.

"We can do anything you want, Callie. You're mine, and I will do everything in my power to keep you happy. Keep you safe," he promises. He kisses me softly.

"Should we head back?" I ask.

He nods. "Whenever you're ready, princess."

Together, we slowly make our way back down the shore. Hand in hand, we talk about all the adventures we're going to have together. The places we'll see. The love that will only grow bigger and brighter over time. We were meant to be together. I've known it for so long. And before long, I'll start to show, and our secret will be out. I can't wait to proudly tell the world all about my love.

As for my dad, he'll come around. After all, who better to trust with his daughter?

His Fertile Groupie

Book Themes: Breeding, creampie, simultaneous orgasms, and a very horny groupie with a dominant jerk.
Word Count: 5320

Ally couldn't believe her luck. After months of following *The Buzz* around on tour, dreaming of the sexy-as-sin singer, he'd finally noticed her. But more than that, he'd invited her to a special gig, on a private island in the Caribbean.

Only eighteen, she thought she'd experienced all of the pain in the world, and she'd found purpose in their music. But more than that, she spent her nights lusting about their front man. Flynt Slader.

That gorgeous man with the kohl rimmed eyes and the soul that spoke to her. His piercing blue gaze stared into the deepest parts of her. She swore all of his lyrics were written about her life, and she knew they could heal one another's broken hearts.

She'd just been getting out of a bad relationship when she

first heard The Buzz come on the radio, with their hit song, and she listened to it on repeat.

She'd even dropped out of college to follow him around on tour. Every night she styled her bottle-blonde hair into a wild mess of curls and she hoped her dark eyes and full lips and tiny bra tops would entice him. Finally, one night, it did, and she was invited backstage.

That was when he invited her to his private concert, on an island in the tropical Caribbean. He'd told her it was a fundraiser, just a small show for a select few very special fans.

He even shelled out for a private jet for her.

But when she stepped off the luxurious jet, dressed in her nicest and sluttiest black dress with her suitcase in hand, she wasn't expecting what she saw as she was driven towards her hotel.

Everything seemed so rustic and quaint, as if she'd gone back in time a hundred years. Even the fine manor that she pulled up in front of, with its colonial styling and large support beams out front, reminded her more of an old historical museum rather than the lavish hotel of the rich and famous.

Yet there he was, Flynt Slade, sat outside with his guitar in his lap, strumming idly as he rocked back and forth on the porch swing.

She couldn't believe her eyes. He was dressed better than he did for his shows, in a nice pair of jeans and a black vest atop a white linen button down. He looked up as she arrived, sweeping his hand through his black hair, making it spike up a bit more.

"Hey, Ally," he said, and she nearly fainted that he'd remembered her name. She inconspicuously pushed up her cleavage, though her push up bra did most of the work. She stepped towards him, her long, slender legs moving gracefully in her high heels.

She was almost over joyed, too excited to exist, and she couldn't help that she went to him faster than she should have, acting like a little girl getting a puppy.

"Oh my God," she said, looking up over the old building. "Is this really where I'm staying?"

"Yeah that's right," he said with a smile her way, that uneven expression so charming on his face. He looked like such a bad boy in every way. So handsome and dashing, a devious looking black goatee, and looks that could kill. Even if he wasn't a musician, he could probably get away with murder on that devilish smile alone.

"We both are," he remarked, strumming upon that guitar idly, producing such a hypnotic melody as he lowered his dark-rimmed eyes down to the instrument.

"Oh my *God*," she repeated, this time louder and with more emphasis. Every bit of control she had was quickly slipping away as she closed the distance between them. She smelled of vanilla up close, her cleavage absolutely scandalous as she stared at him.

"I can't even believe it," she added on with a full scale blush, her tanned skin turning pink beneath her cheeks.

He looked back up at her, though not without stopping at her luscious breasts to stare a while.

"I like to come here to relax, get myself back together after a tour," he said simply, in that dark voice of his that produced such beautiful lyrical sounds. "And a man can't be expected to relax with a fine piece of ass around, now can he?" he remarked bluntly, looking back to his instrument and trying a few more chords.

Ally was such a smitten fan girl around him, so excited that he was checking her out that she barely comprehended his words. When they finally sank in, though, she blushed towards the ground, taking a step backwards and towards the house.

"Oh, yea, totally! I'm so sorry," she said, her luggage resting against her firm leg. "Totally didn't mean to interrupt your music, it's just, I'm your biggest fan and had to, like, thank you for getting me this spot!"

He didn't seem to pay her much mind, just playing some beautiful notes, practicing little pieces of what she no doubt thought would eventually become new masterpieces of his. Until finally he looked back at her in that scandalous outfit.

"Just leave your things out here," he instructed her. "Your place is upstairs, right next to the big one. Mine. You can go up

there, freshen up. Left a few treats in there for you, to help get
you in the spirits before this evening," he stated bluntly, though
an offering of anything from him was something she couldn't
possibly refuse.

Immediately she set down her luggage, backing towards the
door another foot or so.

"Oh my God," she repeated, breathlessly. Right next to his?
There was no restraining the thrill that gave her, blue eyes
widening with such excitement!

"Okay! This evening, right, of course!" she said, though she
had little idea what was in store for her. What plans he truly had
for his willingly little groupie. But she could dream.

"I'll see you tonight, then!" She took another step back
inwards, her breathing so quick before she turned and quickly
moved towards the stairs.

He didn't say a word more, just peered back over his shoulder
and watched her hurry on up the large, curving stairs through the
manor. She saw no other people there yet, but she understood a
true artist like Flynt needed his peace.

When she arrived upstairs, there was no mistaking the place
he meant. There at the center of the upstairs hall was a set of
double doors, old and exquisite, leading the way to what must
have been his room. Then, right next to it a small, single door. It
was unlocked, and she went right in.

Inside, the old colonial style room was small compared to
what his must've been, but lavish and beautiful. An adjoining
bathroom with a large tub awaited her, and there to her right... a
locked door that could only have led directly into his room.

In all her excitement about that, she almost didn't notice the
silver tray next to the bathroom. There, a decanter with some
fluid awaited her, right next to a fancy gold tin. Opening it up she
found inside some pills, and knew immediately they had to be
what he meant below.

She looked at them curiously, fingers roaming over them
before she went to the bathtub and turned it on, letting the hot
steam begin to fill the air.

370

It had been a long flight and she stripped down, looking at herself in the full length mirror next to the bath. Her breasts were large and capped with tight pink nipples, her stomach flat and her ass firm. She was proud of her body and smiled at it before she pulled her hair up into a bun and stepped into the steaming water.

She let it wash over her, breasts disappearing beneath the surface as she kept her hands dry.

With those, she reached towards the pills and the water. She poured herself a glass, the cool drink contrasting against the hot steam, and she held it in her mouth as she popped a pill between her lips and swallowed.

It was risky not knowing what the pill was, how she'd react, but it was thrilling at the same time. A way of learning what type of high Flynt liked.

Little did she know, though, that it wasn't that type of pill at all.

As she bathed she swore she heard someone enter into her room, and assumed it was the help with her bags as to be expected. But by the time she was done and got out of the tub, she looked into her bedroom only to see her clothing gone and an outfit laid out for her on the bed.

Her bags were nowhere in sight, and a peek into the drawers showed nothing of her own.

She assumed it was all part of Flynt's plans, and went to the clothes he'd laid out for her.

Outfit was perhaps being a bit generous, as it was a see-through white dress, a pair of matching high heels, and nothing else more but gold chains. A waist sized one, a neck sized one and four others that looked ankle or wrist sized.

She looked them over curiously, uncertain of what to make of it.

She didn't yet feel any high from the drugs, though the bath had relaxed her and she felt fresh and clean. She'd shaved just before she left, and used the lotion provided so that she was soft as anything.

Even though she was accustomed to dressing sluttily the

clothes provided for her made her blush, and she drew her lower lip into her mouth.

Yet there weren't any other options, and so she pulled on the dress, amazed that her nipples were so visible from beneath it.

There was no way she could go out looking like that, especially without a bra. It felt so scandalous, the way her breasts swayed as she moved.

As the minutes ticked on and the sun began to set, though, she knew she didn't have the luxury of time, and went towards that door that led to his room. Perhaps if she could just ask for her things...

She knocked twice, listening to see if she could hear anything from within.

It was locked to her though and she couldn't hear anything from the other side. For that matter the door to the hall was also locked, and though that should've made her panic she merely reasoned it had to have been for her own security. Right?

She kept herself calm, and decided to take it easy, enjoy the tropical air by the balcony. She wasn't sure how long she sat there before the sound of music came wafting by her, sounding like it was coming from Flynt's room next door, out the open balcony door next to hers.

She went back to the door that joined their rooms, and though her first inclination was to knock, she didn't want to interrupt him in the middle of his performing.

So instead, she gently turned the knob to test it, and surprisingly found it unlocked.

When she opened it up, she saw his massive, spacious room, a giant four-poster bed big enough to fit a family, and then him... sat down by the window.

His vest was gone then, just the shirt on, left wide open, showing his hard, well-toned abs and pecs beneath as he played the guitar. And he looked utterly wrapped up in what he was doing, the random pieces of music from before slowly coalescing into something nearer to a song.

She leaned against the door, feeling quite the voyeur as she watched. She lost track of how long he played as she stood there in nothing more than her translucent dress, the rest of her outfit still resting upon her bed.

The music, as always, spoke to her soul. It touched her in such a deep and meaningful way, and she slumped down a little, closing her eyes as she listened.

At last he stopped and put the guitar aside, casting his gaze her way as he if he knew she'd been watching all that time. His blue eyes ran up and down her figure, able to see her areolas through that white, slinky dress.

"Where's the rest of it?" he asked curtly, his voice rough and impatient.

She started as he spoke, straightening up and glancing behind her to the door she'd just come through.

"Oh, I'm sorry!" she said nervously. "It's just... my clothes? Where are they?" She didn't know why she was so nervous. She'd hoped to be able to fuck him for so long, but dressing in such revealing clothing, clothing that wasn't hers, it made her feel more uncertain.

"I gave you better clothes," he stated bluntly. "Why the fuck would you want the other stuff back?" He sounded impatient with her, and got up from his seat, going over to one of the stands and pouring himself up a drink into a tumbler. He took a sip then looked her over, "You tellin' me you came all the fuckin' way out here just to get hung up about some stupid shit you brought with you?"

He was so crass, so rude, but damn he looked good. His hard body on such display, those tight jeans hugging his firm thighs, his round package, dipping low to show the dark hairs that pointed towards his manhood.

She caught herself staring as she took a step back, towards her room. She felt like such an idiot. A confused little girl, and not the badass sex bomb she pretended to be.

"Oh God, I'm so sorry. I didn't mean to offend you," she said as she went back into her room fully, reaching for one of the gold chains and wrapping the long strand about her waist.

She then repeated it along her limbs, her throat, before stepping into the heels. Though she couldn't stop blushing, feeling so stupid in front of her crush.

When she came back into the room she found him pouring another drink. He cast a look her way, noting the gold chains back upon her.

"That's better," he stated a bit gruffly, leaning his tight, round ass back against the dresser behind him and sliding a hand down over his rocky abs. "Did you take the pill I left you at least?" he asked, and then very unceremoniously undid the top button of his jeans. She couldn't see anything but for the way he slid his fingers down into the gap so lewdly.

It distracted her from his question for a second and she had to force her mind free of thoughts of him unzipping his pants further. At what he'd look like. Smell like. Taste like.

She licked over her lips and forced her eyes away as she finally nodded.

"Yea, but, like, it hasn't kicked in yet," she said confidently. "I took it before my bath."

"It's not that kinda pill," he said to her downing some more of his rum before he jerked his head in a 'come here' gesture. "Take 'em twice a day while you're here, got it?" He instructed as he looked her up and down, "Unless you want me to bring in some other fan who's willing to have some real fun."

"Real fun?" she asked, tilting her head to the side as she walked towards him. "What's it, like... vitamins?" A teasing grin warped her lips as she bit down on the corner of them seductively.

"Somethin' like that," he said, sizing her up with such casual interest as she got up close to him. "They're good for a woman like you," he said of the younger woman, pulling his hand from his pants and casually reaching out to lightly squeeze her breast through her top, and sink his thumb into that fleshy mound.

She couldn't help how broad her smile was, how thrilled she was at his touch. Sure she'd understood all the signs, of her being put in a room next to his, of being forced to dress in such revealing clothes, of being so controlled by the domineering rock star.

Feeling his hand on her, though, was completely different.

"You're not on the pill are you?" he asked, so bluntly. "IUD? Anythin' like that?"

He'd asked her that stuff before he invited her along, and she'd answered him then, but she figured he was being safe.

She shook her head no. She had problems with those types of birth control and always relied on condoms to keep her safe.

"Good," he said simply, rolling his thumb over her growing nipple, teasing that stiff little nub through the thin, see-through fabric of her white dress. "Can't stand fuckin' broads with that stuff," he said, finishing his drink and laying the tumbler down on the stand beside him.

Then, her rockstar crush did such a lewd thing, and he reached his free hand down, popping open another button, then another, tugging down his pants to free that thick, long cock of his. She could see immediately that it wasn't even fully hard yet, but it was immense. Bigger than any she'd ever seen, and he was exposing it to her right before her eyes. Even the two heavy cum-laden balls beneath.

"On your knees and suck it," he commanded her.

She wasn't expecting it to happen like that. She didn't know what she *did* expect to happen, but not that.

The God she'd worshipped for so long, the man she thought understood her soul, commanding her so forcefully.

And yet stranger still was how obedient she was about it. She'd lusted for him for so long that she couldn't resist dropping down, staring right at his cock with such a curious hunger. Her friends would never believe her!

Her mouth opened as her hand gripped the base of his thickening shaft, holding him tight in her fingers. Her tongue poked out, tasting his masculine musk with such relish. Her cunny was throbbing so hard as she went down the length of his shaft, suckling him so eagerly.

Flynt reached out and put his hand upon her head, sinking his digits in through her hair as he began to forcibly guide her actions. His dick was so big, and as it rested along her tongue she could feel it swelling up, thicker, thicker. It soon became hard for her to fit it in her mouth! It strained her jaw just to keep going, but that forceful hand in her hair made sure she continued.

"That's it," he said in a low tone of voice, the husky sound of pleasure on his tongue as he spoke to her. "I didn't fly you all this way for nothin' after all," he said, the tip of his cock probing her throat as he urged her on.

One look up showed his eyes struggling to stay open as she worked that thick cock of his, his chiselled abs and pecs tensed as his chest rose and fell.

She'd never been with a man so huge, and as her airways were temporarily blocked, she gripped his thigh tight, her other hand wrapping around his cock more fully. It gave her a bit more leeway so she wasn't taking him down her throat.

And yet the idea of it made her throb excitedly, and she wriggled on the floor.

A soft moan went over his cock, her pleasured sound so deep that it vibrated his flesh, her tongue working along his veins so intently.

She worked her mouth over his dick so diligently, throwing all her excited enthusiasm into making him moan and twitch with pleasure. He still grasped her head and hair, but finally he groaned and yanked her off his long, hard cock.

"Fuck!" He cursed loudly, "Nearly made me cum, bitch. Careful what you're fuckin' doing." It was confusing to see him so upset at her nearly doing exactly what she thought was her duty, but he looked down at her crossly. "Here," he said, shoving her face in under the shaft to his two large, heavy balls. "Suck these for now."

He was so much crasser than she'd expected and she was delighted by it. As though he had ignited a fire in her loins, and so she went to his sac and suckled it in. His heavy cock rest across her face, and she was once more surprised by its length and heft.

But she turned all that attention she'd paid his cock to his balls, lapping them up so hungrily.

The masculine taste of his loins was so intensely unique; he was all man and as that thick, meaty shaft rested over her face, she swore she felt a trill of excitement course through her. It throbbed, spurted its thick precum that she'd only moments before tasted upon her tongue, but now ran down his length and onto her face.

His girth was so hot, and pulsating with desire as she suckled and licked his two heavy balls, struggling to fit them into her mouth one at a time without grazing them with her teeth.

"That's it," he husked, hand still on her head as he watched her slather his sac with her tongue and saliva. "You're not the brightest girl, but you catch on eventually," he instructed. "I don't want you spillin' any of that seed in those balls until I'm good and ready to give it to you."

His words did a dangerous thing to her, that thinly veiled threat, the questions about birth control, all swirling about in her mind.

And yet she wanted it. So badly did she want it, and she pressed her face more firmly into his sac, her tongue running across his balls so eagerly, dragging her tongue along his flesh.

A low hum went across his flesh as she squirmed, the throbbing in her loins almost too much to ignore.

He shuddered, letting his head arch back as he released a low, lewd moan, all that chiselled, hard flesh of his on display as she slathered over his balls. When his dick pulsed and spurted another jet of precum down its length he pulled her off his balls once more and looked down at her. His gaze was hard.

"Go stand up on the balcony, bend over the railing," he instructed her, tugging her hair to guide her in the direction, though it made her teeter.

Her mind was spinning. She couldn't believe that he was so into her, his hard behaviour only making her want to please him more. She walked as quickly as she could towards the balcony, her arms going to the railing as she leaned over, flushing as the skirt of her dress rolled up over her hips and exposed her fleshy ass.

Her blonde hair feathered over her face, hiding her blush in its golden curtain, and her feet even spread to hip width, inviting him in.

It'd been so long since she had sex, not that she lacked the opportunities.

No, she was saving herself. For him.

He strolled up behind her, staring at that ample, round ass of hers on display, and the sight of her bare cunny bared between her thighs. He swaggered on up behind her, reaching his hand out to stroke along the smooth curve of her two cheeks, then dip down, to touch that warm, wet slit below.

"You are one eager slut," he remarked at the slickness of her cunt, that thick hard dick of his prodding her thigh as he felt her up. "Here's the thing," he said to her firmly, grasping the base of his dick as he walked in behind her. "That pill you took? That was some fertility drugs I had brought in just for you," and he slapped the raw flesh of his dick to her pussy, making a wet smack in the night air. "You know why?" he asked, as if speaking to a child in need of instruction and guidance.

Her mind was reeling, and she tossed her hair over her shoulder as she looked at him, mind swimming with confusion. She may not be a kid, but she certainly couldn't understand why he'd feed her fertility drugs, come to this island and be his little sex toy with so much risk!

Flynt looked at her with that cocky smirk, the same one he wore on stage, except now he was rubbing his raw dick along her puffy, wet slit, teasing her clit with his thick, throbbing cock.

"You're gonna be my lil' breeding bitch," he informed her, and for a moment he very nearly stuck his dick right in her, nudging that broad crown against her plush nether lips.

"I'm gonna dump every load I have this trip right in your lil' pussy. And when I'm done? You're gonna be knocked up with my kid in your belly. You hear me?"

His voice was so firm, so resolute. There was no choice offered to her by the way he spoke, yet her mind reeled with indecision.

And arousal.

To be knocked up by her idol?

Nothing could possibly compare to that, and her eyes widened. She wanted it. Everything in her wanted it. It would be the ultimate thrill, the highest reward a groupie like her could ever want for!

"Yes!" she finally said as her mind stopped tumbling with their thoughts, and her legs spread wider.

"That's more like it," he said, giving a smack across her smooth, round ass to make her squeal, using that moment of opportunity to sink his fat dick into her slick little cunt. The feeling of that thick, veiny girth plowing into her deep and raw making her knees quake.

He was huge, his dick as big as his ego, making her feel every inch of it as he sank right down to her utmost depths to nudge against her womb.

"Fuck yeah, you're gonna like being my personal breeding bitch," he said before he tugged back his hips and gave a lewd groan into the tropical night air.

Perhaps she should have been put off by his rude language, but she sensed the desire running beneath it, and those raunchy words did little more than excite her as much as the sensation of his dick filling her did.

She could barely believe what was happening to her, but she pushed back against him with such eagerness. She truly was his personal little slut, so absolutely soaking wet and wanton for him.

She'd always played it safe before, so careful with sexual inter-course, but there she was, bent over a railing, offering up her raw, fertile pussy to her idol. And he was taking it for all its worth.

His two hands grasped her hips and ass cheeks as he rocked his hips, the warm ocean breeze washing over them both as he pummeled her pussy, sliding that thick, bulging cock into her so deep as he claimed her his.

"This is gonna be your new life, slut," he groaned out amid his moans. "You're gonna live here on my island... gonna pop out as many kids as I wanna have," he insisted, and with each word she felt his dick throb with excitement. He wanted her to be the mother of his children so damn bad.

His enthusiasm was infectious, and for those moments, she wanted nothing more than to do just that. To be whatever he needed, whatever he wanted, and she shuddered violently against his cock.

With every thrust, her pussy clenched him, that thick head pounding so deep into her against her womb, the threat implicit.

"Yes," she gasped out, her head tilted back and her back arching as that white dress pulled up a bit more.

Flynt arched his back, letting loose such a lewd, depraved moan at that clench of her pussy around his dick. His skin developed a light sheen of perspiration, and all that hard muscle gleamed in the Caribbean moonlight.

"Fuck!" He cursed, his hefty balls tightening against him as that first load began to travel up through his shaft like an intensely burning pleasure. "Gonna knock you up, slut," he bit out mere moments before his dick exploded, and all that virile cum blasted out, thick rivulets of creamy spunk filling her up.

As big as his dick was, that rich load of semen matched, pumping her so full as she bent over that railing. He moaned so deeply, filling the night air with his pleasured sounds, pumping her fertile womb full of his seed all the while.

And instead of horrified, she felt so... relieved. Her mind went numb and all that was left was her emotions, that sensation of pleasure that twisted its way through her core.

As his heavy balls slapped against her clit those few final times, she could barely hold back any longer, her entire body excited and so very near to that brink. She brought one of her hands from the railing, moving it between her legs and touching her wet clit, rubbing it roughly.

He felt her bring her hand down, and though he pulled back, he didn't take his dick out entirely. He grasped the long shaft, and pumped it with one hand, squeezing out the last of his seed into her depths, milking it for another spurt. Then another.

"That's it," he told her, stroking her lower back with his free hand. "Cum for me, slut... make that pussy purr and lap up my cum." He knew it'd only enhance the chances of her conceiving his child, and he egged her on excitedly.

She rubbed her clit so hard and fast, and she was so close that it only took a few seconds before that spark ignited in her loins, spreading out so instantly as her pussy drew him in, clenching his cock so tightly.

"Oh Flynt!" she cried out, lust apparent in her tone as she slammed her hips back against him.

He shuddered, feeling that tight clench of her pussy as it reached climax, and it milked another thick spurt of his virile cum right out of him. He grabbed a hold of her, keeping her in place tightly as she quaked and screeched into the warm, breezy night until they were both panting and sticky.

"Don't fuckin' spill a drop," he warned her so grimly, pushing down on her back to arch her spine and keep her pussy propped up in the air. He plucked his dick from her, leaving it to drool his thick cream, but he very quickly scooped her shapely body up into his arms and lifted her.

Her legs were wobbly, and the heels didn't help, so she was grateful for his strong arms about her. He smelled so masculine and she nuzzled into his neck, inhaling deeply.

He carried her back into the bedroom and laid her out upon the extravagant, thick bed, his hard cock exposed as he grabbed a pillow and propped it in beneath her ass.

"Let that pussy drink it in," he told her in that smooth, lyrical voice of his.

And she felt like it was the time to protest, to move away and escape his hold on her, but she didn't want to.

She didn't know it before that day, but she wanted absolutely nothing more than to have that tie to him, to know that they'd created something together, their souls forever linked. And so she lay on that pillow, his cum draining into her eager womb.

And he'd promised to breed her every day of the vacation!

Bad Seed

Book Themes: One night stand, fertile tryst, risky sex with a stranger
Word Count: 4635

I know I look like the part of the perfect good girl. Pencil skirt, neat blouse, stockings, heels, glasses, hair tied back in a ponytail. And I have the grades to prove it. I came to college on a full scholarship and I've held onto it no problem, so far. But... that doesn't mean I don't have bad urges.

Like how I could be sitting in class, and that dreamy English professor just gets my panties so wet they're ruined for the day. I could offer myself to him, and I fantasize about it. About him bending me over his desk, slapping my ass and lifting my skirt.

Heck, sometimes I even imagine him doing it in front of the whole class. Just claiming me as they watch, forcing me to look at them as his dick is rammed into me from behind.

God, that gets me so worked up.

But that's just a fantasy. I can't have that. No professor is gonna do that, and get himself fired.

And of course, I'd get kicked out of school.

So instead I just sit and squirm. And wait for class to be out.

No way the English professor's the bad boy I want him to be. But that doesn't mean I give up. I walk out of the campus, down the busy streets, books in one hand. It doesn't take long to get to the part of town where a girl like me looks *real* out of place.

Me, prim and proper, long legs carrying me over dirty sidewalk, and down a dark alleyway. There's guys here, but they're not like the ones on campus. They're hanging around outside a dingy old bar that's hidden away, and all of them look like the type that either spent time in jail or are working a rough job.

Right away one of them catches my eyes. How could he not? He's big. Tall I mean, and muscular. He's only wearing jeans, shoes and a tanktop, so I can really get an appreciation for how cut he is. Broad in the shoulders, with bulging biceps, thick forearms, and washboard abs that you could grate veggies on. And those tattoos all down his arms? Oh god, icing on the cake.

Makes me weak in the knees just looking at him.

"Hey girl, you lost or somethin'?" says a guy to my right, stepping up to me, leering. God, I love the way men's eyes can just devour a girl.

"No, she ain't lost," said the man I had my eyes on first. "Are you, girl?" he flicked his toothpick onto the alleyway and stepped out from the wall, a wall of muscle himself.

"Oh, what if I was? What if I was just some dumb girl who found herself on the wrong side of the tracks?" I can't help but fight my smirk, my amusement. I wanted them riled up, and I enjoyed teasing them, even if it just has to be by using my words. At least for now.

The big guy is intuitive, though. He doesn't sound cocky or like he's taking a wild guess. He can see that I have no fear in me, despite how prim and proper I look.

"Sounds lost to me," said the man at my right as he stepped closer, very close to grinding up on me as he sized me up from head to toe. He even reached out to touch my blouse, feeling it between his fingers.

"No," said the bigger man, his voice so deep and gravelly as he seemed to see right through me, giving me the shivers. "She knows exactly where she is and why she's come here," he remarked, casually making his way towards me, until he was looming over me from his towering height. Even the muscly man at my right backed off, but I stood my ground.

"You're lookin' for trouble, ain't you doll?" he said to me, his face ruggedly handsome, short dark hair swept back.

I smiled up at him, and it was genuine. Truly, unforgettably genuine.

I mean, how often do you find a man who can read you like a book, just at a glance?

"Is that what they call you around here? I'm tired of finding men where trouble is their *middle* name."

His stony, hardened but handsome face cracked a hint of an uneven smile for me. It made him even more appealing. It made him look scary, even. Well, I guess scarier. He is already the kind of guy most girls would be walking away from as fast as they could.

"That and worse things," he said to me, and without delay, his big, strong hand was on my hip. "You're awful young to be seekin' out trouble here, but... that ain't no impediment," he said to me with a hint of a grin as he began to guide me down that alleyway, around a corner to an even darker corner of the city.

Even the dark alleyways have dark alleyways, I muse while my brain can still think of anything but his hard body and his harder dick.

It was a losing battle, and my knees were already trembling. Not with fear, but excitement. It felt so... wrong. Anyone who knew me would be outraged, disgusted. Especially since I wasn't on the pill, and I knew damn well that this wasn't the type of man you demand wear a condom before he fucks you in the dirty alleyway.

I was also at peak fertility. I knew it instinctively, because I always got even hornier this time of month. To the point that it just starts driving me mental, and I can't think about anything else.

It was hugely irresponsible for so many reasons, and that just made it hotter.

He didn't waste time with words, we were around that corner and he swung me about, pushing my back up against the brick wall as he pressed in upon me. He was like a wild predator, and I'd stumbled into his domain like a doe eyed fawn.

He tilted my head to the side, and his lips went right for my neck as his big, powerful hands felt my sides, slid up over my figure to fondle my breasts through that thin blouse. God, if only my parents and all the prim church and school people could see me now.

I didn't hold back my moan, didn't bite down on my lower lip like I'd have to if I were in that dorm room. That was the best thing. Not having to hold *anything* back. I guess that's what this stranger liked in me, too. He could just finally be himself.

"You take girls back here often?" I asked as I writhed against him, pushing my blonde ponytail away from my porcelain neck, letting him mark me like the slut I was.

He didn't answer me, not right away. He kissed and nipped at my neck, felt my body as he pulled my blouse open. And for a moment I hoped none of those buttons had popped off in the brute act. But then I realized if he had, I'd have an even more shameful walk back. Wouldn't be able to hide what I was up to after this.

God that got me even hornier.

"Yes," he finally said to me as his hands dove into my opened top, those rough, strong fingers sinking into my breast flesh, fondling with a greedy, powerful grip.

I was still wearing my bra since I'd come right from class, a little lacy balconette that left my nipples exposed while pushing my tits up. I liked the way my blouse felt on my nipples all day as I squirmed, but I like his hands on them even better.

"You don't get tired of having to stick it to misbehaving schoolgirls that wander into your neck of the woods?"

His light scruff scraped my skin as his lips made his way to my jaw, then closer to my lips. It made me shiver, everything he did was so rough. Even a kiss was like a jolt to the senses.

"You're not just any schoolgirl, are ya?" he said to me, staring me in the eyes. It was only a split second, but it felt like an eternity. That dark gaze of his holding me entranced before he shoved his mouth to mine, his tongue piercing my lips as one of his hands dipped low again, grasping my skirt and lifting it up.

It was almost embarrassing how wet I was. My panties were soaked, after spending all day in class with my dirty thoughts. And then, meeting him?

Yea, I was filthy, and every moment made me wetter.

My mouth met his back eagerly, letting go of all civility and manners as I lost myself to his body. Everything outside of us drifted away, and all that remained was him and the anticipation of him breeding me like the slut I was.

My parents would disown me if they knew what I was doing. And if I got pregnant with some random hoodlum's baby? Probably the same thing.

But all I could think about was how hot it was when he grasped my panties in his two hands and just shredded them with one tug. There was nothing between my pussy and him now, and he helped himself. Letting his hand touch my slit, feel that fiery heat, that overwhelming slickness.

"Damn. Maybe you are just another little schoolgirl slut in need of some real dick," he said to me as he toyed with my clit, making me moan and writhe. And he took a moment to pull back, to look over my exposed tits, my wet slit, before bringing those fingers up and putting them in front of my mouth.

"Suck," he commanded me.

My baby blue eyes were on him as my mouth obediently opened, and my tongue did all the things to his fingers that I wished I was doing to his cock. Of course, my tongue would have a *lot* less room with his cock, but still. I liked showing him just how right about me he was.

I was nothing but a slut in need of a dick. His dick.

Real dick.

"You like that, huh? But you'll like the real thing even better, won't you," he said to me more than asked, watching me intently as his free hand went down and unbuckled his jeans. My eyes finally dipped once he was taking out that cock and...

It was everything a girl dreams of.

To match the man himself, it was big and long. A thick girth that was ribbed with jutting veins, the tip of it was a dark purple crown that glistened with precum.

"Now get down and show me how bad a girl you are, before I help myself to that hole I really want," he said, as his hand went from my lips to grasp my shoulder, forcibly pushing me down before him.

The alleyway was dirty, my white stockings definitely getting dirty around the knee as I was bent before him. Knowing I didn't have any say just was the cherry on the top. He would take what he wanted, and knowing that just made my clit throb with need.

My mouth opened, my lips eagerly finding the head of his shaft, my tongue teasing him for just a second as I gathered his delicious precum up. I wanted to taste him so bad, to remember this moment forever.

And from the moment I tasted that salty tang on my tongue, I knew I would.

But as much as I wanted to savour my time with his thick, manly cock, he put his fingers through my hair and forced me to lick and blow him at his pace and discretion. That guiding hand taking over as I slid my tongue in around the ridge of his tip, then went down and up his length before wrapping my lips around his shaft.

It was a strain to take him into my mouth, it wasn't used to opening that wide. But I made him fit as he force fed me that thick, meaty dick, and I felt his big, heavy balls nestle at my chin as he rocked my head back and forth.

"That's it. That's my dirty lil' slut. Ain't even worthy of bein' a whore, you're too weak in the knees for dick to risk chargin'," he growled out in his lust laden voice.

He was right, and that only made my honey leak more down my inner thighs, and I had to squirm to try to give my pussy a little pressure. It just needed to be filled so dang bad! Even being choked on his dick couldn't do anything to distract from how much I needed him to fuck my cunny.

I didn't even know where his friend was, if he'd followed. Anyone could be watching me as I kneel on the ground in my prissy pencil skirt curled up around my waist, my blouse torn open, my nipples harder than diamonds. I was so humiliated and degraded and *turned on*.

He shoved his cock down into my throat, that thick beefy length stretching it wide and sealing it shut. I was without air for a while, my nails digging into his thighs, before he finally pulled back and let me gasp for air.

"Get up here," he said, grasping me by my ponytail as he hauled me back up to my feet, which was easier said than done as I gasped. But in the flash of the moment I saw that yes, his friend was there too. Leaned back against the opposing wall, watching me with a glint in his eyes as the bigger male twisted me around and bent me over against the brick again.

The brick pricked my arms, and it made me feel so *alive*. Knowing that I was being watched, that I was going to get knocked up by some bad boy I didn't even know the name of and would likely never see again. My pussy was swollen and red, and I'd made sure to be completely waxed today so that I could feel everything And he, no doubt, could see just what a mess he'd made of me already.

He grasped my ass in one hand, prying my cheeks apart as he admired that sticky mess of my pussy, and the other took hold of his thick, long cock as it glistened with my saliva. He brought it in, and just as I predicted, he made no move to put on a condom. He just rubbed that raw tip along my slit, teased my clit so mercilessly.

"You need this, don't ya, slut?" he asked me in his dark, rumbling voice.

"Please," I begged, no longer even able to tease him and act like I have this all under my control. That was most of the fun. Knowing it's out of my control, knowing that I'm subject to whatever this big, brute of a stranger's whims are. "I need it so bad!"

"I know you do. Just be aware, I'm goin' in raw, and I ain't pullin' out. Whatever happens is on you," he said, though he didn't give me a chance to object. He just split me open on the biggest dick I'd ever seen. I screamed out, filling the alleyway with the sounds of my cry as he shoved so much of that thick, meaty dick up into me, stretching my pussy to its limits, making me dizzy with the sensation of it all.

My arms pushed further into the brick, that painful sensation absolutely nothing compared to the explosion of pleasure erupting within me. I'd gotten exactly what I wanted, but it was even better than I could have dared hope. I had to go up on tip toe, even in my high heels, and my long legs screamed with the effort, but it was worth it.

My pussy clung to him, even though I was wetter than I'd ever been, and my tight little ass pushed up against his pubic mound. I could feel him against my innermost center, and the ache was utter perfection. I'd finally found my Holy Grail.

With both hands free now, he grasped my hips and began to pound into me. No building up to it, no easing in, he used his raw strength to just force his dick through my tight, clenching pussy again and again, at his own pace. My tits were bouncing and swaying beneath me, and he had full control as he made me squeal and moan, his own grunts and pleasured sounds lower, but no less real and sincere.

"That's it... fuck, that's the tightest lil' pussy I've had," he growled at me.

I squeezed him harder at the compliment, feeling his pulsing veins as I ground my pussy against him. I felt like I might pass out, but at the same time, I was more alert and aware than ever before. I screamed as he pounded me, each thrust making my voice warble.

"You gonna make me yours?"

He slapped my ass hard at that, made me squeal again as my cheek stung. He reached up, grasping a hold of my ponytail and twisting my head back and to the side, so I could see him out of the corner of my view.

"You think you're worthy of bein' my girl and not just some

one-time cum dump?" he growled, punctuating his question with another rough slap.

It was so cruel, and yet it was the thing that absolutely obliterated me. I felt my pussy tensing up, betraying me to the stranger. There was no holding back, that was for sure. There was no hiding the fact that his words, his sharp smack, his yanking me around was what toppled me over the brink and gave me the most intense orgasm I've ever had in my life.

He let go of my hair sharply as he continued to hammer into my pussy, even as that narrow little hole grasped his dick oh so tight amid my orgasm. He wasn't impeded by anything, he just helped himself to me at his own pace and time, reaching a hand in underneath me, grasping a breast, squeezing and fondling it, feeling my stiff nipple prod his palm as he grunted and shot off some pre into me.

"Not much to say for yourself,," he growled. "You look like some bookworm, but you fuck like a bimbo slut," he said roughly.

I was still shuddering as a powerful aftershock went through me, and a moan was all I could manage. I wanted so badly for him to claim me, for him to sneak into my bedroom at night and wake me with his cock. But I couldn't even beg him to make me his. It was all too perfect.

He was hammering me towards my second orgasm in no time, everything was so exquisite about the moment. His balls slapped against my clit up until they tightened, getting ready to unload all his seed. And he moaned, gripped me tighter as my nipple was pinched between his fingers.

"You're gonna take it all, slut," he growled, right before he pounded into me a few final times, groaning as his dick swelled and then...

I could feel it. Every pulse of his dick was another thick jet of sticky, rich cum. He blew so many strands of his virile seed into my fertile depths, and true to his word he never pulled out. He just jammed that thick crown up against the entrance to my womb and unleashed it all.

I'm not an idiot. I knew the risks, and I knew that when a girl cums the same time as a guy, those risks shoot way up. Maybe that was the knowledge that sent me toppling over the edge, left me screaming my head off in the dark alleyway as I pushed my ass against him, taking every last drop of his seed.

We both pressed into each other, our bodies melded, his seed trapped deep within me as our bodies slowly uncoiled down from their intense highs. It was the greatest rush of my life, fucked by some rough stranger in a back alley, blasted with his raw cum, watched by some rough thug.

He grasped my ponytail again, wrenching my head back.

"You still wanna be my girl, slut?" He asked me with a growl.

"More than anything," I gasped, forcing my blue eyes on him. I didn't want to mess it up. I didn't want this to be a one time deal. Sure, that's hot in its own way, but I knew that no other dick would satisfy me like his. I was going to be forever trying to find someone who could stand in his shadow.

He studied me, and again I felt like he saw right through me to my core. There was no lying or games with him possible, because he'd ferret out the truth without a word.

"Get down on your knees," he demanded as he let go of my hair then yanked his dick out of my pussy. It made me squeal from the sudden roughness, then whimper from the sad emptiness as his cum drooled out of me and down my inner thighs. "Clean me up, slut. Show me you want to be my girl," he demanded as his cock jutted out, still hard.

My legs were quivering so hard that it was easy to fall to my knees. It forced more cum from my pussy, though, and I brought a hand to my slit, cupping it as my other hand wrapped around his cock, aiming it at my face. I looked at his delicious masculinity for only a second before my mouth was taking him in again, tasting our combined juices upon every single inch of his dick.

He watched me, evaluated me. I felt so scrutinized, tested. But... didn't I say I was a good student? I always aced my tests. And this one was no different, I cleaned and teased his dick masterfully, made him give a few grunts of approval. Until at last I was done, according to him.

"That's enough," he said as I lapped around his balls, cleaning what honey had leaked down around them. And more than saying it, he yanked my ponytail off his shaft. "If you're gonna be my girl, you gotta be more than just some slut," he told me. "You gotta be a whore."

He whistled sharply before I could respond.

"Dino," he called out to the man behind him, who came immediately.

"Yes boss?"

"A hundred bucks'll buy you sloppy seconds," he shot the man an intense look, but already he was fishing out a wad of bills and slapping them into his boss' hand.

It was all happening so fast, but as I watched that money change hands, I could feel my heart begin to pound, my pussy throbbing once more. I looked up at the stranger, the one I still didn't know the name of.

Then I looked at Dino, my smile growing.

The Boss peeled off some of the bills and slipped them into the waist of my skirt as he tugged me back up to a standing position.

"Graduate from being a bad girl to being a good whore," he told me before letting go and backing off.

Dino was already unbuckling his belt excitedly. He'd been aching for this moment since he first saw me, and the fact his boss had got to me first and left me a mess, wasn't gonna be a deterrent for him at all I could tell. He needed a taste of me too.

And even though I knew that what I really wanted was the Boss... If this pleased him, then that was everything I needed. I knew then and there that I'd do anything to get his cock again, and being paid for the privilege of getting what I wanted anyways?

Icing on the cake.

I turned around again, my arms pressing against the brick as I spread my legs, bracing myself.

"My boy Dino here doesn't mind sharing his boss' pets. And I'll even let him raw you too. Though not those other guys, y'hear me?" the boss said to me firmly, as Dino got in behind me, and began to push his hard dick into my wet, cum filled pussy with a squelch of juices and seed.

I nodded my head, even as I let out a wanton moan, my back arching as I took another man into my used cunt. He was smaller, and I was so wet, but that didn't matter. This wasn't about Dino. This was about finding my true calling in life, and I was planning on acing this exam.

Dino wasn't as big as his boss, nor as strong. But still, he hammered that raw cock into me hard and fast, he made me body quake and caused me to moan all over again. And that's what I needed. I needed to feel like a woman. And they did that.

Dino pounded me, made my ass cheeks ripple and quake with each thrust, and got my tits to swaying again. And like his boss, he helped himself to groping my flesh all over, taking handfuls of my tits, pinching my nipples, ravishing me too.

But even as spent and sore as his boss had left me, I loved it all, and it was coming to an end all too soon as Dino's dick began to throb wildly.

I slammed back against him as hard as I could, my body begging for him to finish in me. The idea that he would pull out, deprive me of that sensation of his pleasure bursting into me was awful. I couldn't allow that.

My pussy tightened around him, begging for his seed, milking him with such wanton desire.

Dino didn't let me down, as I was afraid he might. He just hilted himself inside me and let his load burst out, adding to the sticky mess of virile seed that his boss had dumped in me already. I squealed and moaned with excitement, knowing that now not only had one random stranger risked knocking me up, but two had.

It was the filthiest, happiest day of my life.

T his time when I walk down that alleyway, it's not looking like a sweet schoolgirl. Butch--that's his name, I finally learned, after weeks of being his--has transformed me.

When I walk down here now, it's with fishnet stockings and leather, my tits practically bursting out of my top as I make my way over to his side.

He catches sight of me before I reach him, and that dark gaze lights up a little. He lifts his arm and puts it around me.

"'Bout time," he says to me in his gruff way, Dino giving me a nod from across the alley.

I nuzzle in against Butch, wrapping my arms around him.

"I'm late," I say, taking hold of his massive hand.

"I know that, ho," he says to me.

"No, I mean... I'm late. Like, real late... in fact, two months late," I clarify as I guide his hand over to my bare stomach, to let him feel there. I knew that meeting him was fate, and in his eyes, I saw a little sparkle. A faint grin forming on his lips.

"I said, I know," he growls at me before his lips find mine, our bodies melt into one another's once more.

Sugar Baby: Paige

Book Themes: *sugar baby / escort, bareback breed-ing, billionaire*
Word Count: *4909*

David's big, strong hands grasp my hips from behind. I'm laying out on his private little strip of shore-line, sunbathing on the beach in only my white bikini set, my blonde hair pulled to one side.

I was calm and relaxed before I felt that touch of his, the way he felt my smooth, supple skin, then curled his fingers into my thong and began to tug it slowly downwards. But already I can feel my body tingling in response.

Don't get me wrong, being a sugar baby, being David's hot, young little arm candy and sex kitten, it's kinda like work. I have to be looking my hottest at all times, sexy and seductive. I have to be available for him.

Sexually.

That means my little pink pussy has to be wet and glistening when he needs it. But... I get so many expensive gifts. A lovely

Ferrari of my own was the latest one. A thick fur coat for when we're not at his vacation home on the beach.

And frankly, his towering, rock hard muscular body is a treat in itself.

"I don't even know why you bother wearing this bathing suit. We're all alone here, nobody for miles but us," he says in that deep, husky voice of his as he tugs my thong on down entirely, exposing my soft little pink pussy lips, grasping my thighs and gently parting them as I lay on my tummy.

"I like the tan lines... don't you?" I response, pouty lips crooked into a wry smile as I lift my sunglasses and bat my long lashes over my shoulder.

"Yeah," he admits with an uneven grin of his own as his big strong hands feel my legs and fondle my round, bubbly ass. I can only catch a glimpse of his bare, muscular body like this, but I know he's naked, and that dick of his is rock hard and huge, as always.

"I like knowing there's parts of you no one sees but me," he growls, and I smile as I wiggle my ass at him in response.

"Not even the sun," I say with a teasing giggle. He says he just wants me for my body, but that's a lie. If he just wanted my body, he could have it for a whole lot less. He wants the *experience*. He wants my giggles, and my sense of humor, and the way I drive him wild all the time. I'm paid well because I'm the whole package for him.

He swats my ass with one of those big strong hands of his, making the cheek ripple with the impact as I give a little gasp and squeal to it. It's playful, but he loves it. And I love it too, frankly.

His hand slips down, past the crack of my butt, after he licks his fingertips. He touches my pussy, feeling that there's already that natural reservoir of slick honey rising up for him obediently. His every touch having an effect on me. I didn't have to try, too hard at least, with David. He just got me going each time.

"Damn girl, you never let me down. Always such a good little kitty cat, nice and wet for me and my dick," he growls possessively as he teases my clit a bit.

"I don't even have to see you to have a perfect picture of you in my mind. And every time I think of you, well... I can't help it," I say, a half grin on my lips as my long, dark lashes flutter over my eyes. Another nice thing about David... he knows how to touch me. He actually wants to please me, not just have me fake it for his sake.

He leans in over my shoulder, a grin on his face as he bites my slender neck, then my ear, growling with desire as he works my sensitive little clit into a frenzy.

"I forgot the condom," he husked into my ear lowly, and I knew it was a bit of a fib. He never forgot anything, that's why he was so successful in business. At least, not unless he wanted to forget it. "What do you say to me going in raw? And me buying you some new Louboutin's as a reward?" he asks, and I feel his thick, throbbing shaft press against my slit, that bulbous purple crown of his cock nudging bare.

We're both each other's only sexual partner, and we're both clean, but he also knows I'm not on the pill. And it'll cost a lot more than some new heels without a pull out.

He's such a dick sometimes. But he's a dick in a way that I really, really like.

That is to say... he's a considerate asshole, and he knows our relationship is transactional.

"You didn't forget," I say, wiggling my ass a little, teasing him just as much as I'm teasing myself, feeling him sliding against my wet pussy. I don't want to wait for him to go back to the room and grab a condom any more than he does. "But if you think I'm going to risk getting knocked up by your super seed for some heels, you don't know me very well at all."

He grins and chuckles at my teasing, and he returns it by letting that thick cock of his press in a bit, making my slick little cunny lips flower about his tip, feeling my slick honey coat his shaft as he gives a groan. He doesn't risk any further though, doesn't sink right in before he says.

"I'll pull out. Promise," he rumbles, grasping my two ass cheeks, squeezing and fondling them.

He silences me for a moment, that risk he's taking with my body making me thrill with delight and concern, my mind going foggy for a moment. It was never something I thought I'd like, but the added risk and thrill... I shake my head, trying to clear my thoughts.

"Yea, that's what they all say," I pout, pulling away and looking over my shoulder at him. "I'm not taking a lifelong risk for a pair of shoes. That's going to be at least a condo. A nice one."

I get a better look at him like that, his rock-hard body, with those broad shoulders, thick biceps, chiseled pecs and abs. His handsome, broad jawed face, lightly stubbled, with dark hair. And below, oh god, those thick muscular thighs and a huge, pulsating cock above two dangling balls.

"For that kinda deal, I definitely don't wanna pull out," he said, licking his lips. "Tell ya what, I fuck you raw the rest of this day, no pulling out... and the whole vacation house and property are yours," he said, gesturing around the large area, bigger than most parks I knew growing up.

I raise my sunglasses at him, trying to figure out if he was being serious.

A huge place all to myself, worth at least half a mill...

That was a much more tempting offer. I lick my lips, tasting my vanilla lip-gloss as I think it over.

"The whole house? All legal?"

"Yeah, sign it all over to you," he said, sounding sincere. I mean, he was thinking with his dick -- that big, throbbing, hard dick of his -- but he was sincere. He had never backed out of a deal before. No matter how worked up I got him to get him to do so. And right now, I could tell his cock was pulsating with need.

"So, what do you say?" he asks, sliding his hands over my body, taking a moment to feel my breasts before moving back down to my ass and squeezing.

I bite my lip, looking him over. It wouldn't be the worst thing in the world to be knocked up by him. He was rich, generous, and absolutely gorgeous. Plus, he was smart to boot. Those were all good genes begging to be passed on.

If I ever did have a kid, it wouldn't be bad to come from David.

"If you knock me up, you're gonna have to pay up," I grin, and even though I'm still my usual sarcastic self on the surface, my heart is racing. I can't believe I'm even thinking about doing this. I can't believe I'm going to do this! And I can't believe how much I fucking *want* to do this. To take a risk, to feel that ultimate pleasure...

I want to know what his cock feels like, bare and stretching me out. I want to know how it feels when he cums in me. It's all such a rush, such an incredible turn on, and by the time David rubs his cock against me again, I'm absolutely drenched between my thighs.

His ruggedly handsome face lit up with a big, wry smile as I finally caved, his dick jumping with excitement as he grasped me, pulled me back to where I was before I pulled away, and pinned me to the lounging seat beneath him.

"If I knock you up, I'll do more than just pay you," growls, not adding any more to it than that before he pushes his massive cock back up inside me. Only this time, there's no condom, no barrier between us. Just his raw shaft stretching my tight little pussy open, making my pouty lips part with a moan as he fills me up, letting loose his own low roar of satisfaction. And it only felt better each time he throbbed and pulsed inside of me, his excitement straining my narrow little slit as he sunk to my depths, getting balls-deep inside me.

There's so much more sensation, so much more heat now that we're flesh on flesh, and it takes my breath away. I've never taken a guy raw before. Not in all my life.

It's like losing my virginity all over again, and I realize how much I've been missing out on all this time. I almost pass out from the intense pleasure, my body shuddering with such delight. I don't even know if it's all physical. It's like he found the g-spot of my mind, some secreted away kink that could make me cum if pressed just the right way.

It's almost embarrassing that as David is just beginning to fuck me, sliding that big, hard shaft in and out of me, I'm already cumming on his dick. My hot honey coating him as I squeal and moan.

"F-fuck!" I curse, my little pussy spasming around his shaft, squeezing it even tighter and making him grown.

"Damn," he grunts. "No question you ain't faking it," he says, building up his pace despite my natural grasp on his shaft, smacking his groin to my rear as he ploughs into me harder, faster. "Guess we found my lil' kitten's kink," he says, before giving my ass a playful swat.

I want to protest, to be the playful and sarcastic sugar baby he knows and adores and spoils.

But he found his way past all my barriers, and now it's just him and I, raw. Not just his cock. No, he has me bare too. My toes curl and my body presses into his more eagerly, knowing it would be useless to protest. He knows what I like now.

I know what I like now.

There's no going back from this.

He has full control of me, pounding my bubbly butt from behind, filling me with that raw, veiny shaft as it pulses with need for me. My cries are filling the beach air, the sounds of the ocean behind us a light backdrop. He grunts and moans, his own pleasure undeniable as he pounds my little pussy into a tingling mess.

"Fuck, you're always so damn tight," he moans out, shuddering, dick spasming and spurting a little precum into my unprotected depths. "Now I can *really* feel it," he praises.

I shudder with such pleasure, my entire body slamming against his, desperate to feel every bit of his cock. My pussy squeezes him, and each throb of his veins, each pulse of his heart, is shared with me. It's so intimate, so much more taboo than anything else we've done, more than when he tied me up, more than all that bondage stuff we tried. And pleasure shoots from every part of my body.

It's like I'm alive for the very first time, and my cries and moans fill the air as I struggle to find where one orgasm ends and the next begins.

But I get pulled back to reality a bit when it finally happens. That big, Adonis David finally lets himself go, giving into his own desires. Far sooner than usual, because he's got stamina like a bull and lasts forever. No, this time he's tensing, his cock throbbing, and he buries that thick, rigid shaft into me deeply, as far as it'll go, and lets loose a roar of pleasure as he blows that thick load right into my depths.

So much thick, creamy seed flooding me, filling my depths as he shudders and moans. Rich, virile cum filling my womb as he keeps himself locked in tight, grasping my hips and ass.

I lose my fucking mind.

Every part of me is filled with such an intense sensation of wanton pleasure and desire, and there's no holding me back as my pussy milks him of every last drop of his seed. It's like my entire body wants this, and it rewards me with an orgasm the likes of which even my Hitachi couldn't give me.

I'm bucking and shaking and screaming his name, nearly toppling over as I slam against him, making the tip of his cock press as deep inside me as possible.

We both hold that position tightly as he spurts the last of his seed into me, keeping it locked deep inside as we pant and moan. I can feel him twitching inside me as he holds me tight, his powerful body tensed with the act of controlling me, keeping his dick locked in my pussy.

"Fuck that was the most satisfying orgasm ever," he finally said in a loud husk, giving a satisfied sigh as he smacked my round ass again playfully. But then he leaned in and kissed my neck affectionately, nipping it ever so lightly.

"I bet you're already craving for today's next load," he growled in my ear, a cocky grin on his face.

"Asshole," I manage to hiss out without any of my usual vigor, because he's right.

He has the entire day to fuck me raw, and I want to get the most of it. Maybe even more than him.

The sensations of bliss are still flooding my system, my mind still hazy with desire, and I feel like I found a part of myself I'd been missing.

Needless to say... it was the best orgasm I've ever had as well. But he doesn't need to know that.

He's slow to pull out, taking his time, kissing me, spanking my ass, nipping my smooth skin. But finally, he does, and I feel all that thick creamy seed begin to flood out. But he stands right up, then scoops me up into his arms.

"C'mon doll," he husks, slinging me over his shoulder like I was just a little girl. "Time to head back up to the beach house," he says, heading through the sand and up over the stairs into the large place that was but a vacation home to him, but larger than any house I ever lived in.

He took me inside, through the sliding glass door, then across the floor to the thick, plush carpet of the living room, where he finally lowered me down to my feet. And I got to see that big, confident grin on his face.

"Get down on your knees, babe," he says to me, his hand cupping my cheek then letting his fingers thread into my blonde hair. "I wanna see you work for this next load you'll get."

He's always been a horndog, but usually we fuck once, maybe twice a day when I'm here with him. And even that, it's usually spread out through the day. He's never wanted me again so soon after. Or, I suppose, his body couldn't handle that.

But already blood is heading back to his organ, and the sight of it makes my mouth water.

"Already?" I ask, raising a brow as if I wasn't thirsty for him. "You don't want to relax a bit first?"

He shakes his head silently, liking his lower lip as his strong hands guide me down to my knees in front of him. Bringing me to stare at his thick, glistening shaft in all its veiny glory. The scent of his musk and our rutting ripe upon it.

"Can't afford to waste any of our opportunities today to knock that sweet little pussy of yours up, babe," he growls at me with such lust and desire.

When he says it like that, it sends a shiver down my spine, desire making me go stupid again.

How is this so damn hot to me?

What has he done to me?

I look up over his body from the new angle, appreciating every hard ridge of muscle, every throb of his cock as my lip-glossed mouth opens. He loves it when I hold his gaze as I blow him, but instead, I'm entranced by his cock, and what it's awakened in me.

My hand grabs him, my tongue pushing out to run along his crown, tasting my honey on him as I feel his cum dribble between my thighs. Another shudder goes through me, a soft moan silenced on his cock.

He groans lowly as my mouth begins to please his shaft, tasting the salty tang of his cum that remains, making his shaft twitch with rising excitement. He strokes and pets my hair, holding my head as I begin to tease his shaft to full size again. All as he stands there, so tall and towering, watching my every move.

"God damn, I can't wait to shove this dick back inside your bare pussy," he growls, the thought of giving up his prized vacation home so far from his mind. Fucking me raw was worth the trade to him, and then some.

Sometimes, in a workin' girl's life, she realizes she should have asked for more, because she could have gotten away with it. Now is normally when I'd regret not asking for the world, because I realize he would have happily given it to me.

But regret is the furthest thing from my mind.

I stroke his cock, my entire body moving with my arm and head, putting everything I have into getting him as hard as possible, as quickly as possible. I can't even open my eyes to look at him, because I'm taking him too deep and tears are threatening to spill as he presses against my gag reflex.

I don't care.

All I can think about is getting him as hard as possible as fast as possible, and my thick saliva quickly coats his cock as I get him full erect in record time.

He doesn't waste any time after that, and pulls his thick, pulsating cock from my mouth, letting it dangle before my pouty lips, glistening with saliva. He reaches down, taking hold of me as he gets down and presses my back to the thick, soft rug.

"No time to waste," he grunts, getting over top of me as my breasts jiggle with the motions, nearly spilling out of my bikini top. And he positions himself there, grasping his thick cock and then spearing it back inside me with a loud moan, sinking right to my utmost depths. And he wastes no time, thrusting wildly into me, again and again.

My legs wrap around his ass as my head knocks back, screaming in pleasure. My nails dig into his skin, and there's no more hiding how much I love this. He knows. He knows my greatest weakness.

And he's definitely taking advantage of it.

I couldn't be happier.

"You really want to knock me up?" I ask, the words sounding so strange on my tongue.

He doesn't hesitate, locking his steely eyes with mine as he nods, the loud slaps of his hard body striking mine filling the air amid our moans and pants. His thick cock splaying my little slit open wide, making me his.

"Yeah babe," he growls, pounding me harder, making my heavy breasts spill out of my bikini top lewdly. "I wanna fuckin' bareback you every day," he declares with such heady, needy lust. "God you feel so damn good!" he shouts.

The sensation of the air on my nipples makes them even stiffer, aching to be touched, and I bring one of my hands to them, tweaking the stiff bud and making me wince with pain. But it's that beautiful pain that makes my clit throb and my body ache for more.

"You're so dirty," I manage, my words breathy and filled with lust. It's hard to tell if I meant them for him... or for myself. It could apply to both of us, really.

He reaches up amid our wild, rowdy fucking, grasping one of my breasts after pushing my hand away. He takes over, squeezing that thick, supple flesh, tweaking my poor, stiff nipple as his raw, thick cock piston's inside of me so rapidly. Those heavy, cum-laden balls slapping my round ass as he claims me on the floor like we're animals.

His thick, muscular body is glistening with perspiration, highlighting every bulge of his pecs, every valley between his six-pack abs. He's a sculpted fuck machine of a man, towering and strong, gorgeous and so virile. And with the frenzied pace he pounds my pussy, I know he wants nothing more than to knock me up and empty another thick load inside me.

I should never have agreed to this. To take this risk. To become his.

It's wrong, isn't it?

So then why does it feel so right? Why does this feel like everything I've always wanted, and everything I've always been missing in my life?

My calves are locked around him, making it so that he can barely even pull out, and I can feel him pushing his previous load into me again and again, upping the risk of pregnancy with every single thrust. I once read that women have a better chance of getting pregnant if they angle their hips up, and I instinctively grab for a throw pillow, putting it under my ass.

And when I do...

He hits my g-spot just right, and all I can see is a blinding white light of ecstasy.

I have no idea what I'm doing. It's like my mind is taking a backseat to my body, and I'm just along for the amazing, mind-blowing ride.

He bucks with me as I lose it again, and a loud roar of a moan tears out of his throat. He shudders and grasps me tightly, squeezing my breast and waist as I gush slick honey around his cock and over his balls again.

His broad shoulders push back, his muscles rippling as he holds on, but with my pussy tightly clenching around his shaft in my intense climax, he loses all control, yet again. He's shaking as he thrusts, his balls tightening, and he pounds down into me, burying his shaft once more as he empties his nuts into my cunny, filling it with a second, heavy dose of his rich, virile seed.

All as he pants over top of me, like a stunning Greek statue come to life with the power of sheer lust and a need to breed.

We're no longer just client and provider. No, we've both gone way past that line in the last hour, and even with his generous offering of a home in exchange for that romp... I know things can never go back to how they used to be.

I don't want them to.

Maybe I'm not thinking straight, or maybe he's simply opened Pandora's Box, but either way, having him fuck me raw is too good of a treat.

I swallow, panting as I try to get my breath, looking up at him with lidded eyes as he subconsciously bucks into me a few more times. With the pillow beneath my ass, he has such a perfect angle to breed me, and I have to bite my lip to keep from grinning.

What if he really does it?

What if he really makes me his? Permanently?

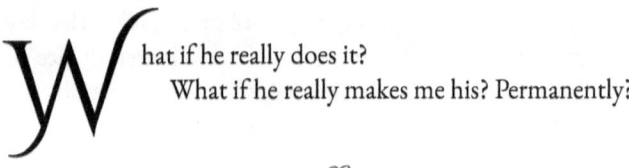

Midnight is approaching, and then our deal technically ends. But we haven't stopped. Not all day. Not for more than a moment's breath.

We've been fucking like teens again, that gorgeous, hard cock of his managing to rise to the occasion again, and again, and again. He holds me up off his bed, grasping the headboard as he grunts and I moan.

It's been a long, slow, tantric last session. He's blown so many loads in me already, but we're determined to milk out at least one more. I can see in his eyes there's no holding him back.

He bites my breast, then licks at my nipple, suckling it into his mouth as our two bodies slowly but firmly grind together. His one big strong hand holding me up a couple inches off the bed.

I've never cum so much in all my life as I have in this one day, and I don't want it to ever stop. He's always been an amazing lover, but today he's taken it to the next level. He's held nothing back, and neither have I.

I stare at him, my body exhausted, my mind a delicious, decadent haze, my pussy filled with his cum, and I feel complete.

How could I ever want a day like this to end?

The slow, unceasing grind of that thick cock into my poor, well-pounded pussy continues. Every throb of that veiny girth still exciting me. Every pulse of his heart travelling through our loins and shared.

He shivers, and he moves his hand down, his thumb finding my clit again. Teasing it. Pressing it. And he groans aloud.

"C'mon... cum on my cock again... just one more time," he growls in command, as the minutes tick by. The two of us both getting so close, so close to something that we're too lost in lust to seriously consider.

A spark travels from his thumb into my body, warmth and pleasure spreading through my stomach and towards my exhausted limbs. No matter how many orgasms crash through me, they're still just as intense, and I whimper and cry with the exquisite bliss of his body on mine.

It's all that's needed to send him spilling over into me too, and a final thick load of cum erupts into me, seconds before midnight, and the deal is done.

We collapse to the bed, panting and sweaty, holding each other. Only then becoming aware of how hungry and thirsty we've become after nearly a full day of uninterrupted fucking. But it was worth it.

T rue to his word as ever, David signed over the vacation home. The beach property. All of it. He did so happily, with a smile on, after calling his lawyer the very next day to draw up the papers.

So now I'm no longer a homeless working girl, sleeping with my sugar daddy, I've got my own lavish place on a tropical beach.

But, true to my concerns, I've got more than just that.

Standing there at the railing, looking out over my beach property, I cradle the heavily pregnant stomach in my grasp. Just one day. That's all it took. I told him that cum of his was super powered.

And as soon as we learned that I was knocked up, he presented me a legal document, promising money for both me and the child for years and years to come.

"There you are," he said, opening the sliding glass door.

Yeah, we're still together.

"I had something for you," he said, coming up behind me, brushing my hair out of the way and kissing my neck, squeezing his arms around me.

"What's that?" I ask as he takes a moment to feel my curves, even cops a quick feel of my breasts, which have swelled bigger than ever.

"Will you..." he begins, and then presents to me a little velvet box on the railing, flipping it open to reveal the ridiculously expensive ring inside. "Marry me?" He asks, his grin so obvious I could hear it in his voice as he pressed in behind me.

"W-... of course," I say, feeling the tears welling up in my eyes.

He squeezes me tight, kisses me then says in a low husk:

"And we won't even use a prenup... as long as you agree to more bareback days," he says with a devilish grin, twisting me around to face him.

"That's a deal I'd be a fool to say no to," I reply, tears glittering in my eyes as I lean up to seal the deal with a kiss.

The Billionaire's Fertile Submissive

⌥

Book Themes: BDSM, Barely Legal, and Breeding
Word Count: 6880

⌥

As my private jet landed on the small airstrip, I looked at all the warmth, the green of the land. This time of year, New York seemed ashen and grey, and compared to this tropical paradise, it might as well have been in black and white. Everything was vibrant and lush, the blue of the sky so bright, the water along the horizon a beautiful sea foam teal.

I'd changed for the flight into a more comfortable outfit, discarding my usual suit and ties and instead opting for plain cotton pants and a half unbuttoned linen shirt. Sunglasses hid my eyes, my brown hair left a bit shaggier and wilder than its usual style.

I was ready to relax for the first time in months. No meetings. No calls. No visits with Presidents and Prime Ministers from around the world, no expectations placed upon me at all.

Stepping from the plane, I looked around with a sense of

excitement and vigor I hadn't had since my much younger days, and there was an extra pep in my step as I made my way towards the classic car that awaited me.

Gleaming and a brilliant blue to match the sky, I took a second to appreciate it before I saw her.

My prized package, all wrapped up in a gauzy dress, looking at me expectantly. She wasn't a local — it didn't make me feel powerful to have a poor woman with few options serve me. No, she'd been shipped in as well, an import from home. I'd ordered her as others ordered movies.

Blonde hair cascaded down her shoulders, her fit and firm body porcelain coloured.

I couldn't help but smile. The agency had delivered me the perfect woman, and as she made her way over to me, she seemed so small and delicate. Her head tilted and those full lips parted as she waited my first order.

Well, that wasn't true. My first order had been that she wasn't to speak unless spoken to, and she was fulfilling that wonderfully.

Pretty and demure, that lovely young woman walked up to sheepishly press against my side, as if she were longing to be my latest adornment. Such perfect white teeth in that smile, such a bright excited glimmer in her eyes. She was mine for the trip, but she didn't look unhappy to be. Perhaps she was pleased to find out her keeper for the trip was handsome and fit, rather than the stereotype of what guy requires her services.

Who could blame her for that bit of relief?

I patted her on the head and motioned towards the car.

"Get into the backseat," I instructed slowly, as if talking to a child. She was legal, of course. I only dealt with reputable companies, after all, and ensured that there'd be no public fallout should they get wind of my excursion. But who can blame me for wanting to treat the little beauty like that?

I turned my back on her, trusting her to do as I'd instructed as I looked to my guard and right hand man. Elliot had been with me almost since the start, and I trusted him with everything. He was already getting my suitcases, ready to load them into the trunk, but I still watched him as my pet lifted her near see-through dress and climbed into the back seat.

Those long, shapely legs of hers were ivory coloured and so beautiful. The kind that just made you want to kiss them, rub your hands along them, all before feeling them wrap about your waist and cling to you.

She slipped in deep to the center of the back seat, adjusting her blonde hair as she waited for me, leaving that slender stalk of a neck exposed facing me.

Elliot finished packing the trunk as I stood quietly watching, just letting her stew in anticipation, to see what she'd do and how she responded to pressure.

But she had the patience of an angel, and I couldn't help but smile as I saw her sparkling blue eyes look at me.

I moved to the back seat with her, the hard seat against my back and ass as I looked to her.

"What's your name?" I asked.

"Angela," she said without pause, but what was most remarkable was just how beautiful that voice was. 'Voice of an angel' didn't do her justice, and it made me regret having silenced her for as long as I did.

She was the whole package, a body that belonged on the cover of magazines and billboards, a voice that should be singing before a crowd. The grace of a lady far her senior in years and social standing. Her every little move so dainty and meticulous as she crossed her legs and let her hands rest over her knee.

"Well, Angel," I said, taking ownership of that name and rebranding her. "I think you're going to have a wonderful vacation." My hand went to her thin, toned thigh, resting atop it and squeezing as Elliot went into the front seat and started us on our journey.

With the windows down, it blew her blond hair away from her perfect cheekbones, the little button nose that made her look so youthful.

She leaned in against me, slender arms coiling about my own as she pressed her surprisingly ample bust to my bicep. She was the full package, and as she gazed up at me with such sparkling eyes, I could see down that dress to the sight of such ample, pale breasts on display.

"I know we will, Sir," she said with such reverence and respect in each word.

I was only a man, and I couldn't control the way I began to swell at those sweet words, at the press of her body to mine. I leaned back, trying to look more relaxed, when all I could think about was getting to the hotel and ravishing her.

She wasn't just any companion, after all. She was chosen for my tastes, and I throbbed again just thinking about it.

Thinking about making her mine.

It was an old colonial style building, settled amongst the trees and overlooking the ocean. Beautiful sand and water spread out before us, the cities and towns hidden by the lush foliage. The sea air blew in, and it was as if all my worries simply melted away. Especially with beautiful Angel still shimmying into me, needy for approval that I never truly gave.

Elliot opened my door, and I held out my hand to help Angel out as I looked upon the great hotel. It could easily house a couple dozen families, but it was far more exclusive than that, and only a few cars were parked nearby.

I strode towards the building with the same slow, measured gait of the locals, taking my time to enjoy the warm sun on my skin and the breeze in my hair.

I felt so relaxed, and yet, I also felt this excitement beneath the surface of my skin. I didn't want to rush, though. I wanted to soak in every moment of my vacation.

"What do you think, Angel?"

She looked like a kid in a candy store, eyes wide and shimmering, excitement radiating from her as she bit her lower lip and soaked it all in.

"It's beautiful, simply beautiful," she said soft and breathlessly. The ravishing young vixen nearly bouncing along my side with her excitement, rubbing against me with her supple, yielding breasts. She was the perfect, soft woman, who looked like she'd ever be in need of a hard, guiding father figure.

"Where are we staying, Sir?" she asked delightedly.

I smiled, taking a moment to stop and point to the east wing. "That's us," I said, "so that we can enjoy sunrise together."

The way her eyes sparkled at that said she was delighted with the response, but then looking at her stare at our place for the vacation, I wouldn't have been surprised if she'd reacted that way to whatever I said. She looked absolutely delighted just to be at my side.

Either she was a really good actress, or she was actually the real deal. An innocent little thing who wanted nothing more than to be taken care of.

A rare and true pet.

I'd find out soon enough, and I draped my arm around her delicate shoulders as I guided her inside.

Beautiful artwork surrounded us in the lobby. It wasn't just the hung paintings, but the marble carvings, the way the ceiling as shaped as if to tell a story, it was beyond lavish. And it wasn't like the high class places in New York, stripped of emotion and personality. It was true artisan work, and I couldn't help but appreciate it.

I was a lover of the arts, and my own condo was filled with colour and passion. It was one of the few things that motivated me to earn as much as I did.

The second thing was the pristine young woman on my arm.

I led her up the marble staircase, listening to her heel click against the smooth stone, the two of us left alone as I showed her to our suite.

We had the entire wing to ourselves. I didn't scrimp on things like this. I worked hard, and I deserved the best, and while the hotel technically housed other guests, I ensured they'd be nowhere near me and my Angel.

The room was adorned in red and gold, the king sized bed nestled next to the large window that looked out over the ocean.

But lavish rooms and high class living weren't the only things the hotel was known for, and I greedily took in the little instruments I'd requested, laid out with care on the bed. A blindfold, five strips of leather with their metal Os, a paddle.

All I needed.

Angel reacted with sheer awe, gazing about as if she'd never seen so magnificent a place before in all her life, and of course she hadn't. Though when her gaze came to rest upon the sight of those kinky implements, her eyes dipped and I could see the blush fill her pale cheeks.

Though sweetest of all was how she clung to my arm a little tighter as she forced her gaze away.

"It's spectacular," she said breathlessly.

I stroked over her shoulder, warm from the heat of the sun, and yet even still, my touch made her skin bump.

I shut the door, locking it.

I didn't want to waste even a single moment with her, and I pulled away from her.

"I didn't give you permission to talk, Angel," I said with a tut-tut to my voice, my eyes flicking to the bed. The sun was higher in the sky now and the room was a bit darker than outside, a warm orange flooding the bed.

"You're going to have to be taught what happens when you speak out of turn."

The poor girl looked mortified. Her round, exotic looking eyes wide and glossy, her face appearing simply aghast. Those pouty lips of hers trembled, about to speak before she realized better and hung her head. Those little hands clasped before her as she awaited her punishment.

What a sweet young thing.

I had to hide my smile, though. My excitement.

That was the hardest part, for me. It wasn't doling out the punishment, it wasn't listening to the girls scream in pain and pleasure, or feeling them wriggle and writhe.

It was trying to pretend it didn't affect me until it was time.

I motioned towards the bed.

"Keep your dress on, but go to the bed," I said sternly, though I'd like to think I wasn't cold about it.

She obeyed perfectly, that beautiful young woman moving with such angelic steps, her dress streaming behind her as she went and tucked the skirts beneath her thighs and took a seat. She glanced over at me with those big blue eyes of hers before hiding back beneath her blonde hair.

I stepped towards her as she settled in, and I hoped her heart was racing like mine.

I had a specific set of instructions for the company that sent her, and so far as I could tell, they obeyed my every word.

My index finger went to her jawline, touching along it and making her look up at me again.

"I want you to be as quiet as a mouse," I instructed as I reached towards the leather collar at her side. My thumb ran along it, the cold metal pressed to my palm. Rubies adorned it all around in an intricate pattern and I smiled at the craftsmanship as I brought it to her throat.

She tilted her head back, chin up as she let me put that collar about her neck, tying it tight about her slender little stalk.

Up close like that I got to appreciate just how long and curved her lashes were, they fluttered before me beautifully as she let me take control. Her anxious swallow straining the confines of that collar, yet she restrained her squirm.

I looked down on her with such appreciation as I went for the next piece of leather, this one suited for her wrist. I lifted her hand from her lap and she kept it in place as I fastened it, the rubies glittering alongside that metal O ring.

I took a moment to feel her slender, smooth arm and smile.

I was so damned excited. The thought of having her, fully, excited me like nothing else. No meeting with the most powerful people in the world, no amount of money, could compare to the way I felt before taking a beautiful young woman for the first time, claiming her for myself.

To feel that milky white skin, with its smooth, flawless complexion. She was a work of art, like a statue carved by the finest of artisans, I wasn't sure such a girl as her could exist before then. But there she was, sitting so demurely, obediently. Offered up to me as I strapped her into the leather, claiming her as mine.

She of course never uttered a word, just cast furtive glances at me as I went about my work, took liberties with feeling her skin.

As I fastened the last one around her ankle, stroking up along her calf with such a calm sense of entitlement, my heart thudded faster and I could barely contain myself. I let her bare feet rest against my thighs, both of them held by my hands, as I looked up at her.

I reached for the blindfold, and beckoned her head towards me so that I could rob her of her sight.

She did just as I wished without a word said, leaning forward and letting me wrap that blindfold about her head, tucking her beautiful blonde hair out of the way. She was so still and quiet, but there through her gauzy dress, I could see the outlines of her stiffened nipples, betraying the excitement she felt as I took my time with her.

Those full, pink lips parted as she breathed heavier, her bosom rising and falling with each breath.

Without her being able to see, I was able to finally smile. To let my eyes trace along her beautiful body and finally let myself seem weak to her utter beauty.

I throbbed in my pants, and I wanted so badly for her to touch it, for her to know what she was doing to me, but that wasn't part of the game. The fun part was seeing how long I could resist. How far I could take her before I simply had to have her.

My hand cupped her jaw and forced her blinded face to me, so that my forehead rest against hers.

"Are you ready, Angel?"

That beautiful swan of a woman gave a light nod, her magnificent voice so soft and light.

"Yes, Sir," she said, ready to offer herself up to me fully, completely. She was the full package, no hesitation, no reservation. She wasn't just mine, she wanted to be mine. Such a rare treat in a submissive.

I smiled and stroked her cheek as I stood. I didn't want to bind her, not yet. I wanted to see what she'd do, how she'd react.

I wanted to give her some freedom, just to see her limits and what she'd do with it.

"Alright, Angel. I want you on all fours on the bed."

She obeyed, but blinded as she was she had to feel her way up onto the bed, her dainty fingers feeling out the rich blankets as she climbed in. That dress of hers didn't cover even half of her thighs like that though, her pert little rear wagging in my face as she bent away from me, bare feet dangling over the edge of the bed.

I liked disorienting them just a little. Making them enter my world, rely on me more.

What could I say other than that it got me hard?

I stood behind her, watching her ass sway with uncertainty, little tremors running down her spine, and I licked my lips as I undid my belt slowly so as not to give myself away.

"How do you feel, Angel?"

She was hesitant to answer me, I could tell, but she obeyed. That soft little voice so sweet and light.

"I'm not sure, Sir... a little nervous," and that much was obvious, with the way her slender limbs shivered now and again. Her much tinier form so frail compared to mine, her skin looking porcelain and untouched in the Caribbean light that streamed through the open windows along with the ocean breeze.

"First times will do that," I said, though I wasn't sure if I intended it to be comforting so much as a statement of fact.

"What do you want me to do?" I asked, and that time I knew I was just curious. Interested.

That question obviously threw her, the poor little dove flinching and faced me with confusion written on her beautiful pale face around the blindfold.

She took her time, wet her lips, leaving them glossy and moist.

"I... I'm not sure, Sir," she said faintly. Though she'd sold her virginity off to a rich man she'd not yet met, and I could see the stiffness of her nipples prodding down through her see-through dress.

Maybe it was just the money, but I didn't believe so. Not

with how selective I'd been, not with how many boxes on the checklist she had to say yes to.

I brought my hand to the back of her thigh, rubbing the backs of my fingers along that smooth, sensitive flesh. "Did you shave like I asked?"

Her blush deepened at that question, and I felt her thighs quiver a little. Those beautiful milky stems in my hand so soft and pure. She nodded her head and said to me softly, "Yes, Sir. Of course."

She'd never miss so big of an instruction as that, but I just wanted to see her reaction.

Especially as my hand trailed up her inner thigh with such a slow, teasing motion, closer and closer to that prize of hers. That little bit of herself that she sold to me.

Though I knew I got more than that. I didn't just want a girl's virginity.

I wanted them to be mine, willingly, happily.

I could feel the gentle heat of her femininity as my hand grew near along her thigh. That soft inner thigh flesh led me up towards it, where her bare little cunny — so smooth from her shaving and slick with excitement — greeted the light brush of my hand.

That momentary contact made her gasp audibly and her whole body stiffen in surprise. She bit down upon her puffy pink lower lip and suckled it into her mouth as she tried her best to remain quiet.

"Did you shave like I asked?"

Her blush deepened at that question, and I felt her thighs quiver a little. Those beautiful milky stems in my hand so soft and pure. She nodded her head and said to me softly, "Yes, Sir. Of course."

She'd never miss so big of an instruction as that, but I just wanted to see her reaction.

Especially as my hand trailed up her inner thigh with such a slow, teasing motion, closer and closer to that prize of hers. That little bit of herself that she sold to me.

Though I knew I got more than that. I didn't just want a girl's virginity.

I wanted them to be mine, willingly, happily.

I could feel the gentle heat of her femininity as my hand grew near along her thigh. That soft inner thigh flesh led me up towards it, where her bare little cunny — so smooth from her shaving and slick with excitement — greeted the light brush of my hand.

That momentary contact made her gasp audibly and her whole body stiffen in surprise. She bit down upon her puffy pink lower lip and suckled it into her mouth as she tried her best to remain quiet.

It was so sweetly endearing, and I couldn't help but throb once again, so eager to feel that tight little pussy around me. But more that even that, I wanted to taste her.

First, however, I had to do what I promised.

I brought my finger, laced with her juices, away from her smooth and untouched sex, hands instead pushing up the flirty dress she'd chosen so that I could look over her pristine ass cheeks. They were so pale, so delightfully gorgeous, and I stroked along her left cheek, feeling her out.

I rubbed it, first. Greedily, letting the soft flesh caress my hand and get the blood flowing to the surface.

She was like a mewling little kitten, half in heat, half awkwardly shy. She didn't know what to do with herself, trembling with the anticipation so innocently, a soft little sigh escaping those pouty pink lips of hers.

"This is for your own good," I said before bringing my hand down.

Crack!

The sound filled the air, and I stayed still for a while as she got that wail out. Her slender throat put to work producing a surprised squeal as my hard hand met her soft, delicate skin.

I felt almost heady with the sensation, greedily taking in her response and letting it ease my troubles away.

Back in the big city, I have a few trysts, when I care to. But overall, my tastes are so selective that regular sex just didn't thrill me. Not in the way that training new subs did. Those with a curiosity and a high price tag.

I brought my hand down again and watched as my handprint marred her beautiful, pale flesh for just a moment.

It wasn't just about the sex. It was never just about the sex, or even the power.

I wouldn't call myself benevolent, but I couldn't deny that a part of me wanted to imprint upon the women I've been with. That I wanted to have an impact that I couldn't have as just a suitor, just another john.

And so I brought my hand down again, shhing her in a gentle and warm manner as my hand stilled on her ass, rubbing the heated flesh.

Her pristine, pale flesh tanned red beneath my hand so quickly, her sensitive body prickling with pain as she cried out again and again, each crack of my palm making that gorgeous girl teeter forward on her slender limbs and reel back in.

It was easy to see that the intensity of my punishment was a bit hard for her to take, but she never relented, never showed a sign of failing me. She was a beautiful work of art, and I was making my mark upon her as she cried out.

I didn't want to take it too far. This was a ballet, and one that I knew needed time before it reached the final, beautiful, marvelous act. I enjoyed every moment of it as I brought my hand down once more, softer this time though it still met her skin with a loud crack.

"Because it's your first time, sweet Angel, I'll let you off if you say sorry."

She was whimpering, quivering before me upon all fours as she did her best to topple face first into the blankets.

"I'm sorry!" she said with little hesitation, her voice wavering a little with the pain she felt rising through her throat into her words. "Please, I'm sorry!" she bleated like a white little lamb.

She couldn't see my smile, or what those words did to me.

I had to watch my breathing so that it didn't get away from me, and I stroked her thigh tenderly.

"It wasn't all that bad, was it?"

"N-no, Sir," she said to me through trembling lips, the pretty little thing clearly enjoying it despite her delicate nature. Her flushed cheeks betrayed the depths of that sweet woman's reluctant interest.

She bit down upon her pouty lower lip, suckled upon it so sweetly as she knelt there before me. Looking utterly desperate for me to claim her, make her my own.

I couldn't help myself. I wanted to see her, and I wanted her to see me.

My hand went to her cheek, guiding her with such a tender, yet commanding, touch before my fingers wrapped around the back of her head, unveiling her to me like a delicate present.

I could see the moisture in her eyes beaded between her long, curves lashes as they fluttered and her gaze shut.

I then guided her towards my mouth.

I wanted to taste her, to feel the warmth of her worried lips against mine as she trembled. My other hand went to her shoulder, holding her aloft.

Those soft lips were pressed to mine, so perfectly smooth and damp. It was such a delight, the loveliest pair of lips I did ever kiss, and I could've savoured them for hours.

That sweet girl made kissing feel new and interesting again, like it weren't the prelude to something but the whole show. Intensely satisfying and exciting.

Especially with how her little tongue probed mine, testing it out, tasting me as well. I couldn't hide the fact that I throbbed beneath my pants at her enthusiasm, at the way she was eager for me despite the pink hue of her perfect ass.

The warm, tropical wind blew the curtains inwards, filling the air with the scent of sand and the ocean, the sound of foreign birds calling in the distance. It was the perfect vacation atmosphere with her kissing me so delicately.

I pulled back, coiling my hand around her ear, thumb rubbing along her cheek.

"How did you envision losing your virginity, Angel?"

Her eyes fluttered open once more and she looked at me,

anxiously gnawing her lower lip a moment before she mustered up the courage to answer me.

"A strong, handsome older man... who guides me, takes me from behind," she swallowed anxiously. "I've resisted temptation..." she said, and I could feel the need in her words. She'd been a good girl for so long; too long.

My hand roamed over her face, tenderly, just getting a sense of that softness of her cheek, down over her jaw and further towards her throat as I smiled.

That's another reason I love these arrangements. They're mutually beneficial. There's no drama for them in giving away their virginity, no boy that's going to play games or judge her for not knowing what to do.

It was simple, and pure, and again I throbbed in my pants as I motioned towards the head of the bed.

"Crawl back into place, honey. What have you done with others, mmm?"

She obediently got back into place, her alabaster skin so perfect and smooth, such sweet glimpses up her dress skirt as she faced away from me, towards the headboard.

"Just... some touching and making out," she said, sounding oh so embarrassed. Her naivety worn like a mark of shame rather than pride, because she was a little too old to be carrying around that innocence still.

My hand traced over her still stinging ass and she flinched, but stayed right where I wanted her. I trailed my finger along the handprint, teasing it as I spoke.

"I'm going to lift my rule for just a little while, Angel. I want to hear every little thought, every little word, said aloud, alright?"

She bit her lip and nodded adamantly, choosing to agree with me silently in such an odd manner. As if not sure what to do with the newfound freedom I'd given her at first.

"Yes Sir," she said, and I could sense her pushing back against my palm just a little bit. Feel the heat not only from her reddened cheek, but from her cunny so close by.

"I... I—" she stammered, struggling with confessing dirty feelings aloud. "I can't help but imagine what you'll feel like.

Inside me," she added on, those last words such a faint whisper.

I leaned back on the bed, my heart beating faster at her shy confession. Was there anything in this world sweeter than an innocent woman speaking dirty?

I licked my lips as I brought my hand along the cusp of her ass, touching her tenderly, teasing towards her slit.

"What else, Angel?"

As my hand neared that cunny of hers, I felt her shudder and heard her give a sweet whimper.

"I— I want you to touch me," she said, her voice a little strained with desire. "I don't want to be ignorant of it all! I don't want to be a virgin anymore," she confessed in such sweet tones, some of her warm slickness touching my fingers as I neared her quim.

I granted her a brush of my fingers against her smooth, shaven slit. She was absolutely soaking wet, and I couldn't help but feel a little bit of pride.

"You're going to have to do better than that, sweetness," I said lowly, just to tease her. To test how far she was willing to go, to see which desperation was worse for her.

She gave a suffering groan, so girlish and soft. It was filled with want and frustration.

"Please," she said, eyes shut, neck arched back as her spine curved in a feline sort of manner. "I want to feel you! Your... your cock," she said, her pale cheeks turning such a deep red as she begged for what she'd never known.

I brushed the back of my fingers against her pussy once more, just enjoying the slippery, smooth feel of her sex. I wanted her to reach her brink, and I knew she was already growing close. She didn't have the words to voice what she really wanted.

"Raw though, right Angel? You want the real thing?"

She was flustered, but she nodded, her vibrant hair bouncing with the motion.

"Y-yes! I don't want my first time spoiled," she said, arching her spine deeper and daring to press her needful cunny back against my fingers just the slightest bit. "I want you to make my first time perfect. Just like I always dreamed! Nothing in between us..." those last words uttered with such a lusty tone.

I intended to laugh, but it came out as more of a growl as I rubbed her pussy, up along her labia and towards her clit, circling there.

"And you want me to cum in you, don't you, Angel? To always have that link to me?"

It was easy to see she'd never been touched directly there before, because as my fingers teased her clit she moaned, shuddered and struggled to resist a flail from the intensity of her nerves being prodded.

"Y-yes! Cum in me! I want it to be real! Complete!" she begged me, that tone of desire unmistakable, unfakeable.

And I wanted to reward her for her good behaviour, but not before I rubbed that bundle of nerves once more, dragging my hand down along her slit and prying her inner labia open. I just wanted to see that perfect, pristine cunny before I filled her up.

She mewled for me as I inspected that perfect, pink slit. The hymen narrow, too taut for her to have been penetrated before. The proof of her virginity right there before me, promising such a tight squeeze when I finally sank into that cunny.

"Please," she begged again. "I don't know if I can wait any longer!"

What a sweetheart. I normally didn't like being rushed, but I was only a man, and her dulcet voice was driving me just as wild. Not to mention the sweet scent of her arousal.

I pulled back and brought my clean hand to my trousers, unbuttoning my pants before standing. I then went to my shirt, watching her as I undid it, letting her see as I throbbed beneath my cotton trousers before I finally stripped.

Watching her squirm, I could see her struggle with resisting moving, her blue eyes flicking to the side even as she tried her best to avoid doing so. She wanted to see my cock. Gaze upon it, know what was about to fill her. And she caught a good glimpse of its thick, vein-lined shaft, pulsating with desire for her. And it made her whimper with need all over again.

I stroked it, once more trying to tease her, to make me need to punish her. But she was so obedient. I don't think I'd ever met a girl like her, and I couldn't help but grin.

I went back on the bed, behind her, bringing my cock to her slit, rubbing my heated member against her labia. The warmth of the air had covered me in a bit of a sheen already, the tropical breeze relaxing me.

She moaned, a genuine, honest, beautiful moan from the very touch of my bare cock against her cunny. My thick, purple crown stretched her hymen gently, working it wider as she quivered and writhed.

"Oh god..." she said, and I wasn't sure for a moment whether she was speaking to me or not, with how she said it. "Please don't stop... I need your cock inside me," she said breathily.

No one could resist her plea, least of all me.

I placed a hand on her ass, parting her cheeks a little as I began to guide myself into her. There was that wonderful, blissful pressure as I eased in and then that final give as I thrust my hips forward, claiming her for myself forever.

I made her cry out, a loud squeal followed by a throaty moan as I sank my thick, pulsating member deep into that tight, once-virginal cunt of hers. And I felt the fullness of just how tight and untouched she was. The narrow clench of her womanhood upon my raw cock, knowing for certain she was the cleanest, most pure little woman a man could ever hope to sink his dick into.

She cried out for me as I watched those puffy pink cunny lips cling to the base of my shaft.

"Oh god... yes!" she said in a quivering voice.

My other hand shifted away from my cock, going instead to her hips on either side as I brought her back against me. I hilted within her sweet, tight pussy and just held her there, luxuriating in her wetness and the almost-too-tight clench as I growled.

Of course, it was all part of what was arranged. Such a sweet, willing virginal woman, who was tested to meet my needs. Yet what made it so good was how genuine it was, her moans, the way her tight little pussy squeezed my cock as I lingered in her, savouring her depths. She was the real deal, not a phony simply in it for the money.

"Please please please!" she wailed wantonly. "You're so big... I need you to take me," she said breathlessly.

I didn't delay or linger any longer. Not with those words tumbling from her lips.

Both of my hands dug into her ass cheeks, pulling them apart as I tugged out before slamming my hips back against her, watching my cock disappear within her again. There was a slight taint of red to my cock, mingling with her sweet, feminine juices, and I began rutting into her full force.

As the hammering blows of my cock reigned upon her, battering her ass cheeks with my groin, thrusting deep to her utmost limits with my throbbing cock, she buckled and fell face first into the pillows. She moaned and wailed, squealing and writhing as my dick plumbed her depths again and again.

"Oh yes, yesss...!" she gave an unintelligible wail and I could feel her body heating up, almost as if her pussy was coiling about me tighter as she wound up towards her climax. "I- I think I'm cumming!" she said, and the way she did so made it sound like she'd never had an orgasm before to judge by.

And I slammed into her harder, the head of my cock hitting against the depths of her body as I brought my hand around front. If she thought she was cumming, well... I'd make certain of that.

My index finger found her clit, that little heated bud almost buzzing with energy, and I pressed against it, circling it with firm motions as I kept hammering my cock into her.

That did her in, the sweet little angel's eyes were shut and she was flailing about, writhing beneath me as she screamed and hit her peak. A flood of warm juices coated my cock and she was like an out of control creature, limbs reaching out, nails digging into the bed sheets as she lost herself to not only her first fuck, but her first climax.

'Ohhhhh!" her voice warbled, "Yes! Yes Sir! God!"

"Yea, Angel," I growled. "Cum all over my cock."

It was hard to resist the way her cunny was tightening around me, squeezing me with such need. As if it weren't just her that needed my seed, but her body as well. It felt so primitive, so lewd, and I knew I couldn't last much longer.

Not against that tight cling of her pussy. The slick grasp of its folds!

She clenched about me, just as her clawing at the sheets tore them down towards her, and she twisted about, moaning and squealing.

"Cum in me! Cum deep inside me, please Sir!" she begged of me, desperate for it. Insane with need for our breeding.

I didn't resist the urge then. It took me not more than a second to find my own end, holding her still upon my dick as I unleashed those torrents of cum deep within her, splattering her insides with my creamy jism.

I growled out something unintelligible, grinding up against her as I brought my free hand down upon her stinging ass.

She seemed almost as ecstatic to have me cum inside her as I was to do it. She cried out with excitement as I flooded her fertile womb with my seed, spurt after thick, virile spurt filling her up as I hammered out every last drop into her.

She shut her eyes, relished it all as she moaned continuously, filled with such deep satisfaction as she let herself be lost to the full experience of her first time. A long, warbling moan passed out of her throat as she quivered and called out for me.

It was sweet, warm bliss and I stayed nestled within her folds for some time, just enjoying the little cries and whimpers and moans of pleasure that kept coming from her. She was such a beauty, and I ground my hips before finally pulling away and freeing my dick with a pop.

But I didn't let her relax. No, instead my hand went once more to her pussy, prying apart those sweet, flushed lips and saw my cream pooling within, threatening to spatter to the bed.

The sweet girl mewled and flinched just a little. Her puffy folds were reddened from being stretched, and oh so sensitive, but she craned her neck and watched with me as that pearly white seed drooled from her slit so beautifully.

"That was magnificent," she said breathlessly, her ample chest rising and falling with her heavy breathing.

My lips curled into a grin as I saw the change I'd brought about in her body, drawing out a little of the cum and rubbing it along her clit just to tease.

She shivered and my grin broadened.

"It only gets better for you from here, Angel. We're going to be spending a lot of time together." My fingers delved into her messy cunny, making her moan once more. "You're my girl now."

Professor's Pet

Book Themes: Teacher/Student, Age Gap, Daddy's best friend, and Breeding
Word Count: 5809

B rittany sat anxiously at her desk. It was the last day of school for the year before exams began, her eighteenth birthday behind her. Yet she knew things didn't look good. Whether she passed or failed entirely rested upon her performance on the exams, and she was just awful at them. Awful at the assignments too, for that matter. In fact, about the only thing she was good at was attendance.

Of course... she had reason for that: school was where the boys were. Where the men loomed over them all.

Mr. Hawthorne closed the door to the classroom, shutting out the noise in the hall before he turned and made his way back towards her.

He was her favourite teacher, for obvious reasons. So big and tall, a fit man who worked out on his lunch breaks, he had a great sense of style to boot. Always in nice European-cut pants, with

431

rich shirts undone a couple buttons, and a shiny vest atop that. Sometimes a fetching blazer.

He wore glasses, but he made them look good, with his thick, luxurious golden hair framing his face. He was twice her age, but always reminded her of the father she'd not had since she was but a little girl.

"Brittany," he said, in that smooth, masculine voice of his as he sat down on the edge of his desk and brought his emerald gaze to bear upon her. "You're not about to pass your exams without help, are you?" That authoritative voice challenged her to defy his logic.

And, of course, she couldn't. Her blue eyes glimmered for a moment before she tried to hide them from him under the long, dark lashes. She wore plenty of mascara to make up for just how fair they usually were, with her natural blonde hair and porcelain skin. She'd tried to tan, but all it had done was given her a cute brush of freckles across her nose and cheeks that she hid with concealer and powder and blush.

Still, they were mildly visible under the harsh glare of the school lights.

"I've been studyin' really hard," she replied, batting her eyes at him flirtatiously. "I just have a lot on my mind distracting me."

"Studying?" he said questioningly, sounding surprised with her, his full lips shifting into an amused grin. He reached out, his long fingers sliding over her cheek before his large palm cupped it. "Why are you wasting time at that, hun?" he said, his glittering eyes studying her, admiring her beauty. "We both know you're not the kind of girl made for that sorta work, don't we?"

She bit in her lower lip, tasting the vanilla lip gloss she loved, and held his gaze. She played a bit shy, but only because she knew it got to him.

She drew in a large breath, her silver chain sparkled along her collarbone, the delicate cross hanging lower beneath the cusp of her white blouse.

"What else am I supposed to do at night, when you're home with a family and responsibilities?"

He gave her a crooked smile as his thumb traced along her

lips, feeling the thick lower one softly as he admired her beautiful features. Wetting his own mouth with his moist tongue, he said, "Now, Brittany, I'm separated, but that's not the point of this talk..." he remarked, growing increasingly enraptured with her by the moment, she could feel it. One thing she did know, just instinctually, was men. "We could come to an arrangement for me to get you a passing grade, but what good would that do you, huh? You'd only bomb your other courses, right?"

She paused for a moment before reluctantly nodding. "Probably."

He was so near to her, she could smell some soft, woody aroma from him, and she leaned in to inhale him deeper into her. Just as instinctually as she knew men, she lusted for them. Was desperate for them.

Him in particular.

He gave her a gentle, tender sort of smile as he continued to softly stroke her cheek, letting his fingertips graze back over her ear and hair. "I knew your mom way back when," he remarked off-handedly. "You're a lot like her. Bet you're just as man crazy as she was, huh?" he said with a bit of a wry grin forming. "You're much prettier than she ever was though." His voice grew progressively deeper and sexier as he spoke and she licked her lower lip hungrily.

"She and I don't talk much about that stuff," Brittany admitted, but she quickly started remembering the comments her mother had made over the years and it all started falling into place. Her lips curved upwards and her cheeks dimpled in such a complimentary manner, a bit smug with the favourable comparison.

"Take my word for it then," he said in that husky, paternal voice of his laced with that added layer of lust. "Now, Brittany. Knowing who your mom is, and watching you very closely every day in class"—and the look he gave her said it all, truly—"I could offer to give you a passing grade if you agree to get down and suck my cock." He let that hang a moment as he studied her reaction. "Or..."

He trailed off there, his fingers curling in her hair and giving just the slightest hint of a tug on the blonde strands.

Her lip trembled at his... request? Demand? It didn't matter. Her stomach still flipped and she squeezed her thighs together beneath her navy-blue skirt.

She was a fairly thin woman, yet she'd been blessed with an ample bottom and full chest that threatened to make the buttons on her blouse pop open at any moment. Her breath caught again and they rose even higher, so deliciously near to his hand, begging to be touched.

"Or?"

He gave her an approving little smile, and his fingers uncurled from her hair as he leaned forward, his masculine musk so clear and pleasant to her as he neared her. He filled his suit so well, she noted, looking so professional yet stunning as he trailed the backs of his fingers along her collarbone and grazed along her breast flesh. "Or you can forget this silly learning nonsense, and focus on what you were made for, darling. You can come over to my place after class, accept you're gonna be a high school dropout, and I'll teach you what you really need to know to survive in the world. How about that, hm?"

"Oh god."

The words slipped out of her throat, so breathy and raw and instinctual, filled with such longing. As if he'd plucked from thin air just what she needed to hear, and her legs squeezed tight again, her pussy throbbing against her panties.

Her throat felt so raw and her stomach was twisted with her emotions.

She wanted that.

"But my mom will be so upset," Brittany managed in protest, but her smoldering gaze dared him to tell her she was wrong.

WIth a shrug of his shoulders he said, "So what? You're eighteen now. High school's behind you, and you can do what you want. Besides" —he gave her a cocky, knowing grin— "she did it when she was even younger than you. I should know, I advised her to do the same back then."

His thumb trailed along her lower lip, pushing the moist

morsel down as he leaned in close to her, those green eyes of his seeming fiery with desire. "If it'll ease your mind, after you come stay with me, I'll go over and calm her down some. How's that sound?"

She swiped her tongue along the salty, textured pad of his thumb, staring at him intensely.

Regardless of what transpired in this classroom, she knew that she would flunk out before the year was through.

And she wanted him so bad.

With his thumb still between her full lips, she murmured, "Promise?"

She watched as his Adam's apple bobbed as he swallowed, seeing and feeling her taste his digit exciting him even further. "Promise," he said, smoothly withdrawing his hand to reach behind him and grab a notepad. He jotted something on it then handed it to her. "Here's instructions to my place. Nice and detailed. Can't be seen giving you a ride home yet, doll, so you come on over after class and I'll start teaching you the only stuff that'll ever matter to you."

He stood up then, dangling that piece of paper before her, a commanding look on his face that said it was no longer an option. The choice was made.

She grabbed for it eagerly.

Brittany never went home, but straight to his place, following the directions on his note.

It led her to a quiet neighbourhood, and then right up to his house, which was a lovely place. It was a bit nicer than a teacher typically had, but then he had a wife before, separated now, so it must've been bought then.

His car was in the driveway, and she recognized it immediately. It was a nice, silver Lexus that looked only a couple years old.

Heading on up to the door, she rang the bell. She was a bit nervous, she had to admit. She'd never done anything quite like this, though she had thought about it so often. Fantasized about following him home one night or hiding away in his backseat, just waiting to pounce on him in private.

She'd fixed up her lipstick and straightened her skirt, but still she stood in those Mary Janes, the navy skirt that just grazed her white knee high-stockings, and her pressed white blouse. She knew it showed off the red, lacy bra beneath if anyone stared hard enough, and it always made her wet to think about.

To know that the boys and men around her were going to their rooms with the teasing glimpses of her cleavage and thighs on their mind.

It felt like an eternity, but a few moments later he appeared there before her, opening up the door and welcoming her in.

"Come on in, babe," he said to her with such a casual air of confident control, gesturing her up the stairs to his living room. His home was well furnished inside, the living room nice and big with a bar on one end. She noted his sleeves were pulled back, showing his thick, bulging forearms, the veins protruding prominently.

She nearly stumbled as she stared, but forced her way up, slowly.

She knew what he could see if he followed just the right distance behind. Those little flashes of milky flesh, so tender and ripe.

"Thank you, Mr. Hawthorne."

He never corrected her, never told her to call him anything else, but after staring up her skirt at the round swells of her ass cheeks as she climbed those stairs, he then very casually placed his hand upon her hip. "I'll get you a drink," he said, his strong fingers sliding down over the curve of her rear and giving her backside a squeeze.

She didn't bother suppressing her moan.

It was a slow, purposeful gesture, and he then walked over to the bar, taking out some vodka and a few other drinks as he went about mixing something for her. "Make yourself comfortable," he said, gesturing around the room, with its two large, plush sofas around a beautiful fireplace and TV; it was obviously meant for entertaining a large crowd.

"Oh, the parties I could have here," she said appreciatively, walking towards one of the couches and taking a seat, crossing her legs at the knee, and staring at him. It was almost like she was seeing him for the first time, her eyes traveling up his body with slow, steady purpose.

She popped open one of the buttons on the top of her blouse, revealing more of that hidden cross as it teased between her cleavage.

As he mixed their drinks he looked across the room at her, a wry smile upon his face. "There'll be plenty of parties here, Brittany, and you'll be here for 'em all from now on." He was so purposeful and matter-of-fact about it, even as his words dripped with heavy sexual meaning. "Your mom used to be a real party girl too. Wasn't how I met her, but it was how I got to know her way back when."

Brittany couldn't help but feel a bit curious, and almost relieved, to hear him say that. It was comforting to know that she wasn't... broken. She'd always looked up to her mom. She always worked hard, even if they didn't always see eye to eye.

Still, she found it a bit odd for her teacher to be talking about her mother in such a... sexual setting.

"Are you still close?"

He finished fixing the drinks, pouring a couple White Russians for them before heading over to the sofa with her. "Not as close as you and I are gonna get, Brittany," he said in a low voice, handing her the drink as he slipped down beside her, putting an arm around her shoulders. He was closer than he'd ever been with her, his hard body pressed up beside her, really accentuating just how much bigger the man was than her.

Leaning in, he inhaled her feminine scent and smiled. "Everything about you is just fuckin' beautiful, doll."

She loved the constant barrage of familiar nicknames, the feel of him... lusting for her. Wanting her.

And yet she knew she wasn't the one in control. She wasn't the one calling the shots.

He was.

She licked her lower lip before sipping the creamy liqueur, her eyelids fluttering pleasurably. "I never thought this is where I'd be tonight. Or any night."

He took a sip of his own drink then laid the glass down on a coaster on the coffee table before reaching over and resting his hand upon her knee. "Never?" he questioned her, as if doubting her. Those strong fingers of his rubbing over her inner thigh as he moved from her knee. "I guess imagination's not your forte, doll. It's okay," he said soothingly, smiling fondly at her.

She smirked back at him, already feeling the effects of the alcohol. Or, more likely, her youthful idea of the effects of the alcohol, combined with her own burning lust.

"I said I never thought this is where I'd be. Not that I didn't want it."

Some music seemed to start playing all of its own accord, or perhaps Brittany didn't notice him start it up. The rhythm of it starting off smooth and getting rather lively before long, though she didn't recognize it at all.

"You know, I've been waiting for this day to come for quite some time, doll," he said in his deep voice, rubbing her shoulder and along her thigh as he edged his fingers beneath her skirt. "Watched you grow up. Saw the telltale signs that you were becoming such a little sex bomb all the time." He gave a big, broad smile. "I don't think you could've turned out any more promising."

She uncrossed her legs and her knees pressed together, that throbbing of her pussy nearly driving her mad as she drank more of the White Russian. It was nerves. She knew it was. Her stomach was flipping and dancing unlike it ever had before, and she was feeling so damned hot.

"Oh?" she practically stammered, and cursed herself for not being better at keeping herself calm and collected. Uncaring of her teacher's desire for her.

He tilted his head, his thick blonde hair spilling to the side as he smiled at her. "Yeah, that's right. I was looking out for you even if you didn't notice it as such," he explained, his hand squeezing her leg as he moved in so daringly close to her feminine heat, forcibly prying her thighs apart enough to graze over her panties. "You're a very special woman, Brittany. A beautiful little airheaded bimbo," he said, as if it were the highest compliment.

"Oh god," she pleaded again, her head tilting back and her long, straight hair spilling over the cushion on the back of the sofa. Her entire body felt like it was on fire, and when he touched her, she barely knew what to do with herself. Her hands shook as she brought the rest of the drink into her mouth, eager for the creamy coolness to ease the scorching heat, but it only inflamed her more.

Mr. Hawthorne leaned over her, his mouth finding her neck and kissing upon her smooth, pale skin as his hand crept up to rub over her panties. His long finger tracing the outline of her slit as he kissed and suckled her neck up towards her ear, where he nibbled her lobe.

She could hear his rising breathing, and his low, lust-laden voice so quiet yet right there against her. "You're a walking, talking dickteaser in the flesh," he husked as he felt her dampness through her panties. "You're pure sex, and you've got no room in that head for anything else, just like you should be."

Brittany made a small noise, but it was incoherent. Halfway between a moan and a protest, her hips writhed against him of their own volition.

Her teacher was touching her.

Mr. Hawthorne was touching her.

Kissing her.

Purring in her ear.

She was putty in his hands as she put the glass on the end table, her body pressed to his eagerly.

He was so different from the way he acted during class, that warm, knowledgeable veneer replaced with bawdy talk and lewd touches. This was the man in his own home, acting with her as he truly wanted to, she realized.

The handsome, dashing man she had a crush on for so long feeling her up, pressing his long, powerful fingers into the cleft of her womanhood. Prying those well-trimmed digits in under her panties and tugging them aside so he could touch her slit bare, with nothing between them. He gave such an expert little swirl of his fingers around her sensitive clit and stoked her excitement so high.

"You were always an obedient girl, weren't ya, Brittany? Just never so good at the follow-through on all that boring school-work," he said in a low, lusty voice, eying her so hungrily.

She was squirming against him without even realizing, her body needing him so badly. Wanting for him so badly.

Her lithe thighs parted and she pulled back from him to stare at him with her bedroom eyes, her lips partially parted. "We shouldn't be doing this," she moaned, and begged for him to tell her she was wrong. Her back arched, her chest lifted, and she pushed herself towards him, her arms wrapping around his neck.

"Shhh." He hushed her softly as he continued to tease and excite her, kissing along her jaw towards her pouty lips where he licked and sucked those luscious morsels. "You leave the thinking to me, doll," he said quite firmly.

He pulled from her, despite her attempts to get nearer to him. Lifting those cunny-slick fingers to his lips he licked and tasted them, his eyes fluttering nearly shut as he seemed to revel in her flavour. "Mm, be a good slut and get down on your hands and knees," he commanded sternly.

Her stomach twisted, but she knew she wouldn't disobey. She couldn't. The way he was looking at her was driving her crazy and she whimpered as she leaned closer to him. But she knew that wouldn't be good enough, that she couldn't beg her way back into his lap and arms.

So she did what every good girl should.

She crawled off the couch and her navy skirt fluttered around her thighs as her knees pressed against the hard floor. Staring up at him beneath those dark lashes, she inhaled deeply and awaited his instructions.

That strong jaw of his squared off in a satisfied grin as he watched her fall to her knees so obediently, and he got up from the couch, straightening his vest as he lowered himself down behind her on one knee. Very casually he reached out, hooked his fingers upon her pleated skirt, and lifted it up, revealing the smooth, round cheeks beneath.

"Such a beautiful ass you've got, Brittany," he remarked just a moment before he casually turned one cheek red with a rough crack of his strong palm.

Her eyes went wide as she jolted forward with shock. "Ow!" She wasn't expecting that, not at all, but then the pain lessened and left a tingly feeling along the swell of her behind and her breath caught.

That was nice.

Letting her skirt rest on her lower back, he stroked his one hand up her spine, like stroking a good pet. The other rubbed over her stinging cheek, prodding those tingling nerves, putting them to the test as he smiled approvingly at both her beautiful body and her acceptance of the spank.

"That's for being such a little cocktease all this time, doll," he said, his fingers curling into her blonde hair, wrapping the strands about his digits as he struck at her ass once more, making the flesh burn hot.

"Ah!" Her eyes widened and then shut, her body folding to his whims, her scalp prickling, and her ass stinging.

Yet she couldn't remember ever being so turned on, so needy. The amount of control, of buildup that he was creating was something unusual for her. She shivered at the tension in the air, at her desire for him to simply take her.

And at the same time, she wanted him to take her to the limit.

His fingers tightened their grasp and he twisted his fist, punching her hair up and pulling back her head as he gave her stinging cheeks a pat, bringing more of the blood to the surface before he cracked his hand against the still pale and unpunished half of her ass. "You're gonna be a good lil' cock sleeve for me from now on, Brittany. Aren't you?" he said in a husky, commanding voice that so darkened the handsome man's words.

This was her teacher. The man who graded her papers, who knew her mother, who went to parent-teacher meetings and talked about her performance.

And now she was down on her knees, her skin stinging from his abuses, and all she could do was want more. Her ass even stuck out a bit more, begging for his harsh hand, even though it tugged her hair more.

Worst still, it all caused her to moan like a wanton whore.

He cracked his palm against her ass again, harder this time, and the sound of it filled his beautiful entertainment room. "I asked you a question, slut. That's a rare opportunity for you to use your words," he chastised as she heard him work his belt behind her. Was he undoing his pants? She couldn't tell, not with him holding her head in place so tightly.

She tried to look, but it only gave her more of that painful sensation to her scalp and she moaned louder. But she knew better than to disappoint twice, and she managed out a meek "yes," just to please him. To make him happy.

Then, instead of feeling the hot flesh of his manhood, he moved her body to the side just slightly, and... the crack of his belt across her ass landed along both cheeks, narrowly avoiding the puffy wet slit between. "That's better," he remarked in his hard, authoritative voice, over her cry of anguish.

She'd never felt something so intense in her life, and her cunny throbbed hot with need. Why wouldn't he just take her? Why was he insisting on punishing her so?

"Please," she breathed, but she didn't know what she was begging for. Leniency? Forgiveness?

Or for him to fuck her?

"Please?" he repeated questioningly as he let go of her hair and reached to her arms. He wrapped her wrists in his leather belt, then tied it up tight, locking them together securely. Grasping the back of her hair, he pulled her head up as he leaned in and bit her earlobe. A low growl rumbled from his throat and he husked out to her, "Please what?" Then a crack of his hand across her ruddy, battered cheeks came fast behind.

"Ah!" she screamed, this time a bit louder, and she hoped that no one could hear how hungry she sounded.

No one but her teacher.

She tested her hands, her fingers playing with the tongue of the belt as she squirmed on the hard floor. She didn't know what to say, what he wanted, and so she just whimpered again. "Please…"

He growled into her ear, "That's the best you've got for me, you bimbo slut? Just a 'please'? Please what?" He was insistent—demanding—and he struck her ass again, though this time after the loud crack of impact he left his palm to rest there upon her cheek, his fingers sliding over her glistening slit, testing her needful cunt. "Even a dumb slut like you has words enough to tell me what you want."

Her mouth hung open and never had she felt dumber. Not when she was failing his class, not when she'd first hit on him and he politely refused.

Never.

It was like all the thoughts simply left her mind, leaving her feeling vacant and a little haze before she licked her lips.

"You," she managed out finally. "I want you."

He gave a harsh little laugh and bit at her ear, tugging the lobe before letting it snap back to her. "You want me to fuck you, is that it? Then say it," he prodded, his fingers stroking over her cunny, swirling about her clit before trailing her warm honey across her stinging ass cheeks. "You're a bimbo slut, use your words like one," he chided, his hand cracking across her cheeks, the moisture of her cunt only making the sting worse.

This was so humiliating, to have him insult her like that. To use such degrading and horrible language.

But she was so fucking turned on by it, she could barely contain herself from turning into a quivering, stammering pile on his floor.

"Please fuck me," Brittany pleaded, her voice so desperate.

"Good girl," he complimented her, and very quickly she heard his fine black pants come undone behind her. A low thud resounded as his heavy cock smacked against her stinging ass cheeks. That hefty shaft bulging with throbbing veins, glistening at the tip with his precum.

He trailed that beast of a dick down along her cunny, teasing her slick womanhood as he grasped her hips with both of his strong, manicured hands. "This has been a long time in the coming, slut," he remarked, letting his digits sink into her flesh before he speared her upon his thickly throbbing manhood, taking her up to the hilt as he nestled his crown against her womb.

Her thighs tightened as she yanked herself forward, trying to balance herself against that sudden thrust and the sharp pain that followed as he went too deep, too soon. It took her breath away, and the feel of his hips against her stinging ass only accentuated her own feeling of pain.

"Holy fuck," she moaned out, her prissy skirt falling back around the top of her ass and his hips as she squirmed.

Those powerful hands of his grabbed her tight and pulled her back into place as he grunted his approval at her tight pussy. "Fuck, you're a good cunt," he growled, and she could feel the instinctual throb of his excited cock inside of her, twitching and filling her so completely. Pushing the walls of her narrow quim outwards so widely as he just enjoyed resting inside her warm, wet confines.

She couldn't believe this was happening. Maybe it was just the alcohol that made her slower to realize it than she should have, but her teacher was inside her. He was oh, so deep inside her, and she swallowed deeply because her stomach was roiling with butterflies and her mind was quickly growing hazy.

"Mr. Hawthorne," she whimpered, wanting him to be gentle, to go slow, and yet... not.

It didn't matter, as he went the pace he wanted.

He tugged back his hips, letting his thick girth slip from her, slick and hot before pounding it back inside with a satisfied grunt. He didn't ease it in her at all, but began to set a slow, hard pace that grew in tempo. The wet slap of her cunt against his groin, the smack of his heavy balls against her clit as he took her in the middle of his living room.

Took her was the right word, as those powerful hands of his grasped her so tight, taking control of her. Making her bound body his to command and use.

Her fingers tightened around the leather belt and her back arched before she gasped.

She couldn't remember him putting on a condom.

She couldn't feel a condom.

Brittany tried to pull away, partially falling off balance but for his strong hands keeping her pressed to him. "Are you... Did you put one on?"

That insistent throb of his cock inside her was so hot and real, so complete, there was no way some rubbery sheath separated him from her. His thrusting shaft pumped into her without a hitch in its rhythm, the loud smacks of his groin and balls striking her uninterrupted as he slapped her ass and reached out to tug her hair once more.

"Don't put your head to thinking, slut," he growled as he fucked her a little rougher in response. "I want the full experience."

Her heart beat angrily against her chest and she knew this was wrong. So very wrong.

He should be smarter than that.

She should have been smarter than that.

So why did her cunny pulse so wantonly, begging his cock into her deeper and deeper despite the stinging of her ass and scalp?

She was gasping for air and couldn't fill her lungs, couldn't clear her head enough to argue with him.

Despite all sense and reason he pounded into her harder and faster, that handsome, civilized teacher of hers fucking her wildly. The sounds of their rutting filled the room as he pushed her head down onto the floor, bending her body to his will as he kept her ass pushed up in the air only to be beaten so mercilessly with his thrusts.

"C'mon, you want this, don't ya, slut?" he growled at her, his voice ripe with need as she felt him swell and throb inside her. Again and again he pulsed so eagerly, and she could feel him tensing, working himself closer and closer to his climax within her abused body.

She couldn't keep track of the thoughts and sensations that

filled her. They came on too hard, too fast, and then left before she could grasp them. Her mouth hung open as she panted like a dog, her body contorting to his whims.

It was a long few heartbeats before she understood his question, and before she could stop herself, the answer fluttered out. "Yes!"

That was just the answer he wanted, and with one hand upon her hips and the other pushing her cheek down onto the floor he rutted into her with a rabid intensity. Again and again he savaged her poor, battered behind, until... she felt him come to to a screeching halt as he pummeled her depths one final time. His body tensed as he came intensely, letting out a loud, wanton moan of satisfaction.

More than that, she could feel the incessant throbs of his manhood as he shot his load right inside her, deeply filling her honey-slick canal. Spurt after spurt of that rich, virile seed flooding and filling her nubile depths.

"Fuck... yes," he grunted, squeezing her hip so tight as he shook intensely.

She thought, for a moment, she might be sick. Sick of herself, of what she'd let this man do to her.

But it quickly passed and she was filled with nothing but relief. Pleasure.

She groaned as he bucked again, weaker this time, and her eyes rolled back partway in her head as she tried to catch her breath.

He was panting over top of her as his cock twitched out its last pangs of release, unloading every last drop into her unprotected cunt. Bending over her, he leaned in and licked her cheek before nibbling her ear and lowly rumbling his pleasure to her.

"Good work," he praised her lowly. "We've got a bit more work for you to do before you're ready to be the star of this weekend's party, but... you're off to a good start, my little bimbo," he said, the name having no bite to it. Just pure praise. Pure approval.

"A party?" she whimpered, and she couldn't make sense of it.

And then, slowly, it began to sink in and she swallowed hard. "What?"

He slid back onto his haunches, but he took her with him, lifting her up off the floor with his hand in her hair and the other arm about her waist. He was still lodged inside her, and she could feel his pearly-white cum slowly dribbling out of her puffy slit as he spoke into her ear. "Going to hold a nice party here, for me and my good friends. And you're going to be the chief entertainment, doll."

She couldn't see his grin, but could feel it, knew it was there somehow as he held her to his lean, fit physique. "Excited?"

She shivered in his arms and didn't know what to say.

But she wouldn't deny the thrill that went down and settled in her core, making her breath quicken and her back push into his more eagerly. Her bound hands pressed against his stomach and she ran her fingers over him as she began to nod.

"Good," he husked into her ear as he nuzzled his cheek to her blonde hair and squeezed her tighter in his arms. "Until then, you've got a lot of practice to put in. You've still got a little too much pretense in you, my burgeoning bimbo," he said with a hint of amusement as he clutched her breast and squeezed it oh, so tight.

Exposed

Book Themes: virgin, breeding, older man younger woman, stripper
Word Count: 5776

The music is pumping, my body is saturated with a shimmery combination of sweat and glitter, and there's pure adrenaline running through my veins. I feel good. No, better than good. I feel like a million bucks, and it doesn't take a rocket scientist to figure out why. The club is absolutely jumping tonight. Every direction I turn my head, there's another flash of hundreds in some guy's hand. I wish I could say I was the kind of girl who doesn't get excited by the sight of a wad of cash across the club floor, but I would be lying. These days, it feels like nothing turns me on quite like money does. Maybe there's just something in the air.

And white-hot electricity running up and down the length of my body as I bend and sway to the pulsating beat. The bass is loud and powerful under my six-inch heels, giving a heady dizziness to my dance routine. My fingers curl around the glossy metal pole, the neon lights casting hues of bright turquoise and hot pink across my body. It only adds to my mystique, drawing in the whiskey-soaked gazes of the men scattered around the stage like lost boys. Their eyes are wide, their vacant looks quickly replaced with stares of pure desire. I lick my lips, running my tongue along my full, plump lower lip, the gesture stretching effortlessly into a winning smile. Turns out, it doesn't take much to reel in one of these guys. They are ready to party and ready to part with a lot of cash in exchange for a little taste of something new, something almost forbidden.

Almost. Except that I'm not *completely* untouchable. There's one surefire magic spell to get me alone in one of those VIP rooms in the back of the club. No incantations necessary, just enough cash to get my heart pounding and my pussy slick. Maybe it makes me a little shallow. But I don't care.

I need the money, and I am more than willing to bend over backwards-- and forwards-- to get it. I spin around the pole slowly, arching my back and letting my legs stretch out. I stand out from the crowd, even among the other beautiful women who work here. My long, curly blonde hair spills over my pale, bare shoulders. My honey-brown eyes smolder in the low light, and once they land on my catch of the night, there's no going back.

I set my sights on a guy at the edge of the stage. He's tall and broad-shouldered, his face obscured by shadow. He's well-dressed, especially compared to most of the frat guys and lonely older men who come in every night for lack of anywhere cooler to go. He looks like he has money out the wazoo, but it's more than his obvious cash flow that has my attention. Something about this guy draws me down from the stage, my feet barely touching the ground as I swish up to him. All I have to do is bite my lip and bat my long lashes and he's mine. He leads me by the hand, totally silent, all the way back to the VIP room. The door shuts behind us and we're alone. Just how I like it. Just what he wants, too, by the way he slides into his chair and waves me over.

Suddenly, all I can think about is his anatomy and mine, the science of blood reallocating, of hormones and endorphins rushing at breakneck speed to keep up with our money-laced tryst. I straddle him, careful not to actually touch him even though my thighs are burning to make contact. I move my hips and trace my manicured nails down his muscular shoulders. Somehow, even though his face is still shadowed, I can feel his eyes on me. Locked with mine as I gyrate and twist. I wonder if he knows how wet I am between my thighs. I wonder if he knows how desperately I want to slip my lacy black panties aside and tug his tailored pants down to his ankles, climb on top of him, and ride him until we're both sore and spent. Never mind the fact that I'm a virgin. Never mind the fact that he's a perfect stranger- - emphasis on the perfect. I want him. My body wants his. And when he breaks the rules to run his huge, powerful hands down my slender sides, I forget all about the lapdance. He pulls me down into his lap and a burst of bright, searing lust explodes in my chest. I lean in to kiss him. I need to know how he tastes.

But as soon as my lips brush against his, my eyes flutter open and the club melts away, along with my irresistible mystery patron. The adrenaline dies down and I sigh, realizing that I'm now staring up at the vaulted ceiling of my bedroom in between the four posts of my bed. I sigh and roll over in the silky sheets, my eyes narrowing at the number on the clock.

Half past nine. I groan and sit up stretching.

"Just a dream," I murmur. Even I'm surprised at how disappointed I sound.

I slide out of bed, my toes curling as they hit the pink carpet I've had since I was eleven. And the sheer number of horse posters hanging there are indication enough that my bedroom is in desperate need of an update. Not that my parents have noticed that. In fact, it wouldn't surprise me at all if they still think I *am* eleven, even though I'm enrolled in college and I'm almost old enough to order my own whiskey at the club.

But who am I to burst their bubble? I don't need their help anyway. I have a plan.

I trudge into my bathroom, which is just as pink and frilly as my bedroom. I strip off my silky PJs and step into the steamy rain shower. I sigh as the hot water hits my bare skin, beading in thick droplets down my naked body. The remnants of my sensual dream come floating back to me, along with a flush of warmth between my thighs.

I can't help but answer the siren's call, and before long my fingers are slowly working my clit. I bite my lip and close my eyes, giving in to the sensations and letting that mysterious stranger come back into my thoughts. I imagine his big hands running down my thighs, gripping me by the hips, squeezing my ass, my slender waist. I shiver at the thought of his hard cock straining to break free, aching for *me*. I reach up and take the fancy detachable showerhead out of its cradle and switch it to the pulse setting, and with a little sigh of pleasure I point the pounding water at my sensitive clit. Leaning against the shower wall, I rock my hips and whimper with need as the showerhead circles that tight little bud of nerves. I'm not going to last long at this rate, especially when I picture my dream-patron unzipping his pants and pulling me down to rut against the growing bulge in his boxers. He's gripping me tight, whispering filthy, pretty words in my ear as I spin closer and closer to the edge. I imagine a low, growly voice calling me 'princess' and telling me I'm a good girl, and that's all it takes.

"Oh my god," I groan as an orgasm vibrates through my whole body. My knees buckle, and it's all I can do to stay upright and finish my shower with my legs all trembly and my heart racing at breakneck speed.

I hop out and wrap a towel around myself, then step into my walk-in closet to pick out a blouse and jeans. In contrast to this modest outfit, I also grab a pair of fishnets, a matching black lace panty and bra set, and some staggeringly high heels, which I toss into a tote bag alongside my purse and school bag. If there's one thing I've learned about living a double life, it's that you tend to accrue a lot of dirty laundry. But it's a small price to pay for independence. I don't need my parents for money, and I don't need a man to make me cum. And thank god, because I'm still a virgin.

Still, I can only imagine how good an orgasm must feel with someone else.

"Someday," I tell my reflection as I towel-dry my blonde curls.

I skip out on a makeup routine for now, but I pack the essentials for later. Right now, I'm just a good student heading off to class. Nothing risque. But tonight, I'm going to don that black lingerie and a smokey eye and feel like a million dollars. I feel so powerful when I assume the nighttime version of myself, like I can conquer the whole world and crush it beneath my platform heels. Today is Friday, which means I can stay out all night and blame it on a study session or hang-out fest with my friends. My parents will have no clue what their little girl is really doing, and that's the way I like it. They'd just try to stop me.

I comb my curls and hoist my bags over my shoulder. I give myself one more quick glance in the mirror before I walk out, and I'm satisfied with the reflection. I look the part of a normal college student... for now.

As I head down the hallway to the stairs, I'm met with several staff members who greet me with a warm but professional, "Good morning, Miss Holloway." I do what I always do, which is smile and respond with politeness. I'm accustomed to this. My father likes to keep a full staff on the property, since he's always jetting off to foreign countries to attend meetings. He's a real estate mogul. My mom is a former supermodel. She attends fashion shows and makes guest appearances all over the globe.

It's always been this way. My parents check in with me all the time and make sure I have everything I need, but they're not here to see the changes in me. They don't see that I'm not their little princess anymore. I used to dream about being a princess, but nowadays... apparently I just dream about big, hard cocks. Talk about character development, right? Not that my parents have noticed I'm not a kid anymore. They don't know anything about my life.

Hence my former nanny, Maggie, who happens to be in the kitchen chatting with Rodrigo, our personal chef, when I walk in. It may seem strange to still have her on staff when I'm no longer a child who needs a nanny, but at this point Maggie is basically family. She's been with our family since I was a toddler, so there are sentimental reasons for her continued position on the staff. But it goes deeper than that. Maggie also keeps an eye on me and makes sure my parents are in the loop. She's their spy. Which means I need to be extra cautious around her so she doesn't figure out my secret plan and go blabbing about it to my mom and dad.

"Good morning, Prissy! Did you sleep well?" she greets me brightly.

It's Priscilla, I want to insist. Prissy is a childhood nickname I can't seem to escape, and one that no longer fits me. But instead of telling her that, I just smile so she doesn't suspect anything is amiss.

"Morning," I reply, reaching for one of the waffles Rodrigo has stacked on a plate. "I slept fine. How are you two?"

"*Bene*," chirps Rodrigo.

"Good. Heading to class?" Maggie says.

I nod. "Yep."

"Bright and early," she remarks. "Which class is it? Fashion design?"

"I've got three classes today," I answer, dodging the actual question.

I make sure to keep my arm over my school bag to hide the spines of my textbooks so she can't see the titles. That's yet another lie I'm carrying. My parents think I'm going to college for a fashion degree, like my mom always wanted. But it's not my passion, it's hers. And I can't fulfill someone else's dreams. I can only push toward my own.

"Ooh, busy day," Maggie says. Her tone is light and casual, but the way she's looking at me I can tell she's angling for a firmer answer. Time to pull out the big guns.

I take out a pink binder covered with a collage of cutouts from fashion magazines and pretend to flip through it for a second. As soon as her eyes land on the binder, her gaze softens. There we go. Easy peasy. I give her another winning smile.

"Well, I better go or I'll be late. Parking is a nightmare on campus," I remark.

"See you later, kiddo!" she replies.

"Actually, I'm going to a study group at a classmate's house tonight so I'll see you tomorrow," I tell her as I hurry out of the kitchen.

"Oh! Okay! Well, be careful and make sure that homework gets done," she calls after me.

"Will do!" I shout back before stepping out into the glorious sunny morning.

Phew. Glad that's over. I hurry down the steps and climb into my Mercedes, tossing my bags into the passenger seat. I drive down the long, winding driveway to the road and finally out to the highway. I glance at my rearview mirror to check the line of cars merging behind me, then turn on some upbeat music to get my energy flowing. Traffic is crazy, probably mostly students like me rushing to class. There are a few cars going the same way as me, including a heavily-tinted black luxury sedan. I wonder what kind of student drives a car like that. Then again, I'm sure all my classmates think it's odd that a nursing student like me happens to drive a Mercedes. Granted, it's an old model since I got it for my sixteenth birthday, but it's still a Benz. I know what kind of stereotypes I'm working against here. Everyone I know thinks I'm going to college for some frivolous degree, but underneath that fashion-mag binder is a gigantic anatomy textbook. I want to learn to be a nurse and take care of other people instead of relying on other people to take care of me forever like my parents expect. I just need a chance to prove I can stand on my own two feet.

Once I get to campus, it's the usual battle for a parking spot. There's a line behind me of students looking for the same thing, including that black sedan. Although, once I miraculously find two open spots next to each other, the sedan drives right past it and keeps going.

"Weird. Guess they decided to ditch class instead," I murmur to myself as I gather my belongings and get out of the Benz.

I quickly put the black sedan out of my mind, focusing on the day of classes I have in front of me. Anatomy, microbiology, medicinal botany. A far cry from the fashion, yoga, and pottery classes my mom insisted on. I smile proudly to myself as I walk into class and take a seat. It's not that I enjoy lying to my family, but I'd be lying to myself if I said it didn't give me a little bit of a thrill. I can't help it. Besides, I'm not using my parents' money for these classes. I'm not touching the limitless credit cards they gave me anymore either. If I'm going to be a nurse and, more than that, an independent adult, I have to handle things myself.

The day runs smoothly and I enjoy my classes. I'm finished by mid-afternoon so I head off to a cafe for a caffeine pick-me-up and a homework sesh. To my surprise, I happen to notice a black car waiting in the drive-thru line outside the window while I work. I do a double take as I see the car slowly pull out of the line and park. I hold my breath, my heart racing. Is this person following me? I strain my eyes to try and see who's at the wheel. I can vaguely make out a dark, large figure-- definitely a guy, and definitely way bigger than most guys, too. I wait to see if he'll come inside to confront me or something. Maybe Prissy would be afraid right now, but Priscilla can handle it. In fact, I make the decision that if he does come in and get in line at the counter, I'm going to pull a power move by anonymously paying for his order. Just to make him nervous. But before I can live out my perfect plot, the car promptly pulls back out and drives away.

"Damn," I whisper.

I'm disappointed. The driver's bulky frame reminds me of the mystery man in my sex dream from this morning and I wanted to get a better look. Oh well. I focus on my homework and get it done in time for me to take a moment's rest before I get back in my car and head across town to my next destination. The sun is starting to sink toward the horizon, casting pink and golden light across the sky. My adrenaline is pumping. This is what I've been looking forward to all day: my chance to prove myself and hustle my own money.

The sun's gone down by the time I pull up to the strip club. I grab my tote bag and quickly make my way to the back entrance. Immediately, all of my senses are hit with the sounds and sights and smells of the place. I can feel the bass pumping from the front of the club, and it gently vibrates the glossy floor beneath my feet, seeming to reverberate through the very walls. The lights are down low, with orange, hot pink, and turquoise hues casting the hallway into a dreamy nocturnal vibe. It's like stepping into another world. I forget about who I have to pretend to be during the day, about how many secrets I'm keeping. Here, nobody knows me as Prissy. In fact, nobody even knows my real name. We all go by pseudonyms here anyway.

I walk into the dressing room and am greeted with a cheerful chorus of, "Hey, Scarlet!" from the other women.

Out on the floor, we may look like competitors for the attention and cash of the clientele, but in the dressing room our true feelings come out. We can be vulnerable here together while we apply makeup, tease our hair into a little sexy volume, and change into our sexy outfits for the stage. We support each other, crack jokes about crappy or ridiculous clients, talk (quiet) smack about management, and help zip or unzip each other's strappy getups.

"How's everybody doing tonight?" I greet them as I open my locker and start peeling off my boring daytime clothes to change into the black lingerie set.

"Katrina got a heavy hitter earlier," remarks Destiny.

"I thought he was going to be a dead end, but turns out there was a bunch of cash in those ugly, stained cargo pants," Katrina laughs.

"Don't judge a book by its cover," I reply with a wink.

"Or a patron by his number of pockets," giggles Juliette.

"Friday night, girls," says Ruby. "We're all gonna rock it."

"Hell yeah," agrees Destiny. "There's a bachelor party out there."

"Easy pickings," I say with a grin.

Once I've amped up my look, I head out onto the club floor, thrumming with excitement. I get onstage after Fiona steps down and I take her place at the pole, wrapping my slender body around the cool metal. I drop my head back and shake out my bouncy curls while I arch my back. The song playing is one of my favorite jams, and I feel sexy and powerful. Every time another dollar lands at my high-heeled feet, I get a little rush. There's a group of guys accumulating at the front of the stage, all of them clearly buzzed and utterly entranced by my undulating body. This must be the bachelor party, and by the looks of it, they came ready to spend. Drunk, attentive, and spendy, just how I like them. Well, except for the bachelor himself, who is definitely drunk but not the friendly kind. I see him shove through the crowd to stand at the side of the stage, watching me with bleary, narrowed eyes. I can hardly tell if he's turned on or angry, but either way I keep dancing and bringing in cash.

When my song is over, I blow a kiss and step down from the stage. My feet have barely touched the floor before I feel a hand grip my arm. I whip around to see that the bachelor himself is in my face, looking me up and down with a hungry gaze. I can smell alcohol on his breath when he leans in close, and it's all I can do to not jerk away from him.

"What's a guy gotta do to get some alone time with you?" he slurs in my ear.

"Let me take you to a VIP room for a lapdance," I reply, always the good hostess.

There are alarm bells ringing at top volume in my head but I can't turn down a paying customer. I gently pull away and gesture for him to follow me as I lead him back. As soon as we step into the tiny room, he shuts the door and lunges for me, his hands gripping my arms as he pins me against the wall. I let out a yelp of fear as I try to fight him off, but he has his hand on my ass and he's so strong.

Suddenly, the door bursts open and a massive figure rushes into the room. It takes me only a few seconds to register that the man ripping the bachelor away from me is none other than the guy in the black sedan! My eyes widen as I watch him grab the handsy bachelor by the collar, throw him against the opposite wall, and I hear a sickening crunch as his fist connects with a jawbone. The bachelor drops to the floor instantly, and I don't get a chance to react before my mystery follower scoops me over his shoulder.

"What are you doing?" I gasp.

"Saving your ass," he growls.

There's no use in fighting-- he's too powerful. He carries me out of the VIP room, across the club, and out into the night. He hurriedly shoves me into the passenger seat of his car and peels off into the night. I stare at him in utter shock.

"Did you just kidnap me?" I splutter.

"Kidnap is a strong word," he replies. "Besides, you're not a kid."

"Who the hell are you? What do you want? You've been tailing me all day!" I retort.

"Good thing, too. You need someone to watch over you."

"Excuse me? I can handle myself, thanks. And my parents will literally have your head on a platter for this!" I snap.

"Unlikely," he says. "Considering they hired me to do this."

My blood runs cold. "What?" I murmur. "Why?"

"You stopped using your credit cards. They want to know where you're getting your money," he explains. "I'm a private investigator."

"My own parents hired a PI to follow me?" I burst out. "And where are you taking me? Wait. Please don't take me home. Look, your knuckles are bleeding from... hitting that guy. Oh god, I'm going to get fired."

"Judging by what I saw tonight, that might be for the best," he says. "Put on that t-shirt in the back seat so you're decent."

I reach back and grab the oversized t-shirt, pulling it on over my head. I get a little thrill when I realize it just be one of his. It's massive on me.

"You're the one bleeding all over the place," I shoot back. "I'm training to be a nurse. You should let me bandage you up. Maybe... at your place?"

"You're serious," he says.

He sounds surprised and honestly, so am I. But I don't feel afraid of this man, despite the fact that he just stole me right off the club floor. I trust him. He did kind of save me. More than that, though... I want to be near him. I can't help feeling like I've met him before.

Maybe even in my dreams.

"It's got to be better than going home," I tell him.

"I'll figure out what to do with you there," he growls back.

My heart skips a beat. It worked! Far from the fear I was feeling at the club, I find myself simply excited. By the time we pull up to his modern, luxury apartment which seems to double as his PI office, my body is buzzing and my heart pounding like mad. He hustles me into the apartment, which is just as beautiful on the inside as the outside. It's meticulously clean, if a little spartan. He leads me through the office area to the kitchen, where I pull up a chair and make him sit down while I find a bottle of alcohol and a washcloth to start tending his bloody knuckles. Being this close to him is intoxicating, and for the first time I get to see him in better lighting. He's even more handsome than I thought when I saw him in low light. As I hold his injured hand in mine, I feel my body getting hot.

"It's really not fair," I say suddenly. "You seem to know a lot about me but I don't even know your name."

"Vince," he replies. "And you can stay here for the night, but I'm taking you home tomorrow. I'll make you a cot on the couch."

"Aren't you worried I'll try to run away or something?" I tease.

"Not if I keep an eye on you," Vince remarks.

I quirk an eyebrow. "All night?"

"If that's what it takes," he answers.

"You were right earlier," I tell him slyly. "I'm not a child. Let me prove it to you."

He crosses his thick arms over that powerful chest and watches me, waiting. I flash him a devilish smile and take a step back. Slowly, I play with the hem of the oversized t-shirt, teasing him with little tastes of what's underneath. He's watching me ever so closely and I can see the fierce desire burning in his gaze. It's a thrill to want and be wanted in the same degree. I've never craved anything the way I crave him. I don't quite know what to expect, but I know I want whatever he has to offer me. I long to feel every part of him.

I run my hands down my body and hold eye contact with Vince while I gently tug the shirt up over my head. I toss it aside and begin to rock my hips. My fingers course through my blonde curls and I let out a soft sigh. I can feel his eyes burning into my very soul while I seduce him. He doesn't look away for a single second while I step closer and drape my arms over his muscular shoulders. I can't help but feel like my sexy dream is coming true. It feels totally surreal. I'm giving my mystery guy a lap dance, but not in the club. Not for money.

For something I've never had before.

And judging by the thick bulge I see, Vince is after the same thing. I sway and gently brush up against him, then peel off my black lacy panties and bra to let them fall on the floor. My fingers traipse down his back as I slide closer. I lean close to tease his lips with mine, bestowing an impossibly soft kiss. My hands move to cup his face and I revel in the sharp cut of his jaw, the rough stubble shadowing there. Every inch of me is on fire for him. I'm acutely aware of his heat, his quiet strength, his scent— everything about this man is addictive to me.

Vince can't resist anymore. His hands grip my slender waist and rove down my thighs. He flicks a fingertip along my wetness, just for a moment, just enough to make me gasp.

He leans in close to raspily whisper in my ear, sending sparks of desire through my body.

"You want to be a grown-up, I'll gladly treat you like one. But you have a lot to learn, don't you?"

I shiver. "Yes. I-I'm a virgin. But please, I want to learn. I want you to teach me, Vince."

"As you wish. On your knees," he growls.

"Yes, sir," I reply breathlessly.

I drop to my knees and watch enraptured as he unzips his pants and pulls them down with his boxers. My heart is pounding. I can't believe this is really happening. His massive, hard cock bounces free and my mouth waters to taste him. I've never wanted anything the way I want him. I've never done this before, but Vince guides me down with his hands pressing gently at the back of my head and weaving through my hair.

"Open your mouth and relax your jaw for me," Vince orders softly.

I do as I'm told, and I'm rewarded with the satisfying sensation of his cock pushing into my mouth and tickling my throat. I groan and feel another rush of wetness between my thighs. I begin to bob up and down on his shaft, reveling in the way he stretches my cheeks and fills me up. He grumbles with pleasure when I pick up the pace. I was made for this. Made for him. I feel him tensing up, but he lightly pushes me back before I can get him to the edge. His cock slips out of my mouth with a wet pop. There's a fierce hunger in his dark eyes as he grabs me and picks me up, my legs wrapping around his waist. He carries me down the hall to his neat, sleek bedroom and lays me back on the king-sized bed. The breath catches in my throat when he moves down between my legs and runs the stiff tip of his tongue along my wet slit. I cry out and he pushes my thighs further apart with his hands, diving in to nibble and suck at my swollen clit.

"Oh, it feels so good," I whimper.

His tongue traces perfect, delicious circles around the sensitive bundle of nerves there while his finger teases my right little opening. Before long, I'm bucking my hips and rocking against his face. The pleasure becomes overwhelming and I go limp as the most powerful orgasm of my life vibrates through me— and it doesn't stop at one. I come again and again with his tongue and fingers between my legs until I'm no longer even coherent.

"Are you ready for me, Priscilla?" he rasps.

I can only nod vigorously and say, "Please."

Vince positions himself carefully, guiding the head of his stuff cock to my aching hole. I press up against him needfully. I hiss with a combination of pleasure and pain when he pushes inside, millimeter by millimeter until he's fully sheathed down to the hilt. My pussy contracts and pulses around him. The feeling of fullness, of being whole is almost too much.

But Vince leans down to gently kiss me while he withdraws and slides back in, gradually moving faster and harder. I'm so tight that we can both feel every twinge. The head of his cock bumps against a secret spot deep inside of me that makes me see stars. My pussy blooms for him, unfolding to let him in.

I know what a risk it is, taking him inside me, without any protection. I don't care. Hell, maybe I even like it. The thought of him knocking me up, marking me as his for all time...

He caresses my breasts, my stomach, my face, while his rod spears into me over and over again. I can feel him starting to lose control and that sends me over the edge. My legs tremble through another climax, and the way my pussy squeezes his cock is enough to bring him over the line with me. With a few more rapid thrusts, Vince tenses up and growls my name fiercely while he empties his virile seed deep inside of me. We shudder together through the powerful waves, clinging to one another. He rests his forehead against mine for a few sweet moments. My heart surges with affection and I feel so completely connected to him on a soul level.

When we're both spent, he pulls out and collapses beside me, tugging me close. I giggle and drape an arm across his chest while we come down from the enormous high.

"Well, if I wasn't a grown ass woman before, I am definitely one now," I sigh contentedly.

"Yes, you are," he agrees with a smile.

"Listen," I whisper sleepily, "I don't want my parents' money. I also don't want them to worry about me. Please let me keep my secret. Just for now."

"I don't need your parents' money either," he answers after a short pause. "I'm not going to turn you in. But I have conditions."

"Go on," I urge him, snuggling closer.

"I'll give you cover and protection if you promise to be more careful and find a less dangerous job. You also have to promise you'll let me help you," Vince commands.

"I promise," I tell him.

"And Priscilla?" he prompts.

"Mhm?" I mumble.

"I think you should start spending your nights here. With me. You know, for safety's sake," Vince insinuates. He traces a finger across my cheek. The softness underneath his words is reflected in his gentle touch. For the first time in a while, I feel truly safe. And happy.

Like this is where I'm supposed to be.

I smile against his warm skin as I drift off to blissful sleep.

Fiona's First Time

Book Themes: Voyeur, Virgin, First Time, Age
Gap, Creampie, Peeping, Breeding
Word Count: 6777

The farm had always been run by us for as long as I can remember. My ma and pa passed when I was just a baby, and so my oldest sister, Rose, she took over. Then the twins, Mary and Lizzy came of age and they started helping out. Then Fiona, she graduated high school, and you guessed it, she started workin' on the farm too.

But I wanted something more than that. I wanted to go away to the big city, to see the flashing lights and a city that never sleeps. I wanted to lose myself in a new place, and meet new people. But Rose, she didn't want that, and neither did any of the others. They were pleadin' with me not to go away for college.

My grades sure were somethin', and I always was the teacher's favourite. Reading far beyond my own level, but our town's library wasn't at all big, and there was still so much I wanted to learn.

So I guess we came to a compromise. I'd stay until I turned 19 at least, and help out on the farm. In return, they were gonna hire me someone they called a tutor, which I guess was just a teacher who would be able to teach me in private. From home.

I wasn't lookin' forward to it, not at all. It was just somethin' I was agreeing to to get them all off my back for a little while when I finally decided to take off.

But Mr. Roberts, well... he made me have some second thoughts, I'll admit.

The first day Mr. Roberts arrived was a pretty momentous occasion for our sleepy lil' farm. My sisters never saw a whole lot of men folk in their day to day, and neither did I for that matter. The local school house was run by the church, and so boys and girls were taught in separate halves of the buildin'. Which meant even in our school days, we never had much of a run in with fellas.

But when he first got there, I watched from my upstairs window. There he was, a dapper lookin' fellow, wearin' a smart lookin' suit the likes of which I'd never seen. I'll admit here and now, my opinion about having a tutor immediately changed. If only a little.

Rose was the one most eager to greet him, though not for the reasons ya might think. She was the boss of the farm, as the oldest, and she had it in her head that she was our protector. And a fella on the farm meant she had some idea that she had to scope him out and make sure he'd be safe to have around.

Even she was a lil' surprised to see such a fancy lookin' fella at our door though. Tall, dark and handsome would be the cliché way of puttin' it. He wasn't big and burly like the few other local farmers we did encounter, he was lean and fair. With a pair of glasses, though they didn't make him look dorky or nothin', lil' bookish perhaps, but that was okay. I loved my books.

I never heard their first talk, but I could imagine how it went, knowing Rose well enough, and their body language.

She stomped on up, past my three other sisters who were there to greet him first. Rose pushed on up to the front, hair tied back in a ponytail, her old work shirt tied up in front, skin tanned and glistenin' from a hard mornings work as she stood there in her jeans.

She was welcomin' him, but layin' down the rules too. She was big on rules, especially for guests. But while she barked and blustered, I could see Mary and Lizzy talkin' between each other with masked excitement, eyin' him up and gigglin'. Then there was Fiona, lookin' stern as she could manage, though that's how she always was. I knew beneath it all that she was just as excited for the touch of change, almost as much as me she wanted sometin' else. Don't think she ever liked bein' the "middle child". Felt she never got enough due.

Which was why when Mr. Roberts started to greetin' them all, takin' Fiona's hand first of all and kissin' the back of it, I could tell she was smitten. Though the twins weren't fussed at bein' second and third place. While Rose would have none of that fancy do!

M y first time meetin' him came shortly after of course. Well, shorts a relative thing. Rose kept him out there for ages, showin' him around, impressin' upon him the importance of his duties to teach me. She could go on a while, I'll tell you.

I swear, she thought she really was my ma.

But this part of the story ain't about me and Mr. Roberts, not yet.

My sisters didn't tend to notice me so much, 'cause I was quiet and kept to myself. Or so they thought. But truth of the matter was, I was a great listener, and I had a knack for sneakin' about, keepin' tabs on what everyone else was doin'. Usually it weren't nothin' too interestin', but with Mr. Roberts on our farm, things took a turn for the interesting, and I wanted to be in on it.

Fiona had changed her clothes since Mr. Roberts first arrived, even though it was only a couple hours later. That weren't like her at all, but then again, Fiona was a different kinda woman altogether when there was a fella involved I was learnin'.

I knew she had an inklin' to leave the farm. We'd talked about it in times past, but she never wanted to do it by her lonesome. And she never wanted to do it with me much either. Fact of the matter was, though she'd never admit it, I think she just wanted to meet a fella and move off together.

Seein' her dolled up in a nice dress as she went out to the guest house confirmed it. She brought a plate with her, holdin' a lil' mini cake she'd baked herself to bring to the man as a dessert.

When Mr. Roberts answered the door, his tie was gone, and his collar undone, but the man looked only more handsome still.

"Oh hello Fiona, sorry, I wasn't expecting company, I was just unpacking and trying to settle in," he said, a bright, friendly smile upon his face as he held the door open. "Come on in," he invited immediately.

Fiona goin' into the tutor's room? Well, that was against one of the rules, and I knew it. Could have screamed bloody murder and Rose'd come running, and she'd chase him out of the house then and there just for invitin' Fiona in. We were all pretty close in age, me and my sisters, but Rose acted like she was fifty when she was only half that.

Now, I know Fiona didn't always get lots of attention, but truth be told, it wasn't her looks. She was a pretty girl, and none too stupid. But she just always was overshadowed by Rose. Or the twins. They teased her somethin' awful at times, so Fiona sometimes acted like she was the loneliest girl in the world.

"Sure, I'd love to Mr. Roberts," she said with a cheerful smile on those ruby lips of hers. She even got dolled up with makeup!

Now, here's about where my knowledge of the situation might be expected to die off, but I knew our farm in and out, better than any of my sisters even. And every place had its own little peep holes or quiet nooks to nose in on, and the guest house was no exception.

"What's that you have there?" he said, eying the little cake with fascination as Fiona waltzed on in, swayin' her hips so wide.

It was a little weird, watchin' her like that, I had to admit. Kinda exciting, though. I just knew somethin' funny was goin' on with how she was movin' and biting down on her lower lip like she was real nervous as she offered him her baked good.

"I made this just for you, Mr. Roberts," she said, as she blushed real bright.

It was a pretty lookin' lil' cake too, I had to give her that. Chocolate, looked like a lil' volcano with some chocolate sauce runnin' down the sides to the base. It set my tummy to rumblin' then and there, but I had more important things to keep track of.

"Wow, it looks delicious! So fast too," he exclaimed in surprise, smiling as he took the cake from her and laid it down on the small table that was his own personal eating nook, just two chairs and a table next to his mini-kitchen.

I was watchin' from my hidey-hole that I crept into from beneath, and I could see it all.

"Would you like to share it with me?" he asked, fetching two forks from the drawer as I studied his room. He wasn't lying, he was fast settlin' in, putting out his suits, a little ornate globe and an array of books he'd brought with them.

I couldn't wait to get my hands on 'em! But it wasn't the time...

Naw, I was learnin' about something different altogether. I was learning about how men and womenfolk talk together. I practiced pressing my lips together like Fiona was doing, but it felt strange.

"I would love that," she said, and even her voice was different. Had a strange little lilt to it. Like it was a bit lower, and she really emphasized the world 'love'.

She went to sit down, but then Mr. Roberts did a surprisin' thing, he took hold of the chair for her and pulled it out, offerin' it up to her like she was some sorta princess or somethin'. Guess he just had some refined manners that the local boys didn't.

"Such a gentleman," Fiona said, and she came over, holding

her red dress up at one side between her index finger and thumb as she sat down more dainty than I'd ever seen her behave. It was such a strange shift in her behaviour, but I couldn't help but be entranced by it. I was learnin' something real different. Like for instance, that beneath her red dress, Fiona weren't wearin' a stitch! Nothin'! I could even see her bush!

"Ah well, when a man entertains a lovely lady in his residence after she brings him a delicious looking cake, he has to treat her right," he said, setting the table, pouring them both up some milk before he sat down with her.

He was pretty smooth, my new tutor-to-be. I wondered if he'd treat me like that, but I shook the thought from my head. I was just the baby of the family. No one wanted to treat me like that, and I never could have thought to make him a cake like that. I should've, though. That would have made him like me loads more and wanna teach me even better.

She crossed her legs and I couldn't see between them no more except for along the sides, her tan legs nice and muscular from all her hard work around the farm. Fiona wasn't a slouch.

She might've chafed at Rose always bein' so bossy, but she worked as hard as any, harder! Just to prove she was as good as any of the rest of us.

They dug into the cake, but right away Mr. Roberts was taken. You'd think he'd just bitten into the most delightfully tasty thing he'd ever put in his mouth!

"Mmm mmm! Oh my, Fiona, you must be the baker of the family," he said with such appreciation, and I bought it, didn't think someone could fake such enjoyment of a simple cake!

But oh, Fiona, she was bright red, and I watched as the top of her foot ran up his shin a little. I thought that was weird, her messin' up his nice pants like that. But he didn't look upset at all, and she was grinning like some fool.

"Thank you for sayin' so, Mr. Roberts, but normally I leave the cookin' and bakin' to the twins. It's only when special company comes by that I like to break out my... culinary skills," she said, her voice like I'd never heard it before, so... enticing and erotic.

For his part, Mr. Roberts reached on over, placed his big hand upon her knee, right at the edge of her dress skirts and gave a squeeze as he smiled.

"A shame you don't get to exercise those skills a bit more then, you're clearly well suited to them," he said with a smile.

And I knew for a fact that Fiona never cared for baking and cooking, heck, she downright loathed it normally! Or at least, pretended to. But suddenly with Mr. Roberts there you'd think she was Martha Stewart! Heck, I wouldn't have been surprised if the twins had baked that cake and she was just takin' credit.

Her foot kept rubbin' on him, and she shimmied a little bit closer to him, bringing the fork to her lips and pressing the cake between them. And she made a sound, but it wasn't a normal dinner-time sound. It was more like a moan, and she was lookin' at him the entire time. That was really strange, I figured, but I didn't know nothin' about this sort of thing.

I'd have to practice when I got to my room, makin' that sound.

They continued a while like that, the two of 'em eating and looking at one another across the table like somethin' was strange. If I didn't know better I'd say they wanted to eat each other more than the cake.

There on her knee, Mr. Roberts' hand lingered, and her foot — still in that high heel I'd never seen her wear before! — kept tracin' up and down his calf.

I knew the cake was done because I heard the forks hit their plates, but still they kept touchin' one another a little.

"Mr. Roberts," my sister began, as if somethin' was on her mind rather serious, "I know you're going to be busy with teaching Lily, but..." she stopped there.

"Go on," he said, urging her as his hand rubbed up from her knee to her thigh, raising her dress a little and letting his palm and those long fingers touch her thigh. "What's on your mind?"

"Well... I was thinkin' you and I could spend some time together now and then. Get to know one another. I'd be ever so interested in hearin' your stories about travel and such. Maybe...

tonight. After the other girls have gone to bed," she said, an impish lil' smile on her ruby lips.

"Fiona," he said and it sounded more like a wolf growlin' than a man speaking, and he leaned closer to her.

"I'd enjoy that quite a lot."

I couldn't believe what I was hearing. Fiona was gonna get her behind tanned if Rose ever found out about this!

Yet there she was, Mr. Roberts barely havin' time to get through the door and she was encin' him off to do things that were strictly not allowed. More than that, her high heeled shoe was left upon the floor and her bare foot trailed up from his calf in between his thighs so brazen like I figured he'd jump up!

But he didn't.

"There's a creek nearby, where the farm gets its water. But there's some trees off to the west, and that's where the old tree house is. You and me can have some private time there, lookin' out over the water... the moon and all above us," she said so sultrily, I had no idea where she got it from!

Mr. Roberts stiffened in his seat a little, and I could see he was breathin' heavier.

"I'll meet you there then," he said.

"After all the lights go out in the farmhouse," she added, smilin' so happily with herself.

I couldn't believe my eyes, nor what I was hearin'. One thing I knew for certain, though. There was no way I was going to miss what was to happen later that night.

T knew full well what treehouse Fiona was talkin' about. I'd spent much of my time up there readin' to get out of chores over the years. Never did I think Fiona would be usin' it for somethin' so... naughty, though.

But soon as the lights went out, I waited for it: the sound of Fiona sneakin' off. It was so soft you'd have to be expectin' it to hear. She was a crafty one, craftier than I gave her credit for, that's for sure.

I went after her shortly thereafter, my PJs nice and thick, so I didn't need to worry none about gettin' cold. But her? I could see her ahead in the moonlight dressed in the same outfit as earlier, but holdin' her heels in her hand until she got to the edge of the farm, and slipped 'em back on.

I had to be cautious, because I didn't know when Mr. Roberts would be comin' behind, but as Fiona got into her heels and waited, I took my station.

Y'see, later on, Rose found out about my secret tree house, and she'd come and drag me back to the farm to do chores. So I created a second little hideaway in the trees. Tucked in underneath the treehouse was a lil' box, obscured by the branches and leaves, where I was able to hide out.

I had to get into the treehouse before either of 'em though, slide the secret hatch out of the way and climb down in. None too soon either, 'cause I heard a giggle and a laugh.

I was beneath 'em again, but this time I had a much better vantage point. My little hideaway was made to avoid Rose, but for that I needed to keep a good eye on her too. It helped that when Mr. Roberts and her climbed up, they turned on a lantern, lightin' them both up so I could see 'em clear as day.

There came Mr. Roberts, a fine back jacket on, but no tie again. He looked slicker than before, and his glasses were gone too. He was downright dashin' without 'em.

"So this is your little fortress of solitude, Fiona, hmm? A nice hideaway," he said with a grin.

It was my hideaway. A little flare of jealousy went up in my heart, but I squished it back down. I didn't have time for none of that. If she wanted to use it, I wished she'd have asked, but I understood why she didn't. I wouldn't tell her if I was sneakin' out after lights-out. That would be a recipe for disaster.

But she was touchin' on his chest, and that made me feel a little jealous too, though I didn't know why. I barely knew the teacher, and I didn't want to be the one touching on his chest. So why did it make me feel weird?

She beckoned him in, biting her lower lip anxiously as he followed after her. From his angle, he could even get a glimpse up her dress skirts, and I wondered if she was still not wearin' any panties like before.

"Just a convenient lil' get away for us, under the circumstances," she said to him, and I noticed her dress was awful low cut. She must've done somethin' to make it even worse than earlier that day, because her breasts were showin', big round mounds swelled up into cleavage from the red dress.

"So why are you so interested in my travel stories, huh? I figured you had to be very happy here on the farm. After all, it was young Lily that's the one trying to get away," he said, already being filled in on that personal tidbit.

I kinda resented being 'young Lily'. I wasn't a baby anymore, and I felt a bit hot and angry, but Fiona started talkin' again and what she said shocked the anger right out of me.

"I've been thinkin' of running off for a while now. You know, really experiencing what the world has to offer. But with you right here, I figured maybe you could just show me."

I didn't understand it wholly, but I knew that tone wasn't to be used in polite conversations.

I saw as Mr. Roberts gaze dropped low, then looked to Fiona and saw her legs were spread, and spreading wider. Her dress hiked up, and from my angle below I could see, she was bein' downright shameless with how she was showin' her flower to the newly arrived man!

I mean, we all had fantasies and such, but this fella had only just arrived, and there was my older sister showin' him her privates so shamelessly!

"Looks like you've got a lot to show me too, Fiona," he said, his voice deeper and huskier than usual as he stared between her legs, making my sister grin and bite down upon her lower lip. "You're as pretty beneath your dress as you are outside it," he said.

I thought it might not go no further than that, but then Mr. Roberts reached out, his long fingers extending to touch along her inner thighs, stroking the backs of his digits along her smooth skin. He traced along her, enjoying the feel of her skin quite obviously.

It sent a shiver down my spine, truth be told. My breath held, and it wasn't that I was scared they'd find me. They were both too distracted for that.

But I just couldn't find my breathing. It was weird, but I could almost feel it myself, that light tracing of fingers along my sensitive flesh. But that didn't stop how wrong my sister was. I wondered if I should stop her, tell her she better get back into the house to apologize to Rose straight away.

But instead I just waited for what would happen next.

"I'm glad ya think so, sir," Fiona said, just lettin' him touch on her! His fingers tracin' in closer and closer to her cunny. He weren't just lookin' at her most private of privates now, he was touchin' 'em! His fingers grazin' along the edges of her puffy, reddened lips, so swole up.

I've seen my own get like that on rare occasion, only when I awoke from a rather... naughty dream. And it looked like my older sis was havin' a doozy by the looks of how red and glossy it was.

"I've been around the world, visited a lot of countries," Mr. Roberts said, studying Fiona's little flower, brushing his thumb against those folds, makin' her shiver and whimper. "But there's more beauty to be found on this simple farm than I've found in all my journeys."

Again I felt that weird little pang, wishin' that he could've said that to me. But instead I was just young Lily, nothing like my overconfident sister and her way with him. She wasn't embarrassed or shy, not at all. I'd never seen her be so up front to someone, not ever.

"You mean that?" Fiona said, brushin' back some of her hair from her face, and I could see she had a touch of blush to her cheeks. She wasn't as brazen as I'd given her credit for, although... only by a bit.

She had the nerve to show off her lady bits to the man, but she still felt at least a lil' embarrassment over it.

Mr. Roberts didn't answer her right away though, and I thought for a moment he'd confess to not meanin' it. Instead, he brought his free hand up, stroked two fingers along the mound

CANDY QUINN

of her bulging breast, then curled them into the cup of her dress. He helped himself to tugging down her dress, exposing her right breast — which was so much bigger than my own! I felt jealous. Then he was stroking about her pinkened areolas, and stiffened nipple.

"It's confirmed," he said with a confident smile, so smooth and undaunted by it all. "Absolutely beautiful."

I was breathing heavier, though I was trying to keep still. It was uncomfortable, cramped like I was, but I barely noticed. My eyes were glued on the two of them, on how they were touchin' each other.

Fiona let out the sound like she did when eating the cake, this low moan, and she pushed her breast into his hand, her legs spreading even wider.

Mr. Roberts leaned in to her closer, his hand workin' at her lil' cunny in such a curiously precise fashion, makin' lil' circles near the top, makin' my older sister moan and whimper some more. While his other hand squeezed at her breast, sank into that fleshy mound and toyed with her sensitive nipple, makin' her flinch now and then.

"Have you ever been with a man before, Fiona?" he asked her, and I almost answered 'no' for her. None of us had!

"Yeah," she said, and my eyes went wide! I had no idea!

But my older sister stared into his eyes, lost in the moment, breathin' heavily as her chest heaved.

"He was older'n me," she continued. "He passes through now and then to sell things to the local shop."

I immediately knew who she meant. Mr. Erics. The travellin' salesman! He worked for some company or another, and he pitched products to Herbert family for their local store. I couldn't believe it! Fiona and Mr. Erics?

"How far did you go?" Mr. Roberts asked, continuing to work at her body.

She couldn't have done what they were doin', not like this. He wasn't ever around long enough for that, I was certain. But then, I'd been certain she'd never done somethin' like this before at all just a moment before.

Didn't she know what Rose would do to her?

It was enough to make me wanna scream, to try to protect her from her bad decisions, but Mr. Roberts was touching her so lovingly, and I stayed put. Part of me didn't want to interrupt.

"We touched some, like this," she said to him slowly, her voice heavy with her lusty breathing. "He took me behind the shop, and we showed each other all we had. We was gonna go all the way... but then he got transferred to a new area," she said with a whimper as Mr. Roberts seemed to find some special way of stroking her.

"So you've never had a man slip his cock into your pussy," Mr. Roberts said, his words so crass I felt my cheeks turn blood red! "Such a shame. We'll have to fix that tonight," he said with such a smile I felt a chill run down my spine.

I wanted to run out, to hide from all this. I was curious, sure, but that language... I couldn't believe my ears. I know there was no way that I'd be innocent, not after seeing what was happening in my treehouse.

But there wasn't a way out. I was trapped, unless I wanted to expose myself, and then I'd be in as much trouble as Fiona for not telling sooner!

"Please," my sister said in a whimper, "please fix that for me, Mr. Roberts."

I couldn't believe my ears! My sister was beggin' for it! For the nasty things that dashing stranger was sayin' to her!

He withdrew his hand from her chest, leaving her breast to fall back to her chest with a jiggle as he began to undo his top. Now, I'd never seen a man naked, not once. But I'd seen one topless a time or two, but none compared to Mr. Roberts.

He was lean, but he was fit. Beneath his shirt was hard, lined muscle, and just a sprinkling of hair over it. He stripped away his shirt to show his statuesque pecs and abs, and my sister and I were transfixed as he exposed himself.

She was the first to break the spell though, reachin' out, and runnin' her hand along his chest, feeling him up with such relish.

"You're so handsome," she said, soundin' younger than me with her excitement.

I had to put my hand over my mouth to quiet myself then, because I was getting really scared and feeling really hot. Not just my cheeks from being embarrassed, but between my legs too. I pressed them together tighter and took in a deep breath through my nose.

I couldn't make a sound. I had to be as quiet as a mouse, even as her hand went lower and lower along his abs.

Mr. Roberts paused his own hands after he stripped off his shirt and jacket entirely, his broad shoulders rotating.

"I'll leave that to you," he said, as my sister's hand got to his belt at his wait.

She nibbled her lower lip anxiously, but did as he said. Her two hands going to that leather belt and unbuckling it, the excitement in her clear as day as she began to undo the man's pants right before my eyes!

"There you go," he said in a deep husk, right before she peeled his pants open... and reached into his underwear!

Dear lord! How'd she manage to do such a thing?!

I'll never know!

Fiona was grabbing at his maleness, right before my eyes, squeezing him and keeping her eyes on his the entire time. She was being so brazen, I couldn't believe it.

And I really didn't understand why my own breathing was getting shallower. It wasn't happening to me, after all, but I could almost imagine it was. I had to shake those thoughts away though. They weren't proper, not at all, and I couldn't stand to think about them.

Then she pulled him out of his pants, though, and my sex throbbed in response. I couldn't believe it. It looked so strange and foreign, that big, meaty stick that she held in her hands. It wasn't like us girls at all, and I leaned forward to get a better look.

That big tool was ribbed with pulsing veins, jutting off its meaty length. It rose up at a slight upwards curve towards the tip, where her stroking hand revealed a big, glistening purple crown! It was... well, magnificent. I never saw a thing like it in my life and yet I immediately knew I wanted it. Craved it.

It was embarrassing to even think that, but it was the truth, and I could feel it down below. Watching those twin balls swing out of his drawers, so heavy and big, I was breathless!

"God, you're a big man," Fiona said breathily, and though I had no point of comparison I felt he had to be! I was wonderin' how he was gonna squeeze that thing into my sister — or me! — and not sure how it could be possible.

He grinned at my sister's compliment, stroking the hairline along her cheek and pushing some of her hair back as he watched her. She was touching his most private of parts, and he was just looking at her like it was all a big laugh or something. That it wasn't nothing to be ashamed of.

I forced myself to take in some breath, because I was getting a bit dizzy, and I had to close my eyes for a few seconds just to steady myself. When I finally opened them again, he was kissing her right on the mouth as she started to run her hand up and down his shaft.

The two of 'em were poised above me, showin' their naughty parts with not an ounce of shame, makin' out and touchin' one another as if it were no big thing. I couldn't hardly believe it, but there it was, right before me.

He pressed Fiona back, laying her out on the floor of the treehouse as he got down over her, in between her legs. Now, that might've made it hard for me to see, but nope! Fiona's legs spread so gosh darn wide that her dress slipped up to her ass, and I watched from beneath as her hand guided him in to her. That big, bulging tip of his pressed to her puffy, wet folds, and they prepared to lock parts just a few inches from my face!

I could smell the soft scent of them both on the air, and maybe that was what was causing me to be so dizzy. My heart was pounding in my chest and I was worried that they'd find me, but they didn't seem to hear a thing over their own heavy breathing.

I wanted to reach down and touch myself, truth be told, but I was a good girl. I wasn't going to do something like that, or something like what Fiona was doing. It wasn't right, but I was transfixed as he started to push into her.

It was like something was stopping him, at first, and I figured it was just too big to fit into that tiny little twat. She made a face like it hurt, but she kept her legs open wide.

"Just break it," she said, and I was scared for her. Break what? Break her?

I wanted to yell at him not to, but what could I do? I was trapped, and I had to stay still and quiet. And even if I wanted to, I couldn't stop him because he bucked his hips forward in one movement, and she screamed somethin' awful.

He stayed still for a second as she quieted down, her body relaxing a little bit and she smiled.

I didn't understand that! She'd just screamed bloody murder and now there she was, smiling like a maniac.

I looked back to where their bodies met, his thick organ splaying her folds so lewdly, his balls pressed up against her ass. Then as he began to pull slowly back, I could see that little trickle of red that stained his bulging shaft. He'd hurt her!

But the way she was moanin' as he pulled back, then thrust in again, said she wasn't hurtin' no more. Fast as that.

Mr. Roberts was pumpin' that big dick of his into my sister right before my eyes, and the pungent aroma of their sex was fillin' the air as they grew faster, more heated.

"Fuck," he cursed so crassly all the time with her. "You've got such a tight hold on my cock, I feel like you're gonna milk my nuts dry in no time," he said, staring at her tits as they swayed with the motions of their rutting.

I puzzled at those words. I didn't know what milking nuts meant, and it took me a second's pause before I decided to look it up when I got back. Try to find it in one of the books I had, though I knew I didn't have nothing that talked about what they were doing.

My lips parted as Fiona moaned back in response, "Oh yea, big boy?"

She obviously understood what he was talking about!

Fiona clearly had more experience with men than me, and I reckoned that the salesman had shown her quite a few things behind the shop judgin' by her familiarity with it all... but I was so focussed on what they were doin'. The slap of their flesh, his heavy balls smacking against her ass, the wet noise of his dick plunging into her cunny again and again.

I was so close I could smell and see it all, every lil' detail! The way her tight little quim swallowed up his dick each time he thrust forward, only for her folds to cling to him as he tugged back. It was gross and yet beautiful in its own way. I'd never seen a thing like it, and I should've been horrified, but hearin' them moan as they did it, I knew there was nothin' but good feelings to come from it all.

"Fuck you've got such a tight little cunt," he said in a deep, rumbling voice. "I'm gonna fill it with so much cum, you'll be bursting," he growled.

I didn't know what he meant, of course, but I knew from the way Fiona was squirming beneath him, begging him with those whimpered, "Yes, yes," sounds, that it was good. It had to be real, real good, and I wanted it too.

I was jealous, and my hand went between my thighs, just to try to stop my bits from throbbing.

I had no idea how long it'd all gone on for, but it felt like an eternity to me. With how my privates were pulsing with need, aching for some relief, I felt like I was ready to die.

Yet above me, I watched my sister get fucked by that handsome stranger, ploughed into by his thick cock again and again, their pace rising. I watched as a curious thing happened, and those big, heavy balls of his began to tighten up, and no longer slapped my sister's ass anymore.

He gave a big, loud groan, and his rough thrusts became erratic, and Fiona cried out loudly, screamin' for him to fill her. Then I watched it all from beneath as if in slow motion. That big dick of his pulsed, and even though he came to a halt, it swelled up as if it was pumping all on its own.

And I began to understand it all better then. He was filling her full alright, and it wasn't long after I found out with what. Because once he pulled back that thick, creamy white spunk began to drool from her puffy lil' slit, and I could see it begin to run down towards me.

I was going to have to move or else it'd drip down and hit me in the face, but I didn't. I don't know, maybe a part of me was just too curious to wanna hide from it, and I watched as those few little drops went down between the cracks, dropping on my nose.

It smelled so strongly, and my nostrils flared.

And then I did something I'm not too proud of. I brought my finger up to my nose, to those little drops, and I smeared them away before...

Before bringing my finger right to my lips, and tasting their combined juices.

As I tasted my first drop of cum, the two of them above me made out passionately. While I was delighted by the salty tang of that milky seed, and another drop landed upon my lips this time where I licked it away, they fondled and felt each other up.

I got so wrapped up in my own experience, fondlin' myself beneath my PJs and tasting his seed, that I got carried away and made a moan myself. It got the attention of the two of them above me and I froze in my tracks.

"Did you hear that?" Fiona asked Mr. Roberts as he felt up her big tits.

"Probably just some animal," he replied, not wanting to be distracted from her body.

"We should get on back before Rose notices I'm missin'," Fiona said, suddenly worried about getting caught again, now that she had the man's cum dribbling out of her pussy.

"Alright," he said and he pulled back from her with a final smack of their lips.

"Thanks for showin' me somethin' new," Fiona said with a blushing grin as she pulled her dress back into place.

"Thanks for the warm welcome," he echoed in response as he tucked his big tool back into his underwear and pants with some effort.

And then, before I knew it, it was all over. They were disappeared back out into the darkness, and I was left in the treehouse by myself, the smell of their sex so heavy in the air. I couldn't believe what I'd witnessed that night, and I figured it was goin' to be the only time I'd ever see something like that.

But following around Mr. Roberts, it didn't seem he was all too content with just one of my sisters, and when I noticed him eyeing up the twins one day, I took to spying again...

Sweet on Her Boss

Book Themes: Age Gap Romance, BDSM,
Boss/Intern
Word Count: 5667

The heat bubbles from the pot on the stove, gently boiling hand-stretched pasta while a fragrant, creamy pesto sauce simmers in a saucepan.

I'm tending the stove with a big wooden spoon in my hand, breathing in the complex bouquet of aromas. I'm in a commercial kitchen, the familiar white and stainless-steel mini universe at the stuffy, steamy back end of a restaurant.

I feel totally at home in this environment.

As a student of the culinary arts, this is the kind of place I spend most of my time. I could whip up a compote with my eyes closed. I could flambe a bananas foster with my hands tied. A kitchen like this is my happy place.

It's weird, though. Despite the warmth of the stove, I still feel a bit of a draft around my legs and ass. I look down and do a double take as I realize I'm not wearing my usual double-breasted white smock, nondescript black pants, and sensible black shoes like I'm supposed to in the kitchen.

Instead, I'm wearing what looks like a stereotypical French maid's uniform, complete with black swishy skirt, frilly white apron, poofy petticoats, and black stilettos. My legs are cross-hatched with a fishnet stocking, black lace thigh garter, and-- oh my god. Crotchless black thong?

This is absolutely not a food-safe ensemble!

In what universe would I be caught dead in this kind of outfit in the kitchen?

But it quickly becomes clear to me that I'm not here under the usual practical purposes. There's no note pinned to the wall over my head instructing me to complete an order. In fact, there's no other sous chef or line cook or even a dish washer. And yet, I realize that I am not alone here.

Before I can turn around to look at who's with me, I feel a warmth at my back. Someone very tall and broad is pressing up against me. I can feel the muscles rippling as he moves and the hot breath on my neck. I shiver with ticklish delight and goosebumps grow on my arms.

I feel my mystery head chef lean in to whisper against the shell of my ear, and his voice is a low, rasping growl that makes me feel small and dainty, a dandelion in the claws of a wolf. I like it. A lot.

"You're a little overdressed for the kitchen, sous chef," he whispers gruffly.

"Oh, am I?" I murmur, still too paralyzed to turn around.

"Yes. I'm going to need you to take your clothes off," he orders.

Yum. I may be a strong, independent young woman, but I love nothing more than a big, tough man to boss me around and make me behave. I dutifully start peeling out of my French maid's dress and apron, letting them drop to the floor.

"Now, bend over for me," he instructs. "You deserve a little punishment."

He reaches around to take the wooden spoon from me and

my anticipation shoots through the roof. I'm already getting tingly between my legs and my heart is racing like crazy.

"Yes, chef," I answer submissively. "Please spank me."

I bend over, poking my taut behind in the air as I brace myself on my arms against the prep counter. I bite my lip when I feel the first solid thwump of the wooden spoon against my nearly-bare ass. The sting is delicious, edging my pleasure with a perfect pinch of pain. I'm itching for another whap of the spoon, but before it can land, I'm startled by a piercing, loud noise.

The kitchen falls away to darkness and I open my eyes blearily. It dawns on me slowly that I'm not in a kitchen at all-- I'm in my bed, in my teeny-tiny Bronx apartment. I look over at the screaming alarm clock to see that it's almost five in the morning, which is my usual wake-up call.

With a dissatisfied groan, I turn off the alarm and flop my arms out across the bed, staring up at the ceiling.

How unfair that I was interrupted from my sexy dream before anything *really* filthy could get going! Still, I don't have the time to wallow in the sheets and maybe fall back into that yummy dream. I have a different dream to tend to-- my hopes of becoming a world-renowned chef one day. And to do that, I have to start by getting my ass out of bed.

I heave my legs over the side of the bed and swing out, trudging to my itty-bitty bathroom across the room.

That's one thing convenient about having a micro-studio in New York City: I never have to walk very far to get from point A to point B, seeing as it's all in the same two-hundred-square-foot space.

I hop in the shower, already thinking about the day I have ahead of me. It's my first ever shift at my new internship, and it's an important one. Because I'm interning at a three Michelin-star restaurant called Brick, under the tutelage of master chef and culinary celebrity Jeff Huntsfield. I need to impress him, or at the very least, not embarrass myself in front of possibly the most crucial connection in the culinary world I've encountered yet. By far. It was a lot of work and dedication winning my spot in the intern program here, so I'm going to show up bright and early with all my ducks in a row.

Especially because I know I'm working against some stereotypes. First of all, even though cooking in general tends to be considered "women's work," the culinary arts world is dominated by male chefs, mostly macho men.

As a dainty, pretty twenty-one-year-old woman, that's one strike against me. Then there's the fact that I don't come from a gourmet, farm-to-table, all-organic background like most of my colleagues. I grew up poor.

My mother worked her butt off to keep me fed and healthy, but there was a lot more boxed mac and cheese than caviar. Among the trust-fund kids and legacy students I often feel like the odd one out. But that just makes me work harder.

What I lack in a solid gourmet background, I more than make up for with a tireless work ethic, unbreakable spirit, and enough ambition to fuel several lifetimes of dedication to my craft.

Not to mention the fact that I just plain love cooking. And eating. And feeding people and seeing their faces light up with joy at something I've created. There's really nothing better, is there?

Well, I remember with a twinge as I step out of the shower, maybe getting spanked with a wooden spoon while bent over the prep counter in a gourmet restaurant kitchen might be a little bit better. But that's relegated to just dreams, not real life.

So I get dressed in my uniform, throw a peacoat over it, and head out into the brisk spring morning to catch a bus to catch the train to catch another bus to Manhattan. Ah, city living.

While I'm en route, I do a lot of mental prepping. I get in the headspace for some hardcore sauteing and chopping and seasoning. I read over current and archived menus from Brick, so that I can visualize and walk myself through each item's preparation.

I turn the flavors over in my mind, I picture the way it will be presented on the plate, and I anticipate the kinds of criticism I might encounter. Basically, I'm a killer student, and I plan to be the best intern the likes of Brick or Jeff Huntsfield have ever seen.

I'm totally nervous, but at the same time, I'm confident. I know I'm a great chef in the making, and it'll be fun to show off everything I've learned in the field so far. Even more exciting? Getting to learn new things under such a talented and well-known chef. It's an honor to work alongside him, and I'm going to make the most of it.

I arrive a little too early, but I don't mind. I wait in the cold, looking up and admiring the appropriately brick facade of Brick, imagining what it'll feel like to be inside. To be a part of the team. I can't wait!

I'm so distracted with excitement, it takes me a second to register the glossy black Mercedes pulling up to the curb. A lanky young man about my age steps out, a cocky smile on his face. He strolls over and gives me a *very* obvious look up and down.

"You a hostess or something?" he remarks.

My face burns pink. "Uh, no. I'm an intern. Starting today."

His eyebrows shoot up and he snorts. "Really? Me, too. I didn't realize the other intern was going to be a girl," he says.

Is this guy for real? What I want to say is, "Well, I didn't realize the other intern was going to be a jerk," but I bite my tongue. I can't let this asshole throw me off my game.

"I'm Ashlee. Nice to meet you," I lie. I offer my hand to shake.

He shakes it reluctantly, making sure to flash his sparkly Rolex in the process.

"Paolo Angelino," he replies. He's looking at me expectantly and then it dawns on me.

My stomach turns. "Angelino? As in, *the* Angelino's in Milan?" I splutter.

He nods. "Now I'm here to learn the family business. Angelino's will be mine someday, once my ancient father finally kicks the bucket," Paolo remarks callously.

Yikes. I make a mental note to steer clear of this guy. He's a spoiled brat from a rich family and he would only get in my way. Thankfully, the door swings open just a few minutes later to reveal a middle-aged woman with the sleekest blonde ponytail I've ever seen, smiling and waving us in.

"Look at those bright young faces! You two must be the new interns. Welcome to Brick! I'm Lori, head of wait staff and front end business. Come on in and get ready to meet the team. Everyone will be arriving soon, including the big guy himself," she chirps.

I smile. Her upbeat but down-to-earth vibe is comforting, especially compared to the energy Paolo is putting out into the world. We both introduce ourselves and Lori leads us through a tour of the front end of Brick.

I'm amazed by the crisp white table linens, the expensive art on the walls, the elegant chairs, and fancy light fixtures. Everything here is somehow both sumptuous and minimalist at the same time. There's a sense of quiet luxury in the air, and the place smells heavenly. Like all of my favorite herbs have gathered to create a specific and glorious bouquet.

"What do you think so far?" Lori asks excitedly as she leads us toward the back.

"It's amazing," I gush. "I'm already so impressed with the dining room, I can hardly imagine what the kitchen will be like!"

"It's quaint," Paolo comments with a shrug. "Not my style, but you know, not everyone can have a long line of Italian culinary prowess to build upon."

Lori's smile doesn't even falter even though I'm personally mortified by Paolo's disrespect. She simply skims right over his words and looks back to me.

"I'm just so excited to work with Mr. Huntsfield," I remark. "I've been dreaming of an opportunity like this for so long."

"Oh, he's a genius. Pay close attention and you'll learn a lot from him," Lori agrees. "He's got a bit of a reputation, but don't worry about what people say. Jeff is a tough guy to work for, but only because he expects the best. If you're giving him your best, you'll do just fine."

"Of course. I mean, I've heard stories, but he can't be that bad, right?" I reply.

"Some of what you've heard is probably true," she chuckles.

"For his sake, I hope he doesn't try to mess with me," Paolo butts in. "I don't think my parents, who own several Michelin-star restaurants across Italy, would like that."

Lori and I exchange eye rolls, which luckily Paolo is too oblivious to notice.

"Well, I think you two are in for a hell of a ride," Lori says as she opens the double doors to the back kitchen.

My heart is pounding when we step inside. My eyes widen and I get goosebumps as I look around the space. Stainless steel, spotless prep counters, the kinds of high-tech equipment and tools I have never gotten to use before. It's beautiful and inspiring to see. Not to mention, it looks a lot like the kitchen in my dream. The restaurant staff are all dressed in immaculate white smocks and standing against the far wall as though waiting for instruction.

And just a moment later, the instructor comes strolling in. I immediately stand up a little straighter and feel my heart race even faster. Holy shit-- Jeff Huntsfield is hot as hell. I did not expect that. Of course, I've looked him up online before, but there are very few photos of the chef himself, just tons and tons of food photography. He's clearly a man who likes to let his work speak for itself, so I'm even more excited to learn from him face-to-face. In fact, the closer to him I can be, the better. Something about him draws me right in; maybe it's his gorgeous, thick dark hair or his perfectly symmetrical, strong features. He's got a jawline that could cut glass. His lips are full, even set in a hard line. His dark brows are furrowed, and his muscular arms are folded over his chest. Everything about this guy screams *control*. This is a man who knows what he wants and how to get it. And he'll lay down the law without hesitation.

A shiver rolls down my spine and I feel a little twinge between my thighs. There's no denying it-- Chef Jeff is a tall drink of water, and I'm one thirsty little intern. He turns his hawklike gaze over to Paolo and me, and it's like an electric current rips through me. I can feel his eyes on me like a pair of hands, feeling me up, taking in every curve and angle of my body.

"Good morning," he says in a low, raspy voice that makes me tingle. "Welcome to another day at Brick. Most of you already know the drill, but I can see our new interns are here today, so let me clarify a few things off the bat. In this kitchen, we work hard. We make magic. We create masterpieces. I take this very seriously, and I assume that if you've made it into this room, you feel the same. I expect nothing but the best from my team, so if you're not prepared to leave here tired and spent, you might as well leave now."

Paolo scoffs quietly beside me. Oh my god. This guy is shameless.

Jeff cuts him a quick, withering glare. "You. What's your name?" he asks.

"Paolo. Paolo *Angelino*," he enunciates pointedly.

Chef Huntsfield's mouth twitches a little, like he might smile. But instead, he says, "You're on onion duty. Get to work." I can feel Paolo's indignation from here.

"And you, what's your name?" Chef demands of me.

"Ashlee Golden," I chirp. "It's an honor to be here, Chef."

This time, he really does smile. Only for a split second, but it's enough to melt my heart.

"Thank you, Miss Golden. You'll be baking bread this morning. With me," he instructs.

My heart skips a beat. He picked me! Already! Jeff gives out more instructions for the whole team and then we jump into action. I spend the whole day at Chef Jeff's side, learning new techniques and tips that broaden my understanding of the culinary world. Everything he says is crucial information and I find myself hanging on his every word. I follow his directions to the letter, no hesitation. I love the way he bosses me around. He's dominant without being cruel. He's powerful without picking a fight. It's pure heaven getting to cook alongside him, and the most difficult part of my day is trying to fight off my steamier, less professional thoughts about the head chef. I keep imagining him ordering me to get on my knees, to bend over for him, to give him whatever he asks for.

By the end of the day, I'm feeling fantastic. Jeff heads into the dining room to make the dinner rounds, chatting and engaging with the last round of clientele for the night like the culinary diplomat he is. Things are winding down, the team is cleaning up, and Paolo sidles up next to me as I wash dishes. Ugh.

"I smell like onions," Paolo complains. "If I get carpal tunnel from chopping onions all day, I'll take my talent elsewhere. I mean, come on. This guy is such a joke."

Anger bubbles up in my chest. "I think he's a genius," I shoot back.

"You just like him because he makes you feel special," Paolo sneers. "And if that's what you're looking for, you should get with a guy like me."

I scoff and wrinkle my nose in disgust. "Sorry, but no thanks. I'm good."

He looks like I just slapped him across the face. He turns beet red and gets in my face.

"You'd really pick that loser over me? Do you know who I am?" Paolo snaps. "I know your type. You're not a real chef, you're just here to sleep your way to the top. What did you have to do to get into this program? Who did you have to fuck?"

Everyone is silent as they watch the ugly scene unfold. I know they don't want to speak up because Paolo has connections. I'm blushing and shrinking away like I might melt through the floor. I'm so embarrassed to have this negative attention on me. I don't want the drama-- I'm here to learn! I wish someone would step in.

Paolo opens his mouth to keep ranting, but then the double doors swing open and Chef Jeff comes striding in with a tense look on his handsome face. His hands are balled into fists and he looks ready to kill. It's intimidating as hell, but... also sexy. The way he's looking at Paolo, I half expect some lasers to demateri-alize the guy.

"Mr. Angelino, it's been illuminating to hear you speak from the heart," he says sarcastically. Paolo's face goes pale. Oh my god. Chef heard every word. "I'm going to do the same. Hard work and loyalty are important to my philosophy. It is my belief that money can't buy talent. It also can't buy good taste. And since you have neither, it's no benefit for me to keep you in my kitchen. You're fired. Don't show your face here again."

Paolo is stunned. He splutters for a response, but nothing comes out of his mouth. Finally, he just rolls his eyes and storms out, slamming the double doors on the way. Then Jeff looks around at the team and waves his hands.

"You're all dismissed for the evening. Thank you for your hard work today. I'll see you bright and early tomorrow morning," Chef declares. Everybody starts to filter out, and I turn to follow them. But then Chef Jeff stops me.

"Miss Golden, you stay," he orders.

I freeze in place. Oh no. Am I in trouble?

When it's just the two of us, Jeff comes sauntering over to me. His enormous size compared to mine makes me tremble a little. Or maybe it's just the mind-numbing level of lust short-circuiting my brain right now. I want him as close as possible. I don't even care if I'm in trouble, I'm just turned on to be alone with him. I can't stop picturing him bending me over the counter, pulling my pants down, and spanking me with a wooden spoon.

"I promise I didn't come here to start drama," I defend myself. Jeff gives me a genuine smile and I feel my worry release.

"I have no doubt you're here for the right reasons. I've watched you work all day. I know talent when I see it. More importantly, I know passion when I *feel* it. Mr. Angelino is responsible for his own drama. Although, I can't exactly fault the guy for asking you out," he says smoothly.

"Me?" I breathe. Oh my god, is this really happening?

"Yes, you," Jeff growls. He steps closer. "Mr. Angelino did have a point: you *are* special, and I've definitely taken notice. I've seen your GPA, your recommendations, your resume. Not to mention, I like the way you take orders, Miss Golden. I look forward to teaching you more."

"Like what?" I ask breathlessly, playing along.

He's close enough now to feel my heat. Jeff knows exactly what I've been fantasizing about all day. He looks me up and down, licking his lips. He slowly starts to unzip his work slacks. I know what he wants and I am salivating to give it to him.

Just like I've been dreaming about all day, I drop down to my knees in front of Jeff. His hands drop to my head, guiding me to him. His cock slips free, already stiff and erect-- and massive. I'm drooling by the time I pull the thick, swollen head between my lips. Jeff groans and rocks his hips forward, pushing deeper inside my mouth to brush the back of my throat.

"Good girl. You earned this today," he

I love the way his cock stretches my cheeks and weighs heavy on my tongue. His fingers wrap around my high ponytail and give it a gentle pull to move me backward a little.

"Look at me," he commands in a low voice.

I flick my eyes up to meet his. Then, without breaking our gaze, he pushes my head back down. His shaft pokes the back of my throat but I don't gag. It feels so good, the fullness, the feeling of being totally at his mercy. Jeff rocks his hips slowly, sliding his cock in and out of my mouth in an increasing rhythm.

"Touch yourself," he orders.

Without missing a beat, I push my hand down the front of my pants and do as I'm told. I moan around his thickness and he responds with a deep groan.

"Very good," Jeff murmurs. "Stay right where you are. Let me fuck that beautiful mouth."

He holds my head with a firm but careful grip as he quickens the pace. He thrusts harder and faster, still taking care not to hurt me. I can feel his strength and control and it exhilarates me. I'm in safe hands, even as he pushes me to my limits. My fingers stroke my clit in pace with his thrusts until we're both dangling at the edge.

"Come for me," he directs. "Now."

It's like magic. I feel myself twitching and pulsing as the most incredible thrill passes over me. The pleasure is so intense I see stars, but I'm nothing if not professional. I keep my composure and suck his cock passionately amid the spasms of bliss. I moan with anticipation when I feel his body tensing up. He's close, and I'm desperate to taste him.

"I'm going to come down your throat, Miss Golden. And you're going to swallow every drop," Jeff commands.

I lock eyes with him, giving just the tiniest of nods to convey my total submission. He grabs hold of my ponytail and keeps me utterly still while he explodes hot, sticky cum in my mouth. I gulp down his seed dutifully, desperately. And when he's totally spent, he pushes me back and I lick my lips.

He strokes my head fondly, then gestures for me to stand up. He leans in and kisses me softly on the lips.

"I knew you were highly skilled, but you continue to impress me," he says. "I can't wait to see what other talents you have up your sleeve."

"I'm eager to learn," I reply.

"Good to hear," Jeff praises. "Come on. I'll drive you home. I know how far you go to get there."

On the ride home, we talk about our shared love of food and cooking. He tells me about his travels, I tell him about my classes. He listens with real interest to what I say, and our conversation keeps me laughing and giddy the whole way across town. Jeff walks me up to my apartment like a gentleman, with promises of an even better day tomorrow. I go to bed still smiling, and fall back into a steamy dream with my head chef.

The next day, I show up early again, and this time Lori lets me in immediately. She has a sparkle in her eye as she leads me back to the kitchen.

"Sorry to hear about your intern partner," she remarks. She doesn't sound sorry at all.

"It *is* a tragedy," I reply.

"But you'll soldier on," she quips.

"I'll find the strength," I laugh.

"Have a good day," she says with a wink. She swishes away and I step into the kitchen.

My day is way better than good. I fall right into step beside Jeff as though we were made to cook together. I prep while he marinates. I peel while he chops. It's a perfect ebb and flow, and the food we cook up together is the best I've ever made. He explains every step to me thoroughly and relies on me without question to carry out his orders. He trusts me.

I love the way he commands me in the kitchen, foodwise and otherwise. We flirt in the smallest ways, just a prolonged look or the faint brush of his hand over mine. I'm positively tingling all day long with his presence so close by. The heat between us only grows higher and higher with each passing moment side by side. By the end of the day, we're both desperate for alone time. The second everyone else is dismissed, we practically jump each other.

Jeff grabs me and spins me around against the wall. His hands encircle my wrists to pin them in place while he leans down to kiss me. I arch my back to press my pelvis against his. I get a tingle of lust when I feel his cock already getting stiff.

"I've been thinking about this all day," he growls in my ear. I get goosebumps from his soft breath on my sensitive neck.

He kisses his way across my face to my lips. He rocks forward to press against me. I can feel myself getting slick between my thighs. My body is responding to him in kind, unfolding for him. I can't help but offer myself up to whatever he desires. What Jeff wants, I want with a desperation that thrills me.

"Me too," I answer breathlessly.

"We work well together," Jeff whispers. "We seem to fit. Like a well-oiled machine."

"I feel it," I murmur. "You can have anything you want."

Jeff pulls back and gives me a smile. "I know. But not here. Come home with me. Let me cook you dinner," he says softly.

I grin. "Okay."

We disentangle and head back to his place. We're both still buzzing from our close encounter, but Jeff shows his control once again. We cook together in his beautiful chef's kitchen— salad and steak au poivre. We share a bottle of red wine and flirt our way through dinner. He tells me all about his inspiration for culinary art: his grandmother. She was a fabulous cook who encouraged Jeff to help in the kitchen from a young age. I tell him about cooking for my little sister and my mom when she was busy working multiple jobs. Our backgrounds are so different, but instead of pushing us apart, it creates extra fascination. Jeff looks at me like I'm something brand new. Unexpected in the best way.

After dinner, he looks across the oak table at me and says, "Third course: dessert."

I frown. "We didn't prepare a dessert."

Jeff stands up and slowly walks over. I hold my breath as he offers his hand. I take it, and he leads me back to his bedroom. It's artistically decorated but cozy. He scoops me up and lays me on the bed, making quick work of my clothes. I bite my lip when he pulls down my panties and pushes my thighs apart.

It dawns on me... I'm dessert.

Jeff leans in and flicks his tongue over my clit.

I gasp and let my head fall back against the pillow while he drags his tongue slowly up and down my sensitive flower. I rock my hips up to meet him in a silent plea for more. He responds with direct attention to my clit, nibbling and sucking at the tender bud of nerves. The rhythmic flick of his tongue is driving me crazy. It's not long before I'm gripping the sheets and moaning with pleasure. I twitch and whimper through the waves of climax, and Jeff devours me like a starved man. Just before I come a second time, he delays my gratification again.

He steps back and strips out of his clothes, keeping his eyes locked on me the whole time. I lay waiting for him, legs wide apart, pussy glistening and ready. I'm aching. I need release. I need Jeff.

He straddles me and presses the swollen head of his thick member against my slick cunny. Jeff pauses for a moment, gazing into my eyes. He's barely holding back. He wants to fuck me more than anything, but he is always in control.

"You belong to me," he growls. "And I'm going to take what's mine."

"I'm yours," I breathe. "All yours."

He pushes inside of me, rocking back and forth until he's fully sheathed. My pussy is twinging and pulsing around him. The pleasure is so intense I can barely think. He's so thick I have to stretch to accommodate him, and with every thrust, the head of his cock presses into my g-spot. I'm on the edge of coming already, and when Jeff grabs my wrists with one hand and pins them over my head, I lose it completely.

With a whimper, I gush slick honey all over his pounding shaft. He grunts his approval and fucks me even harder. He knows I need the release of complete submission. I need to be at his mercy.

"Very good, Miss Golden," Jeff praises. "Come for me. I want that pretty little pussy to feel so good."

I'm dripping wet and tingling with pleasure, which only rides higher with every push of Jeff's hips. With my hands pinned, I can only writhe with indescribable pleasure. His free hand roams to my breasts and he rolls my nipple between his fingers. Every little tweak and squeeze gives me another jolt of electric sensation straight down to my clit.

"You always do as you're told, don't you?" he whispers. His cock spears into me harder and faster.

"Anything you say," I mumble. "Anything."

"Such a good girl," Jeff grunts.

"Your good girl," I answer.

"That's right, Miss Golden. Mine. And I'm going to mark you as mine," he whispers. "I'm going to fill that little pussy with my seed."

"Yes," I gasp. I lock my legs around him, gazing straight into his eyes.

"Tell me what you want, Ashlee," he grunts.

"I want to feel you come inside me. Please," I beg.

Jeff grabs my hips and starts to pummel my cunny hard. I know I'm going to be aching for hours, and I can hardly wait. I want the ache, the physical reminder of this moment. Of my submission.

I offer myself fully to him, and he takes it. He takes me. His cock slams into my g-spot again and again, and when my body seized up in another overwhelming climax, Jeff follows suit. I convulse around his cock as though squeezing out every precious drop. With a few final gentle thrusts, he withdraws with a soft groan. My heart is racing, but Jeff dips down to kiss me passionately. We hold each other through the aftershocks of pleasure, and when we're spent, Jeff drops down beside me.

He pulls me in close with his arm around me. I feel totally safe. Totally at home in his arms. I could definitely get used to this. My big powerful head chef who respects me and teaches me, but also gives me the most explosive orgasms I've ever had.

"We're a damn good team," Jeff says. He kisses my forehead and I giggle.

I answer, "I fully agree."

"We can give it a little time, keep it our secret until you've finished your internship," he muses thoughtfully. "But the moment it becomes possible, we're making it official."

"Really?" I gush.

He nods. "Of course. I will be elated to show you off to everyone. Beauty, brains, the work ethic of twenty people, and a wealth of talent? You're going to be a hit. I'm happy to call you mine."

"I feel the same. I can hardly believe this is happening," I confess.

"Believe it. And I hope you know that our... connection will never interfere with your career. I admire your ambition and I will do everything I can to help you succeed. Your success is my success, and vice versa. We're going to make one hell of a culinary power couple," he remarks.

"I can't wait," I reply happily.

Sheltered Annabelle

Book Themes: age gap, virgin, breeding
Word Count: 6783

I'm sitting with my chin propped up on my hands, just staring across the table at the obscenely good-looking man in front of me.

My eyes are locked on his every move.

My ears are tuned into every word he says.

Although, I have to confess, it is a little difficult to pay proper attention to those words when I'm so focused on the shapes his lips form when he says them.

I can't help but lick my own lips with desire while I watch him. I wonder in the depths of my most shameful fantasy world what it might feel like to kiss him.

I almost don't even dare let myself go there.

I know it's not the time nor place to be drooling over him, but what can a girl do? How can I possibly resist him when he's sitting right there-- so deliciously close and yet so impossibly far.

How would it feel to bridge that small space between us? What if he just leaned in and touched me?

I almost close my eyes to fall into the fantasy, but I remind myself I'm supposed to be paying attention. I'm supposed to be listening-- my future kind of depends on it. And yet, I can't shove off these sexy, pesky little questions popping into my desire-addled mind.

What if we did kiss? Would his mouth feel soft or firm? Would he part his lips or keep them closed? I try to imagine his tongue pressing into my mouth while his big, strong hands cup my delicate face.

I can almost sense his warm palms on my blushing cheeks. I wonder if I could suck his finger into my mouth. I remember seeing that happen once in a movie-- before my parents quickly intervened to turn it off.

They're a little sensitive about that kind of thing. I know they mean well.

They just want my mind filled with good things, not sinful lust that will only corrupt me and distract me from what's really important.

Still, right now, it's hard to fathom how anything could be more important than Levi.

I have been spending time with him for quite a while now. Almost five weeks of sitting across from each other, our bodies close enough together for me to feel his heat. To see the way the light plays across his chiseled features.

To breathe in that delicious scent of masculine body aroma and a hint of classy, manly cologne. I used to think freshly-baked bread was my favorite smell in the whole world-- especially when it's my mom's famous ciabatta. But eau de Levi is infinitely better.

It's damn near intoxicating, which should be enough on its own to tell me how dangerous my feelings for him have become. I don't just look forward to our little afternoon rendezvous, I count down the seconds.

Levi has turned me into the kind of girl who always watches

the clock. It's like everything else in my life is shaped and molded around these sessions with Levi.

Nothing else takes precedent. He's my first thought in the morning and my last fantasy before bed.

Sometimes those fantasies get a little out of hand and I have to shut it down. After all, no matter how much I adore Levi and how desperately I want more, I have to remember who I am. I'm a good girl.

I'm a virgin.

I'm my parents' pride and joy.

I have to control my desires, even when they get so steamy and irresistible that I start to get a little tingly down between my legs.

When I look at Levi, I feel a deep down ache in a place no one has ever touched. Not even me. That's okay. I'm waiting for the right person to show me the way. I wish that person could be Levi. I imagine his hand slipping under my plaid skirt and sliding up my thigh...

"So, given what we've gone over so far, what would you say is the core conflict at the heart of *Hamlet*?" Levi asks suddenly, and the fantasy world pops like a balloon.

I blink rapidly, realizing with a shock of panic that I haven't heard a single word he's said in the last few minutes. I was too busy staring at Levi. Daydreaming about him. I rush to come up with the best answer I have-- lucky for me, I've read *Hamlet* pretty thoroughly.

"Indecision," I answer. "Hamlet is so preoccupied with his own internal world that he can't effectively interact with what's going on around him. Every time he gets a chance to make a change, he hesitates instead."

Levi's gorgeous face lights up with approval. He pats me on the arm.

"That's a fantastic answer, Annabelle. Great job. I can tell you're really taking your homework seriously," he compliments me.

I blush deeply and start to shy away, averting my eyes. Nothing dispels the allure of a sensual daydream like the word 'homework.' I'm swiftly reminded that this is not a date in some intimate, romantic restaurant or something. Quite the opposite, in fact. Levi and I are seated in the stiff, potpourri-scented formal dining room of my parents' house.

This is a tutoring session. Levi is my twenty-five-year-old college prep tutor, and I'm a recent high school graduate preparing to start university in the fall. I'm only eighteen, but even more than that... I've been homeschooled my whole life so far. My parents did a pretty excellent job teaching me, but I still think I have a lot to learn.

"Alright, you ready for a little quiz?" Levi suggests.

I sit up straight and nod. "I was born ready!" I chirp. Oh god, I sound like way more of a nerd than I meant to. So much for looking cool in front of a hot guy.

"I'll name the character and you tell me which play they come from," he says. "We'll start off easy: Ophelia."

"*Hamlet*, of course," I reply.

He smiles. "Of course. Prospero?"

"*The Tempest*."

"Mercutio?"

"*Romeo and Juliet*," I sigh. "My favorite."

"Really? What do you like about it?" Levi asks, leaning in.

I can tell he's genuinely interested in what I have to say, which makes my heart flutter. He's such a brilliant, worldly guy-- it would be so easy for him to treat me like a naive little bimbo, but he's always been so sweet. So understanding.

"I guess I'm just a sucker for a love story," I explain shyly. "There's something about the whole world trying to keep you apart, but your love is too powerful to be contained."

Levi smiles softly. "Love like that doesn't come along every day. And as you've seen from *Romeo and Juliet*, that kind of love has the power to destroy. 'These violent delights have violent ends.' But it has the power to do good things, too. At least, that's what I believe."

My heart is melting. I lean in a little closer. "That's so beautiful," I breathe.

He's about to say something else, when we're both interrupted by the rude ringing of an alarm on Levi's phone. My heart sinks. It's an alarm to mark the end of our tutoring session. It never feels like enough time. I swear, all the other hours pass at a regular pace, but the two hours I spend with Levi every weekday seem to fly by like mere seconds. I'm ravenous for more hours. More time to stare at him. To listen to his velvety, deep voice. To pick his glorious brain and learn bright new things from him.

Levi grabs his phone and silences the alarm, frowning slightly at the screen.

"Over already?" I sigh.

He nods and looks up at me with an apologetic look. But there's something else there, too. Something more like genuine regret. Like he isn't just playing this up for my sake-- he misses me too while we're apart. Or maybe I'm just fooling myself. Am I Juliet?

Or am I Ophelia? I guess either way I meet a pretty unfortunate ending.

"Two hours sounds like a lot at first, but now it's like nothing," he agrees.

"I wish we had more time together," I admit, just as I hear the telltale thumping of my parents coming down the stairs. My heart speeds up to a rollicking beat. I hurry up and add, "More time to learn, of course!"

Levi opens his glorious lips to respond, and when my parents come walking into the dining room, he perks up and smiles. "Don't worry, Annabelle. We'll have plenty of time to cover all of Shakespeare's plays before you start the fall semester at college. If we're lucky, we might even get to read some of his sonnets," he explains in a very professional tone.

My mom and dad look utterly chuffed by his words. They approve of Levi so far, since he's given them no reason to distrust him. They're very, very particular about who I spend time with, but Levi is a winner for sure. So it's a relief that they love his response, since it means they haven't caught on to how into him I am. But I feel kind of dismayed, too, because Levi is so damn convincing as my totally professional, totally hands-off tutor. Either he's a really good actor, or he's just not into me the way I hoped he would be. Maybe I've just been imagining him flirting back with me all this time, after all.

"Sounds like yet another productive session with our little girl," my dad says proudly.

My mom nods, a big smile on her face. "College won't know what hit it!" she chirps.

"Annabelle is already so smart and well-prepared," Levi says. "She's going to be the top student in her class once I'm done with her."

My heart skips again. On the one hand, I love the compliment. On the other hand, I hate the idea of Levi ever being done with me. I'll miss him too much.

"We appreciate how hard you're working hard for our princess," Dad says.

I blush beet red. Ugh, how do they always find a way to make me feel even more like a silly little girl than I already do? Levi packs up his study materials and stands up to leave, as usual. I hastily stand up and follow him to the door, along with my parents.

"See you tomorrow, Annabelle. Don't forget that homework I assigned," he says with a wink in the doorway.

I give him a big grin. "I'll do it right away. See you soon."

"Thank you again, Levi. You're a lifesaver," Mom says.

"Have a good night," Dad says as he closes the door.

I gaze out the beveled glass panel of the front door, just watching as Levi walks down the driveway to his motorcycle. My feet are riveted to the spot, but I wish I could burst out the door and go running after him. I wish I could throw my arms around him and beg him to stay-- or better yet, take me with him. I would die to ride on the back of his motorbike, feel the buzz of the wheels on the road, the roar of the engine. And I could have my arms around him. I could rest my cheek on his strong back and hold on tight while we ride into the sunset.

But instead, my parents interject.

"How was the session?" Mom asks.

"Did you learn a lot?" asks Dad.

I force a smile. "Good. And yes. I did learn a lot. Levi's a great teacher."

"I still don't think you even need a tutor," Mom laughs. "We did an excellent job of homeschooling you, sweetie. You're probably smarter than all the other kids you'll be in class with already."

"Nothing wrong with wanting to be a little extra prepared, though," Dad muses.

"True. Only the best for our little girl," Mom coos. She boops my nose and I shrink away.

"I *am* eighteen, you know," I sigh.

As we're heading to the kitchen to start getting ready for dinner, we all hear the growl of Levi's motorcycle driving away. It makes me swoon, but my parents wrinkle their noses.

"I do wish he didn't drive that death trap," Mom complains.

"I think it's cool," I shrug.

"And that's why we make decisions for you," Dad chuckles. He puts a hand on my shoulder. "You're a smart cookie, Annabelle, but we know best."

"I know, I know," I groan.

They really have been making all my choices for me my whole life. Not only did they homeschool me, but they've pretty much set up all my friendships, sports teams, and community events since I was born. I know they mean well, and they just want me to be safe and happy. But I am really looking forward to going off to university. Finally for the first time ever, I'm going to be in control of my own life.

I have to be careful, though. It was a real fight to get them to agree to let me attend a public college all on my own. And to live on campus instead of at home? Well, let's just say it was a years-long process of convincing them I can handle it. I told them I just want to be competent and independent. I want to stand on my own two feet. And that's definitely true. But mostly, I want to be free. Not only do I want to learn new things, I want to *experience* new things, too. If you know what I mean.

I help my parents with dinner and sit down for a meal of

steak, potatoes, and green beans. During dinner, my parents chat as usual about the neighbor down the street who let his grass grow too high and the lady at the town hall meeting who... did something or other. Honestly, I'm not paying much attention. I'm too busy thinking about Levi. I interject a sentence here or there, just enough to make them think I'm listening instead of daydreaming. But when dinner is finally over, I can hardly go upstairs fast enough. I yell goodnight as I run up the steps. As soon as I'm in my bedroom with the door closed, I release a heavy sigh.

Alone with my thoughts at last. I take a shower and get ready for bed, all the while fantasizing about how different things would be if Levi was here. If he was with me in the shower, our bodies naked and wet and rubbing up against each other. If he was with me in the bathroom-- me on the counter while he kisses me. And when I climb into bed, I imagine him lying there beside me with those beautiful dark eyes and those luscious lips. He's so hot, but he's smart, too. He knows so much about the world. Levi has so much to teach me, and not just about Shakespeare. He's twenty-five, so he's done the whole freshman-on-campus thing already. He knows what it's like to sit in a classroom with two hundred people. He knows what it's like to take a big, scary exam and pass with flying colors. He could really guide me. Show me the way.

I'm a good learner, too. I know how to take instruction, especially after a lifetime of being bossed around by my overprotective parents. If Levi is such a fantastic teacher of college prep, he must be a good teacher in other subjects, too.

This is why I can't sleep. This is what keeps me awake at night. I lie here, staring at the ceiling in the dark, just dreaming about all the things he hasn't shown me yet. The world out there I have barely touched. The parts of *me* that are barely touched. If only Levi was here to slide down under the sheets and cuddle in close. He would slowly kiss me, his hands roving up and down my petite body. I want his hands on my breasts, my ass, my hips, even between my legs. I'm getting slick down there, just thinking about it. How can I sleep when I'm so turned on?

It's tempting to give in to my desires and touch myself to the thought of Levi.I'm just about to slip my fingers under the hem of my nightgown, but I stop myself. I have to be good. I know it's wrong to touch myself like that. I never have, and I shouldn't. Besides, I wouldn't even know how to do it right. Better to leave it to an expert. Someone who already knows what to do, what my body needs. Someone who can guide me along...

I have to figure out a way to get more alone time with Levi somehow. I'm not going off to college unprepared. I need him to teach me *everything*, even the knowledge you can't get from a book. I fall asleep feeling determined.

T he next day, I'm pacing back and forth in my pastel pink bedroom. Every few seconds my eyes dart over to the clock on the wall. It's ticking down closer and closer to three o'clock, the moment of truth. That's when Levi shows up for our college prep session. It's the time when my boring, parent-prescribed life suddenly gets a little exciting, and I need it.

I walk over to my full length mirror and look myself up and down. I inwardly critique my outfit, worrying that it might be too risqué for my parents and too modest to catch Levi's gorgeous gaze. I'm wearing a plaid pleated skirt that cuts off just above my knees, a bright white blouse tucked into the skirt, knee-high socks, and mary-janes. I've brushed out my long, wavy blonde hair so that it falls delicately around my shoulders. I don't own a lot of makeup since my parents are pretty strict about it, but I put on a little mascara and lip gloss at least. I think I look pretty decent, not that I have much to compare with. I just hope my parents don't make me change— how embarrassing would that be?

As I'm looking in the mirror, I hear the doorbell ring downstairs. I let out a squeal of excitement and turn on my heel. I go running down the stairs and into the foyer just in time to see my mom opening the front door to let Levi inside. He whips off his motorcycle helmet and looks straight at me. My heart stumbles over its own beat. It's like an electric volt passes between us. I can feel his intensity from across the room, like we're connected on a physical and spiritual level. His eyes rake up and down my body and he licks his lips. I feel a thrill of delight. I think he likes what he sees. Something is different today, like he's bringing a new kind of energy that I can feel from here. Maybe he really was flirting with me yesterday and it's not just all in my head.

"How are you today, Levi?" Mom asks.

"Great. Even better now," he adds.

He glances over at me when he says it, and I can see the corner of his mouth twinge ever so slightly upward like he might grin, but he holds back. Luckily, my mom is oblivious and doesn't notice anything amiss.

"Hi Levi," I murmur, biting my lip.

"Good afternoon, Annabelle," he replies. "You ready to dive in?"

I nod emphatically. Mom beams at us.

"Well, your father and I will be right upstairs if you need anything," she says.

"Okay," I tell her, forcing a smile.

Finally, she goes upstairs as Levi and I sit down at the dining table with all his books and note cards. While he's setting up, I quietly scoot my chair a little closer to his. I undo the top three buttons of my blouse to reveal my ample cleavage. I un-cross my legs and slowly hike up the hem of my skirt to show more of my thigh. I shake out my golden waves and sit back, waiting for Levi to notice these little differences. My heart is pounding. What if my plan doesn't work? What if it *does* work?

Levi does a double take at me, then looks contemplative for a moment. He's considering me. Considering this. My little hints-- my body language, my outfit, my makeup.

"What are you thinking right now?" I ask softly.

His eyes burn like a fire has been lit inside them when he looks at me.

"'O, she doth teach the torches to burn bright,'" Levi murmurs.

I recognize it immediately as a line from Romeo and Juliet.

"You're beautiful," he whispers.

I'm aching for him. My Romeo. Adrenaline is rushing through my system. What will he do next? I've offered my hand, but will he dance with me? He reaches over and gently lays his big hand on my knee. My heartbeat quickens and it's all I can do to remember to breathe. I'm slippery between my thighs from just this one touch.

"We're going to take a quiz now. And I hope you've studied," Levi says, "because the stakes are high this time."

I manage to nod my head. "Okay."

"What year was Shakespeare born?"

"1564," I reply.

Levi's hand moves a few inches up my thigh and I suck in a sharp breath.

"Name one of his comedies."

"Twelfth Night."

His hands moves a few inches higher, pushing under the hem of my skirt. I can hardly breathe. Levi's eyes are locked on mine the whole time.

"'To be or not to be' is the famous soliloquy spoken by...?"

"Hamlet," I blurt out.

"Excellent work," he growls as his hand inches up my thigh.

My chest rises and falls rapidly while his fingers push underneath the lace of my panties. Goosebumps prickle up across my whole body. My hands grip the sides of my chair, my mouth open and my eyes wide. The ticklish sensation of his fingers on my thigh is nothing compared to the almighty rush of bliss I feel when his fingertips brush across my sensitive flower. I whimper and slump down in the chair, giving in to his ministrations.

"No one has ever..." I trail off breathlessly. "Not even me."

"I know," he purrs back, leaning in. "Just relax, Annabelle."

His fingertips dive between my slick folds, stroking me up and down. It feels so good, the rhythmic pressure working me into a hypnotic state while waves of intense pleasure roll through my body. Every third stroke, he sweeps his stiff fingertips upward to trace a light circle over the tight bud of sensitive nerves that makes me shudder with every breath. I feel dizzy with lust and exhilarated with the constant risk of being caught. My parents could walk downstairs any moment and catch us in the act. But somehow, that only adds to the thrill.

"Ohhh, it feels good," I whisper. I let my head drop back.

"Good girl. Let me teach you how to come," he murmurs.

His fingers work a circle around my clit, and the sharp pang of pleasure just intensifies with every moment. I can feel my body tightening up as eighteen years of purity and innocence fall away. I never imagined it could feel this good. Not in my wildest dreams. I can't believe I've been missing out all this time, but I'm also glad I waited, because Levi is the perfect man to make me a woman. He has so much to teach me.

Suddenly, I feel a different kind of pressure building. Something that makes my heart race and my body perspire. I look to Levi for guidance.

"You're getting closer now," he says softly. "You're almost there, baby."

"I-I need..." I break off, whimpering.

"Shhh, just give in. Let yourself feel the pleasure, Annabelle," Levi instructs me.

And all at once, it's like a bomb goes off inside of me. My pussy pulsates under Levi's fingers, my whole body twitching uncontrollably as shockwaves of mindblowing pleasure flood my bloodstream. I'm adrift in a storm of physical sensations and spiritual awakenings. Levi has to clap a hand over my mouth to muffle my moans of pleasure.

"That's right. Very good," he encourages me in a rough growl.

As I come down from my incredible high, I can see that Levi is just as turned on as I am. His jaw is tight, his body is arched toward me like he can barely hold back, and when I glance down I can clearly see the thick, glorious outline of his cock through his jeans. He's hard... for me! My mouth salivates and I immediately know what I want to learn next.

Levi's hand slips away and I stand up in front of him, smoothing down my skirt. He peers up at me quizzically. I slowly bend down to my knees and start unzipping his jeans, never breaking eye contact.

"Will you teach me?" I whisper.

Levi looks toward the stairs for a moment, then back to me.

He reaches to brush my wavy hair out of my face and cups my cheek. Then he nods and smiles. With my hands shaking just a little with nerves, I work his thick, massive cock out of his jeans and boxers. I stare at it with mingled fear and longing. I admire how huge it is, especially compared to my hands. He's absolutely enormous-- far bigger than I ever expected a dick to be.

"Work the shaft with your hands," Levi guides me softly.

I do so obediently. I slide my hands up and down, slow at first, then a little faster. I revel in the smoothness of his skin, the warmth and weight of his cock. He's hard as steel and I can only imagine what it would feel like to have this kind of power inside me. Plunging into me. Breaking me apart from the inside out.

My mouth is watering when I lean in to flick my tongue around the engorged head. Levi sighs and drops his hand to the back of my head. He applies gentle pressure to guide me to his cock, to take more of him. I eagerly suck his length into my warm, wet mouth. He tastes divine. I love the way his cock stretches out my cheeks and presses all the way into the back of my throat when I take him as far in as I can. He's so massive I can barely do it, but I love the way it feels. I start to bob up and down, every now and then letting him slip all the way out so I can hungrily suck him back in. I take him down to the root, almost gagging myself on his thick cock.

"Oh, that's good. You're a quick learner," Levi sighs. In a barely-audible voice, he adds, "Now, let's try something new. Hold still for me. I'm going to fuck that pretty mouth, okay?"

"Mmm," is my eager response.

Levi holds my head with both hands and slides down a little in the chair. He lifts his hips and pulls back a little, then pushes forward. His cock slams into the back of my throat. I get even wetter when he starts to thrust into my mouth, sliding in and out while he keeps me in place. I can only whimper and moan with pleasure. I love the way he fills me up and makes me whole. I love the taste and thickness of him. I love how he uses me, gives in to his lust and just takes me however he needs to. But just as he starts to move quicker and I can feel his body tensing up, there's a sound from upstairs.

A door opening and closing. Then the thump of feet on the staircase.

Levi releases me and his cock pops free of my lips. I pout as Levi hurriedly tucks himself away and I jump back into my seat. We both turn toward the table as my parents get closer. My heart is pounding-- what if they heard us? What if they know? I'm nervous, but Levi is composed. Thank god one of us can act natural.

"Sorry to interrupt you two," my mom says, looking stressed out.

"There's been a HOA emergency," Dad remarks. They grab their coats.

"An emergency?" I ask.

"Oh yes. That new neighbor down the street painted her mailbox hot pink. Hot pink! Can you even believe it?" Mom snarks.

"We're having an emergency intervention, and we might be gone for awhile. Levi, I expect we can trust you with Annabelle for an hour or so," Dad says.

"Absolutely. She's safe with me," Levi says warmly.

"See you later!" I call out as they slip outside.

Levi and I stare at each other in complete shock for a moment. My parents would usually never leave me alone with a boy. They must not suspect a thing!

"Wow. They really trust you," I blurt out.

Levi smiles. "They should. I'm a good teacher, and you have a lot to learn."

He stands up and offers me his hand. I take it happily. The two of us all but run upstairs to my bedroom, both laughing with exhilaration.

"I've wanted this for so long," I tell him, slamming the door shut.

Levi scoops me up, making me giggle with surprise. "The wait is over, baby."

He carries me to my four-poster bed and rolls me back, unbuttoning my blouse. He leans in to kiss me for the first time and I feel like I might actually faint. My heart is soaring. His lips are soft, even when he kisses me harder. His tongue pushes into my mouth while his hands strip away my blouse and bra. I moan as his hands caress my bare, perky breasts.

"Oh my goodness," I gasp when he gently tweaks my nipples.

It feels like a spiral of fiery-hot pleasure streaking across my frame, straight down to the wetness between my thighs. Levi's hands slip my panties and skirt down my legs while he licks and sucks my breasts. I let my hands comb through his thick, dark hair. His lips kiss a tantalizing trail down from my chest, over my flat stomach, downward to my pelvis. I tighten up as he draws closer and closer to my slippery sex. I spread my legs for him, watching with held breath while he dives in. It's just the two of us now, so I can be as loud as I need. I cry out when his lips suckle my sensitive clit, lathing his tongue up and down to make me convulse beneath him.

"Oh, Levi," I gasp.

His mouth is perfectly warm, his lips so soft and teasing, and when he increases pressure on my clit I almost lose my mind. His tongue dips between my dewy folds to lap up my gushing juices. I've never felt so enthralled before, so totally honed in on every flicker of sensation. Levi's hands rove up to grope and fondle my breasts while he goes down on me. He devours my pussy with delight, like I'm the most delicious, irresistible morsel he's ever tasted. His tongue slides up and down my folds, then he suckles my clit, repeating the same rhythmic process until I'm almost in tears. I need a release, and I can feel it building again, just like before.

"It feels so good. I think I'm almost there," I whimper.

Levi slurps my clit harder, bobbing up and down while I tremble beneath his touch. I cry out as the stimulation gets almost too intense. The pleasure is blinding. Intoxicating. I feel like I'm about to burst everywhere. And then-- I do.

"Levi!" I squeal as I gush sweet honey all over his gorgeous face.

"Mmm, yes," he groans.

It's so intense I almost twinge away from him as he laps up every drop. Every flash of his tongue across my clit makes me gasp. All my nerves are on fire. My mind is a screaming train whistle. My heart is galloping away into the sunset without me. I can't wrap my head around this level of pleasure. It's something primal I never even tasted until today, and now that I know what it feels like, I'm never going back. Gone is the pure, innocent Annabelle. I belong utterly to Levi now, and I want him to corrupt me. I want him to destroy me and remake me as his own.

I want him to take my virginity and make me a woman.

Levi finally wipes his mouth and stands back, looking at me with a dominating stare. I prop up on my elbows to watch him take off the rest of his clothes. When he stands before me totally naked, I suck in a tight breath. He's even sexier than my naive mind pictured. He's strong and muscular, with a body that could crush me and arms that could carry me for miles without tiring. I drink in those well-defined abs, his broad chest, and of course... that beautiful, brutal cock. I lick my lips, begging him with my eyes to come back to me. To come to bed.

"You're learning very quickly today," Levi declares as he saunters over to me.

I nod. "I want to know everything."

He smirks and leans down to kiss me deeply. He straddles me on the bed, pinning my arms down on either side of my head. When he breaks away, his eyes are ablaze.

"You're a virgin," he growls.

I bite my lip shyly. "Yeah. But I'm eager to learn," I assure him.

"Totally untouched. Mine for the taking," Levi says. His hands explore my body as he speaks. He squeezes my breasts and slides down to the curve of my hips.

"I'm all yours. Always have been. I've been waiting for you," I confess breathlessly.

"You want me to fuck your sweet, tight pussy, Annabelle," he says. It's not a question.

I nod eagerly and arch my back to meet him.

"Please. I want... I want you to be my first. My only," I admit in a small voice.

"Nobody will fuck you like I can," Levi hisses between

gritted teeth. "I care about you, Annabelle. I've thought about this for a long time."

"Me, too!" I burst out. "I've never been more sure of anything in my life. Please, Levi. I need you. I need your cock inside me."

Levi grabs his thick shaft and starts to tease my aching cunny with the tip. He rubs himself on my clit to make me twinge and moan. I rock my hips, thrusting toward him, begging with every inch of my body.

"Trying new things can be a little painful sometimes," he reminds me.

"I'm not afraid of the pain," I tell him. "I know what I want. I'm eighteen now. And I want you."

Levi lines up the head of his cock at my desperate little hole. I hold my breath while he gazes at me for a long, powerful moment. Then he bends to kiss me just as he shoves his massive cock inside my virginal cunny. I cry out with combined pain and pleasure, and he swallows down my cries. He rears back and gently pushes into me again, doing this same technique over and over again to work me open.

"Fuck, you're so tight," he growls.

"I'm sorry," I whisper.

He smiles down at me, like a wolf about to devour his prey.

"It's a good thing," he assures me. "You feel so good, Annabelle."

"I want more. Give me more," I plead.

I'm addicted to his cock. One little taste and I want him to tear me apart.

"Such a good girl, but so bad," Levi teases.

He pushes deeper into me and I can only shudder and wince. It feels so fucking good, even with the tinge of pain. That only makes it feel more delicious. I'm so tiny compared to Levi. He could easily shatter me into tiny pieces, and I'd let him do it. Gladly.

"It's so big," I groan wantonly.

He sheathes himself entirely in my pussy, pushing so far as to knock against some tiny barrier inside me. I feel him pull back, then plunge forward. I get a sharp pang of momentary pain that makes me whimper, followed by wild pleasure.

"Yes, Annabelle. Good. Open yourself up for me," he commands.

I spread my legs further and wrap them around his waist, pulling him in. Locking us in each other's embrace as his cock spears into my twitching virginal cunny again and again. He hits some deep, dark place within me I never knew existed. With every powerful thrust of his hips, I get another intense rush. He picks up the pace, slamming into me repeatedly. His swinging balls smack hard against my bare ass while his hands play with my tits.

"Yes! Yes! Yes!" I burst out. "It feels so good-- oh my god!"

"You want my seed deep inside your little pussy, don't you?" Levi groans.

"Oh yes, I need it!" I plead.

His cock slides in and out of me faster and harder. I love the wet splash of his hardness plunging through my gushy flower. I can feel my juices running down my thighs, collecting on my pink bedsheets. Levi's hand reaches down between us to rub my clit while he pounds my pussy. It's almost too much to handle-- the flashes of intense pleasure combined with the thrill of being used, being controlled, being owned by this magnificent man. This feels so much more amazing than my steamy fantasies. Nothing in my dreams could top the reality of Levi pumping that thick cock in and out of my virginal cunny. All those years of waiting, aching, longing for someone to show me what I need.

"Oh my god," I gasp. "I'm so close again."

"I'm almost there," he groans. "Fuck, you feel so good."

His cock plunges inside of me deeper than ever before, and I cry out. The world goes black for a split second, then comes back in scintillating light. Levi grips me tight as he pumps into me erratically. He's losing control, on the verge of orgasm. I squeeze his cock with my pussy, begging for his precious seed. I want every last drop. I want him to make his forever mark on me. I want to belong solely to him.

"Oh, Annabelle," Levi growls as he bends to kiss me again.

I cry out with climax just as his lips collide with mine. At the same exact time, I feel him tense up and release. His shaft pumps me full of his hot come, mingling with my own juices as we ride out the waves of pleasure together. We moan and rock and cling to each other. The high is almost too much to believe. Nothing has ever felt like this. I'm exhilarated and exhausted, flushed and finished. When he empties every last drop inside me, Levi finally withdraws. He lays down beside me and pulls me close to kiss me.

I snuggle into his warm, muscular body as his arms fall around me. I rest my cheek against his chest and listen to his steady heartbeat. I'm beaming, so happy I can barely function. Levi strokes my hair and kisses me all over. It makes me giggle.

"So what did you think of today's lesson?" Levi teases.

"It was *everything*," I sigh happily. "But... can we do it again?"

Levi laughs softly. "Of course we can. We can do it as many times as you want, for as long as you want. I'm yours, Annabelle. From the first moment we met."

"And I'm yours," I gush.

"As soon as you go off to campus, you'll be my girlfriend," he says.

I'm on cloud nine. "I would love nothing more."

"We might have to keep this our little secret for now, though," Levi muses.

I nod. "Oh yeah. Definitely. But I don't mind. I kind of like the secret."

"Me too. Just the two of us," he says, kissing my forehead.

"Romeo and Juliet," I sigh.

"But with a way better ending," Levi smiles.

I grin and press into him, happier than ever. "Way better."

The Fertile Foreign Exchange

Book Themes: Age Gap, Breeding, Creampie, and Foreign Exchange Student

Word Count: 4406

S ending my son off onto a foreign exchange program had to be the best decision of my life. Though I had no idea when I signed up for it, it'd lead me to the most intensely erotic moments of my life.

Nope, when I said goodbye to my son, I thought it was to have to put up with another terror of a young man, looking to cut loose in his college years in a whole new country. Instead, when the time came to pick up Aren from the airport, I was greeted with the most breathtaking of sights.

It wasn't some scruffy Scandinavian punk coming up to me, but the most delicate looking of beauties I'd laid eyes upon.

Then there was me, standing there with that sign, speechless as she approached and removed all doubts.

Her smile could melt an iceberg with those rosy lips, and the fairest skin I've ever seen. There wasn't a freckle anywhere to be seen, those blue eyes crystal clear and blonde hair so bright.

I found myself fantasizing about touching it, reaching out and grabbing one of those braided pig tails, but I resisted the urge.

Instead I returned her smile as she pulled her pink suitcase up next to her.

She wore a summer dress even though it was only May, and still admittedly chilly. Her shoulders were bare, the yellow fabric accenting her long legs and nipped waist.

"Are you Mr. Chandler?" she asked in that accented voice of hers.

"That I am," I said a little delayed, dumbstruck by her beauty. "Aren?" I asked, even as I reached out to alleviate the young woman's burden. Hell, she could've been the wrong person entirely and I'd still have helped her heft that suitcase out of the airport, just as an excuse to prolong our encounter.

She nodded, her beautiful face dipped from me for a moment, giving me a chance to look over the large swell of her chest.

When she caught my eye again with her baby blues, I swear she'd caught me, her skin pinkening just a little before she relinquished her suitcase to me, her index finger brushing over my coarser digit.

"I'm looking forward to staying with you," she said finally.

I was doubly unsure of how to respond to that, my mind so wrapped up in that gorgeous young lady, her pristine skin and seeming sweetness. I lifted her bag and gave her a nod and a bright smile.

"It'll be just the two of us, so you shouldn't have to worry about time for study or getting to know the country," I said, but the only thing my mind was on was how I'd get to spend the next few months with this beauty.

And how I might even be able to accomplish something more than merely spending our time together.

After all, it was the expectation that I'd be spending a lot of time with her, showing her around, teaching her all about America. Driving her wherever she needed to go...

I couldn't help my growing bulge, or my widening grin, as I led her to my car.

The drive back was a struggle to keep myself in check and to summon up all those skills of casual flirtation, which had atrophied in my time with my ex-wife. But when we got back to my spacious home, I took her on up to the spare bedroom, which had been prepared for her arrival.

"Here you go," I said, pushing open the door, showing her the queen sized bed, the simple yet elegant furniture and drapes. "Had I known I was getting a beautiful young lady to stay with me, I would have made sure it prettier itself to compliment you," I remarked, laying down her suitcase at the foot of the bed.

Her giggle was like music as she padded into the room. She was barefoot, now, her legs not hidden beneath stockings or tights. It was just nude, honest flesh, as she felt the cold, hardwood, beneath her feet.

"It's beautiful!" she said earnestly, her arms going out as she did a spin, revelling in the space.

Yet it gave me a chance to revel in how her skirt flew up, unveiling more of that pristine, milky flesh.

I couldn't help but grin like a fool at that sight, she was stunning, happy, like a cheerful nymph that frolicked about my home, making it feel alive again.

"My room's right across the hall," I said pointing to the other door. "So if ever you need anything during the night, you know where to find me," I explained with a smile, wanting her so badly to disturb me with a very particular kind of nightly need.

"So with that," I said, rubbing my hands together, "you hungry?"

That was how we started out, and luckily the skies were bright and sunny, so she spent little time studying in the face of asking me to take her out and show her around. Chauffeuring a beautiful young minx like her about was a sweet pleasure.

She was always so meek, so willing to go along with my suggestions. I always wanted to take it a step further, but the sense of wrongness held me back. Sure, she was a beautiful young woman, but she was under my care. A surrogate daughter for a few months that I was supposed to look after and protect.

And with her kindness, it seemed she needed protection. She was always asking for coin to hand to the beggars, for an extra sandwich for our picnics so that she could share with anyone who looked to be in need. They stuck out to her, she said, and didn't find it fair that we could have so much while others had so little.

It all changed, though, when we caught a burglar in the house.

Arriving home to the dark and finding a huge, intimidating man in my house wasn't the sort of thing either of us were expecting after a day at the museum.

By rights that should've been terrifying for me. I didn't own a gun and I wasn't a violent man. But something came over me then, and my instincts as a man to protect sweet Aren took the fore, keeping any fear for myself at bay.

I leapt at the man before his surprise was up, and I managed to grab a hold of him and force him to the floor. Like I said, I'm not a violent man, but I keep fit and in shape, and so I was able to get him down and keep him there despite his struggles. There was little of an altercation, and the burglar managed to only get a few smacks at me before it was done and over with, and I got him pinned securely to wait for the police.

That was the exhausting part, because then the adrenaline wore off, and it was just tedium. But the moment they left, I went to Aren, concern for the sweet young girl ripe in my eyes.

"You alright?" I asked, reaching a hand out to rest upon her bare, milky shoulder.

She had been screaming during the fight, I remembered that much, and she was looking like a wounded little bird, startled and scared as she trembled against me. She'd been so strong in front of the police, but now her eyes watered and she went into my chest with a sob.

I wrapped my arms about her, pulled her delicate frame in against me, holding her soft form to my hard chest. My hands roamed over her back and shoulders, rubbing and trying to comfort her as her smaller body heaved with her upset.

"It's okay," I said to her reassuringly, and in that fatherly kind of manner I kissed the top of her head, felt the brush of that perfect blonde hair against my lips and face. "You're safe with me," I assured her, and she was. I'd kept her safe throughout it all.

She stayed there for some time, allowing me to breathe in her scent, to feel strong and as though I were a pillar of security.

Though I don't think I'd ever forget what happened when she pulled away, her watery eyes up at mine.

"I don't want to sleep alone tonight."

Those words. Whatever they did to me, they summoned forth from me more of that male part of me that strove to be a protector. Someone who looks out for the weaker, and Aren, with those puffy blue eyes, watery from tears, was weak and in need of help then.

I scooped her up in my arms as if she were but a feather-stuffed pillow case, and carried her on upstairs.

Sex wasn't on my mind then when I did that, but when I got to my bedroom, and brought her in to my king sized bed, in that well-appointed room, I laid her out and was struck once more by her beauty. How perfect that pale little delight was.

"You'll sleep with me," I said in a firm, hard voice, a protective — even possessive — edge to my words.

She was still in another of her summer dresses — that seemed to be all she brought for the trip! — her feet bare. It looked almost like a nightgown, and she made no protest or move to change first. Instead, she looked up at me, one leg pulled up at the knee, the other rested against the bed.

Her braids caressed her throat as she nodded.

"Yes, Mr. Chandler," she said in deference to my order.

Maybe what I did next was way out of line, but something in me said that she needed more than that. More than merely being next to me for safety through the night. More than my protection. She needed a man to not only protect, but soothe. To defend her and comfort her.

So I leaned in, and I brushed my hand along her cheek, pushing back one of her braids before I pressed my lips to hers and gave her a tender, loving kiss.

Just as I'd thought, her body didn't startle. Instead it softened, a sigh passing from her lips against mine. Her hand went to my arm, touching me so gently, as if just to have a connection and remind herself of my strength and presence. The way her thumb rubbed along my bicep, how she melted into my kiss...

I couldn't have asked for better.

But as much as I desired her in the nubile flesh, she was in need of me, the comfort a strong, older man could provide. So I did what we both yearned for, and I got down atop her, lowering my broad, masculine frame slowly as we kissed, our lips smacking.

She tasted like honey and heaven, such pristine perfection in every way. Her tongue moist and almost cool compared to my own, I just couldn't help but give a deep, husky groan. My arms swelled with the effort of hefting my weight over top of hers, and she felt the bulge of my bicep.

She was still the meek little darling I'd picked up at the airport, in need of my care, and her fingers squeezed around my arm. She let out a moan into my mouth as her legs spread, making room for me between them.

She was shy, I could tell that much by how she kept trying to hide her eyes, to not let me see the flush of her cheeks, or the way her body was softening to mine.

But where she was soft, I was hard. My muscles were firm, my dick a solid pillar then. All that exhilaration of earlier, of getting to protect this fair young maiden, it had filled me with more desire and virility than I'd felt in my entire life. Even the stiff ones I'd popped as a teen paled by comparison.

I rubbed one hand along her thigh, felt her smooth, creamy flesh as I pushed her sun dress up to her hips. I felt like a god among men then, and she was my Aphrodite. The sounds of our lips softly smacking filled the air, and I couldn't help myself but press my bulge in against her, and roll my hips, grinding my groin against her.

Aren looked up at me with uncertainty for a moment before her eyes fluttered shut and her rosy lips parted. I loved how she felt against me, that sweet, foreign exchange student so nubile and youthful. Her skin was like cream, so soft and delightful as my hands went further and further up her hips.

She was breathing nearly as hard as I was, our heartbeats racing against one another's.

My hands pressed up beneath her dress, felt the waistband of her panties before moving on past to delve up, over her broad hips to her slender waist. She felt like heaven to touch, that was the gods honest truth. I could've gotten lost in just exploring her body for eternity, if I wasn't in such an insatiable mindset thanks to the events of that night.

I'd conquered the enemy in my efforts to protect a woman, and now she was mine. That was the stuff of pure masculinity, like a man always yearns for, but so rarely comes.

"I've never done this," she said in her accented voice, and it gave me a moment of surprise. Though it was quickly countered by how her arms wrapped around my neck, as if she were afraid that'd make me want to leave.

As if I could.

Her legs were already spread for me, my cock hard and throbbing against her clothed pussy, and she felt too sweet to pass up. My testosterone was flooding me, and I ground into her as her lips once more found mine, her tongue lashing against me.

I curled my fingers along her hips, into the waistband of her panties and found myself peeling that garment away from her cunny. The slick dampness of her moistened folds making a wet sound as I tugged the cloth away and slid it on down her legs.

I took one look at that pink little slit and felt my dick throb so hard it risked popping free of my pants on its own. Instead though, I focussed myself, and peeled off my own shirt, tugging it up over my head and shoulders, revealing my broad torso, bulging with muscles across my abs and pecs.

I began to work my belt as I gazed down at her tenderly.

"I'll take care of you," I promised her in a deep husk.

Her pussy was swollen with blood, puffy and bare of hair but for a sweet blonde tuft above the slit. It was so wet, and she didn't shy away from my gaze. She may have been a virgin, but there wasn't shame as I stared at her. I let my eyes trace down her face, over her full lips, her large breasts and down to that heated little slit.

She was gorgeous, and I wanted to see so much more of her. All of her. So as I took off my belt, I looked up at her eyes.

"Take off your dress," I ordered, not unkindly. I smiled to take any bite out of my words, and her hands tentatively reached for the sides of her dress. She shifted into a sitting position, pulling the material up over her flat stomach.

Her skin was perfect, and as she took the dress over her head, unveiling her large breasts, held in place by her white and pink flowered bra, they were even bigger than I'd imagined.

She shifted, the breasts bouncing a little as she looked at me.

I undid my pants and shed myself of them, letting my thick, muscular thighs loose, but then more importantly, I tugged down my boxer-briefs. That thick bulge that drew her eyes soon became the full on sight of my bare cock, the broad shaft tumbling out, ribbed by the ridges of my thick veins.

I reached out as she gaped at my manhood, my powerful hands undoing her bra and peeling it away. I wanted to free those tits of hers, and the moment they fell free, so perky and large, I sank my fingers into them, squeezed and kneaded them, enjoying the supple feel of those perfect mounds of flesh.

Her body was so responsive, nipples prodding into my palm as she moaned.

One of her hands went down, resting between her thighs, teasing over the soft flesh as if she wanted to play with herself. But I was paying far more attention to the one that was reaching out for me, for my cock, curious fingers reaching out to touch it as she shimmied closer to me.

I watched as her slender little digits coiled about my cock, feeling out that thick, veiny instrument as I gave a low, gravelly moan. The heat of my shaft pulsed against her palm, the girth stretching her fingers open wider as I leaned down over her.

I kissed at her breasts, again, then again. I took my time, teased around the edges of her pink areolas before giving a light suckle to her stiff nipple. Only stopped once I'd tugged it back and let it snap into position once more.

She gasped, but her nipple stiffened further, and her hand along her thigh couldn't resist anymore.

I didn't think anything could match the sight of her in her nude glory, but the fact that her fingers went between her thighs and began stroking at her pussy was sublime. Her hand wrapped around me more firmly, though she didn't quite stroke me. No, she was just feeling me throb against her.

My mouth left her nipple as I pulled back and watched as those fingers played with her wet folds, teasing herself. She struggled to find that little clit of hers, and I brought one of my hands to her wrist. Holding it tightly, I changed where her finger lay, forcing the middle digit right over the throbbing nub.

I watched her face as her mouth dropped open in delight, her moan so much lustier as she ground against her finger. I dove down and collected her nipple in my mouth, tugging on that heavy tit with my teeth, her supple form yielding to me as she let out a loud cry.

She was so close, so very close, but I had all I could take, and I grasped hold of her dainty, feminine body and pulled her down the bed a few inches, to get her before me just perfectly. I lowered myself down, letting the thick, purple crown of my cock glide against that virginal little pussy. I couldn't suppress the deep, throaty moan, my desire too intense even for me then as I rolled my hips forward.

I stretched that sweet girl's hymen around my cock, and I pressed on into her, sinking deeper and deeper into her nubile depths. My gruff, thunderous moan filling the air as I sank my dick into her raw and unprotected. No girl's first time should be spoiled with a condom, and what we were doing was raw, animalistic. It was nature at its core. A strong, older man, looking out for a nubile young woman. We had to play it out like it was meant to.

And her sweet little pained moan was all I needed to know I made the right decision. Her fingers retreated a little as I pierced her, but she was so wet and turned on that the pain faded quickly. Just a pinch before I forced myself in further, taking away her innocence, as her legs wrapped around my hips.

"Ah!" she said with a gentle tremor to her figure, her arms going above her head as my darker body sunk into her pristine, pale form.

She was an unreal beauty, like a goddess carved from white stone. And I fucked her, slowly pumping my hips, stretching her tight little cunny with each pass of my thick, veiny cock. I moaned, revelling in the sensation of her moist, warm pussy stretched taut about my dick, my heavy balls slapping against her ass as I built momentum.

It was her first time, but for me, it was my finest time. I made love to that sweet girl with all the devotion a man could muster. She felt exquisite, and I leaned down to kiss her pouty, ruby lips repeatedly as my hard ass rose and fell with each thrust into her fertile depths.

I was her safety, her security, and she clung to me, understanding that all so well. Her soft, buxom form pressed into my large bed...

I'd never felt better, that sweet little pussy wrapped around my dick, her slickness pulling me in. Her long legs wrapped about my hips, cautiously, uncertainly, but as my large hand went to the side of her thigh and held her there comfortingly, she calmed.

Her wide eyes were still upon me as her mouth met mine,

again and again, tongue swirling against mine as she let out the sweetest little groans of delight.

"My sweet little Aren," I said in a deep, gravelly voice, filled with such desire and caring. We'd not known each other long yet by that point, but after just that brief moment downstairs, where we were man and woman at our most primal, I felt a bond with her that boiled deep in my blood.

I groaned loudly, filling the air with my deep, basso voice as I fucked her. Her moist cunny smacking to my groin as I plunged deep, filling her up with each new thrust. All the while, my manhood strained the limits of her taut little pussy with each throb, my pleasure mounting just as I mounted her faster and faster.

She felt heavenly, especially when her hand went between us, touching once more to that hidden bundle of pleasure. She touched against it where I'd shown her and I saw her entire body light up. Her cunny clenched me, begging me in deeper.

I wanted so badly to cum in her. I hadn't had a woman raw in a long time, and I'd forgotten how good that bare sensation was, and as she twitched around me, I thought I might blow, right in her fertile depths, but I held back. For now.

I wanted to see her cum first, right on my cock. To make her feel so good, so that she'd always come back for more. So that the next few months, I could expect to have the prissy woman riding my cock like a pro. I'd teach her to be perfect for me, to take that virgin woman, to fill her with my seed, to breed her and make her mine for all time.

I made her body rock with my thrusts, those thick tits jiggling and swaying atop her chest as I ploughed into her utmost depths, filling her up again and again. It was hypnotic, watching her body move with mine, responding to my motions, my desire.

With a deep, husky moan I felt my dick spurt a little precum into her, and knew I wasn't long for the finale. But I did my best to savour every moment inside her tight little virginal pussy. I grasped a hold of her thigh breast and continued to pump my dick, angling it just right to give her the most stimulation.

"Cum for me Aren," I beckoned to her in a deep husk.

God, just the thought of how she'd feel, cumming on my bare dick, was enough to make me spurt a little bit more. A warning that soon, she'd be bred by me, owned, just as it should be.

She shivered at my words, her fingers rubbing herself more urgently as she began to quake and then there was no holding her back.

Her head tilted towards the pillow as she cried out, her body trembling as her pussy tightened around me. It was milking my cock, and there was no way I could hold back, and so we dove into the forbidden bliss together.

I arched my neck back and let loose a deep, bellowing cry as I felt the fire of sensation travel up my shaft and explode outwards. My thick, virile seed flooded her depths, filling up her nubile womb. I pressed into her deep and hard, jamming the tip of my cock up against her cervix and unleashing all the rich cream I had.

There was nowhere else I could have willed myself to blow my load them. We were man and woman, raw and natural, rutting wild with the need of nature broiling in our veins. I had to fuck her, breed her, and she needed that comfort from it.

I shuddered all over, giving a thrust, then another, quaking from pleasure and desire as I finally lowered my lips to kiss at hers through the final throes of our moment together.

She took all of my seed, her pussy still vibrating against my cock, coaxing more and more fluid from me like the ravenous young woman she was. Her body wanted this more than anything, and she let out a low moan of pure desire.

Her fingers stilled at her clit, the other arm going around me and pulling me in closer.

We embraced, her slender arms about me, my thick, muscular ones about her. We held each other, cradling one another's form in the afterglow of our love making. I kissed her passionately, all over her, from her lips to her cheeks, down her neck to her shoulders, then back up.

We laid there like that for some time, lost in each other's bodies.

She was sore after her first time however, and she went to

sleep eventually, her in my arms, her beautiful blonde head rested upon my chest.

But as I lay there, drifting off into sleep, I couldn't stop my smile, feeling her nude body pressed against mine, and knowing her pretty little cunny was filled with my cream.

Quinn and Her Boss

⚬

Book Themes: age gap, BDSM, boss / employee,
dom / sub, bimbofication
Word Count: 8006

⚬

I am thirty-thousand feet up in the air en route to the sleepless city of Las Vegas, and I have never seen such a beautiful sight.

Believe it or not, I'm not talking about the plumes of white clouds swathed across the sapphire blue sky outside the round airplane windows.

The beams of sunlight warming the fluffy clouds creates a lovely effect.

It does look like we are hurtling across heaven right now, this high up on a clear day, but that's not the sight that has me reeling.

That has me shifting in my seat and drifting off into little fugues of fantasy. I love flying, and usually I can just zone out and rest my eyes while I'm in the air, but today there's a massive distraction in front of me that I just cannot ignore even if I wanted to.

Which is unfortunate, because I'm on a mission today.

We have a massive work engagement tomorrow morning and I need to be on top of all the details.

If only I could pay attention to said details instead of gazing in awe at the hottest guy I have ever seen in person.

He's my boss, Daniel Horne.

He's a big-shot CEO with ten years of experience and success under his belt, to whom I play secretary and personal assistant. I am the girl who books his meetings, manages his schedule, and makes sure all the ducks are in a row.

He's the big idea guy and I'm the girl who makes it happen from behind the scenes.

Truthfully, I've been working for Mr. Horne for almost six months and this is the first time I've actually been in the same room as him.

He's a very busy man and he doesn't spend much time at the office, which is usually my territory. Today, though, I'm tagging along to play support for Mr. Horne, to make sure everything runs smoothly.

I love this job, especially now that I've got the amazing opportunity to work alongside my masterful, gorgeous boss on this particular plan. I've had a respectful work-crush on the guy for months, but he's even more charismatic in person.

I steal another glance over the stately mahogany work table at the gorgeous man sitting across from me. My heart skips a beat, just like it does every time I look at him.

My eyes are wide, my mind swirling with contradicting thoughts. Such as: *oh my god, stop staring*. And: *oh my god, I never want to look away*.

I don't even want to blink, for fear of missing one moment of admiring him.

He is absolutely the most handsome man I have ever seen, even more so in person than he is in photographs. (Of which there are very few-- he's a man who prizes his privacy.)

His sharp, moss-green eyes are locked onto the stack of work papers in front of him on the table. His thick dark brows are furrowed in deep contemplation, while his coif of sleek black hair is artfully pushed back out of his face.

And oh, that face.

He has a strong jaw, a straight nose, and sharp cheekbones. There's a perpetual slight shadow over his jaw. I can see that he's the kind of guy who can grow a beard between morning and evening.

I wonder what it would feel like to run my fingers over that stubbly jaw, breathe in his masculine scent. I lick my lips as I check out his muscular body which is barely concealed by his tailored, high-end suit. God, I can't stop staring at him.

I hope he doesn't realize my crush. I'm sure he usually dates supermodels and stuff, not a lowly secretary like me. While he commands a room, I sink into the wallpaper.

I'm shy and quiet, maybe what some people might call mousy. I have long, straight, honey-colored hair I usually wear in a ponytail, and blue eyes which are always slightly hidden behind my tortoiseshell glasses.

I dress modestly and keep to myself for the most part. So a guy like Mr. Horne would never go for me, but every time I feel his feet brush against mine under the table or he locks eyes with me, I get a little rush. Every tiny moment of contact makes my heart beat faster.

I lean back in my cushy leather seat and look around the interior of the private jet. Everything is stylish-- glossy wood grain, creamy leather, sleek chrome. I've flown a hundred times, but always in coach.

Never like this.

Mr. Horne's jet is less like a plane and more like a flying mobile office. Every detail is perfect, with a hint of opulence that makes perfect sense considering Mr. Horne's wealth empire. This cushy conference room seven miles in the air is probably the closest thing to intimate quarters I'll ever get to share with him. He's a hard guy to pin down, and even harder to get alone. Hell, I don't even know what I'd do if I did.

But what an interesting path for my thoughts to follow: the

two of us joining the proverbial Mile High Club together right here on this private jet. I can picture it so clearly. Mr. Horne would put down his stack of papers and look over at me with a burning lust in those piercing green eyes. He might give me a knowing smile, or maybe just remain serious and composed. I bet he would take charge of the situation just like he takes charge of every situation. He's a powerful man who doesn't take no for an answer and always gets what he wants by sheer force of will. Perhaps he would go straight for the throat and sweep everything off the mahogany table and take me right there in the middle of everything. The flight crew would have to watch or avert their eyes. I feel a tingle at the thought of them watching. I've never considered myself much of an exhibition-ist, but something about Mr. Horne makes me want to try new things.

Maybe he would be more subtle, though. I imagine him standing up slowly, brushing his fingertips across my shoulder as he makes his way back to the surprisingly spacious bathroom. A silent command for me to join him. I picture myself standing up and walking back there with my heart pounding. All that exhila-ration and anticipation. All these months of admiring him from afar, being intrigued by his eloquence in emails, his charisma in meetings, and his sense of total control. He fascinates me. I'm impressed by his every move. I would love a chance to show him my gratitude for this amazing job. To show him how much I truly do admire him. I would get down on my knees in the jet bathroom, open my mouth, and take his cock as far down my throat as I can manage.

I'm starting to get really turned on thinking about his thick shaft heavy on my tongue. I'm tingly and wet imagining his moans and grunts of pleasure. His approval, which I desperately crave. My pussy aches for him, for release. I'm so distracted by my fantasy, I can't focus on work. I'm of half a mind to excuse myself for a quick "nap" so I can surreptitiously touch myself under a blanket and get this sexual frustration taken care of. I'm thinking of ways to work in the excuse when Mr. Horne's deep voice cuts the silence.

"Quinn, do you have last period's charts in your binder?" he asks.

I shake myself back to reality, feeling embarrassed. I hastily reply, "Yes, sir. I have them right here. Organized by date and amount."

Still blushing from being caught off-guard, I hand over the charts.

"Thank you," he says, looking them over.

I sit here totally frozen. I wonder if he noticed me zoning out. He's so astute and such a good people-reader that I can't help but worry he might have read my mind. What if he could sense the dirty thoughts in my head? I'm sure that sounds crazy to everyone else in the world, but they don't know Mr. Horne like I do. In the six months I've been his secretary, I've seen him take on projects that could have easily blown up in his face, but he makes it all happen. He instinctively knows what people want, what they fear, what they need. He's a master of negotiation. He can sense someone's strengths and weaknesses within minutes of meeting them. It's how he's built such a successful empire from the ground up. His charisma makes people want to follow him, and his intimidation factor makes people get the hell out of his way. He is the epitome of a natural-born leader, even though he prefers to mostly work alone.

He's a lone wolf who has connections everywhere but doesn't keep anyone close. So for me to be close enough to accompany him on this work trip is important. It's a testament to how well we work as a team. Mr. Horne is the headline and I am the fine print.

"These charts are pristine. Good work," he says.

I feel like I'm floating above my chair, I'm so buoyant with joy.

"Thank you, sir!" I gush.

"You continue to prove yourself invaluable, Quinn. It's unusual that anyone stays in my employment for this long. Most people tend to burn out or can't handle the pressure. I see a lot of potential in you," he tells me.

I'm in shock at his kind words. Mr. Horne is a great employer who pays exceedingly well, and he's a good man at heart. But I know how rarely he doles out praise. This is a big deal.

"I can't tell you how much I appreciate that, Mr. Horne. I respect your opinion above all others," I confess. "I know I still have a lot to learn from you, too."

He gives me a flash of a brilliant smile that makes me feel weak in the knees. Good thing I'm already sitting down or I might crumple to the floor like a deflated balloon. Mr. Horne gazes at me for a long moment, like he's really looking at me for the very first time. My body burns under his gaze. I have been trying to earn a moment like this for six months now. I've worked myself to the bone to impress him, and finally he's starting to take notice. Even though we aren't physically touching, his stare is so intense, it feels like there's nothing between us. Like he can see straight through to my thumping heart which beats always and forever for him.

"This meeting with Tyson Cooper will be a great learning experience for you," he goes on. "He is notoriously difficult in the corporate world, but there are ways of working with even the most unhinged client. Make sure you take notes on strategy during the meeting. You're a sharp young lady. You don't miss a single detail."

Another compliment. My heart is soaring.

"I do my best, sir. As for Mr. Cooper, I've studied up on his background, so I have some idea of how this might play out," I tell him.

"When dealing with someone like him, it's good to go in strong. Know your talking points backward and forward. Know your audience, too. Mr. Cooper is no philanthropist. He is a narcissist with a massive inheritance. Focus on the benefits *he* will receive as a result of his investment in the company. That's what he cares about," Mr. Horne explains.

"That's the impression I got from what I read, too," I agree.

"We're going to have to be on our best behavior for this one, even though he certainly won't. In fact, as I'm sure you've discovered in your research, we will likely have to see a less... professional side of the business," he intimates.

"He sounds like a total party animal to me," I admit.

Mr. Horne chuckles. "You're right on the money. I'm apprehensive about doing business with a guy like Cooper. We have little in common. I built this company from the ground up, while his wealth comes directly from a hefty inheritance."

"Maybe we can use his silver spoon in our favor," I pipe up.

He grins at me and I feel all melty inside. "That's the spirit. Don't let this man's reputation intimidate you. I'll be right beside you the whole time," he assures me.

"I'm not afraid of anything with you around, Mr. Horne," I blurt out.

My face burns hot. Oh god, I've said too much. But before either of us can say anything else, the flight attendant comes swishing over.

"Sorry to interrupt, sir, but the pilot would like to inform you that we will be landing in approximately half an hour," she relays.

"Wonderful. Thank you," he replies.

She nods and walks away. Mr. Horne and I start preparing to land. We chat a little more about strategy and business matters while we pack up our materials. The whole time, I'm trying to not think about how much I want to kiss him. That should be the very last thing on my mind right now, but god, he's just so irresistible. The more I talk to him, the more I admire him. I don't understand how someone can be so kind and so commanding at the same time.

When the private jet lands, we gather our things and walk down the flight steps to the tarmac. It's a beautiful afternoon in Las Vegas, Nevada. The desert sun beats down hot and unyielding on our heads as we climb into the hired black luxury sedan to take us to the hotel. I can finally pry my eyes away from Mr. Horne briefly as we ride through the bright, vivid city. The number of bright lights and flashing neon signs is almost dizzying to the eye. Casinos and resorts loom high and opulent over the busy streets. Everything is manic. Everything is intense. I'm fascinated by all the sights and sounds of Vegas. It's so exciting to be here, and sitting next to the man of my (secret) dreams, too!

We chat as we ride across town, discussing in further detail how we expect the meeting tomorrow to go down. He peppers me with questions, and I answer them all thoroughly. Mr. Horne is impressed that I can keep up. Not only can I handle my business, but I can help handle his. We lay out the game plan.

"When we reach the hotel, we can retire to our rooms for the evening," Mr. Horne explains. "The meeting is first thing in the morning, so we'll need to be fresh. We may not get a second chance at this. We have already had to reschedule several times because of Mr. Cooper's unreliability. What was his excuse last time?"

"Well, according to his secretary, he did too many vodka shots, overslept, and missed the meeting time by a few hours," I remind him.

"Yes. He is the definition of a flake," Mr. Horne sighs with disdain.

"Speaking of his secretary, it sounds like she's been in tears every single time I've spoken with her to reschedule. Poor woman," I groan. "I can't imagine what that's like."

Because I'm lucky. I have *you*, I wish I could tell him. But I don't.

"I am reluctant to take him on as an investor, but he does have the kind of liquid wealth that could considerably boost the company's profile," he reasons.

"Of course," I agree.

"I think a good night's rest is all we need to prepare," he asserts confidently.

"I booked us two rooms at a luxury hotel," I say. "Most of the accommodations were already reserved, but I lucked out. Good thing, too, because I don't think Mr. Cooper's secretary can take another reschedule."

Mr. Horne laughs. "Fair point. And good work landing the rooms."

As we ride across town to the fancy hotel, I'm glowing with his praise. It feels good to get something right amid the madness of scheduling a meetup with a loose cannon like Cooper. A nice, comfy hotel room with all the stops pulled. No detail left unfurnished. It will be the perfect place to lie low and rest up for tomorrow. I'm happy to provide Mr. Horne that comfort.

Within a few minutes, the hired car pulls right up to the curb in front of the stately hotel. The architecture of the exterior suggests an Art Deco style. The building is immensely tall and impressive, with an Old Hollywood charm.

"Your destination, sir," the driver says.

"Thank you," Mr. Horne replies.

He gives the driver a wad of cash far more than the fare, and then we step out into the sizzling Vegas late afternoon. The sun beats down hard on the gleaming white sidewalk and splits orange and gold through the sky as it slowly sets. Even from outside, I can hear jazzy music playing from inside the hotel. Mr. Horne puts out his arm to usher me in front of him.

We walk through the glossy doors of the hotel into the main lobby. The interior of the place is even more opulent than the outside. My jaw drops at the vaulted, beveled ceiling and the bubbling water feature front and center before the check-in desk. There's a faint smell of lavender in the air. From down the hallway comes the familiar symphony of upscale bar sounds. Tinkling glasses, low conversation, bar stools scraping lightly across the floor. I can picture it even without seeing it-- everything wooden or shiny, with dim light. Atmospheric as hell.

This is totally not the kind of place where I usually stay. I'm not a five-star gal quite yet. More like a settle-for-two lady. I'm excited to see what our rooms will look like. I'm going to have a bed to myself, a bathroom to myself. Tons of time and privacy to let my mind wander back to where it was on the flight. Maybe I can finally give myself a little release.

We step up to the check-in desk, where an attractive older woman with steely gray hair and a perfectly-pressed uniform sits waiting for us with a smile.

"Welcome. Do you have a reservation?" she asks.

"Yes, should be two rooms for Horne," I pipe up.

"Okay," she says. She types something into the computer and nods. "Right! The two-room master suite for Mr. Daniel Horne.

Let me get you the room key and a pamphlet of the services we offer here at--"

"Wait," I interject. "That is two separate rooms, right?"

"A luxurious master bedroom with a stylish separate sitting room, yes," she chirps.

I glance up at Mr. Horne in a panic. He looks curious, but not enraged.

"I'm sorry. I must have messed up when I made the booking," I blurt out. "It's meant to be two bedrooms. Two beds, two everything."

Her smile falters a little. "Well, the sitting room does have a full-sized sofa bed. Extra pillows and sheets can easily be arranged."

My face burns. I feel like I'm going to sink through the gorgeous tiled floor.

Mr. Horne steps in calmly. "Could I just buy a second room for the night?"

She looks apologetic as she types on the keyboard. She blanches and says, "My apologies, sir, but we are solidly booked for the next week and a half. Many of the hotels in this neighborhood reserve quite quickly."

I turn to Mr. Horne, ready to fall on my sword.

"I can just find a room somewhere farther from the city center. I'll get up extra early tomorrow and catch a cab over here in the morning," I suggest.

"No, no. You should experience the same level of luxury as I get," he insists. "It's only for one night. You can have the bedroom. I have no qualms about a pull-out couch."

He turns to the concierge with a smile. "We'll take that room key now."

"Right away, sir!" she says cheerfully.

I'm still mortified as we ride the elevator up and follow down the hallway to our suite on the top floor. But Mr. Horne remains cool as always.

"Are you sure about this? I don't want you to have to pay for my mistake," I implore.

He chuckles. "I don't consider sharing my space with you for one night to be the kind of mistake worth punishing you for, Quinn," he says gently.

He slides the key card and opens the door. My eyes go wide as we step into the most lavish suite I have ever been inside. Everything is perfectly designed, perfectly curated to be modern and yet classically beautiful. We walk into the sitting room first, which looks like a film noir postcard. Daniel sets down his overnight bag as I wander into the big bedroom. I stare around in wonder at the luxurious surroundings.

"It's magical," I breathe.

"Looks comfortable," Daniel says.

I whip around to see him in the doorway. I wince.

"You should sleep in here. I'll take the sofa bed, Mr. Horne," I offer.

He shakes his head as he walks up to me. He takes long, slow strides. His eyes look me up and down. Suddenly, I am very aware of how alone we are. The door to the suite is shut. Locked. It's finally just the two of us together, for the first time ever. My heartbeat quickens as he gets closer. He stops with just a foot or so between us. I can feel the heat radiating off of his body, smell his musky scent. I want to lean in and close the space, but I stand frozen.

"We're sharing a hotel room together. I think we're on a first-name basis now," he says. "Call me Daniel."

"Daniel," I repeat breathlessly.

His green eyes are focused on my face. Like he's reading me.

"I must say, it has been a pleasant surprise getting to know you in person after so many months of long-distance synergy," Daniel says.

"Oh. Well, thank you, sir. I feel the same way about you," I admit.

My whole body is on fire. He raises one large hand to brush back a loose tendril of hair out of my face. His fingertips on my cheek make me suck in a tight breath. It's like crackles of electricity under my skin where he touched me. I feel it down to my core. I feel it tingling between my legs.

"Reliable, clever, hard-working; you're invaluable, Quinn,"

he compliments me. His fingers trace along my cheekbone slowly toward my lips.

My pulse is galloping. "And I'm in awe of you, sir," I confess. "I want you to know I am fully dedicated to my job. I exist to make your job-- your life-- easier. I love it."

"Yes, you do. I can tell," Daniel murmurs. His fingers brush along my lower lip.

"Which is why I'm so sorry about the sleeping situation. I can't believe I messed it up. I will do anything to make it up to you, sir. *Anything*," I assert.

"You already do a fantastic job of making my life easier, and you're forgiven for this slip-up. But if it's penance you're looking for, I have an idea," he growls.

He presses his thumb against my lips. My eyes are locked with his. The world around us melts away. I gently part my lips and he pushes his thumb inside. I flick my tongue around his thumb and suck on it deeply, never letting my gaze slip. His free hand reaches down to unzip his pants. I hold my breath with anticipation as he tugs down his pants and boxers to let his cock bounce free. He pulls his thumb out of my mouth.

"On your knees," he commands.

My heart is about to burst out my chest. I slowly kneel down on the plush carpet and look up at him for guidance. Daniel strokes the length of his thick, massive cock. He must be over nine inches by the looks of him. My mouth salivates with the need to taste him. I open my mouth and reach out with my tongue to flick over the salty bead of precome at the glistening tip. Daniel looms over me. I feel like I've finally been put in my place-- I've always served him, but this gives me an even better chance to show him my gratitude and admiration. I take his cock in my hand and begin to pump up and down. I love the sensation of his silky skin sliding under my palm. He twinges and stiffens in my loose grip. His hands drop down to gently play with my hair. Daniel runs his fingers through my long ponytail, every now and then giving it a playful tug that makes me even hotter. He is fully in control, my dominant master. Exactly as it should be.

I take him into my mouth and let his full weight rest on my

tongue. He emanates heat and a masculine scent that drives me crazy. I take him in one inch at a time. I groan and sigh with satisfaction around his cock in my mouth. Finally, I have him down to the root. The pulsing head of his engorged shaft brushes against the back of my throat. I cough ever so slightly, then regain my composure. I want to do the best job possible. Well, the best *blow*job possible.

"Stay right there for me, Quinn," Daniel orders in a gruff voice.

His hands gently hold my head while he rears back. His cock slips almost all the way out of my mouth before he thrusts back in. I moan, feeling myself get tingly and drippy underneath my panties. It feels so right, having him stuff my mouth full of his thick cock. I worship him with my hands and tongue. I slurp and suck with gusto. I let him hold me steady while he picks up the pace. His cock pokes harder down my throat. With every thrust, I feel Daniel tensing up tighter and tighter. He's getting so close.

"Just like that, baby," he grunts between gritted teeth.

"Mmmnh," I mumble back.

He grabs my ponytail and uses it sort of like reins, controlling me so that he can fuck my face just the way he wants to. The way he needs to. His hips snap back and forth while he pummels my throat. Drool drips down my chin. I can feel my juices soaking through my panties by now. Nothing feels as good as one of my holes filled by Daniel's glorious cock. With a few more rapid pumps, he holds me in place and comes in my mouth.

"Oh fuck," Daniel groans.

His come shoots down my throat and I gulp down every drop like it's the most precious gift I've ever received. He releases his grip on me and his cock slips out of my mouth. I wipe my lips and look up at him for approval. Daniel offers me a hand and pulls me to my feet.

"Wow," I breathe. "Thank you, sir."

"Indeed," he says, smirking. "And thank *you*. Look at us. The night's barely begun and we're already bonding," he teases, zipping himself up again. "Maybe sharing a room together isn't such a mistake, after all."

He's looking at me in a way that says we've got much more to come. A whole night to ourselves. He reaches out to stroke my cheek, his green eyes peering into mine. The heat between us is only growing exponentially by the second. We can sense how badly the other wants more. More touching. More closeness. Just as it looks like he's leaning in to kiss me, both of our phones start blowing up with notifications.

We whip around to grab them off the bed.

"I have, like, ten emails and voicemails from Cooper's secretary," I gasp.

"Me too," Daniel says with a frown. "Looks like Cooper wants to reschedule again."

"For tonight?!" I exclaim, reading the email. I look at Daniel in horror. "Tonight?"

"Right now," he confirms. "He's downstairs in the hotel bar."

"Oh my god. What do we do? We aren't supposed to meet until morning!" I panic.

Daniel remains calm. "He's trying to pull a power move, catch us off guard. But we're ready, Quinn. We've been prepping for weeks. We can handle this."

"Okay," I tell him. "I trust you."

He smiles and kisses me on the cheek. "That's more like it. Now, let's go. We don't want to keep this human trash fire waiting for us. The longer he's down there, the drunker he'll be."

We hurriedly get freshened up and dressed for the evening. I'm still riding the high from sucking Daniel's suck as I put on my smart little black dress and light makeup. I take my hair down and brush it out, letting it fall in loose waves around my shoulders instead of my usual tight, no-nonsense ponytail. When I step out of the bathroom fully dressed and ready, Daniel does a double take. He raises an eyebrow and lets out a low whistle that makes me blush.

"You look absolutely beautiful, Quinn," he says. "Cooper won't know what hit him."

We gather our presentation materials and head down in the elevator. As the floors ding by, my pulse is racing. It's been an action-packed day. Flight, arrival, crossing enormous professional and sexual boundaries with my gorgeous boss, and now a last-second, uber-important business meeting at nine PM on a Thursday in a hotel bar?

No problem! I'm nervous as hell, but with Daniel at my side, anything is possible.

We walk into the bar together and immediately notice a big, goofy-looking guy in oversized basketball shorts and a stained jersey with a fancy blazer over it sitting in a corner booth. As soon as he sees us, he jumps up and waves us over, still chewing peanuts from the little bowl on the table. Also on the table are an assortment of empty booze glasses. This is going to get interesting, I can tell.

Daniel leads me over to the booth. With a handshake and his most authoritative business tone, he greets our client. "Good to meet you finally, Mr. Cooper."

"Yeah, yeah, you too," Cooper replies loudly. His blurred eyes land on me. He grins and points at me. "And who is this fine young lass?"

"This is my secretary, Quinn," Daniel answers. "She's been working closely with me on the proposal we have for you tonight."

"Cool, cool. Take a seat, bro. I'll get us a round of shots," Cooper says, standing up to get the bartender's attention. "Jager-bombs over here!"

"That won't be necessary," Daniel says as we sit down at the table.

"Ah, come on. We're in Vegas, baby! Live a little," Cooper insists. "So what's this deal about again? You want my money, but why?"

We launch into our full presentation, complete with charts and notes and everything. It's as detailed as it can be, considering that it's taking place in a hotel bar. And considering how little of the table is left open amid the empty glasses and bottles. Daniel and I do our absolute best to keep steering the conversation in a businesslike direction. But it becomes readily apparent how little

Cooper cares about business. He's not here for work, he's here for play.

He makes inappropriate comments about everything. He does shot after shot, even though we are pointedly not partaking. He belches every few minutes and interrupts without shame. He even hits on the waitress-- and me. I can feel Daniel's patience growing thinner and thinner. He's getting angry, and I'm so embarrassed I've been blushing nonstop the whole time.

Finally, after about an hour and a half of unsuccessfully trying to force Cooper to talk business and stay on topic, something in Daniel changes. He sits up straighter and an almost disturbing calm comes over him.

"Anyways, so I tell my lawyer, 'Whatever, bro! Do what you gotta do to get me off scot-free. But if you think I'm gonna stop trashing hotel rooms just because one judge called me deeply irresponsible, you're out of your mind.' That's the thing about having money like me: you can do whatever the fuck you want," Cooper says smugly.

He looks at me and licks his lips. "*Whoever* the fuck you want, too."

Daniel brings his fist down on the table, hard. Cooper and I both jump with surprise.

"That's quite enough for me," Daniel says firmly. "Mr. Cooper, it's been an enchanting time getting to know you this evening, but I am no longer interested in doing business with you. My secretary and I thank you for your time, but--"

"What?" Cooper blurts out, looking indignant. "You're quitting on me?"

"I can tell when a negotiation has reached its expiration date," Daniel explains. "We're done here. Have a good night, Tyson."

Daniel stands up to leave and I follow suit. Cooper is staring open-mouthed at us. I have to admit I'm almost as shocked as he is. Cooper jumps up, wobbling on his feet.

"Nobody tells me no," he threatens, waggling his finger at Daniel.

Daniel looks down at his finger, then slowly pans up to his

face. He looks mildly disgusted, like Cooper might just be a cockroach on the floor.

"You'll regret this, Horne!" the spoiled playboy shouts.

Suddenly, everyone is looking at us. Cooper is a brat throwing a tantrum.

"Doubt it, Cooper," Daniel says smoothly.

Tyson shoves him hard in the chest. Daniel hardly even wavers, but I gasp. Cooper is trying to start a real fight with him! Rage bubbles up inside of me like never before. I jump in between them and puff up to my fullest height, still several inches shorter than Cooper, but with as much venom as I can muster.

"How dare you talk to him that way? Don't you lay a finger on Mr. Horne! He's twice the man you'll ever be. He had to earn everything himself while you got handed everything. You're a spoiled brat and you should be so lucky as to invest in our company!" I snap.

Cooper and Daniel are both surprised for a moment, then anger fills Cooper's eyes. He makes a lunge for me. I squeal with fear, but Daniel intercepts. He easily grabs Cooper's arm and twists it around. The spoiled investor yelps in pain as Daniel twists him down to the floor.

"Pleasure doing business with you," Daniel remarks sarcastically.

He steps over Cooper, who is curled up on the floor like a petulant child, and strides out of the bar with me following close behind. As we step into the elevator, we see the security team rushing into the bar, no doubt to take care of Cooper, who is now howling. The elevator doors slide shut and we're dropped into silence.

Daniel and I turn to each other and there's a split second of hesitation before we pounce. He grabs me by the face and kisses me deeply on the lips. He pulls me close so I can feel every hard muscle of his frame pressing against mine. His tongue presses into my mouth and I moan, undulating my hips to grind into his pelvis. I feel his hard cock stiffening between us. I almost wish I could blow him again right now, right here in the elevator. But we don't have time.

The doors ding open and we spill into the hallway in a mass of groping hands and desperate kisses. Daniel flashes the key card and the door falls open. He closes it behind us and scoops me into his arms. I giggle as he carries me off to the bedroom.

"You stood up for me," Daniel says in a low voice.

"I know you didn't need me to, but I just got so angry!" I confess.

Daniel smiles and lays me back on the cushy king-sized bed. The sheets beneath me are silky and fragrant. The bed is ultra comfortable, and after the day I've had I could probably get some delicious sleep here, but not right now. I'm wide awake and focused on the gorgeous, powerful man standing at the end of the bed. He looks at me with lust. With hunger. This man is going to eat me alive. I hope so.

"Still, you put yourself in danger to preserve my honor," Daniel croons.

I watch as he methodically strips out of and folds each piece of clothing until he's naked in front of me. I'm in awe. He's even more muscular than I expected. His clothes, while tailored to a T, can't do his body justice. Those bulging biceps. His rippling chest and defined abdominals. His cock stands erect and gigantic, taunting me. My mouth waters and my pussy tingles with desire.

"I think it's my turn to show my gratitude," Daniel says as he approaches me.

I can hardly breathe as he grabs my legs and quickly tugs me to the edge of the bed. I bite my lip while he hikes up my dress. He reaches up underneath to hook his finger under my panties. He pulls them down my legs and lets them drop. He wrenches my thighs apart and kneels down between my legs. I brace myself on my elbows while he flicks his tongue over my exposed clit. I cry out and try to instinctively close my legs. I'm so turned on, I'm a hair trigger. Every light little touch is like fire. But Daniel shows no mercy.

He suckles my clit, interspersed with strokes up and down along my dewy slit. I rock my hips up to meet him with every flick of his tongue. I'm trembling with pleasure already. My breaths come short and fast while Daniel makes messy work of my pussy. He devours me hungrily and laps up every drop of my honey. When he carefully slides two fingers inside my tight hole while he licks my clit, I explode.

"Oh my god!" I burst out, coming all over his face.

"Mhmm," he groans appreciatively with his mouth full of pussy.

I fling out my arms to grasp onto the sheets. I steady myself while the world whirls around me in a haze. My body is burning inside and out. Every cell is screaming for mercy and more at the same time. Daniel eats me out like a starved man at a banquet, and those two fingers gently hooked inside of me stroke my g-spot over and over again. That fleshy, soft place inside me where unspeakable pleasure lives. He perfectly positions himself to hit it, timed with his tongue's strokes up and down my soaking flower. He nuzzles and nips at my tight bundle of nerves until I'm whimpering his name.

"Oh Daniel," I breathe, tossing my head side to side. "It feels so good."

"Good, Quinn. Keep that pussy wet for me," he commands. "You want more than just my fingers, don't you?"

I nod, eyes wide as saucers. "Oh, yes. Please," I whisper.

"That's my girl," Daniel purrs.

He grabs me and pulls me up to my feet. He yanks my dress up over my head and tosses it on the bed. Daniel kisses me hard, his hands sliding up and down my naked body. His hands caress my ample breasts and toy with my sensitive nipples until they're perky and stiff. I lean into his touch eagerly. I want him to know my every inch, and I want the same from him. I want to know Daniel inside and out. Our bodies will learn each other's patterns. I am always ready and willing to learn from the master. *My* master. My boss. My sir.

He spins me around and, still kissing me, walks me backward to the wall of floor-to-ceiling glass windows. The view overlooks the wide, sparkling neon city of Las Vegas. Even in the late evening, it's only just now coming alive. The streets below teem with cars and people, tourists with their eyes trained upward to take in the skyscrapers and whimsical resorts.

If any of them has a pair of binoculars, they're in for a real treat.

Right now, my plump ass cheeks are pressed against the glass for the world to see while Daniel ruts against me. His leg is wedged between my thighs. His cock brushes against my hip while I grind my slick pussy on his bare leg. His hands grope my breasts and explore my taut stomach, my smooth arms, the enticing slope of my sides. He even plays around with his massive hand around my throat. Soft pressure, just enough to make me feel exhilarated but not uncomfortable. Daniel kisses me again and again as tension ratchets up higher between us. I ache all the way deep inside. I have a void, an emptiness that can only be filled by the man I desire.

He leans in to whisper at the ticklish shell of my ear, "I want the whole world to see that you belong to me."

Daniel grabs me and whips me around so that I'm facing the window. He comes in behind me, his cock pressing between my ass cheeks while he feels me up. His hands grip my taut ass, my curvy hips, while my breasts push against the cool glass. Daniel runs a fingertip between my legs, making me shudder. I brace my arms against the window and push back against him to beg for more. I wiggle my ass to tease his cock. I look back over my shoulder at him, lashes lowered and eyes longing.

"Ready for me, Quinn?" he growls roughly.

"Yes, sir," I reply.

That's all he needs to hear. Daniel positions the thick head of his cock at my slick opening. I suck in a tight breath and hold it while he circles my cunny with his shaft, smearing my juices around. I whimper and clench for him. I need this more than anything.

His cock pushes inside of me slowly at first. I shiver and moan with every inch. Daniel grasps my hips and shoves his full length into my aching pussy. This time, instead of just a gentle brush of my g-spot, it's like a battering ram. I cry out.

"Oh my god! Yes!" I gasp.

"Hold on tight, baby. I'm going to fill you up," Daniel grunts.

"Yes, please! Make me yours," I whimper.

He smacks my ass hard while he pounds into me. Every resounding slap makes me shudder with pain, followed by a rush of pleasurable endorphins so intense I can barely remember to breathe. I can't wait to see those red handprints all over my ass later. Proof that Daniel owns me, that he is my master. And hasn't he always been, anyway?

He rears back, sliding almost totally out of me. I pout for a second, missing the wholeness of his thick cock shoved inside of me. I feel empty. Desperate. And then he pushes back into me, hard. I see stars. His hands move up my arms to my hands. His fingers interlace over mine as he fucks me harder and faster. He holds me close, kissing my neck, my back, my shoulders while his cock pounds my aching cunny. I'm gushing over and over again, the orgasms spilling over into each other. I'm so overwhelmed with bliss I can barely think. But luckily, I don't need to think. I just need to feel.

"You like that, hmm? Feels good in your tight little pussy?" Daniel groans.

"Ohhh, yes," I pant. "I can't--stop--coming!"

Another gush of juices runs down my leg. I'm shaking and vulnerable. I've never given up so much of my power for someone, just given in completely to his will. To his care. I know Daniel will take care of me. He knows what I need and he's the only one who can give it to me.

"Such a good girl," he growls. "This pussy is all mine."

"All yours. Only for you," I insist.

He fucks me harder. Every thrust is a hard punch against my g-spot. When Daniel reaches around to play with my clit, I'm done for. Yet another powerful orgasm washes over me. I drip slipper juices all over his hand and his cock. My honey runs down my thighs and drips on the expensive hotel floor. I stare out over the twinkling city while Daniel plows into me from behind. Every thrust gets harder and more desperate as he hammers closer to the edge. I clench the walls of my pussy around his thickness, encouraging him even more. Finally, he rests his forehead against my back and grabs my hips tightly.

"Fuck," he groans as his cock pumps thick, precious seed deep inside of me.

A sense of satisfaction so complete it verges on euphoria comes over me. I'm smiling and limp when he slides out of me. My mind is dazed, my body totally spent. Daniel wraps his arms around me. His body is hard and hot behind me, pressed up against my back. He peppers my shoulders and face with kisses. We look out over the big city together as we come down.

"Beautiful, isn't it?" Daniel murmurs. "Almost as much as you."

I speak up softly, "Well, we didn't exactly do what we came to this city to do."

Daniel smiles and gives me a squeeze. "Business is business. Truthfully, the company will continue to flourish and grow with or without the capital from guys like Cooper. Our investment may have fallen through, but I certainly wouldn't consider this a failed mission."

I catch his drift and turn to grin at him. "I guess we could write it off as a team bonding retreat or something," I giggle.

"By the time we board our flight back home tomorrow, we'll have forgotten all about Tyson Cooper," he asserts. "But this? The two of us? That I will never forget."

"The feeling is mutual," I tell him, feeling utterly free. My heart races happily.

"We're going to make a very strong partnership," Daniel says. "If you'll stay on."

"I'll do anything!" I chirp eagerly.

Daniel cups my face in both hands and kisses me on the lips. "Oh yes. I believe that. But feel free to get creative proving it to me anyway."

I stand on tiptoe to kiss him again. "Will do, boss."

"That's my girl," he whispers. "Now, come on. Let's go get cleaned up, dirty girl."

"Yes, sir!" I salute playfully.

He gives me a soft smack on the ass to shepherd me off to the bathroom for a luxurious shared bath. I can hardly believe the sweet dream I've stepped into.

The rest of our evening is full of soft touches, long conversations, and endless laughter.

It's almost three in the morning when we finally snuggle up under those silky sheets together. It's hard to close my eyes when the most handsome man in the world is lying right beside me. I don't want to miss a second, because I know the fantasies that visit me at night are nothing compared to the real thing.

But I remind myself we will have all the time in the world. Countless trips just like this one.

My business-savvy master and me, traveling the world and making deals together.

Who cares if we lost Tyson Cooper-- when we've gained so, so much more?

Fertile Model: Lights__On__Lydia

Book Themes: virgin, breeding
Word Count: 5619

The sheets were so crisp and white, Lydia felt like she was leaning back into a cloud.

A smile of soft elation spread across her face as her powder-blue eyes absently counted the tiles on the ceiling.

There was crown moulding in the corners, pillars bridging the archway to the bathroom on the other end of the top-floor suite.

The bed had tall-rising posts from which veils of gauzy, sheer curtain hung gently waving in the breeze.

Lydia liked to keep a window cracked when she came to the city like this.

Even though she was a country girl used to sleeping amid the gentle buzz of insects and wind through tree branches outside her cozy townhouse, there was something so alluring about the city soundtrack. It would keep her awake most of the night, but then again, she wouldn't have been able to sleep through the excitement anyway.

This was a much nicer hotel than she was accustomed to. She couldn't help but wonder what kind of man could afford a place like this--and for two nights!

It made her feel tingly between the thighs, picturing a big, strong hand reaching into a fine leather wallet to pull out a thick wad of cash.

Then the same hand sliding down the back of her floaty summer dress, sending goosebumps down her spine. A little shiver she could not hold back, and just the hint he was looking for. The go-ahead. The proof in the pudding.

That faint indication that she perhaps might be in this business, in this room, in front of this particular camera lens for more than just professional reasons.

It was an unspoken, untouched conversation. An exchange that could be tipped to one side with just the soft, nuanced nudge in the filthy direction.

Just a slip of the strap down her shoulder or a tilt of her head, the flutter of her lashes, a gaze that lingers longer than necessary to focus the lens.

Lydia gasped, realizing with a little pinch of hot shame that she had been holding her breath, too focused on the fantasy unraveling vividly in her head.

She sank back into the pillow and sighed, letting her hands trail down the front of her white lace bodice. She had picked up the frilly top from a thrift store, and the black skirt she paired it with had come from a friend's closet back home.

Sure, there were glamorous bits and pieces of her occupation. Hair and makeup on a very good day, designer digs and duds on the best days. Lydia loved being all gussied up with makeup artists flitting around her with various brushes and sweet-smelling, high-end products.

She loved having a hair team arrange her luscious tresses into even more stunning looks.

And the excitement of being assigned a stylist to pick out her clothes and dress her to the nines was potent. It kept her coming back for more, even through the much-less exciting and much more common experience of lowkey, low-exposure shoots she normally landed. So she lived as though she had a foot in each world: the high-gloss fashion editorial world and the lifestyle-slash-boudoir content of her daily gigs.

One foot in a Manolo Blahnik, the other in a consignment shop mary-jane, at least proverbially speaking.

She kicked her feet gently back and forth as she stared straight up, careful not to let the filthy bottoms of her shoes grime up the white sheets.

In stark contrast, the silky panties and thigh-high stockings under her thrift-store clothes were high-dollar items.

Of course, it was easier to afford nice things on someone else's budget.

When a client required a prop or clothing item beyond her reach, she had the option of seeing if the photographer might supply it-- or even better, add a little extra to her bill. If there was anything her scrappy single mom had taught her, it was how to make the most of what she was given.

And what Lydia was given... was a soft, curvaceous body with broad, rounded hips and full, perky breasts. Her stomach was a pale, flat plane, but not so toned as to be hard to the touch. There was only the gentlest impression of the well-worked abdominal core muscles underneath her alabaster skin.

In fact, just about everything about Lydia was soft.

Like silk stretched ever so tautly over feather pillows. Her friends often sweetly described her as "extremely huggable." Lydia melted into whoever she was close to, like she was even hungrier for touch than they were.

Maybe there was even some truth to it.

That was saying something, because she had the kind of body that men really liked to look at. That they could not *help* but to look at. Coupled with a stunned double-take, most of the time. It was impossible for her to go out without the stares and the whispers following close behind.

Lydia was kind of used to it, but it gave her a thrill every time.

She could tell by the look in a man's gaze as he looked at her that his fingertips were downright itching to touch her, to lightly trace every rounded edge of her supple body.

She often imagined the exact same thing they did, rough, calloused fingers gently tweaking those perfect, pale-pink nipples, sending a branch of electricity through her whole body.

Making her back curl into a perfect arch, her thighs parting to let those hands wander wherever they so desired.

Theoretically, of course. It was all just a moving picture in her head, but it was real, too. She could only imagine what these men wanted to do to her, but it wasn't hard to get it right, even as innocent as she was.

Lydia was unpracticed, but even she knew the hunger they felt for her, their mouths watering to taste her sweet lips, on her face and between her flawless thighs.

But it wasn't just her outer beauty that drew them to her like love drunk flies to sweet, sticky honey. Lydia put out into the world a sort of quiet, magnetic energy that drove men wild.

They wanted to figure her out, to chart every curve and memorize every place that made her sigh when touched. She was the most tempting puzzle. The most precious code to crack open. Pretty as a picture, but not just as easily captured.

From the moment they caught sight of her, these guys wanted to get her in frame-- whether it was a picture frame or the frame of a cushy bed. Lydia was not totally naive; she understood that the answer was more often than not 'both.'

But she was careful. Maybe more so than she even needed to be. She couldn't help it. She was shy. The world of sex was something she bordered alongside but never crossed into-- not in real life, anyway.

Lydia was cautious about setting boundaries, about keeping her professional work... professional. As much as she could, at least. It was half out of self-preservation and half out of shyness.

She could use the excuse of her working reputation as a shield against having to give herself over, body and soul, to someone else. In her head, though, it was a different story.

Fantasies weaving intricate webs of desire and longing as her fingertips fluttered softly and familiarly between her thighs.

Daydreams stealing her focus and catching her in an infinite, starry-eyed loop.

Sometimes it even struck her in the middle of a photoshoot. She would cast her soft gaze toward the camera and surprise the photographer with the quiet intensity of her look. Like she could melt glaciers with such heat.

It helped that the camera lovingly hugged every slope and line of her body and her angelic face, making magic on film and digital like a superpower she could wield against the world. She looked good in any kind of fashion, any style, any flavor. Whatever size and brand of muse the photographer needed her to turn into. She was it, and well on her way to becoming an It Girl, too.

All she needed was one big flash, one loud, unignorable bright spot that would cast her into the supernova level of stardom. Maybe one day it would come.

Lydia would be on a billboard. She would really be something. At last, she could solidify her identity and persona to the public, mold her reputation as she truly desired. But for now, she had to wear many labels, put on many costumes. She could be herself, but only underneath the mask she wore for pictures.

Luckily for Lydia, she was an effective chameleon, happy to shapeshift with the mystical power of makeup and styling to suit whatever the shoot called for.

High fashion one day, street style the next. Glam in the streets, barefaced beauty in the sheets.

Metaphorically, of course.

She had a face that took well to makeup, but she glowed with natural softness, too. All in all, she was an easily marketable product, able to succeed gracefully at every gig.

But for all her talents and charms, there was no beating around the bush. There was a sort of unspoken truth she had to confront: the *real* money, the *real* notoriety, would come falling in the second her clothes came off.

Not that she had done that yet, not all the way like so many models she knew.

It had crossed her mind so many times, the idea of increasing her fees for decreasing her modesty. She knew it paid to loosen up and lose the clothes, but that was a line she had yet to cross-- not just in front of a camera, but in front of another person, period.

Lydia, for all her coquettish poses and attitudes that were so convincing in a camera frame, was a virgin.

Some people didn't believe her.

That was to be expected.

Some people were all too eager to believe.

That was even more expected.

But the truth of the matter was that she remained untouched by hands other than her own. And at the quivering age of eighteen, she was all but on fire with untapped lust.

It used to be easy for her to put those occasional naughty thoughts aside. But it was like the closer she inched toward true adulthood, the closer those thoughts inched in.

The harder it was to ignore her deepest, most blushing desires when they breached the surface of her mind. She was always pushing them down, pushing them away, pretending not to feel herself getting wet every time one of those hot, older men moved in closer to her, one eye squinched and the other hidden behind a viewfinder. She was the view to find, but only ever to be viewed.

Not touched.

Not even when the tension in the room reached uncomfortably hot levels.

Not even when the urge to just peel off the layer of clothes separating stiff cock from slick pussy was almost overwhelming. Oh well, she always thought as she walked away from a particularly almost-steamy shoot.

At least she could hold onto those memories in her mind, revisit them when the mood struck. She was a virgin, but she also had an awfully active imagination.

It was a frustrating combination to deal with, from her perspective. At least right now she had a little time to herself before the photographer showed up... and the luxe hotel sheets did nothing to discourage her.

Her fingers slipped under the hem of her silky panties and smoothed lightly over the warm mound between her thighs. She bit her lip, inhaling sharply when the tip of her finger ever so delicately grazed the tight bud of nerves at the hood of her flower. She was wet before she even touched herself.

These days, it felt like she was constantly teetering on the edge. Every flash of the camera, every twist of her body under harsh lights, every night spent awake tossing and turning while rampant fantasies tore through her head... it was all getting to be too much for Lydia. She needed a release.

"Oh," she squeaked, feeling a rush of endorphins through her body.

Her fingertips circled her clit slowly, catching a gentle, lulling rhythm. The model's beautiful blue eyes rolled back in her head and closed, lashes fluttering.

Her cheeks flushed like pale pink roses. Her slender body arched in a perfect semi-circle with her head tilted back.

Her fiery red hair spilled out around her like a halo on the soft white sheets. Some of the curls slid down to gather at her shoulders as she bit her full, pouty bottom lip.

Lightly at first, then a little harder. She applied the same technique with her fingers between her legs. A tingle of pleasure rolled up through her body at the flutter of her fingers across her aching clit, but she momentarily lost her breath when she rubbed a hard, tight circle around it.

Soft or hard, two urges always fighting inside of her. The softness she expected. But her longing to be touched with less caution and more force came along with some insecurities.

She felt dirty for wanting it, but feeling dirty kind of just made her want it more. It was a vicious cycle, and it kept her eternally on the edge.

Lydia was in a never-ending foreplay and guilt routine in her own mind and, indeed, her own body. Which led her to moments like this: desperately touching herself on the hotel bed while she waited for her professional colleague to show up, which could happen at any second.

The thought both chilled and thrilled Lydia completely. She could get caught. Like this.

Fingers circling her clit while her panties became dangerously slick-- what if the photographer could see her arousal in the photos? What if he could see her arousal... there. In person. During the shoot?

"Oh god," she whimpered. Her heart stumbled at the notion. Caught. Exposed.

She had to be oh so careful. A momentary lapse in modesty could undo her. Lydia knew she had to stop. Were those footsteps she heard coming rhythmically up the hall?

Was someone-- someone large-- approaching the door? Surely he would have to knock, right? He wouldn't have a key to the room. Or would he? After all, he was the one who paid for the room.

Her stomach dropped at the unmistakable sound of the door handle jostling. She let out a little yelp of surprise and hastily pushed her skirt down, pulling herself up to her feet.

He wasn't knocking!

In fact, he wasn't using a key either.

The door simply creaked open, pushed by the edge of a large black boot. Lydia's wide blue eyes slowly panned up the statuesque shadow in the doorway. She swallowed hard, her whole body stricken rigid with shock.

As he stepped forward into the light of the lamp, Lydia stepped back instinctively, like a trembling fawn shying from a grizzly bear. But when she saw his face, she could hardly believe her eyes. He smirked, one eyebrow raised.

"Not what you expected?" he said in a low, growly voice.

Lydia was totally tongue-tied. "I--I, um. I didn't--"

"Lock the door. You didn't lock the door," the man quipped. He nudged the door shut behind him, never taking those blazing brown eyes off of Lydia.

"I thought I did," she answered meekly.

"Mm, well, next time you make sure," he said, still eyeing her like she was the most delicious dessert he had ever seen. "Good thing I'm the guy who was supposed to show up here today. Not that you know that."

Lydia frowned. "Are you?" she asked.

The guy chuckled, all fear melting out of Lydia's body as the tiny laugh lines deepened around his eyes. Suddenly, he wasn't so scary. He was ruggedly handsome.

Tall, broad in the shoulders like an athlete, his plain white shirt barely containing the muscles that rippled underneath. And he was smiling. It was like a beam of sunshine right to the heart. Lydia found herself smiling back.

He held out his huge hand for her to shake, still grinning.

"I'm Noel. Nice to meet you," he said.

Lydia's shoulders relaxed and a smile flickered across her face. "NoelEyeFilm85," she said shyly. She took his hand, trying not to gawk at how his downright dwarfed her own delicate hands.

The photographer nodded. "Yep. That's my dorky social media handle," he said.

"No worse than mine," Lydia giggled.

"Oh, I think LightsOnLydia is a pretty cute handle. It suits you. At least I think it does," Noel mused.

Lydia's heart thumped. She found herself desperately curious as to what this almost-stranger thought about her. She was hungry for his approval.

He was already more affable than some of the aloof, self-absorbed photographers she had shot with. He was definitely more handsome. In fact, Lydia caught herself doing double and triple takes at him. The tables were turned for once.

"Oh? You think so?" she asked, strangely a little breathless. There was a glimmer in his brown eyes.

"Well, I can't know for sure if you're a lights on or lights off kind of girl, but I'll take your word for it," he tossed back, just as casually as anything.

It even took Lydia a second to realize what he was implying. Her cheeks flushed pink. Before she could even formulate a response, he walked to the bed.

Lydia turned slowly to look at him, still in awe. The bed? Why was he going to the bed?

He shrugged off his bulging black backpack, letting it fall gently on the sheets. Oh. He was just putting his stuff down. Of course. That made sense.

Noel hummed under his breath as he looked through the bag

of equipment, taking out the usual suspects. He had a slick, well-kept, but easily portable setup.

All good signs, from Lydia's perspective. He looked like he truly knew what he was doing, unlike some of the bumbling, nervous amateurs she had worked with before. What a relief.

He turned and quickly raised an old-fashioned-looking camera to his eye, effortlessly squaring Lydia in frame. She startled, sweeping the hair out of her eyes. She was nervous. Why?

"Don't worry," Noel murmured. "I'm just testing the light for my settings here. You don't have to look pretty yet. Although, I don't think you have a choice with a gorgeous face like that."

Lydia was flustered. It wasn't like she was new to compliments. She got them all the time from photographers, makeup artists, random strangers. But coming so smoothly from Noel's lips, it brought new feelings. The tingly kind.

"Oh. Thank you," she murmured. Her cheeks flushed pink and she fought the reflex to look away.

"And that body? I bet you look good in anything," Noel went on. "I can see why you make an excellent model. Most of the work here is already done; I just have to capture the masterpiece in front of me. But don't worry, I'm pretty good at what I do."

His tone was utterly casual, like he was describing the weather, but it was having all kinds of unseen effects on Lydia. Or at least she hoped they were unseen. Between her thighs, her petals were trembling and dewy with need.

There was just something about Noel, the way he spoke so brazenly and unabashedly about her body.

He lowered the camera and smiled, his eyes twinkling bright. Damn, she thought. He even had two perfect dimples. So symmetrical. So handsome.

"You've modeled, too," Lydia blurted out.

Noel raised an eyebrow and took a step closer.

"Good eye. But that was a lifetime ago," he said. "I prefer to stand on this side of the lens."

"Why?" Lydia asked.

He smirked. "I guess I just prefer to feel more in control. I like to capture beauty in a tiny square. And I'm obsessed with the technical side of things."

"I feel more in control when I'm being watched," she replied, then immediately blanched when she realized the possible double entendre in her words.

Noel laughed and stepped closer. The breath caught in Lydia's throat. He was so close now, only a bulky camera's length between them. She could feel the heat radiating off of him.

"I could watch you all day long," he said softly.

Lydia's eyes widened and her heart began to pound. "Really?" she breathed.

The camera clicked and a little light puffed on for a moment, snapping a photo. Lydia blinked in the bright light.

"Sorry. Your face... I just had to," Noel laughed. "You're stunning. I can't stop noticing that you're different."

"Different?" she pressed.

"In a good way," he assured her. "I mean that you are just as beautiful in person as you are in a photograph. Most people are either-or. But not you."

"Thank you. I think," she replied. "Are you this nice to all your models?"

"I can be nice to anyone. But something tells me you need something more than nice," he insinuated.

"Like what?" Lydia murmured. She felt her nipples twinge and stiffen underneath the fabric of her lingerie.

"Look," he said, setting down the camera. He turned back to look at her with something akin to mischief in his gaze. "I've been waiting for the right model to do this with."

"Do what?"

"A sort of passion project I've been holding onto for a long time. A self-study, full exposure. But I won't do it alone. I need someone to match my energy. Someone who is an expert in her craft."

He quickly closed the space between them and softly cupped her face in both of his giant hands. She felt so small and vulnerable with him this close, towering over her. A little thrill rolled down her spine. As nervous as she was, she didn't want him to stop.

"It's been forever since I stepped in front of the camera, and you are the perfect model to take into this self portrait project with me. Do you accept?" he asked.

She knew how crazy it sounded. How dangerous. If any of her friends described a situation like this, she would've advised them to leave. But there was something so authentic about Noel. And irresistible.

"You feel it too," he murmured. "I can tell."

"I-I do," she admitted. Her body burned for him. He smirked back down at her.

"You're smart. You would run if you were afraid. If you didn't trust me. If you didn't want it just as badly as I do," Noel asserted.

She bit her lip. He was right. It was all moving so fast, but it felt fine. Better than fine. Exhilarating.

"This is insane," she said. "I-I don't normally do this kind of thing."

"I know. I don't either. But I'll take good care of you," he said. "It'll be a fun journey together."

He hooked an arm around her waist and pulled her flush against him. She felt his hard cock, huge and stiff against her soft thigh. He spun her around and walked her backward to the bed. He leaned down to press a button on the camera. A record button. She knew it was. And for some reason, she didn't care.

After all, there was truth to what she'd said: she did very much love the idea of being watched. Recorded. Forever caught in the act. Every inch of her body was silently crying out for intimacy and danger and risk and so, so much reward. She saw all of that and so much more waiting for her in the enchanting depths of Noel's eyes. He caught her in his arms and leaned in close, his lips hovering not even a full inch apart from hers.

"I ask again," he whispered. "Do you accept?"

Lydia nodded. "Yes. I accept."

"Good girl," he growled.

Noel dove in and kissed her hard, stealing her breath as she folded into his arms. She felt the tall brick wall of her defenses start to crumble and fall to tiny irregular pieces. There was a veritable cacophony of alarm bells ringing in her head, nearly screaming at her to be more careful, to remember her smarter instincts. To think with her head instead of the pulsating warmth between her soft thighs. But there was no use in applying reason or rhyme to what was rapidly kindling between Noel and Lydia in the hotel room that night. For once, there was no violent yanking of the chains that bound her to demure isolation. She was not recoiling from a fiery touch this time. She was not politely rejecting the sloppy advances of some lonely camera guy or insomniac photo editor. She was acquiescing happily to a personal project.

Although, she wondered to herself through the fog of lust crowding her mind, maybe she ought to do her due diligence. While she diligently did whatever Noel wanted to do to her.

"So this project," she gasped between fervent kisses as he pinned her down on the bed. "Tell me more. I-I want to know what I'm performing in."

Noel pulled back slowly and gazed at her, his brown eyes lidded with desire. A devilishly handsome smile spread slowly across his face.

"You really are a good girl, aren't you? A real good girl," he mused.

Lydia swallowed hard. He was eyeing her with equal parts awe and hunger.

"I'm a professional," she replied.

"Oh, I could see that from the moment I saw your photo," he said.

"Really?" she breathed.

He dipped down to kiss her again. "Yes. And then walking into this room and seeing you here, in the flesh, just as magnetic and captivating in person as on celluloid... I knew you were even more than I bargained for. You, LightsOnLydia, are something special. The one I've been hoping to find. I didn't go looking for you, not consciously. But here you are."

"Here I am," she agreed with an exhilarated smile.

He had her totally at his mercy, pinned beneath his massive, powerful frame. She was so delicate and dainty under him, her soft curves a profound contrast to his hard body. He rocked his hips ever so slightly and Lydia gasped.

She felt his hard cock straining through the fabric at his crotch, lightly brushing across her mound.

When he heard her whimper, he pressed against her with more purpose, eliciting another soft moan. He was pleased... and so very, very turned on. He had found his muse, the one to explore this videography endeavor with.

"I'll explain," Noel offered. He grasped her wrists with both massive hands.

Lydia arched her back to meet him, making his cock twinge.

"This will be the first in a series. Our debut video, the one to kick it off. Every new installment, I will find a new way to please you. A new way to connect your body and mine," he explained. "I know we've only just met, but that's kind of the schtick."

Lydia was on fire. She found herself desperate to get rid of the thin fabric separating the two of them on the bed. She needed to be closer to him. Skin on skin. She wanted to feel it all, one thousand percent. Still, though, she forced herself to be as rational as she could in between totally irrational waves of passionate need.

"We're making... porn?" she hissed. The word felt unwieldy on her tongue. In fact, she wasn't sure if she had ever even said it out loud before. What was it about Noel that made her so brave, so reckless?

"Some people might see it that way," Noel admitted. He bent to nip and whisper in her ear. Lydia shivered and felt another little gush of honey between her legs. "But I see it as art. We are two artists coming together as strangers to make an explosion of creative juices."

"An explosion," Lydia repeated, biting her lip.

"Two bodies converging in the ultimate tableau. Getting to pay around in the sandboxes of one another's minds, free of predetermined hangups," he went on, pausing to graze his teeth lightly across her throat.

"Uh-huh," she squeaked back, utterly frozen in place by the shivers rolling up and down her spine. "Sandboxes."

"I have a tendency to get a little metaphysical when I talk about art sometimes," he admitted. "My bad."

"No, no. I love it," Lydia blurted out. "Please. Don't stop."

"I won't," Noel growled back.

And he didn't.

Even as he went on explaining the technical side and the aesthetic details of his project involving Lydia, he artfully slid his hands back up her arms and down the sides of her quivering body. He lifted the lacy hem of her lingerie and peeled it up He stopped to bend down and kiss her while the garment was up past her head but still binding her arms.

"It's the ultimate performance art. The testing of two bodies in a vacuum, a neutral overlapping location," he said as he slipped off his shirt and jeans.

"Like a hotel room," Lydia supplied.

"Exactly," he said, grinning. "See, you get it. Already. Of course, you do."

"But if we're recording right now, and talking about it out loud..." she trailed off.

Her thought process stopped short when Noel's hand slipped under the elastic waistband of her panties and between her soft lips. She uttered a faint moan and closed her eyes. Noel was lucid, though his voice was rough with lust, as he went on.

"It's all very meta, I know," he said. His fingertips circled the tingling bud of nerves at the hood of her flower. "But when you've been behind the camera and in front of it for as long as I have, you start to question everything. Lose the facade. Get real."

"Are we getting real?" Lydia murmured.

Noel looked her straight in the eye as he tugged down her panties and his own well-fitted underwear in one smooth pull. She could see the fire blazing in his stare. It was clear: there was something more than just professional chemistry between them. Maybe this was what it was all about. Maybe this was the crux of her lackadaisical foray into modeling, that every flash and every pose had been a stepping stone to this moment.

"Yes. We are," Noel growled.

And with that, he sheathed the full length of his swollen cock inside of her, and Lydia's mind went white-hot like a flash. Her body tensed up for a moment as he pushed inside, the walls of her pussy clenching tightly around him, pulling him in deeper. He held her hand with his left and her waist with his right, holding her in place while he picked up the pace.

"We are experiencing each other without plan or prejudice. No bias, no expectations beyond whatever we create together in this room," he grunted.

Lydia was even more turned on to hear the roughness in his voice, how obvious it was that his feelings and sensations were distracting his philosophical endeavors. He bent to kiss her again, their tongues probing as he rocked in and out, harder and faster with every stroke.

"Feels like magic," Lydia gasped, her body starting to shake all over.

"It is magic," he agreed.

Goosebumps prickled sharply down his arms and legs, both of them hurtling violently toward a gripping climax. Lydia felt something rise up inside of her, something she had never experienced before. It was like something had taken over her body and mind, her very soul exposed like a raw nerve.

The thick head of Noel's cock slammed again and again into that deep, dark ache within Lydia's cunny. Every stroke brought branches of white-hot lightning through her body. She hooked her legs around his waist tightly and held him close, her perfectly-manicured nails raking down his back as his cock pounded her toward oblivion.

"Yes. Oh my... oh my god," Lydia whimpered, her head falling back limply.

"That's right. That's my good girl," Noel groaned.

"Oh, right there. Right there!" the model yelped. "I'm... oh my god!"

"Oh fuck," Noel gasped, feeling her clench and convulse around him. Lydia was coming, and she was both totally out of body and yet more in tune with and comfortable with her body at the same time. The waves of throat-clenching pleasure rocked her hard, her mind short-circuiting as she gushed slippery juices all over Noel's cock.

He followed mere seconds after with a low groan, his hips pistoning rapidly back and forth while he speared into her, pumping every last drop of his thick come inside of her aching pussy. He slid in and out of her a few more times, milking himself into her before slipping out and gracefully collapsing next to her.

They both stared at the ceiling for a moment, their hands grasped between them on the come-soaked hotel sheets.

"It was a pleasure making art with you," he said, smirking down at her as she rested her chin on his chest, fingers stroking her hair.

She giggled. "Most definitely a pleasure," Lydia sighed.

"And only just the start," he said.

Lydia beamed. She could hardly wait for the second installment of their project.

His Muse: Kiara

⌒~~~⌒

⌒~~∽~~⌒

Book Themes: virgin, first time
Word Count: 6410

⌒~~∽~~⌒

I t is an absolutely divine day outdoors as I stroll across the expansive grounds of the bed and breakfast where I make my home. Summer heat warms my body while the breeze plays around my bare legs and ankles.

My curly hair bounces around my shoulders with every step while my hips swing from side to side. The land stretches out over rolling countryside for at least an acre.

The property is edged on all sides by thick forest stretching on for miles and miles. The sky above is a dense sapphire blue, dotted with whimsical little plumes of white cloud. The sunshine streams through the branches of trees arching over me like the soft arms of an embrace.

My eyes follow the flickering of sun reflected off of dewy grass and the shadows playing on the ground. Dappled light sparkles on the damp clay earth between the tree branches. When

I peer off into the distance, I can see the bluish peaks of mountains emerging from the mysterious fog over the tops of trees.

It's a beautiful little snowglobe of a world, all mine and tucked away from the rest of everything else.

Strolling around the grounds, it's easy to imagine that you're all alone in the world. Just a tiny person at the foot of magnificent mountains.

Maybe some people would be intimidated by that, but I love it. I soak up the feeling of being so small and insignificant in the grand scheme of things. Nothing makes me feel so grounded and at peace the way being out in nature does. I love to be surrounded and engulfed by natural sounds and sights.

The chittering of a small animal in the brush. The melodic, repetitive song of a bird perched with its tiny feet on a flowering branch. The whirl of wind through the trees, making them sway and crack. I can close my eyes and just listen to the multi-layered symphony of animals, plants, and elements all around me.

Who needs a white noise machine when you're entrenched in real white noise all the time? The quiet makes you even more in tune with what you do hear.

Every little detail stands out. Every little detail matters. I love knowing I'm just another little thread in the great tapestry of the mountains around me. I'm just like the singing birds or whirring insects. This is my home just as it is theirs. Living in harmony with nature is such a benefit of where I live.

Not to mention the privacy of living in such an isolated rural area.

It's so pleasing to know that I could pretty much walk around the property stark naked and nobody would notice. I could strip off my long, flowy thrifted dress, kick off my comfy hiking boots, drape my bra and panties over the clothesline, and go prancing around the orchard like some kind of mystical nymph.

Not that I have ever actually given in to that strange desire, but if I wanted to, I could do it.

I wonder how it would feel as the sun beats down on my bare

shoulders. I imagine how it might feel to have the sunshine kiss my back, my stomach, my ample breasts.

To feel the breeze wrap around my naked form and give me chills up and down my spine. I look down into my basket, full of herbs, vegetables, apples, and wild-growing strawberries collected from the orchard and garden. There are stalks of aromatic basil, lavender, dill, and parsley.

I have a shiny collection of juicy heirloom tomatoes and bright green zucchini, even one thick, dark eggplant at the bottom. The teeny berries lay dotted across the top, daring me to pop one in my mouth, feel the sweet but tart juices run down my chin. I wish I could lie down under the comfortable shade of an apple tree, in the soft grass and blanket of flowers growing underneath it.

I picture myself doing so but not alone-- with a mysterious, handsome stranger who kisses me with sticky berry lips while his hands brush back my soft, honey-colored curls. He can sense the loneliness in my heart. That heavy sense of longing that I carry with me all day and night.

Don't get me wrong, there are definite upsides to living out here essentially by myself, privacy included. But sometimes I feel like a princess locked away in a tower, just waiting for my sexy prince to storm the castle and release me from my self-imposed bondage. I am available.

I am full of piqued desires, building and building for the past few years of living out here. But I am always so out of reach. So rarely does anyone come out of the city and up to my lonely place on the mountainside. Usually, if there's a vehicle chugging up the long, winding dirt road, it's because I have a guest booked for the time being.

Nobody comes here by accident, and only a select few come here on purpose either. Just other people looking for the same peace and quiet I live with daily. People retreating from their big cities choked with sirens and smog out to the countryside where the air is clean and smells of a misty mountain morning.

Usually it's a middle-aged couple of empty nesters or a retired loner. Occasionally I'll get the odd family vacation or lone wilderness hiker. My guests usually don't stay for very long. The spotty cell service and lack of anything non-nature-related to do make for a perfect short visit. I don't mind.

I'm an introvert by nature who likes her space, so my social gauge is satiated quite well by the minimal, polite interactions I have with my guests during their stay.

But nothing quite compares to what I really crave, what I long for in my deepest fantasies.

Even though I am twenty-five with my own land and business in the form of my bed and breakfast, there are... other areas of my life in which I'm less established.

For one thing, I remain a virgin.

My body is untouched by the hands of another-- except for the one or two sloppy makeout sessions I had with boys in high school. And does that even count? Other than that, I am pristine.

I guess you could say I'm saving myself for the right one, but when I live in the middle of rural North Carolina by myself with only the woodland creatures, my beloved mystery novels, and my guests for company, it's hard to imagine when and how I might even meet the right one.

Still, I can picture him in my mind's eye. Dark blondish hair, cheekbones cut from glass, a warm smile with dimples, soft eyes that peer right into my soul. I have been dreaming of the same prince for so many years. The same bed and breakfast where I live and work now was my childhood home.

I've been here almost all my life, dreaming of the same man. I used to sneak away out to the orchard for a private place to read a dirty book or sit and stew in my imagination.

As a horny teenager, I would curl up under a tree and just daydream, my thoughts as far away and untouchable as the clouds above. I had to hide from the watchful eyes of my parents back then, but today is a different story.

I run the place by myself since my parents retired to Florida, and this weekend is an anomaly-- no guests are booked at all.

So it really is just me by myself, surrounded by miles of empty countryside. No one to see me lie down in the soft grass.

No one to hear my moans as I touch myself, eyes closed and heart pounding.

I bite my lip. It's so tempting. And why not? Who would stop me?

I set down my harvest basket and gently kick off my sandals, stepping barefoot onto the dewy grass. I let out a little sigh of contentment.

I feel safe and sensual with the soft green blades folding under my foot and between my toes as I walk to the biggest apple tree. I flash back to memories of lying beneath her swaying branches, just breathing in the fruity, floral aromas. I bend and recline back onto the mossy ground. My heart begins to beat faster as my hands wander my body in search of earthy pleasure.

All the while, I imagine my mystery prince alongside me. I replace my hands with his and imagine him feeling me up.

I cup my breasts through the slick fabric of my dress and arch up into my own touch. My nipples stiffen under my fingertips, sending sensitive spirals of pleasure through my body when I trace them lightly with my fingertips.

My body warms and blooms for my imaginary stranger.

I spread my legs and slowly pull up the lacy hem of my dress, higher and higher to expose more of my milky-pale legs. I can feel my flower getting dewy like the grass around me. I unfold for my hands-- for his hands. I stroke my sensitive mound over my cotton panties. My lips fall open with a sigh.

I brush over my clit and rock my hips upward as I imagine my prince dip down to kiss me between my thighs.

I can almost feel his warm lips and wet tongue between my aching folds. He could smell my sex, my desire, my longing. He could take me right here in the middle of the orchard, just bend me to his pleasing with no one around to see us.

And yet, though I know how private this property is, I still feel a faint rush of exhibitionism for being partially nude outside. There is very little risk of being caught in a compromising position, but that tiny potential is enough to add an edge of danger to my fantasy.

But just as I'm about to slip my fingers underneath my

panties, I'm interrupted by a very unnatural sound-- my phone dinging. It sounds especially out of place with the background hum of real nature sounds.

Nothing out here resembles a digital notification.

But I don't have any guests booked for this weekend, and it's the slow season anyway. No responsibilities, no new faces to greet and entertain. No one needs me right now. I belong only to myself... and to the handsome stranger in my dreams.

I close my eyes again and take a slow, deep breath. I suck in the taste of honeysuckle on the breeze. I hear the faint crackle of grass blades bending under my limbs.

I feel my curls splaying out into the tiny wildflowers and moss and apple tree leaves under my head. My prince is kneeling down over me, his hands pinning my wrists to the spongy earth while he leans in to kiss me on the lips.

I arch my back.

He bends to meet me.

His lips trail down my cheek, my neck, my collarbone. His hand slides up under my dress and I fall open for him.

DING!

My eyes open again. "You just had to ruin the mood again," I groan.

I sigh and push myself up into a sitting position. It might very well be something business-related, so I might as well check. I grab my phone from the basket.

My eyes go wide. I have a new, last-minute booking. Not just for the night. For the *month*. Someone wants to rent the largest of my four rooms, the upstairs executive suite, for an entire month! Oh, and he's checking in tonight.

"Holy cow," I murmur, getting to my feet in a daze.

That's a lot of money. This guy has to be pretty well-off to book the executive for that long. But more importantly, I have a lot of work to get done in preparation!

I snatch up my basket and hurry through the rest of the day's little harvest before rushing off to the bed and breakfast to start the pre-guest cleaning process. I can't help but smile as I wash the sheets, scrub the floors, and make sure there's not a particle of dirt or dust to be found. I truly love this place.

It's full of bright, shiny memories for me. There are four bedrooms, each with an adjoining bathroom. The executive also has a sitting room and a balcony. Add to that a massive chef's kitchen, a living room, and a formal dining room.

It's a sprawling old Victorian with vintage touches throughout the interior, including some knickknacks from my childhood. Every piece of this house is steeped in nostalgia for me, even after we renovated the place to be a little more business-like.

I remember my brothers and I running up and down the beautiful staircase playing tag.

My dad reading a newspaper in the living room. My mom and I laughing in the kitchen.

This house is always home to me, even when I went off to college. I'm the youngest, so once I moved out, my parents turned the house into a quaint, cozy bed and breakfast.

I got my degree in business and hospitality, came back home, and took over the reins when my parents retired to Florida. I've been happily running things ever since.

It does get lonely, even with my guests coming and going. It's rare that anyone stays long enough to form a meaningful bond, and even rarer that I would let myself reciprocate.

I keep things professional. Besides, nobody who checks in here is Prince Charming material for me. To be honest, the closest friend I have out here is my fluffy gray tabby, Gravy. She winds around my feet meowing at me while I work. That makes me smile, too.

Later that afternoon, I stand in the conservatory out front of the house where the check-in desk is located. The sun is just starting to slope toward the horizon.

I can see the sky streaked with gold and lilac through the glossy windows. It's a beautiful sight, but my mind is distracted with nerves. It's not unusual for me to get a little anxious just before a new guest arrives-- you never know who you're going to get.

I want to do my best to please every guest who comes here, and some guests are higher-maintenance than others. It's all fine with me, though. I genuinely love this job and enjoy making people feel at home in *my* home.

But for some reason, the butterflies are extra fluttery tonight. I keep checking the clock and squinting down the long driveway. I don't know what kind of person to expect.

The room's booked under Steve Jones, which is such a common name he could be anybody. But whoever he is, he's staying with me a whole month. I might actually get to know this guy.

I'll have to be in-tune with his wants and needs the whole time, anticipating his desires as often as possible.

In the three years I've been running this place, I've never had a negative review. I plan on keeping it that way. So whatever Mr. Big Spender wants, he gets.

I see a flash of headlights in the near distance and my heart almost leaps out of my throat. A big truck is rolling up the driveway. That has to be my guest, I think to myself excitedly. I can hardly keep my cool while he parks his truck and steps out with a single roller suitcase in tow.

"Whoa," I mumble to myself.

This guy is a total dreamboat. He's tall and broad-shouldered, and I can tell he has a chiseled body underneath his jeans and button-down shirt. The sleeves are rolled to his elbows to show off those strong forearms.

He walks with such confidence.

As he gets closer, I can see his thick dark blondish hair and, oh my goodness, chocolate-brown eyes that make me melt. He looks like he could have stepped directly out of my own fantasy world.

Like he's coming to sweep me off my feet and kiss me under the apple tree. In all my time here, I've never had a guest who looks like *that*. When he makes eye contact with me, I freeze up. He comes through the front glass door and gives me a big, reassuring smile as he stands in the doorway.

There go the butterflies again.

With every step closer he takes, I feel my heart pounding faster. Who is this handsome stranger and why is he all the way out here?

"Well, hello there," he says, in a voice so warm it makes me smile.

"Hi," I squeak out. "Welcome home. I mean, welcome to *my* home."

My cheeks are blushing so hard I bet he can sense the heat waves radiating off of me. I feel utterly flustered by this extremely gorgeous man standing before me.

"Thank you. Happy to be here. I should be under the name Steve Jones," he replies.

"Yes. Got it," I answer. "Executive suite for... a month."

He grins. "Looks like we're going to be seeing a lot of each other."

My heart is racing. Adrenaline pumps through my veins just looking at him. How is this man real and where did he come from? More than that-- how am I ever supposed to get my work done with his gorgeous face and banging body distracting me?

"Seems that way," I smile back.

He holds out his hand for me to shake. "Arlo Worth," he says.

I cock my head to the side, confused. "You're not Steve Jones?"

He chuckles. "Sorry about that. I tend to use an alias when making reservations. Prevents people from looking me up before they get a chance to meet me."

"I'm Kiara Golding," I introduce myself. Then, it's like a timer goes off in my head. His name is finished percolating in my memory and I jolt with surprise.

"Wait-- oh my god. You're Arlo Worth? The author?" I splutter.

He nods humbly. "That's me."

"You're my favorite! I've read all your mystery novels, like, three times each," I gush.

How did I never realize how hot my favorite writer is? I can't believe I've never looked him up. I just assumed he was some eccentric old man with a bushy white beard or something, not this young, strapping Adonis standing in my conservatory.

"Thank you very much. I'm glad you enjoy them. I sure enjoy writing them. In fact, that's the main reason I'm here," Arlo explains. "My agent wants me to produce the next instalment of my series, and I've been looking for a peaceful, quiet place to do it."

"If it's peace and quiet you want, then you've definitely come to the right place," I remark proudly. "I've lived here almost all my life and I don't think there's a more beautiful corner of the world than this one."

"I believe it," he beams. "Good to hear I'm on the right track. Oh, and my apologies for the last-minute booking, by the way. I selected this bed and breakfast on a whim. Well, more like a gut instinct, I suppose. It just felt right."

My heart soars. This place is so special to me, and it makes me happy to know that Arlo recognizes how special it really is.

"Come, I'll take you to your suite," I beckon.

I lead him through the beautiful old house and upstairs to his room, giving him a brief tour along the way.

"So, you said you've been here a long time?" he asks me conversationally.

"I grew up here, actually," I reply. "Lots of fond memories on this property."

"I can feel it. This place has history. If only these walls could speak," Arlo muses.

He sets his suitcase on the bed and looks around approvingly.

"What a beautiful space. And that desk in the sitting room will be a perfect writing nook. I can see this was the right choice," he says. "I'm going to get a lot of work done here."

"I'm already dying to read it," I tell him as I turn to leave. "But I'll try not to let my fangirl status get in your way."

"You don't have to keep *too* far away, though," Arlo says with a wink.

Oh my god. Is he flirting with me?

I bite my lip as I hover in the doorway. "My bedroom is just down the hall. You know, if you need anything," I add quickly.

"I'll definitely keep that in mind," he replies pointedly.

"Take your time getting settled. Dinner tonight is beef bourguignon with apple pie for dessert," I remark. "But if you're too tired--"

"I'll be there," Arlo assures me.

"Okay. Uh, great. See you then," I say awkwardly.

I tear myself away with great effort and close the door behind me. As soon as the door is shut, I heave a sigh. I can't believe it! My favorite author just so happens to be staying here with me... for so long, too! My mind is running in circles as I think about how hot he is, how badly I want him. My body is still teetering on the edge from earlier. I got myself all hot and bothered just to be interrupted. But damn, what a beautiful interruption. Arlo Worth, brilliant novelist and genuinely good guy, right down the hall from me. It's not lost on me how much he resembles the prince of my dreams. It has to be coincidence, right? Or is it fate?

I head downstairs to start prepping for dinner. All the while, Gravy waddles around and watches me. It's damn near impossible to focus on cooking when I know Arlo is just upstairs, but I force myself to get it done. Within an hour or so, the big house is filled with delicious aromas. Arlo comes sauntering downstairs looking relaxed and happy as I'm setting the table.

"Damn. This looks incredible, Kiara," he says, letting out a low whistle.

"Take a seat wherever you like. I'll bring you a glass of wine-- red okay?" I offer.

"More than okay. Fantastic. But it's just the two of us here; you might as well take a break and eat dinner with me. I would really love the company. Come on, we can share the wine," Arlo suggests brightly.

My heart skips. "Well, I can't say no to that," I answer.

We sit down to eat. The conversation flows as easily as the red wine.

"I love this place. The nostalgia, the memories, the peace-- it's like my own little world out here. But I guess it can get a little lonely sometimes," I admit.

"Funny how loneliness can find you no matter where you

go," he contemplates aloud. "I'm from Chicago, so I'm the opposite of isolated. And yet, I still manage to feel alone, even when surrounded by people. Still, the city has always been inspiring to me, until lately. I think I just needed a change of pace. Besides, my next novel is set in a small town, so I think this place will be inspiring for that process. If I'm going to write about a rural village, I need the experience of living in one."

"That's why you're here for a month," I fill in the gaps.

He nods. "I want the full experience, or as close as I can get."

"How exciting," I sigh happily. "I can't wait to read it. Your books are always so romantic and captivating."

"I appreciate that," he replies.

"Oh, and your protagonist is such a dreamboat. I have to admit I've always had a little bit of a fictional crush on him," I laugh. Oof, maybe I need to slow down on the wine.

Arlo grins. "I'll let you in on a little secret: the hero of the story is kind of based on me. You know, loosely. I write what I know, what I feel. It's the love interest that always trips me up, to be honest. It's hard to find the right inspiration for a character like that. They never live up to real life. To a real woman. You know, like you."

"Like me?" I breathe.

"No fictional love interest ever stands up to the real thing," he says, shaking his head as he looks at me fondly. "Never as beautiful or authentic. The perfect girl next door."

The way he's gazing at me tells me that he's no longer talking about a made-up character. He's talking about me. I blush deeply and take another sip of wine.

"This girl next door isn't quite as enchanting as most of your love interests," I deflect. "The most exciting thing I do is a walk in the woods. Or dancing in the kitchen with my cat."

Arlo finishes off his glass of wine, then stands up and offers me his hand. I take it, eyes wide, as he pulls me to my feet. He lifts our hands and tucks the other one at my hip. I let my own arm fall to his back while he slowly guides me through a dance. My head is foggy with wine, but my body is fully alert. I am viscerally aware of every light touch of his fingers on my skin. I feel his warmth, I smell his masculine scent. We're so close together, just slowly spinning while the professional distance between us shrinks away.

"You're a better dance partner than my cat," I murmur.

"Good to hear," he chuckles softly. "That's not all I can do, though."

He leans in and kisses me. My whole body freezes up for a moment while white-hot desire soaks through me. My body burns to be closer to him. His lips are soft, even as he kisses me harder. His tongue pushes into my mouth and I let it, moaning while his hands slide down my sides. He gropes my taut ass, the slope of my hips. He strokes my face and pushes back the messy curls spilling into my face. I melt into him. I've never felt this kind of high before. I want to offer him everything-- whatever he wants of me. His hand hikes up my dress and slips down between my thighs. I moan my pleasure into his mouth as he strokes my slick sex through my damp panties. I rock against him, totally at his mercy.

"Nobody has touched me there before," I mutter.

"Does it feel good?" Arlo whispers in my ear.

I nod helplessly. "Yes. Oh, yes."

"I know something even better," he says.

Arlo scoops me up and puts me on the kitchen counter. He tugs down my panties and tosses them aside before bending in to devour my pussy with his lips. I toss my head back and moan while he flicks his tongue around my sensitive clit. His hands massage my thick thighs, grab my ass. He licks up and down the length of my flower until I'm almost sliding off the counter, I'm so wet and trembling with need. All these years of waiting for someone to show me what true pleasure feels like. All this time, alone and aching for touch. Arlo is magic. He knows exactly what my body needs, even before I do. He suckles my clit and uses the rigid tip of his tongue to circle the tight bud of nerves until I feel an overwhelming push of bliss. I tighten up, my hands white-knuckling the edge of the counter as my pussy gushes sweet juices all over Arlo's impossibly handsome face.

"Oh my god! Arlo!" I cry out.

He groans his appreciation and laps up every drop until I'm out of breath and clutching at him. He wipes his mouth and stands up, looking pleased with himself but still wanting for more.

I stare at him wide-eyed. I can't believe this is really happening. We just met! But the connection between us is undeniable. He's everything I've always longed for, and he looks at me the same way. It must be fate that brought us here together. Whatever the reason, I'm done waiting around. The moment of my release has come, and I plan to take full advantage of it. No more holding back, waiting like a patient, pure virgin for someone to come take my innocence and make me a true woman. I know what I want and Arlo wants to give it to me. I can feel it in the way he takes me by the hand, when he leads me up to his suite. As we go, we're stumbling over the steps and laughing, stripping off our clothes to leave a trail of discarded clothing in our wake. We can hardly get to the bed fast enough.

"You are insanely gorgeous, you know that?" Arlo growls as he tears off his boxers.

I can't stop ogling his thick, massive cock. My mouth waters. My cunny aches. I need to feel him inside me. I need to taste him.

"Not as gorgeous as you," I breathe as he saunters up to the bed.

He leans over me and kisses me deeply on the lips. His hands cup and play with my breasts while my own hand wanders down to the stiff shaft bobbing between us. I wrap one tentative hand around him and start to slowly stroke up and down. He's rock-hard, but his skin is soft and warm. I love the way he feels under my fingers. Like velvet. Arlo pushes into my hand, encouraging me. I know what I want.

I gently nudge him to lie on his back while I settle in between his legs. I bend down to eye level with his cock and then flick my gaze up to his face, looking for an answer.

"I've never done this before," I admit.

"Just do what feels right. Don't be afraid," Arlo urges me.

His hand strokes my curls while I lower myself down. I reach out my tongue for an exploratory lick.

I lap up the bead of shiny pre-come glistening at the tip of his cock. I salivate when the salty come hits my tongue, and I can't hold back anymore.

I slurp his thickness into my mouth and moan at the ache of his girth in my cheeks. I pump him up and down with both tiny hands while I suck his cock. Arlo groans and pushes up to meet my mouth. I take him down to the root and let my hand gently massage his heavy balls.

I love the way his length pushes into the back of my throat, making me almost cough. It makes me feel complete to have him inside me, filling one of my holes. It's a thrill to suck him off. My whole body is tingling and I'm so wet between the legs I can feel my pussy dripping all over the clean bedsheets.

"That's so good, Kiara," Arlo purrs.

I move a little faster, pumping him harder while I gag myself on his shaft. Arlo's hips thrust just a little to meet me, like he feels so goddamn good he can't resist.

I love it.

I want him totally out of control. I want him to explode inside me. I want every drop for myself.

But just before I can get him all the way, Arlo softly pushes me back. His cock slips out of my mouth with a slick pop and I pout at him. He smiles and sits up to kiss me.

"Don't worry," he whispers in my ear. "I'm not finished with you yet."

He pins me down on the bed and straddles me. I peer up at him, licking my lips. He strokes his cock with one hand while the other strokes my soaking pussy. I arch my back and beg him to fuck me.

"I've been waiting so long for this," I murmur.

"The wait is over," Arlo assures me.

He kisses a trail down my neck, along my collarbone. Every inch of me is covered in chills. Every little kiss, every touch sends me reeling. I'm pushed to the very edge. I need to release the pent-up desire I've been holding tight for years. Arlo understands without even needing to ask. He can sense how much I need him inside me.

He holds the thick head of his cock at my aching slit. I push into him, feeling the overwhelming rush of endorphins as he slowly pushes into me.

With every inch, I get a mindblowing concoction of pleasure tinged with just the faintest delicious edge of pain. My virginal sex splits open for him bit by bit as he tears me apart in the best possible way.

"You're so tight for me," he growls.

"You're my first," I admit breathlessly. "You're the only one."

"That's right. I'm the only one," he agrees fiercely. "I am yours and you are mine. This pussy, this body, all of it belongs to me."

"Yes, oh god, yes," I babble.

He's pushing deeper and deeper inside me until he hits a barrier. His fingers circle my clit while he pounds deeper and harder. I feel him shattering my virginity and I love it.

I love the way it aches at the same time as it feels like heaven. Before long, I can feel his tip brushing against my g-spot-- a part of me no one has ever touched. Not even myself.

"You're perfect. Perfect for me," Arlo groans.

"It feels so good," I whimper.

"That's right. Give in to the pleasure, Kiara. Feel it all," he urges me.

He fucks me harder and faster. I bite my lip and close my eyes in the waves of pleasure.

"Look at me," he commands, and my eyes fly open.

I stare up at him with wanton longing. His two fingers tease my clit while his cock spears deep inside of me, pummeling my g-spot with every deep, claiming thrust.

I can't believe it; the star of my dreams, the man I've been wishing for all these long years of solitude-- he's really here.

He's really taking my virginity and making me belong solely to him. It's more than I ever could have imagined. I never want it to end. I feel that tightness within me constricting once again. I'm getting close to coming all over his thick cock.

My cunny aches and contracts with every powerful push of his hips. I wrap my legs around his waist and pull him down to kiss me while we lock in together like two puzzle pieces. Perfectly made for one another.

Perfectly shaped for ultimate pleasure and satisfaction. We were made to make love like this. I have no question about it anymore; this is fate, plain and clear.

As he pounds my pussy, there's a wet, slushing noise deep inside me. I feel a powerful, delicious burning from within and I know I'm on the very edge.

I dig my nails into the smooth skin of his broad back and drag them down, scratching him just enough to leave a mark. Arlo responds by nuzzling my neck with deep, biting kisses.

He sucks my sensitive skin and makes me moan uncontrollably while he bruises me up. I can hardly wait to look at myself in the mirror later and admire my marks. Proof of our tryst. Proof that I belong entirely to Arlo.

"Oh, that feel so good. Arlo, I'm going to cum," I pant.

"Good girl. I'm right behind you, Kiara. Don't hold back," he growls.

He picks up the pace and slams into me harder and harder. The ache is overwhelming. The pleasure spills out everywhere as I gush hot come all over his cock-- but it doesn't stop there.

I never even knew it was possible, but I can't stop coming.

As soon as one lightning-sharp orgasm shudders through me, there's another one right behind it. My fingers twist in the sheets and I can only hold on for dear life as Arlo claims my pussy. His cock pounds climax after climax out of me until finally he's grasping at me, losing his own control. I grit my teeth and clench my pussy, tightening my grip around his glorious cock to bring him closer.

"Kiara," he murmurs, like my name is a precious magic word.

I feel him stiffen up and slam into me one last, powerful time. His cock pumps his seed deep within me, and every resounding thrust pushes his come deeper inside. We moan and cling to one another as our juices mingle together inside me.

He pumps his cock in and out of my clenching pussy a few more times before he withdraws and collapses beside me.

He tugs me in close and peppers my face with kisses, making

me laugh. I nuzzle up to him and feel totally safe in his arms. We lie there in perfect satisfaction while the rain drizzles cozily on the window.

"Wow. I have to say, this place has the best service of anywhere I've stayed," Arlo teases.

I giggle and gaze into his eyes. "And you're the most intriguing guest I've ever had."

"It's only day one," Arlo reminds me. "I have a whole month to show you just how intriguing I can be. I have so much to teach you. So much to give you."

"Suddenly, a month doesn't feel long enough," I confess.

Arlo smiles and kisses me again. "Well, luckily I can write from just about anywhere. So let's just say that one month might stretch on a little longer. There's nothing back at home in the city that could even hold a candle to you."

"Are you saying you'll stay?" I gasp excitedly.

He strokes my cheek and nods. "For you, Kiara, I would go anywhere anytime. There's no need to look any further. I've found my inspiration and it's right here beside me."

"I can't wait to start our story together," I whisper.

Arlo cuddles me close. "We already have."

His Muse: Layla

Book Themes: age gap, bdsm, millionaire
Word Count: 6309

S unlight streams in through the large windows on the far
side of the airy conservatory on the top floor of the luxury
hotel.

Rippling golden afternoon rays play across the curves and
angles of my naked body.

Shafts of light cast long, dancing shadows on the far wall as
the clouds drift by in the blue sky beyond the windows.

I remain perfectly still as I lay artfully draped over a black
velvet chaise lounge.

The air is cool enough to make goosebumps pop up on my
skin and stoke my soft, pale pink nipples into perky points, but
the heat of the sun keeps me warm enough to stay comfortable.

The light spills over my ample breasts, soft and milky white.

Even though my tits are weighty and plump, they stand up
on their own like two perfect globes of plushness.

The light illuminates my taut, sculpted stomach and barely-visible rib cage.

I have my arms reaching up and bent over my head, exposing my underarms and the narrow slope of my sides.

My back is slightly arched like I'm stretching, to add more visual interest to my pose. One of my legs is drawn out along the tufted texture of the lounge while my other leg dangles daintily off the side, with my gently curled toes touching the cool wooden floor just enough to keep me balanced and comfy.

It's important that I stay still, so it's even more important that I find a pose that is both intriguing and sustainable for at least an hour.

It's in moments like this that I feel most grateful for the hours of yoga I put in every week to stay in shape and keep my body in artistic movement. One can barely even see the rise and fall of my chest with my steady heartbeat. I'm good at what I do.

The only real detectable motion in my pose comes from my honey-brown eyes, which scan the room for interesting things to look at while I'm stationary and bored.

In the brightness of the light, I can see sparkles of dust floating half-suspended in the air, which lends a subtle ethereal glow to my presence. I love the feeling of being completely nude. No sharp clasps or itchy tags or uneven hems to distract me. No too-tight bra to leave angry pink marks in my ribs.

No worrying about whether my outfit is making a good impression or not.

This is my true self: naked, authentic, always real. My body is my temple, and sometimes others come to kneel at my altar. Right now, I am the centerpiece of a room full of onlookers.

I can sense their eyes roving across every delicate slope of my body, drinking in the angles and shades, the textures and shadows. I am a piece of art behind glass in a museum-- visible to all and accessible to none. Only for your eyes, never for your fingertips.

Not even my own fingertips, in fact. No matter how turned on I am by the languid nudity of my own body and the lustful stares of my audience, I have to stay in this stiff position. I cannot allow my hands to fold down and explore my body.

No fingers tracing a line down between the swell of my breasts and my flat stomach. No hands spreading my soft alabaster thighs apart to dip in between.

No stroking the dewy, needful flower that aches down to my core with untapped desire. It's an exercise in patience and self-restraint. I'm turned on by all the eyes watching me and the hands furiously stroking the canvas to evoke some likeness of me to take with them, to study and love in the privacy of their own homes.

I can feel the desperate stares. I can taste the salivating mouths.

I can hear the longing in an occasional gasp or sigh. I am splayed out fully nude for the crowd to drink in. It gets me wet between the thighs to think about their own delayed gratification, to wonder how many of them will rush home with aching balls to find a quiet place to think of me.

To mentally stroke their hands over my soft body. They commit me to memory to explore my pleasures later in privacy. You can't take me home, but you can paint my picture, and for some that's close enough.

Still, I wonder how many of them can tell how turned on I am, too. Can their critical eyes chart the slight skip of my heart or the faint aroma of my soaking cunny.

Will it disturb the professional stillness of the space if they notice my juices drip ever so slowly down my thighs?

Are they fascinated by the way my round, bouncy bum gently presses into the black velvet of the chaise? The softness makes me want to touch myself more-- to stretch out like a cat and curl up in my own pleasure.

I would let the others stay to watch. Maybe they could paint me in desperate, keening motion instead of this frozen position. I have no doubt that some of them are here just on the off chance that could happen, hoping for some strange twist of fate that will bring me close to them.

I am off-limits entirely, just another tool in the room like a paint brush or a color-splattered palette. I might as well be a statue, albeit one imbued with warm, vibrant flesh instead of cold marble.

As my eyes surreptitiously scan the room, I see many of the usual suspects. Old retirees with too much time and money on their hands. Stressed-out art students who could probably barely afford the supplies needed, much less a session like this.

There are two couples here on a whim, a bizarre date of two people focused on my body instead of each other's.

That one kind of turns me on even more. And then, of course, there are the perverts. The scruffy, too-quiet guys who spend way more time ogling my bare breasts and pussy than actually putting oil to canvas.

But apart from the regular types, there's another painter here who is less easily categorized. He's in the very back of the room, dressed in a sleek black suit.

I can tell even from here that it's tailored to fit him like a glove, and it's expensive. I can't see his face because of the canvas in front of him on the easel, but he emanates a mysterious vibe that has me intrigued.

I wish I could sit up a little and get a better look at him, but I'm not supposed to do that. I'm the one on display, not him. Still, I've done nude figure modeling many times for extra cash, and the room has never held a vibe quite like this one. Something is different this time and I know it has to do with that mystery painter. Every time I catch a fleeting glimpse of his face and hair, I feel a pang of familiarity.

Who is this guy?

Where do I know him from?

I can't put my finger on it.

As I'm scrutinizing him from afar, something mystical happens: his eyes meet mine. I feel an immediate shock through my body when his moss-green gaze pierces me straight through to my very soul. I feel a heat rising in me.

The urge to lick my lips or bat my lashes at him is overwhelming. I want to rub my hands down my body and entice him closer.

I want to crook a finger to beckon him over, let him learn my curves with his hands rather than by oil paint. Judging from the way he's staring at me, he wants the same thing. What is this connection we're feeling right now? This never happens to me in these gigs. Am I just imagining it? Will my mysterious painter just disappear into nothing at the end of class like everyone else?

Just then, the organizer of the session, Fred, calls out, "Okay, everyone. Time's up. Please put down your brushes and paints. I'm going to come around and take a look at the beautiful art you've all been creating during this time."

He looks over at me with a nod and I smile back. I've worked with this guy before-- he's always professional and hands-off, just as I prefer. I finally get to put my arms down, pull my legs up, and stretch out my achy body.

Fred brings me my silky robe and I slip into it, feeling satisfied with a job well done.

Now I can just sit back and watch the brief critique process before the session lets out. The instructor strolls around the class, giving everyone commentary.

"Oh, what an interesting use of color," he says. He moves on to the next two, a couple who are beaming proudly. "Excellent work, you two. I can tell this isn't your first rodeo."

While Fred goes around the room, I can only focus on one person: the man in black. I am both fascinated and intimidated by him at the same time. I crane my neck to get a better view and I'm stunned to see that his face is just as handsome as his fine suit. He has dark brows, green eyes, and an air of control about him.

He's staring openly at me now.

Totally unabashed. Those green eyes drink in every inch of my body, making me blush and look away. It takes a lot to make me blush these days, but this guy is something special.

My hunch proves right when Fred makes his way over to the mystery guy's painting and he outright gasps and clasps his hands over his mouth. It must be either really bad or really good.

"My god," Fred breathes. "The hues, the textures, the brush strokes, wow! This is absolutely... just completely... a masterpiece! Sir, do you mind showing the class?"

"Not at all," answers the man in a low, commanding voice that gives me shivers.

He turns the easel to face the rest of the group, including me. Murmurs and gasps ripple throughout the room.

My jaw drops.

This isn't just some haphazard sort-of-likeness of my body. This is a full-on artistic smorgasbord for the eyes. I'm an art student myself, and I can tell instantly that this guy is no hobbyist. He's a master painter. A true artist. Fred rants and raves about the painting, but my mystery man remains cool and collected, even humble.

"I can't seem to say enough about this work," Fred gushes. "It reminds me of the fleeting but moving paintings of the infamous Alexander Sargent before he disappeared from public life and turned reclusive."

"I've heard that critique before," the artist says evenly.

"I mean, the resemblance is really uncanny," Fred continues. He stares at the canvas utterly flabbergasted. "How did you create this level of depth in such a short session?"

"Must be beginner's luck," is the sardonic answer.

Fred chuckles in disbelief. "Beginner? That's funny."

"Are you, like, somebody famous?" pipes up one of the art students.

"Oh my god, don't ask that," quips the other student, with a jab to her ribs.

Fred claps his hands once to draw attention and then announces, "Sorry, everyone, but we have to start clearing out. The next workshop is scheduled for this room."

Amid disappointed murmurs, the group gathers up their stuff and start filing out, Fred in the lead. That leaves just me here, putting my street clothes back on, and... my heart skips. The mystery painter is walking over to me, like the rules don't apply to him. But as he gets closer to me, I start to think maybe the rules *don't* apply to him.

Maybe this guy is beyond the rules.

He has a deeply calm but commanding presence. He's a man fully aware of his abilities. He knows he's the apex predator in any room, but he doesn't let that make him cruel. It gives him enough confidence to get what he wants. And right now, it looks like he might want me.

His eyes survey me like a piece of moving art while I pull on my panties, bra, floaty dress, and beat-up boots. He watches every moment without hesitation. Unashamed. His brazenness makes me wet. I wonder if he can tell.

"You're a fantastic model," he comments. "The pose was inspired."

"Thank you," I reply, blushing. "You made me look very good."

"I appreciate that. It's decent. Nowhere close to your real beauty, but I would love the opportunity to try again," he says casually.

"What?" I murmur. Now I'm totally taken aback.

"I'll cut to the chase. I am a man of extraordinary means. I have the time, money, and desire to pay you very well in exchange for private figure modeling," he reveals.

My heartbeat quickens. There's a part of me crying out that this could be a potentially dangerous situation, and if he was anyone else I might say no. But I can't help but feel drawn to him. My body feels a pull to his. I want more time with him.

Alone, even.

I want to know what's underneath that fitted black suit. Is his body as sculpted as his face is handsome? The little flicker of danger does little to scare me off. If anything, it makes me want him more.

"I'll pay you ten per session," the artist says.

"Ten?" I repeat, confused.

"Thousand," he clarifies.

My eyes go wide. "You're kidding, right? That kind of money could help me pay off my tuition fees and... more."

"So you'll accept?" he quips.

I nod. "Of course!" I answer.

"Wonderful," he says. "Your name?"

"Layla Cassatt," I tell him.

"Beautiful," he says. He hands me a business card. "Text me

at that number and I'll give you instructions. Our first session will be tomorrow afternoon at my in-home studio."

"Okay. I'll be there," I breathe incredulously.

"It's a date," he confirms. He starts to walk away.

I reach out and put my hand on his arm. It's like an electric jolt of warmth passes through me instantly, and I know he feels it too. He turns to look at my hand, then in my eyes.

"Yes?" he prompts me softly.

"What use does an artist of your talent have for a beginner's class like this?" I ask him.

He smiles. "When you can't find inspiration in the usual places, it's time to try new places. And it worked. I found you. I'll see you tomorrow, Layla."

I watch him leave, still frozen in shock at the whole exchange. But the next workshop is shuffling in and I have to catch a bus to get to class anyway, so I hurry out. As I rush to catch the bus, I wonder if I'm being too reckless. I mean, I could really use the money. Plus, I'm so intrigued by him I couldn't pass up the chance to get to know him more.

I climb onto the bus and look around to find my friend Elisabeth waving at me from a seat near the back. I light up at the sight of her, even though we ride together pretty much every day. I plop down beside her happily. We chat for a bit about classes (mostly me) and parties we've attended (mostly Elisabeth).

Then she asks, "How was the gig?"

"Good. Mostly amateurs, but there was one guy who... I swear, he could be a real artist," I confess. "And get this-- he gave me his business card. I'm supposed to text him to set up a private figure modeling session with him."

Elisabeth's jaw drops and her eyebrows shoot up. "What? Who is this guy?"

I fish out the business card and lay it down on my bag. The name emblazoned in silvery lettering is *ALEXANDER SARGENT*. My heart stops for a moment.

"Wait a second..." I mumble. The name is familiar.

"Holy shit!" Elisabeth whispers. "Alexander Sargent? As in, the artist who got super famous at a young age, produced, like, a

BE MY FIRST

million priceless works of art, and then disappeared from the scene and became a recluse for the past ten years?"

"Oh my god. I didn't even recognize him. He was so young when his career blew up. He looks different now," I fumble. I can't believe this!

"Different how?" she prompts.

"He's older. Dignified. Mysterious. He's a man who makes an impression," I gush.

Elisabeth grins. "Sounds like you've got a crush already. Well, my two cents: he's hot, you're hot, you need the cash. Go for it. But be careful, okay? If anything gets weird, you let me know right away and I'll come kick a famous artist's famous ass."

"Thanks, Lis," I laugh. "I'll keep that in mind."

We head off to class, and for the time being I force myself to put Alexander out of my mind and focus on studying. It's not easy, but I get it done.

The following day, I'm nervously waiting to catch a bus to Alexander's place. I'm wearing my favorite little black dress and strappy heels. Sure, I'm just going to take it all off to model for him, but dressing up a little bit gives me a boost of confidence I definitely need right now. I can't help but feel a pit in my stomach. My heart is racing already. In fact, it's been pumping away like crazy since I first met Alexander yesterday. I could barely get a wink of sleep last night because my mind was so filled to the brim with thoughts of him. My brain circles around and around, replaying our interaction. I hyperfocus on his perfect, mysterious black suit. Those sharp green eyes that don't miss a thing. That face so handsome it could've been carved from marble and kept in a fancy museum. He's so devilishly hot and intriguing to me. I want to figure him out. I want to know what makes him tick. What makes him interested in someone like me. I don't know much about him, and I'm already going to his place. Alone. On paper, it sounds like a bad idea, but I'm fascinated. I have to get to know him. Besides, that amount of money is impossible for me to turn down.

I wonder if he'll match up to the reputation he garnered in the media. I remember what Elisabeth said about him being a former artistic genius turned mysterious recluse. And even more than that, I hope I can match up to his expectations of me. I know I'm an attractive girl with a body that makes you look twice. I'm also an accomplished nude model who can rock a pose. But he's paying me so much and I want him to get his money's worth. Hell, for what he's paying me, I'll do just about anything. I'm already taking my clothes off for him; what else could be on the menu? Me? Him? Both of us?

I lick my lips, feeling my body warm to the idea of going above and beyond what he asks me for. It would be so damn sexy to have a distinguished, powerful man like Alexander Sargent bossing me around, controlling what I do. I ponder what kinds of poses he will expect from me. It turns me on to think of giving him all the control. Letting him move me and mold me as he so chooses. I'm his plaything, bought and paid for.

Just as I'm wondering if the bus is late, a black luxury sedan with darkly tinted windows rolls up the curb in front of me. I frown in confusion, but the driver rolls down the side window.

"Layla Cassatt?" he asks.

My eyes go wide. "Yeah, that's me."

"I am Mr. Sargent's chauffeur here to collect you for a private meeting," he explains.

"Oh! I didn't know he was sending a car," I reply. "Thank you."

I climb into the back and settle in for a comfortable ride to the mansion. When we arrive, I'm amazed at the beauty of the private residence as we wind our way up the long driveway. The building is made of stone, with flowering vines climbing up the walls. It looks like some half-forgotten villa in the European countryside or something. I'm instantly fascinated by the exterior and curious about the inside. The chauffeur leads me up to the front door, where I'm passed off to a formal butler.

"Come with me, Miss," he instructs. "I will show you to the studio. Mr. Sargent is already waiting for you there."

He takes me through the vaulted foyer of the mansion, and

I'm immediately overwhelmed by the opulence of the place. Everything has a restored vintage feel, with sparkling chandeliers, priceless works of art on the walls, mid-century modern furniture and decor that could've come straight out of a design catalogue. I follow the butler up a winding grand staircase, feeling like my heart might burst out of my chest at any moment. I've never been so nervous and excited at the same time. We go down a long hallway and then the butler opens a door for me into a spacious, beautiful room with wide windows along the far wall. It's starting to gently rain, and the drops pattering on the glass makes me feel cozy. I can see all the usual signs of a professional studio-- lighting, tools, canvas, supplies, the whole package. This is definitely a legitimate operation here. And some of Alexander's own art is hung up on the walls. I recognize them from my art textbooks. I can't believe I'm not only in the same room as these works of art-- I'm in the same room as the artist himself!

"Here you are, Miss," the butler says, and disappears behind the door.

I look around to find Alexander sitting in a leather armchair, looking much less formal and even hotter than before. He stands up and strolls over to me. I can only stare. He's wearing jeans and a shirt that shows off his strong arms and hints at the powerful body underneath the fabric. That chiseled jaw and sharp cheekbones make me weak in the knees. A living legend is walking up to me with his beautiful green eyes looking me up and down with clear approval. He holds out his hand for me to shake.

"Good afternoon, Layla. I hope you found the journey here comfortable," he says.

I smile and nod. "Definitely. Thanks for the ride."

"No muse of mine should ever have to take the bus," Alexander remarks. "Now, let's get started, if you don't mind."

"Of course. I'll, uh, take my clothes off," I suggest.

"Very good," he replies. He gestures to a stylish cream-colored sofa. "This is where you will be posing. I'm thinking you can do something similar to the pose you selected for yesterday's workshop. I will guide you into the right position."

I strip out of my clothes, reminding myself inwardly that he's already seen me naked once, so it shouldn't be as nerve-wracking this time. I neatly fold my clothes on a chair and then drape myself onto the cream sofa. I stretch out like a cat in a sun spot and then Alexander takes over. He gently takes my hands and arranges them so that one lays flat against my chest and the other is artfully arched around my head. He moves my legs so that they're both slightly bent on the couch. Then he arranges my long coppery hair around my shoulders. With every light brush of his fingertips, I feel a heat gathering within me. I'm already getting slick between the thighs and we've barely begun. Alexander sets up his canvas and supplies and starts painting.

"This must be an unusual occasion for you," he comments from behind the easel.

"Not my usual gig," I agree, trying not to move too much. I want to be perfect for him.

"I don't know how much, if anything, you know about me," Alexander prods.

"I know that you're a master painter. I know you gained a lot of fame ten years ago and then you just kind of disappeared," I answer. "But I don't know why."

"Sometimes the brightest lights burn out too soon," he says cryptically. "I pushed too hard. I worked myself to the bone and the recognition became too heavy. I was painting a lot, but I was spending even more time doing press events, signing autographs, attending galas. It was simply too much. I became uninspired. I don't make art for the money or fame, although I have to confess I have garnered a considerable amount of both. I do it for the magic of creating. I do it for the passion of capturing something so beautiful and alive in the stillness of a canvas."

"Wow. That's poetic," I breathe.

"When I embarked on my ten-year sabbatical, I assumed I would never find that kind of passion again. I started looking for inspiration in the least likely places. Then I hit the jackpot. I found you. Suddenly, all the inspiration, all the desire came rushing back to me," he reveals with a devilish smile. "I knew then I had to make you mine. All mine. My muse."

"Me?" I murmur, shocked.

"You felt it, too. The connection between us," he points out correctly.

"I did. I do," I admit.

"I need passion and authenticity. I need truth and beauty. Layla, you are everything I thought I'd never find again," Alexander explains. "Could you move your hand from your chest to your thigh, please?"

I do as I'm told.

"Now, take your other hand and lay it on your other thigh. Spread your legs for me. Let me see that beautiful pussy," he instructs.

My heart skips as I follow his commands. This is swiftly becoming less professional and more sensual, but I don't care. In fact, I'm desperate for his next demand. I part my legs and display my dewy, slick pussy lips. Alexander gazes at me with lust in his green eyes.

"Touch yourself, Layla. Don't worry about the pose, just focus on your own pleasure. Stroke your clit with your fingers," he commands in a low voice.

Still watching him, I dip my fingers between thighs and circle my stimulated clit. I sigh and arch my back, warming to the sensation. I'm getting off on the exhibitionism, showing off my body and my pleasure to this famous near-stranger. I hardly even care about the money anymore. I desperately want to please him, to be the perfect muse. Alexander is rubbing himself through the front of his jeans as he watches me. That only turns me on more. I play with my soaking pussy and feel my pleasure mounting higher and higher.

"Tell me how it feels," Alexander commands.

"It feels good. I'm so wet," I confess breathlessly. "I think I'm going to come."

"Not yet, Layla. Not until I say so," he orders. "But don't stop. Keep touching that pretty little cunt for me."

I whimper with need. I'm hovering at the edge, so turned on and slick I'm dripping all over this expensive cream sofa. "Please, Mr. Sargent. I need it," I murmur.

"Not yet, my muse," he replies. "But don't stop touching that clit."

He sets down the palette and walks over to a cabinet. He pulls out a cord and comes strolling across the room to me. With every step closer, I feel my anticipation ratcheting higher. Every cell of my body is on fire. Is he going to touch me? I'm full to bursting already. I rub my clit in rhythmic circles while he looms over me, slowly unzipping his jeans to let his massive, glorious cock bounce free. My mouth waters with want. My pussy is tingling. I need to come.

"Please. I'm almost there," I plead.

But Alexander isn't finished tantalizing me. He takes my hands and, to my surprise, he binds them with the cord, tying my wrists behind my back. My pussy aches and twitches for touch, but I can no longer reach anything. I'm fully at his mercy... and I love it. He strips off his shirt, pants, and boxers to reveal his perfect nude form. He's muscular all over. Strong arms with bulging biceps. A broad chest with hard pecs. A flat stomach with well-defined abs and a dark, curly happy trail leading down to the most magnificent cock I've ever seen. My lips ache to taste him. My cunny twinges to be filled with his thickness. I know even the lightest touch could send me over the edge, and Alexander knows it, too.

"I want all that pent-up passion," he encourages me as he kneels between my thighs. "Whatever you feel, let it out. Don't hold back, Layla. I certainly won't."

He pushes my legs farther apart and dives in. His warm, wet mouth envelops my overstimulated clit and I reflexively thrust against his face, crying out. His hands rove up and down my milky pale body to grope my plush breasts and plump ass. His tongue flicks over my clit and he pushes two fingers inside my clenching little hole. Immediately, I explode all over him, gushing sweet juices everywhere as my body spasms uncontrollably.

"Oh my god!" I gasp. "Oh, it feels so good."

"Mmm. Perfect, Layla. You taste so sweet," he murmurs, peering at me from between my thighs. He fingers my tight cunny while he licks and suckles my clit, making me shudder through orgasm after thunderous orgasm. I'm tingling from head to toe and fully intoxicated with chemicals of desire. I want nothing more than to feel every inch of him on every inch of me.

"Let's try a different pose," he says suddenly. He pulls away from me and I whimper, needing him close. But I don't have to wait long.

With my hands still bound behind my back, Alexander looks down at me. He strokes his thick, heavy cock in front of my face. I open my mouth and stick my tongue out in a silent plea.

"You want to taste this cock, don't you?" he eggs me on.

I nod vigorously. "Please."

Alexander cups the back of my head with one hand and guides his length to my waiting lips with the other. I suck him down eagerly while he presses my head. My cheeks ache to accommodate his girth while the thick head of his shaft brushes into the back of my throat. I love the feeling of fullness, of having one of my tight little holes filled with Alexander.

I bob up and down on his cock. I love the way he slides in and out, almost making me cough with every powerful thrust. He's pumping his hips now to pummel his cock down my throat, slipping in and out with wet, slurping noises. I devour him desperately and he holds my face still while he fucks my mouth. He uses me like a little sex toy. I am his servant, his mistress, his muse. I am nothing but a font of inspiration and pleasure for him to tap into. I am fully under his control. My hands are tied and my mouth is full of cock. I love every second of it.

"That's perfect, Layla," he groans through gritted teeth. "Take that thick cock in your beautiful little mouth. Let me pound your throat."

I moan around his thickness while he fucks my mouth. I can feel him getting stiffer and his thrusts more erratic. He's starting to lose control and I eagerly suck him down in hopes of getting a throatful of precious come. But instead, before he can ejaculate down my throat, Alexander pulls back. His cock slips out of my mouth with a slick pop and I lick my lips, looking at him with confusion.

"Time for a new pose," he tells me.

"Anything for you," I answer obediently.

"Good girl. My perfect muse. Turn around for me, let me see that ass," Alexander commands. With my hands still tied, I manage to flip around. I stick my ass up in the air and bend my face forward, spreading my legs to tease and draw him in.

Alexander grabs my ass with both hands. He squeezes and gropes me while the slick, velvety head of his cock brushes against my hole. I back into him in another wordless plea for him to fuck me. I wonder if the whole city can see us through the big wall of windows. I don't mind. In fact, I hope they can see me. It only adds to the riskiness and sexiness of the moment.

My mysterious artist gives my ass a hard, resounding smack. I moan and tremble all over. My cunny gushes honey as I anticipate more. Alexander rubs a tight circle around my asshole while he rubs the head of his cock against my clit. When he pushes inside of me, I let out a wail of mingled pain and bliss. His thickness spears into me from behind and the walls of my cunny expand and contract around him. He sheathes himself entirely inside me and grabs my hips with both hands. He rears back and slams into me so that the tip of his shaft pummels my g-spot deep within. All the while, he fingers my bum and smacks my ass cheeks, adding even more nuances of pain and pleasure to the concoction.

"This is exactly the inspiration I've been looking for," Alexander growls. "Give me every drop of your passion, Layla. Show me your raw side. I want to know you inside and out."

His cock pounds into me with wet slaps and I feel tears of intense stimulation in my eyes. It's almost too much to bear, but in the best way. I am viscerally aware of everything-- the rain on the windows, the cord snug around my wrists, Alexander's length spearing me, splitting me with every merciless thrust. He grabs a fistful of my sleek red hair and pulls it while he fucks me from behind. I push back against him, begging for every stroke. When he reaches around to play with my burning clit, I almost collapse with delight.

"I'm so close," I whisper.

"Excellent. Come for me. Gush all over my cock, Layla," he orders.

I explode with a little squeal of pleasure. My cunny squirts thick honey all over his thick cock while he pounds me harder and faster. He doesn't let up at all. He yanks my hair, smacks my ass, and fingers my tight little asshole while he destroys my pussy. I squeeze myself around him to urge him closer to the edge. I want him to feel as good as I do. I want to prove to him how good a little muse I can be, how much pleasure I can give him.

"Are you ready for me to come inside you, my muse?" Alexander teases.

I look back at him with wide, imploring eyes. "God, yes! Please come inside me!"

Alexander's hands explore my body while he loses control. He caresses my swinging, ample breasts. He massages my clit and gropes my ass. He grabs my hips and uses them as leverage while he fucks me deeper than before. I can feel him splitting me open, wrecking me from the inside just the way I want him to. He slams into me several more times and just as I'm screaming through yet another mindblowing climax, he comes, too.

"Layla!" he bellows as his cock spills thick, precious seed deep inside my cunny.

I twitch and whimper through the shockwaves of pleasure. My pussy is clenching around him, squeezing out every last drop into my womb. He's marking me. Claiming his territory. I am his muse, now and always. I can think of nothing I would rather be. After he finally slides his thick, spent cock out of my dripping pussy, he unties my wrists. He kisses the soreness away sweetly, then helps me up to my feet. I stand there, wobbly and over-whelmed while Alexander cups my face and peers into my eyes like I'm the most precious thing he's ever seen.

"You, my muse, are everything," he murmurs.

He leans in and kisses me on the lips. Fireworks explode in my mind. My body goes slack and I have to lean into him to stay upright. Alexander strokes my hair, cradles me against him. He kisses me again and again while his hands caress and hold me. I've never felt so safe and desired. When we come down from the high, he wraps us both up in a silky sheet and we cuddle on the sofa together just watching the rain pitter patter on the windows.

"I think my sabbatical has come to an end," Alexander remarks with a smile.

"Really?" I reply excitedly.

"I've found my inspiration in you, Layla. Your passion, your beauty, your obedience. You are just what I've been searching for, and now you're mine," he says.

"I am yours. For as long as you want me," I declare.

"I'm planning an entire series of nudes for which you will be my model," he tells me. "I think we're going to be spending a lot of time together. How does that sound?"

I snuggle into him happily. "It sounds wonderful. Picture perfect."

His Muse: Stella

Book Themes: age gap, coworkers, celebrities
Word Count: 5866

The smell of whiskey hangs sweet and sticky in the hot air, mingling with plumes of thick smoke from the cigars and pipes my customers are smoking.

From a particularly smoky corner of the saloon comes the plinky tones of an old piano playing out a jazzy tune. Throughout the rustic wooden interior, men are gathered in small groups to chat about whatever menfolk chat about.

Horses.

Territory.

Who has the quickest draw in all the land.

I take it all in from my prime position behind the long, notched wood bar counter. I have eyes on the whole place, which is a good thing, since the saloon is the first place outlaws tend to go when they roll into our quiet, dusty town out in the plains.

I have to make sure everything runs smoothly. I have to figure out how to keep the peace even among these trigger-happy cowboys.

I'm the saloon girl, the barkeep, the babysitter of sloppy drunks and the listener of bombastic stories.

And of course, I have to fight off my fair share of suitors-- to put it kindly. Sometimes, it's kind of fun to flirt with a ruggedly handsome traveling salesman or a cowhand. I love the attention, even though it can get a little annoying from time to time when someone won't take the hint.

But tonight, I'm trying to drop hints. Because across the crowded saloon, partly obscured by curls of white smoke, is the sexiest man I've ever seen in my life.

He's intimidatingly tall and broad-shouldered, with a muscular frame that could easily trounce any one of these other cowboys in a brawl.

He's dusty from travel, but he still manages to look gorgeous through all the grime. I've had my eye on him for the past half hour. I glance at him every chance I get, between refilling people's beers and wiping down the counter.

It's getting late here, and the nightly party is starting to ramp up. There are even a few people up and dancing, still sloshing their mugs of beer around in the process.

That'll be another sticky mess to clean up in the bright, revealing light of dawn. But that's a problem for future me. Right now, I have something much more pressing on my mind.

Because that impossibly handsome cowboy has stood up from his corner table and is now sauntering up to the bar.

To me!

My heart pounds as I watch him approach out of the corner of my eye. I'm trying not to give away how intriguing I find him. As the saloon girl, I have to maintain some degree of inaccessibility. I have to keep boundaries, otherwise all of my lonely-heart patrons will pester me until the end of time.

But I can tell before this guy even reaches the bar that it's a different story here. I can't resist him. I couldn't deny him anything. My body is getting warm and tingly as he leans in and rests his elbow on the counter, his clay-brown eyes smoldering as he gazes at me. There's something of a smirk playing about those luscious lips, and when he gives me a full-blown smile, I nearly swoon.

His eyes flit down to take in the curvy slope of my hips, my cinched waist, and my ample cleavage on display in my corseted dress. My cheeks burn, but I try to remain collected.

"Well, hello there," I greet him. "How are you on this fine evening?"

"Much better now that I'm lookin' at you," the cowboy drawls.

I smile. Oh lord, this man's a smooth talker. And I'm a goner.

"Why, aren't you sweet. Can I get you another ale?" I offer.

He reaches across the bar and lays a large, work-calloused hand on my arm.

I feel an immediate shockwave of delight at this gentle touch. I'm getting slick underneath my petticoats already. The cowboy runs his hand up my arm to my shoulder, then his fingertips trace lightly across my exposed collarbone.

The whole time, I'm completely frozen. The spark between us is instantaneous and powerful. I've just met this guy and I would already bend over and give him whatever the hell he came here for. Where is my restraint? Where are my morals?

"Can I get a tall glass of you instead?" he asks suggestively.

I bat my eyelashes. "That depends. Can you hold your liquor?" I tease.

"Why don't you and I go upstairs and I'll show you just how well I can hold it," he says.

I know exactly what he's getting at, and I want it, too. We're about to head up to the bedroom for a rollickin' good time when suddenly, the bustling saloon, the handsome cowboy, and all my sexy excitement melts away around me.

I close my eyes for just a second, and when I open them again, the saloon is gone.

In its place, I can make out the details of a dressing room trailer in the weak light of morning. I sigh and sit up on the comfy pull-out couch that has become my makeshift bed leading up to filming day.

I'm not actually a saloon girl in 1890s Colorado.

I'm just an actress about to play one in a movie.

In fact, instead of a blanket covering me, I've got a stack of assorted script pages scattered across my body. Proof of a late night spent poring over my lines and committing them to memory. Hours of blocking actions and adjusting my inflection. Playing the role alone in my dressing room trailer.

I probably should have gone back to my apartment for a real night's sleep, but what can I say? I'm the kind of actress who throws herself headfirst into her role.

From the second I was cast as Florence Rose, saloon girl and fresh-faced love interest of the male lead, Jasper Clayton, I've been tapping into her character whenever possible. Apparently, now I've even started dreaming as Florence. I get a little shiver of delight at that. The more like Florence I can feel, the better my portrayal will translate on screen.

I need my audience to really believe I'm her.

And part of being Florence is being in love with Jasper. So when I think about it, I would actually be getting into character if I were to... pick up where my dream left off.

I close my eyes and lean back on the pull-out couch. My hand slips under the hem of my comfy pajama bottoms. I bite my lip as my fingers trail down toward my dewy flower.

As soon as my fingers gingerly brush over my clit, I get chills over my whole body. I'm already so wet, just from the briefest flirtation in my dream. But what if I had actually gone upstairs with Jasper to the spare room, to that bed with the rattling metal and the straw mat?

Maybe not the most comfortable place to make love, but I know Jasper would make it magical. I can imagine the cowboy pushing me against the wall, wedging his leg between my thighs to grind against my slick pussy while he kisses my lips.

I imagine his hands groping their way up and down my body in my swishy dress and petticoats. How he would have to gather the skirts with his arm to reach underneath and touch me, pulling back two glistening fingers.

I see him raising those fingers to his lips. He sucks off my sweet juices with a look of pure need on his handsome features.

I lick my own lips and reach down slowly for the thick, mouthwatering bulge at his crotch.

Suddenly, there are two sharp knocks at the trailer door and I nearly jump out of my skin.

I hastily whip my hand out of my pants and rush to the sink to wash my hands as my eyes frantically search for the clock. It's almost eight in the morning, and the table read starts at eight-thirty. I was so distracted with lust, I lost track of time.

There's another knock, and then someone's assistant says, "Table read in thirty, Miss Swanson!" through the door.

I call back, "Okay, thank you! I'll be there!"

Thankfully, I've had my day-one outfit planned for a week now. I pull the cute-but-cozy t-shirt and designer jeans out of my closet, paired with some stylish sneakers. I wash my face and brush my hair in a hurry. I decide to go for a natural look and just rub on some lip balm and moisturizer. It's a table read-- I don't have to look perfect.

Although, as I exit my trailer and rush off to the writer's room, it does dawn on me that I'll be meeting most of the cast for the first time today.

Including the incredibly sexy and well-respected actor, Eli Daniels, who is playing Jasper Clayton.

My heart skips a beat remembering that little fact. Eli is going to be my love interest, which means I have his incredible reputation and body of work to match up with. Don't get me wrong, I'm a great actress. But so far, people mostly know me as a former child star who acted in a lot of daytime TV.

They don't realize I took a break from acting to get my degree and learn about myself as a person. They don't know the journey I've taken to lead me back into show business. I'm sure they don't expect me to be the hard-working, ambitious woman I've grown into. But I'm going to prove to everyone just how seriously I take my craft.

Which means I have to impress the likes of Eli Daniels.

If only I could stop fantasizing about him long enough to *make* an impression. Because from the moment I step into the writer's room, my eyes are locked on him.

My god, he's even better looking in person. He's wearing a button-up shirt, but half the buttons are undone to reveal his muscular chest. The sleeves are rolled at his elbows to show off his strong arms, and his perfect, thick dark hair looks artfully tousled. Like the most professional bedhead I've ever seen. I take my seat across from him, in between two older actresses on the cast.

I notice immediately that Eli's gorgeous brown eyes are locked on me. He looks me up and down approvingly, then gives me a warm, welcoming smile that makes my heart skip. I smile back at him and avert my eyes down to the script in front of me. He makes me nervous and giddy at the same time.

He's just as handsome and impressive in person as he is onscreen. How am I going to keep my composure with this chiseled hunk right in front of me?

We all go around the table and introduce ourselves briefly, and then we jump right into reading lines. The whole time, my heart is racing. Eli is the big, shining star of this production, whose face will be all over the billboards lining the streets of Hollywood.

I listen excitedly while everyone goes through their lines until it gets to the scene I'm filming today with Eli. It's our characters' first time meeting in the saloon.

"Welcome to the Half Moon Saloon," I read out my first line in a perfect cowgirl drawl.

"Well, aren't you a sight for sore eyes," Eli purrs. His voice gives me goosebumps.

"You look like you've been ridin' for a week," I reply.

"Don't worry, sweetheart. I've got enough stamina to go all night, too," he remarks with a roguish wink. I blush.

"Can I pour you an ale?" I ask.

"How 'bout a tall glass of you, pretty thing?" he flirts.

We're just gazing at each other now. We both have the lines

memorized, and we can't look away. I'm drawn to Eli like a moth to a flame. I wonder if he feels it too.

"There's an upcharge for off-menu items," I flirt back.

"Well, then. Lucky thing I just came from California. I got gold enough to buy this saloon and everything in it," he boasts. "What's your name, girly?"

"Florence Rose," I answer. My heart is about to burst out of my chest.

"Nice to make your 'quaintance, Miss Rose. I'm Jasper Clayton. But you can just call me Sheriff," Eli drawls. "Though I do prefer Jasper when you're hollerin' my name tonight."

"And scene," interjects the director, who looks positively delighted.

Everyone applauds us for a job well done, but Eli has eyes only for me. And the feeling is definitely mutual. As the cast disperses for a break before we start filming, I try to rush after Eli, but I don't catch him before he's swallowed up by a waiting horde of rabid fangirls outside.

I watch as he's consumed by the starry-eyed crowd, a little disappointed. I wanted to really meet him, really introduce myself before our first on-camera scene.

But I don't get much time to pout, because suddenly I feel a hand tugging on my arm. I look over to see my long-time best friend and current makeup artist, Jenny, smiling at me. My spirits instantly pick back up.

"Hey Stella!" she chirps, leading me away to the hair and makeup trailer.

"Hey Jen!" I reply brightly. "How are you?"

"I'm awesome! So excited to be on-set with my best friend in the whole world. Can you believe it? We used to daydream about this moment and now it's finally here!" she gushes.

"I know, right? We've come a long way from performing on that kids' variety show together when we were eight years old," I giggle.

"Now, look at us: you're a bonafide actress playing opposite to *the* Eli Daniels, and I'm living out my dream of being a profes- sional makeup artist," she sighs happily. "I'm so excited to do your makeup every morning. We'll have so much time to hang out!"

We enter the hair and makeup trailer and get situated in between a couple other actresses and an extra. Jenny takes out her colossal bag of professional-grade makeup and gets to work on my face, to take me from fresh-faced to full-faced.

"So, how was the table read? Tell me everything!" Jenny exclaims.

"It went so well," I smile. "I was up all night studying my lines and I got it perfectly right. And Eli is such a dreamboat. I was getting hot and bothered just sitting there."

"Ooh, juicy," Jenny gasps. "Is there, like, real chemistry there?"

"Maybe too soon to tell, but it sure feels that way to me," I admit in a lowered voice. I don't need the other cast and crew in here to know just how hot for Eli I really am.

"Well, don't you worry. I'm going to make you look totally flawless. If he couldn't keep his eyes off you this morning, he'll be drooling over you once I'm done here," she quips.

I grin at her. "It's so nice to have a friend around. Someone who really gets it."

"It's a cutthroat world out here in Hollywood," she agrees as she dabs at my face with a makeup sponge. "This industry pits us girls against each other, but not you and me. You make your career in front of the camera, and I'm way happier behind the scenes, making it all come together. Crazy how we both get to follow our passion!"

"It's a dream come true," I sigh. "I'm so proud of us."

We chat and gossip throughout the morning as Jenny gets me camera-ready. She hangs out while the on-set stylist does my sexy saloon girl hair. I tell her all about the script, the table read, and lots about Eli himself.

I can't seem to stop thinking about him. Maybe I'm taking my method acting a little too far-- maybe I like him a little too much. But I can't stop myself. Eli Daniels is utterly irresistible, and I'm just another starstruck young woman in front of him.

I feel a twinge of something like envy when I think about

him surrounded by all those female fans. But I remind myself that *I'm* the one playing his love interest, not them.

When my hair and makeup are done, Jenny walks me over to Wardrobe so I can be fitted into my flouncy petticoats and cotton dress with a scoopneck cut to show off my cleavage. They add in my shiny black boots and some fake (but realistic) gunslinger accessories.

By the time I'm called to set for my first scene, I'm looking and feeling good. I'm totally in character and ready to perform, even though I still have a little giddy nervousness in my heart.

That's a good thing, I tell myself.

Use the nerves.

Channel that energy into playing Florence Rose the very best I can.

An assistant guides me to the soundstage where the crew have built the 'saloon' interior. I situate myself behind the convincing bar counter and wait for the scene to begin. Everyone goes quiet. The studio lights glare down on me with incredible heat. I can feel every pair of eyes locked on me.

It's the moment of calm before the storm, but I can handle this. I'm just excited to get started! And... to see Eli again.

When he comes strolling through the saloon doors, my jaw almost drops. Eli is suited up in his historically-accurate, highly-detailed cowboy outfit. He looks like he's been riding a horse and roping up criminals in the dusty plains. He looks like the action star of my filthiest dreams. It's easy as pie to play-act like I'm attracted to him because, well, I am.

We run through the lines we practiced this morning at the table read, both of us fully committed to our characters. We fall into our roles perfectly, and I'm getting an adrenaline rush from performing with him.

Everyone is watching us flirt and make eyes at one another. I can't deny that the exhibitionist aspect of filming kind of gets me hot. Especially when it's Eli I'm filming with. I'm so into the scene I can almost ignore the crowds of people watching. It's just the two of us: Sheriff Jasper Clayton and saloon girl Florence Rose.

"Though I do prefer Jasper when you're hollerin' my name tonight," he drawls again.

This time, we keep going. I give him a sassy look.

"You've got one hell of an ego, Sheriff," I retort. "And I sleep alone."

"Trust me, Miss Rose: we won't be doin' a lot of sleepin'," he flirts.

Oof. How I wish it was really Eli saying this to me.

"Look, mister. You may have a shiny gold badge on your chest, but in my saloon, you're just another thirsty customer," I quip back with a serious attitude.

"Aw, don't be like that. Don't give me a hard time," he croons.

"Your 'hard time' isn't my problem," I clap back, swiveling on my heel to ignore him.

"Cut!" the director barks. "Well done, you two. Excellent work."

As the crew start shifting things around to film a scene with some other actors, I hurry after Eli, eager to catch him this time. He looks down to see me gazing at him and grins.

"Great job, Stella," he says, still walking. "You killed it."

"Sorry for getting so sassy with you," I stammer awkwardly. "I would never talk to you like that outside of a scene."

He laughs gently. "I know. No offense taken. You're a damn good actress."

I feel like I'm floating on air.

"Thank you. You're amazing," I reply breathlessly.

"Besides," Eli goes on, "I've had far worse things said to me both on and offscreen."

"Really?" I gasp, walking alongside him. He towers over me as we head back to Wardrobe together.

"Oh yeah. One time I had an actress slap me across the face. Wasn't in the script, either. She just didn't take it particularly well when I turned her down for a date," he chuckles.

"Wow," I breathe, eyes wide. "Sounds like that might've made it a little awkward on set."

"I'm used to it," he shrugs good-naturedly. "But I can tell it'll be different this time around."

"How so?" I pipe up.

Eli gives me a glittering grin.

"Because *you're* different. You're serious about your craft. You're focused. You're a natural talent. I appreciate that, as a fellow actor," he compliments me.

My heart swells like it might burst.

"Thank you so much," I gush. "That means a lot coming from a well-respected performer like you."

We step into the wardrobe trailer and get changed, with little privacy curtains between us. I steal a glance at his silhouette through the curtain and nearly choke on my own lust. He's incredibly built. He looks like a mythical hero. I would climb him like a tree.

"You're a seasoned actor, yourself," Eli reminds me. "I think we can both learn a lot from each other."

"I would love to hear any advice you have to offer. I am always trying to be better," I tell him.

"You know, I have an idea," Eli says. "I have a red carpet event tonight in support of my charity. There will be all kinds of producers, directors, performers, movers and shakers. Lots of well-connected people with a combined wealth of experience. You should come with me."

My jaw drops. "Wha—really?"

"As my date," he adds casually.

I might just ascend to the clouds, I'm so delighted. My heart is racing as I hurriedly nod.

"I would love that!" I blurt out a little too loudly. "I haven't been on a red carpet since I was ten years old at that movie premiere."

Eli chuckles. "Perfect. Time for you to make your second debut, then. I'll pick you up at eight tonight. Wear your most fabulous dress," he adds as he walks out the door to his next set.

I stare after him dumbfounded for a moment before the wardrobe ladies descend on me like vultures to help me find something to wear tonight. Thank god. After they fit me for a beautiful, floor-length shimmery green dress and strappy gold designer heels, I rush off to the makeup trailer. I tell Jenny about the gala and she excitedly agrees to help me get ready for the event.

Later that evening, I'm in my bedroom staring at my reflection in the full length mirror. My every curve is hugged by this slinky green gown, my legs look extra chiseled in these strappy heels. My long blonde hair is perfectly styled in classic Hollywood waves, my makeup is on point. Jenny gave me this incredible waterproof (and kiss-proof, she pointed out) red lipstick that makes me look like a retro screen siren. I look damn good.

But that doesn't keep me from feeling super nervous, especially when Eli shows up in a glossy black Mercedes with a chauffeur to pick me up. He opens the side door and ushers me into the sleek leather interior.

"You look absolutely divine," Eli says.

I blush deeply. "Right back at you."

And it's true: he's dressed in a perfectly tailored black suit with a gunmetal gray tie and shiny black shoes. His dark hair is swept back, and he's smoothly clean shaven, making his chiseled features stand out even more. He looks good enough to eat. I wish I could get a little taste...

But before long, we arrive at the event. Flashes of bright camera lights threaten to blind us as we step out of the Mercedes arm in arm. I cling tightly to Eli as he leads me down the red carpet. All eyes are on us. All lenses are focused on us.

It's clear that Eli is the man of the hour, after all, it's his event. His charity.

And I am the luckiest woman in the world getting to be his arm candy for the evening. The magical night only gets better and better as we flit from one little social group of well-connected people to the next.

We mix and mingle with the best of them, and Eli introduces me to a bunch of important names in show business. And the whole time, Eli is whispering in my ear, holding me close with his arm around my shoulders or my waist, giving me little tidbits and secrets of the trade mixed in with tiny flirtations.

It's enough to get me giddy and fluttery in the chest. The chemistry between us is undeniable and I know he's feeling it too. Every time he looks at me, I sense the growing heat there.

"Having fun yet?" Eli whispers in my ear.

I get a delicious shiver from his warm breath on my ticklish neck. "Are you kidding? This is the best night of my life!" I reply.

Eli's hand slips down the slope my slender waist to rest on my hip. Then he murmurs in my ear, "If you want to get out of here, I can show you an even better time."

My eyes grow wide and I feel myself getting dewy between my thighs. Does he mean what I think he means? Does the famous Eli Daniels want to take me home tonight?

Suddenly, I have zero interest in this gala. I just want to be alone with Eli. I stand on tiptoe to whisper back to him, "I'm ready to go when you are."

I mean that in every possible way. Eli catches my drift instantly. He takes my hand and gently pulls me through the tipsy, rich crowd and out into the balmy LA night. His chauffeur drives around to pick us up and we pile into the back. Eli rolls up the partition and turns to me with hunger in his dark eyes.

He cups my face in both hands and dives in for a passionate kiss, his tongue darting into my mouth. I moan and lean into him eagerly. His hands slide down my body to feel me up.

His fingers toy with my perky nipples through the thin fabric of my dress while his other hand slips underneath the bottom hem and cups my dewy mound. I rock into his touch while he kisses me, tasting of wine and heaven.

He hikes up my dress and moves down to crouch in front of me. I watch with mouth agape and eyes wide as he pulls down my panties and takes a deep, luxuriating breath. His eyes flick up to my face and I give him a nod.

"Please," I murmur.

That's all he needs to hear. Eli dips down to swirl his tongue around my clit and up and down my slick folds.

I whimper and clutch the edge of the leather seat, tossing my head back in delight. The stiff tip of his tongue teases my aching, virginal hole in between delicious attention to my clit.

His fingers join the party and slide inside of me— not too far, just enough to stimulate the bands of sensitive muscle at my opening while he sucks and nibbles at my tight bundle of nerves.

My hands drop to his head and hold him there as the car rolls down the road. I'm thankful for the dark tinted windows and the partition— the only things separating us from the prying eyes of others. Again, I'm struck with the tingly risk of being caught, and it just adds to the thrill of the moment.

We want each other so badly we can't even wait until we get home. Eli devours my aching cunny, lapping up my sweet juices as my climax approaches.

"Oh, Eli," I whisper.

"Mmm," he replies with his lips against my clit.

The vibration of his mouth is enough to push me over the edge and I burst hot, slippery honey all over his face and fingers. I cry out and buck my hips, but Eli doesn't miss a second.

He laps me up hungrily. Desperately. And when he wipes his mouth and pulls my dress back down, we're already at our destination.

Eli dismisses his driver and grabs me, all but carrying me into his massive, luxury mansion in the Hills. I hardly get a chance to be impressed by the incredible decor, high-quality furniture, and impeccable ambiance.

Eli takes me straight to his bedroom upstairs, a lavish space with a massive king sized bed and adjoining master spa bath.

Eli is stripping off his tailored suit and yanking his tie while I stare in shock at his gorgeous body being slowly revealed.

"I'm a virgin," I blurt out suddenly.

Eli smiles and saunters up to me, fully nude. His glorious, gigantic cock bounces slightly in the free air and my mouth waters for a taste. He slips the dress straps off my shoulders and unzips it down the back. The dress falls to the ground.

"I know," he says softly. "I could feel that from the moment we met. I can also feel how badly you want me. How much you want to give me that virginity."

I nod slowly, staring at him.

"How can you tell?" I mumble.

He kisses me deeply, then pulls back to say, "You're an incredible actress, but some things just can't be disguised."

I swallow hard. "It's true. I do want you."

"Ask and you shall receive," Eli replies. He scoops me up and carries me to the bed, laying me back with care.

He straddles me and bends to kiss my lips while his hands rove down my body. He caresses my breasts, tweaks my sensitive nipples. He slips down my panties and plays with my pussy with his fingers.

I'm still wet and dripping and ready for him. I decide to be brave and reach down between us, wrapping my hand around his thick, warm cock.

He's hard as glass and so, *so* big. I stroke him up and down, loving the way he feels in my hand. I love even more the groans and sighs of pleasure that fall from Eli's luscious lips.

"I want a taste," I venture quietly.

Eli immediately turns around and to my surprise, he straddles my face so that his cock brushes over my lips.

I open my mouth to pull his thickness inside, warm and wet and inviting. Meanwhile, Eli goes down on me, showing no mercy as he licks and sucks my stimulated clit.

He gently thrusts his hips so hat his enormous length pumps in and out of my mouth. It's a new and exciting sensation, especially when the tip brushes against my throat. I taste the salty precum, fee his girth stretching my cheeks. He fucks my throat while he devious my cunny until he's tensing up and I'm on the verge of another climax.

With a few more expert strokes of his tongue, I explode in a second orgasm, crying out his name.

Eli pulls back and whips around, his cock popping out of my mouth. He grabs me and flips me over onto my knees on the bed. I look back at him, almost drooling with need. He lines up the head of his engorged cock at my ready opening and swirls around it, teasing me and making me want him even more.

"Fuck me," I whimper. "Please, Eli."

"Hold on, Stella. I'm going to pound that perfect little virgin pussy," he grunts through gritted teeth, and with one powerful thrust, his cock sheaths deep inside my shuddering cunny.

I feel him rock back and forth and my pussy clenches around him tightly, pulling him in. I feel so complete and whole with his shaft poking past that thin little barrier inside me.

He's pounding the virginity out of me with an animalistic need. I arch my back and push back against him to show him how ready I am, how much I want this. It feels so fucking good, like blinding flashes of mingled pain and delicious, irresistible pleasure.

My body blooms for him eagerly. I can't wait to feed him explode inside me. I want his precious seed deep within my womb. I want him to make me his for all the world to see. I want to be the lucky girl he chooses forever.

"You feel so tight. So good for me, Stella," Eli purrs. He kisses along my spine while his cock spears deeper and deeper into me.

I shiver and whine with need. When he reaches around to stroke my clit with two fingertips while pounding me from behind, I nearly collapse with the intensity of the sensation.

"Oh god! Just like that!" I exclaim.

"Good girl. So good, Stella. Come for me. Come all over this thick cock," he commands.

Just like magic, my cunny gushes and squirts everywhere, drenching is both and the bedsheets beneath us. I'm dizzy with pleasure and incoherent with lust.

Nothing makes sense.

Nothing needs to.

All that matters is his cock buried deep in my pussy, pumping closer and closer to orgasm.

To giving me that greatest gift any man could give.

Eli strokes my clit with one hand and gently pulls my hair with the other to hold me in place while he pummels my insides with that glorious cock. He slams into me again and again, and before long I'm losing control. My legs are shaking, my heart is pounding, and I can feel him get so close.

"Come inside me," I beg. "I want your come."

"Hold still, baby," he orders softly. "Oh yes. Just like that. Stay right there."

He grabs my hips for purchase and pounds into me hard and fast. He loses all control and, with a long shuddering groan, his cock bursts its delicious seed deep inside my womb.

He pumps again and again, filling me up so full I can feel it leaking down my thighs to stain the bed. Eli withdraws and flips me over gently. Then he bends down to kiss me before scooping me up and carrying me into the en suite spa bathroom.

He runs me a hot bubble bath and cares for me kindly and intimately while we come down from the high together. I'm on cloud nine, and neither of us can stop laughing and grinning with delight.

"Wow," I breathe.

"Wow, indeed," Eli agrees. "I think we should make this a more regular occurrence."

"Yes, please!" I cry out.

He chuckles, eyes all shining.

"One thing's for sure," he begins. "This might be the most extreme method acting I've ever done."

I laugh, feeling utterly blissful. "I think our onscreen chemistry might just be an award winner if we keep this up."

"We make a damn good team," he says.

"Yes," I sigh with a happy smile. "We do."

Fertile First Time Tourist

Book Themes: Barely Legal, Breeding, and Virgin
Word Count: 5469

Parents, what a drag.

I'm done with high school and suddenly I'm expected to pack up and ship out to some Ivy League college, to compete with eggheads and boring blabber mouths. A whole bunch of dull try-hards. Sounds like hell, if you ask me.

But my parents didn't ask me. Okay, well they did. But for once they didn't listen. And so here I am, facing the prospect of flying across the country to do yet more school work in just a couple months.

I couldn't imagine a bigger downer for my summer vacation.

And that was how I managed to get a simple vacation out of them.

Somewhere nice, somewhere hot, somewhere Caribbean.

Mom and dad were both busy with business meetings all summer, so they couldn't take me. That meant that they would only agree to let me go on my own, if it was somewhere safe, and

I got a full time tour guide. I agreed — reluctantly! — but when they said they were sending me to Cuba because it was so safe, I didn't know what to make of it. Isn't that where communist terrorists come from or something?

Well, if it was, it sure didn't stop it from being beautiful. Because from the moment I started flying over it, I was impressed. And I don't easily impress, trust me.

Landing down and going through customs was a bore, but then on my way out of the airport... there he was.

You see, my parents insisted on a full time tour guide, but I got to pick him myself. And I looked around online, and found the perfect one.

Romy.

Pictures didn't do the man justice. And neither did the endless reams of gushing — frankly fangirling — reviews left by countless women for him. It was easy to see why such a massive hunk was so popular.

The heat when I arrived was intense, but Romy stood there in a white button down shirt, gently flowing in the breeze, with a pair of khakis on. Simple, right? Except that white shirt was practically see-through, and what was there to see was worth it. Bulging pecs and abs, a hard body to just die for. With dark hair, and handsome good looks like out of a movie, Romy trampled all expectations.

"Miss Julia?" he said, his voice tinged with such a delightful accent as he flipped his sunglasses up and revealed his sparkling, dark eyes. "I am Romy, your personal guide."

I'd originally looked for someone who didn't speak English — better to be seen than heard, right? — but with his reviews, well, I figured I could shut him up easily enough.

Though now I didn't want him to stop.

"That's me!" I said with a flirty flip of my hair that I knew drove guys wild. I had a nickname in school, one no one dared call me to my face, but I knew it anyways.

Cocktease.

I actually loved it.

It was what I was.

What I still am.

Romy had a way of making even the most adamant cocktease want to give in though.

"More lovely than mere pixels can convey," he said, reaching out to take my hand in both of his, the smooth hard skin of his fingerpads so delightfully well-kept yet masculine. The smell of some sort of coconut-y aftershave upon him, but oh so light.

"I hope your flight was pleasant. Or at least as pleasant as flights can be," he remarked, his voice husky and deep, but so beautifully lyrical in that Caribbean accent of his.

I couldn't have been more pleased with my choice, especially as he pressed his plush lips to the back of my hand.

He was a few years older than me, but definitely in his prime.

He had no idea what I had in store for him.

For us.

"Come with me, I'll take us to the hotel, you'll love it, I promise," he said, and I believed him. He had a way about him that made a woman want to trust him after all.

I was told that Cuba was all old fashioned cars, and that sounded awful to me. But when we got to his vehicle, it was actually shiny and modern, very comfortable. He put my things into the trunk, and then offered me a seat inside. It was a two-seater, very swanky with a convertible roof. I'd tell you the name of the car, but I don't know dick about them, hun, sorry.

The sun shone down so bright and lovely as he drove us along the coast, the heat would've easily been too much for me but there was always a lovely breeze off the ocean adding to the wind that whipped by.

We chatted on the way, those beautiful lips of his having no shortage of interesting things to say. He told me all about his life on the island, growing up. And while I usually nodded off during such things, I actually wanted to know more about Romy's life.

The hotel itself was pretty nice, in Havana itself, not in one of those touristy resorts everyone else was going to. I'd heard all the resorts were filled with nothing but stuffy old tourists, and who wants a vacation like that? The hotel was an older style, well kept. Though everything was looking so much sunnier with Romy guiding me along.

He took my things up to my room for me and I got a glimpse of the large, spacious area, and the big king sized bed. There was a balcony overlooking the ocean, and the sight was delightful.

"I hope you approve," he remarked, placing my luggage down and showing me about the place. "I picked this all out for you myself," he said, and it's true. I hired him to look after all the details of my trip for me.

My parents spared no expense, not after how much I pleaded and begged and bargained. If they wanted me to do well in College, I argued, I had to be well rested and prepared.

So the hotel was likely one of the best in the city, but I still looked around it like I was used to nicer things and places. I didn't want Romy to get too swollen of a head. Not yet.

"Oh, it'll do fine."

The smile he gave me held a sparkle, and it was like he could read right through me and see I was more than approving of it all.

"If you are hungry," he remarked, opening the balcony doors open wide, "I can have food brought up, or we could go down-stairs and eat. Or I could even show you some lovely spots to dine around town. I know all the best, either way," he boasted.

"Oh... I suppose I might as well have a taste of the town," I said. Even though I was practically starving by that point, he made his knowledge of the town sound so intimate, I just wanted to rush out and see what he had to show me.

The streets of Havana were beautiful, old fashioned but lively and well kept. The kind of thing I probably wouldn't have appre-ciated if not for the handsome man guiding me down the streets to the lovely restaurant overlooking the historic city.

Everything was so tall, but it wasn't like home. The side streets were narrow and filled with people and colour, and the main streets were flooded with noise. Beautiful, shiny cars drove by in outlandish colours that would've been gaudy if it didn't seem to fit in with the city so well.

A bunch of schoolgirls in blue rushed ahead of us, glancing

back at Romy and giggling before they took off down a side street. Some people glanced at us as we walked at a leisurely pace that I wasn't quite used to but it seemed that was how everyone walked. Leisurely.

To get to the restaurant itself, we had to climb these winding, narrow stairs, and I thought for a moment on how strange it seemed. But once we got to the top, it was a beautiful place. Old fashioned but classy, with a live band and some other, well-to-do tourists sitting down with locals, talking, enjoying drinks and good looking food.

"I think you should try the special," Romy said to me, nodding with a smile to the manager or owner before guiding me to a table and pulling out the seat for me. "I hope you eat meat," he asked, "because the pork here is excellent."

I wasn't a very adventurous eater, truly. Though something in me made me not want to admit that. Which was, honestly, a first. Usually everyone knew how I felt just as soon as I did.

I brushed some of my straight, blonde hair behind my ear, looking at him. Just drinking him in.

What my parents didn't know, was that I had a plan. A plan so that I never had to go to school again.

I smiled seductively at Romy. "I'm sure it'll be fine."

He ordered for me and the meal was delightful, the drinks delicious, the music so calming and pleasant. Yet it was the company that truly made the evening special.

"I have a confession to make," Romy said, smiling at me across the table as we savoured our drinks as the sun slowly made its way to setting.

"What's that?" I asked, batting my long, curved lashes at him as I tilted my head back, letting my blond hair slip away from my slender neck a little.

"You are far younger and more beautiful than my usual clientele, Julia. By leaps and bounds unmeasurable," he said before raising his mojito to me in toast.

I couldn't help but feel smug at that, and I let the top of my foot graze against his calf as if by accident.

"Oh really, Romy?" I purred, leaning in and letting my shirt fall away from my chest a little bit.

He held my gaze for a moment, but then very casually let his eyes dip down. The way he took a peek at my breasts made it feel as if he wasn't letting me get away with pretending to be so casual about it. It was like he turned the tables on me with but a few simple facial expressions. Pulling me out of my hiding spot to gaze at me with such casual interest.

"Luscious and ravishing," he stated so calmly in that smooth, charming voice of his.

His accent made it sound even more exotic, and he certainly had a way with words that none of those dumb boys at school could ever dream of. He was way too calm and in control.

And that excited me.

My lip quirked into a smile and I watched him for a moment. "Thank you," I said before taking my straw back into my mouth, finishing off the rest of my drink.

We were walking on out, through the darkening streets of Havana when I had to put my arms about his for support. The drinks had been so strong, stronger than I was used to, but any excuse to cling to his muscular arm for support was welcome.

I could feel the bulge of his muscles, the veins rising up on his flesh. He was so well sculpted, nothing just for show about this hunk of a man.

"We could go enjoy some of Habana's night life," he remarked, looking to me from the corner of his gaze. "But maybe your trip here has been long enough already, and you could use some rest. Tomorrow I am going to take you into the jungle, after all. Show you a beautiful spot in the mountains that you will just adore."

But the salsa music was already spilling out onto the streets, and I could feel it in my hips, my bones. I wanted an excuse to get close to him.

It wasn't that I needed to seduce him. I knew what guys were like. If I'd asked him to take me back to the hotel and bone me without a condom, he totally would. Probably wouldn't even be bothered that I was still a virgin.

No, wanting to dance with him had nothing to do with him and everything to do with me.

"Naw, let's go dance!"

Romy looked at me with a wry smirk, some mild surprise on his face at my sudden brazenness.

"Dance you say?" he remarked, and I thought for a moment he might try to talk me out of it. But instead, he guided me off our path and took me down a different road. "I know just the club," he said with a smile.

It wasn't hard to tell where he was taking me, the lights and sounds of the club were apparent from far away. The beautiful music and gorgeous people spilling out into the streets even, as we approached. It was such a remarkable place!

Again, Romy seemed to know people, the man at the door let us both pass with barely a word, just some friendly hand gesture between the two of them. We headed on in, the thrum of the music and the sights of so many stunning, scantily clad people grinding, swaying and cutting amazing moves all around us.

It was unlike anything I'd ever seen, and the music was already thrumming in my veins, making me feel so hot in all the right ways. Like I was invincible.

I dragged him towards the small, free spot on the dance floor, my soft hand in his before I tugged him in. My arms wrapped around his neck, and instantly my hips started swaying.

I knew I had a good body. My parents paid for a personal trainer for me since I was fourteen, and I didn't skimp or cheat.

If you ever met Helga, you wouldn't either. She was an Amazonian woman, and mean as they come, but she whipped my ass into perfect shape.

The perfect shape for Romy's big hands to cup and gently squeeze, which was exactly what he helped himself to as we began to dance. The handsome, smiling man showing no sheepishness in holding me so personally, and for a moment I debated whether it was just the hot Latin nature of the place, or if it was all him and his charming bravado.

Either way, worked for me!

He certainly showed no lack of moves on the dance floor, his ripped body moving with such ease and masculine grace.

"You dance well," he said to me with a smile. "Especially for such a pretty, fair girl from away," he tacked on playfully.

I was letting myself fall for him. Really fall for him. Forcing those barriers down as I enjoyed the music pumping through our veins.

I pressed my breasts into his hard chest, looking up at him with a devilish smirk.

"That's not all I do well," I taunted, though honestly, the furthest I'd gone with a guy was hand stuff.

Romy didn't know that though, and he grasped hold of my hips and spun me about, sliding one hand up to grasp mine before pulling me back in against him. We moved with the music, our bodies twisting and turning, until my rear was pressed up against his groin, and we were grinding so shamelessly in the middle of the club.

So shamelessly that Romy made not an effort to hide the thick bulge that quickly grew to a full — and startlingly impressive — size against my two cheeks.

I even swear I heard a low groan over the sound of the music.

And I know I said it wasn't for him, and it wasn't. But his reaction, that's what I needed. To know that he wanted me. Not just a little, but that he couldn't think unless he had me.

I got off on the power, on making guys want more and then pulling away.

But instead, I ground against him closer, my mouth parted as I lifted my arms up, wrapping them around him and drawing his head in towards my shoulder so that I could feel his breath on my ear.

There he was, held in thrall to me as one of his big, muscular arms went about my waist. I could feel his bulging, hard forearm press into my tummy as his fingers splayed and slid down over my mons atop my dress. He hovered his mouth so near to my skin I could feel the warm, moistness of his breath.

He felt glorious, hard, tall and broad, like a man should be. And he rocked his hips in tune with me, grinding his manhood into me as we swayed and danced. Until finally those lips of his dared brush against my earlobe, my neck. A soft, light kiss.

My tummy flipped, and I felt a tingle between my thighs. It wasn't anything explosive, but my body certainly didn't seem to care that it was *just* a kiss.

No, my body was responding like he'd just managed to find a hidden part of me, a sensitive and secret place, and open it with such expertise...

I was losing at my own game, but then, that was the plan. To let myself give in to passion, and do what felt right. What felt natural.

For once.

And Romy was the perfect man to let go with. Those big, strong hands rubbing over my flesh, soaking me all in, appreciating every inch of my body. Every little brush of his fingertips was like fire and ice, exciting and calming at once.

Before long I lost all connection with what I was doing, there were only the pleasurable sensations of our two bodies contacting, with no clear idea of where I stood, or that I was even a distinct being, separate from him. It was like we'd both just... evaporated into tingling, excited energy.

Mere moments of clarity got through, and I heard myself moan as Romy's lips tugged my earlobe into his mouth, and he suckled upon it.

It was like a warm chill went through me, my nerves responding with such eager delight.

My panties were already soaking wet, and I wanted him like I'd never wanted anyone before. My lips parted, and I panted out, gently, "Let's go."

His grip upon my hips tightened for a moment, and those strong fingers sank into my flesh right above my womanhood, slowly pulling my dress up fractions of an inch. Then finally he let go, and spun me back around, looking into my eyes with his intense gaze before he began to lead me out.

His hand was around mine as he guided me, taking me into the cool night air, which made my overheated skin tingle. No sooner than we were free and clear in the open, he put his arm around my back and pulled me close, guiding me towards the hotel.

No words passed between us, but once we were in the elevator, he pressed me up against the wall and kissed me on the lips. Hard, passionately.

He still tasted of the minty mojito, and my tongue lashed against his, hungrily. He was a skilled kisser, and his hands roamed over my body, over my clothes, and it felt like such a long ride up to the top.

My arms around his neck, we practically fell out of the elevator when it arrived on my floor, nearly crashing into a couple waiting for it. I giggled as I tugged Romy's hand, leading him into my room.

The door shut behind us, and I was suddenly glad he had the foresight to leave the balcony windows open, because I was still so hot and the cool air was helping keep me from passing out with the heat of desire.

It was mere moments before we were toppling over onto the big, king sized bed. That strong, hard body of his over me, my hands running along his broad shoulders. The swell and throb of his manhood against my cunny and lower belly as he lifted a knee and loomed over me as our lips smacked moistly.

I didn't want to tell him I was still a virgin and give him cause to stop or slow down, but at the same time, I was a little worried. Would it hurt?

But those thoughts were quickly swept away as his hand cupped my breast, squeezing it firmly and not treating it like a radio dial. He was paying attention to the whole mound, and that just brought my arousal to the next level.

"Fuck me," I begged him, my voice low with lust.

His lips moved from mine, making their way on down my neck as I arched it out to the side. He undid his shirt all the while, so that his white cotton top came undone, and his dark tanned flesh was bare for my wandering hands to appreciate. To feel the smooth skin and its light peppering of dark hairs.

He raised my dress up to my hips, then let his thumb trace along my lace panties, on in towards my mound, where he traced the outline of my labia, all the way down my slit, making me mewl in response.

He was perfect.

Our child would be the cutest little thing, I just knew it.

My legs parted and my entire body flushed with heat as he revealed more and more of my skin to his gaze. The buzz of the mojito had mostly worn off, but was replaced with my lust for him. I hooked my hands in to each side of my panties, beginning to strip them down.

Romy watched my unveiling so intensely, his gaze glued to the sight of my glistening slit, licking his lips as he watched their reveal. He helped me at the end tug those panties away before reaching to his own belt. He unbuckled it, then lowered his pants, showing the large bulge of his manhood.

He knelt upon the edge of the bed on his knees, those thick, muscular thighs showing as he then reached into the waistband of his briefs and slowly peeled them away. The big, pulsating shaft that sprang free was glorious. So much bigger than any of the boys I'd played with and teased over the years.

Though before he bent over me, he reached into his pants pocket and pulled out a condom.

That was not the plan.

My brows furrowed and I placed my hand on his wrist, holding it away.

"We don't need that," I said, pulling my panties off my feet and bringing my other hand between my legs, petting myself lewdly.

He looked at my dainty hand at his wrist, then back to my eyes. He pondered for a moment, perhaps taking measure of me. But then his decision was made.

The condom was tossed aside, and he got over me, his big, broad body suspended over mine as he leaned in for another passionate kiss. He brought his free hand to my hip, stroked his fingers on down across my thigh, until he was tugging my leg up to his hip and letting that big, beefy cock of his slide along my bare slit.

"As a warning," he said, his voice husky, deep, and ripe with desire, "I can't see me being able to pull out of you."

"Good," I purred, and I swear, I was nearly passing out with need and excitement. It felt like we'd been making out and touching one another for an eternity, and my body was on high alert. I couldn't wait to find out what it felt to have a man inside me, and I reached out, gingerly touching his hardness.

The big shaft twitched against my hand, and I could feel its pulsating hotness so distinctly. He was immense! Put all the boys I teased to shame, and I stroked back along his length gingerly, watched the glistening purple crown as it flared near my wrist.

My gentle, exploratory touches elicited a big, lusty groan from the man, and his eyes nearly shut. Instead though, he splayed my legs open wide as the pleasant air breezed on by us, and I used that big tip of his to tease at my sensitive clit.

"Mmm," he let loose in a big groan. "Your little pussy is going to look so perfect stretched around my cock, chica."

My eyes rolled back in my head and I thought I was going to pass right out. His seductive words, the way he was making me feel, it was all so good.

I moaned out loud, grinding against him wantonly. "I need you to fuck me," I said, trying to sound commanding but instead sounding so breathy and small.

It was only my first night there, and already I was splayed out, putty in Romy's hands. He took hold of my hip in one hand and angled his own torso, pointing that big, hard dick right along my cunny.

"I'll fuck you, baby," he growled out, then began to push himself into me. That thick tool stretching my cunny open wide, breaking my hymen as he let loose such a deep moan. "So goddamn tight!" he declared.

I screamed a little, because it fucking hurt like hell for a moment, even though I was so wet, so turned on. I bit down on my lower lip to try to hide a bit of my pain, but as he rammed inside of me, I couldn't help but emit a few little whimpers.

Once he was deep inside though, and my little cunny was stretched wide about his shaft, there was only the pleasure of being full for the first time in my life. Being completely whole, with a man deep inside me... it was bliss.

Romy reached his hand up to my breast, tugging down my dress to expose the supple mound and squeeze it so masterfully as he began to tug back. My narrow sleeve of a quim clung to his girth, and he groaned, but then he was soon thrusting back into me, pumping his girth inside again and again.

"So tight... so damn tight," he groaned out aloud.

"So... big," I managed to pant out in kind, my head swimming as my eyes rolled back in my head. I arched my back, pushing my breast into his hand as I took all of his cock between my spread legs. My slickness helped, after the pain ebbed, and I knew that after this, I'd be addicted.

Just watching him work at me, his body undulate as he thrust, that eight-pack of abs moving so sensually... seeing thick, corded muscle shift and bulge so gloriously. All as my body experienced every delightful bulge and throb of his organ inside me.

Each new thrust brought a slap of his heavy, cum-laden balls against my ass, growing louder with each rougher thrust into me.

Once he warmed me up, no longer was he treating me like a delicate doll. No, he was pounding into me, making all of my body feel alive. I screamed, uncaring who might hear, as my fingernails dug into his shoulders, keeping me rooted in place against him.

The panting, moaning and screaming we made together carried out the window into the streets of Havana, but on we went. His big, beautiful form glistening with a thin sheen of perspiration, highlighting his hard musculature as he pounded me into the lush mattress.

This man I'd only met a few hours before, was taking me so passionately all on my parent's dime. It was intense, and I couldn't help but reach out a hand and rub it all over his bulging, muscular chest, adoring the grooves of his sinew.

He felt amazing, and I clung to him, my legs wrapping around his back and clinging to the cusp of his ass, forcing him in deeper. Letting our bodies grow hot and sticky against one another as I lost all rational thought and simply succumbed to the illicit, exquisite pleasure.

"You feel so good," I whimpered.

He growled out his words, "So do you," and brought his hand from my thigh up to my hip. His thumb reached in, and with an expert touch he began to circle and prod at my clit, stoking my fires higher, bringing me closer to true bliss.

His balls tightened, and he pounded me harder, faster, building up to a bigger frenzy.

"I'm going to cum in your little cunt," he seemed to roar. "Cum for me. Cum on my cock," he commanded.

It was... sublime. I'd never felt anything like it, and it only took seconds before that bundle of nerves started to feel strange. Tingling, the sensation growing stronger and stronger until it was like a wave crashed over me and I was lost at sea, just bucking and screaming beneath my Latin lover.

Romy pounded into me all through it, fucking me like a wild animal lost to passion. My moist cunny juices flowed about his girth and our bodies smacked with a loud, wet crash each time he hammered into me. He continued like that, stoking my fires, teasing my clit and drawing out my orgasm until finally, just as the fog of pleasure began to clear enough for me to see clearly...

I got to watch him lose himself to his own satisfaction.

He thrust in roughly, his dick spasming as he stretched my pussy wider. Loud moans bursting from his lips as he abruptly began to spew his load. Thick gouts of virile seed firing deep inside me as he thrust in to the hilt and coated my womb in his cum.

He knew just as well as I did the risks we were taking, the risks we both wanted to take, in part.

My toned legs tightened around his ass as he came, holding him into me so that he couldn't try to pull away.

I bit down on his shoulder, muffling my cries, my sound of pleasure, against his warm, salty flesh.

His spine was arched, and he stayed imbedded in me as my pussy drained his manhood dry of every little drop of seed. He shuddered and groaned, squeezing and kneading my breast as he continued to flick my clit and make me squirm and writhe.

"Ohhh fuck yes," he husked out. "Your pussy is heavenly."

I was panting for breath, almost too sensitive for words as I licked and suckled at his flesh. He was so perfect, so exquisite, and even though my entire body was singing, I couldn't stop grinding against him, taking me to that point of explosive bliss once more.

Even as the last of his seed was milked from him into the narrow canal of my cunt, I shuddered, moaned and spasmed. His magnificent hand working my clit, bringing me to such a boil as he watched, enjoying the jiggle of my breasts, the way my face flushed a bright red at the oncoming of my second orgasm.

"Cum for me," he husked so charmingly. "Cum on my dick."

My entire body was shaking, like a vibrator, and my pussy clenched him so hard I could feel his body pulsing with life.

"Oh God," I cried out as I hit that peak again, and felt the rush go through my body, flooding his dick in my sweet juices.

He moaned and rocked his hips, grinding our bodies together as I rode out my second, intense orgasm. I was a sweaty, messy heap, and as I gazed up at my big, buff hunk of a lover... I realized my vacation had only just begun.

So that was just the start of my trip. But here I am, ready to see my parents again for the first time in a while.

Oh, there's so much more to tell about my trip, but sorry. Right now my mind is on something more dire...

"Sweetie! It's so good to see you again," mom says, and dad comes in for a hug.

"How's college?" dad asks.

"Are you doing well?" mom chimes in, the barrage of questions endless.

"I need to drop out," I say, and their faces look horror-stricken.

"You can't!" mom cries.

"You've barely even started!" dad protests.

But now I'm reaching down, cradling my stomach with one hand, and the tiny swell there as I whip out the test stick in the other hand.

"I can't stay. I'm preggers," I say, and lord help me, I can't help but smirk a little despite the aghast look on their faces.

Tending to His Fantasies

Book Themes: Bareback, breeding, boss/employee
Word Count: 6662

Damn, it's hard to focus with a face like that in front of me. The guy sitting directly across this high-top table has the most striking bright blue eyes, and I swear they can burn right through to my very soul. My whole body is tingling just from sitting this close to him, and the heat is growing between my thighs. I can't help it. My eyes follow the rugged lines of his body, the contour of his muscles pushing against the fabric of his t-shirt.

His arms are almost as thick as logs, plus he has those delicious wide shoulders and a broad, powerful chest. His hands are casually folded on the table counter, and I can tell from the scars and calluses on his skin that he's not afraid to get his hands dirty. On top of that, he's one of those guys who clearly look tall even when he's sitting down.

Even though he's been seated since the moment I walked into

the bar, I know he would tower over me if he stood up. The thought makes my mouth water. I lick my lips, imagining how it would taste to press my lips against his, to push my tongue into his mouth. I could lean into his herculean frame and feel his pectorals and abs hard against my own slender, willowy body. I'm a pretty delicate-looking woman to begin with, but next to him? I look like a dandelion next to a hundred-year-old oak tree. There's something so sexy about being overwhelmed with his size. I love knowing that a man could easily toss me around, bend me to his will, take me wherever and whenever he wants.

Ooh. Yum.

Now, don't get me wrong; I'm a strong, confident, independent woman who can handle her own shit. I'm from the big city and I'm no stranger to struggle, to being condescended to or underestimated for my size and dainty appearance. It comes with the territory. I know what I look like. And I have the stones to back it up. But that doesn't mean I'm too proud to let a man boss me around-- at least in the bedroom. He could throw me like a pillow and I would let him. He would tell me what to do in that growly, authoritative tone and I would obey like the good girl I am.

It makes me almost giddy to think about what he might order me to do once I turn over control to him. What if he asks me to drop to my knees and suck his thick, weighty cock? What if he tells me to strip off my clothes and turn around for him, real slow? What if he just throws me on the bed and jumps me, taking me the way he wants, the way his body needs? He could fuck me hard and fast and make me come again and again, gushing all over his shaft while he pounds me mercilessly...

"Nicole? Are you all right? Should I repeat the question?" interrupts the *other* guy sitting across from me, next to the subject of my deepest, darkest fantasies. His name slowly bubbles to the surface: Joey. He isn't half bad to look at, himself, but he's not the big hulking man of my dreams. Which is probably why I'm having trouble focusing on him while the hottest dude alive sits next to him. And the sexy guy's name?

It's burned into my brain from the first moment I sat down. Leo.

My cheeks flush bright pink as I shake off my fantasy. I have to pull my head out of the gutter and get back to reality, especially since I'm kind of in the middle of something important. Oops. My imagination tends to get away from me sometimes, but this may be the first time I've actually had a full-blown zone-out during a job interview. I guess that's just a testament to how sexy this dude is.

"Uh, sorry. I guess the jet lag is catching up to me a little bit," I laugh. "Could you say that again? My bad."

Joey smiles graciously. Phew. I think he bought it.

"I was asking how your flight was," he says with a wink.

Oh, thank god. A fluff question.

"It was fine! Long, but not bad. I drank a ginger ale and finished a chapter," I reply.

"A chapter?" prompts Leo in that growling tone that makes me shiver in a good way.

I smile and nod. "Yes, I'm a writer."

"And a bartender, I hope," says Joey. "Judging by your resume in front of me," he says, shuffling through the papers on the table.

My heart skips a beat. My life on paper in his hands. I have to pay attention.

"Right. Of course," I reply quickly. "A classic combination bartender-writer."

Both of them chuckle.

"Well, you'll certainly meet some interesting characters working here," Joey remarks. "You're new to town, but you'll realize pretty quick that it's a special kind of place."

"We're a little biased," Leo comments.

"I actually picked this town specifically because it feels special," I tell them eagerly. "I did a lot of research to find a charming small town in a quiet location with beautiful surroundings. This place ticks all the boxes."

The joy gleaming in their eyes at my statement makes my

heart swell. I can tell these guys are really proud of where they come from.

"Well, then," Joey says, leaning in. "I'll tell you a little about the Magnolia. We like a laid-back atmosphere and a friendly face. Most of our patrons are regulars, and pretty much all of 'em are locals. I guess you could say we get a lot of local color."

"Sounds like a dream," I gush.

He grins. "We like to think so. It's a great place to work. We're coworkers, but we're friends and family, too. You know, Leo and I bought this bar four years ago right out of college."

"We met in business school," Leo adds.

"You two seem young to be bar owners," I comment.

"We've both been hustling since high school and worked our way through college, too," Joey answers proudly. "When we had the money, this place came up for sale, right in the heart of our hometown. Seemed like fate. So we jumped on the opportunity, and here we are today."

"That's awesome. I'm impressed," I reply.

"Back to you, Nicole," Leo says. Oof. Hearing him say my name gives me goosebumps. I hope he doesn't notice. I pull down my sleeves to hide it better.

"Go for it," I prompt him.

"What's your favorite drink to make?" he asks.

I light up instantly. "Ooh, that's a fun one! Well, back in New York, I used to make this signature cocktail I called 'a walk in the garden' which has a bunch of floral notes that are bold and fresh and energizing for the springtime," I ramble.

Joey and Leo exchange somewhat skeptical expressions, then look back at me.

I feel a zing through my body. Those piercing blue eyes have me hypnotized. It's like time slows down every time he looks my way. God, I'm almost trembling.

"A walk in the garden? Can't say I've heard of that one," Leo remarks.

"I'm intrigued. What's in it?" Joey asks.

"Let's see. Creme de violette, butterfly pea flower tea which gives it an all-natural bluish tint, lavender syrup, gin, and honey. Some of my absolute favorite ingredients," I reveal.

"Wait. Butterfly *what* now?" laughs Joey.

"Butterfly pea flower," I clarify, tucking a loose lock of hair behind my ear to focus better. "It's a sort of tea that originates in southeast Asia. It's got a lovely flavor, but the coolest thing about it is that it turns everything a blue-purple color. It's beautiful."

"Where does one even find something like that?" Joey asks.

"Southeast Asia, apparently," Leo quips.

"No, I mean a cocktail like that," Joey laughs. "It says on your resume you've been a bartender for two years at a place called... Evangeline's Apothecary."

"That a pharmacy or something?" Leo jokes.

I grin, loving all the gentle ribbing. "It's a trendy bar in Soho. Lots of indoor plants, funky light fixtures, candles, expensive art on the walls. You know the place."

Joey and Leo chuckle. "Well, maybe not so much. You won't find any *apothecaries* out here in the sticks, but I'd like to think we still put together a mean Manhattan," Joey says.

"Now, that I can definitely believe!" I chirp happily. "Back in New York, it was exciting getting to mix and mingle with the beautiful people. Pouring up drinks for actors, models, CEOs, fashion designers, Wall Street suits, all of that. Folks with way too much time, money, or ego to really relate to. It was eye-opening and taught me how to wheel and deal with people far outside my own social circle. I wouldn't trade those experiences for anything. But honestly, I'm looking forward to the change in pace and atmosphere. City living was fun, but I'm excited to make this place my new home. In fact, I feel at home here already."

"That's good to hear. I have no doubt you'll figure out how to connect with the locals 'round here. Just about everybody you meet is a friend. Not a lot of drama, but we don't get bored either. Always something fun to do, always good memories to be made," Joey beams.

"I can't wait to start building my own memories here," I sigh. "And I just met you guys, so there's a good memory to start with!"

Joey looks tickled to death at my enthusiasm. I can tell he's one-hundred-percent sold on me. Ready to hire on the spot. Score! But Leo, otherwise known as The Man Of My Literal Dreams, seems less convinced. But then, that might just be his resting stoic face. RSF.

He leans forward, steepling his fingers on the table. "Now, Nicole, I hope you don't take this the wrong way, but I've got to ask. How the hell would you ever end up in a town like this if you're used to that fast-paced, high-risk New York City lifestyle?" he asks thoughtfully.

A smile spreads slowly across my face as I warm to this new, delicious subject.

"Basically, I've been trying to write this damn romance novel for going on four years now. It's seen me through college and bartending in Soho, but it's never been the right time to sit down and work on it in earnest. But even more importantly than the right time, it's never been the right place," I begin, already excited to talk about it.

"The right place?" Joey echoes.

I nod. "Exactly. As much as I loved the city, it never inspired me with the kind of sweet but rugged romantic feel I've been dreaming about. I would sit down at my laptop in my Brooklyn apartment and stare out the window at the city below, just watching the cars go by, hearing all the honks and shouts and alarms wailing. Sometimes I liked the noise. It was invigorating to feel like I was just a tiny cog in a gigantic machine. But it didn't make me think about romance. It didn't give me those warm fuzzy feelings I need to write this book and do it justice, you know?" I conclude.

"And you think you've found the place now?" Leo prompts. His blue eyes look more like calm cerulean waters than frigid ice, and it makes my heart skip a beat.

"It's beautiful here, with all the colorful foliage and the local waterfalls and the historic buildings. It's a quiet, safe community with lots of parks and a quaint farmer's market. Crime rate is low. Neighbors take care of each other. There are endless trails to hike through the forests surrounding the area. I could go on," I giggle.

"Sounds like you've done your research," Joey remarks. I can tell he's impressed.

"Yes. I really think this town is where my story's meant to begin," I smile. Good closer. Now time to bring it back full circle. "And that's why I would love to work here."

Joey and Leo exchange nods, then stand up to shake my hand. I hastily get up and reach for Leo's, my whole body hotter than a habanero when his rough, rugged hand closes over my smaller, delicate one. He gives it a solid squeeze and I'm almost melting before I remember to shake Joey's hand next, a big goofy smile on my face.

"Safe to say you're hired," Joey declares. "Can you start tomorrow? Five PM?"

"Absolutely!" I chirp back. My heart is racing with excitement. I got the job!

The job here... with the hottest guy alive. Phew. It's going to be even easier to think about hot, steamy romance than I expected!

I say my most polite goodbyes and head out to get in my little compact car in the parking lot. I turn on some upbeat folksy music and putter across town to my rental cottage on the edge of the woods. It's an adorable house, just a one-bed, one-bath unit, but it feels spacious compared to the tiny apartment I had in Brooklyn. The lot is surrounded on three sides by trees, making it feel extra private. I trot up to the front door and fit the key, taking a deep breath as I step into the cottage. It smells woodsy and warm, with a hint of something like cinnamon. Just like home. I shrug off my jacket and head into my kitchen to pour a glass of wine. After all, I just landed a job. I should celebrate!

I run myself a fragrant bubble bath and settle into the hot water, with one arm poking out to hold my glass of wine, of course. I close my eyes and sigh as the steam and aromas cloud around my face. It feels incredible on my tired muscles and tense nerves. I'm a pretty chilled-out person in general, but moving from NYC to this small town has still been a stressful leap to make. But I just need one good, relaxing evening to refresh, and I'll be back to my usual self tomorrow. I take a deep sip of wine, set it on the edge of the tub, and let the hot water soothe my body into a lulled, sensual state. My mind wanders through the events of the day, inevitably spiraling back to Leo. The way he asked such interesting questions and seemed to genuinely care about the answers. About me. The way his bright blue eyes smoldered and those hands... even folded on the table I could tell how strong they are. The hands of a man who isn't afraid of a little hard work, to literally get his hands dirty. I wonder how those fingers would feel on my naked body, on the parts of me nobody ever gets to see...

I imagine his hand pushing slowly through the thick layers of bubbles into the hot water, his calloused fingertips trailing down the slope of my leg, across to my inner thigh. I bite my lip, envisioning the look of barely-contained lust on his handsome face, the way his muscles ripple as he reaches down between my legs. I arch my back to meet his imaginary touch, ticklish but arousing as he strokes my sensitive flower. He strokes between my pink petals to circle around my clit. I shudder at his soft touch and lift my hips to meet him, encouraging him to do more, to push further. In reality, I have my own hand between my thighs, my own fingers stroking my stimulated clit. But I'm a writer, and it's easy to let my imagination do the work for me.

I picture Leo giving me a smirk when I start to whimper. The pleasure is ratcheting higher and higher. I'm sliding quickly toward the edge, with Leo's powerful hand coaxing and guiding me there. My lips fall open in a gasp.

"Oh, Leo," I whisper.

And the climax comes shuddering through me, making me writhe and moan in the bath. My fantasy ebbs away and I pull myself out of the bath, all relaxed and pruny. I finish off my wine, traipse off to bed, and fall into the deepest slumber of my life. Good thing, too, because I have a big day tomorrow.

. . .

The following evening, I am so excited to start my first shift at the bar that I can barely contain myself. It's been a good day-- I finally got to sleep in and catch up on that nasty jet lag. I spent the day unpacking and relaxing, getting accustomed to my new digs. The cottage is a perfect place to make my home, the perfect setting to write that long-awaited romance novel. At four o'clock, I get dressed, put on my cutest vintage dress and knit cardigan paired with some kitten heels I picked up at one of my favorite thrift stores in Manhattan. I head out to my little car and drive across town (a stunningly short distance) to the bar for my first shift. The drive isn't long, but it's definitely scenic. Everything is green and overgrown, like the forest is bursting at the seams to overtake the small town and disappear it away forever. I love it, the feeling of being surrounded by nature and peace and quiet. It's exactly what I've been looking for.

I'm smiling ear to ear when I pull up and park at the bar. I turn off the engine and take a deep breath to center myself before I pop the door open and walk across the parking lot. My heart skips a beat when I see Leo working the door. He's wearing a tight black shirt and black pants, all of which does little to hide his bulging muscles. His bouncer scowl lightens up into a familiar smile when he sees me, and I almost melt in place.

"Good to see you, Nicole," he greets me, letting me through.

"You, too," I reply. And god, do I mean it.

I sidle up behind the bar and immediately meet my coworker for the night, a woman in her mid-thirties with bleached blonde hair and gray eyes.

"Nice to meet you," she says with a grin. "I'm Liz. Head bartender. Don't tell Joey and Leo, but even though I'm not a co-owner, I pretty much run the place."

"Well, I'm glad I get to learn from the best, then," I chirp. "I'm Nicole."

Fortunately, the first hour or so of our shift moves slowly. We only see three patrons during that whole time, and all of them are blue collar locals who seem downright enamored with Liz. I can see why. She's got a sharp wit, a devil-may-care attitude, and one hell of a memory for recalling details about people. She knows everybody's go-to cocktail before they even sit down at the bar counter. She racks in the tips, with me learning alongside her. The two of us quickly establish a sisterly connection, which I love. In fact, I'm digging Liz so much I'm already considering basing a side character in my novel on her. Liz is a great trainer, and by the start of the second hour, I feel totally prepared to jump right in. I'm adjusting so well! Maybe I dress a little different, maybe I don't have the same local accent, but I'm fitting in great.

I'm having a fantastic time bonding with Liz, chatting with the patrons, and taking every possible opportunity to look over at Leo working the door. I can hardly keep my eyes off of him. The fantasy world I've built up around him is only getting more detailed and lush by the minute. It's so reassuring to know there's a big tough guy like Leo across the room, ready to jump into action and protect us all. Although so far, everyone has been so friendly, it's hard to imagine a situation that could call for those muscles in action.

It's easy to get wrapped up in the ebb and flow of busy hours, between nine and midnight when all the late-night workforce comes trickling into the bar. It's different here, making simple drinks like rum-and-cokes or whiskey sours, compared to the complicated, ten-ingredient cocktails I used to make at the Apothecary. But it's so much fun. I hardly notice time passing, until finally one in the morning is rolling around. Soon, my shift will end. I'm already in my own head trying to decide whether I have the courage to chat up Leo before I go home for the night.

But my fantasy is interrupted when a guy who's been sitting at the far end of the bar for a couple hours suddenly slides down to an empty seat directly in front of me. He's scruffy and wearing a leather jacket, plus an arrogant smirk on his face. I can smell the whiskey on his breath even before he leans in. He's been here awhile and drinking the whole time.

"You're not from around here," he points out.

"Good observation," I reply brightly.

"You need someone to show you 'round. Give you the grand tour," he slurs.

"I actually love exploring on my own," I tell him. "Can I make you a drink?"

"Can I buy you one?" he shoots back.

"Not on the clock," I quip. This is getting old already.

"Well, what about off the clock?" he says, sounding more aggressive now.

"Sorry, I'm new in town and not looking for anything--"

He slams his fist on the counter, making me jump back, eyes wide.

"Damn it, woman. Just say yes!" he snaps.

"Take a lap, Travis," Liz breaks in sternly. He opens his mouth to argue and she holds up one finger to shush him. "I said *take a lap*, Travis."

Still grumbling, the guy angrily storms off. Liz turns to me with a sympathetic frown.

"So sorry about that. He's usually just annoying, not aggressive," she says. "Your shift is over, anyway. You did a fantastic job. Glad to have you on the team."

I smile, my previous nerves relaxing a bit. "Thanks, Liz."

"Of course. Anyway, you can just slip out the back," she instructs me. "That way you don't have to deal with Travis again. Have a good night, Nicole. See you tomorrow!"

"See you!" I whisper.

I turn around and hurry out the back entrance. I'm bummed that I'm missing the chance to potentially chat up Leo, but oh well. There's always tomorrow. I had a great first day here, barring the last five minutes (thanks, Travis). I'm smiling as I jangle my keys around my finger, walking through the lot toward my car around the front. I'm already thinking about tomorrow, about what outfit I'm going to wear.

I hope I pick something that catches Leo's gorgeous blue eye.

But I'm shaken out of my sweet ponderings by an almost animalistic bellow coming from the direction of the front entrance. I whip around, eyes wide, to see that Travis is at the door. His face is all red, his hands are balled into fists, and he's shouting hoarsely after me, barely restrained by Leo's powerful arms.

"Come back here, you citified bitch!" Travis yowls. "You ain't too good for me!"

I stand there, totally frozen. I can't believe this is happening. My cheeks burn with embarrassment. Why did he have to single me out? Just because I'm new here?

"Sir, I warn you not to talk like that to a lady," Leo growls at him.

"I'll talk to that townie slut however I damn well please!" Travis spits back. "Call off your rabid dog!"

"Strike two, man. You're going to want to back down," warns the bouncer.

"I'm sorry I offended you," I call out to him, my voice a little shaky.

Travis scoffs. "Don't worry, baby. I can fuck that disrespect right out of you!"

"Strike three, Travis. I warned you," Leo snaps.

He pins one of the guy's arms behind his back, but in that split second, Travis hurls a booze bottle in vaguely my direction. It shatters into shards of sharp glass at my feet and I yelp, jumping back. I look up just in time to see Leo punch Travis in the jaw with a stomach-churning crunch. Travis drops like a fly and Leo pins him to ground, knees on his chest and both hands locked around the man's wrists. Travis is groaning and writhing in pain but Leo has a look of pure calm and control on his handsome face.

He leans down right into Travis's face and snarls, "Go home, take a cold shower, go to bed, and don't show your face around here for a week. Spend that time thinking about how much of a damn jerk you are and figure out how you're gonna fix that. Oh, and you better find a way to make it up to Miss Nicole here, because she's one of us now. And I protect my own."

"Okay, okay, I get it! Let me go, man," Travis pleads. He's like a dog with his tail between his legs. It's kind of satisfying, in a guilty way.

Leo lets go of Travis and the guy goes stumbling off to call a cab. To my surprise, Leo strides up to me and says gruffly, "Follow me."

"What? To where?" I ask. My voice is still trembling. In fact, I'm shaking all over.

"My truck. I'm taking you home," Leo says.

"I-I can drive myself," I say half-heartedly. Leo gives me a kind smile.

"You're shaking like a leaf. I'm driving," he says. And that's that.

We climb into his big silver truck and head across town to my quaint little cottage. The whole drive, my body is ringing. I feel like I'm on fire just sitting next to him in the front seat. I find myself wishing the center console would disappear so I can slide up closer to him. I want to feel his skin on my skin, his muscles hard and powerful against my dainty, smaller frame. I want to know everything about him. What makes him tick, what makes him hard. I lick my lips as I look over at him in the dim light of a passing streetlamp.

We get to my house and he pulls up, turns off the engine, and turns to look at me, those blue eyes smoldering. I want him. So badly. I don't want him to leave just yet.

"Thank you. For driving me home, for having my back, for... everything," I tell him.

"Just doing my job," he replies, but we both know that's not exactly true.

"Do you drive all the new girls home?" I tease as we step out of the truck and make our way to the front entry.

He smiles. "Only the excessively beautiful ones," Leo remarks.

My heart skips not just one beat, but possibly three.

"You think I'm beautiful?" I reply, cheeks pink.

"Yes. Would you like me to prove it to you?" he growls.

The door shuts behind us and suddenly we are all alone. In my house. Where no one can see us. I bite my lip and saunter up to Leo, trying to hide how fast and hard my heart is pounding. I blink up into his eyes and see the same fiery desire burning there, too. Adrenaline has us both on fire, and even the slightest tip in that direction could take us past the point of no return. I'm booking a one-way ticket. I'm all in.

"Yes. Prove it," I goad him.

"As you wish," Leo grunts.

He scoops me up in his arms like I'm a feather pillow and carries me off to the kitchen, where he sets me on the counter. He's tugging at my dress, his hands roving up and down my gentle curves, groping and stroking all the way. I tilt my head back and moan as he slides a hand up my dress. His fingers brush across my damp panties and I cry out. I rock my hips to meet his touch, and when his other hand slides up farther to caress my breast, I nearly lose my mind. It feels so fucking good-- his fingers tweaking and rolling my sensitive nipple while his other hand cups my moistening mound. The heat between us is undeniable.

I grab his lapel and pull him in close to kiss him. The moment our lips collide, a sensation of fireworks explode behind my eyes and I feel my whole body bristling with erotic energy. His tongue probes into my mouth, dancing against my own as we kiss again and again, our bodies moving closer together until he has my panties on the floor and his fly unzipped. I reach down to feel his growing heat and weight between his legs. Oh my god. It's massive. My mouth salivates with anticipation, almost as wet as my pink folds. I wrap my hand around his thickening shaft and sigh with approval as I begin to slowly slide up and down.

Leo groans and closes his eyes for a moment. It makes me smile. I love to see him giving in and losing himself to the pleasure I give him. I want to get him so hot and bothered and needy. I want him desperate to fuck me. To pound my little pussy and pump me full of his hot, precious seed. Leo's large, calloused hands gently push my thighs wider apart. He dips down to flick his tongue over my clit. I whimper and press myself against him while he slides his tongue up and down my sensitive flower. I tremble and bite my lip.

"Oh, that feels good," I whimper.

He hums an affirmative against my clit, sending delightful bolts of pleasure up through my whole body. I love the way his tongue lathes smoothly along my slick folds, then flicks and circles my clit to complete the pattern. Leo is a damn expert, or maybe he just happens to know what I need. Either way, it doesn't take long for that magical tongue to have me shaking and clinging to the counter for dear life. I cry out his name and buck my hips, but he doesn't let up. My first climax shudders through me and is immediately followed by another, then another. He laps up every honey-gush drop like he's ravenous for it, like my come is the sweet elixir he's been hunting his whole life. And when he slips two thick fingers deep inside me? I see stars.

He hooks his fingers to perfectly reach my g-spot. He strokes and pets that deep-dark spot with velvety touches, never pushing too hard. Just enough stimulation to get me twitching and keening, begging him for more.

"Leo," I gasp, head tossed back. "I'm gonna come again."

"Good girl. Come for me. That's exactly what I want," he growls.

Right on cue, my cunny gushes. *Hard*. I nearly slip off the counter when I squirt hot, slippery cum all over his fingers and tongue. I can feel him smile against my clit, his tongue caressing me through wave after wave of intense orgasm.

"Yes. Oh god, yes," I mew weakly. "Please, Leo. I-I'm shaking."

I can't tell if I'm too overstimulated and want him to stop for a moment, or if I'm just getting warmed up and want him to never, ever stop under any circumstances. But Leo knows me better than I know myself, because he then stands up and puts his hands on my curvy hips. With those piercing blue eyes locked with mine, he tugs me a couple inches closer to the edge of the counter to kiss me hard. It turns me on to taste myself on his lips, on his glorious tongue. My cunny still twitches from the intense, delicious attention she got, and I'm ready to give him what he gave me. So I gently push him back a notch and slide down off the counter.

I give Leo a seductive wink before I drop to my knees and tug down his boxers to let that gigantic cock bounce free. I'm nearly drooling by the time I lean in and flick my tongue around the swollen head. His skin is velvety smooth and utterly irresistible. I pull his full, thick length into my mouth and hear his gratifying groan. I take him in inch by inch until my cheeks are aching to hold him and his tip is tickling the very back of my throat. I use my hands to pump and swirl his shaft while I bob up and down on his cock, slurping and suckling, enjoying every filthy moment of this much-needed blowjob. I love the weight of him on my tongue. The way he stretches my cheeks and makes it ache in the best way possible.

As I pick up the pace, I feel his hands drop down to rest gently on my head. I smile around his thick pole and let him hold my head in place while he fucks my face. I open up my throat to let him pound deeper and deeper, drool dripping down my chin. I've always had a bit of an oral fixation-- maybe that's why I like mixing fancy drinks. Just something sweet to sip on and keep my mouth busy. But no cocktail could possibly hold a flame to Leo's cock. I let him fuck my throat, loving every filthy-sexy second of it while his fingers tangle lightly in my hair.

"Mmm," I groan, feeling him start to tense up in my mouth.

He's close. Very close. I know all I'd have to do is suck him faster, work up a perfect tandem with my swirling hand and suctioning mouth, and he'd lose it. Shoot that glorious load down my throat. But no-- Leo isn't done with me yet. He pulls my head back and his cock slips out of my mouth with a wet pop. I lick my lips and peer up at him, awaiting instruction.

"Get back up here," Leo grunts.

"Yes, sir," I reply.

I hastily stand back up, just in time for Leo to grab me and spin me around. He essentially pins me to the counter, bending me over. He sidles up behind me and I smile devilishly when I feel that rock-hard cock against my plump ass cheek. Leo gives my ass a resounding smack that makes me whimper with mingled pleasure and pain.

"Again," I beg.

He smacks my other ass cheek, even harder than the first. It stings in the best way. And when he grabs my hips and ruts against me, I can hardly wait for more. I tease him a little, shaking my ass to entice him.

"You're a dirty girl, aren't you? Is that what they teach girls like you in the city?" Leo growls as he gropes my ass and feels me up from behind.

"I guess you could say I'm a natural learner," I tease back.

"You ready for me, baby?" Leo groans.

His fingers circle my tight cunny, spreading my thick honey to make sure I'm nice and wet for him. The perfect pussy, swollen and pink and dripping with desire.

"I was ready the moment I met you," I whisper over my shoulder.

Leo kisses a soft line up my spine and whispers in my ear, "I could smell it on you."

I shiver. Ooh, he's dirty. I love it.

"Can you smell it on me now?" I say coquettishly.

"Absolutely. It's intoxicating how badly you need this cock inside you," he replies.

"Then give it to me. Please, Leo. I want it. I want you," I murmur.

I feel the thick head of his rod press against my tight opening. I spread my legs further apart and poke my ass out, showing him how very ready I am.

"Take me, Leo. Do it now," I beg.

"Stay right there, baby girl. And hold onto that counter for me. You might need it," he warns. With that, he pushes his massive cock inside me, spearing me wide open with every progressive inch.

I cry out and tremble and clutch at the kitchen counter while he holds my hips in his strong hands. He braces himself that way while he pistons his hips back and forth, that monstrous cock shoving deeper and deeper inside me until I'm seeing stars burst behind my eyes. It feels so fucking good. So damn *right*. Like we were made for this. For each other. He reaches around to play with my clit while he pounds me from behind. My pussy twitches and clenches around his thickness. We fit just perfectly. We move in excellent rhythm. Everything feels so well-coordinated, almost like a dance. But it all comes so naturally. Like we've been fucking each other for years and we know exactly what the other wants. What we need.

Leo and I give ourselves fully over to the tsunami of bliss crashing over us. He spears me from behind, his fingers circling my swollen clit while I use the leverage of the counter to push back against him, clenching my cunny around his shaft for added pleasure.

"I'm close," he groans through gritted teeth.

"Me too," I whimper. "Don't stop."

Our pleasure ratchets higher and higher until we're both moaning and gasping for air, clutching at each other while an all-powerful orgasm splits us in half. Leo explodes inside of me, his cock pumping thick spurts of delectable seed deep within me. I tremble and whine through my own heart-stopping climax. His cock twitches and my cunny clenches, making both of us weak and spent. Leo kisses the back of my head and slowly withdraws.

"Holy wow," I murmur, turning to face him.

He cups my face and kisses me with astonishing sweetness compared to the raunchy act we just did together. Those blue eyes soften when he smiles at me.

"You're beautiful," he says. "And that..."

"Was incredible," I fill in eagerly. "Do you want to stay the night? Please?"

"I'd love to," he agrees.

We drop off to bed, curled up in each other's arms under the afterglow. We fall asleep with smiles on our faces, and when we wake up together in the late morning, we make love again. This time it's slow and gentle and romantic. Just the kind of love-making I want to write about in my novel. Then we laze around for the rest of the day, watching baking shows (Leo's secret guilty pleasure) and wrestling (my own secret hobby), cooking together, sharing stories, just getting to know each other. It's heaven.

By the time we roll up to the bar for our shifts that night, we're holding hands. We know we're a thing now. Everyone notices, but nobody says anything. They just give each other pleased, knowing looks. I kiss Leo at the door and head over to the bar.

As I slide up next to Liz to start my shift, she gives me a wink. "Looks like somebody had a good night," she whispers.

I smile, unable to tear my eyes away from the gorgeous hunk of man guarding the door, keeping us all safe and protected from the wild world outside.

"You got that right, Liz," I say happily. "And more than that... I think I finally found the inspiration for my romance novel."

Hook-up with the Billionaire

Book Themes: billionaire, mistaken identity, affair, light bondage, dom/sub
Word Count: 7233

I feel like I'm on top of the world as I sit at the bar counter in my slinky black dress.

The night is young, the fancy drinks are flowing, and I'm in a sky-high mood tonight. It's pouring down rain outside, but in here it's nice and comfy.

I'm supposed to be here just for one little celebratory mojito in light of the interview I landed for work tomorrow.

You know, just a brief moment to exhale between my packed schedule of writing, interviewing, editing, and attending meetings with the rest of staff. I'm a busy woman with a lot on my plate, and I don't often give myself a break.

So tonight is meant to be just that: a little break before I dive headfirst back into work tomorrow morning.

At least, that's what I've been telling myself. Two hours later, I'm still here. Listening to the muffled chatter of mostly-polite conversation mixed with distant soft music. Breathing in the haze of expensive drinks and expensive cologne.

This is where the beautiful people go to see and be seen.

So, naturally, as a curious young woman in search of a good drink and hopefully a good story, I had to check it out. The place does not disappoint. I have definitely been seen-- there are several men in the bar who have eyed me up and down, offered to buy me a drink. The usual moves. And the people-watching potential is just incredible. Everywhere I look there are couples getting cozy, single people tipping back shots to combat their nervousness as they mingle.

There's just something special about tonight, something in the air. Like anything is possible if I just keep my eyes open and my heart ready to accept whatever the evening brings. I raise my mojito to my lips and take a minty sip. I shiver with delight as the delicious liquid courage tips back down my throat. I feel it burn pleasantly all the way down to my chest.

The extra boost helps keep me from looking too nervous while I sit next to the absolute most gorgeous man I have ever seen. The two of us have been trading secretive glances for the past hour while we slowly sip our respective drinks. Mine, a dainty mojito with extra mint. His, what I've observed to be top shelf scotch. I've noted other details, too. No ring on his finger; maybe he's single. His phone is on silent, but it lights up frequently. So he's a busy man, but he has his boundaries. He doesn't let work control his life. He's the one who's in control.

I'm a journalist, so I tend to notice every detail. It's easy enough, from those little starting points, to spin the web of a really strong story. Right now, I'm off the clock. But I can't help noticing every little thing about this guy. He fascinates me. I want to know more.

He looks strangely familiar, like I've seen a photo of him in the paper or on the news before. The guy certainly looks like he would be at home in front of a camera, with a face like that, carved by the hands of angels themselves. He has perfectly coiffed dark hair that sweeps back impressively from his forehead and temples. There's the faintest shadow of stubble on his chiseled jaw, and every time he smiles, I get a glimpse of bright white teeth and adorable dimples that make me weak in the knees. Those bright blue ocean eyes have me captivated. He makes my heart flutter, but I have to stay composed. I can't let him know how intensely I'm feeling him. Gotta play it cool. He glances over at me and flashes that winning smile.

"Coming down in sheets out there," he remarks.

"Good thing we're inside," I reply. "Safe and dry."

"I bet you'd look good soaking wet, though," the handsome guy flirts shamelessly.

I bite my lip and flutter my lashes at him. My heart is pounding.

"Stick around long enough and you might find out," I toss back.

He smiles and scoots in closer. I can feel his heat radiating off of him. I can smell his unique masculine scent, musky and mouthwatering. With him so close to me, it feels like every cell in my body is tingling.

"So what brings a girl like you to the bar tonight all by your-self?" he asks.

"I'm celebrating. I have a great work opportunity tomorrow, and I'm excited about it," I confess to my gorgeous stranger. "What about you?"

"What a coincidence. Tomorrow is a big day for me, too," he says. "I don't know if it's going to be a good thing or a bad thing, though. I guess you could say I drink to forget."

"Well, in that case, maybe I could give you something different to think about," I offer seductively. This is so unlike me! "At the very least, a little distraction."

He moves in a little closer. My whole body is on fire, and it's not the rum in my system. I move in, too, to meet him. To show that I am just as ready and willing as he is. For whatever may come next. I'm tired of spending all my late nights coffee-buzzed awake, writing into the wee hours of the morning. All by myself except for the ever-present ding-ding of my phone with news updates and emails. I need a little distraction, too, and I I think I know where to find it.

The man places his hand on my bare knee through the slit in my black dress and I almost melt at his warm, velvety touch. I meet his glorious oceanic gaze and see a fire building there. The lust he feels for me is matched by my own. We're not fools-- we can both feel it. The inevitable closing of the space between us. The undeniable magnetism that draws us together.

"You are more than a distraction," he murmurs gruffly. "You're the whole show."

"And just as entertaining, I'd like to think," I purr back.

"Oh, I have no doubt about that," he growls.

His hand moves ever so slightly up my thigh and I suck in a tight breath. His eyes never leave my face. He looks gratified at his ability to make me feel things. And boy, is that an understatement. I'm feeling a lot of things. Most notably, the tingly, achy need between my legs. I long to be touched, to be taken.

I know he can feel it, too. Burning through my skin under his fingertips.

"Maybe we should find a place a little more private," he suggests. "You know, so we can properly celebrate your achievement."

"Where should we go?" I breathe.

His face is mere inches from mine. I could touch the tip of my nose to his. I could just lean in and capture those perfect lips in a passionate kiss. I'm waiting for a sign. I'm waiting for him to make the next move. Those blue eyes flit down to my lips for a split second. The breath catches in my throat and the world goes blurry around us. I think he might kiss me.

Instead, he turns to give the bartender a meaningful nod. The bartender slides over immediately. Whoever my mystery hottie is, he certainly seems to have some authority about him. Part of me wants to know more about him, but an even bigger part of me is turned on by the anonymity of our connection. We don't need to know each other's names to have a good time together. It's sexy to hook up with a hot, hypnotic stranger. Why make it more complicated? Let fate be fate.

"Bruno, I'd like to take this gorgeous young woman to the VIP room," he says to the bartender. My eyes widen as he slides two hundred-dollar bills across the counter. The bartender deftly pockets the money and gives him a key card.

"Yes, sir. Last call in one hour," Bruno replies in a low tone, then buzzes away to help another customer.

The hand on my thigh gives it a tight squeeze. He lets go when he feels me shiver and flashes me that confident smile. Before I get a chance to say a word, he takes my dainty hand in his much larger one. His fingers all but swallow mine as he pulls me to my feet.

I'm only a little wobbly with mojito haze as he slowly leads me across the crowded bar toward the VIP room in the back of the building. As the night deepens, the music is becoming louder, with a driving beat. The room is pulsating with resounding bass and moving bodies pressed up against one another in the dimly-lit, moody space. Exhibitions are lowering. The nervous crowd is coalescing into a mass of writhing, lustful dancers and flirts. The vibe in the bar is infectious. Everywhere you look, there are steamy fateful connections. Right place, right time for a righteously hot experience.

I am no exception. Why not? I'm celebrating.

My handsome suitor pulls me along behind him as we approach the VIP room. People just naturally scoot out of his way left and right. Without question. Like we can all sense that he's the one in control. It's absolutely fascinating to watch. We get across the bar to the nondescript black door with a card lock. He slides the key card and the green light flickers. He pulls open the door and tugs me inside with him, shutting it behind us. The VIP room is dark and magical, with colored turquoise and pink lighting that lends an otherworldly feel to the room. There are a couple upscale designer sofas and a modern coffee table with colored LED lights flashing along the underside. Above it hangs a chandelier with scintillating panels of glass that catch and scatter the sparkling rainbow of lights across the dark walls. We can still hear the muffled sounds of crowds outside. But on this side of the door, we have the room all to ourselves. Just me, him, and the dancing lights.

"Whoa. This is actually beautiful," I admit, looking around the room.

He closes the space between us and cups my face in both hands. His bright blue eyes pierce through to my soul. I feel weak looking at him. Now that we're alone, the connection between us makes even clearer sense. There is something in him that needs something in me, and I am desperate to give it to him. He walks me backward and pins me against the wall.

I let out a moan of pleasure when he dives in to kiss my neck. His warm breath tickles my sensitive skin and I writhe under his touch. His hands hold my wrists to the wall on either side of my head. I can feel the thin wall vibrating with sound from outside. Just a few inches of concrete separate us from the prying eyes of the crowds. We're so close to the action, almost close enough for someone to hear us, to feel our heat burning through the wall. You need a key card to get in, but the door isn't locked, per se. It's the perfect balance of privacy and light exhibitionism that gets my heart pumping and those endorphins flowing. We could get caught. We probably won't, but we *could*. And that's more than enough to make me hot.

His lips trail up my ticklish neck to breathe gently against the shell of my ear. I shiver and moan as he moves up to swallow my cries. His lips collide with mine and his tongue pushes into my mouth to explore while his hands hold my wrists flat. He wrenches a leg between my thighs to spread my legs open wider. He pushes up until his body is flush against mine. I can feel every hard edge and rippling muscle of his perfect frame. His broad chest and powerful arms. His taut, chiseled abs. And most delicious of all, the thick bulge at the front of his designer jeans. I kiss him more passionately while he ruts against me. His cock is long and hard against my pelvis. My pussy aches to have him closer.

"I know what it is you need," he whispers.

He rocks against me again and I whimper. Every time I feel his shaft straining to break free of his jeans, straining to be touched by me, it's all I can do to keep from ripping his clothes off. Not that I'd have the choice, since he's got my hands pinned.

I arch my back and roll my hips to meet him, to show him that I want this as badly as he does.

"I'm yours, then," I insist breathlessly.

He raises an eyebrow. "You're offering."

"I guess I trust you," I shrug.

He releases my hands and steps back for a moment. He looks me up and down.

"Take off that pretty black dress," he commands in a silky voice.

I obediently slip the straps over my shoulders and reach to unzip the back. The form-fitting fabric slides down my body into a crumple at my feet. I stand in front of him dressed only in my barely-there lacy bralette and panties and black heels.

"Even better," he murmurs. Then he closes in on me. One large hand pins my wrists at my chest and the other slips between my legs.

"Oh," I sigh as his fingers stroke my wetness through the thin lace. I tremble at his touch. My clit is swollen, my pussy soaking wet and begging to be filled.

He kisses me deeply. I moan into his lips as his fingers slip my panties to the side and reveal my dewy flower. He circles my clit with two rigid fingertips. My knees buckle, and I have to summon my strength to stay up. The pleasure is so intense. He slides his hand down and teases my achy hole.

Twitching like his fingers are electrified, I murmur, "Mmm, yes."

"Yes, sweetheart. I'll give you exactly what you need," he growls.

He slides those two fingers inside of my slick opening. He hooks his fingers ever so slightly to reach that soft, earth-shattering place deep within me and stroke it. He dips in and out of my soaking pussy, making me cry out and tremble with every stroke. My own juices are running down my legs. Then he begins to rub his thumb over my clit while he fingers me, and all I see are bright lights dancing in my eyes.

"Oh my god!" I gasp, "I'm coming!"

"Yes, you are. Good girl," he rumbles.

I gush all over his hand as my body writhes and twists in his grip. He gently withdraws his fingers and raises them to his lips, licking them dry.

As the haze of climax starts to wane a little, I notice him unzip his jeans and pull his cock free. My mouth waters and I know instantly what is expected of me. What I want most. With my own juices still dripping down my legs, I kneel down in front of him.

I look up at him and slowly open my mouth. Begging without a word.

He smirks down at me and grabs my head, bringing my face closer to his massive, stiff cock. I'm salivating as I suck the thick head into my mouth. I moan at the way he pushes out my cheeks to fit him. I take inch by inch until he's poking the back of my throat.

"That's right, sweetheart," he groans between gritted teeth.

He gathers my hair in one hand and gives it a gentle tug to guide me back. His cock slips out of my mouth with a wet pop. I'm already licking my lips for more. I lean in again and take my time to really explore his cock. To worship it properly. I rub my lips up and down the underside, flick my tongue around the swollen head. I reach up to wrap one hand around his thick shaft and work his length in tandem with my mouth. I make pass after pass, my cheeks hollowing out to fit him. I suck him harder and faster, my body tingling to give him more. To do a good job. To get his approval.

I taste the bead of precome at the tip of his cock. He's stiffer than ever, and I can feel his body tensing up around me. His grip on my hair tightens as he begins to thrust his hips back and forth in small strokes. He slides his cock in and out of my open, wet mouth.

"Stay right there for me, baby," he commands gently.

I do as I'm told while he picks up the pace, pumping his cock down my throat. My hand wanders down to play with my slick pussy while he fucks my face. I'm already on the verge of coming again.

"That's so good. You'll take every last drop, won't you, baby?" he purrs.

"Mmmm," I respond with my mouth full of cock.

The vibrations of my voice push him over the edge. He grips my hair tightly while his cock spurts hot, slippery seed down my throat. As I swallow down every precious drop, my own pussy gushes all over my own fingers.

"Good girl," he grunts.

Once his cock is emptied inside my mouth, he pulls back and deftly composes himself. I take a dizzy step up and wipe my mouth. He quickly moves to help me, bringing me my dress.

"Lift your arms," he prompts me in a sweet voice.

I lift my arms so he can slip the dress over my head. He tugs it down into place, fitting snugly around my curvy frame.

"You're spectacular," he murmurs, peering deeply into my eyes.

"Thank you," I mutter.

He leans in to softly kiss me. And then we hear the bumping bass of the music cut out and the bartender's voice calls out, "Last call!"

My handsome stranger smiles and squeezes my hand. "Sounds like our time is up."

"Yeah, guess so," I agree.

"Maybe I'll see you around here again sometime," he says. Is that hope in his tone?

"I don't usually come here, but I-- I would. You know. Sometime," I fumble.

He touches my lips with his fingertip. "Fate served us well once. Let's try it again."

With that, he turns and steps out of the VIP room. I stand there, totally dazed and stunned by his sudden departure. I laugh to myself as I wait a few minutes, then excuse myself separately from the VIP room. I smooth my hair back down as I slither back to the bar to pay my tab, only to find that someone under the name *Harry* paid it for me already. I don't see my guy anywhere. A clean break. I can appreciate that, even though there is a part of me that already kind of misses him. But that's crazy, right? It was just a hookup. Nothing more.

I catch a cab home and fall right into bed, setting an alarm for my dream interview in the morning. I drift off to sleep within seconds of hitting the pillow, and I sleep like a baby.

The following morning, I am cozied up at a corner table in my favorite local coffee shop. I have all my pre-interview research notes, my recording device, my highlighters, even my lucky purple pen all spread out across the table. I got here a half hour early just to make sure I could get all my moving parts set up for my big interview with an important man. It's such an honor to be able to interview someone who so rarely opens himself up to media attention. I have to use my time and opportunity wisely. I need optimal results here, so I'm not taking any chances. I have to be organized.

I'm also tossing back espresso like nobody's business, because last night was... a lot. I slept hard, and I still feel like I'm a wee bit hungover. As I'm re-organizing my notes and going over my questions, my mind inevitably wanders back to that VIP room. To my handsome one-night-stand. Blue eyes flashing, his hand on my wrists. The smell of his skin. The taste of his cock in my mouth. The way he took control. He's a mystery to me. Only a name: Harry. And who's to say that's even his real name?

I'm kicking myself for not getting his number. It was an amazing time, but it had to come to an end. As much as I'd like to be cool about it, I want to see him again. That's what I get for trying to be mysterious. Oh well. At least I have him tucked away in my spank bank forever now. Whenever I want, I can drift back to his hand gripping my hair, his lips on my neck...

I'm jolted out of my steamy thoughts by the tinkling bell above the coffee house entrance. My eyes go wide and my jaw drops when I see the familiar outline of a gorgeous man in a relaxed button-down and jeans. That swoopy dark hair. That broad-shouldered build and chiseled jawline. I do a double take, but the image remains the same.

That *has* to be the guy from last night at the bar! But how? What are the chances of us both ending up at the same coffee shop at the same time right after our first intense encounter at the bar last night? I'm speechless as I sit here, staring at him.What does it all mean? Is this fate intervening to give me a second chance with him? Or just a potential distraction from the interview ahead of me?

I glance at the clock. Harrison Archer, the billionaire philanthropist I landed an interview with for my column, is supposed to be here by now. He's a busy man, I'm sure, with all the charity work he does. But I did think he would be punctual.

I'm fidgeting in my seat as I gaze at last night's love affair from my corner table. He looks around the cafe as he stands in line to order his drink. My eyes dart back and forth between the clock and the man. Where the hell is Harrison Archer? And why can't I focus on that instead of my gorgeous one-night-stand? Once he gets his coffee, he squints around the place like he's looking for something. Or someone.

It hits me with a jolt: what if he is Harrison Archer?

I realize that for all I've read about him, I never found out what he looks like. He's a very private person, so he's hard to pin down to begin with. The guy turns to lock eyes with me in the corner and he looks stunned. He comes sauntering over to me, my heart pounding with his every step. He cocks his head to one side, looking bemused.

"Excuse me. Miss Kitts?" he asks.

My face burns bright pink. I nod. "Yes. That's me. Mr. Archer?"

He smiles broadly. "You got me. Looks like fate wasn't done with us yet."

Damn, he looks delicious enough to eat as he sits down across from me.

"So, um, I'm not sure how to proceed. I mean, I'm not going crazy, right? You are the guy I met at the bar last night. Harry," I add in a low voice.

He leans in and nods. "Yes. That's me. I prefer Harrison, but I use different names around town sometimes for privacy's sake."

"You're a very private person," I remark, getting back to interview mode. "Tell me a little more about that."

Harrison smiles and leans back in his chair while I start taking notes.

"I've always liked to keep to myself. That's part of what drew me to day trading. I liked working in solitude and being beholden to only myself. When I earned enough money to start really giving back to the community, I decided to do it as quietly as possible. I don't seek validation or praise for my charity work. I can afford to help, so I do," he explains.

"Tonight, you're opening a new library. Most people would jump at the opportunity for good PR," I comment.

He shrugs. "Well, Katy, the truth is that I'm not most people. There are other highs I prefer to chase," he says slyly.

"You take a lot of necessary risks as a day trader," I suggest.

"I suppose that's true. If you're new to the game. But at this point, I know what I'm doing. I'm in full control of my finances and what I do with them," he declares. "I think you understand firsthand how disciplined I am."

I avert my eyes bashfully. I'm a hard-hitting journalist, but this guy has me squirming in my seat. Every time I catch those blue eyes or see his strong muscles move under his skin, I'm transported right back to that VIP room.

How can we talk business when we can't stop thinking about pleasure?

Throughout the entire interview, we interweave little flirtations with the real questions. We try to keep it mostly professional, but every time our knees touch under the table, I lose my train of thought. Still, by the end of our hour together, I have pages on pages of notes. Plenty to create a full article.

"Time's up again," Harrison relays as he checks his wrist watch. He looks over at me with a confident grin. "But this time, let's not just leave it up to fate to bring us back together. I have no doubt that would happen, but let's not wait around for it. I have a proposition for you."

"Oh?" I breathe. My pulse is racing.

He takes my notepad and pen and writes out his phone number, then hands it back.

"There is a black tie gala tonight at the library grand opening," Harrison explains. "How would you like to be my plus-one?"

"What? Oh my god. I would love that," I splutter.

He grins and shakes my hand as he stands up to leave. "Perfect. Text me at that number for details. I'll pick you up around seven tonight. Sound good?"

"Absolutely. Sounds magical," I gush.

"Good. See you tonight, Miss Kitts," he says with a wink.

As soon as he's gone and I've mostly recovered from my shock, I gather up my things to leave. I head out and go straight to the office for a post-interview meeting with my boss, Dalton. I'm feeling pretty stoked from my interview, so when I stride into Dalton's office, I carry myself with confidence. He lights up at the sight of me from his desk, where he's essentially drowning in notes. It's organized chaos, but we all make it work here at the paper.

"Hey Katy. How did it go?" he asks as soon as I step into the room.

I grin. "Fabulously. In fact, he's taking me with him to the gala tonight."

Dalton's wiry eyebrows shoot up. "What? How did you manage that?"

"I have my ways," I reply simply.

He looks to be in awe, which is just how I like it. You know, it's funny: any other time, I'm a strong, independent, confident woman who doesn't let anyone boss me around-- not even my actual boss. But when I'm around Harrison, I melt into a goopy puddle of submissive obedience. Duality of woman, I suppose.

"I assume you can use those *ways* to get an even deeper scoop on Harrison Archer at the event tonight?" he suggests.

"I won't disappoint you," I assert as I turn on my heel and walk out the door.

I need no better excuse to pursue Harrison. Hell, I was going to go after him anyway. I certainly could never just forget about him, not after the connection we've formed together. I head home to work on notes for my article and get ready for the event tonight.

I'm standing on my front porch, anxiously checking the time. My ride to the gala should arrive at any moment. I take a deep breath to remind myself that I got this. I really went all out for this event. It's going to be teeming with high-status attendees, and I need to fit in as best I can. So I'm wearing the most expensive dress I own. It's a sleek, form-fitting navy blue gown with bell sleeves and deep, daring cuts in front and back to expose my smooth, white skin and my ample cleavage. I added in a silver necklace and taupe heels to amp up the look. But under-neath my silky dress, I have no panties and no bra on. That part is more for me. I want to feel sexy and carefree tonight. I want my confidence to glow from within.

Plus, you never know what might happen between Harrison and me. I still care about getting the story right, but I'm much more interested in spending time with Mr. Archer.

Right on time, a glossy black luxury sedan pulls up to my house. I take a deep breath and catwalk down the driveway in my teetering heels. I slide into the spacious back seat next to Harri-son, who looks absolutely heavenly. His expensive suit is expertly tailored to show off his perfect body. His hair is perfect, not a swoopy dark hair out of place. He's totally smooth-shaven, and when he gives me a bright smile, I melt a little bit.

"You look absolutely beautiful," he tells me sweetly.

"You look like a million bucks," I reply.

"Together, we'll be unstoppable," he chuckles.

He reaches over and takes my hand, giving it a little squeeze. I'm bubbling over with excitement. During the drive to the event, we chat and snuggle up together. I instantly feel at home with him. This is where I'm meant to be.

We pull up to the library grand opening to find a fully-involved, elaborate, upscale gala in full swing. As soon as our car door opens and we step out arm-in-arm, cameras flash brightly all around us. The crowd cheers and applauds us as we make our way into the building. It's a total adrenaline rush to have everyone staring at us and whispering, looking fascinated. Everyone is curious about us, but most people are too intimidated to approach us.

"You're the man of the hour," I whisper to Harrison.

"It may be my gala, but they're all looking at you," he murmurs back. "I don't blame them. There's nothing in this world more beautiful than you are. Especially tonight."

I blush and give his arm a squeeze. We start our tour of mingling with the crowd, sipping champagne, taking hors d'oeuvres from silver trays, and flirting shamelessly in between. It's a truly opulent affair tonight, with only the finest decor and fare. There's even a live jazzy band complete with braver couples spinning and whirling on the dancefloor.

Everywhere I look, I see the faces of major names in journalism and media. Real connections who could help pave the trail for my career. With Harrison at my side, we can network with the best of them. He sings my praises and drops hints that I should be a writer to keep an eye on. I form all kinds of priceless connections that will help me later on, all thanks to Harrison. Even when people come up to congratulate or thank him for his philanthropic work, Harrison is humble, even while speaking with a tone of real authority.

"What's the point of having the money if I don't put it to good use?" he explains during one such conversation.

I beam at him. I am so proud to be on his arm tonight. People not only admire him, they respect him. He's earned that, every bit. I'm more than just impressed; I'm really starting to fall for this amazing gift of a man. We've been sipping champagne and holding hands throughout the night. Standing close together. Touching in small, secret ways that slowly build up our desire over time. A few hours in, about halfway through the event, our interest in the gala is starting to wane, and our interest in each other is booming off the charts.

Harrison whispers in my ear, "What do you say we get out of here?"

"I say you read my mind," I reply giddily.

With my heart racing like crazy, we walk out into the crisp evening air. The black sedan pulls up and we slide into the back seat.

"Back to my place," Harrison tells the driver. Then he quickly rolls up the partition.

He whips around to pounce at me. He pins me back in the seat, straddling me with his powerful body. He kisses me passionately while I loosen his tie. His hands rove up and down my body. He gropes my breasts and toys with my sensitive, tingly nipples through the silky layer of my dress. He drags his lips down my cheek to my neck, where his teeth dangerously graze my sensitive skin. I roll my back and arch toward him, moaning. Harrison slides a hand up under my dress. His fingertips slink up my ticklish thighs to my bare, dewy cunny.

"Oh, no panties. Such a perfect little whore for me, aren't you?" he murmurs.

"Just for you," I breathe.

His fingers circle my clit and stimulate the tight little bud of nerves while he continues to explore my body and kiss my neck. He bites bruising kisses into the hollow behind my ear, the soft spot where my neck meets my shoulder, and even one purplish bloom on my collarbone. I love the desperation in his biting kisses. I love how badly he wants me. And I can hardly wait to gaze at those love marks in the mirror later and run my fingers over them, remembering how good it felt to receive them. He rocks against me and I feel his hard cock straining to burst free. It makes my mouth water. I want to feel him closer, always closer.

Harrison slides down in the seat and hikes my legs over his shoulders. I look down at him in awe as he pushes my dress up. He bends to breathe in my womanly scent.

"God, you smell delicious," he groans.

He dives in to capture my stimulated clit in his mouth. I cry out and grip the seat. His warm, wet mouth suckles my clit while he flicks his tongue over the most sensitive part. I rock my hips against his face, meeting every stroke. When he slides a finger inside my aching cunny, I nearly lose control.

"Oh my god," I shudder. "I'm so close."

"That's right. Let me make you feel so good, Katy," he murmurs between bouts of devouring my dripping pussy.

The tension is building inside of me. It's like something so tightly wound is getting tighter and tighter, threatening to explode. The pleasure mounts higher and higher, until I'm dangling at the very edge. But just before I can come, Harrison backs down a little.

"Nnnh," I whimper.

Harrison strokes my inner thighs with both hands. He looks up at me devilishly.

"You want to come, don't you? You're right there," he teases in a gravelly voice.

"Mmm. Please," I mumble.

He dives in to lick and suckle my clit again. I'm instantly on that precipice again, almost about to come. Once again, he senses it coming and stops before I can release. By now, my cunny is pulsating with need. One little stroke and I might snap.

"Almost, baby. Almost," he assures me.

The car pulls up to an absolutely breathtaking townhouse. It's a luxurious brick walk-up, the stately front illuminated by glowy streetlight. We all but spill onto the sidewalk together in a mess of kissing and groping hands. Harrison dismisses the driver and we rush up the steps to his front door. We shove inside and close the door behind us, both grasping at each other.

Harrison scoops me over his shoulder and carries me through his spacious, airy house. Everything is professionally decorated and furnished with only the best. I'm amazed by my surroundings as he carries me down a long hallway filled with expensive art. He takes me straight to his luxury master bedroom. There's a king-sized bed with crisp white sheets underneath a sparkling chandelier. Along the wall are several massive floor-to-ceiling windows that reveal a glorious view of the private courtyard. Beyond that, the city lights glimmer and glow at the edges of the windows. It's a beautiful space, but I'm not distracted by it for long.

"This is gorgeous. What a lovely place," I tell him.

He lays me back on the bed and starts stripping off his tailored suit, watching me with the fiery gaze of a predator surveying his next meal. I am but his helpless, submissive prey, and the thought of that turns me on like nothing else. I belong totally to him.

"Take off that dress for me," he commands.

"Yes, sir," I reply playfully. I kick off my heels and slip off my blue dress to reveal my body totally naked except for my expensive necklace.

"Lay back and spread your legs," he orders. "Grab your ankles."

I do as I'm told, spreading myself wide open for him. I lick my lips and watch him with rapt, lidded eyes. All my focus is honed in on him. He pulls down his briefs and his massive, beautiful cock springs forth. I follow its perfect, rigid length with my eyes. I wiggle my ass and pull my legs tighter to stretch myself for him in a wide-open invitation.

"You've wanted my cock inside you since the moment we met," Harrison growls.

"Yes," I agree readily.

With one hand stroking his cock, he reaches out to run one exploratory finger down my slick folds. I shiver and keen with need. He licks my juices off his finger.

"So wet and ready for this cock, aren't you?" he murmurs.

I nod vigorously. "So ready."

"Almost," he says.

He walks over to the bedside drawer and takes out two lengths of silky cord. I am utterly entranced while he binds my wrists to my ankles. He steps back to admire his handiwork: my body, splayed open and totally at his mercy. The restraints pull gently at my skin and only intensify my desire. I am his little fuck toy. His mistress. Whatever he needs me to be.

Harrison straddles me once more, hovering over me while he lines up the head of his cock at my slick hole. I wiggle what little I can to encourage him. He runs his hands up my thighs and back down. His fingertips trace my wet slit, making me shudder. I'm already so on the edge. Every faint touch brings me hurtling closer.

"I'm going to fuck your tight little pussy now," Harrison commands. "I'm not going to hold back. Can you handle it?"

I nod, biting my lip. "Please, sir. I can take it."

He circles the head of his cock around my hole. I groan and tilt my head back. The same velvety pleasure resumes, and just as I'm about to come, Harrison pushes the full, thick length of his shaft inside of me.

I cry out his name. The world goes black for a moment while the overwhelming shock of pleasure edge with delicious pain rips through me. I convulse and tremble through the first orgasm, already hurtling toward the next. Harrison's long, hard cock spears into me hard and fast. Every stroke slams against my spongy-soft g-spot deep inside. I feel myself getting wetter and wetter. His shaft pounds into my dripping, splashy pussy while I helplessly lie on my back with my legs and arms out.

"How does that feel, Katy?" he grunts.

"So-- fucking-- good," I choke out between pummeling thrusts.

It feels like he's pounding into my very insides. Every inch of his thickness is buried deep inside me, and my pussy can't handle it. The combined hotness of being restrained and fucked by a mysterious, handsome billionaire is more than I can take.

He rubs my clit while he fucks me, and when one hand snakes up to wrap around my throat, I feel like I've died and gone straight to heaven. His fingers press expertly against the sides of my neck. He knows exactly how to toy with my breath without actually harming me. The restriction of oxygen only makes everything ten times hotter. Every stroke feels deeper. Every pass of his fingers around my clit feels like a ring of pleasurable fire. My cunny is twinging and twitching through wave after wave of multiple orgasms. I'm gushing everywhere, just a fountain of sweet honey while he destroys my insides with his massive dick.

He squeezes my throat and leans down to kiss me, so that I'm starting to get those little black dots at the edge of my vision while yet another powerful climax tears through me.

"Oh god, it's never felt like this before," I gasp.

"That's right. That's my good girl. Come all over this cock," Harrison groans. "I'm close, Katy. I'm going to pump you full of my seed. Tell me you want it."

"I want it!" I exclaim.

"How bad?" he teases, but I can tell he's barely holding back now.

"More than anything," I choke out. "Please."

"That's what I like to hear," Harrison growls.

He grabs my hips to steady me and hold me in place while he fucks me harder and faster than before. He pounds my pussy until he's moaning my name and twitching uncontrollably. His cock empties a thick, hot spurt of his come deep inside my cunny. I can hardly tell where my juices end and his begin. When he's finished, he pulls me close to him and kisses me on the lips.

"We make a good team," he murmurs in my ear.

"Yes, we do," I agree.

We're both on cloud nine. I feel amazing. Like I could fly. Not that I'd want to-- I am exactly where I want to be. As we lie there enshrined in golden afterglow together, we talk about our past, our present, our future. About how fate aligned to bring us together, and we are helpless to stop the tides of destiny. Besides, we never want to be apart for long. Never again. Now that we've found each other, we know what we're supposed to do. We're meant to love each other, to make one another better and stronger, to grow together.

"We are going to make one hell of a power couple," Harrison chuckles.

I smile up at him, happier than I've ever been.

"Damn right," I tell him. "And the story's only just beginning."

Innocent Tease

Innocent Tease: Punished

Book Themes: *Age Gap Sex, Virgin, Older
Man/Young Woman, Spanking, Flogging,
Religious Themes, Priest Sex, Oral Sex, and
Creampie*
Word Count: 8071

T he schoolhouse stood as one of the oldest buildings in the center of town, a large wood structure that dominated the intersection of the dirt roads that led off down the country routes, towards farms in four directions. It was silhouetted by the forest behind, while in front of it was the local shops that provided just about all the town's needs. Few people actually lived in the town itself; most were farmers out on their plots of lands, somewhat isolated from one another except when they gathered at the center.

Amy adored the schoolhouse though, it was her favourite place to be, for even though many of the other kids didn't take it seriously, it was where she was exposed to worlds and ideas that just dazzled her.

That was why it was so hard to say goodbye.

She'd stayed longer than most of the other children, who mainly gave up the moment they were allowed to go back and work on the family farm full time. But she had graduated, and it'd be all official very soon.

It was her last day, and she had an appointment to meet with her teacher bright and early before class began.

Amy tugged up her tight, navy skirt, the pleated bottoms brushing against her mid-thigh. She was fit, her legs tanned and lean and far too long, the socks pulled up to her knees and black maryjanes scuffed and worn. Her white blouse was translucent, the outline of her simple white bra visible as her large breasts threatened to pop open the buttons.

Her bra offered no real support or comfort, other than hiding her chest from beneath her shirt, and she pulled on her navy jacket over her shoulders. That, too, didn't fit well and wouldn't button in front, but it was required as part of the uniform.

Besides, with as cold as that June had been, she needed the little extra warmth it provided.

Her brown hair was pulled back in a french braid, leaving her tanned face free of the wisps, her blue eyes all the more startling because of it.

She didn't bother to wake her father from his slumber, as there was still frost in the air and he needed the extra sleep. Her breath curled from her lips, nipples stiffening beneath her blouse, so apparent from beneath her sheer bra.

Amy didn't know what her teacher expected of her, but she hoped it was good news. News of a job, of a future. She couldn't procrastinate any longer, not with her father getting up there in years and her mother passing two summers before.

She walked the five miles to school, watching as the sun crested over the forest, slowly illuminating the glittering world, and easing the chill in Amy's body. She walked quickly, satchel slung around her back, as she listened to the birds wake and chirp their song.

When she arrived inside the schoolhouse, she found her

teacher there. The dashing middle aged man was the finest bachelor in town, many said, and that was strange because he was well past the point he should have settled down.

With a pair of glasses perched upon his nose, and a thick head of blonde hair, he was always smiling. His strong jaw prominent as he glanced over at her, head lifted from his work the moment she entered.

She was cold, shivering a bit as she shut the door after her, grateful for the warmth as she set down her bag.

"Amy!" he exclaimed happily, rising up from his desk to come around and meet her. "Thanks so much for comin' in early," he said, his tweed jacket open, showing his crisp shirt and tie beyond. It was a simple outfit, which marked him as the town's teacher as if that was even necessary in such a small place.

She lived in a town with only 400 other people, and most of them were farmers with rough hands and year round tans.

"Hey, Mr. Muran," she smiled in return, her cheeks flushed from the early morning chill, walking towards his desk. He'd taught her for so long, since the next nearest town was over an hour away and there were so few students. It was glorified home schooling, but she wouldn't have traded a minute of it.

Especially since she got to see *him* five days a week.

He reached out and clasped her hand in his, before he did a very peculiar thing and pulled her in for an embrace. It was a chaste sort of thing, proper, but all the same... to be pressed into his tall, hard body was an experience she had trouble complaining about.

"Congratulations," he said before pulling back, a big smile upon his face. "I know it's not official until the end of the day, but... I'm just so excited for you. And the possibilities that may come for my brightest student." He said it all with such conviction, so proud of her. It was hard to believe.

But she was trembling and hoped he'd think it was only due to the cold, then keep her in his arms just a little bit longer. He was so warm and smelled so clean. Not of hay and manure like so many of the farmers around.

"Thank you," she managed, breathily, as her eyes fluttered up at him.

"But I don't know what I can do next. My father needs help on the farm and..." she trailed off, trying not to let her morose mood sour his celebration for her.

He rubbed her slender arm through her jacket and nodded.

"I understand you've got some obligations at home. You need a paying job, right?" he said, with a faint smile. "That's just where I might have some good news," he said, then gestured around him. "How'd you feel about being a teacher?" he asked, brow raised, an expectant, burgeoning smile upon his face.

"A teacher?" she asked, her nose crinkling as she looked up at him, head tilted to the side. Her french braid ran over her shoulder, along the navy blazer and grazing over his fingers.

"I don't have any college, though."

Her teacher shrugged his shoulders.

"This is a small country school, college isn't necessarily required..." he explained, "especially not for a teacher's assistant." He cracked a smile at her, looking quite excited by it all. "The school's small, you know that, but we don't have any teachers good with handling the youngest children, right? That's where you could come in, Amy."

He sat back upon the corner of his desk and folded his arms, he looked so confident and sure, like he'd solved all her problems. Her saviour.

She tried not to part her lips in her excitement, not get too caught up in it, but it was difficult not to let her excitement bubble over. She was thrilled, and quickly threw her arms around his neck, her large breasts pressing into his chest as she almost crawled up in his lap.

Her sudden lunge set him off balance but he managed to regain his position and balance back out as he touched his big, strong hands to her waist.

"Hey now Amy, just a sec," he said, unable to fight his grin as he grasped her rather firmly, a tight, comforting sort of hold around her waist. "There's just one thing you have to do," he said to her in that calm, instructional tone he'd used to teach her all her life.

She backed away from him, just a little, her vibrant blue eyes seeking his out as she tilted her head curiously.

"Anything, Mr. Muran," she said, and meant it with every fiber of her being.

His handsome face contorted and he stood back up. With a slow once-over, he seemed to inspect her, a mischievous look crossed his face.

"As you know of course, the school's budget is tight. We're funded almost entirely by the township, and the local parish. So though we have tentative approval for a new teacher's assistant, there are two people you need to meet with first, to convince you're the right candidate," he said with a proper amount of gravity to the statement.

"Okay," she agreed, without hesitation. A way out of being a farmer and still able to provide for her father? There wasn't any question in her mind that she'd do what she had to in order to convince them.

"You're going to have to meet with Father Mackay at the parish church. He's the first one you'll have to convince. I'm sure it shouldn't be a problem, right? How could anyone not fall for you upon first sight?" he remarked with a grin.

"Sure," she nodded easily, her heart thumping louder as she realized she was still standing so near to him, chest brushing against his with her eager breaths.

"Who else?"

Her teacher gave her a momentary look before he spoke, as if bracing to deliver the news.

"The mayor," he said softly. "And I know he's been a bit of a nuisance for your father in the past, but hopefully he doesn't hold their feud against you. Which he shouldn't. That was ancient even when it started, had no business exploding up like that."

Amy had never quite learned the reason for why the mayor and her father had such an ongoing rivalry, though it had all started shortly after her mother passed away. Her father had always been a gentle man, so it didn't make sense to her that he became so enraged towards the man who ran the town.

But for all her curiosity and enthusiasm at school, she understood her father's desire not to talk about it or let it hurt their time together so she'd never pried.

Still, she let out a soft sigh and nodded at her teacher, fingers lightly brushing over her braided hair.

"What should I say, then?"

He gave a shrug but smiled reassuringly down at her, the angle causing his glasses to slip a bit and he had to push them back up the bridge of his well-shaped nose.

"I trust you know how best to warm a man's heart, Amy. You've never had any issue winning my admiration or appreciation, after all," he stated, reaching a hand out to place upon her slender shoulder and squeeze it gently.

Those words warmed her heart, then swam into her loins as her breath caught for just a moment. How long had she had a crush on him? She was only just a girl, so awkward and shy. But he'd had no small hand in bringing out the woman in her, and she nearly soared at his compliments.

"And then we'd work together? Every day?"

"Every day," he repeated cheerfully, letting his hand slide down her arm to grasp her hand with his. Those long fingers of his wrapped about her dainty digits as he squeezed. "I'd very much like that, wouldn't you?" he asked, brow raised. "No longer have to be teacher and student, it'tll be a real, adult kind of working relationship. We could even go to lunch or dinner together."

Her knees trembled and her head was bobbing up and down stupidly before she even realized it.

"I'd *love* that," she stressed, her breath so warm as she looked up on him affectionately. "I mean, I'd do anything," she continued, her smile growing with every passing moment as excitement filled her. There was no way she'd let either of them turn her down.

She needed that job more than life itself.

His own smile showed he was almost as excited himself. A big toothy grin upon his face, bigger than she'd ever seen it. And her Mr. Muran was not shy of smiling! He gave her hand another squeeze.

"Good. So Father Mackay wishes to meet with you this very morning, and hear exactly why it is you feel you're up for the task of being assistant teacher. Then once he gives you the approval... it's down to the mayor."

He gave her such a warm, confident smile.

"I know you can do this, Amy," he said softly.

There was no part of her that wouldn't make it happen, and she gave him a firm, resolute nod, her face serious.

"Would it be too early to go now, Mr. Muran?"

He smiled so handsomely down at her and shook his head.

"No, Father Mackay is an early bird sort of guy. Up before anyone in this town, I'm sure he'd appreciate punctuality. That's why I asked you to meet me so early today." He leaned in and spoke to her in a conspiratorial sort of tone, "We gotta get these fellas in their weak spots and get 'em hard." He winked at her, that act alone so... adult so... strange.

He then inspected her outfit, ran his hands along her arms and tried to adjust it just a little, though the tightness of that undersized outfit gave little wiggle room.

But the feel of his warm hands on her, it elicited a very obvious reaction; her nipples tightened between the thin fabric of the top and the sheer material of her barely-there bra. Her cheeks flushed bright as she looked at his face, praying he hadn't noticed.

"I'll go right now, then," she half asked, half stated.

"It's best you do," he said to her with a nod. "Go on then," he remarked, and did a very special thing altogether. He leaned in and kissed her forehead softly. "I know you won't disappoint. You never have," he said, just before he turned and walked back behind his desk. Leaving her to stand there, overwhelmed.

Her blood burned hot as she turned and picked up her backpack, her heart stuck in her throat.

She couldn't disappoint him. Not after that tender kiss.

Outside the cool air nipped at Amy again, but it was a relief with how hot and flushed she felt. She made her way on over towards the parish church, which stood almost as big as the school house. It was a little ways away from the center of town, but it was nowhere near the distance of her walk from home, so she hardly felt it was a big deal at all.

She pushed in through the big front doors of the church and looked into its great, cavernous hall. No sight of the Father about as she walked on down the carpeted aisle.

Her father and her hadn't attended since her mother passed on, and she'd assumed it was simply too painful for her dad.

Before then, though, they'd gone together as a family, once a week like clockwork, and she made her way towards where she remembered the office to be. She let down her satchel outside, heart pounding as she sucked in a deep breath, petting over her outfit.

She knocked on the door, hoping it was loud enough, but her nerves and shyness turned it into soft little pulses against the wood.

"Come in!" came a voice from inside, and she opened the door and moved on in. Instantly a wave of heat blasted her, the Father having a cozy fireplace lit high to keep the cold at bay.

He sat by the fire with a book in his lap, but upon seeing her his eyes widened and he shut it closed.

"Young Amy," he said with much surprise. He was an older man, with ruddy hair that had silver streaks through it. He was undoubtedly handsome, though he had the build of a farmer himself. A strong looking man, he filled his frock rather well.

"It has been so long since you have been in the Lord's house," he said as he rose up and smiled at her warmly.

She shut the door behind her so as not to let out the heat, but instantly she felt the desire to take off her jacket, the warmth almost overbearing.

Still, Amy smiled brightly in the face of her discomfort, doing her absolute best to seem chipper and cheery.

"Father," she said, walking towards him, bowing her head just so.

"It's been too long," she agreed.

"Oh, you sweet child," he said as he reached out, and placed his hands upon her arms just beneath her shoulders. He rubbed her thoroughly there as he sized her up. "You've grown so much in so few years," he stated, sucking his lower lip into his mouth. He was nearly as tall as Mr. Muran, and an imposing figure next to her. "I really wish I saw you more often, child."

Amy looked up at him from beneath her dark lashes, her braid rested along her neck.

"Me too," she said truthfully. It was her father's decision, after all, that she not attend on Sundays, and she was, if nothing else, obedient.

"Mr. Muran told me you were expecting me?"

"Am I needed?" he said, his head tilted to the side as he sized her up once more. Then realization sank into his emerald eyes, and they widened. "Ahh, it's you then, isn't it?" he asked, eyes alight with some strange fascination. "Take off your jacket, and come sit, child," he beckoned her, gesturing to the small sofa across from his seat, next to the fire.

She was relieved at the opportunity to remove the navy jacket, placing it on the coat rack next to the door. The heat had already flushed her cheeks as she went to the sofa, scooping up her too short skirt as she sat down.

"Thank you," she murmured, her eyes deferred respectfully.

"Ohh, what a lovely girl," Father Mackay said, touched by her little motions, and he reached out to lightly trace his fingers over her cheek. "So respectful. You were a prime member of our flock, you know that? It saddened me dearly to see you plucked from our congregation," he said before sitting himself not in his former seat, but right next to her on the sofa. The rather large man an imposing figure beside her.

She half smiled, nodding at him, though she'd not say a word against her father. For all his sorrows, he cared most about her, and it was difficult for her to fathom having anyone better in her life.

"I've missed it," she confessed, and raised her gaze for only a second. "It always relaxed me."

"Ahhh, that pleases me to hear," he said to her, his voice deep and yet smooth. He had a soothing voice, to be sure; it served him well in giving mass or simply preaching to the congregation.

"I was afraid I had driven you away," he remarked with a playful wink, his two hands coming up to grasp her slender shoulders. He rubbed them gently at first, very carefully. "You look very tense now, so perhaps you needed more relaxing, is that the true reason you came?" he said in a playful tone of voice.

She let out a soft giggle, shaking her head as she looked up at him, all gentle sweetness.

She bit in her lower lip, drawing it into her mouth before she spoke. "I'm sure I wouldn't mind that, Father, but I mostly came about the, uh, job. At the school?"

He tilted his head back, the Father's mouth opening in a silent 'ahhh' as he continued to rub at her shoulders, moving the worn fabric of her town a little as he rubbed with those strong hands.

"You wish to help teach the little ones for the years ahead, is that it?" he said, a gentle smile upon his face as he smiled at her. "A big responsibility. Not just work wise, but morally."

She nodded, looking up at him with such large, wide eyes.

"Oh, I know, Father," she promised. "A huge responsibility. But you know I've always been passionate about school and learning. I think I could really help there."

Her shoulders relaxed with the massage, a light sigh even punctuating her sentence.

The Father guided her back against the sofa, urging her gently into a more comfortable position as his hands worked upon her.

"Ah, I know you were always a clever girl, my dear," he said to her softly, his voice quiet, almost a murmur. "But... it was the wishes of the church to have someone with... an active role in the congregation. A devout soul, to pass on some of the values of our Lord."

He looked at her, his emerald eyes rolling down over her tightly wrapped form in a faux innocent manner.

She thought it a bit strange, the way his hands touched upon her, fingers working away at the tension in her back. But the headiness to his words, she'd never heard him use that tone while preaching, and it gave her pause.

"Father, once I'm self-sufficient and able to attend again, you know I will," she vowed.

"Oh, I know it, child," he said to her fondly, his voice so sincere and gentle. He even scooted over the sofa toward her a little closer, nestling in against her. "But the Lord asks that we make sacrifices for Him. That we take actions in His name to show our devotion," he said, a sympathetic look upon his face. "What sort of leader for our flock would I be if I ignored that?"

"Is there... someone you have in mind?" she asked, her voice so airy as she looked up at him, paranoia in her gaze even as he moved so near to her. His warmth amplifying her own.

The Father wet his lips and very carefully ended his rubbing, taking his hands from her shoulders as he smiled and reclined back.

"Well my child, when people stray from the flock... it can be hard to tell if they are still truly devoted to our Lord. Willing to do whatever is necessary to spread His word," he says, sounding so genuine and heartfelt. He reached a hand out to rest upon her knee, right beneath the hem of her skirt. "Are you, my child?"

"Of course," she said, aghast he'd even, for a moment, doubt her faith. Her resolve!

She nearly trembled beneath his touch, fear beginning to work its way into her heart. She'd been strong until then, certain that she could sway him to support her. Yet the way he was talking, she was becoming more and more concerned that she couldn't.

He could even see her shaking with how pronounced it was, and he reached back out, put his arms about her and rested them at her shoulders.

"Oh no, my child, don't quiver in fear," he said with a gentle smile. "The Lord does not close a door without opening a window," he said in that reassuring yet authoritarian voice of his. "If you wish to show your devotion, I may be able to give you that opportunity. That is... if you are willing to take it," he said, tilting his head down as he gave her a scrutinizing look.

"Of course! I'll do whatever you want! Come every week, without fail. I know daddy won't be pleased, of course, but he'll understand. It's for the good of the town. For all the children!" She didn't mean to sound over dramatic or like a martyr, but she was incredibly passionate, and she looked over his eyes, his smile, her brows furrowed so sternly.

"That's good," he said with a serious expression and a sympathetic nod. "But in the meantime, I need something special from you. An act of contrition for all your missed time from the house of our Lord," he said, and he stood up, walked over towards his desk.

"You know, so many of the Saints suffered for our Lord. What I ask of you is but a tiny sliver of their penances," he explained as he moved to look through his drawers.

And Amy was nodding, leaning forward on the couch as her skin stuck to the material, the heat gathering beneath her knees.

"Yes, Father, of course. You know my devotion, of course," she said, her words coming out quickly and passionately.

He smiled over at her as he bent down, fishing a long, leather implement from his drawer. She recognized it immediately as a tool that was used to discipline the very unruly students at Sunday school.

"Then you will bend over my desk, lift your skirt and offer your mortal flesh to the Lord's tender mercies, won't you?" he said, testing the implement against his other palm with a slight smack.

She stared in disbelief, her eyes flicking between him and the tool, her body stiffening slightly. It was far too warm in the room, the fire still crackling away, and she felt a bead of sweat trail down her spine, making her shiver.

"Father," she said, her breath panted a bit from the heat, the confusion.

And yet she stood, her arms folded beneath her chest as she glanced to the door. "I don't know if that's, like, appropriate?"

The Father furrowed his brow at her in confusion.

"Not appropriate, my child? Not appropriate," he moved towards her just a couple footsteps, his looming presence a little more imposing. He looked at her with a dark sort of expression, his voice growing harder, "Saving your soul, giving yourself over to God, and making up for your shortcomings is... beyond appropriate."

He was so tall, and when he spoke to her like that, it seemed to be all the more apparent.

"It's just, aren't I a little old for that?" she pressed, her head tilted to the side and letting her braid snake along her bicep. Her heart raced as her brows furrowed with confusion, with anxiety. She wouldn't let something so simple stand between her and her job, though.

"You're right," he said to her as if conceding a point. "It's the sort of minor punishment for a child. But you have been away from the flock for a while now, and you are a woman. In every way," he remarked, his eyes roaming down over her voluptuous figure as he spoke. "We will do something more special, but first..." he pointed the leather strap at his desk with such authority.

She was weak to his commanding presence and she took a step forward, arm over her stomach as she looked back at him curiously. Then another step. And another.

It was difficult for her, but she was so afraid of not getting the job she desired and had dreamed of ever since she was a little girl.

"And then you'll endorse me for the position?"

His demeanor shifted, "Put your fate in the hands of our Lord, and you shall have the life you deserve, my child." He intoned those words so solemnly, so comfortingly, it was hard to believe anything but. Even though the Father was brandishing a weapon, that large man standing there so ominously. Such a big, brute of a man.

Most of the men of the town were hard, worn that way by decades of hard work. But never had she felt so frail and dainty, only the curves of her hips and ass and breasts giving a bit more size to her.

But even though she flushed and felt so terribly embarrassed, she obeyed.

She leaned over his desk, her large breasts pressed into it as she looked at him over her shoulder, skeptically.

"That's it child," he said soft and encouragingly as he stepped in behind her. He kept that gentle demeanor, and reached to the hem of her skirt. She could feel him grasp it at her thighs as he delayed just momentarily.

"To take on a position of authority such as a teacher, one must first be prepared to humble themself," he stated just before he lifted her skirt and exposed the round curve of her rear.

Only her panties hid her from him as he inspected her.

She couldn't remember ever feeling so flushed and embarrassed in her life, but she understood it. That it was part of the 'humbling' he spoke of. Knowing that her flesh wasn't hers to control and own, that it was God's to do as He may.

And the Father was his representative on earth.

But still, she couldn't help but wriggle, trying to hide from his gaze.

She could hear the Father mumble a prayer, it was all so official. Right up until the leather strap slapped her pale ass cheeks. The skin so milky light there, unlike her arms and legs. The hard crack resounded upon her skin and he let loose a sigh, watching as her skin turned red from the smack.

Tears sprung to her eyes at the old, familiar sensation. It felt so much sharper, though, than she recalled. So much more intense.

"No no, this won't do," he said to her, sounding disappointed.

She trembled on the desk, her hands holding her up as she tried desperately to stay in position, her maryjanes pushing her up a couple inches.

"What?" she asked in a quivering voice, trying to look at him. "What won't do?"

"The strikes have to be upon raw, bare flesh," he said to her so matter-of-factly. "Your panties," he explained without her asking, "They are in the way. They'll have to go if you hope to have absolution for your sin of deserting the church."

There it was, that demand. So crass, so simple.

Yet she knew that was different from her childhood, and she rose up, turning to face him and shaking her head so desperately.

"That doesn't make sense," she said softly, her ass smarting from that one blow. "Father, please, I'll do anything, but... I don't understand."

The Father's face turned cross.

"The Lord gives us everything, child. He gives us life, He gives us love. He gives us the food on our plate, the air in our lungs. All he asks is faith, faith Amy," he said to her, repeating it, and he sounded so controlling so ominous. "Faith is belief unquestioning. And *you* — child — ask far too many questions. How can I entrust the children to such a woman?" he asked, looking almost angry at her.

She shrank before him, her eyes widening. She'd never seen him like that before, and certainly not so upset at her. He'd only ever been kind and generous, and she wondered, then, if she was simply being irrational.

Something within her said no, that she should simply leave, but she thought back to her teacher, at how important it was to him that she pleased the Father and the Mayor.

So she turned back to the desk, and, burning with shame, hooked her fingers into her panties and let them drop towards the ground, unveiling her pinkened sex beneath the light bit of fur, clenched between her thighs.

Though as she bent over, there was no fully hiding it with the way her body naturally flowered before his eyes.

"That's better," he said in a low husk, and though she couldn't see him, he eyed that precious slit of hers, reached a hand out and very nearly touched it. "Don't move," he told her instead, and he pressed his free hand down upon her lower back. "You have a lot to make up for. Not just your absence, but your doubts. Your questioning."

The next crack landed against her fully bare backside raw and hard, the third smack even grazed her dainty pink folds and made those delicate lips sting.

She let loose a wail, her body so unused to such sharpness.

She was a tough woman, used to grueling hours on the farm, but that pain was utterly different.

Her head lurched back and she tried to move away, to flee from him and his wicked sting, but he held her too roughly. All she could do was shimmy that rounded ass, with the red markings lancing across it as she whimpered.

"Father!" she cried to his punishment, tears making her vision murky.

"Shh," he said to her, bending over her form. "Hush my child, there are but forty seven more to go," he said to her, his fingertips trailing over her bottom sweetly. Those thick, long fingers touching her bare, rouged ass cheeks in a gesture that seemed to be intended to calm her, ease her suffering.

But that wasn't a possibility. Forty seven?

She could barely have handled those three without becoming an utter wreck, and she trembled so violently, flicking her braid to her back as she looked at him with those pools of blue eyes.

"Father," she began to plead, her youthful face contorted as though she were going to protest. But she knew what was at stake. And fifty lashes was a small price to pay for her future, and her eternal soul.

"Please make it fast," she finally said.

"Ask and ye shall receive, my child," he said to her, and the subsequent lashes came on fast. One, crack! Two, thwack! Three, four, five... on they went until her ass was stinging and she couldn't help but cry out and he stopped.

"We aren't even half way there yet, my child. Do you not have it in you to bear this penance for your Lord and Saviour?" he asked her, his hand rested upon her burning ass cheek, stroking along that smooth, stinging flesh.

But her entire body was quaking, her knees threatening to give out as she tried to push herself forward, away from the punishment. She couldn't take anymore, her face contorted in pain and anguish as her breath was so hard.

She wanted so badly to have the job, his acceptance, but she couldn't take another of those lashes.

"Please!" she said simply, and she didn't even know what she was begging or pleading for. For there to be another way.

"Hush my child," he said to her softly, reaching his free hand up to push her hair back from her face. "There is but one other way, my child. One simple way and you can have all the Lord's blessing, and walk out of here with your head held high. You just need to offer your flesh up, without question... without regret. Can you do that? Can you hand yourself over so willingly?" he asked, sounding so sweetly interested in helping her.

Perhaps it was her naivety that had her agreeing so quickly to his demands, or else just a desire to not feel any more of those cracks against her tender ass. She looked at him so pitifully as she nodded, her lips dry beneath her tongue as she licked them over.

"Good girl," he said to her, and he laid down the leather strap. Though what he did then confused her, though she dared not ask a question.

He circled back around his desk, and opened a drawer. Out of it, he pulled some ropes. Very skillfully he wound one about her wrist, and then tied the other end to the leg of the table. He repeated this with the other arm before going back around before her.

"Think hard on our Lord, my child, and it'll all be over soon," he said as he worked open his frock.

The Father was insatiable. After all that time watching her pale cheeks turn red, when he pulled open his black vestments his dick was bulging and ruddy, throbbing with need as he looked down upon her poor, abused cunny lips.

"This child offers herself up to the Lord, and through me... He accepts," and with that, he pushed his hips forward, brushes that thick, purple crown against her bare folds, teasing them with the pre-cum glistening tip of his manhood.

She let out an incredibly startled cry, so uncertain of what was happening. She was a virgin, never touched, and his sudden press made her feel so many conflicted, confusion emotions.

She tried to shift away, but those bindings...

Amy couldn't move, couldn't do anything more that bite down on her lower lip and feel him so wholly against that most sensitive part of her body. She was throbbing so hotly with a longing she didn't understand, her cunny pulsing with a need that Amy didn't have words for.

She had never indulged with boys in all her years growing up, had always been a good girl. So when the Father pushed through her hymen and stretched that barrier taut about his dick, it was the first time she'd had a man inside her.

He let loose such a deep, satisfied groan, his cock swelling inside her. He clutched onto her ass and hips, and sank right to the very hilt in her. The large, husky man trembled with the overwhelming pleasure of her cunny.

It was even more intense than the lashings, though in an entirely different way. Her mind sparked with sensations and she let out another cry, her pussy throbbing about him as he took her virginity so rudely.

Yet his lashings, her humiliation, it had wettened her for him, and made her grow hot. Another bead of sweat ran down the hollow of her throat between her collarbones before soaking into her too tight top, her skirt flipped up over her hips.

Father Mackay bent over her, his fingers moving through her hair as he tugged back just slightly. He kissed the back of her head and murmured to her quietly.

"You have been a very good girl all these years, Amy," he said to her so appreciatively. "The Lord will reward you for this... I swear it," he said, tugging back his hips and beginning to pump into her. The thrust of his cock sent his balls swinging pendulously up against her cunny as he rocked, such lewd, low moans filling the air as he took her atop his desk.

He was her priest, the one who'd always taught her right from wrong, and even though her stomach was twisted with confusion, she still trusted him.

That what he said, what he was doing, it was only right. Only just.

But still she couldn't stop her quivering atop his desk, the rope biting into her limbs as she panted against him. Every time his hips slammed against her ass, another shock went through her, and she couldn't stop herself from whimpering.

He sank his fingers into her hips and ass cheeks, made her flesh dimple about his digits as he squeezed and rutted into her. He was huffing, panting hard as he fucked her atop that desk, made her little knees tremble.

That thick cock of his plowed in deep, its bulbous mushroom tip stretched her out with each thrust, eased her little virginal cunny wider, trained it to take him better as he fucked her so enthusiastically.

He even held her braid like a reign, as he felt himself tense, his balls tighten beneath him.

"Oh fu—" his words were cut off, and he trembled against her.

So close.

Yet she didn't know what he was close to, nor why he almost used such foul language to describe it. But she was slamming back into him, even as her ass smarted, feeling some strange, carnal need that she couldn't explain or understand.

It was just pure, physical need, her mind too fuzzy from the pain to protest. Her higher faculties had taken a break and she just simply *fel*T everything to such an extreme.

Those little pushes of hers back against him, presses of that supple ass against his groin, helped teeter him over the edge. The Father gasped and shuddered, his dick swelled up as the seed of his loins welled up and then...

"Take it," he groaned out just a moment before his creamy cum shot forth from his bulging crown, and flooded her depths. Such a rich flow, coming in spurt after spurt to fill her fertile, virgin pussy full of its first load.

He bucked erratically, shivered over her as he moaned with ecstasy.

It was very nearly too much for him to bear.

And even more so for her, so lost in a confused fog of sensations, her mind unable to put the pieces together. He'd taken her so lewdly, so quickly, and without any pretenses.

Her body longed for more, even as it ached with the strain and pressure as he pushed up inside her so deeply.

The Father sunk down atop her as his orgasm slowly

subsided, his pulsating cock loosing the last of its cream into her until finally he stilled. His panting breaths in her ear as he made sure every last bit of his cum was deposited into her depths.

"You did well, my child," he said breathily, slowly pushing himself up. "There is but one more thing left for you to do, and you will be free to go. With the career as a teacher ahead of you," he explained, slowly pulling his shaft from her sopping wet folds, leaving them gaping and drooling his seed.

He rounded the desk and went before her, that glistening shaft in front of her mouth.

"You'll pay final homage to the Lord, and thank him for his gift inside of you by cleaning his implement," he said with that hard, authoritarian edge to his voice again.

He taunted her so well, playing on all of her hopes and dreams, but her mind and body were both filled with a fog. She was so uncertain of herself, of what just happened, of what he expected from her.

Yet it felt... good.

Strange, confusing, and so damned good.

Her blue eyes went to him, wide, looking up along his cock and staring, having never before seen one, the scent thick in the air.

The Father grasped her head, wound her braid about his wrist and then pulled her mouth in. That slick, glossy crown of his nudged to her pink lips, then pushed beyond. He sank himself in over her tongue, and gave a low, satisfied groan.

"That's it," he husked softly, "no teeth. Just lick and suck." He began to rock his hips slowly in time with his hold upon her hair.

The sweet tang hit her tongue and she was so unsure of herself, of what to do, but she took his instructions seriously, winding her tongue around the underside of his cock. She tasted her own sweet nectar, combined with his muskier fluid, and curiosity got the better of her, making her seek out more of the flavour.

Father Mackay took her enthusiasm well and began to pump into her mouth faster, his balls smacked against her chin as he built up speed. He grasped her hair tight and felt that tool of his throb once more. The girth of his organ swelling out against her tongue, stretching her mouth a little more as desire resurged to his shaft.

She glanced up at him before she was forced to close her eyes again, feeling him throb so deeply in her throat.

Before entering his chamber, she'd been an innocent school girl, just hoping for a job.

But he'd changed her. Introduced her to something she never knew she'd been missing, and it sent a tremble through her bound form. Her tongue worked over him, cleaning him of their taint, exploring his hardening flesh with her moist mouth.

Yet the more she moved her moist, wet tongue about his throbbing cock, the more it became apparent he'd not be contented with just a cleaning. He shoved his dick between her plush lips, grunted and moaned so lewdly as he filled her mouth with his shaft.

The large, husky man shuddered as he moaned out, his dick throbbing erratically. He was more than twice her age, well past his youthful years, yet she managed to get him hard for her twice in a row. Managed to kindle that need in him yet again.

"Fuck I'm gonna cum again," he rasped so crassly, the Father speaking such filthy words in his rapture.

And she knew his words were wrong, but his tone of voice... She couldn't hide the way it made her body react so lewdly, her tongue probing him more eagerly and curling about this head before he forced her down further until he touched against the back of her throat and made her gag, then caused thick saliva to coat him.

That new layer of viscous spit coated his shaft, made the thrust of his manhood easier. He continued to plunge deep into her mouth, probing her throat just a little, until he started to buckle over her once more. The once gentle and passionate preacher had changed.

Oh, he still held passion, but it was of a different sort. And all for her. Her flesh.

"God—" he choked off, tensing up as he pressed his veiny

member into her deeper. "Gonna cum again," he said, and nary a moment too soon. For the thick gouts of his second cumming came quickly after, rich salty seed blasted across her tongue and over the roof of her mouth.

It was another confusing act, the sensation overpowering to her as she struggled not to choke on it. It was hard for her to take it all, to not sputter, but she'd remembered what he'd said. That she was to clean his tool.

And so as soon as his hips stopped, she went back to it, licking him so lewdly and cleaning him of not just his own cum, but trying to lave up her spittle as well.

That attentive cleaning made him twitch and moan, that dedication to obedience made him pet her hair and cheek.

"There you go, child," he husked softly, watching her cheeks dimple and swell in succession as she cleaned him up. Until finally, she was done to his satisfaction and he tugged back his hips and let his stiff member bob before her. "You did very well," he said, tucking himself back into his frock.

Yet she didn't know what she'd done. Her mind swam as she looked up at him, as if she'd find guidance. Which wasn't strange. After all, he was the man who'd helped to raise her into the woman she was, even though she hadn't attended in so long.

But all her core guiding principles were instilled in her because of him, so his compliment caused her to smile.

The Father bent down and began to untie her binds, freeing her hands one at a time.

"You clearly remain devoted my child," he said to her with a gentle smile. "And you have the churches endorsement, truly," he remarked, clasping her hands then and helping her rise up once more, and let the trickle of his pearly white cum run down her inner thighs.

She rubbed her wrists, moved around the desk and into him on uncertain legs, as if she might topple were it not for his strong hands holding her up.

"What did we just do?" she asked softly.

There were no televisions to corrupt her mind, and she'd been kept oh so sheltered from all bawdy talk. Yet she knew that was a place people weren't to touch, not even her, but now she wondered why.

"You saved yourself for the Lord, my child," he said to her with a gentle hand upon her back. "And He is proud. But your sacrifice is between Him and us, understand?" he said, brow raised at her in question. "You'll say nothing to anyone else about what we did here. Yes?" He tilted his head and studied her hard.

She nodded her head, ever the obedient young woman, and took in a deep breath.

"Yes, Father," she said softly. "I won't say a word."

"Good," he said, and calmly guided her over toward the door, leaving her panties back behind them, upon his floor. "And I expect to see you here every Sunday from now on, my child. Bright and early, before everyone else. You still have some lost time to make up for," he said with a smile and a rather jovial disposition.

"Of course, Father," she agreed, looking over him as if seeing him for the first time, flushing as she gnawed her lower lip. "Every Sunday."

Innocent Tease: Pleasure

Book Themes: Age Gap Sex, Older Man/Young Woman, Creampie, Breeding
Word Count: 6501

Amy was still in a daze when she walked out of the parish church, her first time with a man but moments earlier. The sun had official risen on the day, bright and high, and the town was actually starting to come to life along with the warmth. She could see the students filing into the schoolhouse where she'd spent so many years of her life.

She wanted to rush back there and ask her teacher, Mr. Muran, for advice. Everything that had happened with the Father had been so confusing. Leaving her head a mess. Yet she knew she still had one more man to convince before she could get her job as a teaching assistant. And then she'd work side by side with Mr. Muran.

The town hall, small as it was, sat right there but a stone's throw away.

She made her way on over, pushed her way through the door

to find the secretary just settling in, the older woman looking up with surprise at her.

"Oh, good morning Amy," she said, because of course everyone knew everyone in that little town of hers. "Shouldn't you be at school? It's your last day before summer break, but I never took you as the type to miss anything," she said in a warm, kindly fashion.

"Mr. Muran has requested I speak to the Mayor, Ma'am," she said respectfully with a soft bow to her head. Her blue eyes flit upwards as she smiled, that brown braid still coiled around her neck.

She tugged the navy blue blazer over her chest a little tighter, though with how large her breasts were and how ill fitted her school uniform was, it was impossible. The navy contrasted against the tan of her skin, and she set down her book bag.

"Would you be able to check if he's available?"

"Oh," the woman said simply, sounding a little saddened. "Sorry to say this, dear, but the Mayor's out of the office today. He went fishing with an old friend, you see," she remarked with a gentle smile. "Off by the lake, down from the river," she stated. "So you'll have to try back tomorrow. Should I book you an appointment?" she asked.

"Sure," Amy said with a smile, but she had other plans. She'd simply go down and convince him that very day. There was no way she could sleep if she didn't have it resolved.

She rolled up on her toes, her maryjanes helping her be a bit taller than normal, as she felt the air brush past her bare slit.

After a brief arrangement of an appointment, Amy set out with her backpack on. She headed to the river, which wasn't hard, since everyone knew where it was. All the farms in the area had little drainages off from it to fuel the crops on their land after all.

Off into the woods, she trekked over the ground. The mary-janes made things a little harder on her than normal when she went for walks in the wild, but sheer determination pushed her on. The heat of the sun however grew, and the chill of that morning was long gone by the time she found the river itself.

Following the babbling river she finally had to stop after nearly an hour, and take off her jacket. She was sweating and needed some relief from the exertion and the sun.

She sighed as she tucked her blazer away, but even that white blouse was warm and she had to fan herself. She glanced towards the water, then around at her surroundings.

Surely no one could blame her if she took a brief break from her walk to cool off in the river.

She rolled her white knee socks down over her calves and unbuckled her scuffed maryjanes, stepping out of them both. Her legs were tanned from working in the fields in her shorts so often, the curvy limbs firm and yet soft all at once. She unbuttoned her blouse, revealing the paler skin beneath as she shrugged it off to her own relief.

Her bra was simple of make, delicate and without padding, not as though she needed any. Her breasts were large and full above her nipped waist, and she folded the shirt to lay atop her bag.

Though she remembered that she wasn't wearing any panties and frowned, looking at the glittering water so longingly. She wanted to take a quick dip, but couldn't get her skirt wet...

She stepped nearer the edge of the river, and dipped her bare toe in, her body instantly responding to the chill with goosebumps up her arm. As she let the rest of her foot sink into the water, her nipples hardened as well and she let out a sigh of relief.

How often had she swam in the river? Yet always she'd had on her bra and panties.

Her eyes glanced around once more before she stepped in a bit further. Perhaps if she just let the water caress her legs it'd cool her off enough to continue on her trek.

For all her cautious looking about though, she'd missed the sight of an old familiar face sat down upon the rocks nearby. Mr. Kerny, her father's friend, lounged by a rock not far from her, and saw every moment of her casual reclining.

He was a big man, a hard working farming with sun-bleached hair and a rock hard body that was more tanned than her own. He sat nearby, partially shrouded by the shrubs and rocks along the river, but when he stood up... the towering man was hard to miss.

Especially since he wore no shirt himself, and left all those hard, rippling pecs and abs exposed to her view. Reminding her of why she'd had a crush on him back before Mr. Muran became her teacher and stole her fancies away.

"Amy?" he said in his deep voice, a smile on his face as he strode along the river closer to her. "Damn girl... I didn't recognize you at first," he said.

"Mr. Kerny!" she gasped after she spun about on the slippery rocks, nearly losing her balance and tumbling into the water. She caught herself just in time, but ended up standing, awkwardly, as her arms tried to cover her torso.

Her entire body blushed, her chest and face turning such a deep shade of pink.

"I didn't see you there."

His work pants were rolled up to his knees and he splashed into the water at her fumbling display, rushing in to put his thick, muscled arms about her for security.

"Damn girl, you gotta watch out," he said, ever one with the foul language. Her father had said that's why he'd quit inviting Mr. Kerny around, but Amy had her doubts. After all, her father had no problem with it all the years she was growing up. Why the sudden change?

Though such thoughts were far from her mind as the towering, tanned man held her against his stunning physique, looking at her with warmth and joviality.

"I'll be a pig's son if you ain't the spittin' image of your ma though," he said affectionately, the older man having but the faintest crinkles near the corners of his eyes, still looking so fit and youthful in his masculine strength.

She soothed at his warm touch, at the fact that he gratefully wasn't far enough away any longer to see her half nude body. The familiarity of his scent flared her nostrils and she couldn't help but smile at his compliment. Not a day went by she didn't miss her mother, and being compared to her was so welcome.

"Thanks," she said softly. "Sometimes hard to remember what she looks like now."

Mr. Kerny raised a hand up to touch her tanned cheek, his hard thumb stroking over her skin as he smiled down at her so fondly.

"Only look in the mirror," he said with a fond smile, that thick arm about her bulging with such rock hard muscle that twitched into her flesh, pulling her in against him a little tighter. He looked entranced by her, and not only because he was lost in the memory of her mother. He held her tight and leaned in close.

"Your ma and I were real close growin' up," he said to her in a low husk. "Always was so sad she went with your pa over me. But I never did lose my wild streak until too late," he said, though judging by all her father said about him, the man never did lose his wild streak. Only hid it better.

She felt so safe in his arms, and after the confusing meeting with the priest, she needed someone like him. She relaxed into his arms, though still she felt that embarrassment and desire to run and grab her clothes.

But he'd been so kind, and she didn't want to be rude.

"They never told me that," she said thoughtfully, and was uncertain how she felt about her mother having chosen between the two of them.

"Aw, I was just one among many," he said with a bright smile to her, "your ma had the pick of the town, and then some." He grinned down at her affectionately, his blue eyes twinkling in the daylight reflecting off the river as he stroked her cheek on back to her hair, where he played lightly with her braid.

"She was the prettiest, sweetest gal in the whole town, and beyond from what I've seen," he stated sincerely, though with how he looked down at her, she felt like he was saying it about her instead. Every word of it intended for her rather than her departed mother.

It only made her flush deepen.

"I should really go," she said softly. "I'm supposed to go find the Mayor."

She took a step back, but with how the rocks were slippery

and the way the man held her, she slipped forward, her face impacting against his hard chest and making her cling to him tighter.

"Ah!" she squeaked out in surprise.

Mr. Kerny was quick to pick her up though, his arms grasping at her tightly, though through the tussle an embarrassing thing happened, and his hand went up her skirt to rest upon her bare ass cheek, with nothing between them.

"Whoa, easy now!" he urged with a big smile despite his surprised look. "C'mon," he said, and very nonchalantly he scooped her up in his arms and carried her out of the water as if she weighed nothing. Though the downside was he carried her to *his* side of the river, away from her things.

Her leg kicked as her skirt fell away from her ass, water trickling down over her calf and off her toe as she looked at him. He was a really good-looking man, though that just made her skin prickle and her heart thump louder and she had to look away.

Mr. Kerny laid her out upon a rough blanket he'd been using on the other side of the river, next to his fishing equipment that'd seemingly gone unused. He bent his knees and very gingerly handled her like a delicate doll, smiling all the while he got down onto his side next to her.

"It's crazy to see what a woman you've grown into after all these years," he remarked, and he reached out, touching his hand to her thigh, that warm, strong masculine presence of his comforting.

And yet it was something more as well, and though she relaxed, she swallowed down her misgivings.

"Thanks, Mr. Kerny," she said, her legs prickling coldly as the water evaporated from them and cooled her flesh.

"Why don't you come around anymore?"

His face fell a moment, but the big, cheerful grin she knew spread back across his broad, rock-jawed face again in no time and he reached up to pinch her chin just lightly.

"Not because I don't wanna see you," he remarked fondly, though his eyes had a hard time lingering on her face as old. That blue gaze of his constantly drawn down over her body as his hand stroked along her tanned thigh down to her knee, then up again.

"Your pa don't much care for me no more," he said with a shrug of those broad shoulders. "Guess it was your ma that softened him to me in the first place," he said, though that was hard to believe with how the two men had got along before, always joking, laughing, having so much fun.

But she shook her head sadly. There were things she understood that she didn't know, but that didn't stop her curiosity. Yet she constantly felt like if she dug deeper into the sudden change in her father, she'd rather just not know.

Her hand rested atop his as her skin dried and she let out an exhale.

"I'm supposed to talk to the Mayor and he's out fishing. You seen him today?"

Mr. Kerny shook his head and gave her thigh a warm squeeze as he leaned in so very close to her. His head was propped up on his palm as he lingered so close, giving her time to appreciate his masculine beauty. The way his brown work pants hung so delightfully low, she could see the lines along his hips that formed a sort of V-shape towards his groin. His light blonde chest hair even came down to a little arrow pointing the way to his manhood below. A topic she was now more acquainted with.

"Ain't seen nobody but you today," he explained with a soft smile, leaning in closer to her still, his gentle musk on the air as his bicep bulged beneath his head. "An' after seein' you, I don't care to see nobody else," he said with a cheerful grin, his every word, his every look, having a way of making her feel like she was the only woman in the world.

She flushed so brightly, feeling her heart flutter in her chest as she tried to pull away, laying back fully on the blanket as she smiled up at him.

"I really should go find him," she murmured. "It's really important, otherwise I wouldn't have come all this way."

"What, really?" he said with a bright, white-toothed grin, the broad, handsome man rising up over her as he pressed her leg down. "More important than reconnectin' with an old friend?"

he said with a light tickle to her soft inner-thigh. "'Cause I remember a time when you was cute as a button but had a crush on me," he stated as he got over her, that hard mass of muscle on full display. "You'd never rush off on me in those days."

The fact that he'd noticed made her skin go molten red and she had to close her blue eyes in horror. She squirmed uncomfortably as her breathing quickened and she bit down on her lower lip.

"Crush?" she asked, after letting the flesh pop free of her mouth.

"Yeah, I knew you had a lil' crush," he said, his strong hand moving up her thigh, pushing up her skirt so slowly she didn't even notice. "Didn't say nothin' though, 'cause I didn't wanna embarrass my favourite girl."

He supported himself on one thick arm over her as the other ended up flipping up her skirt, exposing her cunny, that little slit still puffy from her first time.

"I've missed seein' ya, Amy. Especially so now that I get ta see what a fine, full grown lady you've become," he said in a lower husk, the familiarity still there, but the jovial nature of his voice replaced by something deeper. Desirous.

She felt the fabric shift, the air sweep against her sex and she gasped as she looked at him. She wanted to shimmy away, to disappear into the blanket, and yet all she could do was stare at him, her lips parted in confusion.

Her thick legs pressed together, trying to hide that puffy, wet slit, her hand moving to flip her skirt back down.

"What're you doing?" she exhaled.

It was too late though, because he looked down and saw she wasn't wearing a stitch of clothing beneath her skirt. Even caught a glimpse of that little pussy of hers, and his eyes lit up with it.

"God Amy," he said as if in shock, and she thought he'd pull away, apologize for getting carried away with himself. Instead he reached up and cupped her cheek, then leaned in to place a warm, passionate kiss upon her lips. That tongue of his prying its way through her lips to kiss at her and fence with her own moist muscle as he loomed over her.

She was so startled that she could do nothing more than bend to his wishes, her blue eyes large and filled with shock.

Yet she remembered back to her childhood, to thinking about him for all those long, winter nights. Dreaming of him touching her, kissing her...

Her heart raced as she relaxed — only slightly — as she tasted him and then pulled away, sucking her lower lip into her mouth.

He rubbed along her cheek, back to her braided ponytail, and then lowered his body down, that hard muscular mass pressing to her large breasts as he licked his lips and stared into her eyes.

He plucked another kiss from her mouth, moved his hand down over her bare shoulder, along her side to cup her breast, squeeze that over-ripe mound, feel its soft, yet supple flesh through the thin fabric of her barely there bra.

"You awoke a beast inside of me, Amy," he said in a deep, low husk.

She didn't know what that meant, but something in her recognized that tone, and her body throbbed with desire even as she tried to shimmy away. Her nipple, though, hardened beneath his touch, stretching out that barely-there material.

"Mr. Kerny," she whimpered, but she didn't want him to stop. Yet she did, all at once. It was so confusing.

He squeezed her breast one final time, then slid his hand down to grasp a hold of her thigh and pull her back down to him those few inches she'd shifted away. He was so strong, there was no resisting him even if she fully wanted to. It only grew harder and harder to summon up that desire to resist as she looked down over his hard body, saw that obscenely growing bulge in his brown work pants.

"Your ma and me couldn't be together Amy," he said to her, "but don't mean we can't." He had her beneath him again perfectly, and he grasped a hold of her tightly to keep it that way as he leaned in and kissed her hard and deep.

"I can't be with you," Amy breathed out, her brows tilting upwards, and her breath quickening. She had a life to lead, a job to get!

Her lower lip trembled, though, and she lifted her head to

kiss him back, just a soft, childish peck. Her mind was awash with emotions, swirling so dangerously as she tried to sort them out and figure what was right and what was wrong.

"Sweet Amy," he said as he ran his hand back up her tanned thigh, above the tanline as her skirt was nudged back up to expose her little cunny. "Yes you can, I'll show you how. and nobody needs to know about it," he said as he rose up and began to undo his pants. All it took was that one button, and they practically burst open, to reveal that thick, obscenely large shaft beneath.

If there was a beast in him that she awoke, it was certainly that cock of his. It was bigger than the one that Father had, of that she was certain. It throbbed thickly, the foreskin at the crown rolled back a little to show a big, purple tip slick with precum.

Her eyes widened and for a moment it was as though all of her blood rushed from her head, leaving her to swoon.

She stared at him so lewdly, unable to take her eyes from it even as her mind and body were swirled with confusion and anguish. She was so damned uncertain about what to do, of how to respond, and she finally managed to raise her gaze to his face.

Her eyebrows were pointed up in confusion, unable to still the tremors that ran through her.

She barely even registered when he reached out, and moved to undo her bra, his strong hands and his animal lust for her leading to him breaking the garment, letting her thick tits spill out across her chest. Though that only exposed a deep growl from him.

"Fuck Amy, I take it back," he said, and cupped one of her exposed breasts, squeezed and fondled it. "You're even hotter than your ma ever was," he said right before he lunged in and wrapped his lips about one of her engorged teats, licked at her pale pink nipple and areola in his hunger.

She squealed, loudly, her spine arching and her body betraying her as it pushed that hefty flesh towards him eagerly.

It was a surreal sensation, and her body was exploding with such desire and lust, even as she tried to fight against it. She didn't know what had happened with the Father, hadn't had time to contemplate it, but this was wholly different.

Her body squirmed against him as her nipple stiffened against his eager tongue, that stiff peak pressed to his wet muscle.

Yet, had it not been for the Father introducing her to carnal things, she'd likely not have reacted at all as she did. Would have found the surprise and shock within her to pull away. Instead, Mr. Kerny had her beneath him and ravaged her soft, supple flesh with his needy hands and hungry mouth.

She could even feel that thick, throbbing dick of his bump against her inner thigh as she lifted it up, feel it nudge to her lower stomach and smear his slick, precum over her skin as he suckled at her thick breast.

She flushed so brightly at the sensation of pleasure as it kept shooting through her, unbidden, and she tried to shift away, but she didn't want him to let her.

Her bare foot pressed against the blanket, as if she could somehow stand with his bulk atop her, but she knew it was fruitless.

More than that, she wanted it to be fruitless.

There was some part of her that had been awoken earlier that day, some carnal part of her mind and body that longed for a man's touch.

The Father had taken her for God, but Mr. Kerny? He'd take her for who she was. Pure and simple. That should have bothered her more, but it only made it sweeter. He lusted for her without question, longed to have her.

He squeezed her tighter, kept her pinned there as he pulled his mouth back off her tit, leaving it to jiggle as he looked her over.

"I need you right now," he said, pushing down his pants another couple of inches, to let his thick balls spill out as well before taking hold of her two legs, and spreading their smooth flesh wide before him. "I need to feel you around me, Amy," he husked roughly.

She was helpless against him, her body so yielding as those soft thighs were pried apart and that puffy pink sex was unveiled.

She looked up at the heavens and wondered what she was to do, but there was only silence, her sexual excitement having numbed her brain.

Her school skirt still flipped up around her stomach she looked down her body at him, terror and desire mixed in her expression.

"We shouldn't be doing this," she protested.

He kissed her, silenced her protests with his mouth as he brought his heavy bulk down upon her once more, that thick, pulsating shaft throbbing against her cunt as he ground his hips against her. A low, vibrating moan travelled through his throat and across to her mouth as he felt the slick moisture of her quim.

When he broke their lips apart he quickly kissed her again then said:

"Nobody'll know," and he prodded his thick cock to her cunt, slowly began to squeeze its girth into her recently deflowered pussy. It was a slow motion, taking time to stretch her little flower around his raw, hard cock, but he was intent on making it happen, and his hard, pecs and abs tensed with the motions as he gripped the base of his dick, pushing himself into her with a low, lewd moan.

Her eyes widened, as if she had no way to stop it and she were simply watching it happen from the outside.

But oh, her body sang as it sunk into the blanket, her eyes fluttering closed as he began to impale her. She was still sore, but soaking wet, and it let him ease that thick cock into her so much more easily.

The innocent, naive woman taken by her childhood crush, and writhing beneath him in pleasure.

Mr. Kerny filled her up in a way that the Father couldn't have. He sank to her utmost depths and let loose such a deep, satisfied moan, so hard and masculine. He throbbed inside of her, the vein-bulging shaft stretching her further as he savoured that tight clench of hers for a while.

"Oh Amy," he moaned, "just like yer ma..."

Then without further delay, he tugged back those rock hard hips of his and pulled his dick back. She was wrapped so tautly about his girth she felt like he might tug her insides out with him, but instead it just felt so intensely good, and soon he was pumping into her, his beastly lust building him to a quicker rate promptly.

Her thighs were still pressed back in his hands, the soft flesh and flexible limbs held taut as her eyes rolled back in her head.

She was filled with such an intense mix of sensations and emotions, but most of all, there was desire. Need. The way he made her feel...

The Father had awoken something in her, and Mr. Kerny was only giving it more steam. She couldn't restrain the peppered moans and the little cries as he rut into her so crassly on the banks of the river.

As his brutish rutting grew faster, harder, her thick tits swayed atop her chest, rippling with each impact of his hard body. Those bulging pecs and abs of his twitched with the motions of his muscles, and he shuddered over her, such a big, strong man brought to such a quiver by the power of her soft, feminine body.

"Amy," he moaned her name aloud again, his heavy balls smacking against her ass as he thrust harder, filling her completely as he took her legs and wrapped them about his tanned waist. "I want you so bad, sweetie," he husked.

His words, his voice, they both sent a thrill through her body, her affection for him reignited by his passionate embrace. Her arms worked their way up and around him, hugging her chest to his as her breath came out in little pants and whimpers.

She scarcely felt like she could have pulled herself away from that situation, but once he was inside of her, pumping his thick manhood with such precision, she couldn't have imagined ever wanting to end it.

Even with her ass and cunny still smarting, and his thrusts doing nothing to alleviate that, he felt so damn good.

Mr. Kerny wrapped his arm about her waist, pulled her up off the ground just a little, held her there, her breasts mashed to his chest as he pumped, angling her body just right so...

She could never have fathomed such a feeling. So intense! So unlike anything she'd ever experienced, it made her feel like putty in his hands the way he took her. So much more expert than the Father had been with his intent to exact penance.

She was confused, bewildered by what was happening to her, but she wanted for more. Craved him, even as it hurt, as it felt so wonderful.

Her breathing was shorter, choppier, gulps of air into her lungs as she whimpered. Her large breasts were flattened to his chest, her head tilted back in the throes of ecstasy. Her mouth trembled and she pressed it to his, silencing her lewd sounds.

He groaned hard, his chest rumbled and she could feel his dick swell within her, straining her little cunny as he fucked her so hard and fast. He was a big, meaty powerhouse of solid muscle, a lifetime of hard labour bulking him up into such an immense man.

He struck at her just right, even as she could feel him tensing up, getting closer to his own release, a feeling she was fast growing intimate with despite her newly lost naivety.

"Cum on my cock like a good lil' girl," he roared in command to her as their lips broke apart again. "Cover my dick in your lil' girl juices!" the beast in him demanded.

His crass words were jarring to her, but they called to her flesh as she ground against him so wantonly, nature taking over her body. Her lungs gasped for air and she felt her limbs tense as her nerves coiled within her.

It was as if her pussy knew what he wanted her to do, and it throbbed more aggressively and her eyes flew wide as she felt the waves of pleasure crash over her.

Then as he felt that tensing and squeezing of her pussy around him, his eyes shut tight and he let loose a deep, strained groan as he throbbed inside of her, swelling up until he was following her into bliss. His thick cock shooting its rich, creamy seed deep into her, splattering the entrance to her womb with that virile pearly essence as he let loose such a loud roar of satisfaction.

She whined at the intense sensations as it made her toes curl, her limbs stiffen and body tighten as she came atop his cock. Her juices flowed down upon his member, mingling with his seed as he filled her so fully.

"Ohh," she panted out, her voice warbling and hoarse.

Through the tumult of their climax, he had lifted her off the ground entirely, held her in his arms and bounced her atop his thick cock. Only slowly did she come to a halt, her skirt bouncing up, revealing her bare ass as he pumped her full and felt that warm fluid run down to his balls.

As they slowly halted, he leaned in, kissed her passionately, again, then again, squeezing her to his hard chest all the while.

She trembled against him, filled with so many emotions as she tried to catch her breath, to regain her senses and understand the implications of what she'd just done before simply letting them slip away.

Instead she simply basked in the afterglow, her mind so wondrously blank.

Mr. Kerny wrapped both arms about her snugly, clasped both of her full ass cheeks in each palm, and pulled her up and down his shaft those last few times, milking the very last spurts of cum from his dick into her fertile depths until he finally stopped.

He lowered her down, rested her gently to the blanket as he bent over her, giving her a few soft kisses.

"Thank you, beautiful," he husked in a raw, hard voice. "Bein' with such a gorgeous sweetheart reminds me of old times," he said with a smile, his eyes heavily lidded as he slowly pulled his length from her, that long, glistening dick leaving her pussy gaping and drooling his seed.

She was so exhausted, her body worn and tired, but she wouldn't pull away from him. He felt so tender and safe, his strong arms holding her so gingerly, and she was afraid that if he let her go, she'd simply float away on a gust of wind.

She gnawed her lip as she looked at him, her blue eyes lidded as she tried to hide her soft smile, her breath slowly returning to normal.

"You're welcome, Mr. Kerny."

He kissed her again, then again, the two of them making out on the blanket in the warm sun, all memories of the morning chill long gone as Mr. Kerny's large body pressed upon her once more.

At long last, he got up off her, kissed his way down her chest to her belly and rose up.

"Here," he said, taking her skirt off her, "we should clean you up." And with that he simply lifted her nude form up and carried her back into the river.

Her arms wrapped around him, feeling as light as air with the ease in which he moved her. With all that strength in his arms he cradled her carefully and lowered her down into the stream to wash away the thick spunk that pooled in her cunny.

The cool water lapped at her folds, chilling her burning flesh and staving off the exhaustion she felt. She gave a soft, lazy smile, her arms covering her breasts modestly, as if he hadn't so recently been suckling upon them.

Mr. Kerny knelt down in the cool water, holding her there upon his lap with one arm as the other went down over her stomach, his thick fingers probing her puffy folds.

"Sorry about the mess, Amy," he said with that broad, warm smile on his handsome face, "lemme get it for ya." He pushed his two digits into her pussy, cleaning her of that thick, creamy mess, but more urgently he rubbed at her sensitive little clit and leaned in to kiss her mouth.

He was working her little quim more than anything else, and he showered her with such affectionate kisses all the while, his big, warm mouth working against hers, his tongue exploring all the while.

He felt so good, his thick fingers delving into her still throbbing pussy, making her gasp and writhe against him. She kissed him back with those amateurish little licks and pecks, her body shivering as she held herself to him.

It was so embarrassing, so titillating, and she blushed at his lewd touches that made her body grind into his hand.

The large object of her childhood crushes held her so securely as she shivered and quaked. His hand around her back came in around to grasp at one of her breasts, despite her attempts to hide them. He squeezed that fleshy mound and worked her little clit in tiny circles as their lips smacked.

Though it was clear his goal was not to clean her so much as satisfy and tease her all the more, he accomplished both as he brought her body to increasing heights. A low groan rumbling from his chest as she felt his dick still hard against her ass.

Her cunny was still so sensitive after he'd toppled her over the edge and she tried to squirm away from him but it was futile. He was holding onto her so securely, even as he groped her, and she couldn't shy away from that pleasure.

Not as it exploded within her core, tightening her pussy around his fingers, squeezing him with all her might as she screeched and writhed so dangerously.

The comforting Mr. Kerny held her tight, his strong arms resisted her flailing as she came again in his arms. His hold was unbreakable, and he kept her in his grasp all through the mind blowing sensations he caused, until at last, she felt the world spin and realized he was carrying her.

He held her body up out of the water again and brought her back to the blanket to lay her out gently with a broad smile on his face. And a long, thick cock dangling hard once more before her.

She gazed up at him, mind still in a haze as she smiled. She blocked the sun with a hand as her eyes dropped to his member before something dawned on her and she let her hand drop back to her side.

The sun was directly over him.

It must have been almost noon!

Her eyes widened and her lips dropped open as she grabbed for her skirt and her bra in her wet hands.

"It's so late," she gasped. "I was supposed to speak with the Mayor!"

This time, despite his raging lust for her still apparent, he let her get up and watched her with some confusion. His wet pants were still upon his thick thighs as he rocked back, and saw her slip her skirt back on, then struggle with her broken bra.

"Sorry about that," he muttered a bit sheepishly. "I'll buy ya a new one!" he offered, the idea occurred to him. "A present. I'll...

pick one up in town and y'know... we'll see each other again," he said with a broad grin on his face.

She tossed it aside with a nod to him, a frantic smile on her lips.

"Yes, okay, I'd like that. Can you carry me over to my things now?" she asked, her tone urgent.

That request seemed to elicit an even bigger grin from him, the large, muscular man eager to be of service to her.

"Yes miss," he said, scooping her back up into his arms, making her thick tits jiggle as he carried her back through the water over to her things. He put her down gently, "I'll come a callin' on you for that date the moment I get that new bra."

He looked downright overjoyed at the prospect.

She grabbed for her blouse, pulling it on over her bare chest and quickly buttoned it up, petting down her navy skirt as she smiled at him.

She couldn't help that she was a little excited as well, and not just for the new bra.

"I'm... sorry I have to go. It's just very important."

Mr. Kerny leaned in, put his arms around her and gave her a final kiss goodbye. Though in the process he squeezed her ass over that navy skirt and pressed his throbbing manhood into her.

"Of course, sweetheart," he said, pulling back away and giving her rear an encouraging pat. "Go on, and I'll be seein' you soon. Promise ya that," he said with a wink. "Now run along before I can't help myself and keep ya another hour or two."

She grabbed her bookbag and, with a fleeting look behind her, scampered off down the river.

Innocent Tease: Dirty

Book Themes: Age Gap Sex, Older Man/Young
Woman, Creampie, Breeding, Blowjob
Word Count: 5,403

A my was left to wander down the river by herself, albeit a little lighter after being deprived of her bra. The warm midday sun shined down upon her, and made wearing her jacket uncomfortable, though without it her white blouse proved rather see through, displaying the sight of her pinkened areolas beneath.

If only she'd noticed.

Instead she carried on down the river over the grassy earth towards her destination, oblivious to everything but the warmth upon her face and shoulders. That was, until she stumbled upon the mayor. He was the person she had to convince in order to get a job teaching at the school, and after taking her punishment from the priest, and running into a childhood crush, her day had quickly gone from exciting, to confusing, and back again.

The mayor was a striking man, tall and lean. He stood at the river near the lake, casting his rod out into the water. He wore a hat to keep the sun out of his eyes and protect his pale face, but Amy knew him well, having seen him around enough.

His sleeves were rolled up to his elbows, showing his leanly muscled forearms. He was older than her father, she was sure, with silvery hair, but he was handsome and well taken care of. He didn't look his age in his chiselled face.

Amy paused as she watched him, reaching up to touch her auburn french braid, angling it over her shoulder and letting it rest along her white blouse. She still wore her navy school skirt, knee highs pulled up, and scuffed maryjanes on her feet.

Her father was a farmer, and though she'd attended school until she was eighteen, she still wasn't ready to follow his life. She was far too curious and intrepid for that. So all she had to do was convince the mayor to let her be a teacher's aide and all her dreams would come true.

She cleared her throat to draw his gaze, her sparkling blue eyes upon him.

"Sir?"

"Just a second," he said in a low husk, not jumping at her sudden interruption as he seemed to have heard her approach. He took his time, angling his rod and then pulling back... nothing. "Darn," he cursed so gingerly, the mayor ever a careful speaker.

"Now what can I help you wi--" he turned but his sentence was cut off mid-word as he stared at her. "Amy," he said, her name breathed out on a soft exhale. He'd not spoken with her directly in years. Her father had too much of a problem with him. Going way back, before the others even.

Though Amy wasn't aware of it, it wasn't just seeing her after so long that made him stare at her in surprise. It was the lewd display she made, with her rather ample breasts showing through her pale, see-through top that caught the majority of his attention.

She smiled so brightly, oblivious to the way his gaze trailed, how her shirt was barely held together under the strain of her buttons. They couldn't afford new clothes often, so when she hit her growth spurt, she was forced to make due. Even after her breasts grew to a nearly unwieldy size.

"Hi Mr. Aaronson. I... hope you don't mind my interruption?"

His face lit up with a broad smile, that wasn't even entirely due to the lewd sight of her exposed breasts.

"Of course not, Amy," he said, reeling in his rod and then laying it carefully aside as he turned to her. He pulled his hat off, showing his sleek, silvery hair beneath as he approached her. "It's been a long time, sweetie, hasn't it?" he remarked, unable to take his eyes off her.

"Yea, I've been real busy with school and things," she agreed, her head deferred to him, gaze down towards her scuffed maryjanes.

"That's actually what I came to talk to you about. Mr. Muran might have mentioned my graduating?"

It took him a moment to clue in, but then he finally did and nodded his head.

"Oh yeah!" he said with a smile, his mind working as little slower with the nubile young woman before him, so enticingly beautiful. "God though, Amy... I didn't hardly believe it until just now," he let out a whistle, "damn if you ain't the spittin' image of your ma back in the old days. Only..." he lifted his hand and was about to remark on her breasts before he thought better of it. "Prettier still!" he said instead with a smile.

She flushed, the compliment warming her as she stared at the grass. She'd forgotten how nice he'd always been to her, growing up, before she wasn't allowed to speak with him as often.

Her fingers ran along her braid idly as she rolled onto her toes, then back down to her heels.

"Thank you, Mr. Aaronson," she said softly.

"Now then, a pretty young girl like you's not playin' hookie is she?" he asked with a playful tone as he stepped right up to her, towering over her as he reached out to place his hands upon her two arms and rub over them softly. "'Cause looks to me like you're up to trouble, Amy," he remarked with a wry smile.

She shook her head urgently, a blush going through her at his words. She'd been getting into a lot of trouble, but had done her best to clean up and rid all traces of the other men's lusts.

She swallowed, unable to look at him as her cheeks burned red.

"I have permission to miss today, Sir," she promised. "To come speak with you. I... know you handle the budget for some of the things with the school and I've been tasked with convincing you that I'm the right woman for the job."

"Well," the mayor said, looking down over her once more, unable to tear his gaze away from those lewdly displayed breasts as they strained the fabric of her top. "You've certainly gotten off to a great start, Amy... though I must say, I'm pretty surprised by how brazen you've become. Though... I suppose I shouldn't be."

He reached out, and helped himself to undoing her top, letting the first button pop open.

"Your mother was just like you," he said warmly.

Her blue eyes widened in shock, her thick lips falling open as those large breasts strained against the give of her top. Her breath quickened and she took a tentative step backwards, her head tilted to the side.

She didn't know what to make of it, of his words, of the way he was behaving, and yet her skin responded, prickling with heat and interest.

"Sir?" she asked, the word so soft.

"It's okay Amy," he said with a warm, reassuring voice as he followed after her. "I was gonna support you for the spot anyhow, all you had to do was ask," he stated as he reached back out to pop another button of her top.

"But hey, this'll really make me excited to do so," he stated, tugging her top open to let her thick breasts spill out against her chest, his hand reaching in to cup one of those supple mounds.

"Oh damn," he said with a blissful smile on his face, "nothin' quite like these." His fingers sank into her breast flesh, making it bulge about his digits.

She was shocked into silence, not even moving away from his hands, though she blinked. His behaviour had stunned her, that warm, affectionate tone pairing with his sudden touches. She didn't know how to react, and she worked her gaze up to his, filled with such curiosity.

Her heart beat hard in her chest, her nipple instantly hardening beneath his palm. She almost felt as if there might be something she was doing wrong, enticing so many men to want her that day.

She didn't understand it, and yet she couldn't make herself move from him. He might become offended, and withdraw his support for her!

The tall, slender mayor fondled her breast so affectionately, worked her soft yet supple flesh, even gently pinched her pinkened nipple between his thumb and index finger. He reached up and cupped the other nubile mound as well, looking down at those two tits in his hands as he licked his lips.

"We've all missed your mom, Amy. It's so great to have you coming into your own now," he said as he got down onto one knee and held aloft that breast of hers as he leaned in to lick at her teat before placing his lips around it and suckling softly.

She didn't understand his words, the implications behind it.

She didn't have much time to ponder it, either, as he groped her so freely, her body responding of its own accord. She whimpered as her head tilted back, a soft utterance let out towards the heavens as he licked her clean flesh.

Not long before she'd been washed in the river by her old childhood crush, and now the mayor was sullying her flesh with his eager tongue. But she couldn't help how good it felt, how much she wanted and desired more, her skin prickled with excitement.

She dared not look down, to see that silver-haired fox suckle at her teat with carnal hunger. Working that pale mound in his warm, moist mouth as the other he worked in his hand, kneading its supple flesh, only to then switch and bring his mouth to that one instead. It left the other tit to feel the warm air upon the saliva glistening mound.

He gave a low groan of excitement as he grew ever more enthusiastic with her, getting lost in his desire for her gorgeous young flesh.

Her knees were growing weak and wobbly, and her body trembled with such urgency, such need that she was only recently becoming familiar with.

Not but eight hours ago she'd been a virgin, ignorant to the touch of a man. Yet the dam had broken, and all that pent up lust that had been simmering beneath the surface had rushed forth.

A soft moan pressed from her lips, even as her brows furrowed in confusion and angst. She couldn't stand any longer, her legs like those of a fawn as she moved, settling herself onto the shore, her head rolling back as her calves pressed into her thighs.

Mr. Aaronson moved with her, positioning himself atop her as he suckled at her teat, groped her breast and then let his hands roam over her form. He was hungry for her, as Mr. Kerny had been before him. When he plucked his mouth from her breast, she could see the hunger in his eyes.

"You're a naughty girl, Amy," he remarked as he pushed his hands up her thighs, revealing her lack of panties beneath, seeing her puffy, reddened slit there. "But don't worry," he said as he began to undo his own shirt, showing off the lean, hard muscle beneath, "I like bad girls."

She was so pliable against him, submissive to his motions, even as she shrank from his words with uncertainty. Amy'd barely had any time to process what had happened with the priest and Mr. Kerny, but she couldn't hide her own arousal, her desperate curiosity.

She stared, watching him as he moved against her and then himself, with such an intense gaze, trying to drink it all in.

Despite his status as mayor, his pale body was hard and muscular, very lean but cut. His pecs and abs showing prominently, with an obvious indent along his hips down towards his groin. And then when he freed his manhood, that impressive shaft bobbed free, so very stiff and erect for her, criss-crossed with thick veins.

"You pretty little vixen," he remarked with a bright smile, so obviously delighting in her as he rests a hand upon her knee and starts to slowly pry her thighs apart. "You could get anything you want with those big tits of yours, and you know it." He spoke in a velvety voice, looking so entranced with her.

And Amy was like a deer in headlights, uncertain of what to do, if anything. Her world had been shaken upside down so quickly, her morality left in tatters along with her innocence.

It was as though once the veil was lifted from her eyes, she couldn't help but become more enchanted and interested in the world. She'd always been a curious girl, and had grown into an interested and thoughtful woman, and being exposed to so many new sensations and feelings in such a short time was an absolute rush.

The mayor laid her out upon the banks of the river, splayed her legs open and got in between them. He held his manhood in one hand, and propped himself up by grasping her breast in the other.

"Ohh, I've not had a good fuck since your dear mother left us," he said as he licked his lips, guiding his dick up and down her slit, toying with her slick cunny, teasing her sensitive clit. She was still a little sore from losing her virginity, from being pounded by Mr. Kerny's big dick not long before, but still... the excitement and pleasure that rose from her loins was dizzying.

Her head tilted back and she let out a sound of mewled pleasure, her body to tense as she was posed like a doll. His words flooded her head, dizzying her, and her whimpers grew louder, more passionate.

She wanted it. Even if she was confused and conflicted, it didn't stop her interest, the way she craved him. Her lips dropped open as she sucked in a breath, biting down on her lower lip to quiet her little whimpers.

Once the older man was inside of her everything but their fucking ceased to exist. It was just the throb of his dick inside her tight cunny that mattered, the way her narrow little canal squeezed his shaft and made him moan aloud.

"Ohhh fuck," he groaned out, the words so deep and heavy, "you've a sweeter little pussy than I even imagined!" He exalted her cunt even as he began to rock his hips, pumping himself into her slowly on the banks of the river. That lean, hard muscle over-looking her twitching and tensing as he moved.

She cried out, her body so sore and yet it only made the sensations more intense. Both good and bad. She couldn't silence herself in the face of that as her large breasts rocked against her ribs with each thrust.

Her legs pressed into his sides, holding him there as she cooed, "Mr. Aaronson," affectionately.

His dick pumped into her raw, nothing between her and the older man as he thrust his shaft in deep with each push of his hips. He squeezed and fondled one of her breasts, forcing his eyes open to watch in awe as that big, round tit melded to his touch, until his hunger overcame him and he lunged in for it, licking at her teat with a ravenous desire, suckling upon it as he pumped and thrust.

She arched her back, shoulders and head digging into the shore as she forced her tit into his mouth, that tongue brushing against her feeling so amazing.

Her body was on fire, alight with new sensations and she couldn't help but squirm and writhe beneath him. She was acting every bit the wanton slut, even though she'd been so inno-cent to a man's touch until that very day.

Innocent not only to their touch, but to all things about them. Despite what they'd hinted at about her mother, she'd never so much as touched a boy inappropriately or had one do that to her. She'd had crushes, innocent little crushes, but that was it.

So to be experiencing the third man in a few hours to be fucking her raw, unprotected and uninhibited was beyond her imagination.

Yet there he was, the mayor as dashingly handsome as he was, his hard chest on display as his pale, throbbing cock vanished into her cunny, only to pull back out glistening with her honey, again and again.

"Fuck," he groaned aloud, his dick swelling inside her, pulsating with desire, "you're the most beautiful girl in town, and I've never felt so damn good before!"

She was so wet, none of those nerves or hesitations doing anything to weaken her arousal. Her arms went around him, and for those few blissful, wonderful moments, she felt complete. Her worries melted away and was simply left in that carnal embrace, her body grinding into him so lewdly.

It was as though it responded of its own accord, that sweet clench of her pussy, the hardening of her nipple, all completely out of her control. Her purred moans filled the warm, spring air as her legs latched onto him, tugging him inwards.

In so little time, three strong, older men had awoken her desires, and the latest one reaped the greater reward. Pistoning his cock into her with such passion, feeling her legs tug him in and urge him on as his balls slapped noisily to her ass.

The lake was theirs, their pants and moans carrying across its waters as they rut noisily. He was captivated with her, tugging upon her nipple, suckling away before he tugged back and let that elastic teat snap into place.

His eyes trained back upon her chest, watching those thick tits circle and jiggle as he thrust harder, and harder.

Her head was spinning, dizzy with lust as she cried out, again and again, craving more. She was so much lewder about it, even as she tried to keep biting down on her lip, silencing her moans. But it was harder to calm those delightful sounds when he hit against her just so and made her cunny sing.

Mr. Aaronson's chest developed a light sheen of perspiration, that hard muscle gleaming in the midday light that reflected off the lake. He tensed and quivered, pounding her cunt as he clearly barreled towards release himself.

"Fuck! I'm gonna cum in you," he blurted out, his silver hair a little tousled by his fevered rutting, only making him look better to Amy's eyes however. And despite the tension in his body, it made him strike into her so deliciously right.

She still didn't have a great grasp of what that meant, but the way he hammered into her was perfect, so she didn't care. He could do whatever he wanted to her, that warm flood of blood thrumming against the surface of her skin and making her cheeks redden.

It was embarrassing to enjoy what he was doing so much, for she felt like it should be bad and wrong, but it felt so damned good.

When he shook atop her almost violently, and gave a long, strained moan, it was sweet bliss. The delightful pinnacle of their time together as his dick twitched inside her and then spewed his rich seed up into her fertile depths.

She didn't grasp the repercussions of it all, she just knew how good it felt — for herself and him — and the way he looked so beautifully pleased. And then, how he struck inside her cunny just right so that he brought her over the edge along with him at the exact same moment!

Her head was thrown back as her back arched, shoulders lifting off the beach as that powerful sensation jolted through her. Her pussy clenched and vibrated against his cock, her throat warbling so beautifully as her senses exploded.

It was an explosive, dizzying moment and she couldn't even be sure of how long it lasted, she only knew when it ended, he was panting atop her, fondling her large breasts and kissing at her neck and shoulder. She could feel the thick, creamy slickness of all his seed dribbling out of her cunt, for though the mayor wasn't as big as Mr. Kerny by any measure, he'd made an incredible mess of her quim.

"You're an incredible young woman," he said, breathing heavily, looking down at her with such bedroom eyes even after he'd gotten his rocks off.

She blushed, her eyes darting to the side in embarrassment at his compliment. He could do such lewd things with her, to her, and yet his words were the things that most made her belly flip. She smiled, his weight rested upon her as she took in panted breaths, trying to come back to reality.

"Mr. Aaronson," she said softly, reaching to try to push her school skirt down as if that would hide the creamy mess of his leavings between her thighs.

"Oh, so bashful," he said, sounding delighted by her. "So scandalous, yet still blushing adorably," he remarked, reaching up to stroke her cheek tenderly, he leaned in and gave the corners of her lip a kiss before he pulled out, leaving her dribbling such a thick mess.

"Do you know how to clean a man up proper, Amy dear?" he asked, reclining back onto one arm, his still stiffened shaft glistening with a mix of her honey and some smears of his creamy spunk.

And she had an inkling of an idea. To clean his tool, as the Father had said to her in the parish. Yet the reminder of what she'd done, of the taste... It still lingered in her mouth and she felt herself blush brighter.

But instinctually she licked her lips, even as she looked away bashfully.

"Come on," he beckoned her, reaching out to stroke her hair. "Not nice of you to entice a man, make a mess of him and leave him sullied," he said, as if it was all her fault, and that mess about his dick was her doing. The tug at her hair added to the importance of that task.

Her braid was coiled about his fist and she couldn't do anything to resist, even if she wanted to. He stripped her of choice and let her simply do what felt right, without worrying about how it made her seem.

Her mouth parted as she got on hands and knees, her mouth drawn to that male organ, tongue pressed to the lower row of her teeth as she looked up at him with those bright, blue eyes. She wanted to see if she was doing what he expected.

"That a girl," he said encouragingly, holding her long, braided ponytail like a leash. He watched as her mouth and tongue met his organ, and he gave a low, rumbling moan in appreciation. "I knew you wouldn't disappoint," he said, his hard chest rising and falling before her, drawing the eye to his etched muscles.

She tasted her own tang, mixed with his muskier seed, and closed her mouth about it and let her bright blue eyes flutter closed. She let herself experience him, instead, through touch and taste, her tongue trailing along his crown in curious exploration.

He reclined back, lounging up on his folded arm as he watched her work at his cock, that rigid pole twitching against her mouth and tongue, losing none of its hardness as she worked it. The sight of her bent over him, those ripe tits dangling as she suckled his manhood kept the older man rock solid as he watched, spurting some more of his precum into her mouth.

"Either you're a natural cocksucking whore, or you've been practicing, sweet Amy," he remarked to her with a deep, moaning voice.

She made a soft noise, muffled by the flesh of his cock, and her lower lip pressed against him wetly as her tongue darted upwards. She followed the taste, licking him like a lollipop and finding the little hints of flavour as she held him upright with her hand.

Mr. Aaronson twitched at her oral ministrations, wrapping her braided ponytail around his fist to tug her in closer, pull her down around his dick further. He reached his free hand out to pet her cheek and feel the bulge there from his manhood inside her mouth.

"Ohhh Amy," he said aloud, his words all deep and pleasure-laced, "you're a sweet girl. When you're working at the school, you'll have to make sure to pop by the town hall and see me now and then. I've got all kinds of things I'd like to do with a natural slut like you," he declared so casually.

His words electrified her body, making her writhe as her tongue whorled along the underside of his shaft. He was clean and free from the fluids that she was supposed to gather, but he kept tugging her in and so she didn't stop.

Her wet muscle traced along the veins, feeling them out as they throbbed against her kittenish tongue, her eyes fluttering at his words.

Mr. Aaronson groaned loud and lewdly in time with a thick, throbbing in his cock that stretched her mouth open wider. He was relishing the oral affections so deeply, every little flick or lash of her tongue eliciting a vocal response from the dashing older man.

"You can come sit in my lap in my office," he said in that deep, throaty voice, so peppered with pleasure, "pull out your tits and show your appreciation for your new job. And I'll suck those beauties until you're sore," he declared.

Her nipples responded right away, hardening so tight and aching for his mouth, even as her body flushed with shame at the natural response.

Her pussy throbbed and her hands went to his thighs, holding herself there as he guided her movements with her braid.

Her lips were full and flushed from the friction, and she teased some of his flesh into her mouth before letting it go with a pop.

Mr. Aaronson groaned aloud at that, and his lean, hard chest heaved and undulated.

"Clean the balls now too, girl," he bid her, watching with such relish as those two, ripe tits dangled down, capped with such hard nipples. "You can't half-ass a cock-cleaning, you know? You've got to gently lick and suckle that nutsac."

Her eyes opened, looking up at him with such confusion, his cock lodged in her mouth. She swiped against his flesh again before he dragged her head up off his member, leaving her lips glistening and full.

"What?" she asked, breathlessly.

His brows furrowed, and he looked confused that she didn't get it.

"Down here, girl," he said, reaching down and cupping his two balls as he head her down, directing her mouth to them. "Lick and suck, but do so very gently," he guided her to them. "You can handle that like a good little girl, can't you?" he asked, brow raised in challenge at her.

She swallowed, her eyes still upon him, his cock throbbing gently and hindering her gaze as she was so near his loins. Her tongue poked out, curiously, and ran along the textured flesh, surprised at how it responded. It wasn't firm and hard like his cock, but gave against her mouth, and she had to press herself into it more lewdly.

His reaction wasn't quite the same as when she suckled his cock, but it was a definite positive. He tugged at her braided ponytail again, pulling her into his groin as he shivered with delight.

"That's it," he said lowly, "that a girl."

She found that flavour once more, hunting it down with her tongue, her lips, her mouth, devouring him with such hungry excitement. The flesh gave to her and she chased it, her nose pressed to his skin, his cock resting against her cheek as she so ravenously cleaned him.

The mayor moaned in delight, and his dick throbbed excitedly, smacking against her face with a wet thud.

"Come on, just a lil' more..." he beckoned her lustfully, absolutely ravenous for the sight of her slathering over his balls, his dick pressed to her pretty, youthful face as she worked his organ.

The older gentleman was turned depraved with his lust for her, she realized, his features usually so warm and serious looking simply lascivious as he watched her work his cock and balls. His shaft spurt a little precum against her face.

She made a soft sound that hummed through his textured sac, eyes shutting once more. She couldn't look at him any longer, with such dark intents in his gaze. Yet never did she still the licking of her tongue, feeling him out wetly. Every time he encouraged her, she worked a little bit harder until she was sucking his sac in between her lips, tongue running along it.

He was fast reaching his limits however, and he brought his free hand from her to his dick. As she licked and suckled gently upon his balls, he began to pump his slick, saliva-glistening shaft up and down, beating it right before her face so crassly.

"I've got another lil' gift for you, Amy," he said breathily, his dick spurting more of that precum out over his purple crown.

She felt his knuckles brush against her cheek and moved down between his thighs further so he couldn't hurt her accidentally. Her lips still sucked in his flesh, even though her tang no longer resided there, simply covering him with her saliva as she hummed against his flesh in response to his words.

He wasn't satisfied with her moving away though, and he tugged her back up over his dick.

"Stop," he told her, ordering her in place, "Stay right there."

He grunted, his fist pumping so fast over that shaft as he worked himself up into a frenzy. She got to watch as he worked that cock up and down, and then in a deep, throaty moan... he came.

She got to see it all, the thick, creamy white jet of his cum shooting out, splattering across her face. Only then did she close her eyes, unable to see the rest of it as those gouts of creamy spunk lanced across her cheeks, nose, lips and chin. It was so much, even after his recent climax, and those heavy balls of his seemingly packed such an impressive amount of cum.

She let out a soft squeal, her tongue reaching out to free her lips of his seed, instinctually trying to clean herself up. Her tanned skin was laced with white, some of it dripping down her chin. She pushed herself up, onto her haunches, and a few droplets splattered down along her chest.

The mayor watched it all with such glee, seeing that little splatters of his spunk dribble onto her thick tits, he gave a deep, rumbling moan as he pumped out the last spurt onto those mounds purposefully.

"That's a good, good girl," he cooed to her affectionate, and she felt his cum-slick cock press back to her lips, unable to see with her eyes still shut. "Just one last little cleaning to do there, sweetie," he said, wanting her to wipe away the stray spunk that lingered upon his crown.

She ran her tongue along the sensitive tip and let out a soft murmur of exhausted affection as her grip loosened on his thighs.

She was so tired after such a long day of carnality, but she wouldn't fail him then, licking him until he was free of his taint.

When at last his glans were clean, he plucked his dick from her lips with a pop and tucked it back into his pants. With a deep, satisfied sigh he patted her cum-free hair approvingly.

"Very good, girl," he said almost affectionately, looking her over, her blouse undone, tits hanging out, face covered in his seed. "Be sure to stop by and see me regularly, right? Since we'll be working so close to each other now."

Part of her felt thrilled.

With his approval, and the priest's, she had claimed her dream job, working next to her crush.

And yet her mind was a haze, fingers going to her cheeks and gathering some of his cum, drawing it into her lips. Perhaps he was right. Perhaps she was just a natural slut.

A smile quirked her lips.

She couldn't wait to tell Mr. Muran.

Innocent Tease: Claimed

*Book Themes: Age Gap Sex, Older Man/Young
Woman, Impregnating Creampie, Unpro-
tected Sex, Blowjobs, Simultaneous Orgasm,
Pregnancy Sex, Teacher/Student, and
Breeding*
Word Count: 5,388

Amy was left braless, pantiless and sore by the activities of the day, but more than that, she was happy. She'd gotten what she was after, and her dream job was now hers; an assistant teacher working under her crush, Mr. Muran.

Despite how long the day had been, and how physically exhausting it'd been fucking her way to her answer, she practically skipped her way back to town through the woods. All the way, her mind rang with the joy of knowing she'd not have to go back to work at the farm, that she'd have a career doing what she loved instead.

Right alongside the man she fancied.

On her way back through town, she met some of the smiling

faces of the other townsfolk. They appeared more chipper and gossipy than usual, she noted, more of them stopping to try and chat with her. She'd not experienced such enthusiasm from them since her father pulled the two of them back after her mother's death.

She had no time for chit chat, however, and she politely excused herself each time to make her way to the school house.

Class was already ended by the time she got there, the students already gone, and — she worried — so might Mr. Muran.

Entering into the building, she called out through its simple halls.

"Mr. Muran?" her words echoing through the corridors. There were only a few classrooms, the town just wasn't that big after all. So it didn't take long for him to hear and respond.

"Back here in the classroom, Amy," he called back from behind his desk, grading some tests.

She couldn't help it. She ran, her smile so bright and enthusiastic as she came to the door, skidding to a stop as she held onto the frame, her maryjanes slipping a bit on the floor.

"Mr. Muran!" she panted, her cheeks red and her large, braless breasts heaving from the jog. "They said yes!"

Her french braid was messed up, brown hair a little fuzzy along it, her navy skirt clasped around her hips and her socks pulled up high. None of her clothing fit all that well, the busty young woman almost bursting out of her near see-through top, but her tanned cheeks were flushed with innocent excitement.

Her teacher was such a handsome man, tall and broad shouldered, but lean and good looking. He had short hair that looked so much more styled than the other men of the town, and glasses that clearly came from a boutique of some sort well beyond their town's limits.

Dressed in his nice sport coat and tie, he looked up at her from his desk with surprise. Finding that busty young woman panting and grinning at him so excitedly.

Though even the lewd sight of her didn't distract him too long from his own excitement at her words.

"They did?" he said, standing up, placing down his pen. "That's... that's great!" he exclaimed, pushing back his chair and moving to her with open arms. "Congratulations Amy!"

"Thank you!" she said, bounding into the room, her breasts jostling before she wrapped her arms around him tightly, her fresh scent of the lake and spring air mingling with something more carnal. Something she didn't even know about until he'd set her on her task.

He could feel those thick, supple mounds press into him, detect that scent on her, and as they embraced his hug went from innocent to... something a little more. His hands dipped down to the edge of her skirt and he pulled back to look her over. Able to see her breasts so clearly without her bra beneath that top, the pink of her areolas showing through.

"You have become such a woman, Amy," he said approvingly, his handsome face stretched into a warm, almost fatherly smile. "And I was lucky enough to see it happen here in my classroom."

She didn't pull away from him, her excitement almost too much to contain, causing her to bounce before his very eyes. Those ripe breasts of hers rose and fell in her enthusiastic vibrations, unable to stand still for even a second.

"I just can't wait to start!" she said, before that frown marked her lips. "I guess not until school's back in session though," she pouted.

"Well," Mr. Muran said, hesitant but then reaching one hand up from her backside along her nipped-in waist, brushing alongside her hefty breast. "We can take the summer for... special lessons, y'know? To prepare you for your new work," he offered, licking his lips as he watched her. Those full breasts bouncing before his very eyes.

"How does that sound, Amy?" he asked with an expectant smile.

And she was nodding before he even finished his sentences, thrilled with the prospect. She'd always been the teacher's pet, had such a crush on him for years, and being able to work alongside him for ever was a prospect she couldn't have been happier about.

So she looked up at him with sparkling blue eyes, only vaguely aware of the way his hand was playing against her body.

His strong hand was brushing alongside her thick breast, and the older man couldn't help himself. She felt so delightfully soft yet supple, so perfectly feminine and nubile. He was enamoured with every little bit of her.

"It's hard not to see you as such a beautiful young woman now, Amy," he remarked, licking his lips again slowly, habitually. "And to notice how much my own feelings have changed," he said, looking down over her.

"Changed?"

She seemed... worried! Frantic even. Despite the closeness, the way he looked at her, she was still too frightened at the possibility of losing him, of what they could have had. She was too innocent to realize that he meant: changed for the better.

She stood up straight, her head cocked and her french braid trailing over the large swell of her breast.

Staring at those two thick mounds, so clearly visible through her top, he couldn't help it. He swallowed anxiously and squeezed her hip and the side of her bust in his two hands and shook his head.

"I dunno if I'll be able to stand teaching you all summer, just... just the two of us," he said, struggling with his own moral compass as he stared at her beautiful figure, drawing his eyes slowly back up to her face.

But Amy looked... crushed by that!

It was hard to even comprehend the swirl of her emotions, of how rejected she felt for those moments, even as he helped himself to her body in such a casual manner.

"Mr. Muran," she said softly, her voice so crestfallen. "I swear, I'll be the best student."

His brow furrowed, his handsome, strong-jawed face looked so troubled.

"No, it's not that, Amy," he said with such concern, holding her in his arms still. "I just... I don't know if I can teach you any longer and be responsible about it. It's... it's so hard," he remarked, struggling with how to explain his lust for the young woman in a way that wasn't crass and lewd.

"Responsible?" she asked, clearly not understanding what he was saying. Her hands went to his chest, concern on her face as she looked up at him. "Mr. Muran, I believe in you. I think we'll work together really great."

His two hands grasped her tight, pulling her against him as he trembled a little, unable to help himself.

"Ohh Amy," he muttered lowly. "I can't be around you all summer, just the two of us... not with the beautiful young woman you've become," he looked down her top, through the open buttons. "I won't be able to restrain myself," he said frankly.

"Restrain," she paused, "yourself?"

She licked her lips.

Her body, if not her mind, understood what was happening, what he was getting at. Her skin prickled beneath her blouse, the nipples stiffening so obviously as they showed through the translucent white.

"I just..." she paused again, "I just don't want to spend all summer without you," she asked, more than stated.

"Amy..." he murmured again, wanting so badly to kiss her lips. "You're not my student any longer, not officially at least. But I want to be with you in a way that teacher and student shouldn't ever be," he said, his thumb daring to rub along the mound of her breast just a little, sampling that young, supple flesh.

"I won't be able to think straight as long as you're here with me, and I can't touch you... feel you," he swallowed anxiously, "have you."

Her bright blue eyes widened, her plush lips falling open in shock as she looked at her handsome teacher. The man she'd had a crush on for years, the one she thought of when she was falling asleep, and the one who was on her mind upon waking.

"You... want me?" she asked softly, nervously.

"So badly Amy," he said, his other hand sliding back from her hip to her ass just a little, stroking the curve of that ample backside as he fondled her breast in the front. "I thought I could resist, but... seeing you now," his eyes flashed wide. "I need you," he stated firm, his voice so rough with lust. "I need to know what it's like inside you."

She couldn't believe her ears. Her heart was racing, so much excitement and affection bubbling over. Those other men, the ones who had touched her, sullied her, given her such thrills and pleasure, they were all different.

Mr. Muran was the one who could make her belly flip and her breath catch in her throat, and she stared up at him, stunned for such a long few seconds before she brazenly pushed her mouth to his.

He grasped her tight then, their lips mingling, his tongue shoving past her lips to fence with hers. His hand slid down around her ass then up in under her skirt to touch her bare ass. He helped lift her that bit of extra height to add in their making out, though it wasn't long before her ravenous teacher tugged at her shirt in his excitement, popping the buttons apart to free her heavy tits and squeeze that supple mound within, letting his fingers sink into its young flesh.

She squeezed herself against him, her entire body rubbing against his as she kissed him harder, more passionately. For years she'd fantasized about what he'd taste like, how he would kiss, and though her own touches were a bit more furtive and much less refined, there was a desire there that exceeded his own.

Fingers moved to his neck, arms wrapped about his as she pressed her heavy breast into his palm.

She'd fucked three men that day, the only three men she'd ever screwed. But then at the end, her teacher, her true and greatest crush, was grasping her, holding her so tight, his hands upon her bare flesh as he kneaded her breast and squeezed her ass.

Their mouths intertwined for so long, tongues lashing against one another again, and again. Until finally, he broke away and looked down over her exposed chest, the tanlines that showed her pale tits meeting her sunkissed flesh.

Without warning, he began to pull off his jacket, loosen his tie.

"I need to have you, Amy. Right now," he said as he pulled

open his shirt, showing his lean muscled chest, peppered with dark brown hair. He was so hard, the bulge seemed to threaten to burst through his trousers.

Her eyes widened, drinking him all in with such thirst for him, for his body, and her hands went to his exposed chest eagerly. With her other lovers, she'd been soft, slow. Like an object to be used, that derived pleasure from obedience.

But with him, her curiosity and longing had burned within her for so many years, she couldn't hold back her desire to explore him, fingertips running along his chest, over his hair, such reverence there.

He wasn't as big and muscular as Mr. Kerny, but he was lean and hard, his body felt so cool beneath her fingers, and she watched as he undid his belt and lowered his pants. The bulge in his underwear prominent.

"C'mon," he said and pushed his exam papers from his desk, making room for her as he guided her there to sit. "I need you so bad, Amy," he said heatedly.

She'd only lost her virginity earlier that day, but already she was learning. Or, perhaps, she simply wanted him so badly that she instinctually knew what to do, and she brought her fingertips to that bulge. Her legs spread atop his desk, her sweet pussy kissing his wood as her school skirt rose up over her hips, exposing that red, flush little slit.

Mr. Muran groaned lewdly as she rubbed at his cock through his cotton underwear, and he chased her lips, kissing at her madly as she reached in and pulled his manhood free. He was so thick and hard, his dick throbbing with its veiny length heated and stiff as timber.

"You have no idea how badly I have been wanting to do this with you, Amy," he said, sliding one hand up her thigh, lifting her skirt to expose her bare pussy below, the other fondling her thick, young tit, hefting its impressive weight. "I've fantasized about having you atop this very desk every day for so long," he said in a deep husk.

She couldn't believe it. She didn't.

There was no way she could easily accept that he was as

enamoured with her as she was with him, but it didn't matter. She clumsily stroked him, her motions so beguiling in her naivety as she squirmed atop his desk.

She was splayed before him, her swollen pussy red with need, and she tilted her head back as he kissed lower over her throat.

"Mr. Muran," she whimpered. "Me too!"

That confession of hers made him moan, the low sound becoming a growl almost as he bit and kissed his way down her neck, making his way toward her twin tits. Those two heavy jugs the object of his affection then as he lifted one and suckled at it hungrily, prolonging the entry of his manhood into her pussy that much achingly longer.

His hungry mouth made that mound of flesh jiggle as he suckled her sensitive teat. He'd not been the first to do it that very day, but when he did it was somehow more special.

And not just for how he swirled around the crowned top, the ease in which he suckled her to fullness. It was the affection, the true desire beneath it. To him, she wasn't just a woman following her mother's shadow, but her own person.

Her fingers went to his hair, pressing him into her soft breast harder as she ground atop the table, filled with such wanton lust. She was making a mess, her pussy juices staining the desk, but it didn't matter to either of them.

Her teacher was touching her, tasting her! And she could feel his manhood throb so excitedly for her, spurting its slick precum in anticipation of when he'd finally slide into her raw pussy. The two of them were quivering with anticipation for that moment, but Mr. Muran was insatiable for her tits.

He switched from one teat to the other, suckling that to full stiffness and making her mewl and squeal in the process. It was only after a long, enthusiastic suckling that he at last pulled away and gently guided her back.

"I need to be inside you Amy," and his eyes went over her, drifted on down to see the sight of her bare little pussy, not even her panties covering those puffy red lips, so sore from the three other men who had pumped and fucked it that day.

And though she was tender, there was nothing that could

make her want for him less. The heels of her maryjanes lifted, hooking into the desk as her soft ass moved forward, bringing her pussy just off of the desk as she looked at him with such animal lust.

She touched his dick, using it to tug him closer, pressing the crown to her puffy, swollen slit.

At the feel of her slick, bare pussy against his dick, Mr. Muran shuddered before her. His eyes rolled back and he clung to her so tight, as if trying to find some measure of restraint to resist, but coming up with none.

"I shouldn't," was all he muttered, but he did. He did it so deliciously, sinking that dick into her tight little cunny. The fourth man that day, but the most special by far.

His shaft throbbed so thickly, and he moaned aloud with excitement, unable to helping rocking his hips, giving her a first pump of his dick as he struggled to continue kissing her amid their first fucking.

Oh, she was so tender, and it caused her to gasp and retreat a little, but she was hooked into the desk, holding herself against him as much as she could as he pushed that throbbing shaft into her. He was such a beautiful, masculine specimen, and it was all happening so fast, but she didn't care.

She couldn't wait another second for him, her entire body filled with so much lust, her mind hazed with love.

His shirt slipped from his shoulders and hung from his elbows as he began to pump into her more regularly. His hips working, that round ass of his rising as his abs tensed and undulated. He was fucking her with such raw passion, because he wanted her and had for some time.

All the while she saw that beautiful male physique of his rock into her, his pace grew, his hands grasping a hold of her thigh and breast, pressing her back to the desk as he grew more and more insatiable.

"Fuck I've never felt so good in all my life," he choked out in a groan that made his body shudder.

She leaned back fully on the desk, her back pressed into his papers as he grabbed her thighs, equally pulling her into him and thrusting into her. Each smack brought a little gasp of pain, but she couldn't help but want more, to feel him so fully, into the hidden depths of her body.

"Mr. Muran," she moaned, her skirt flipped up over her stomach.

He groaned so lewdly, his face contorted with overwhelming pleasure as the sounds of their fucking filled the classroom. The same place she'd spent so many years learning under him, now she was pinned beneath him, taking his cock in deep.

Her breasts jiggled before him, each new hammer thrust of his dick making her chest ripple. He forced his eyes open to watch that delicious motion as best he could, though it only heightened his own arousal, made him tremble, his dick swell and spurt pre.

"I dunno how much longer I can last," he groaned out, the pleasure such a strain on his body. He was racked by the sensations.

And though she wanted it to last so much longer, to feel him riding into her so deeply, it was hard for her to fight her own need. The fact that she was so sore, of course, but also her desire to see him pleased. To watch his face contort in ecstasy and feel him pound into her, battering against her depths.

She squealed at the thought, as he tugged her closer again, her large breasts bouncing with every thrust as she was only able to make out a strained, "Yess!"

Her teacher fucked her harder, even if his motions grew more haphazard and uneven. He was losing control of even himself as his pleasure mounted, spiralling towards his end as he pounded her just-recently-virginal cunny.

"I can't pull out!" he choked out the words before burying himself into her, jamming his shaft right in to the depths of her pussy and blowing his load against her fertile womb. It was intense, for him and her, and though he didn't know he wasn't the first to do so that day, to her he felt like the first to truly matter.

He bucked and spasmed atop her, thrusting his cock a little

more as he pumped out all he had into her raw, unprotected little pussy.

The heels of her hands dug into the desk as she cried out, her body on fire with the intense sensation as she gasped for air. He felt so amazing, and she forced herself to watch as his face contorted with pleasure, because of her. Because of her body.

It was a high, and she wouldn't soon forget that look he gave her once he settled, his gaze holding hers so intensely.

M onths later, it was still etched in her mind.

The entire summer had been spent together, her teacher he remained. Instructing her on how to handle the duties for her new position. Instructing her on how to be a good lover.

School was set to start, and as instructed, she showed up bright and early to get things ready with him. Though most of their prep time was taken up in other things.

Cradling her continually swelling belly between her knees, she knelt before him, his dick in her mouth as he looked down at her, moaning and quivering as his hands stroked her hair.

"Oh fuck, that's it," he told her, petting her, coaxing her alone. He'd been teaching her to be such a pro at sucking dick, and she'd gotten so damn good at it. "Such a good girl," he approved through in his moaning voice, forcing his eyes open once more to watch her suckle upon his stiff prick.

She had no way of knowing who's baby it was inside of her, but in her heart she felt it was his, completely.

She ran the tip of her tongue along the lining just beneath his crown before diving back further down his cock, feeling him press against the back of her throat. It was a feeling and a sensation she relished, and with each passing day, she enjoyed it just a little bit more.

It was easier, now. He didn't leave anything to guess work, simply told her what she needed, and she always obliged him. It was what she lived for, was happy to do, and her every motion spoke to that passion she still had for him.

The look on his face, the sound of his pleasured voice, it all made sucking his dick such a delight for her. The salty little spurt upon her tongue as he guided her back off his dick was an added treat.

"Okay, careful," he said, peeling her lips from his throbbing dick. "Not yet," he said, breathing heavily in his fancy brown suit, ready for the first day of classes.

"Get up," he instructed her, taking her hands and helping pull her to her feet in her high heeled shoes. He took his time, looking her over in her short skirt, her blouse strained not only by her pregnant belly but her thick breasts, all the more full from the milk that was engorging them.

"Damn you are so incredibly beautiful like this," he said so sincerely.

She blushed at his compliment, never tiring of his sweet words, his delicate touches. She was so passionately, blissfully in love with him, and she leaned in and up to press her lips to his, tasting his mouth with her tongue.

Her fingers pet down her skirt, running out any of the little wrinkles as she looked up at him, her brown hair pulled back into a high ponytail that she thought made her look professional. It also gave him a little bit of a leash, should he want it, and that worked well for the innocent woman turned debauched slut.

"I dunno if I'll be able to resist from keeping you in this state from now on," he remarked, his arms reaching out around her, one cradling her belly, the other her ass, fondling those supple cheeks. "Maybe I'll keep you knocked up from here on out," he said sweetly, letting his hand round the curve of her belly to softly knead her swollen breasts, the mounds fleshy and tender from being so full.

She'd been curious, since that first day, if rumours of how she'd gotten the job had touched him, if he knew of her promiscuity, but it never came up.

She wasn't certain how he'd have reacted, but she was so tender hearted towards him, filled with such affection and attentiveness that she barely left his side any longer, if she could help it.

And she had to admit, she liked how swollen her breasts looked atop her firm stomach, her body softening in such a supple and womanly fashion.

"Did you do like I told you?" he asked, a smirk upon his face as he reached down, and without waiting for an answer he very slowly raised reached down and raised that skirt, lifting it up to expose her bare little cunny slit. "Perfect," he said, sliding his hand in between her thighs to rub at her slit softly. "Just like our first time," he said approvingly, letting one finger slip into that slick little pussy of hers.

She sucked in some air, her body so turned on from pleasing him, from so willingly being his little mouth slut. Her darkened areolas stiffened beneath her tight shirt, her legs spreading a little as his finger delved within her slick, fleshy walls.

"Sir," she gasped, her eyelashes fluttering downwards.

With his dick still throbbing hard and exposed, he stood up from the edge of his desk and directed her.

"Bend over," he said firmly. "This load's for your little pussy, even if it's already too late to plant another seed there," he said, smiling at her wryly as he guided her hands to the edge of his desk, positioning her just as he wanted her, those heels helping push her ass and cunt up to just the right height for him.

He got around behind her, lifted her skirt to expose her ass, that little pussy.

"So damn fine," he muttered.

Her hands clasped her former teacher's desk, holding herself aloft as her swollen pussy was presented to him. It was slightly darker, both with her need, and from her pregnancy, and was glossy with her juices.

She looked over her shoulder at him, that ponytail whipping along her face.

"I need you, Sir," she pleaded, pushing her ass and cunny closer to him. "Take me."

"I know," he said simply, reaching out and grasping her ponytail, wrapping it about his hand as he sank his dick into that little pussy. It was still so tight, and wrapped deliciously about his dick as he began to pump his cock into her. His pace more careful and slow with her belly so fully of child.

"There you go," he said in a deep, throaty groan, followed by a loud sigh of pleasure. "You feel so damn good," he mutters lowly.

She squealed a little as he went in so deep, plumbing her depths with such angled precision as she wiggled her soft ass against his hips.

He always felt so good. She never tired of the feel of his body against hers, of the way he made her sing out.

Her cries were warbled by the way he tugged her head back slightly, but she enjoyed that too. The little prickle of her scalp, the way he claimed her as his. And she so desperately wanted to be his. All of her childhood fantasies had come true, and she was still so utterly thankful.

Mr. Muran — as she still thought of him — pumped into her, smacking his groin to her ass as they fucked against his desk. His balls swung up pendulously to smack against her clit and mons, and he tugged back on her hair, keeping a tight reign on her.

"Your first task as— as teacher's assistant," he began, panting and finding his words interrupted by the pleasured moans, "is to get me off... before class starts." He licked his lips and gave her ass a smack of his palm, "Better hurry. They'll be gettin' here before long, miss Amy."

And even though she knew he was having her on, trying to entice her, she responded as if it were more than mere words, but an earnest warning. Her ass slapped against his hips as she gasped and gulped for air, her breasts rocking and the tender mounds aching with each thrust. Yet the ache only caused those darkening nipples to harden as she tightened her cunny around his thigh cock.

Her little squeeze did just the trick, it made him moan aloud, filling the room with the sounds of his pleasure. He didn't have much more left in him, he couldn't have; Amy had been sucking him off for some time. Toying with his balls upon her tongue, suckling on his prick. His cock was sensitive and bound to blow any time.

All the same, he made each moment count, and he reached around beneath her and her pregnant belly, teasing her little clit.

"Show teacher how fast you can cum for him," he muttered in command, wrenching that ponytail a little tighter, tugging at her scalp as he shuddered and his nuts tightened, taking him so close to his limit.

Oh those dark, devious words matched with that skillful touch... She'd been teaching him to please her, in her own amateurish way. After all, he'd spent quite some time learning her body, and it was with all that practice that made her gasp.

It wouldn't take long, just a few seconds of his fingers rubbing along that soaking, throbbing nub before her grip tightened on the desk, holding herself just barely aloft as she gasped and then saw that explosive spark behind her eyes, like fireworks being let off in her body and making her cunny vibrate around his stiffness.

It was so intense she could barely even sense the moment when her teacher's dick exploded and he let loose a deep, booming moan that filled the room. His dick spurt its load, thick long creamy strands that filled her already pregnant pussy. So much of his cum filling her up, overflowing her as he rocked his hips and pumped out all he had into her.

"Ohhh fuck...!" he muttered, his words gravelly and harsh as he shuddered, all the contents of his balls dumped into her depths.

"Mr. Muran!" she cried out, her entire body trembling with such bliss. Her orgasms had only been getting stronger along with her pregnancy, or perhaps just with his skill, but whatever it was she was eternally grateful as her knees trembled with the power, the aftershocks thrilling through her as he pounded into her and laced her with his cum a few more times.

"Ohhh, Mr. Muran," she said as she let herself go downward, resting her body more fully across his desk.

They were both panting in the afterglow of their climaxes, and only after a long while relaxing did he slowly pluck his dick from her cum-filled cunt. He tidied himself up, put his cock back in his pants then came to her, helping her stand back up right, leaving the cum to drool down her inner thighs.

"The students are coming," he said with a smile. "Here," he instructed, handing her papers. "Distribute these to all the desks."

She took them in her hands, her face brightening as she looked at him so affectionately.

She had her dream job, her dream lover, and the best life possible.

Recommended For You

For a full list of all my books, or to browse by length or kink, please visit my website!

https://candyquinn.com/books

Free Exclusive Story

LUST LESSONS: BELLA

She has the hots for teacher

Mr. Wright is totally off limits. Not only is he her teacher, but he's also her brother's best friend.

Bella has never wanted anyone more. At first, she just wants to tease him. She doesn't wear panties, and practically begs him for the big D — detention — just to prove to him how good she is at being bad. But he wants more than a tease. He wants to claim her fertile, innocent body, and neither of them can resist their forbidden desires.

TEASER

By the time the bell rang and the other students rushed out, Bella's fantasies had her wound up tighter than a knot. Her bare pussy was dripping on her chair, and she slipped out of it eagerly.

"Well, Mr. Wright, you got me alone," she grinned.

Clark gave her a cautionary look, before he went to the door and shut it tight then locked it.

"You really chose an... interesting way to get yourself in trouble, Bella," he said to her as he returned from the door, shaking his head at her in surprised disbelief, a soft chuckle escaping his lips. "But you always were a little terror of a tease," he said as he made his way back towards the class windows, beginning to slide the curtains shut.

"You make it sound so sweet," she giggled, sitting on his desk. She pulled her white skirt out from under her, crossing her legs as she watched him shut the curtains. "I just did what felt natural."

Get your free copy of Lust Lessons: Bella, and so much more! All you have to do is subscribe to my newsletter.
http://candyquinn.com/newsletter

Become Candy Obsessed

For over a decade, I've been writing the hottest, naughtiest stories I can think of, and I'm addicted. I love to explore the forbidden, the taboo, and the over-the-top sexy. Each story starts off with a sizzle, giving you that nice build up, and that perfect release.

Discover new, secret fantasies, or just indulge in those sticky-sweet guilty pleasures. I'll never judge! Make sure to follow me on your fave site so you never miss a new release.

Plus, if you **sign up for my mailing list**, you'll get updates on my new books, bundles, giveaways, and several **free, exclusive books.**

CONNECT WITH CANDY!
candyquinn.com
candyquinn.com/newsletter
candy.quinn.erotica@gmail.com

FOLLOW ME EVERYWHERE!

facebook.com/candyquinnromance

twitter.com/sexycandyquinn

amazon.com/Candy-Quinn/e/B00K187NCE

bookbub.com/authors/candy-quinn

www.ingramcontent.com/pod-product-compliance
Lightning Source LLC
Chambersburg PA
CBHW020240030726
47499CB00001B/1